Jocelyn,
Happy Solstice
2005

Joy

With Love,
Amber

Joy

Naked happy Girls

new york undressed sexy private home innocent natural sunny erotic real & playful
by Andrew Einhorn

GOLIATH

Contents
Inhalt
Sommaire
Contenido
Indice

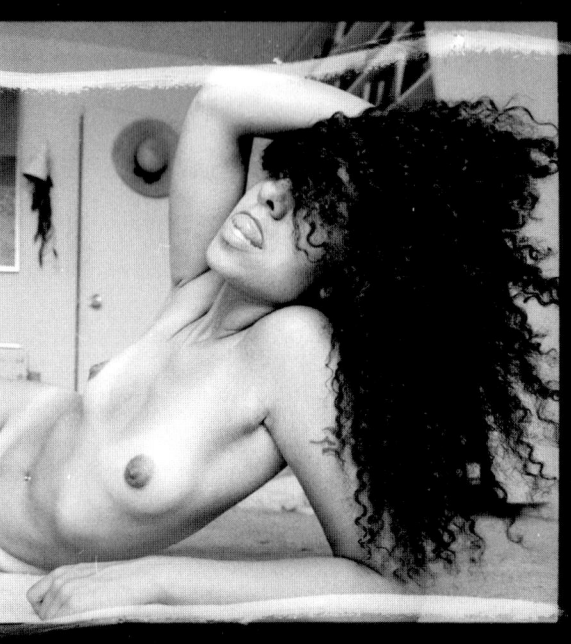
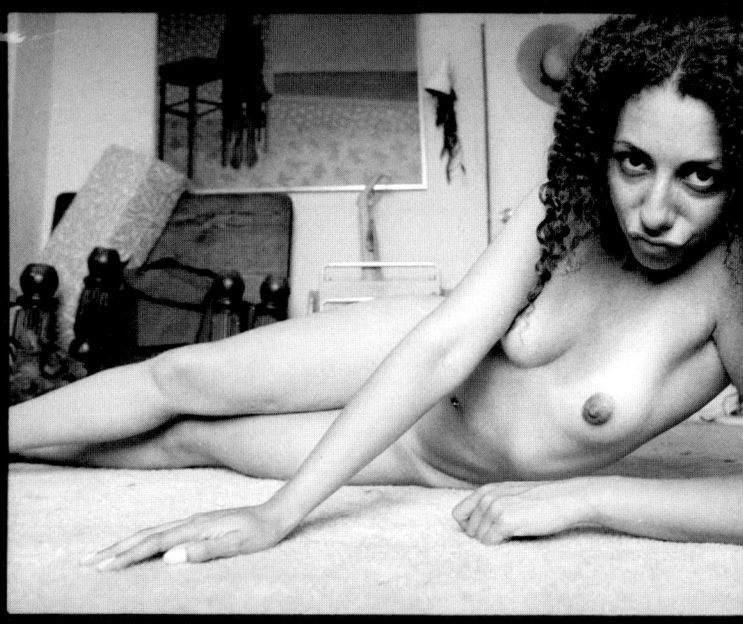

4

Naked happy Girls *English*

As any New Yorker will tell you, one of the best and worst things about living in this city is that you can walk down the street bawling your eyes out and no one will bat an eye. Hell, you could be naked and bawling if you liked, and you'd still garner barely more than a second glance. The second-best thing about living here is meeting people who flagrantly break the rules of non-engagement. Andrew Einhorn is one of those people. A self-professed "nice Jewish boy" from the suburbs," he has made a career out of approaching passersby. And not just approaching them: He asks them to get naked. This being New York, some of them actually say yes. But as they say on TV, don't try this at home; you probably couldn't pull it off.

Einhorn's success — he has a book of photographs to show for his efforts and his nose has yet to be broken — is based on more than just a willingness to ask. It's knowing who to ask (Einhorn says he can spot a good model by the way she walks, the way she holds herself), and more importantly, how to ask. He exhibits a genuine interest in learning (and telling) their stories, and he has an uncanny knack for putting strangers at ease. He's even managed to sweet-talk a few waitresses into disrobing, and everyone knows they-'re the toughest broads this city breeds. And he does it all on rollerblades.

What you'll see in these pages is that the women remain at ease even after shedding their clothes. They're at home, both literally — almost all the shoots took place in their own apartments — and figuratively. They wear that unfettered look that says, this is how I'd move, how I'd smile, how I'd lean back on my bed, even if I weren't unclad in the presence of a near-stranger and his camera. Einhorn prides himself on being "the king of comfort," and it's no surprise to learn that he used to shoot kids' fashion and has a penchant for snapping his models' pets, as well as the occasional barmitzvah.

Einhorn has a photojournalist's eye for plot — the details in the frame that hint at the same woman ten minutes before or after the shoot, throwing on a robe, making a cup of coffee, watching TV. And like a good reporter, he lets his subjects speak for themselves, rather than using them as actors in a story he's already contrived. Fortunately, he's not encumbered by a journalist's responsibility to stay neutral: He'll share a few beers, hand her the camera, maybe even get naked if she thinks it'll even the playing field. Einhorn actually likes the women he shoots, and you can tell they can tell. No moody nudes, these: They look warm, they look playful, and they're giggling. They're, well, they're happy girls. And they're naked.

Emma Jane Taylor ("The Em & Lo Down," Nerve)

Des jeunes filles nues, heureuses   *French*

Tous les New Yorkais pourront vous le confirmer : ce qu'il y a de pire et de meilleur dans cette ville, c'est qu'on peut hurler à se faire éclater les poumons sans que personne n'y prenne garde. On pourrait être complètement nu et hurler mais les passants se contenteront de vous jeter un coup d'œil dérobé. Et encore autre chose fait qu'il est particulièrement agréable de vivre dans cette ville : ce sont les habitants qui se font un malin plaisir de ne respecter aucune règle lorsqu'il s'agit de prendre des engagements. Andrew Einhorn fait partie de cette catégorie. Il se désigne lui-même comme le « gentil garçon juif des faubourgs » et il a construit sa carrière en abordant des passants. Mais il ne se contente pas de les aborder. Il leur demande de se déshabiller. Et New York ne serait pas New York si certains d'entre eux n'avaient pas accepté. Mais comme on nous le répète sans cesse à la télévision : n'essayez pas d'e faire autant chez vous. Il se pourrait que vous ne puissiez plus en vous en passer.

La recette du succès d'Einhorn – il a publié un ouvrage de photos qui prouve qu'il a du succès et témoigne de sa réussite exceptionnelle – n'est pas tant fondée sur le courage qu'il a de demander à des passants de se déshabiller mais bien plutôt sur le fait qu'il sait parfaitement à qui il doit s'adresser (Einhorn prétend pouvoir reconnaître un bon modèle à sa démarche et à son maintien). Mais le plus important est bien entendu la façon de poser cette question. Einhorn fait preuve d'un réel intérêt pour la vie de ses modèles (et il veut représenter cette histoire) et il a véritablement l'art de mettre un étranger à l'aise qui n'a plus dès lors de fausse pudeur. Il a circonvenu quelques serveuses jusqu'à ce qu'elles se déshabillent et pourtant nous savons tous à quel point, d'habitude, on peut se casser les dents sur les serveuses. Et Einhorn se déplace toujours en rollers.

 Dans cet ouvrage, vous découvrirez des femmes qui savent rester tout à fait décontractées, même une fois déshabillées. Et elles sont « chez elles » au double sens du terme : non seulement parce que les photos ont été prises à leur domicile, mais aussi au sens figuré. Et elles nous disent avec un regard insouciant : regardez, je me comporterais exactement de la même façon, je rirais et je prendrais mes aises sur mon lit de cette manière si je me faisais prendre en photo toute nue par une personne que je connais à peine. Einhorn est fier d'être le « Roi du bien-être » et personne ne sera surpris d'apprendre qu'à l'origine, il a été photographe de mode pour enfants, avec un penchant très prononcé pour les animaux domestiques de ces enfants et la Bar-mitsva.

Einhorn possède le regard du journaliste-photo pour les bons plans, pour les détails de l'image qui montrent la même femme dix minutes avant ou après la prise, lorsqu'elle enfile son peignoir, fait du café ou regarde la télévision. Et, tout comme un bon reporter, il laisse la parole aux personnages qu'il photographie au lieu de les traiter comme de simples acteurs dans une histoire imposée. Et fort heureusement, il n'est pas gêné par l'engagement pris par tout bon journaliste de rester neutre : il n'hésite pas à boire une bière avec un de ses modèles, à lui confier sa caméra et parfois il se déshabille lui-même s'il pense que sa séance-photo risque d'être un combat inégal. On sent qu'Einhorn aime vraiment les femmes qu'il photographie et elles le lui rendent bien. Ici, il n'y a pas de modèles nus de mauvaise humeur : elles sont extrêmement chaleureuses, enjouées, rient sous cape et sont – tout simplement - heureuses. Et nues.

Emma Jane Taylor ("The Em & Lo Down," Nerve)

Nackte, glückliche Girls *German*

Jeder New Yorker wird bestätigen: das Schlimmste und zugleich Beste an dieser Stadt ist, dass man sich die Lunge aus dem Hals schreien kann, ohne dass jemand darauf achtet. Man könnte nackt sein und dazu noch brüllen, mehr als ein flüchtiger Blick von Passanten ist nicht drin. Das zweitbeste daran, hier zu leben, sind die Menschen, die völlig ungeniert sämtliche Regeln brechen, was das Eingehen von Verpflichtungen angeht. Andrew Einhorn gehört zu dieser Kategorie. Der selbsternannte "nette jüdische Junge aus der Vorstadt" hat seine Karriere darauf gegründet, sich Passanten zu nähern. Doch nicht einfach nur zu nähern. Er bittet sie, sich auszuziehen. Und er wäre nicht in New York, wenn nicht tatsächlich einige von ihnen tatsächlich ja sagten. Doch wie heißt es im Fernsehen immer so schön: Machen das bitte nicht zu Hause nach. Es könnte passieren, dass Sie nicht mehr davon loskommen.

Einhorns Erfolg – er hat einen Fotoband, der seinen Erfolg beweist, und er ist damit noch nicht auf die Nase gefallen – liegt nicht nur in seinem Mut begründet, zu fragen, sondern vielmehr darin, wen er fragt (Einhorn behauptet von sich, ein gutes Model am Gang und an der Haltung zu erkennen). Am wichtigsten ist natürlich, wie man die Frage stellt. Eichhorn bekundet aufrichtiges Interesse an der Lebensgeschichte der Models (und daran, diese Geschichte darzustellen), und er hat ein echtes Händchen dafür, einem Fremden die Scheu zu nehmen. Ein paar Kellnerinnen hat er so lange umgarnt, bis sie sich entblätterten, dabei weiß jeder, dass man sich an Kellnerinnen normalerweise die Zähne ausbeißt. All das macht er auf Rollerblades.

Sie werden in diesem Band auf Frauen stoßen, die auch dann noch ganz locker sind, wenn sie sich ausgezogen haben. Und sie sind im doppelten Sinne des Wortes "zuhause": einmal, weil die Aufnahmen in den eigenen vier Wänden stattfinden, und auch im übertragenen Sinne. Und mit unbekümmertem Blick sagen sie: Seht her, genau so würde ich mich auch bewegen, genau so lächeln oder es mir auf meinem Bett bequem machen, wenn ich nicht splitternackt von einem mir fast unbekannten Menschen fotografiert würde. Einhorn ist stolz darauf, der "König des Wohlfühlens" zu sein, und da überrascht es niemanden, dass er ursprünglich Fotograf für Kindermode war, mit einer Vorliebe für die Haustiere der Kinder und das Bar-Mizva-Fest.

Einhorn hat den Blick des Photojournalisten für gute Plots, für Bilddetails, die die gleiche Frau zehn Minuten vor oder nach der Aufnahme zeigen, wie sie sich den Morgenrock überstreift, beim Kaffeekochen oder beim Fernsehen. Und wie ein guter Reporter lässt er seine Objekte für sich selbst sprechen, statt sie wie Schauspieler in einer vorgegebenen Story zu behandeln. Und zum Glück wird er auch nicht von der journalistischen Verpflichtung gehemmt, neutral zu sein: mal trinkt er mit dem Model ein Bier, ein andermal übergibt er ihr die Kamera oder zieht sich sogar selbst aus, wenn sie der Meinung ist, es wäre sonst eine ungleiche Schlacht. Man spürt, dass Einhorn die Frauen wirklich mag, die er fotografiert, und die Frauen spüren das. Hier gibt es keine schlechtgelaunten Aktmodels: Sie strahlen Wärme aus, sind verspielt, kichern und sind – einfach glücklich. Und nackt.

Emma Jane Taylor ("The Em & Lo Down," Nerve)

Ragazze nude e contente *Italian*

Ogni newyorchese lo confermerà: il peggio e contemporaneamente il meglio di questa città è che ci si può anche estrarre i polmoni dalla gola senza che nessuna se ne dia per inteso. Si potrebbe essere nudi e in aggiunta anche urlare, ma più di un'occhiata veloce da qualche passante frettoloso non si riuscirà ad ottenere. E la seconda miglior cosa del fatto di vivere qui sono le persone, che violano tutte le regole in modo completamente disinvolto, per tutto ciò che riguarda l'assunzione di obblighi. Andrew Einhorn fa parte di questa categoria. Il "giovane ebreo gentile della periferia" come lui si è definito, ha fondato la propria carriera sul fatto di avvicinarsi ai passanti. Ma non semplicemente avvicinarsi. Li prega di spogliarsi. E non sarebbe a New York, se non ci fosse qualcuno che effettivamente dice tranquillamente di sì. Tuttavia, come si sente dire spesso in televisione: non fatelo a casa vostra. Potrebbe accadere che non riusciate più a venirne fuori.

Il successo di Einhorn – c'è un volume di foto che dimostra il suo successo, e non gli si è ancora rivolto contro – non è dovuto solo al suo coraggio di domandare, bensì piuttosto nel fatto di chi sceglie per porre tale domanda (Einhorn dice di se stesso di essere in grado di riconoscere un buon modello dall'andatura e dalla postura). La cosa più importante è naturalmente come pone la domanda. Eichhorn dimostra un vero interesse alla storia della vita della modella (e al fatto di raffigurare tale storia), e ha una vera mano fatata nel rimuovere ogni vergogna a una sconosciuta. Ha circuito talmente a lungo un paio di cameriere fino a che queste non si sono spogliate, mentre è noto a tutti che è proprio con le cameriere che ci si rompe le corna. E tutto ciò lui lo fa sui Rollerblade.

In questo volume vi imbatterete in donne che sono ancora completamente abbandonate, anche se si sono spogliate. E sono "a casa" nel doppio senso della parola: da un lato perché la ripresa ha avuto luogo fra le loro quattro mura, me anche in senso astratto. E con uno sguardo indifferente pare dicano: vedete, mi muoverei esattamente in questo modo, sorriderei esattamente in questo modo oppure mi metterei a mio agio sul mio letto anche se non venissi fotografata, completamente nuda, da un fotografo che mi è quasi sconosciuto. Einhorn è orgoglioso del fatto di essere il "re del farle sentire a proprio agio", e non sorprende nessuno scoprire che egli in origine era un fotografo di abbigliamento per bambini, con una preferenza per i piccoli animali domestici dei bambini e per la festa di Bar-Mizva. Einhorn ha lo sguardo del fotogiornalista per le buone inquadrature, per i dettagli delle immagini, che mostrano la stessa donna dieci minuti prima o dopo lo scatto, mentre si infila la gonna del mattino, fa il caffè o guarda la televisione. E come un buon reporter lascia parlare da soli i suoi soggetti, non li tratta come attori in una storia già predefinita. Ma per fortuna non rispetta sempre il dettato del giornalista professionista di essere neutrale a tutti i costi: una volta si concede una birra con la modella, un'altra volta le consegna la macchina fotografica o si spoglia anche lui, ma solo se lei e s'accordo, diversamente sarebbe una battaglia impari. Si avverte che Einhorn ama veramente le donne che fotografa, e le donne lo sanno. Qui non c'è nessuna modella di cattivo umore: tutte irradiano calore, sono svagate, ridono sommessamente e sono – semplicemente – contente. E nude.

Emma Jane Taylor ("The Em & Lo Down," Nerve)

Felices chicas desnudas *Spanish*

Todos los neoyorquinos lo confirmarán: lo peor y a la vez lo mejor de esta ciudad es que podemos gritar a pleno pulmón sin que nadie nos preste atención. Podemos ir desnudos y además vociferar, pero lo máximo que nos puede ocurrir es que un peatón nos eche un vistazo furtivo. Lo segundo mejor de vivir aquí son las personas, que totalmente insensibles violan todas las normas respecto al cumplimiento de las obligaciones. Andrew Einhorn pertenece a esta categoría. El autodenominado "simpático joven judío de los suburbios" ha basado su carrera en la aproximación a los peatones. Y no sólo en la aproximación. Les pide que se desnuden. Y no estaría en Nueva York si realmente no hubiera algunos que dieran su conformidad. Pero como se suele decir tan bellamente en televisión: por favor no imite en casa esa conducta, pues puede ocurrir que ya no se pueda desprender de ella.

El éxito de Einhorn – tiene un rollo de fotos que lo certifica y todavía no se ha percatado de ello – no se basa únicamente en el valor que despliega al preguntar, sino más bien en la persona a quien pregunta (Einhorn afirma de sí mismo que es capaz de identificar una buena modelo por la forma de andar o por su actitud). Lo más importantes es, lógicamente, el modo en que se formula la pregunta. Einhorn proclama su sincero interés por la trayectoria vital del modelo (y por representar esa trayectoria), y tiene auténtico destreza para quitar el pudor a alguien que desconoce. Estuvo seduciendo a un par de camareras hasta que se desnudaron, y todo el mundo sabe que normalmente con las camareras se puede uno estrellar. Todo eso lo consigue él sobre ruedas.

En esta cinta se encontrarán con mujeres que se sienten plenamente desinhibidas incluso después de desnudarse. Y que se sienten "en casa" en doble sentido: primero porque las tomas se realizan dentro de las cuatro paredes propias, y segundo también en sentido figurado. Y dicen con ojos despreocupados: mirad, yo me movería exactamente igual, sonreiría idénticamente o me pondría en la cama con la misma comodidad que si no me estuviese fotografiando en pelota picada una persona casi desconocida. Einholz está orgulloso de ser el "rey del bienestar" y a nadie le sorprende que en sus orígenes fuese un fotógrafo de moda infantil con cierta predilección por las mascotas de los niños y por la fiesta Bar-Mizva.

Einhorn tiene ojo de periodista fotográfico para buenos entornos, para los detalles figurativos que muestran la misma mujer diez minutos antes o después de la toma, sobreponiéndose al arrebol de la mañana, preparando el café o viendo la televisión. Y, al estilo del buen reportero, deja que sus objetos hablen por sí mismos en lugar de tratarlos como artistas de cine en un guión preestablecido. Afortunadamente tampoco se ve cohibido por la obligación periodística de ser neutral: lo mismo se toma una cerveza con la modelo que le entrega la cámara o incluso se desnuda si ella piensa que la batalla tiene que ser en igualdad de condiciones. Se percibe que Einhorn hace reales a las mujeres que fotografía y ellas se dan cuenta de eso. Aquí no hay modelos que actúan de mala gana: antes bien irradian calor, juguetean, serpentean y son simplemente felices. Desnudas.

Emma Jane Taylor ("The Em & Lo Down," Nerve)

Skye · I met Skye one night when we were both filming the same band. I photographed her in her west village apt, just after she bought two kittens and two nipple rings. Skye was very easy to photograph, because everything she did was sexy. Skye is a photographer, artist, and musician.

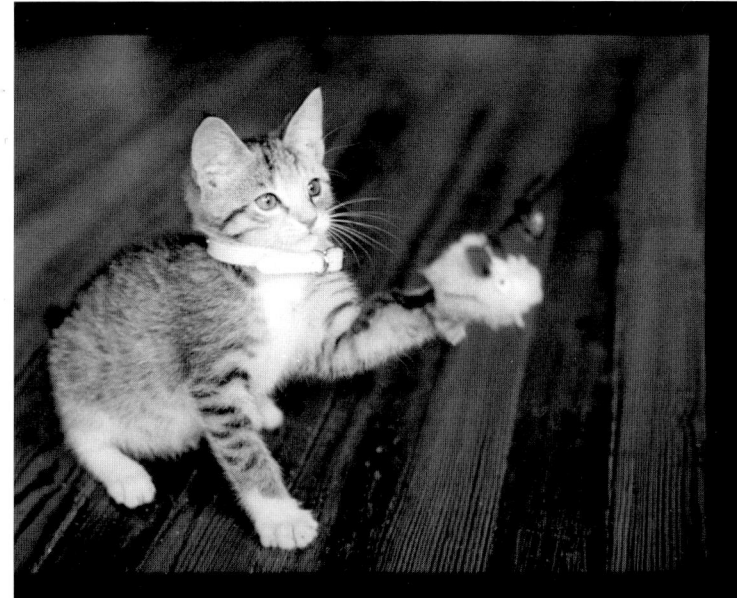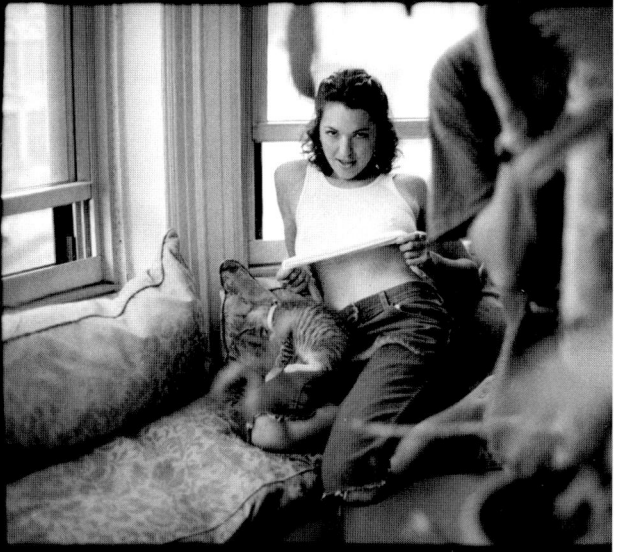

3 ▷ 3A 4

8 KODAK 5063 TX 9

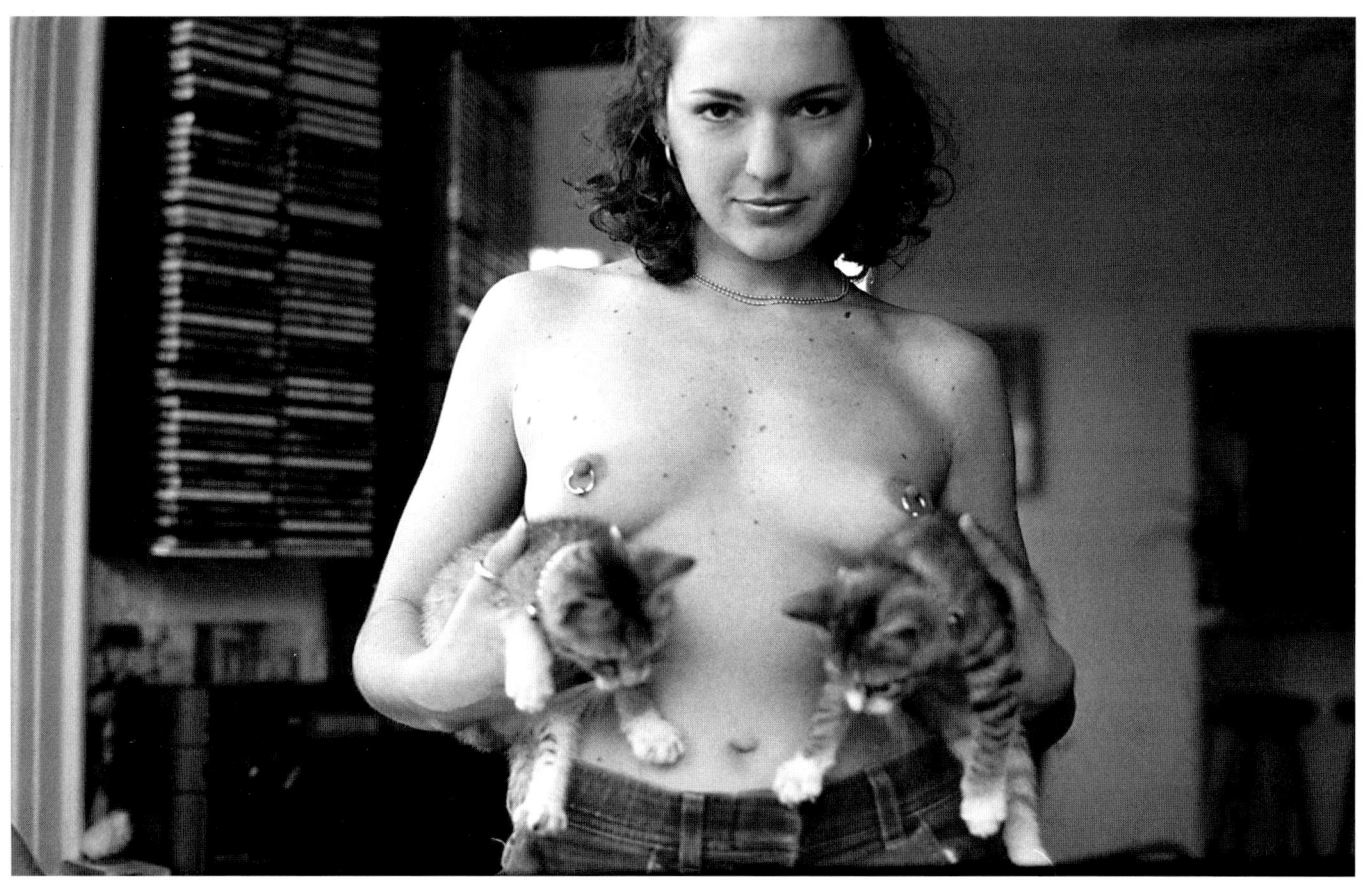

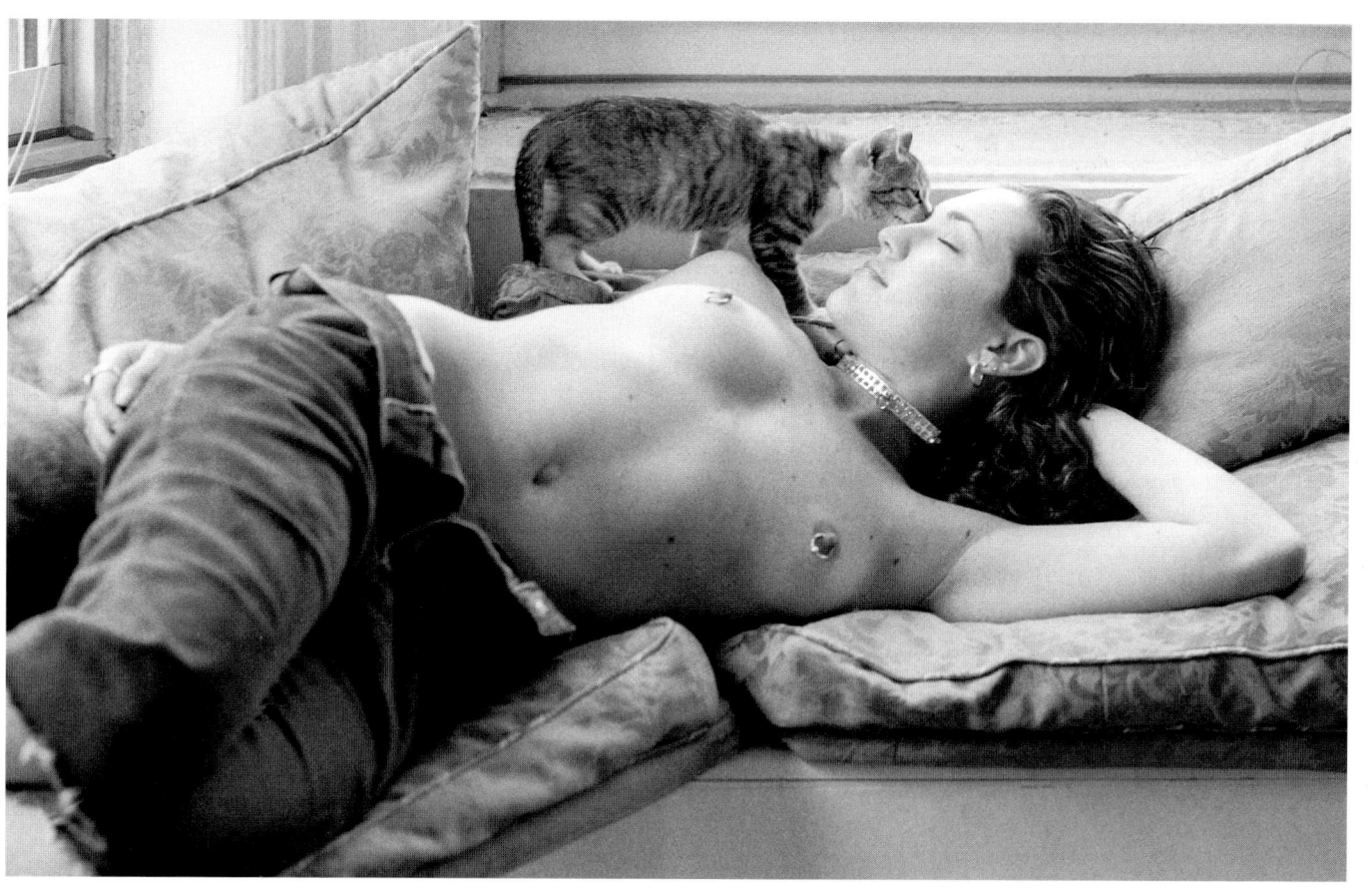

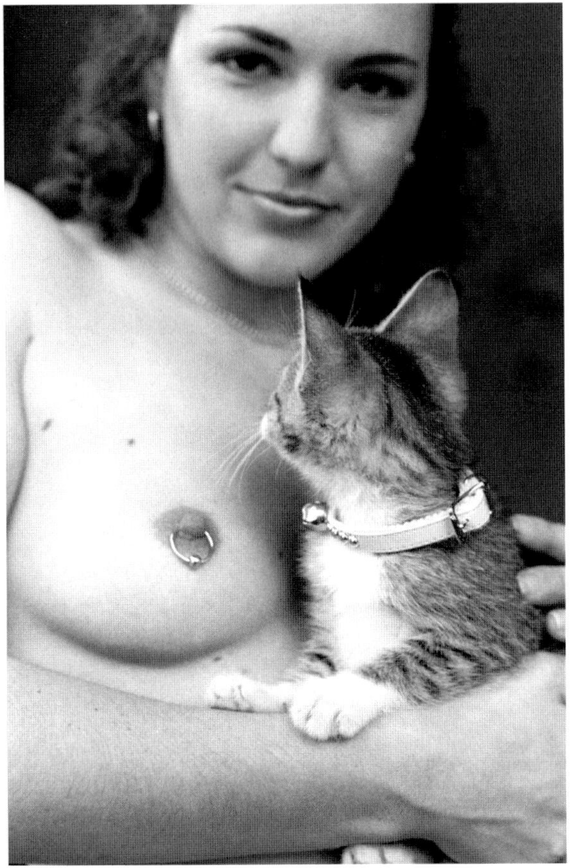

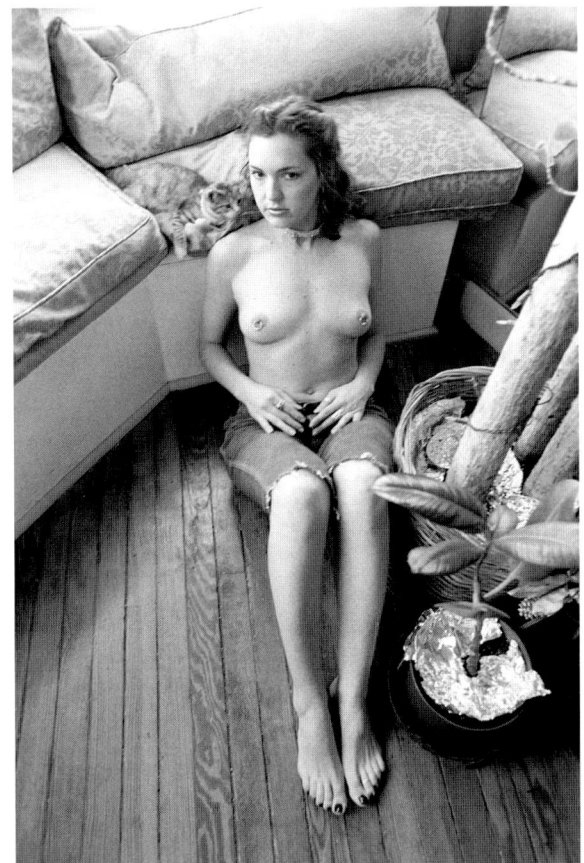

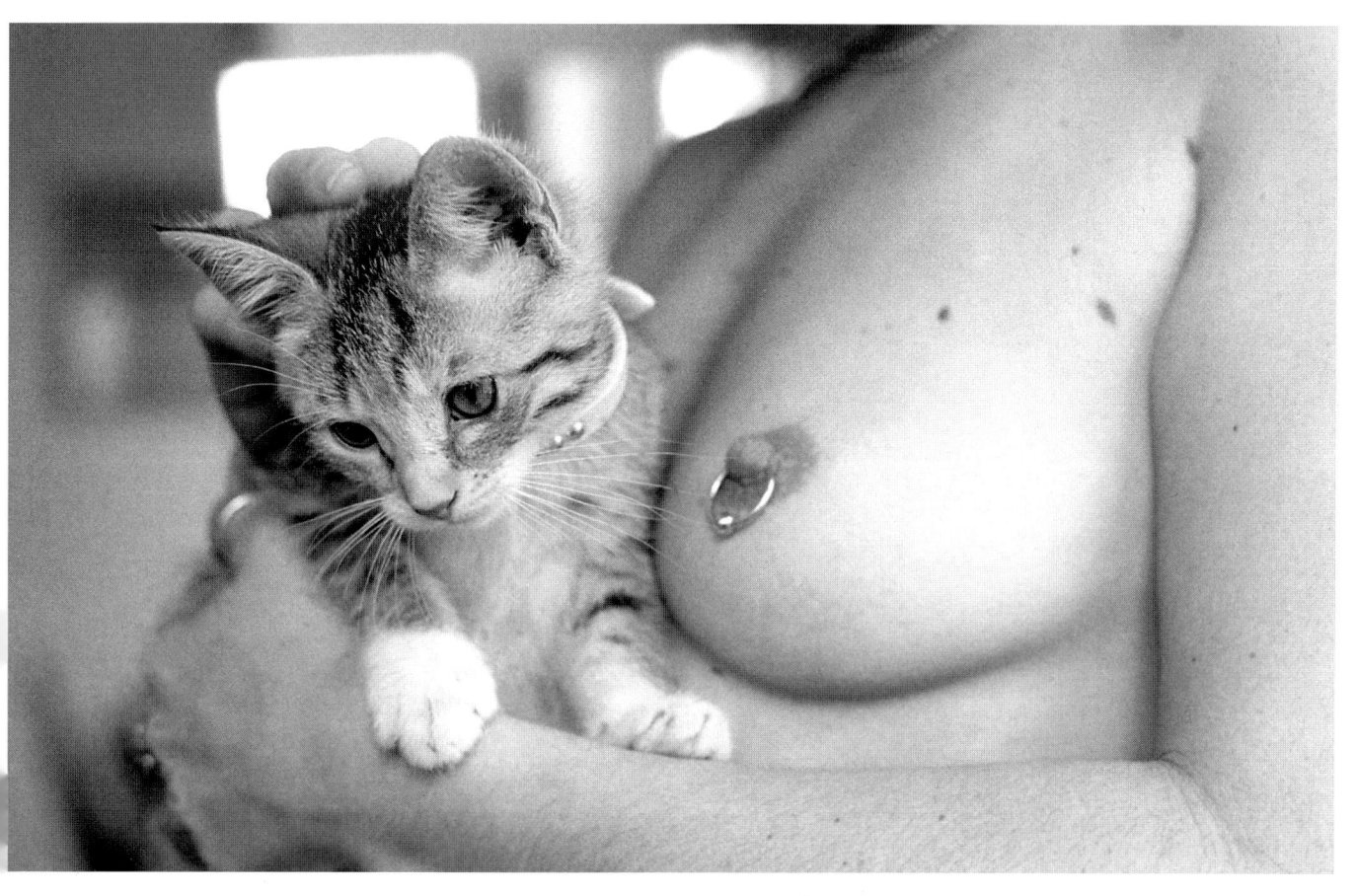

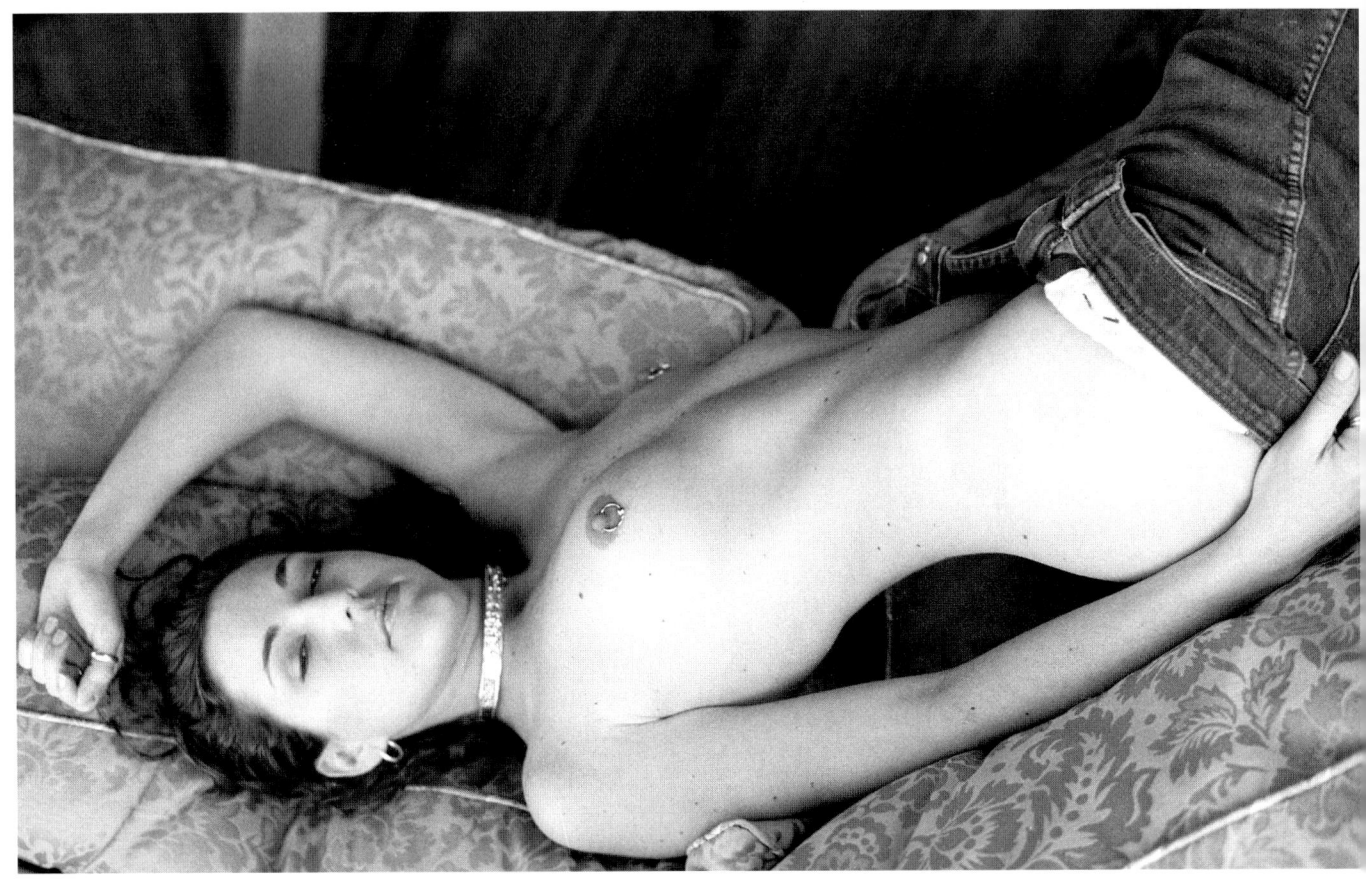

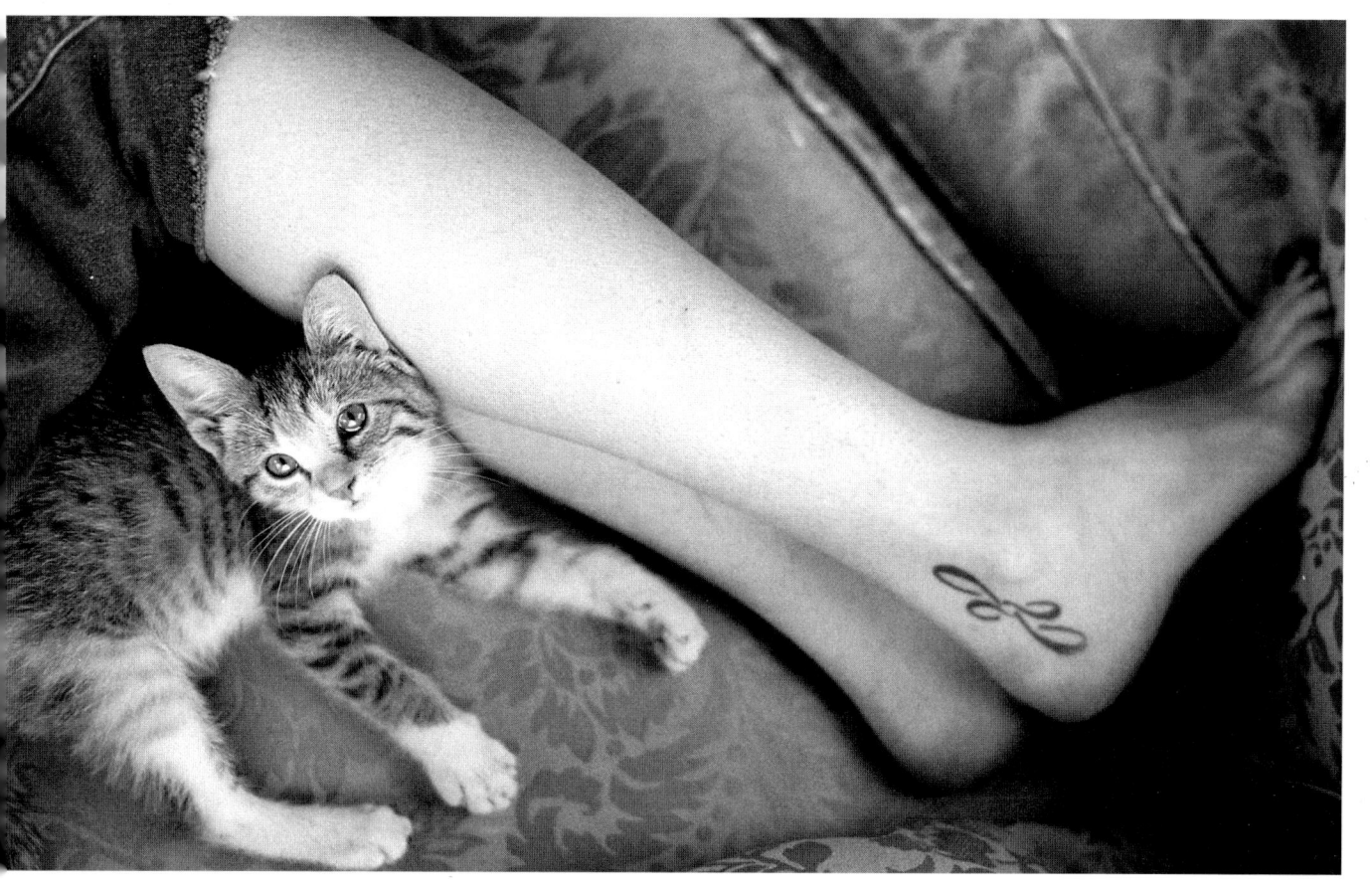

Alysa · I first met Alysa at 5am, when she was posing nude for another artist. I photographed her in her west village apartment, with her cat named "Walker." We had a really fun day together, and she took photos of me as well. Alysa was a former dancer, and later became a Pilates instructor.

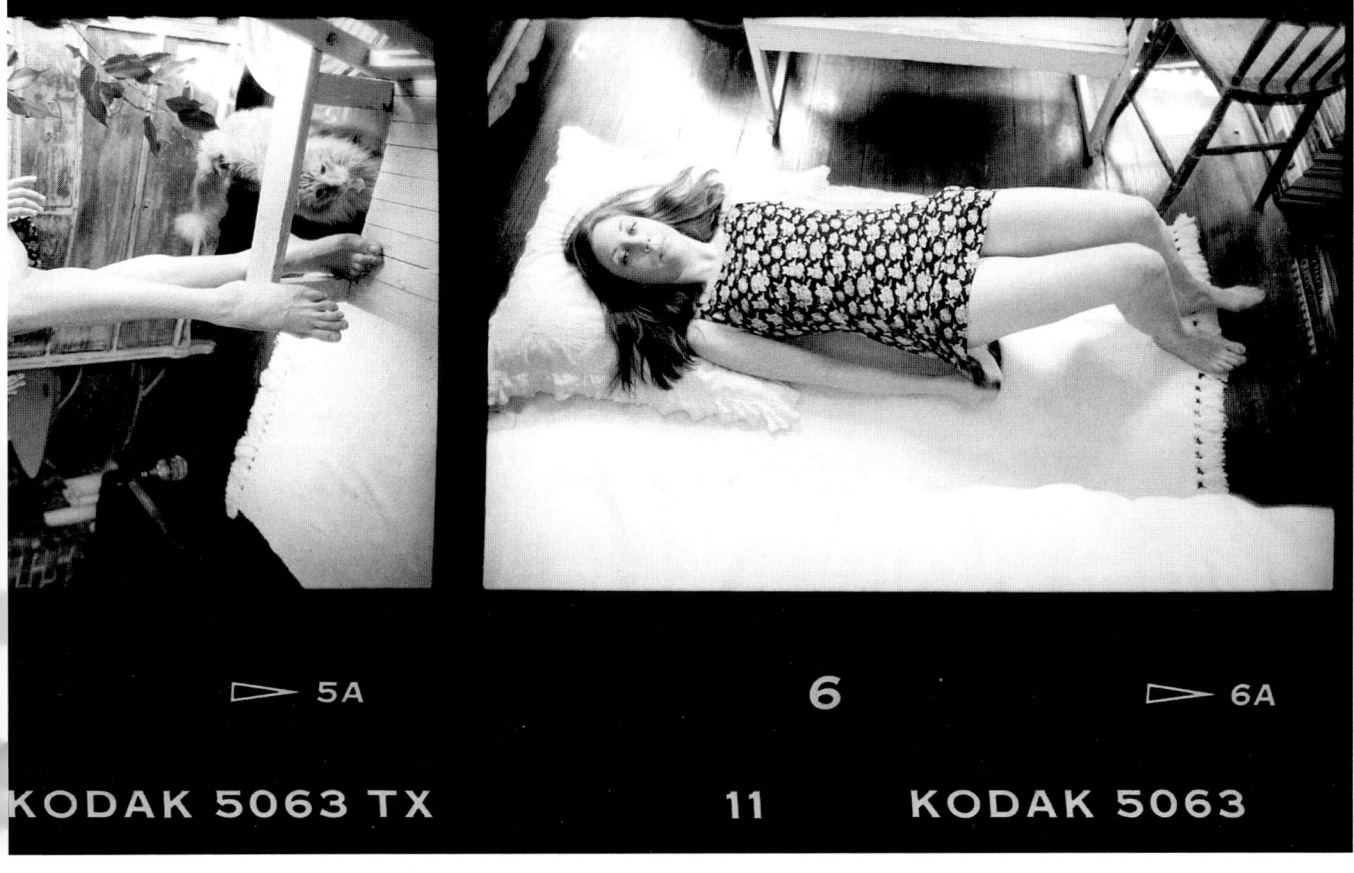

▷ 5A   6   ▷ 6A

KODAK 5063 TX   11   KODAK 5063

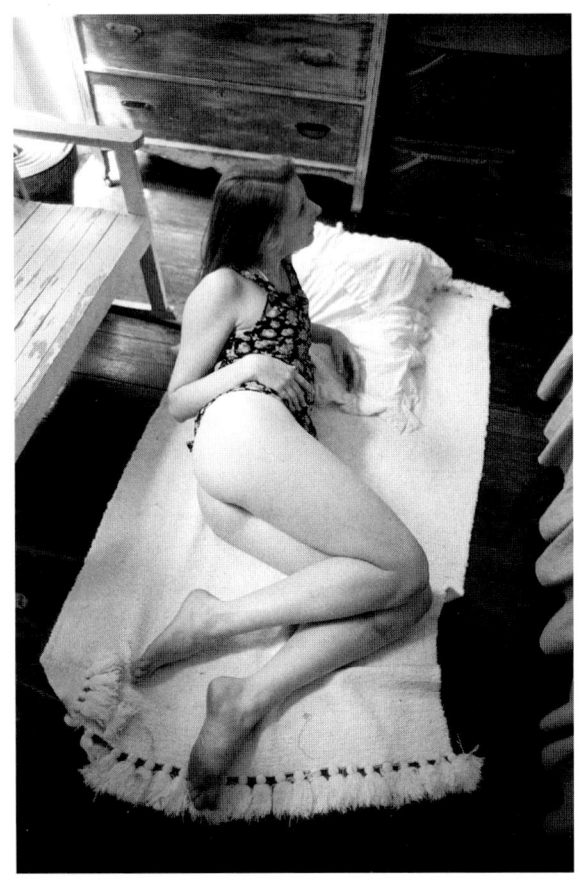

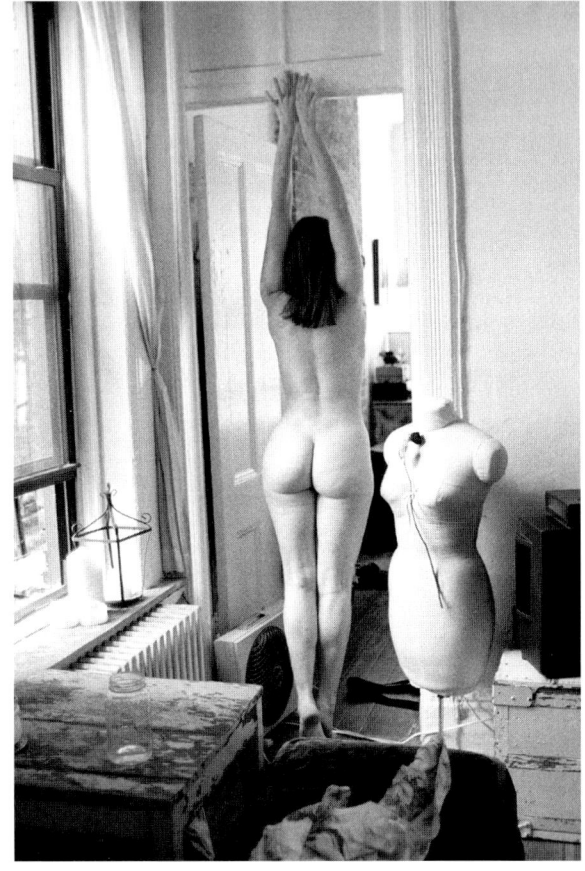

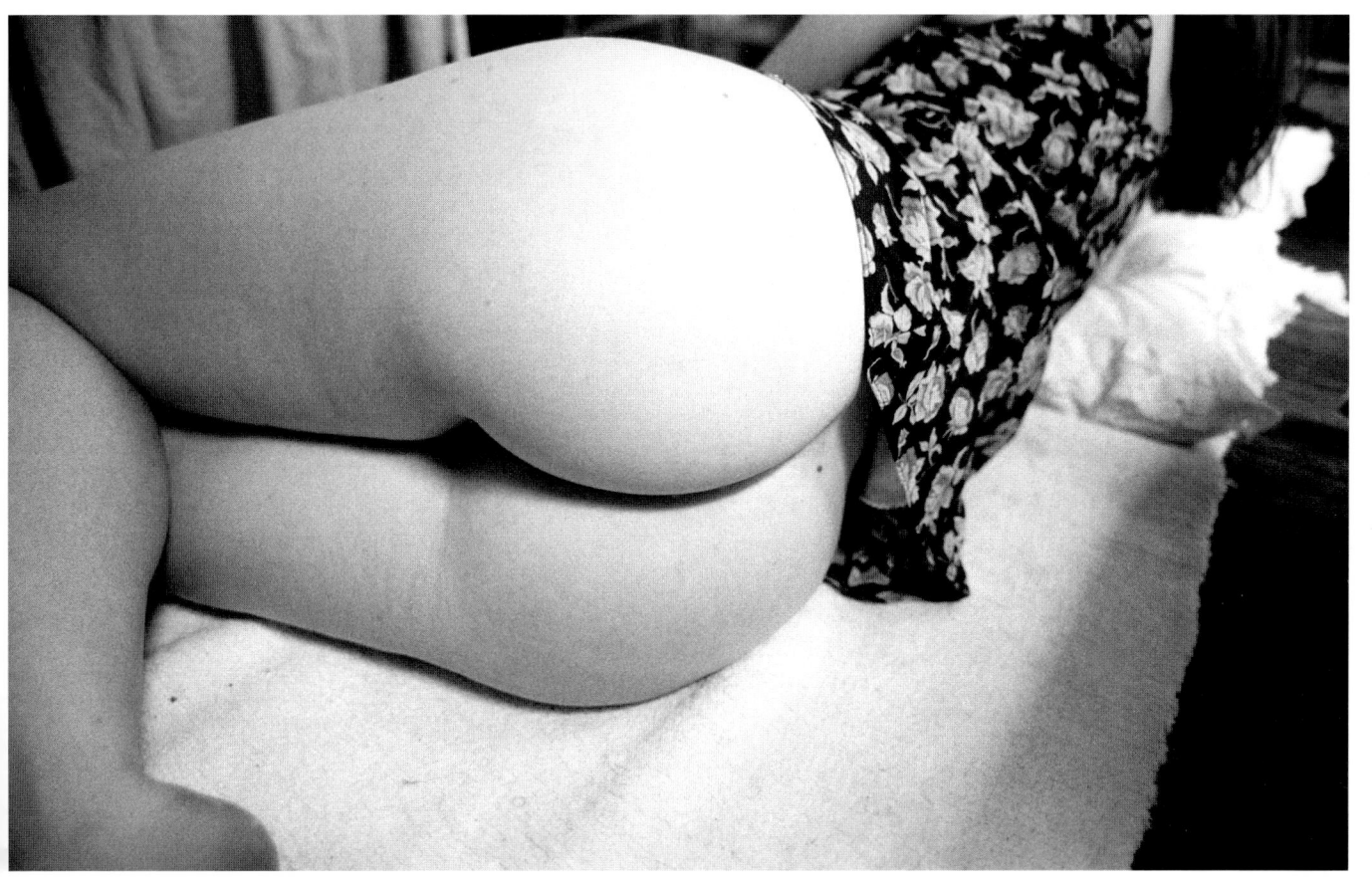

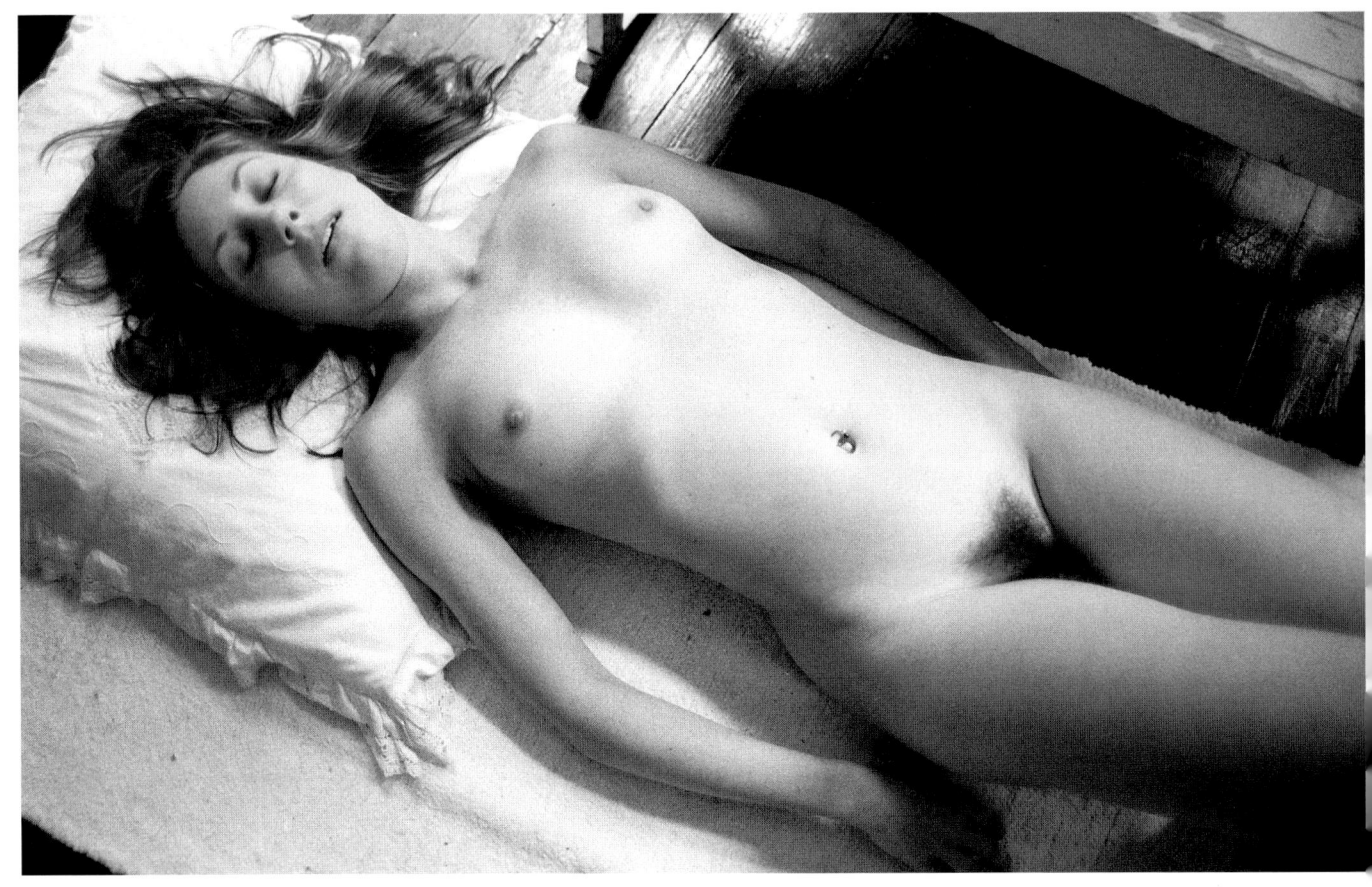

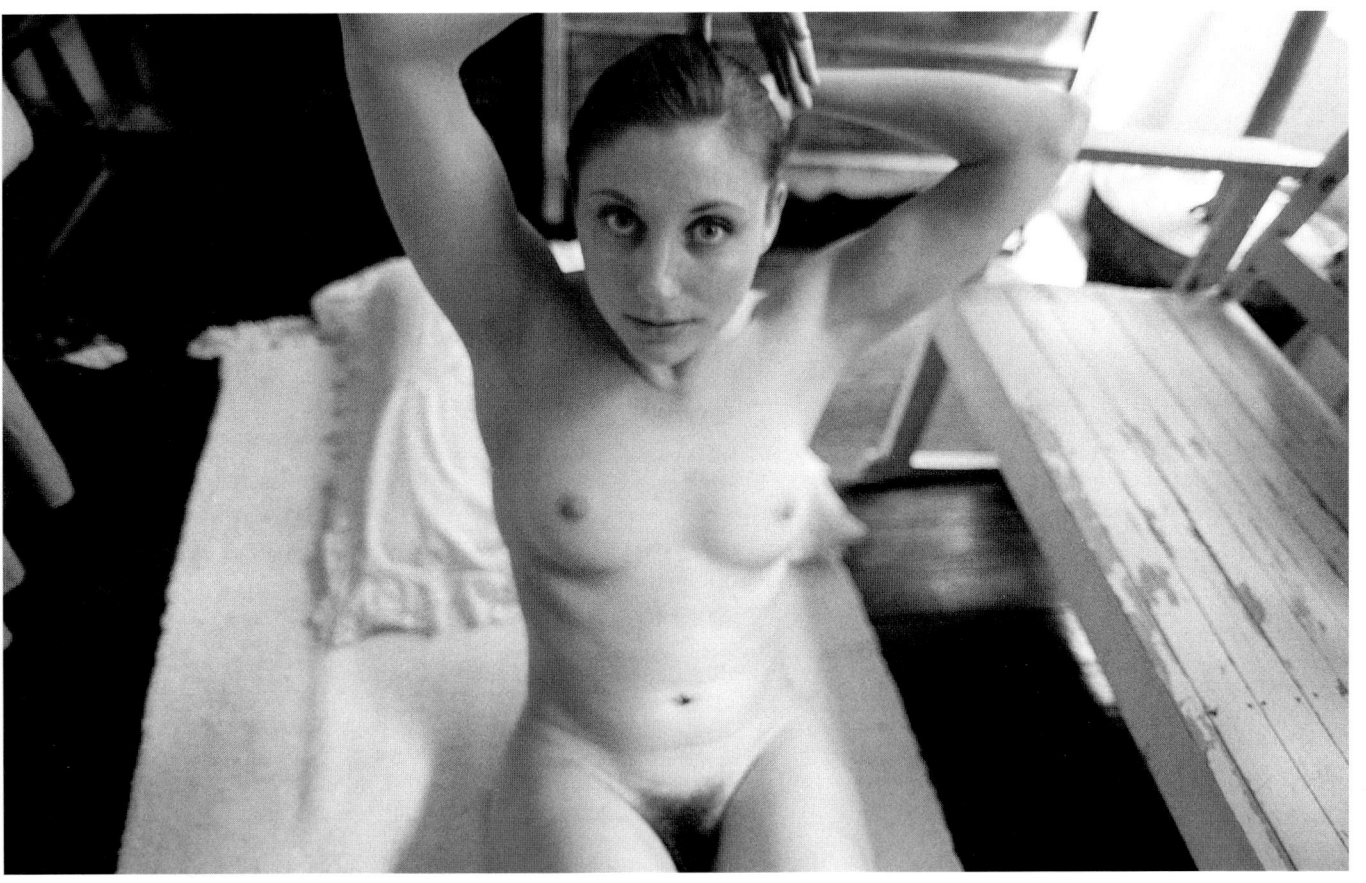

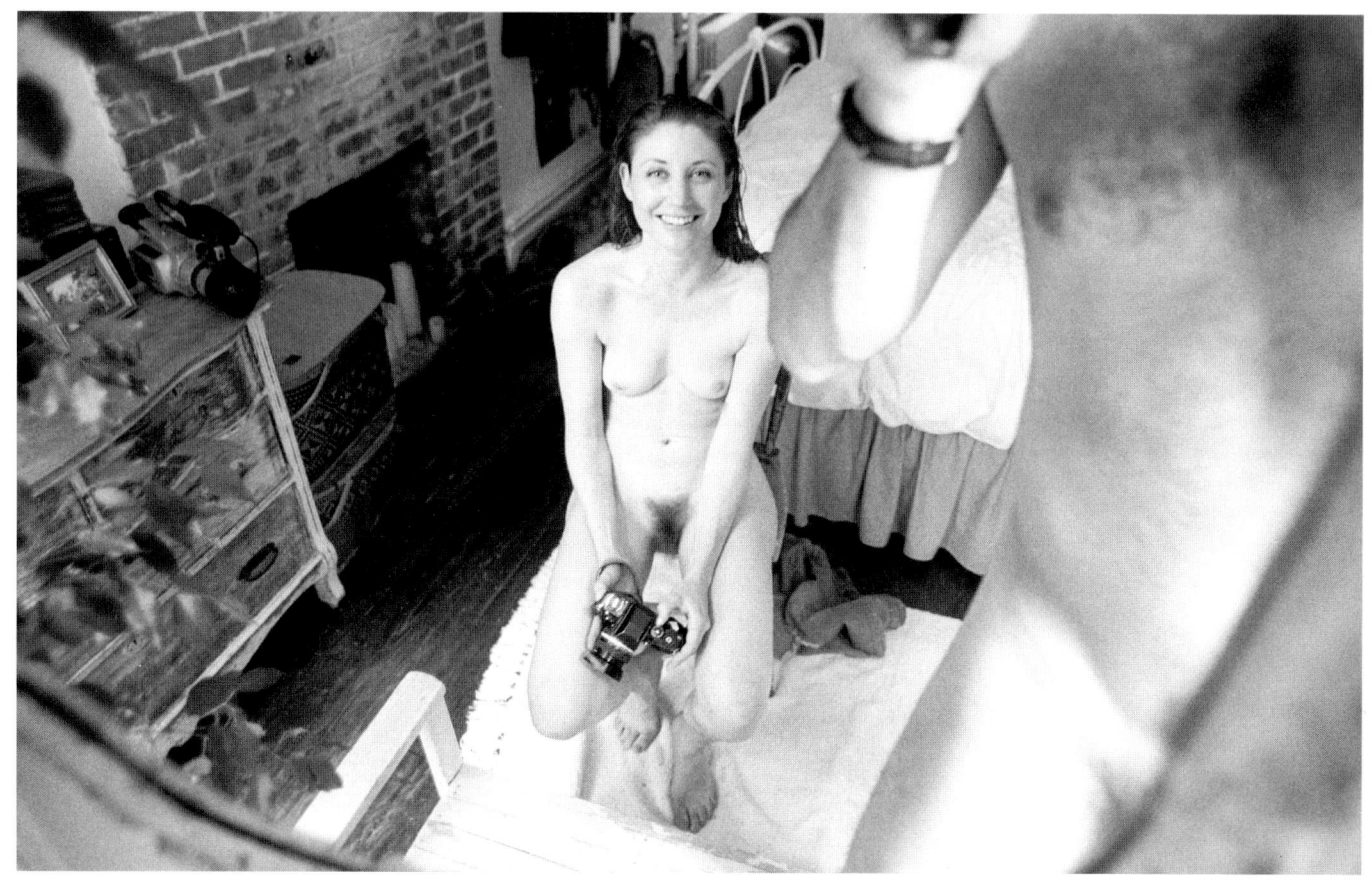

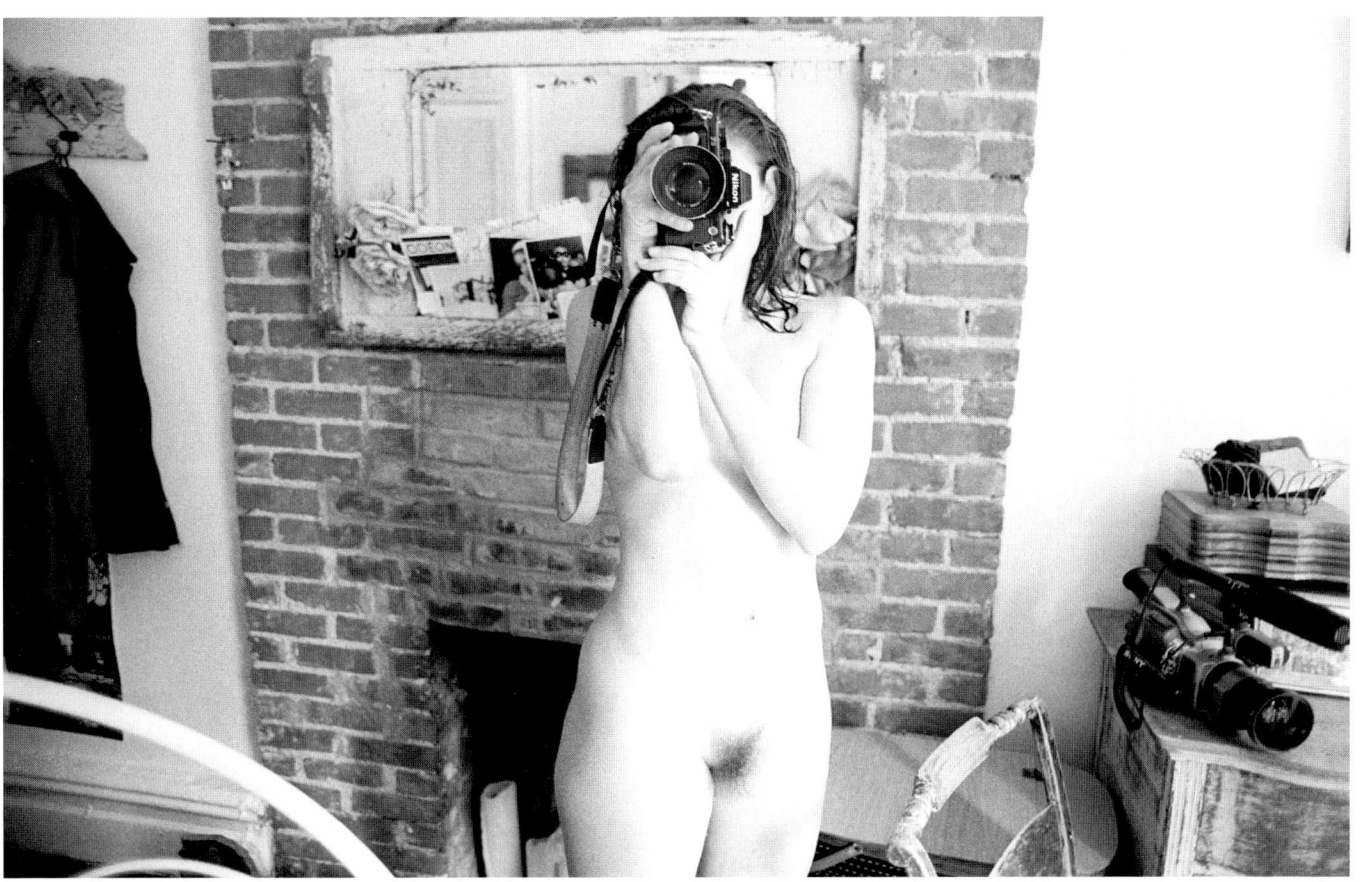

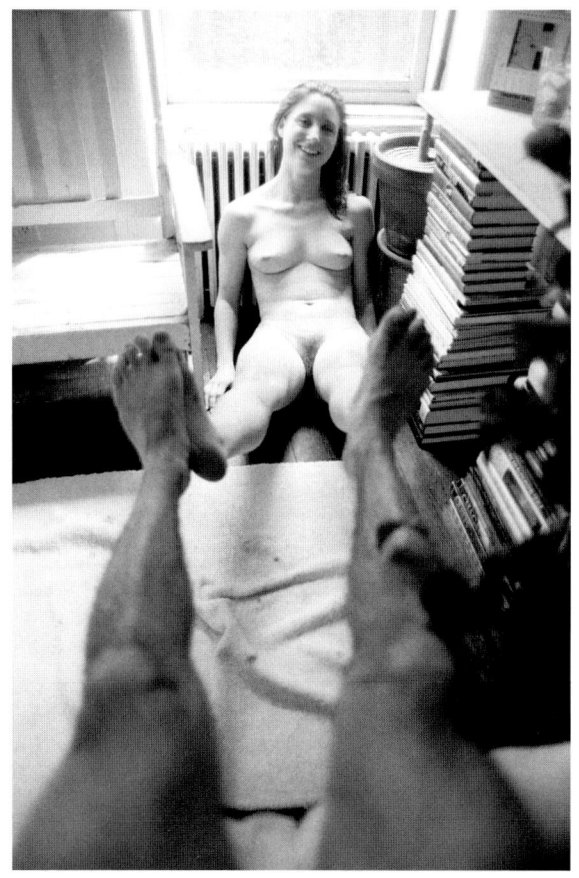

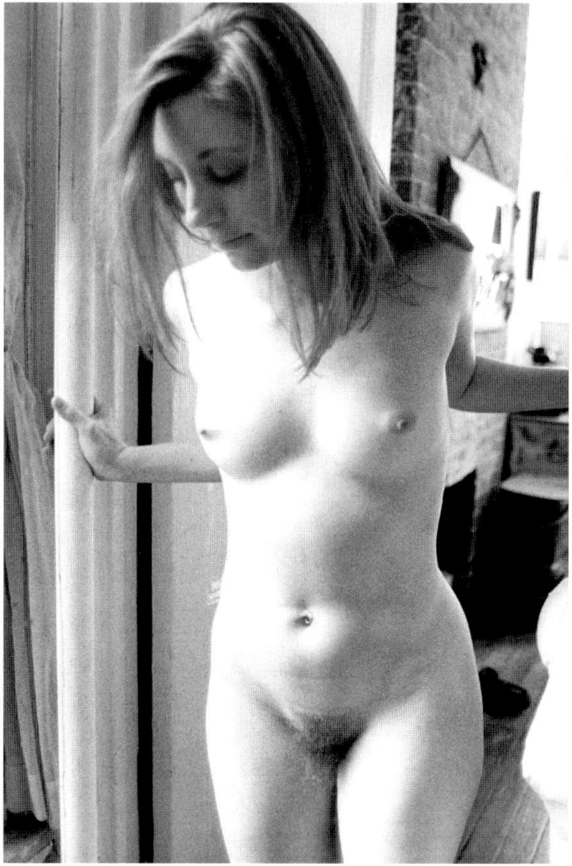

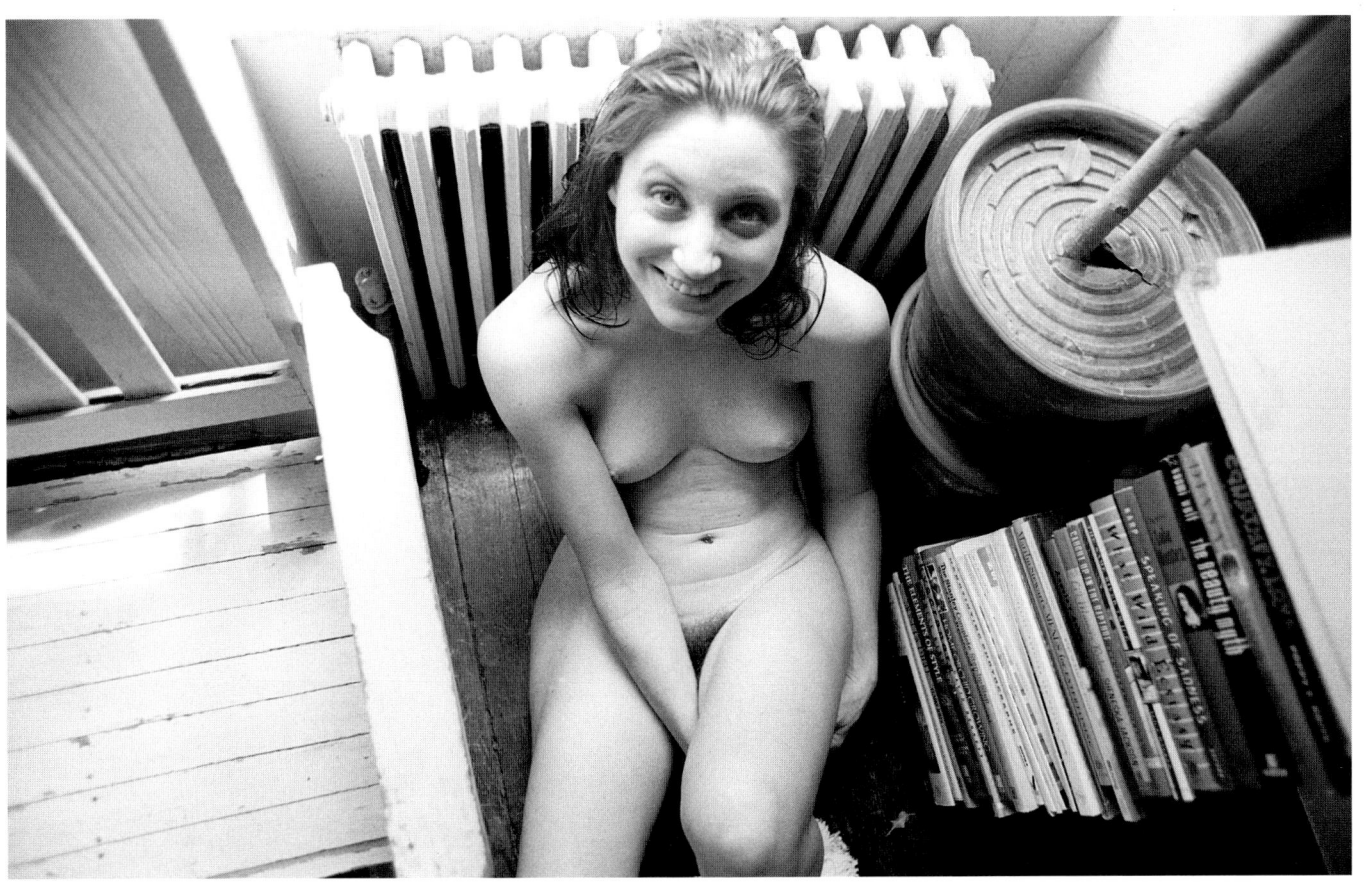

Andrea · I didn't know Andrea until I went to the "Burning Man" festival with her in 1999. I photographed her in her Bay Ridge, Brooklyn apartment. Andrea smoked cigarettes, laughed a lot, and kept hiding from the windows so the landlord wouldn't see her naked. She is an artist, loves pistachios and red wine, and has a fairy tattoo on her thigh.

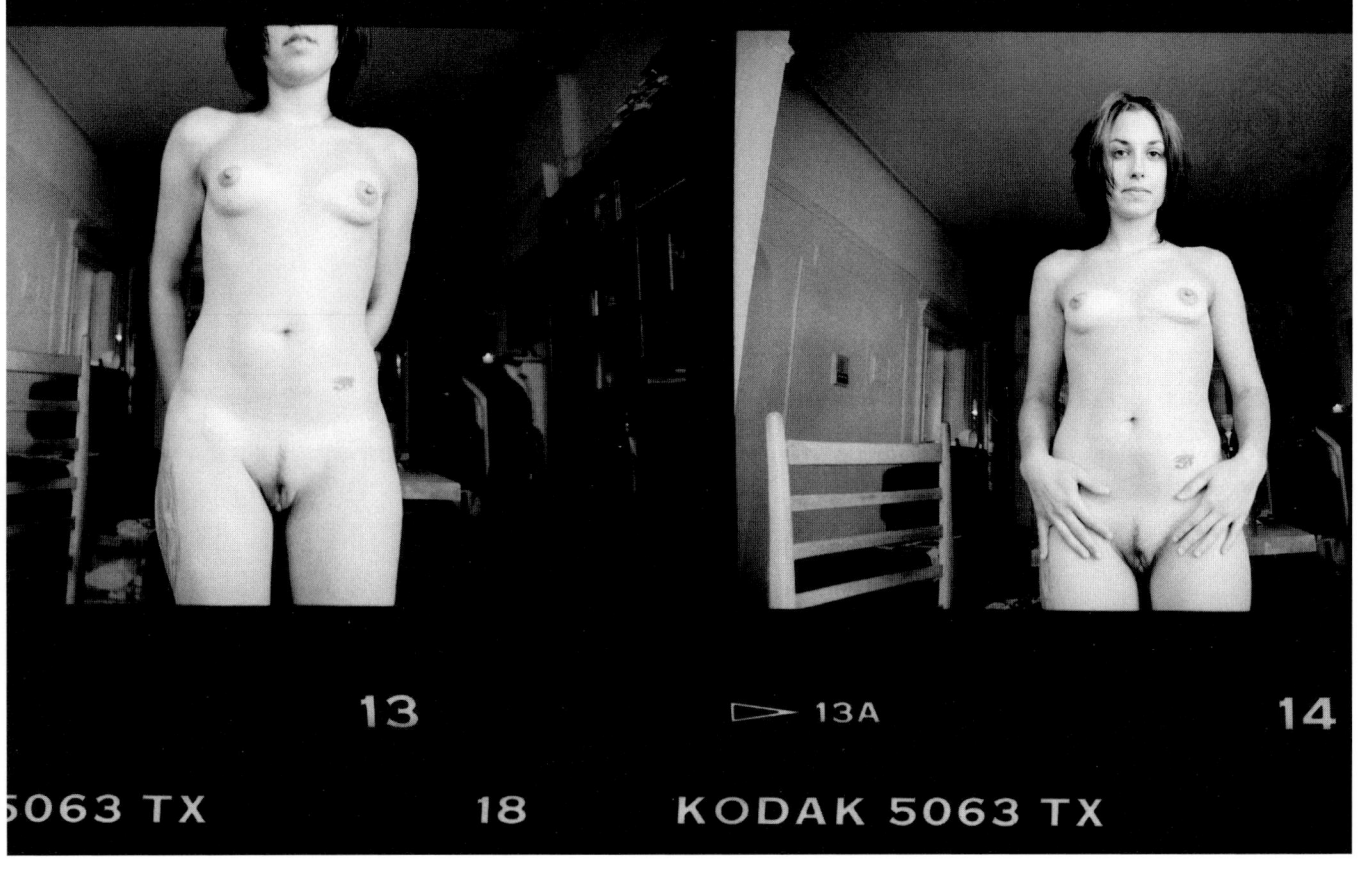

13 ▷ 13A 14

5063 TX 18 KODAK 5063 TX

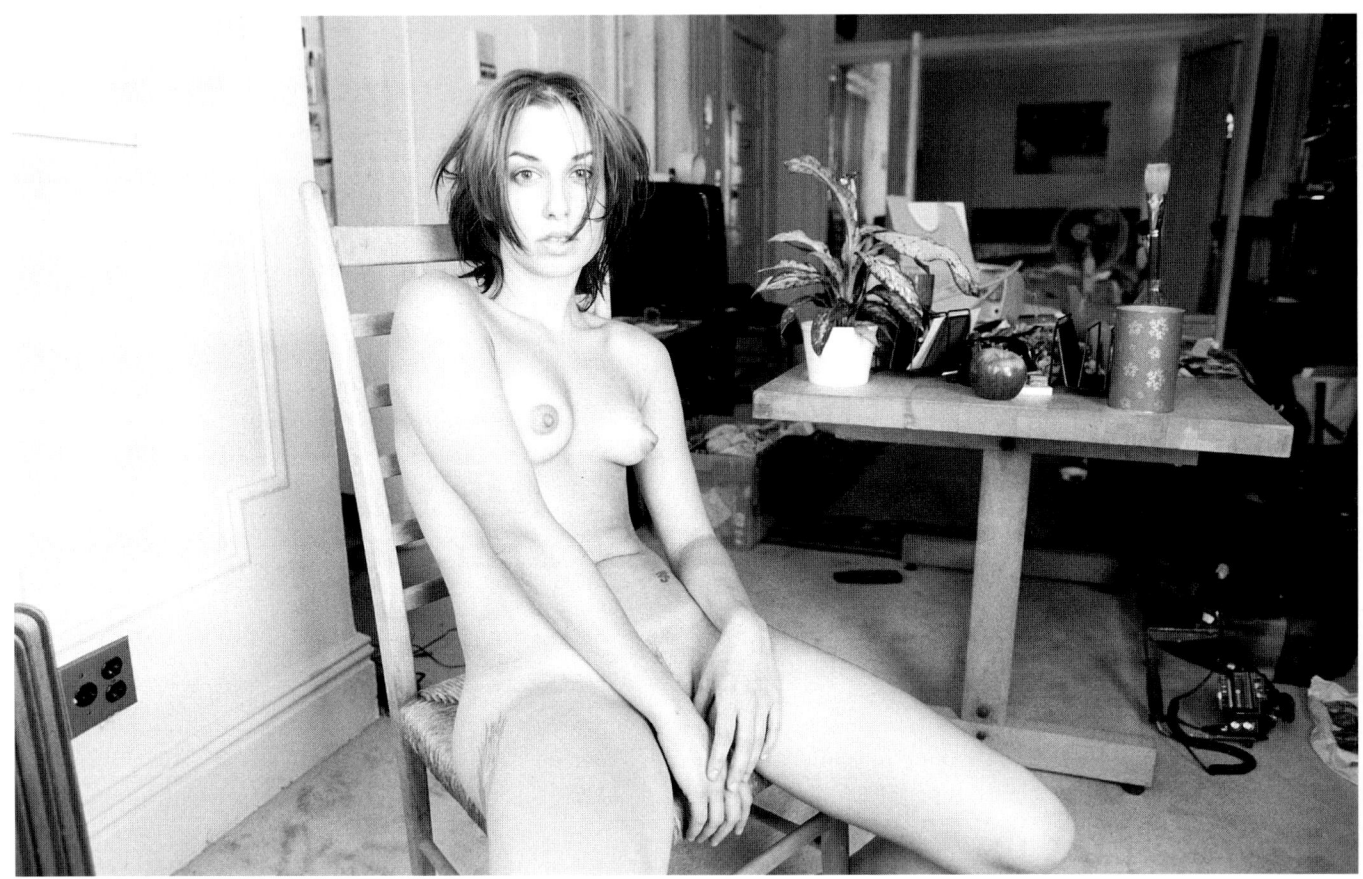

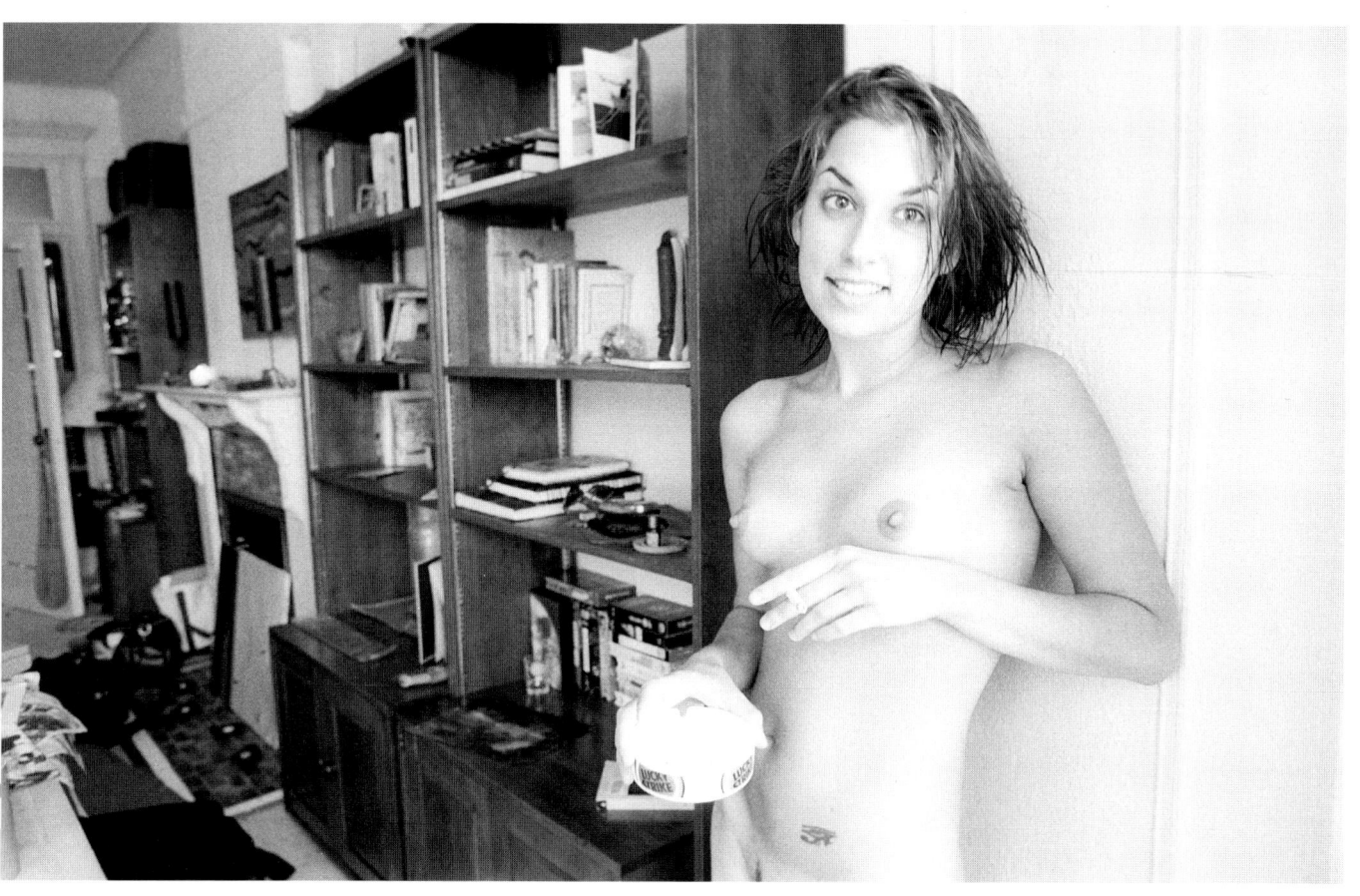

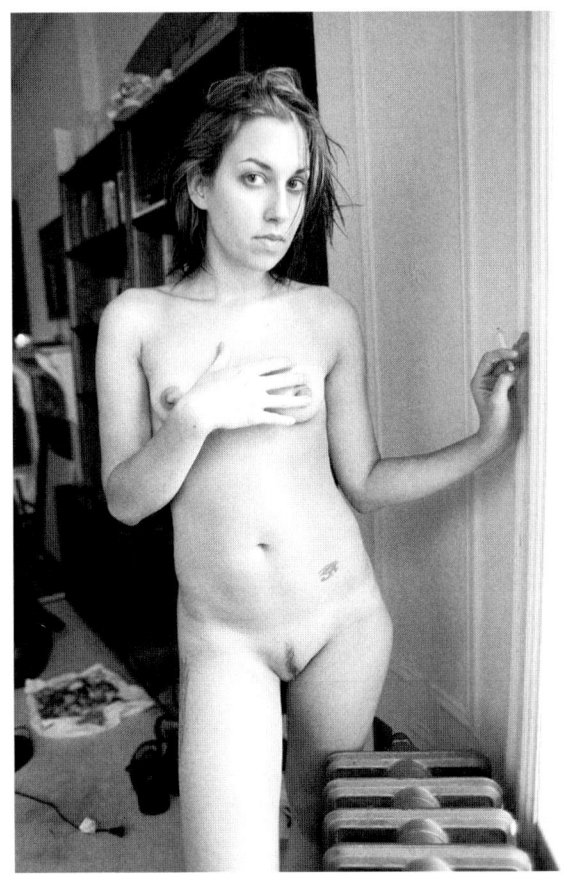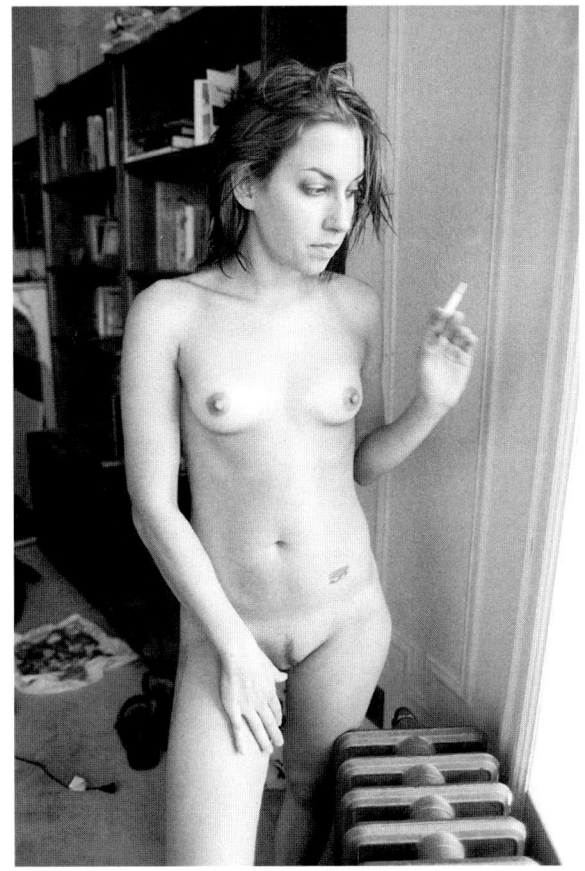

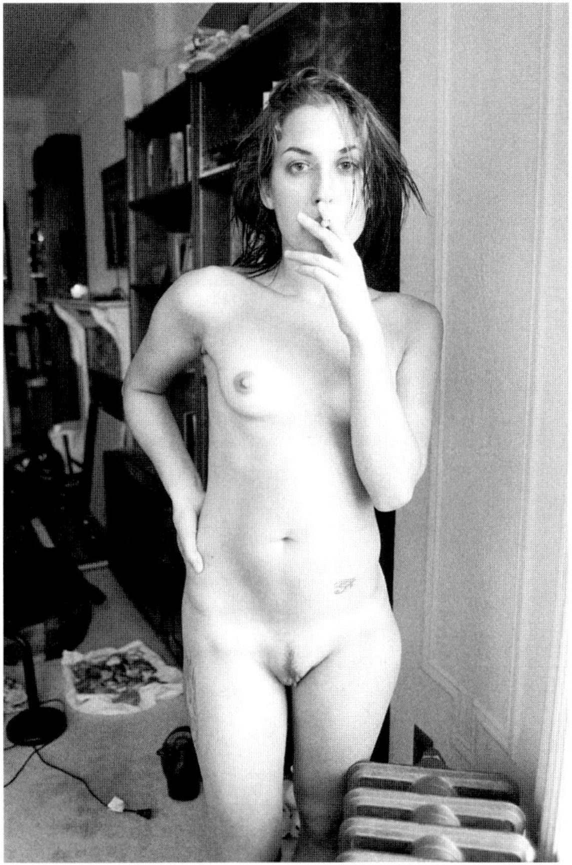

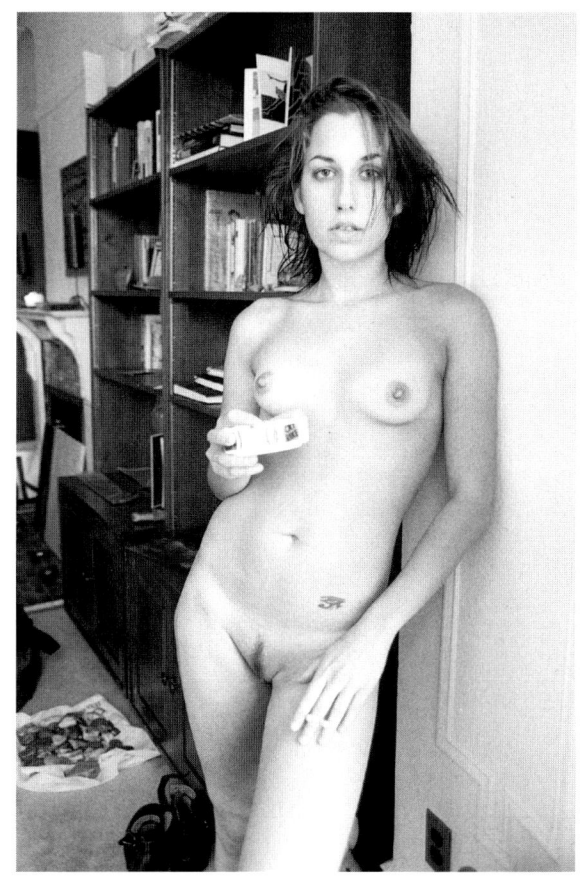

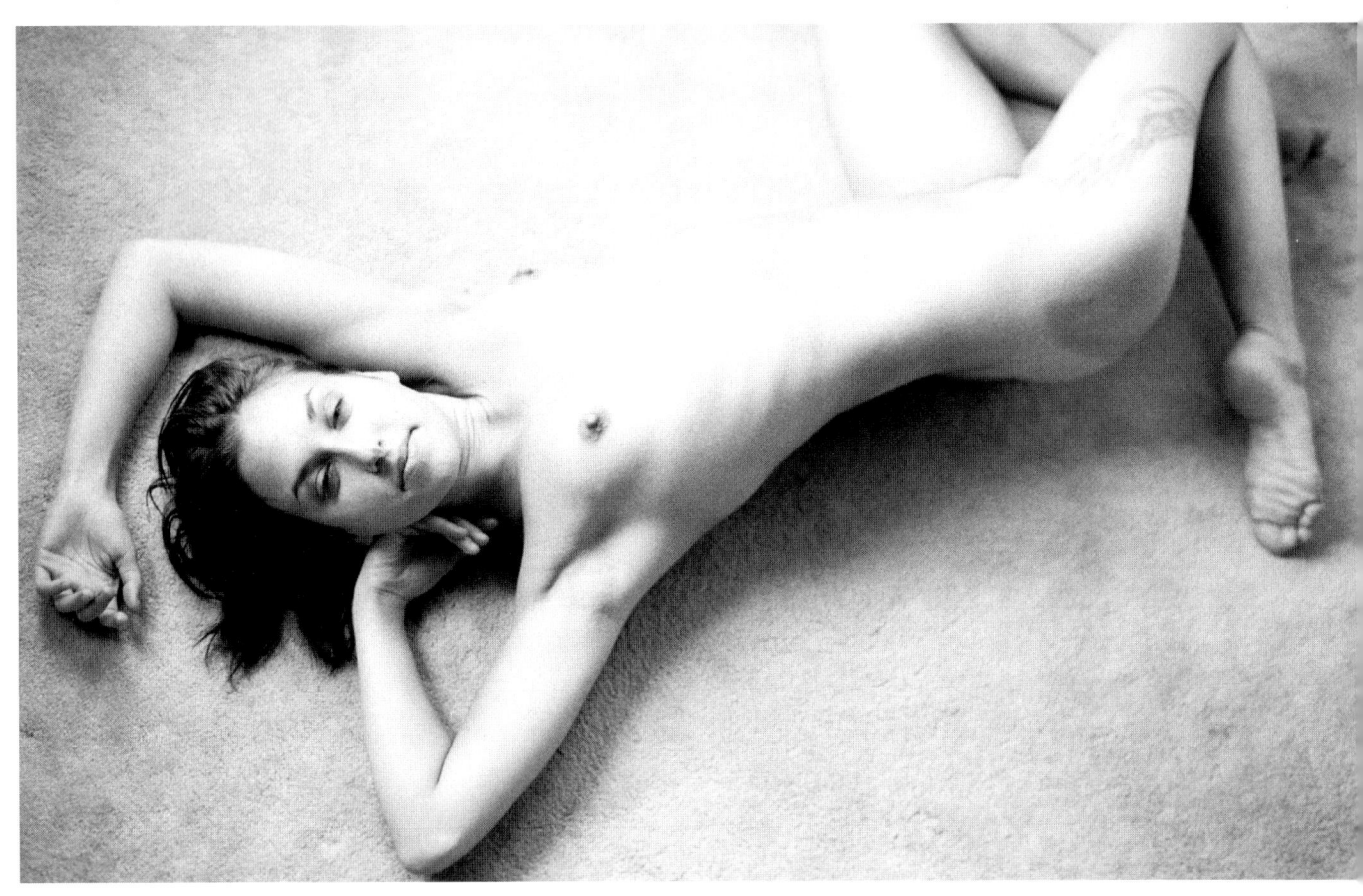

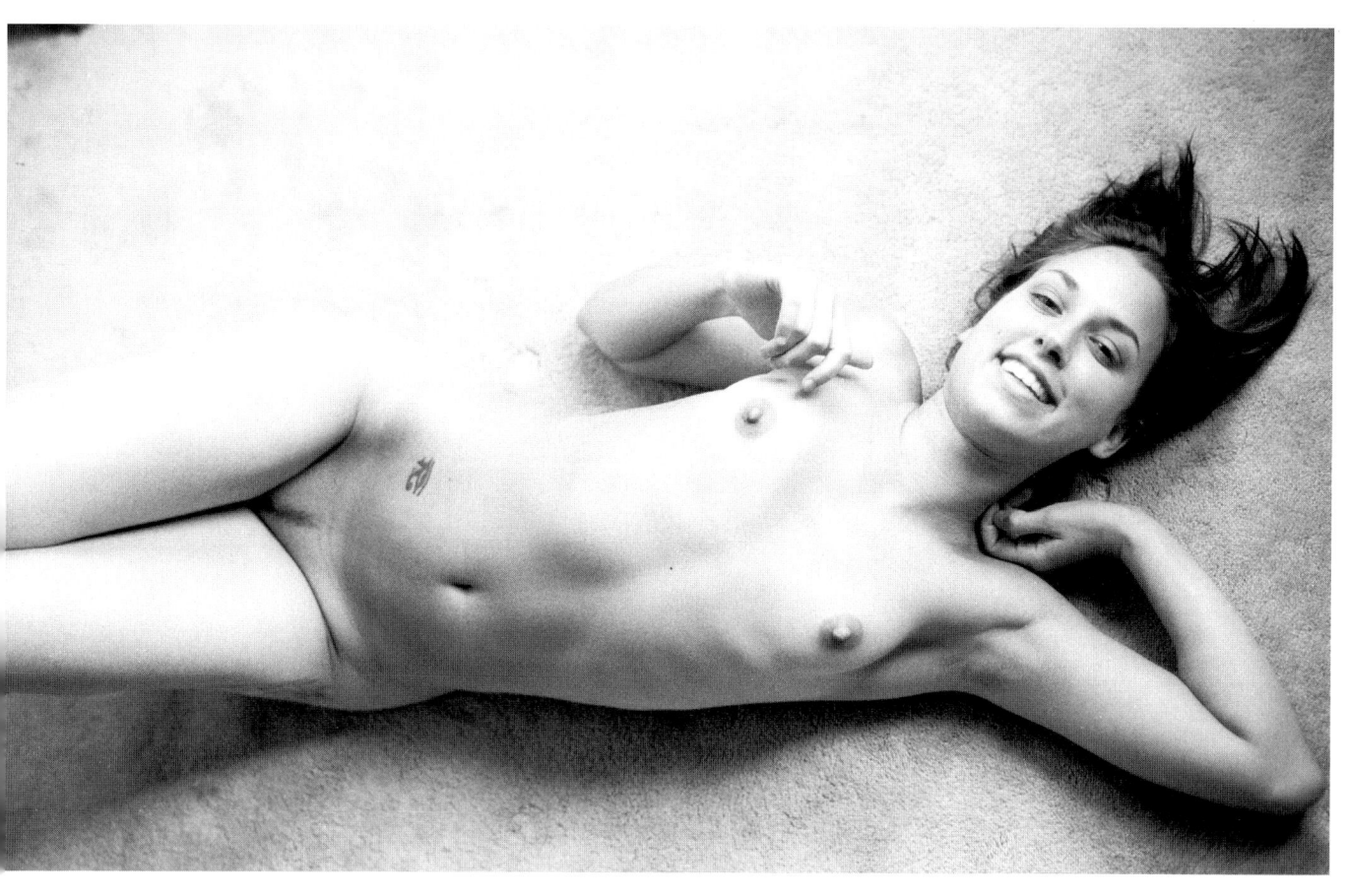

April · I met April at a media company where she worked in midtown Manhattan. She's originally from Indiana. I photographed her in a bright corner of a photographer's studio in the West Village. We drank 3 wine coolers and photographed each other. April has great legs and a better vocabulary.

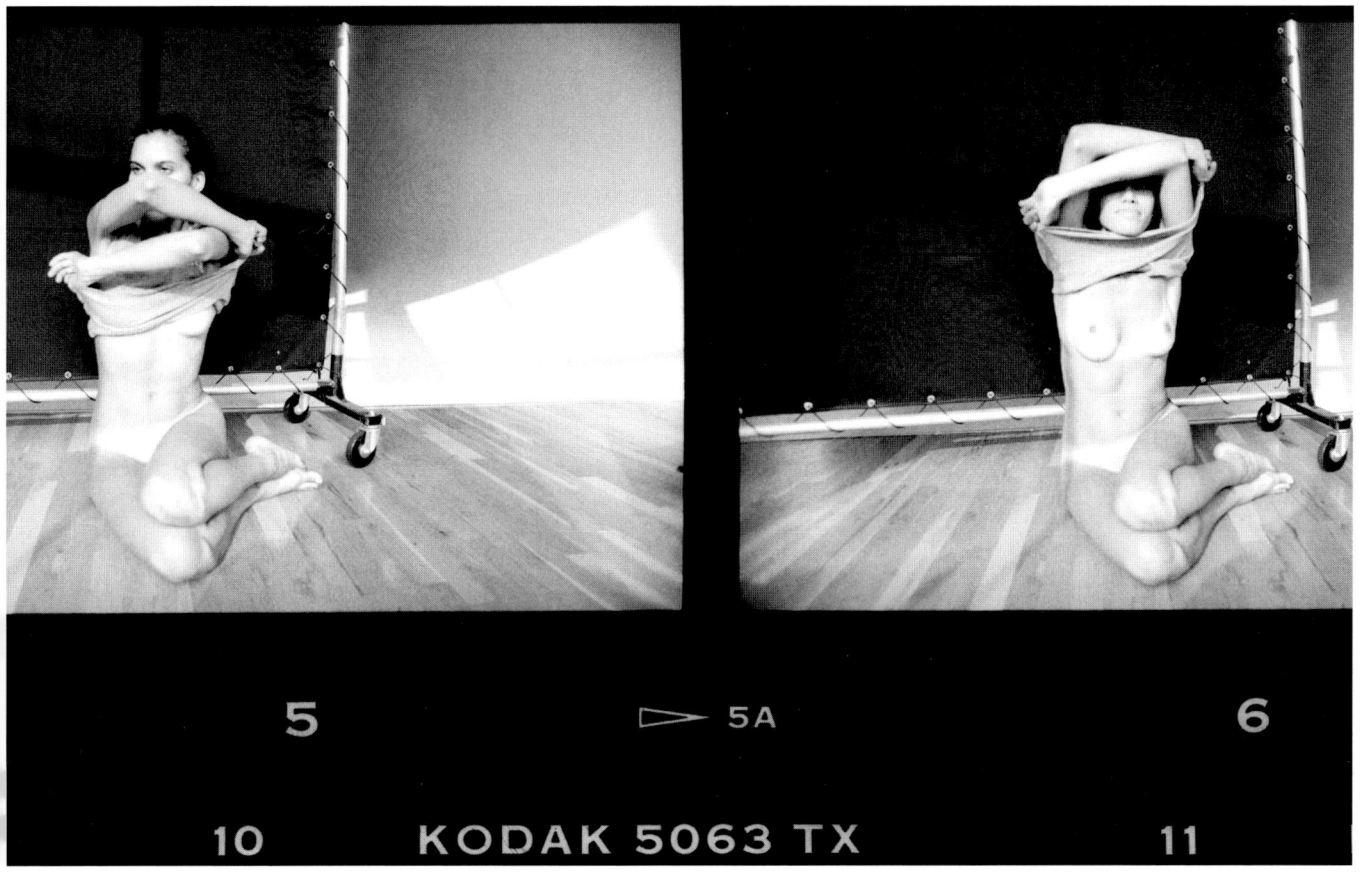

5   ▷ 5A   6

10   KODAK 5063 TX   11

37

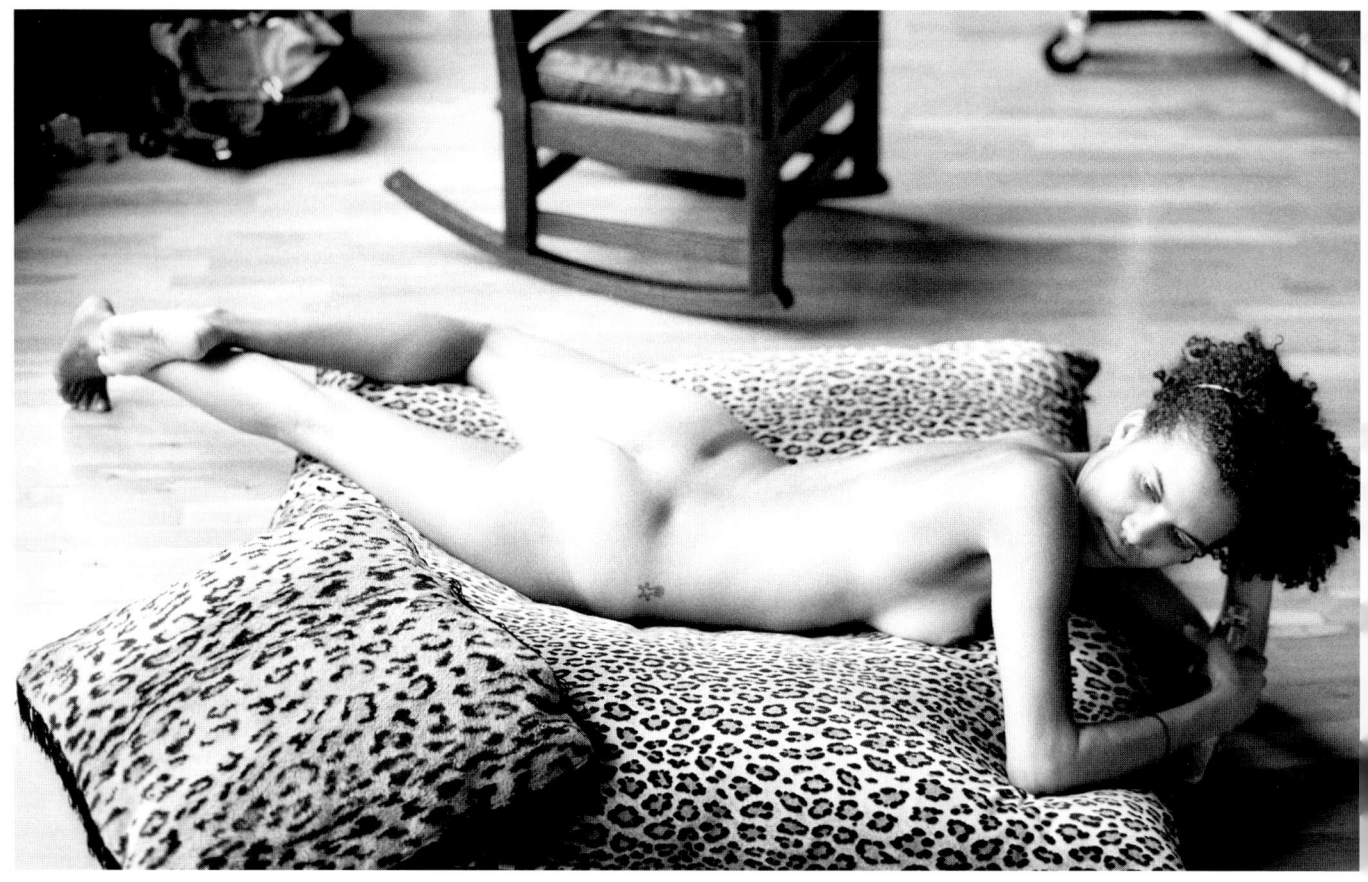

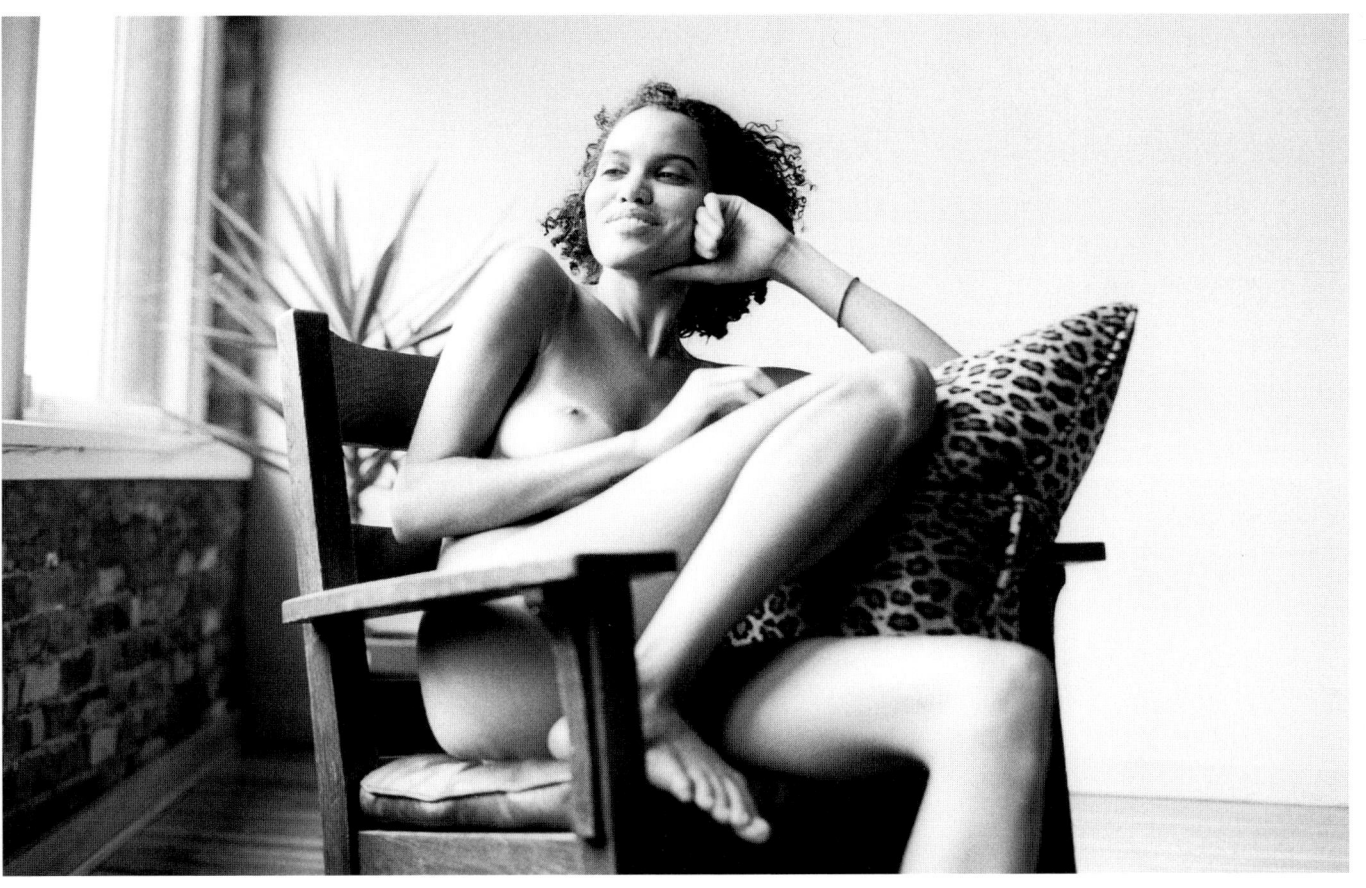

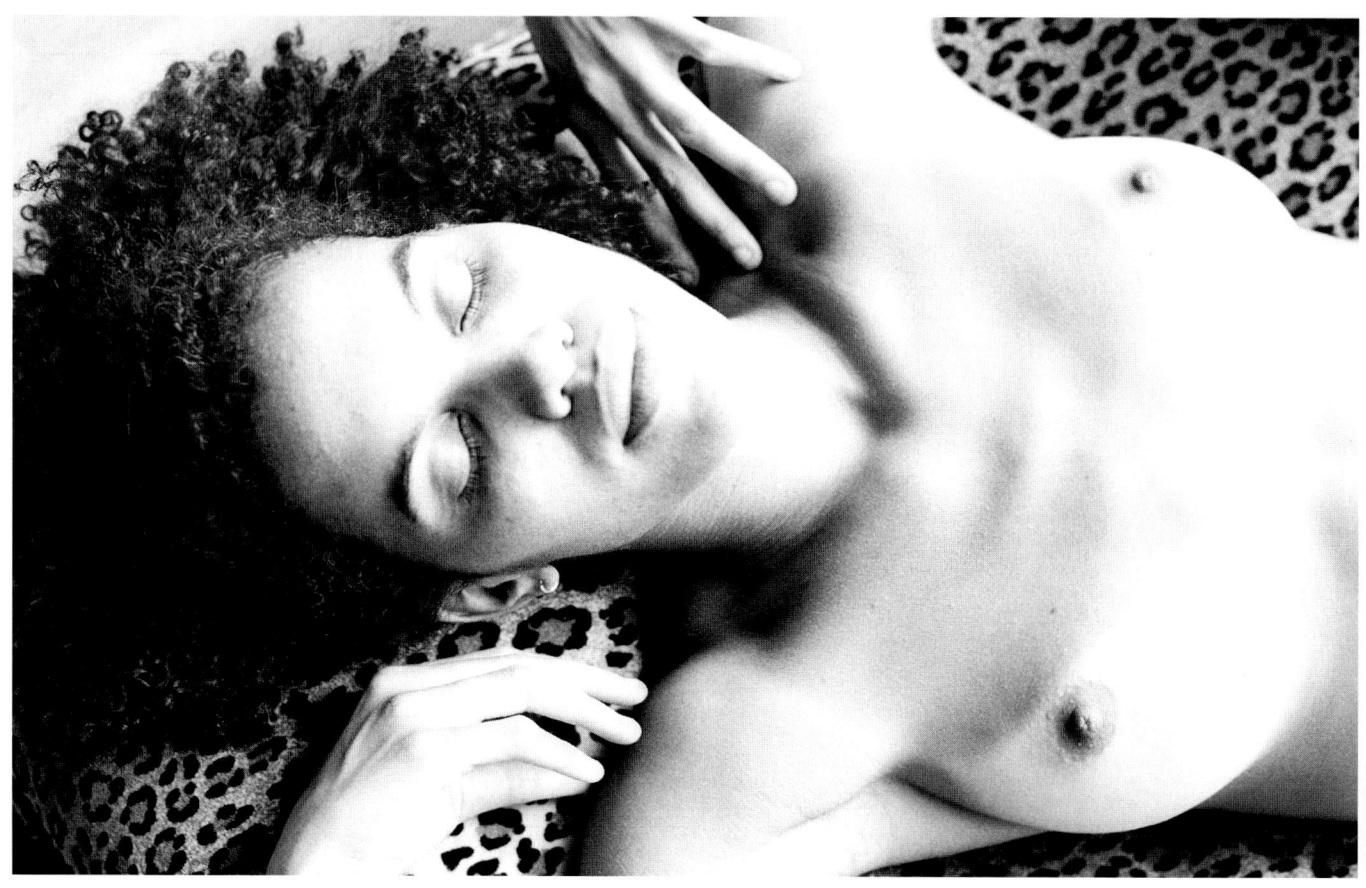

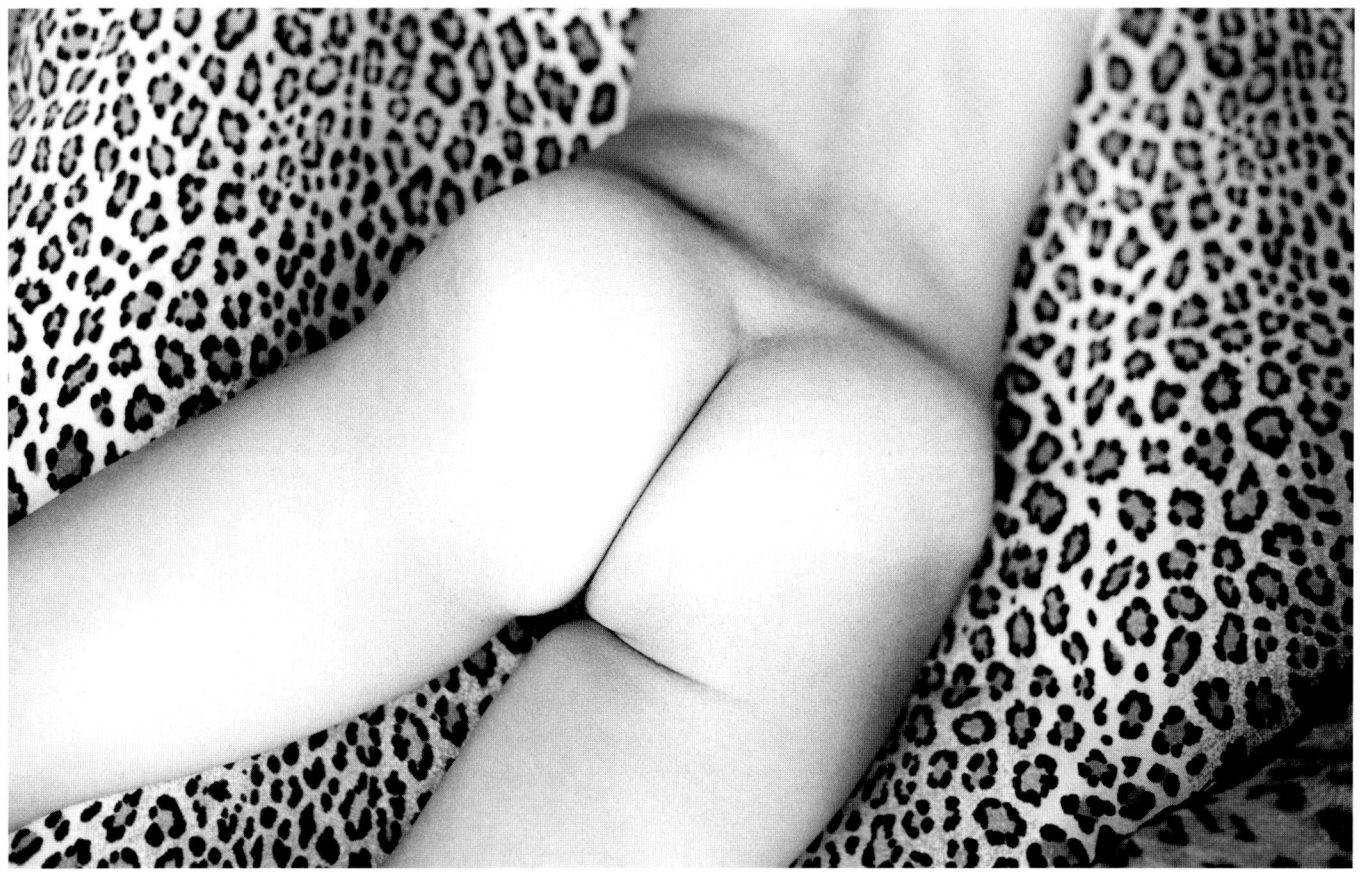

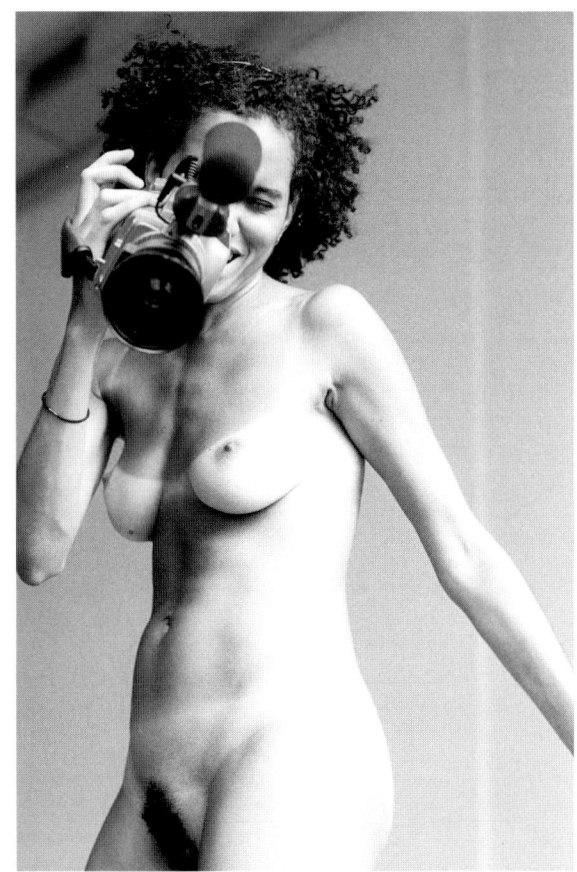

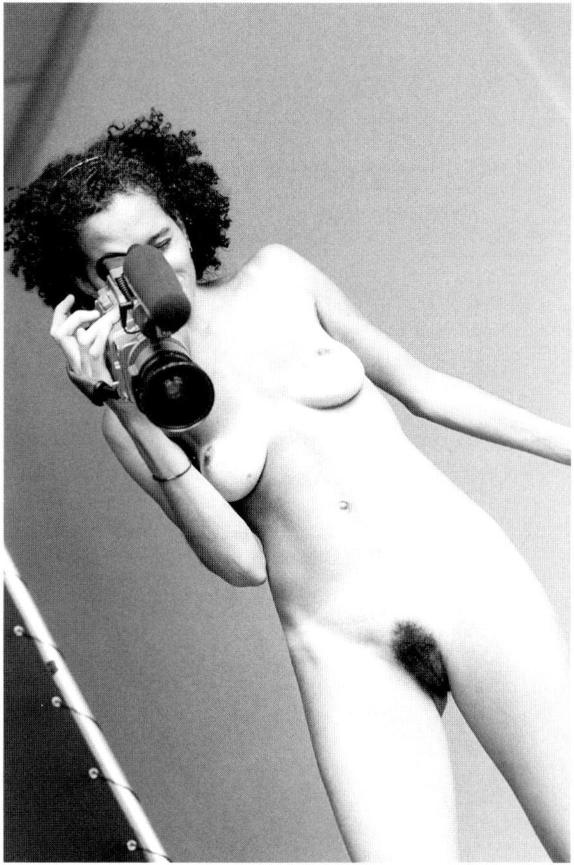

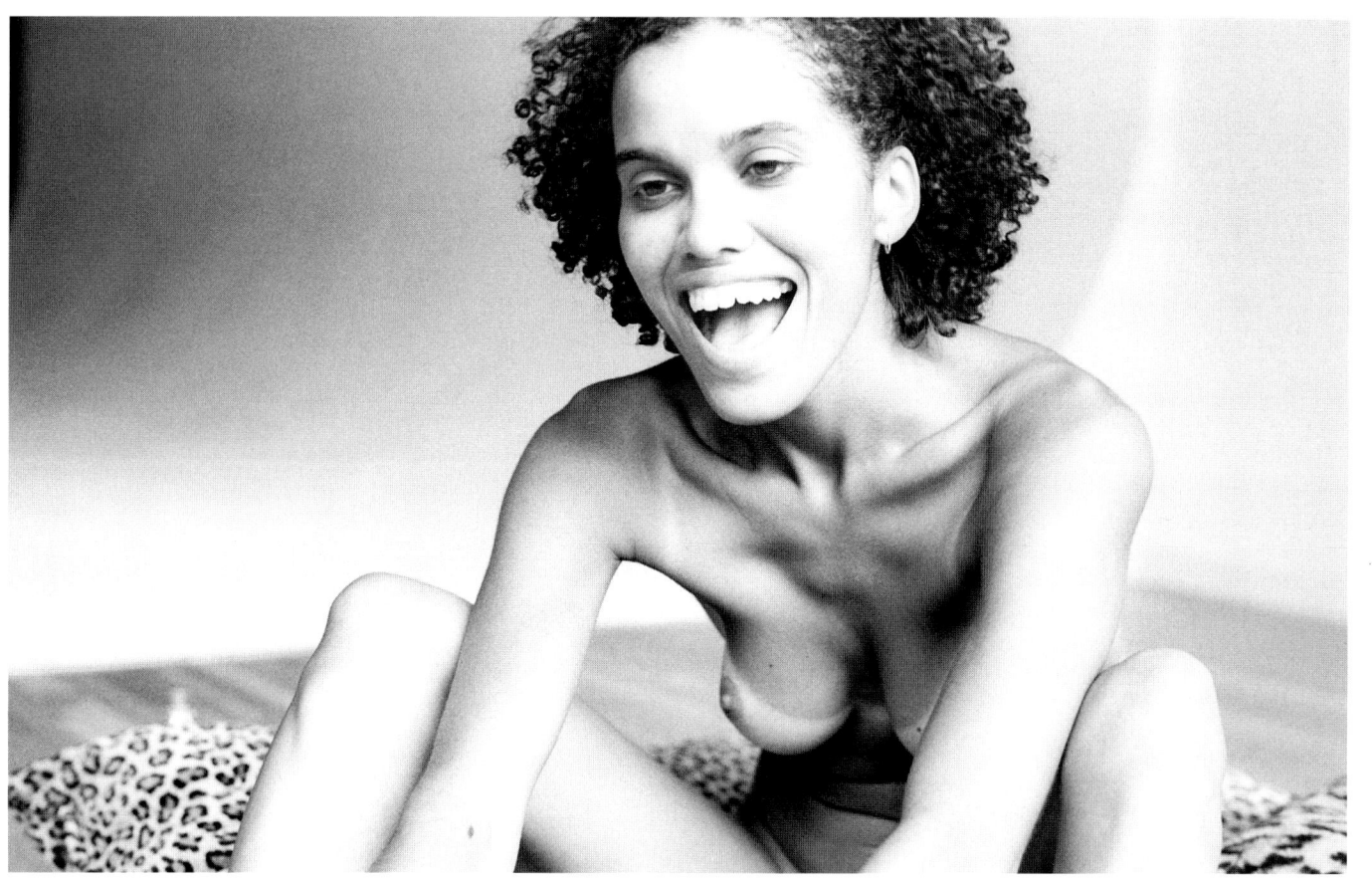

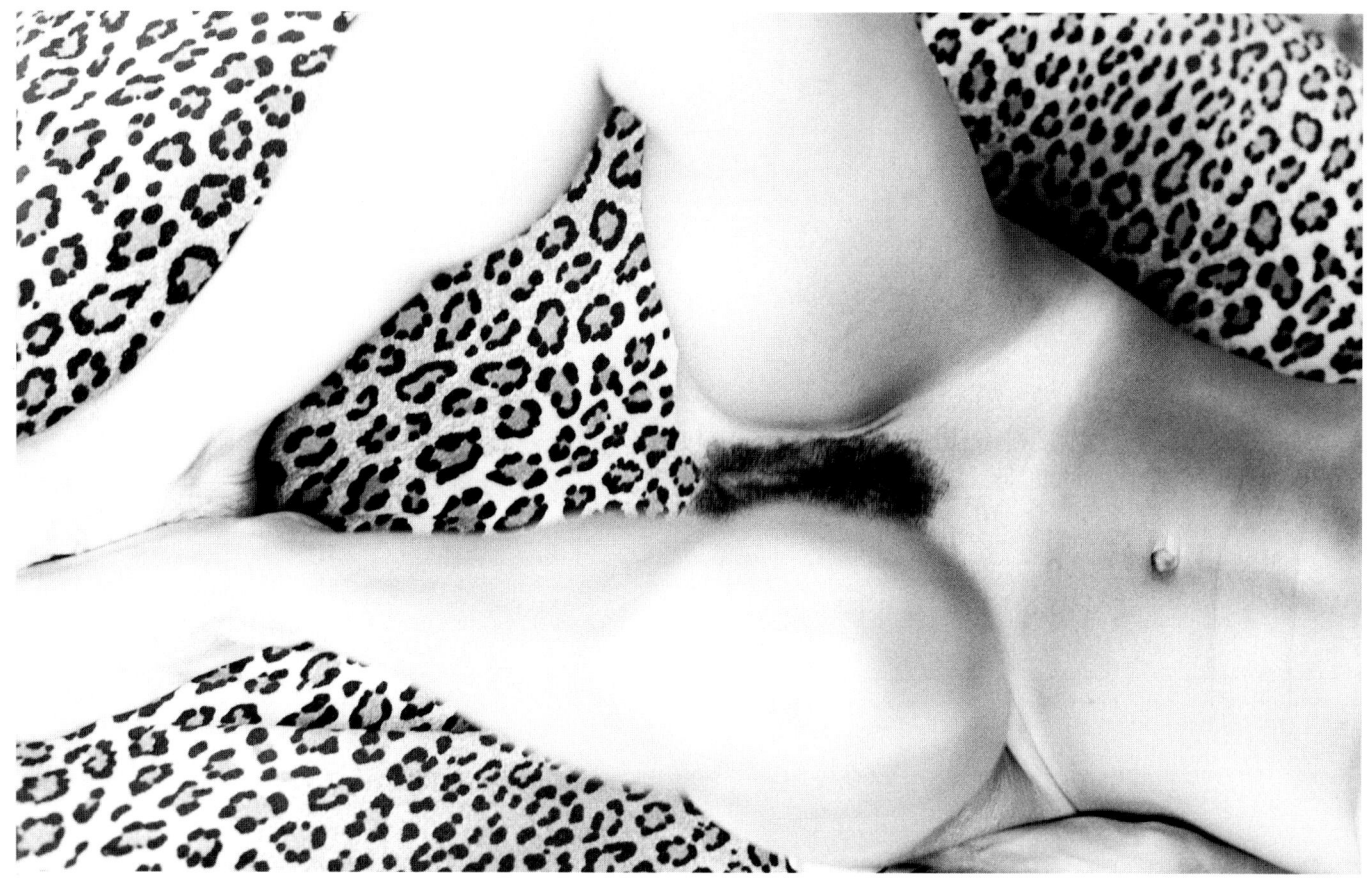

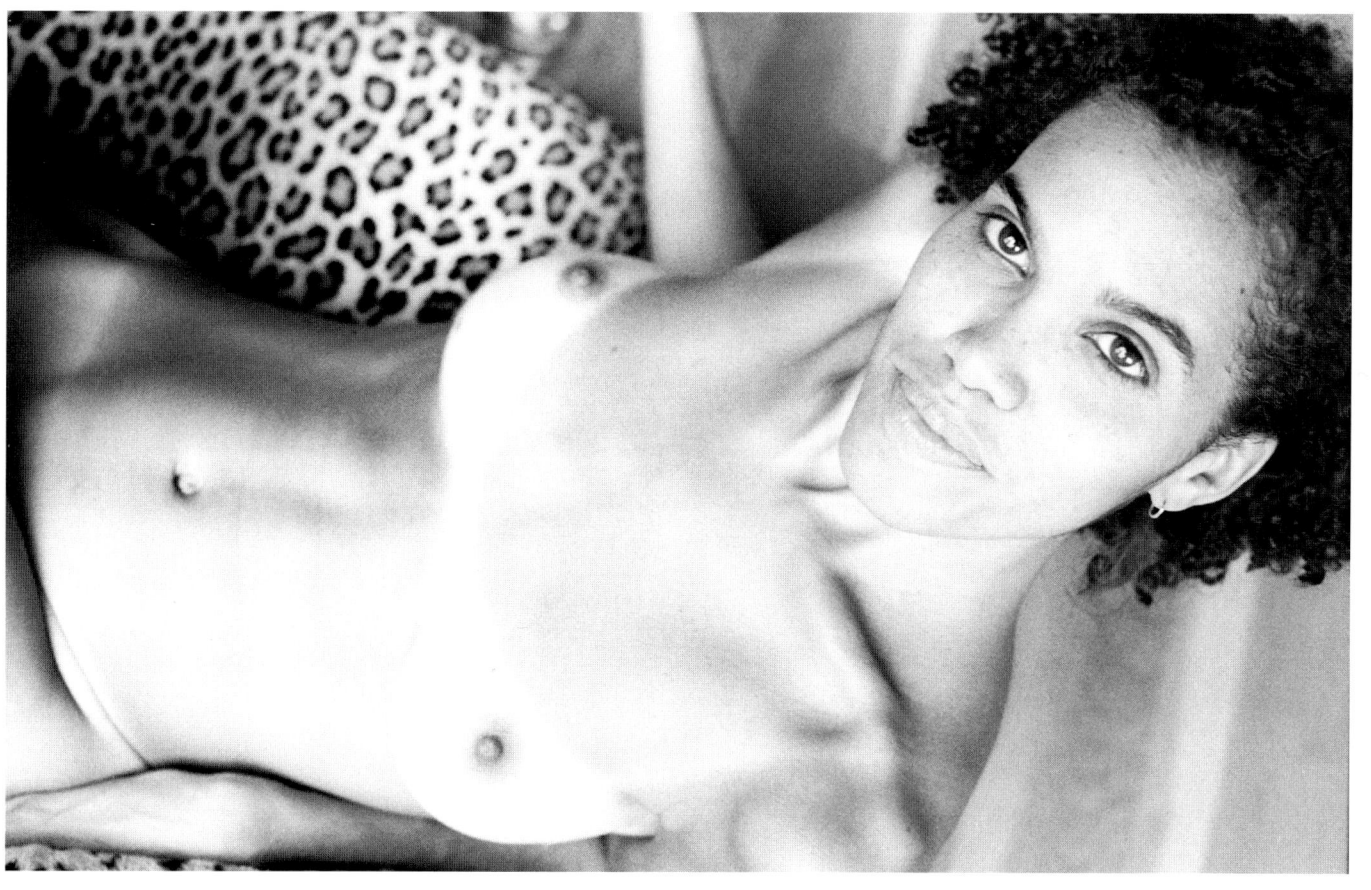

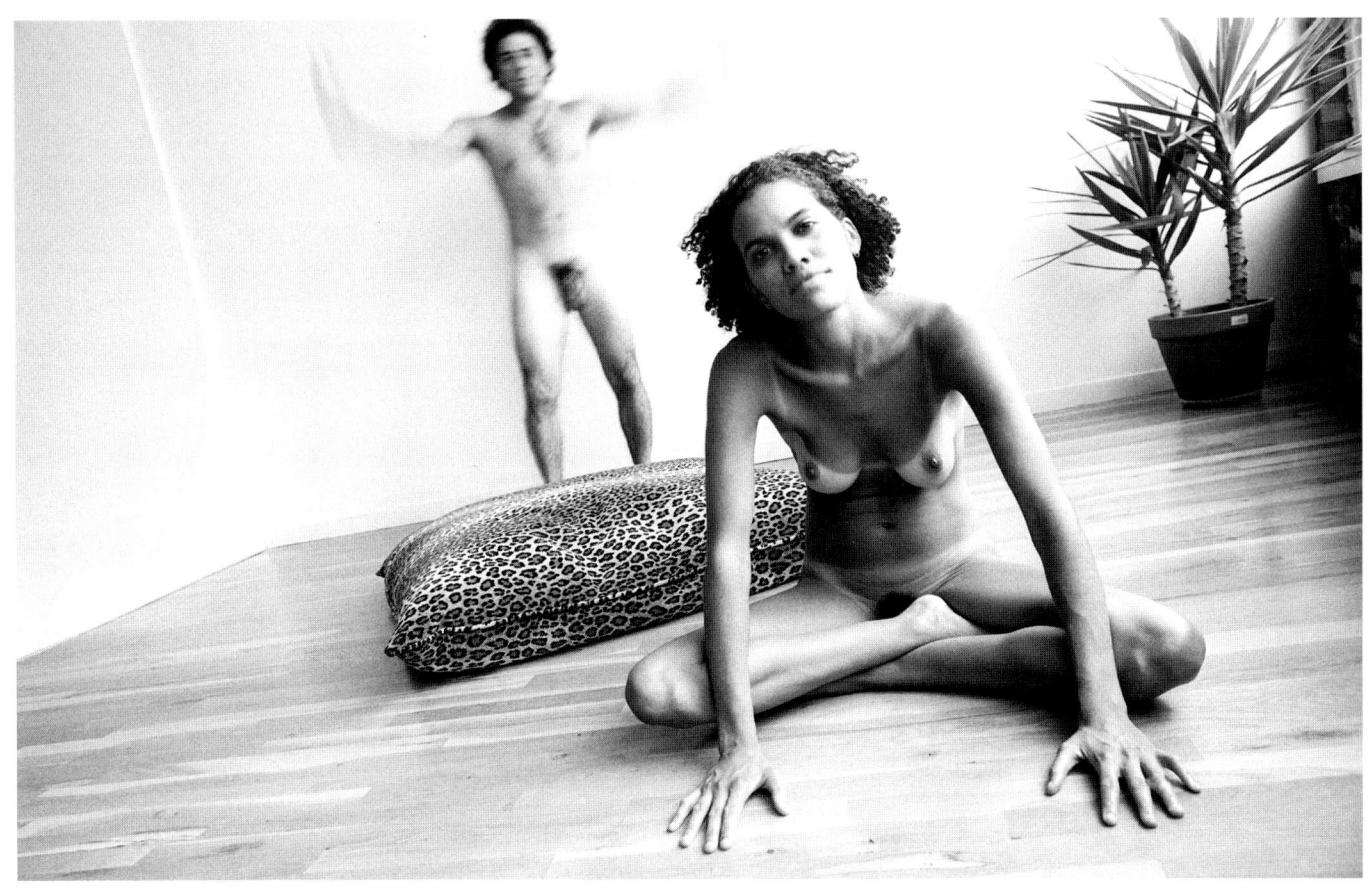

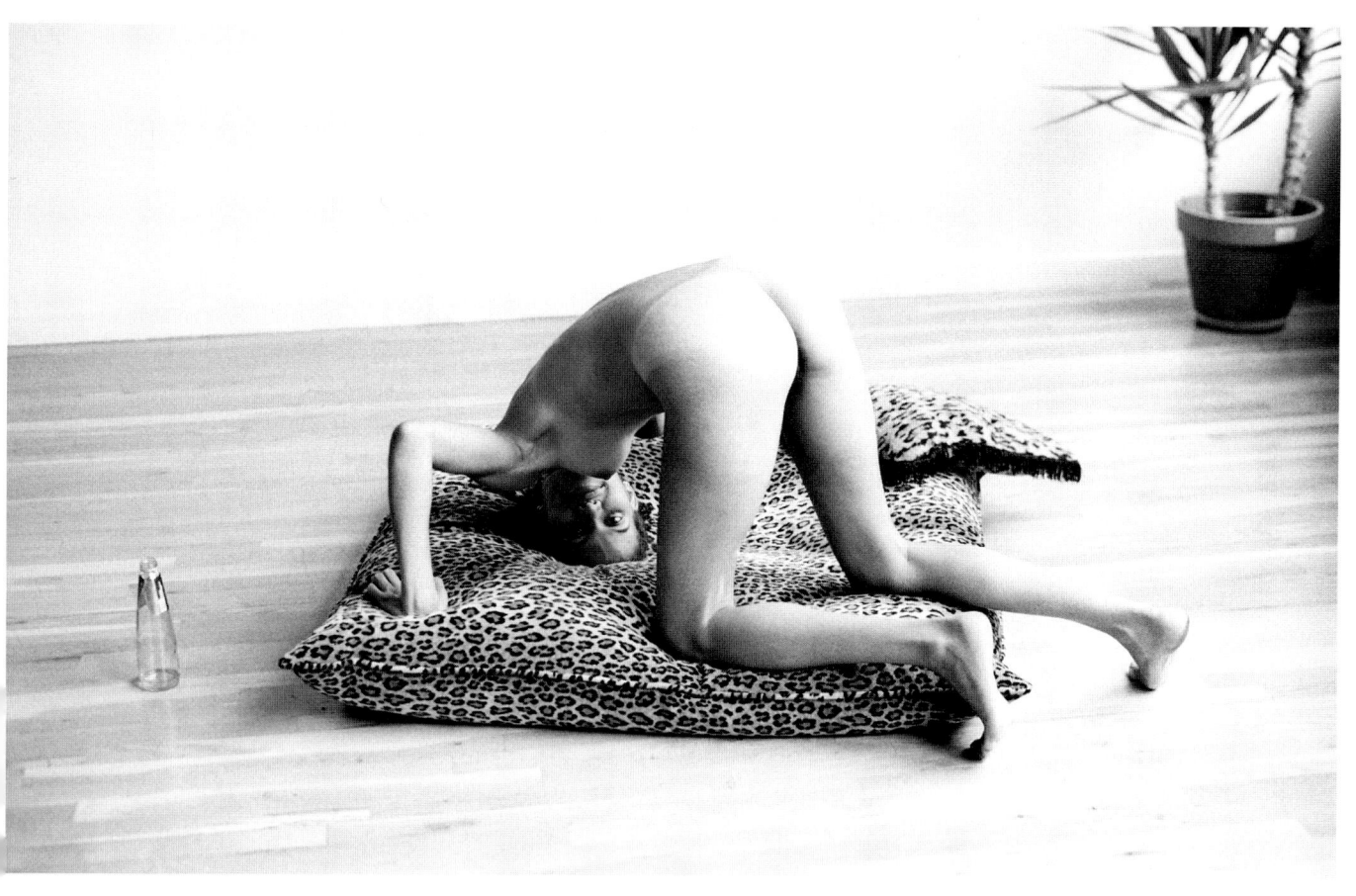

Bex · I met Bex in a small cabaret theatre in Manhattan. She reminded me of a young Bette Midler. Bex is an actress, comedian, dancer, writer, director and singer. I photographed her in a friend's high-rise apartment near central park. We drank a little and smoked a little, and went out on the balcony. I took lots of pictures of Bex singing.

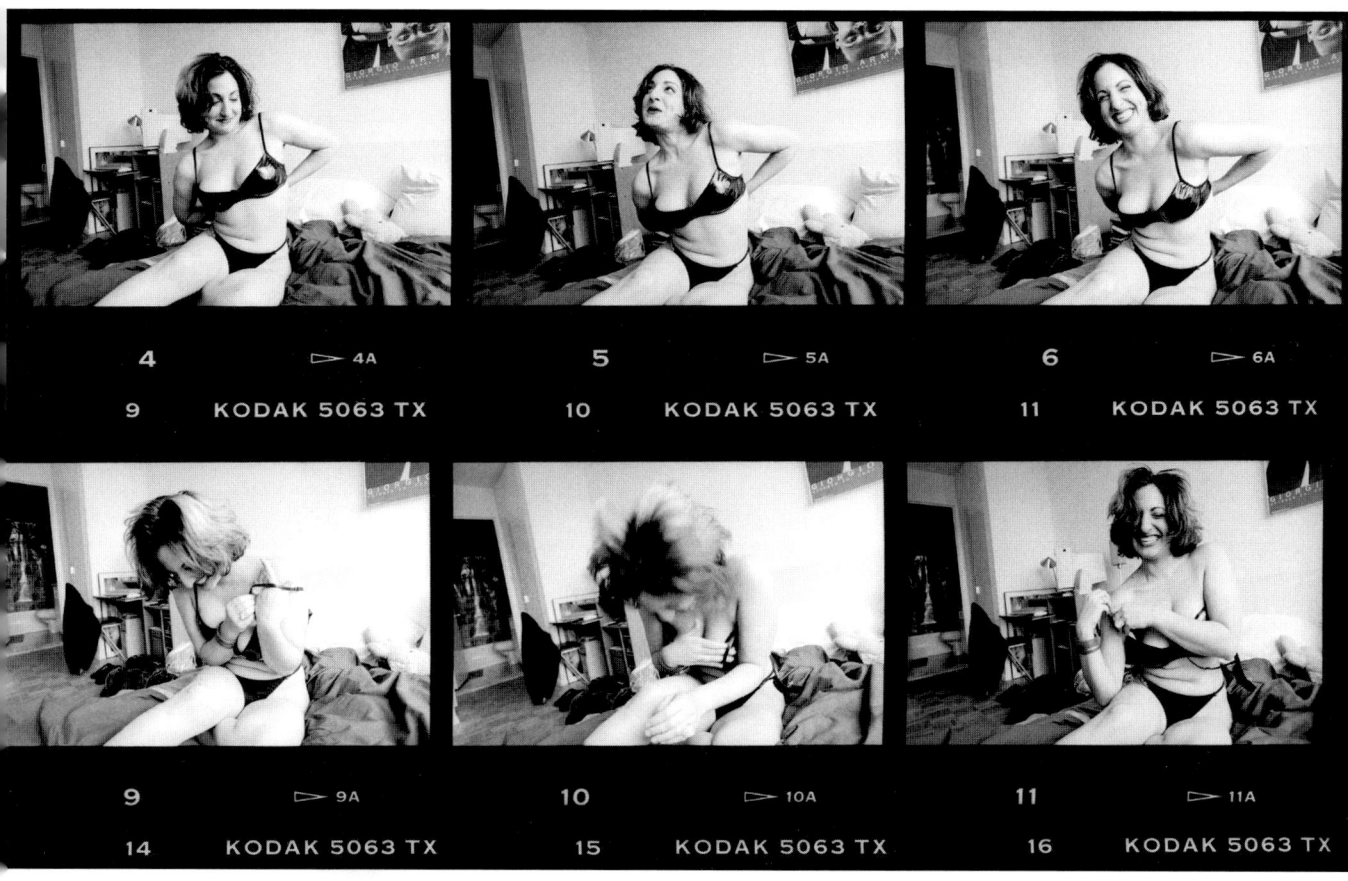

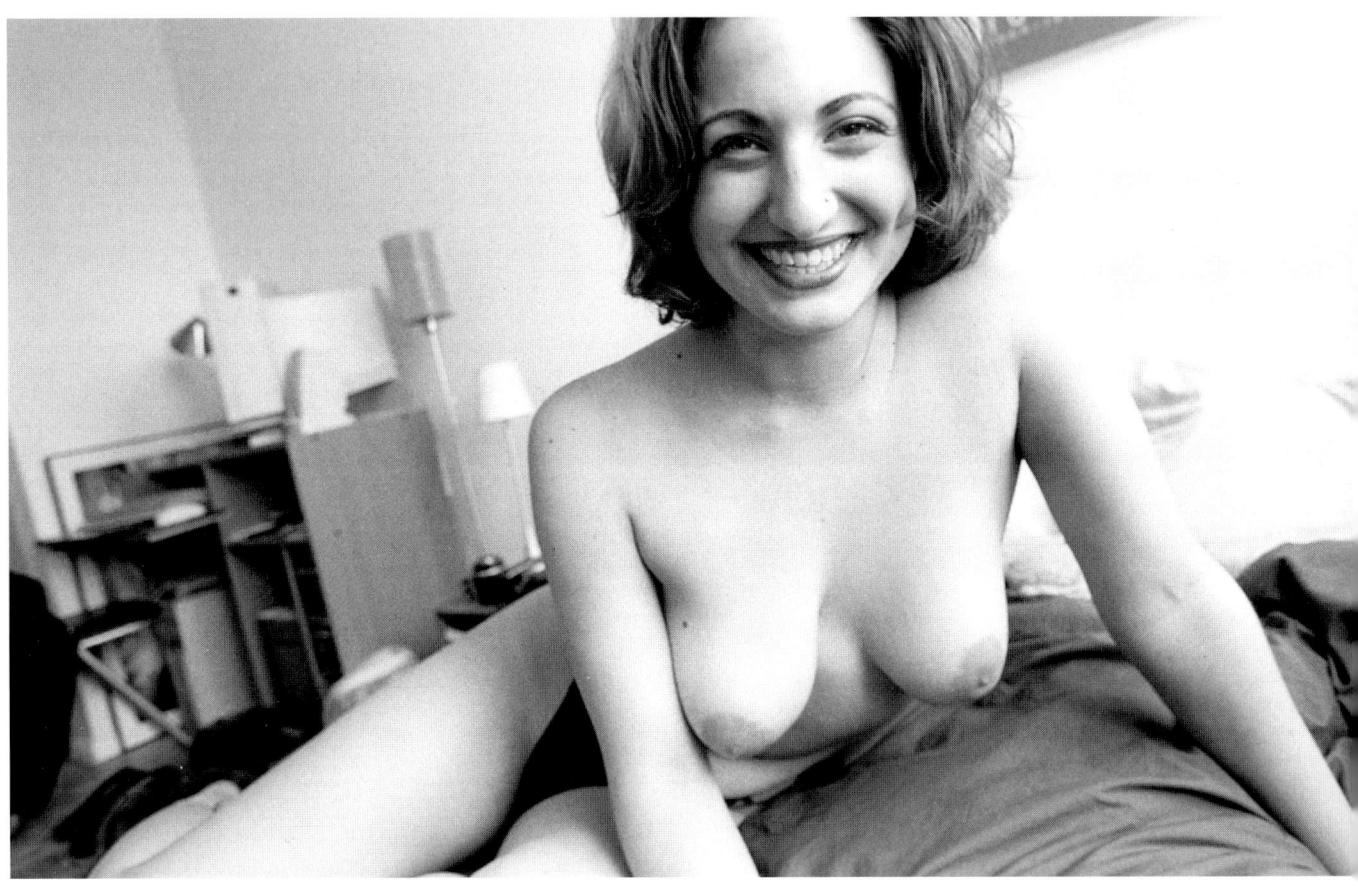

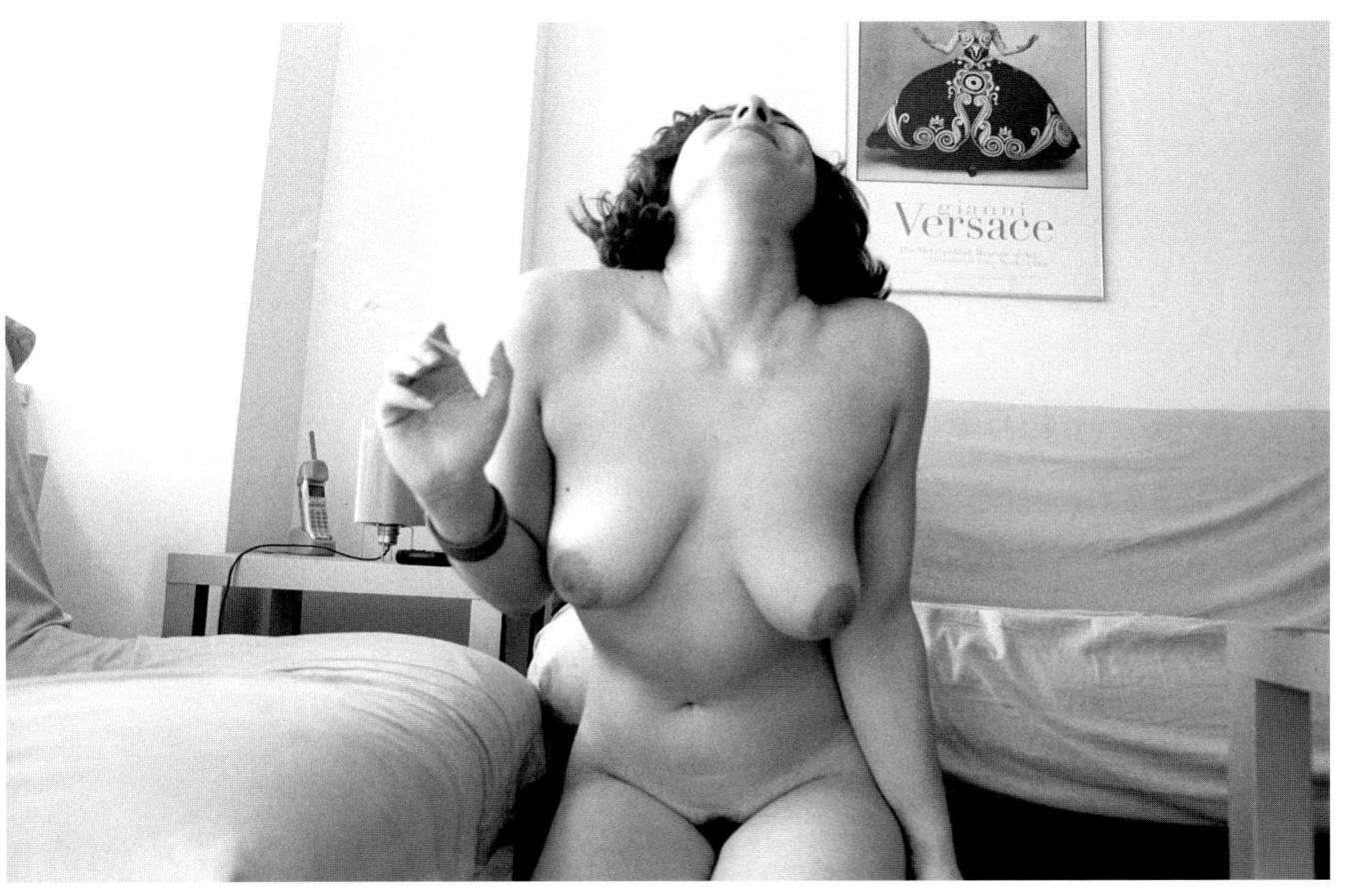

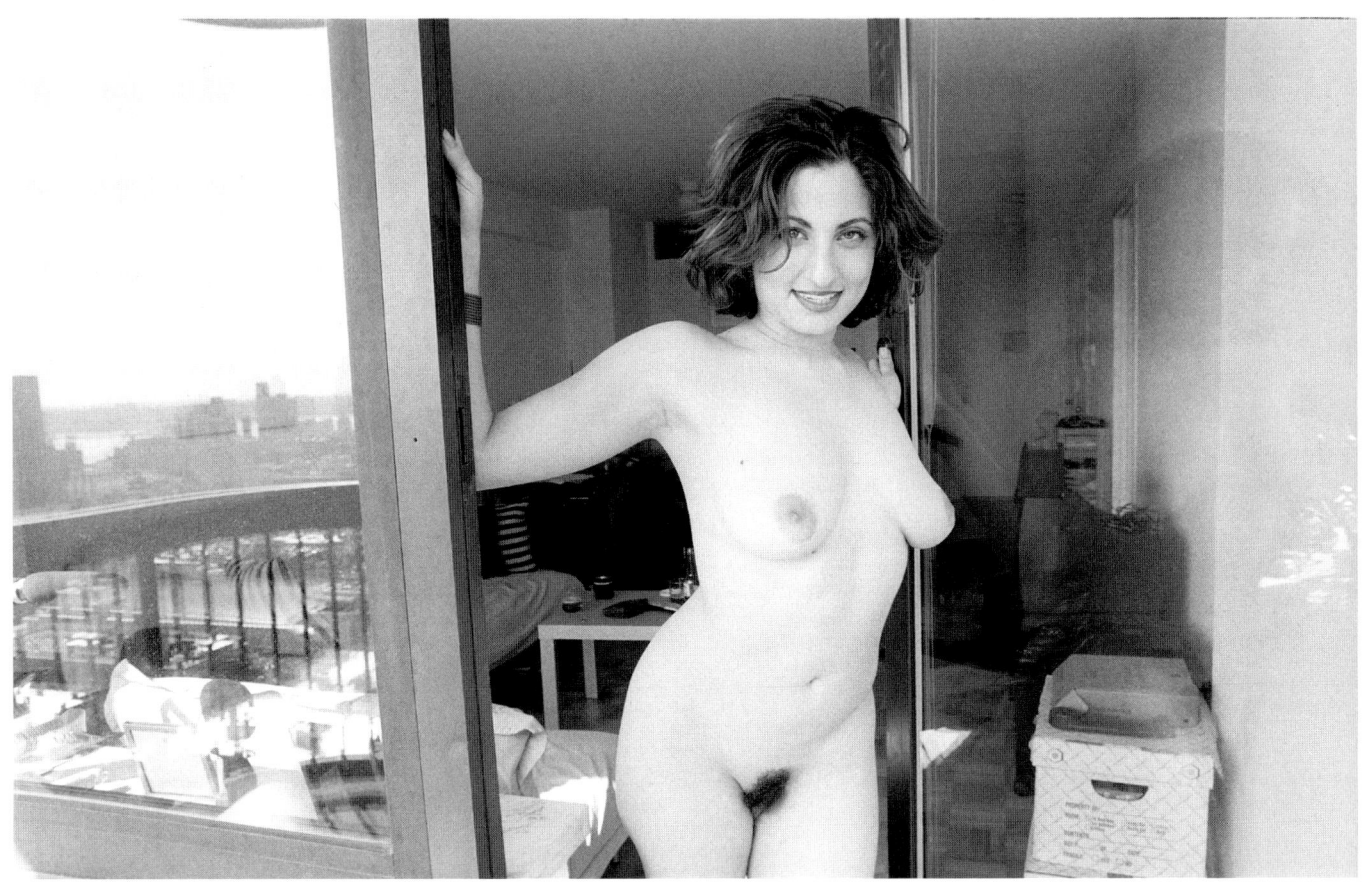

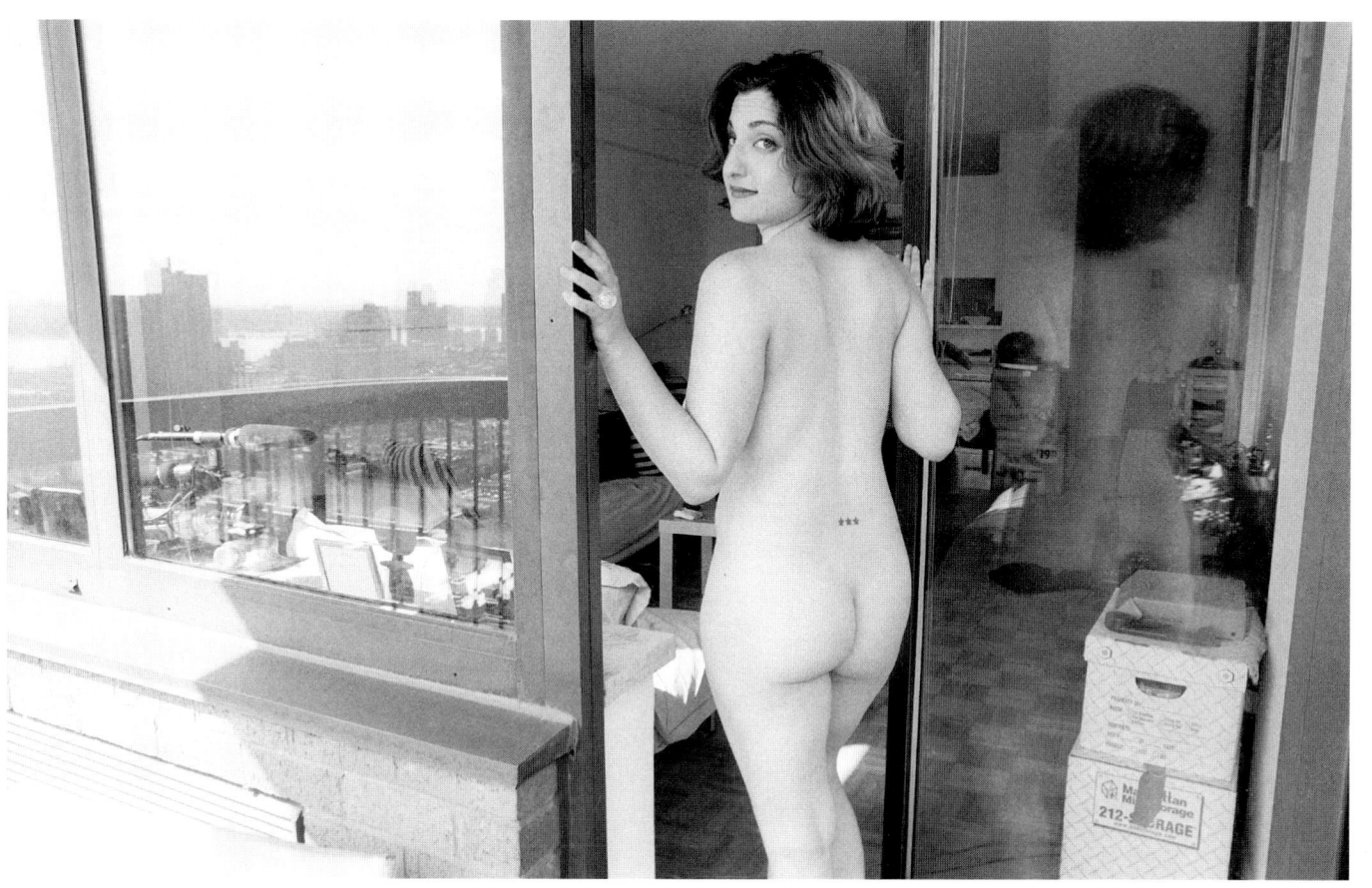

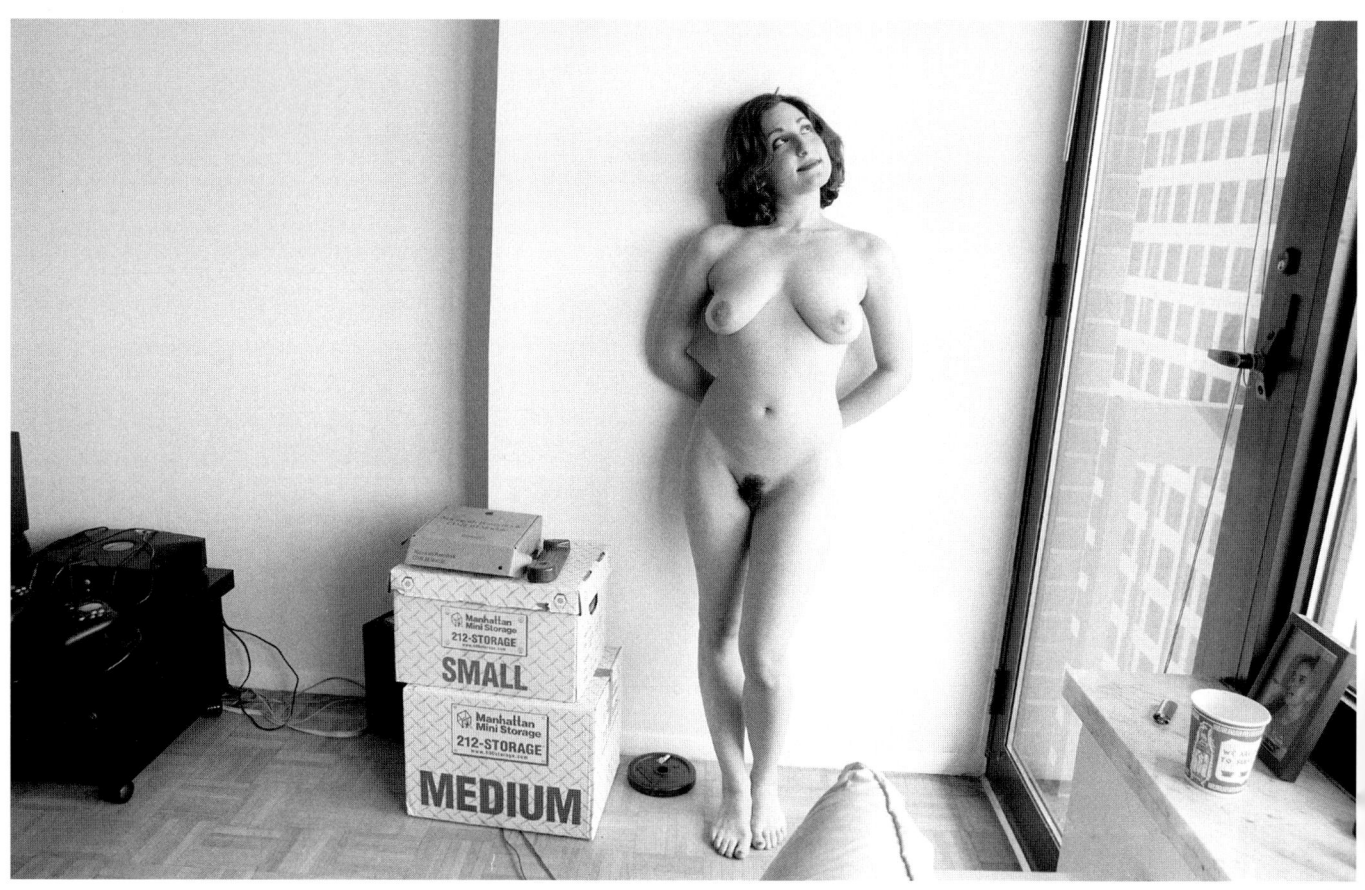

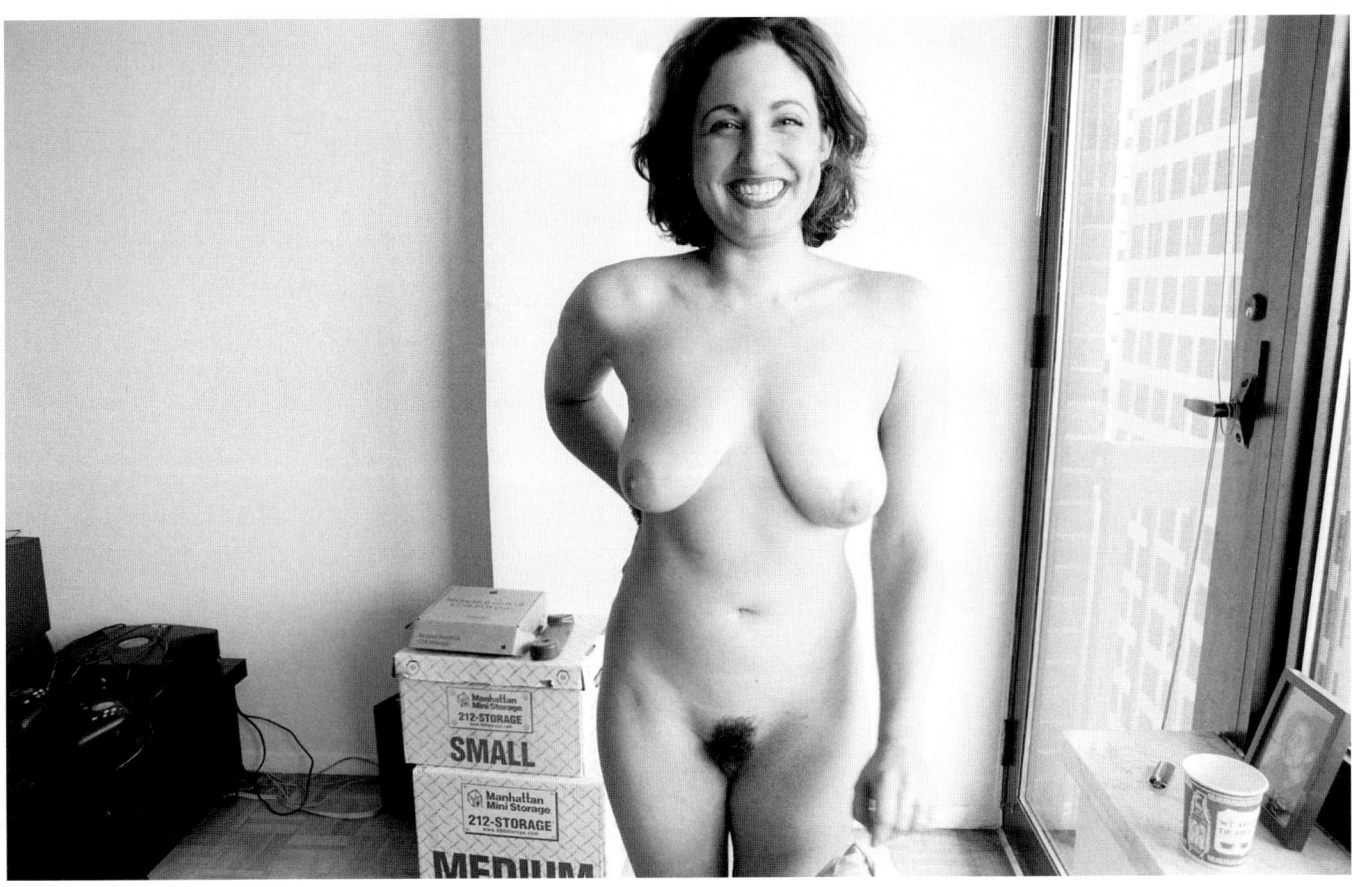

Cara · Cara was a friend of Julia's. I met her at an internet company I used to work for. I photographed her in her East Harlem apt. Cara was a bit more serious than most models, but had an angelic face. For the last roll, she climbed into bed and almost went to sleep.

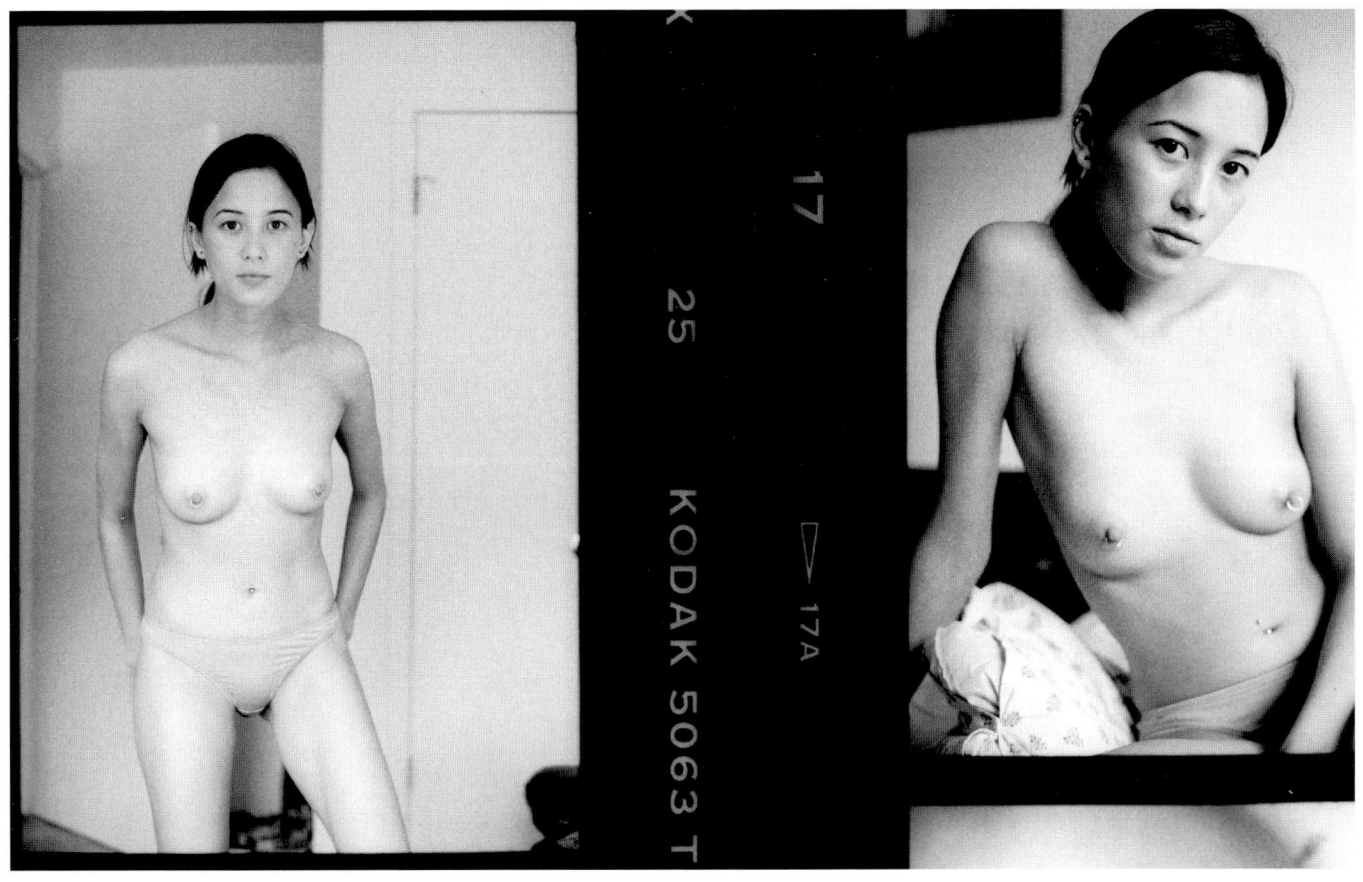

17
25
KODAK 5063 T

17A

57

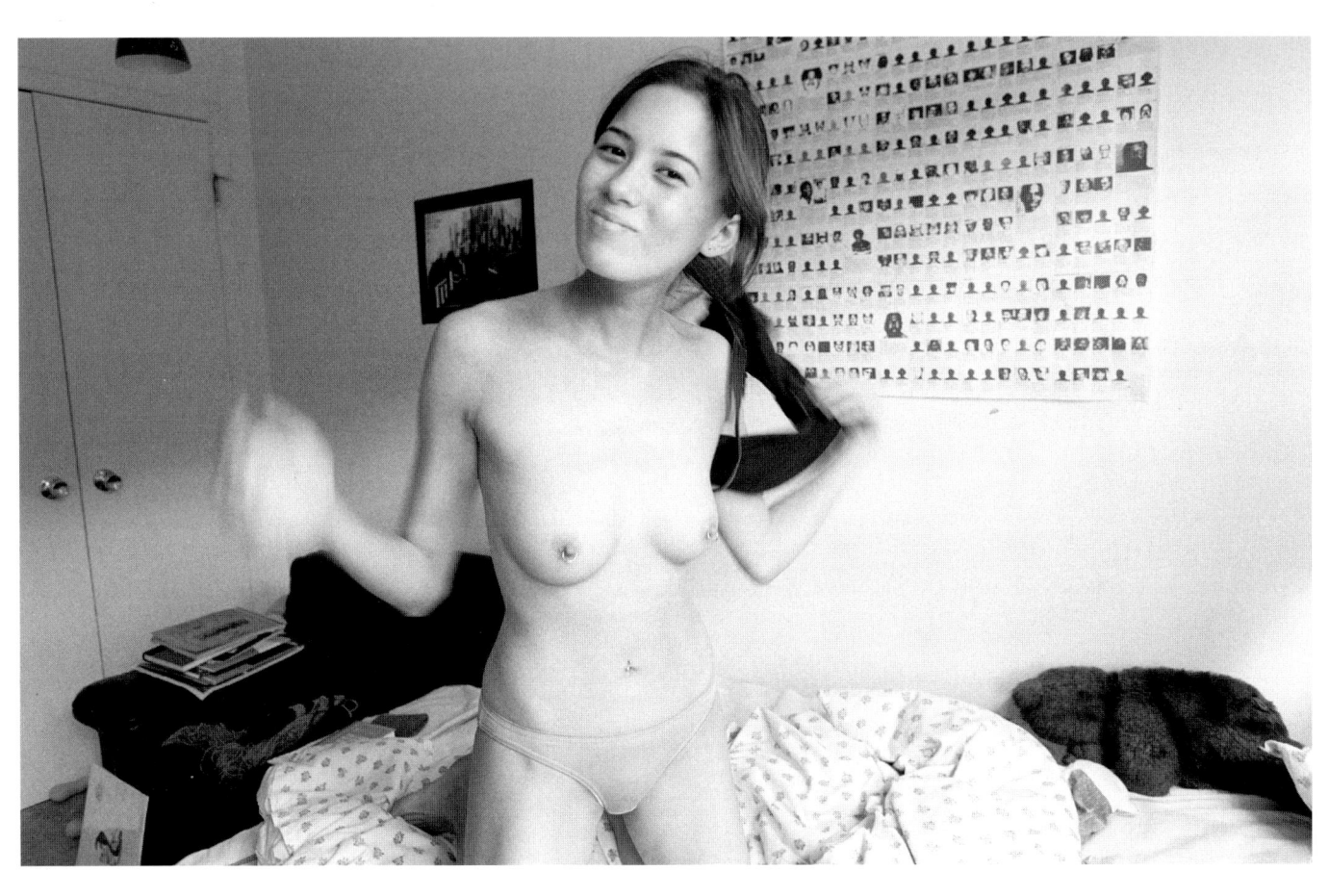

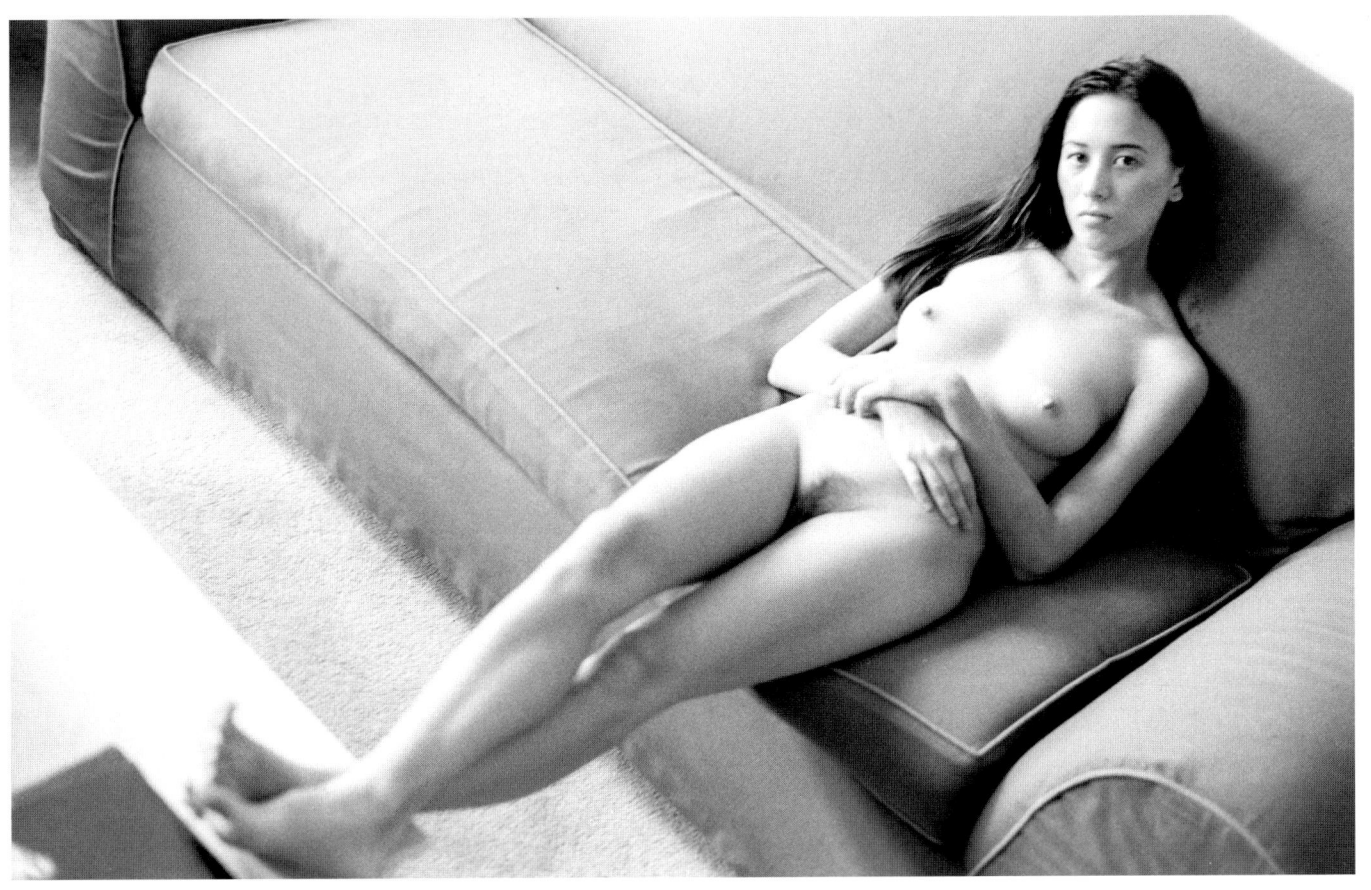

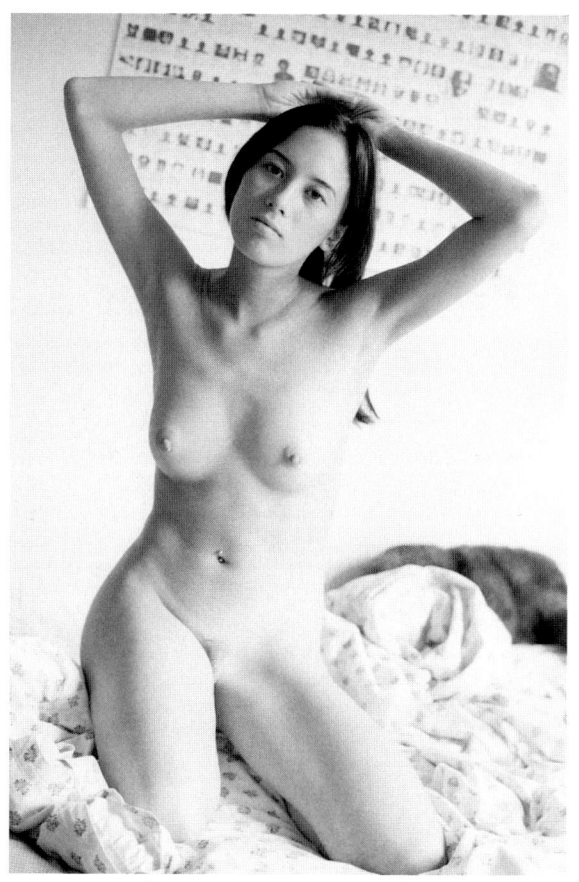

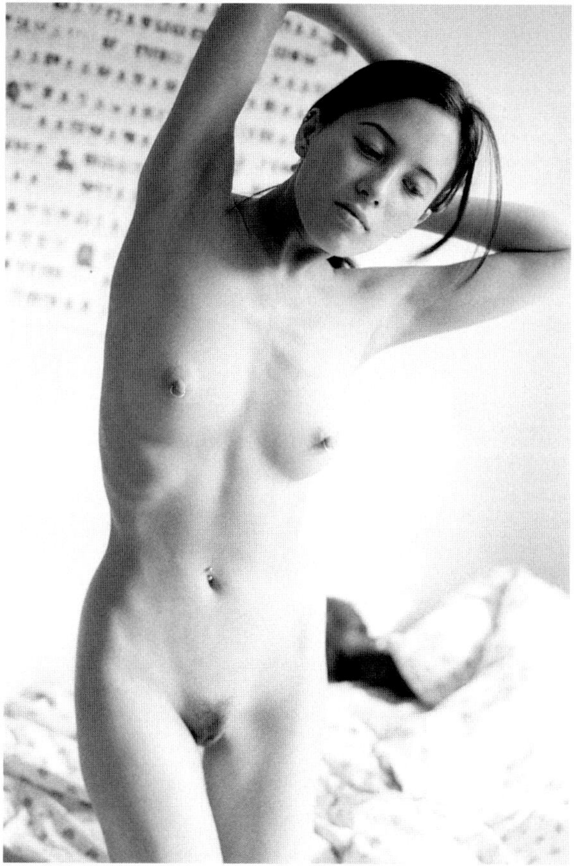

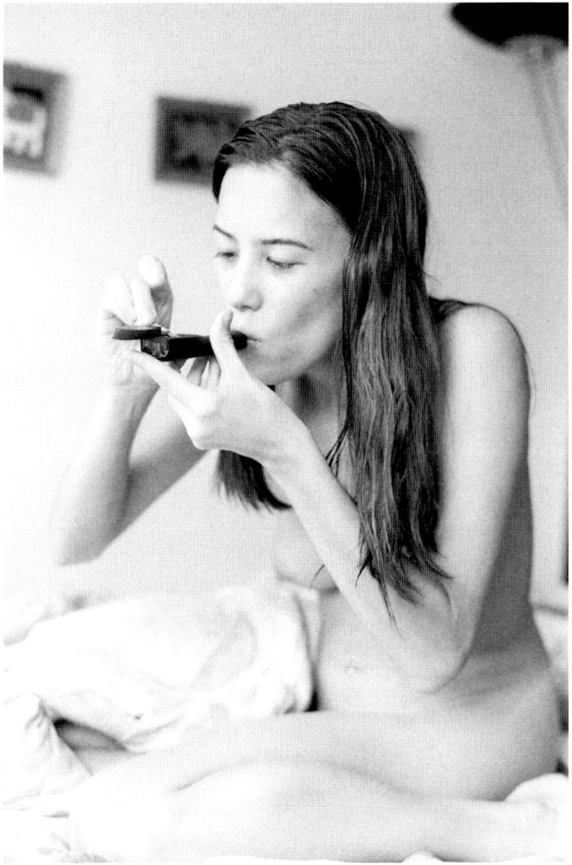

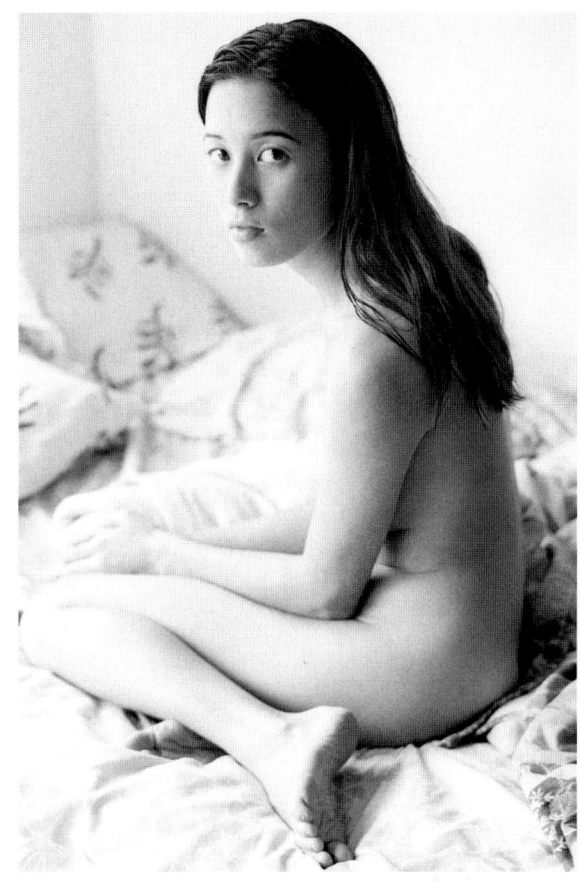

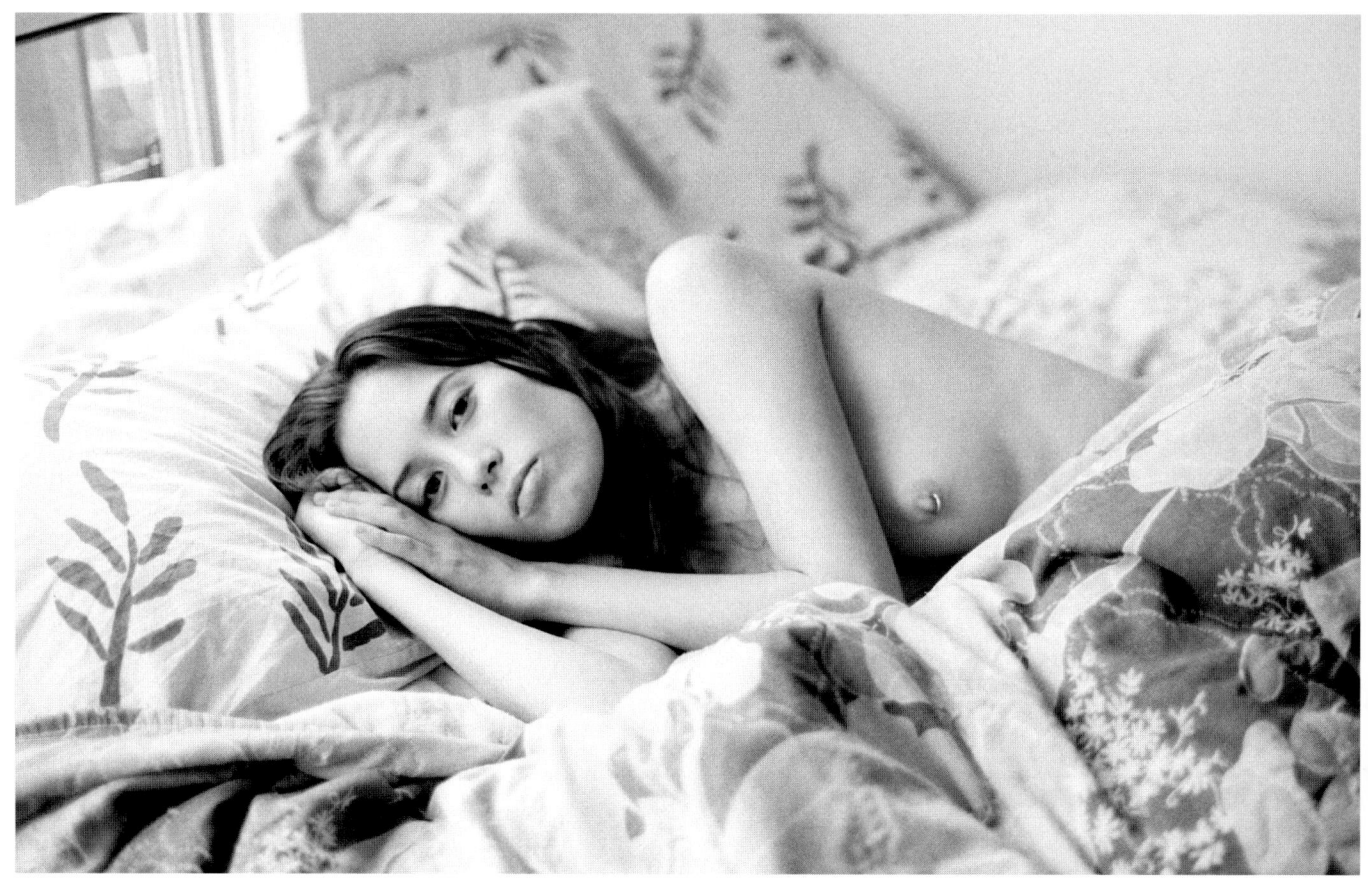

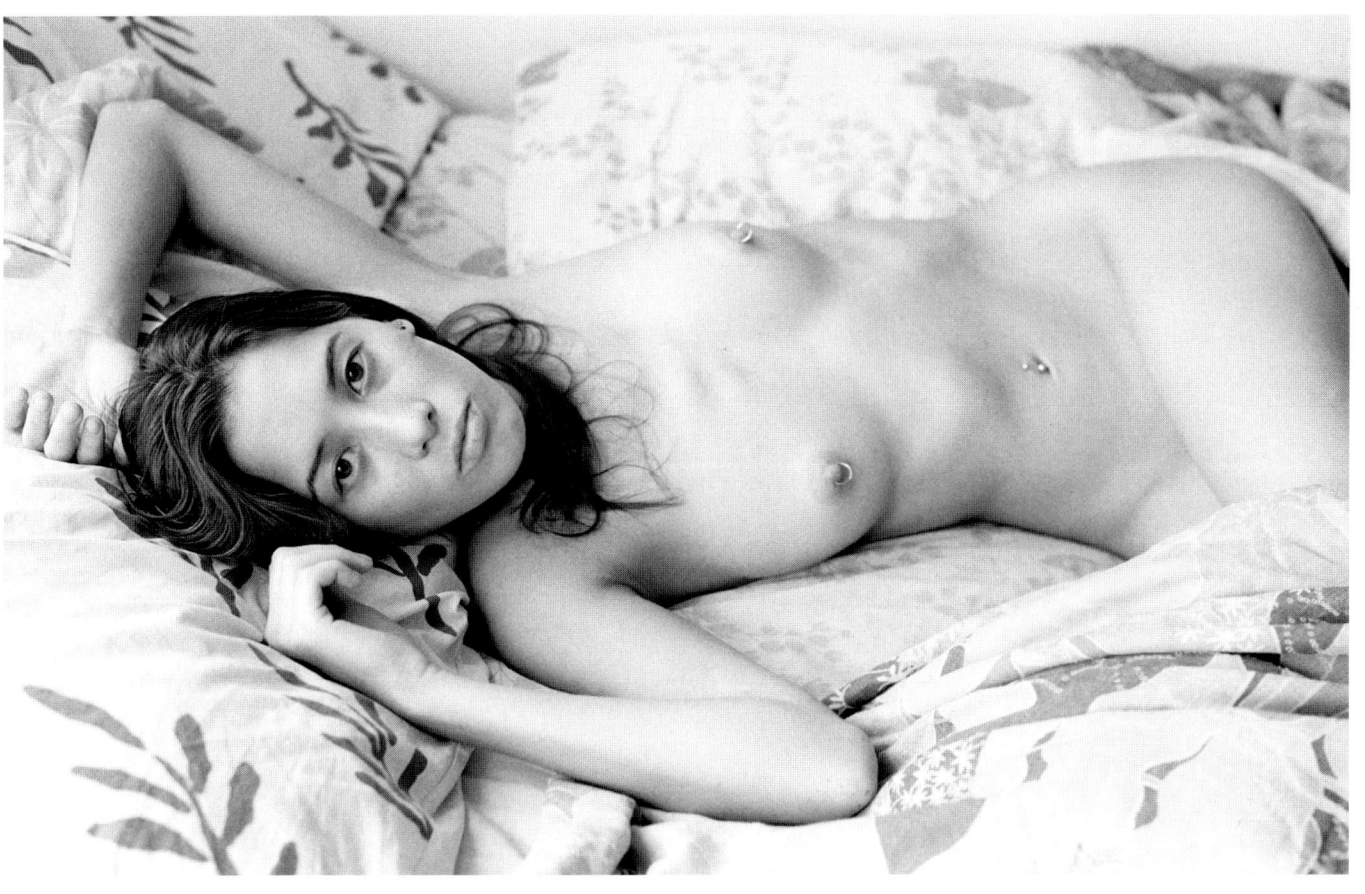

Charlene · I met Charlene at a club called the Flamingo East. She was a social butterfly and nightlife diva. I photographed her both outside on a pier, and in her Manhattan apartment. Charlene had just died her hair, and told me that people were much more intimidated by her as a blond, than as a brunette. Charlene is an artist who paints giant pin-ups.

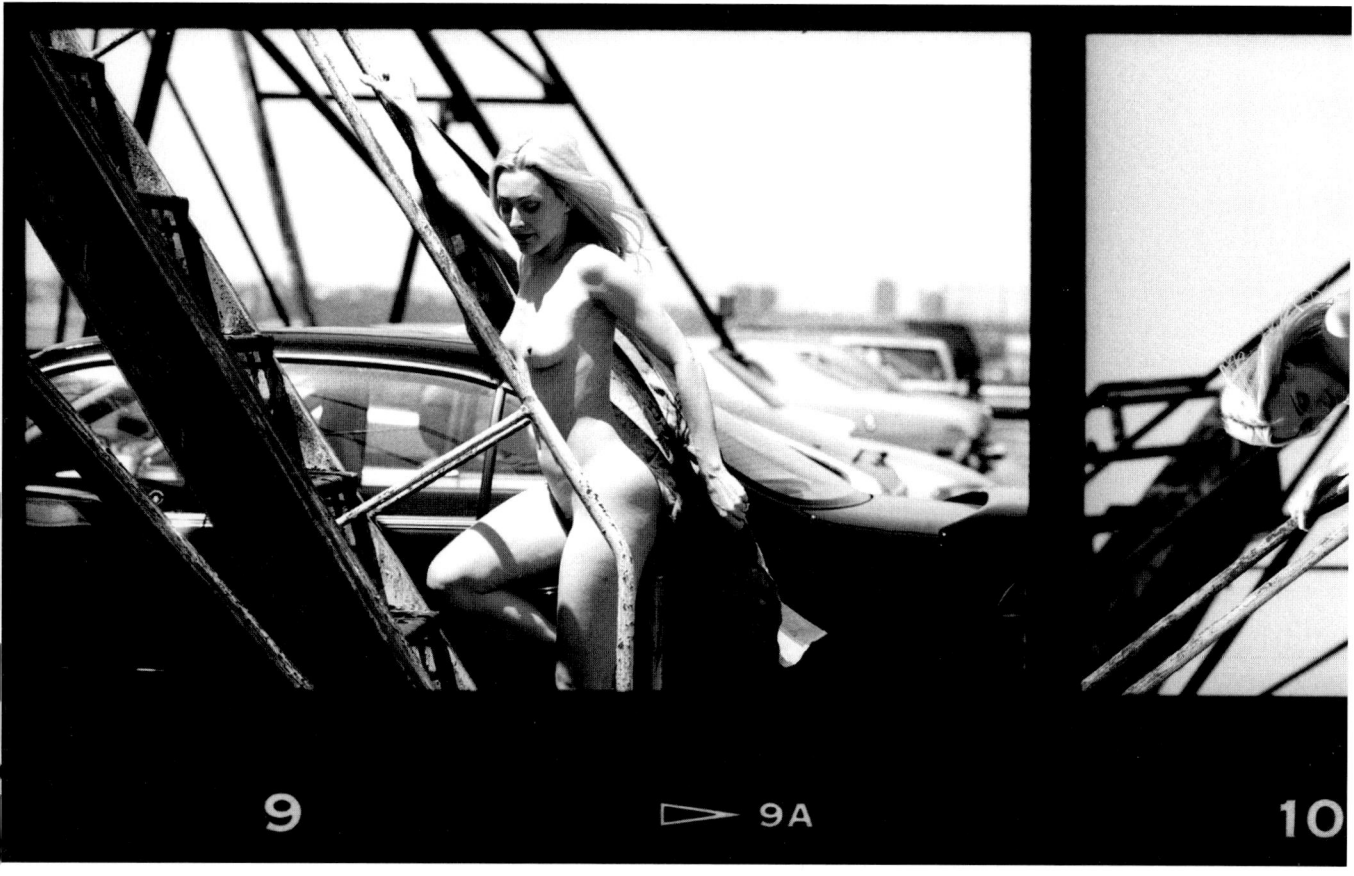

9   ▷ 9A   10

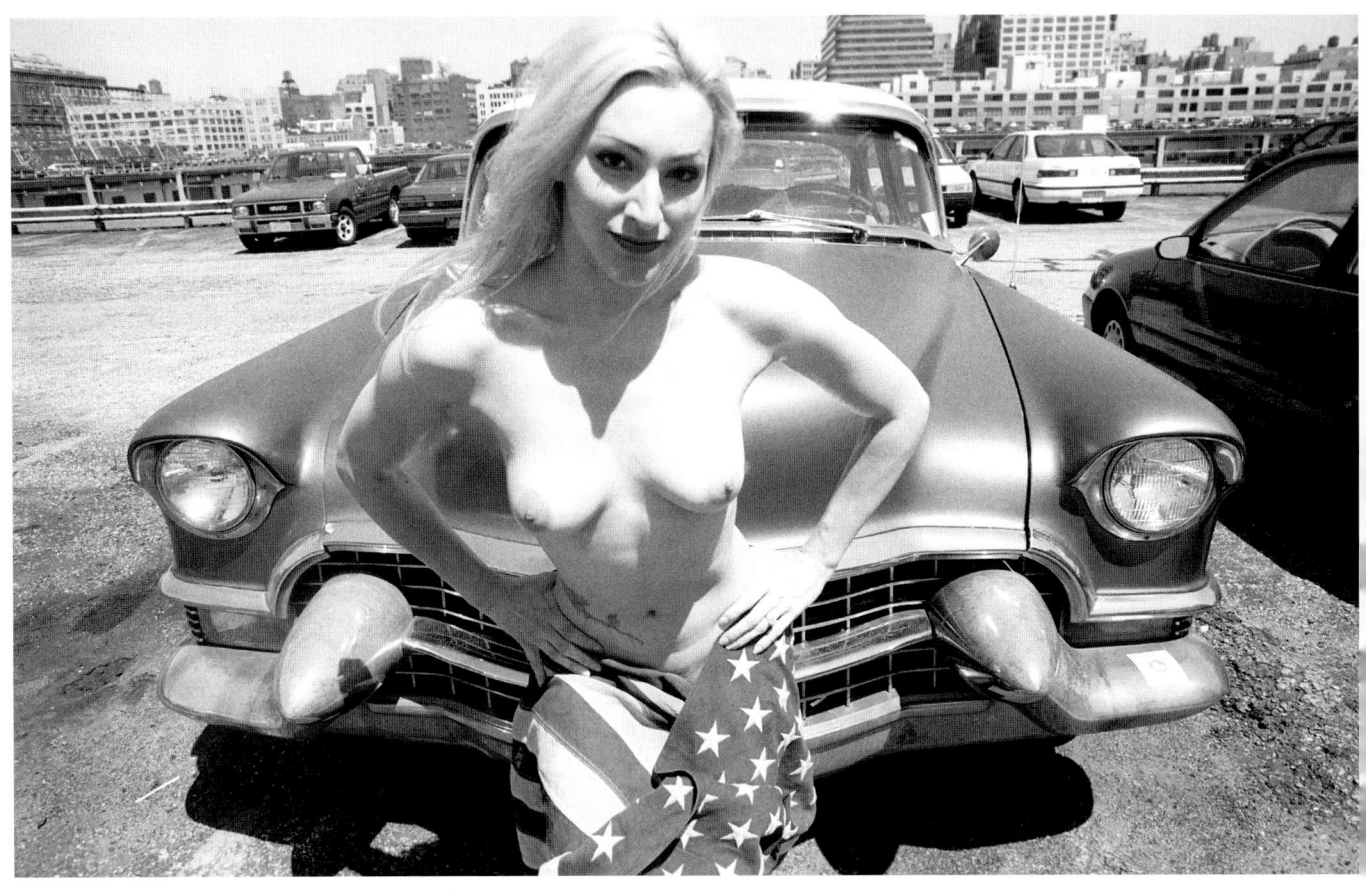

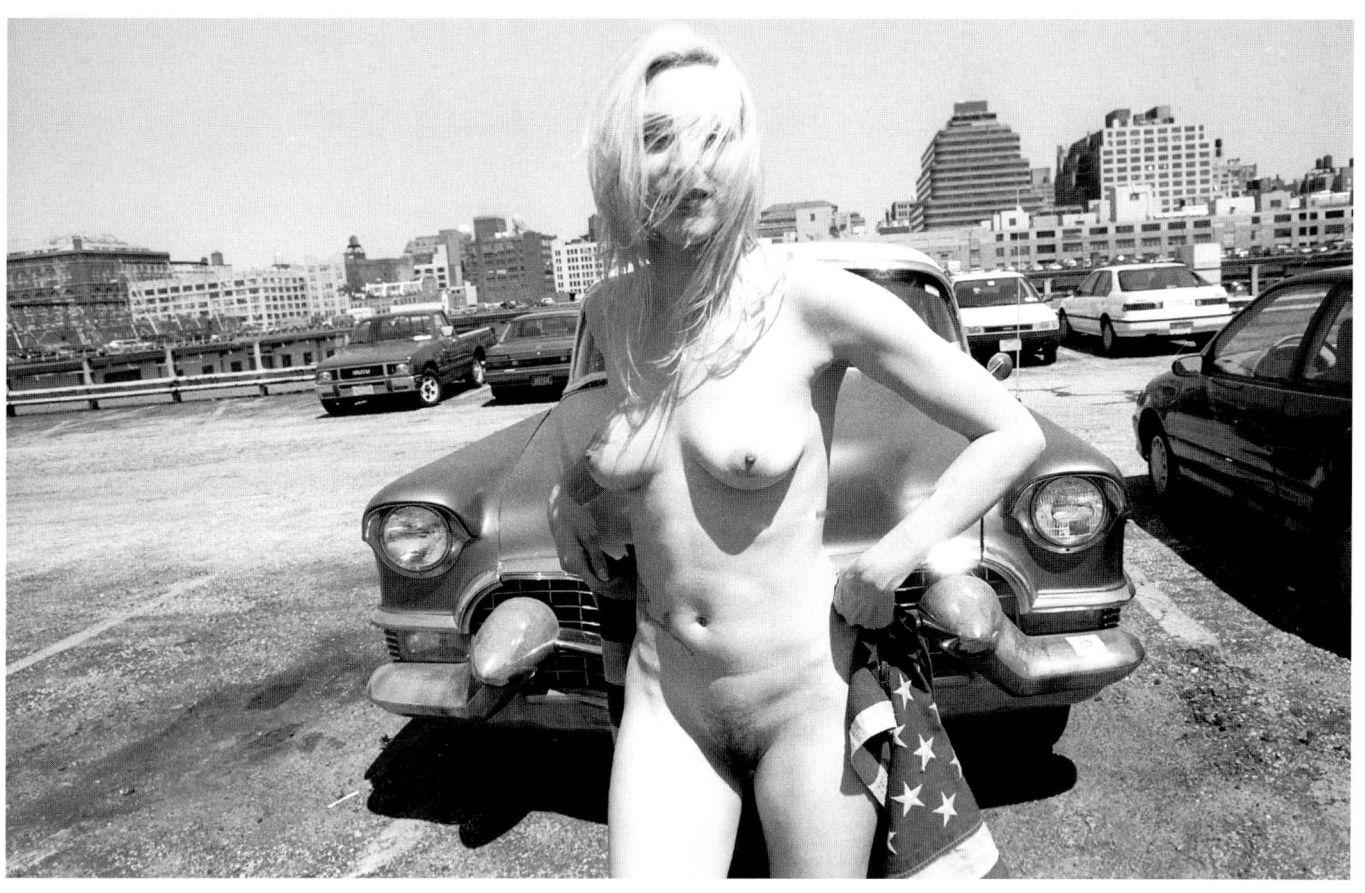

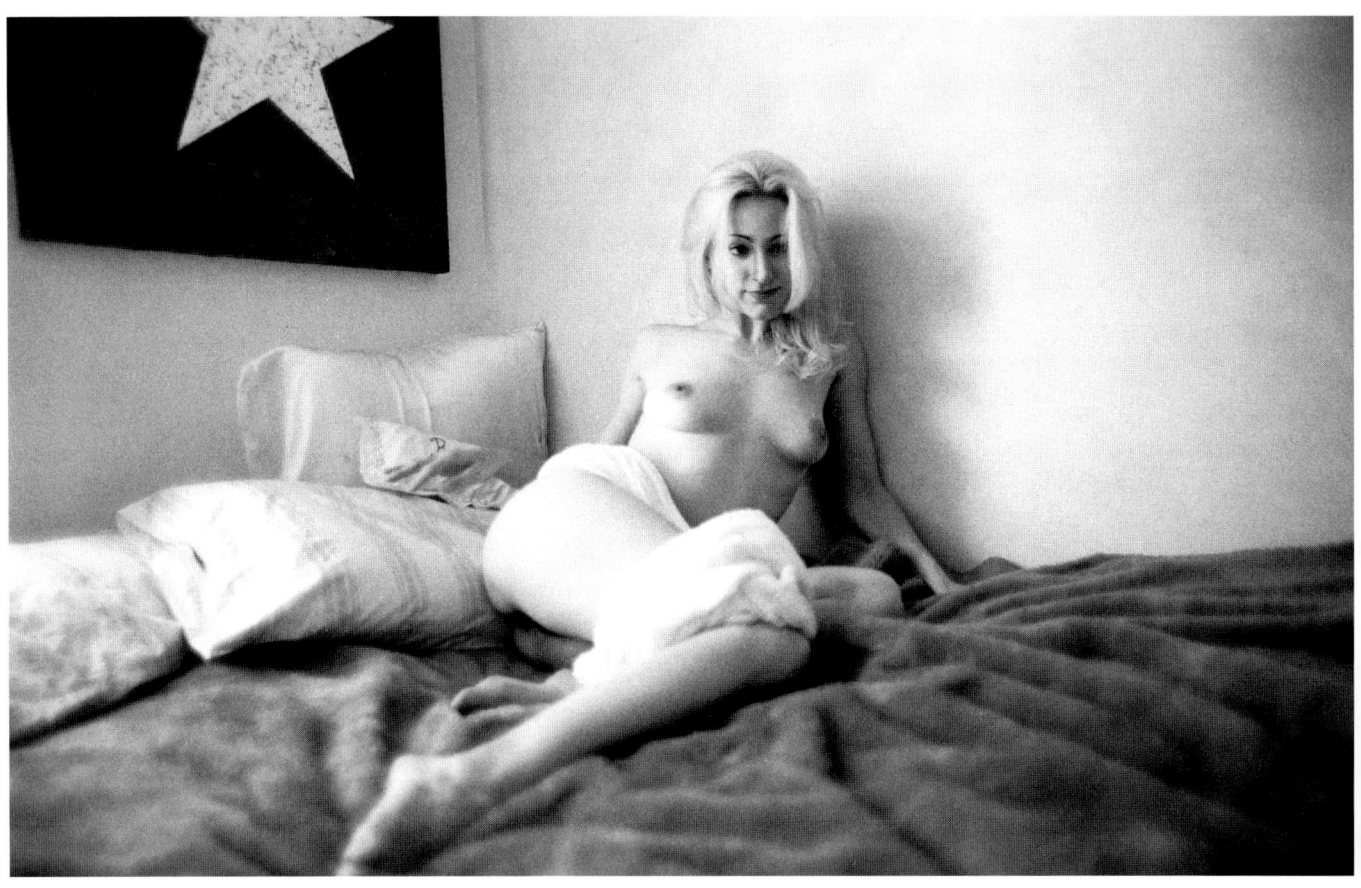

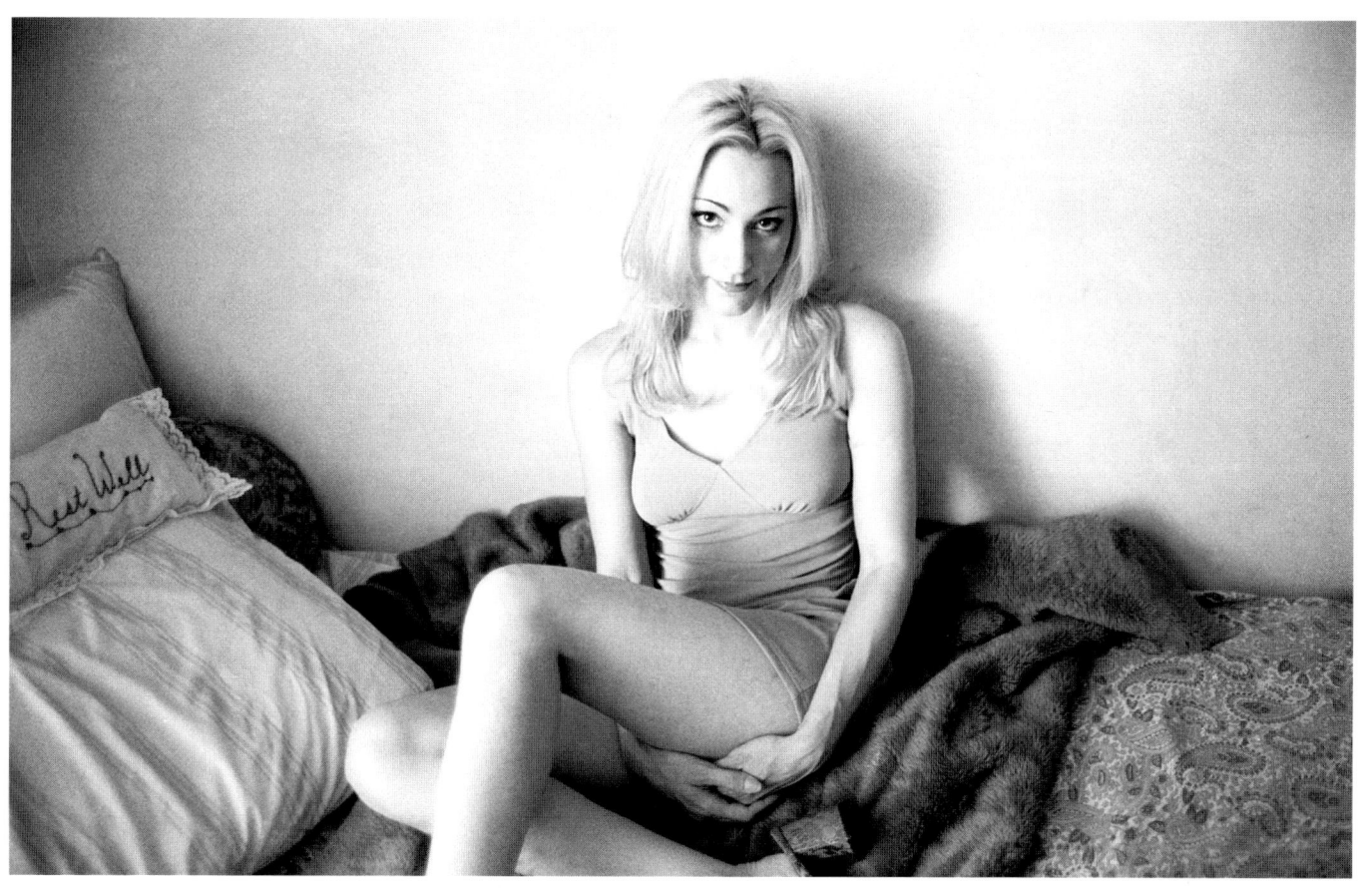

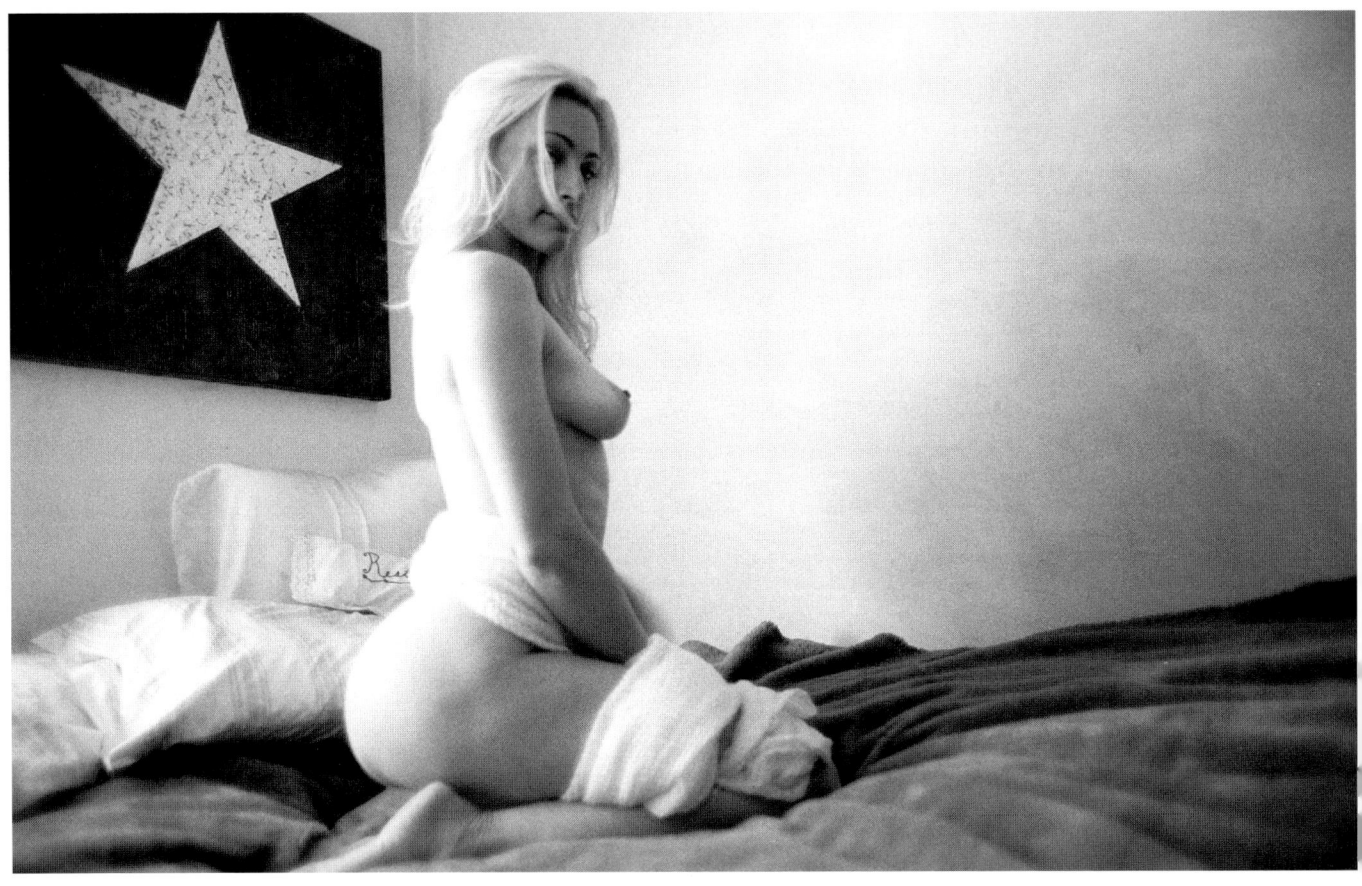

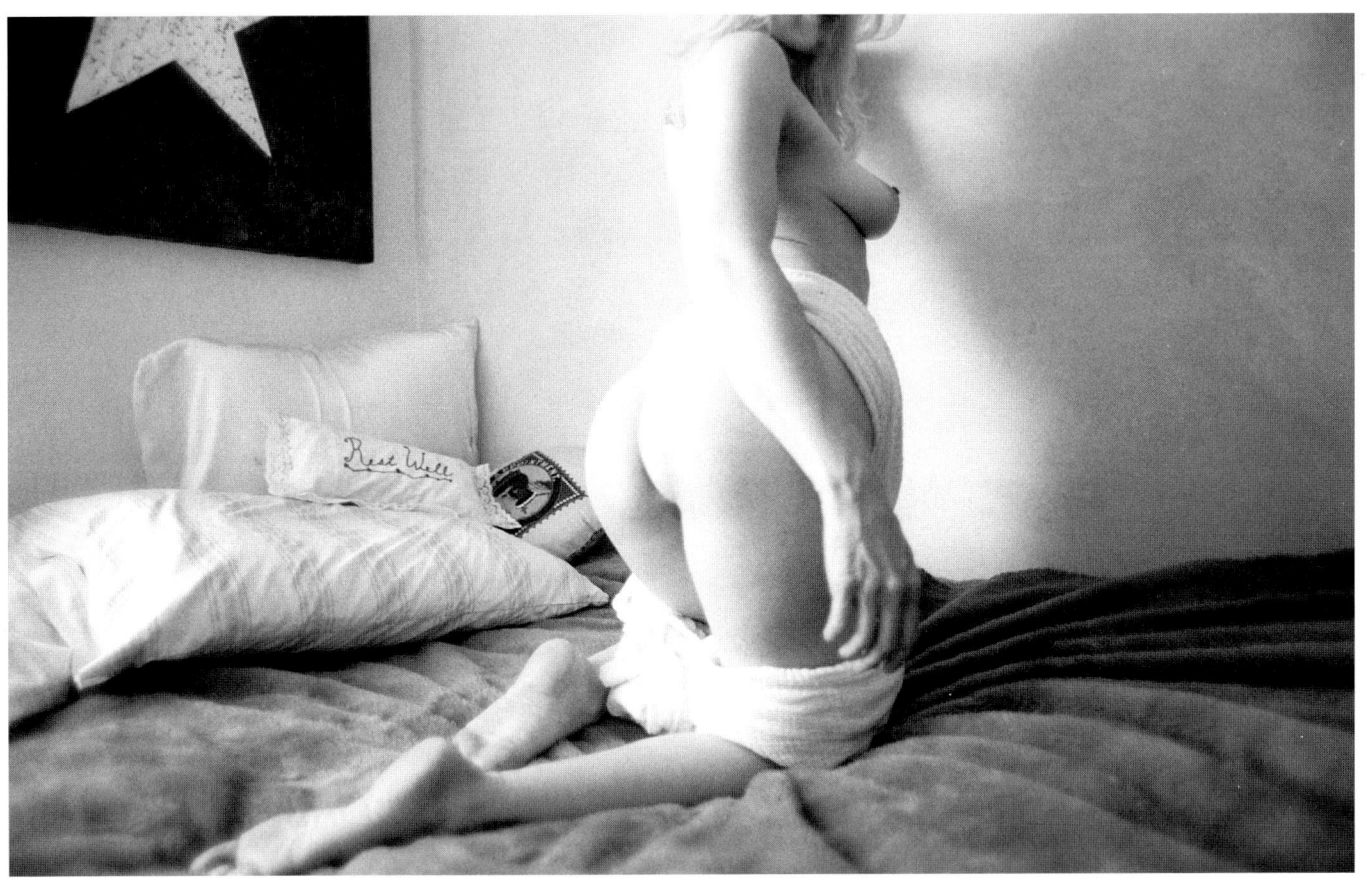

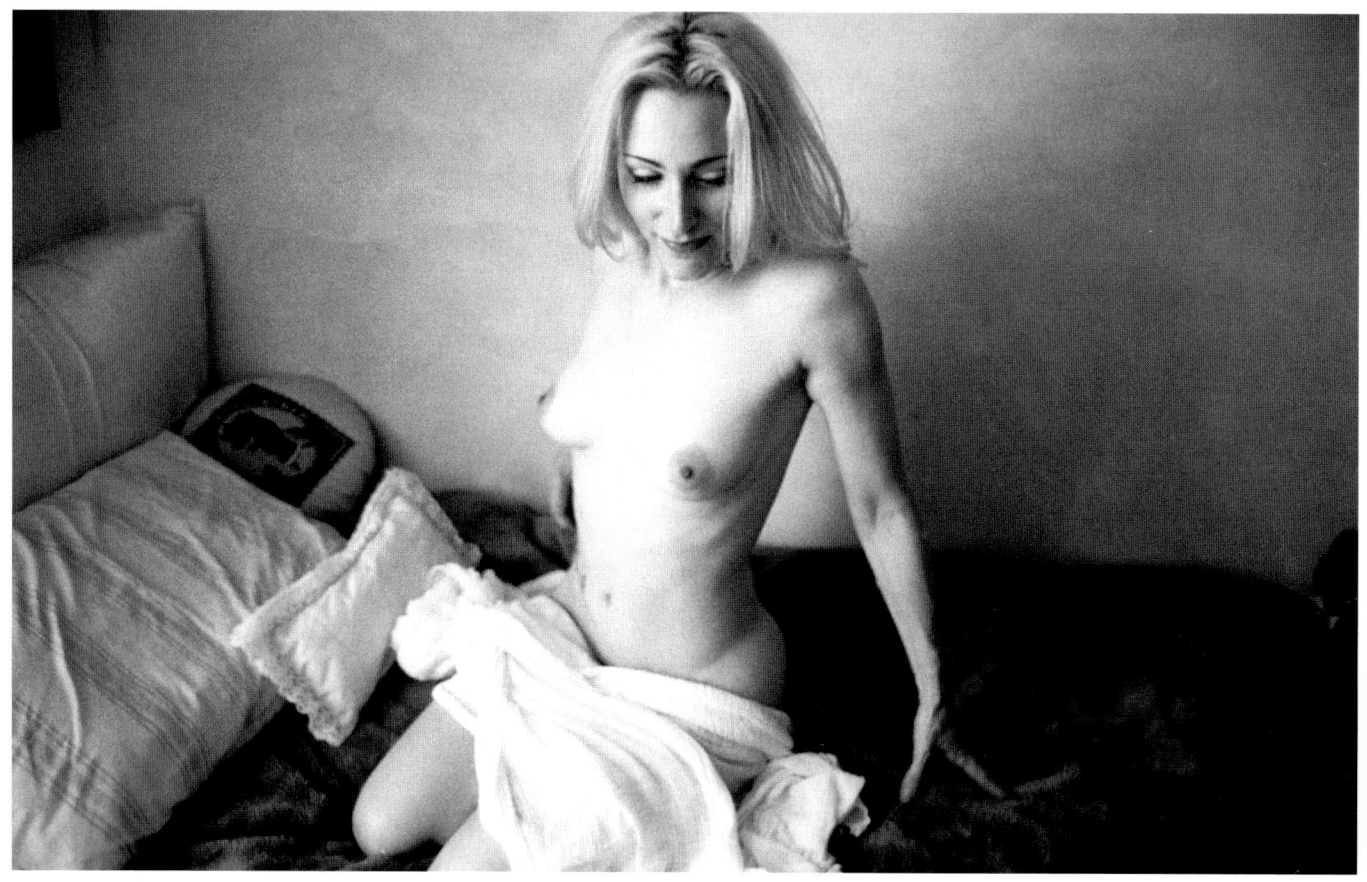

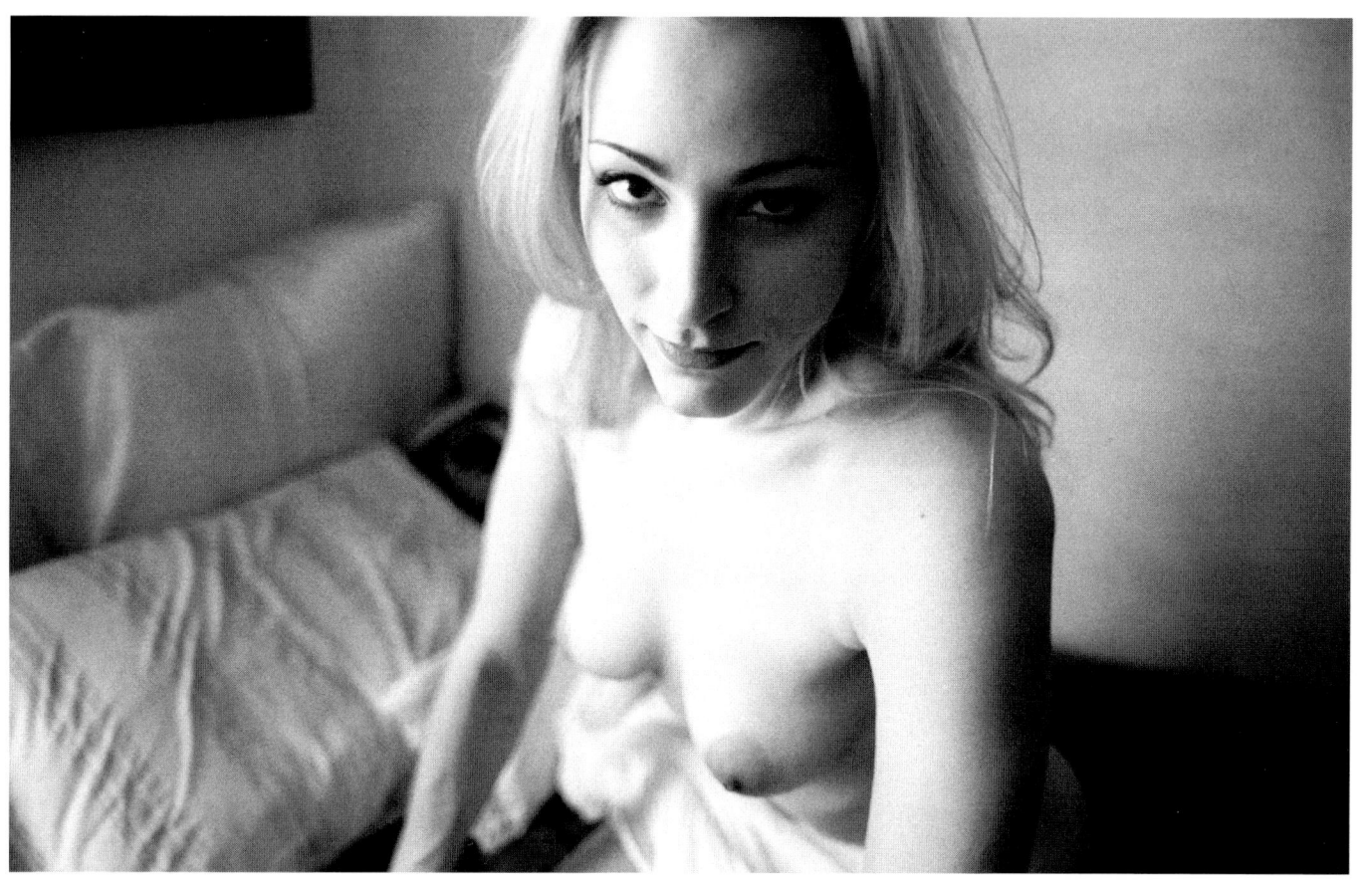

Christina · Christina is from LA, but I met her in New York. She's an interior designer. I photographed her in her LA apt, with her Cat "Pia". Christina was one of the sexiest people I've ever photographed. Every move was sensual, playful, and seductive. Her apt was like a small bright, cabin, and made a great studio.

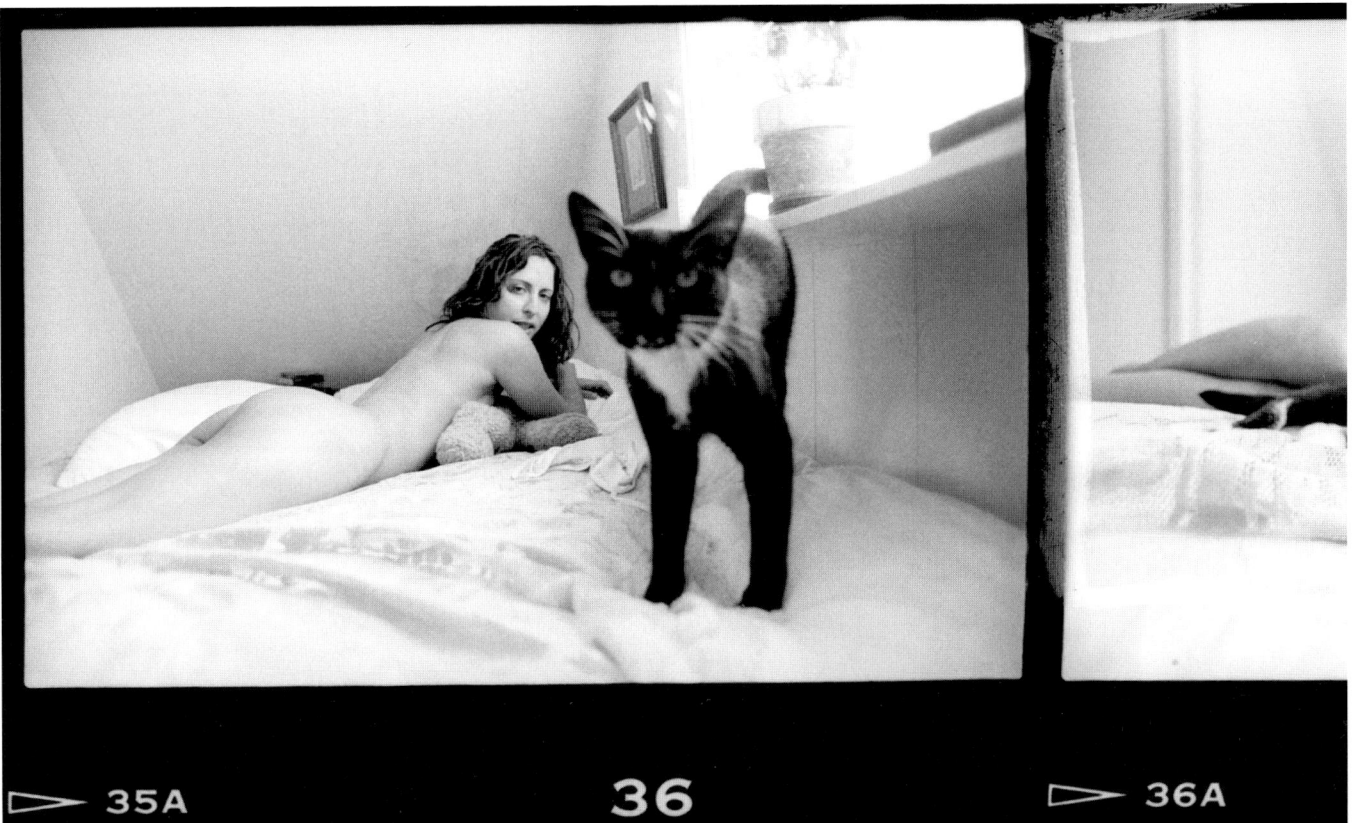

36

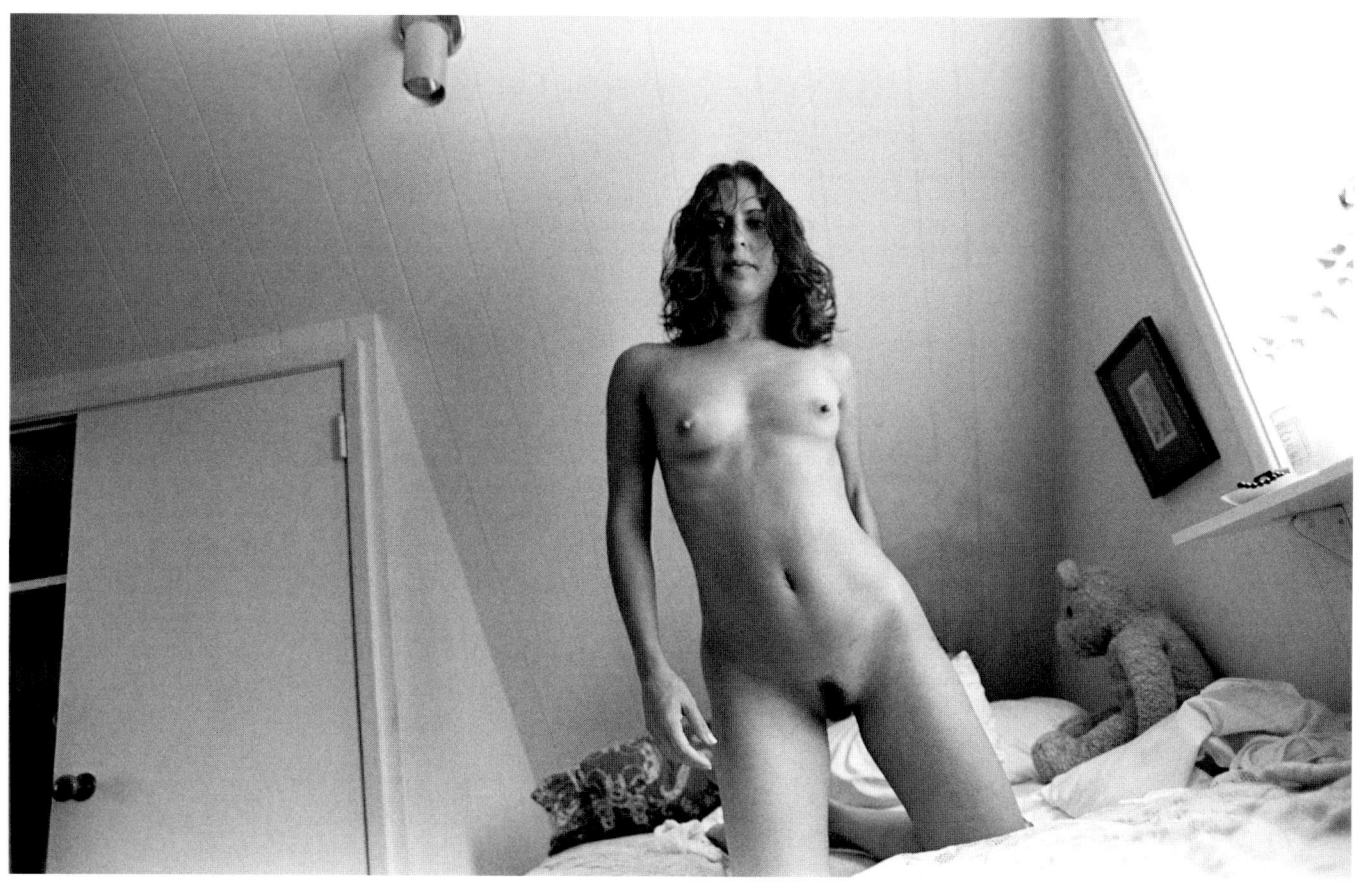

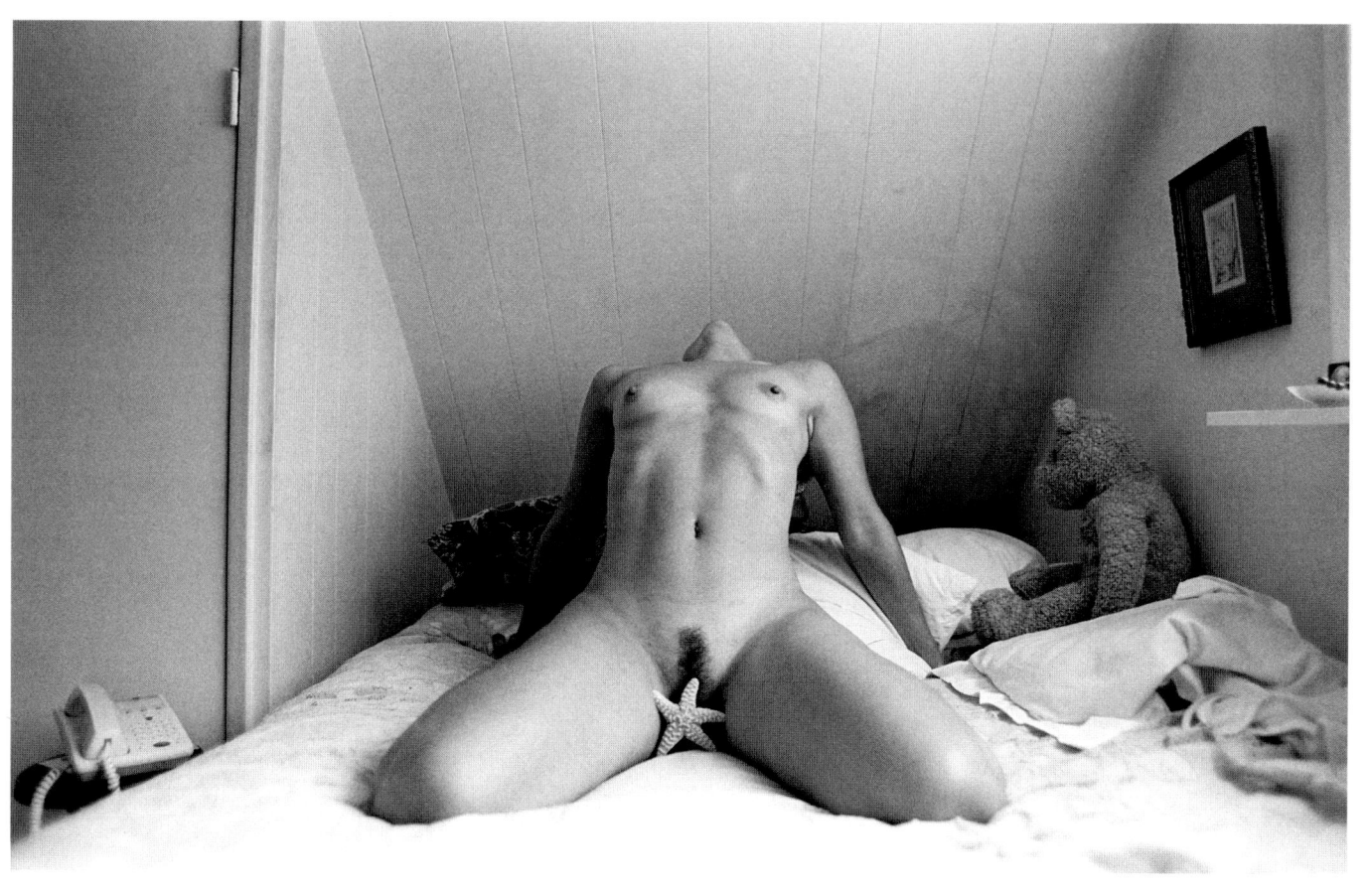

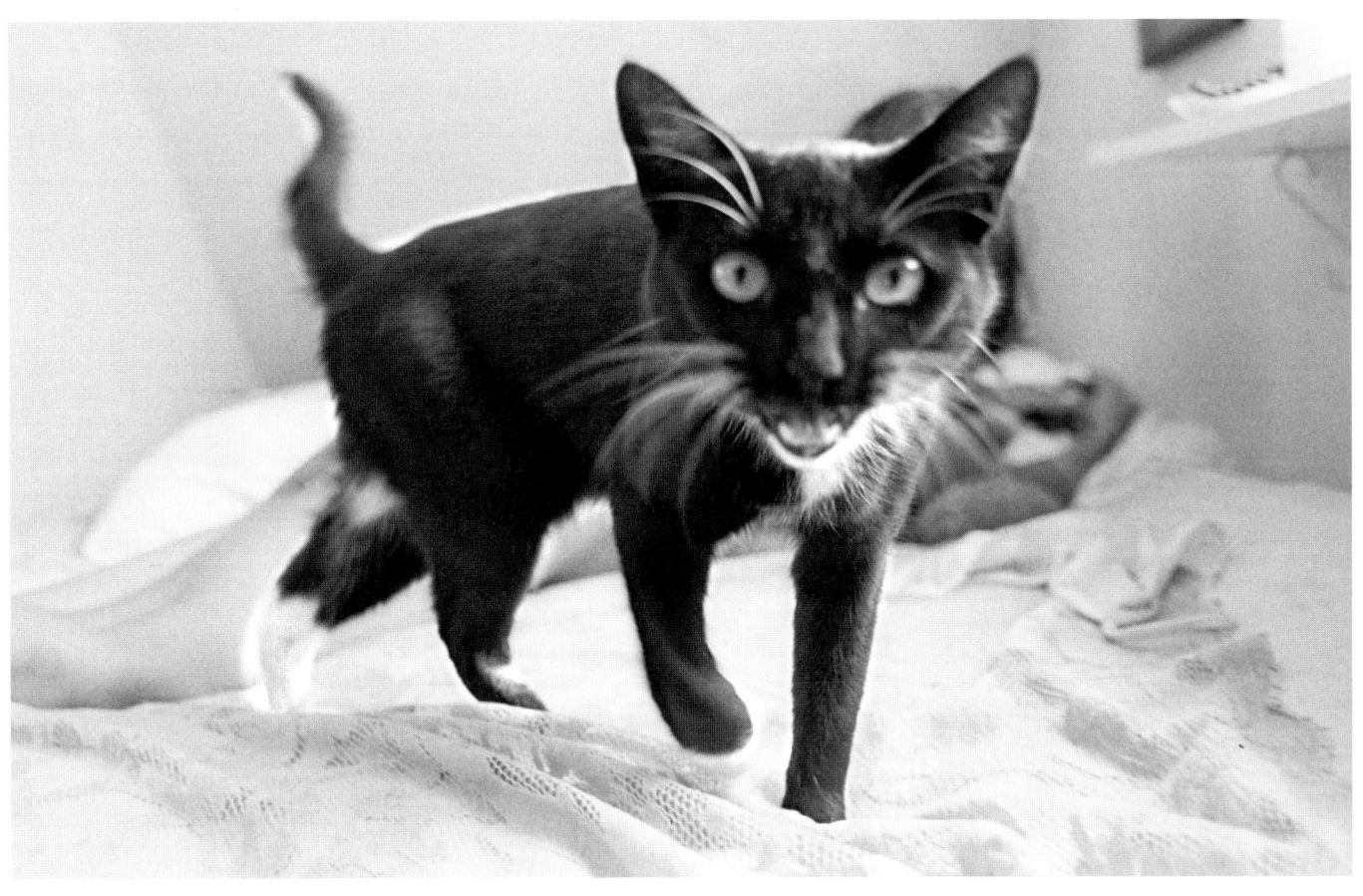

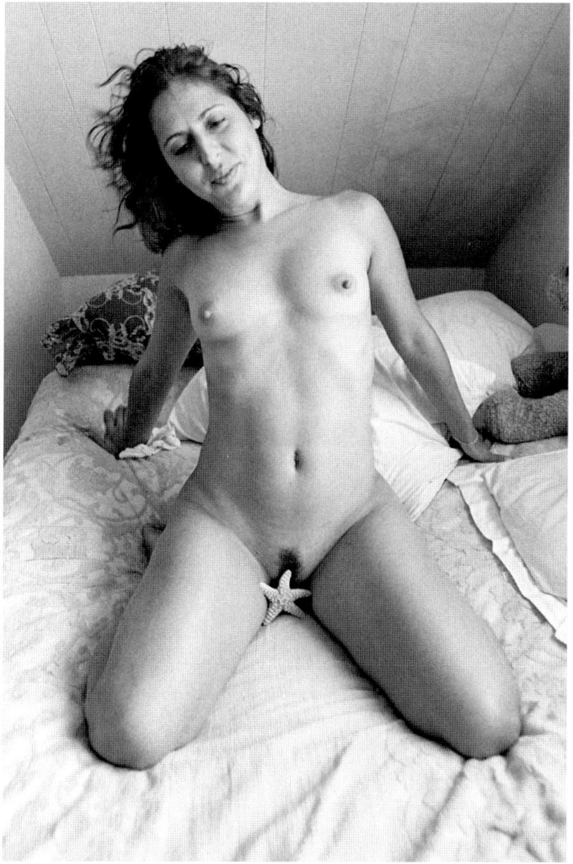

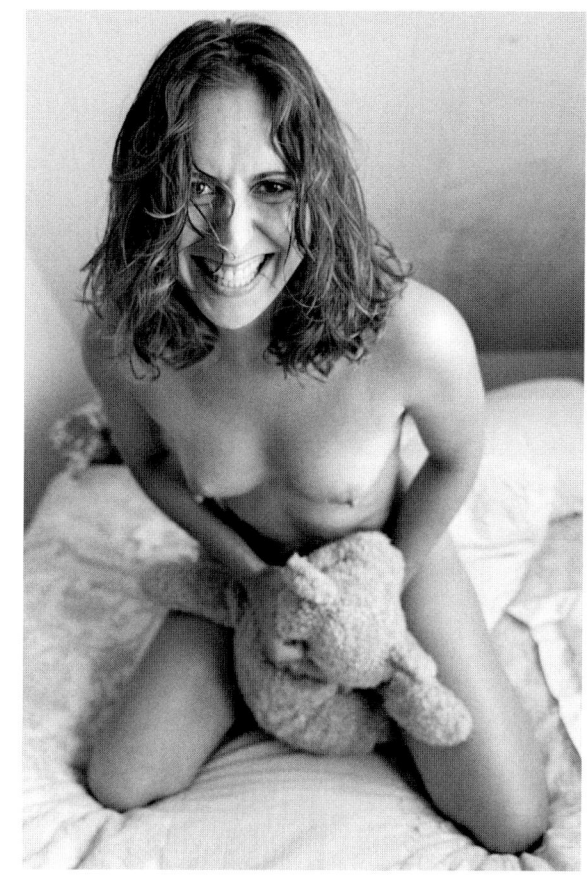

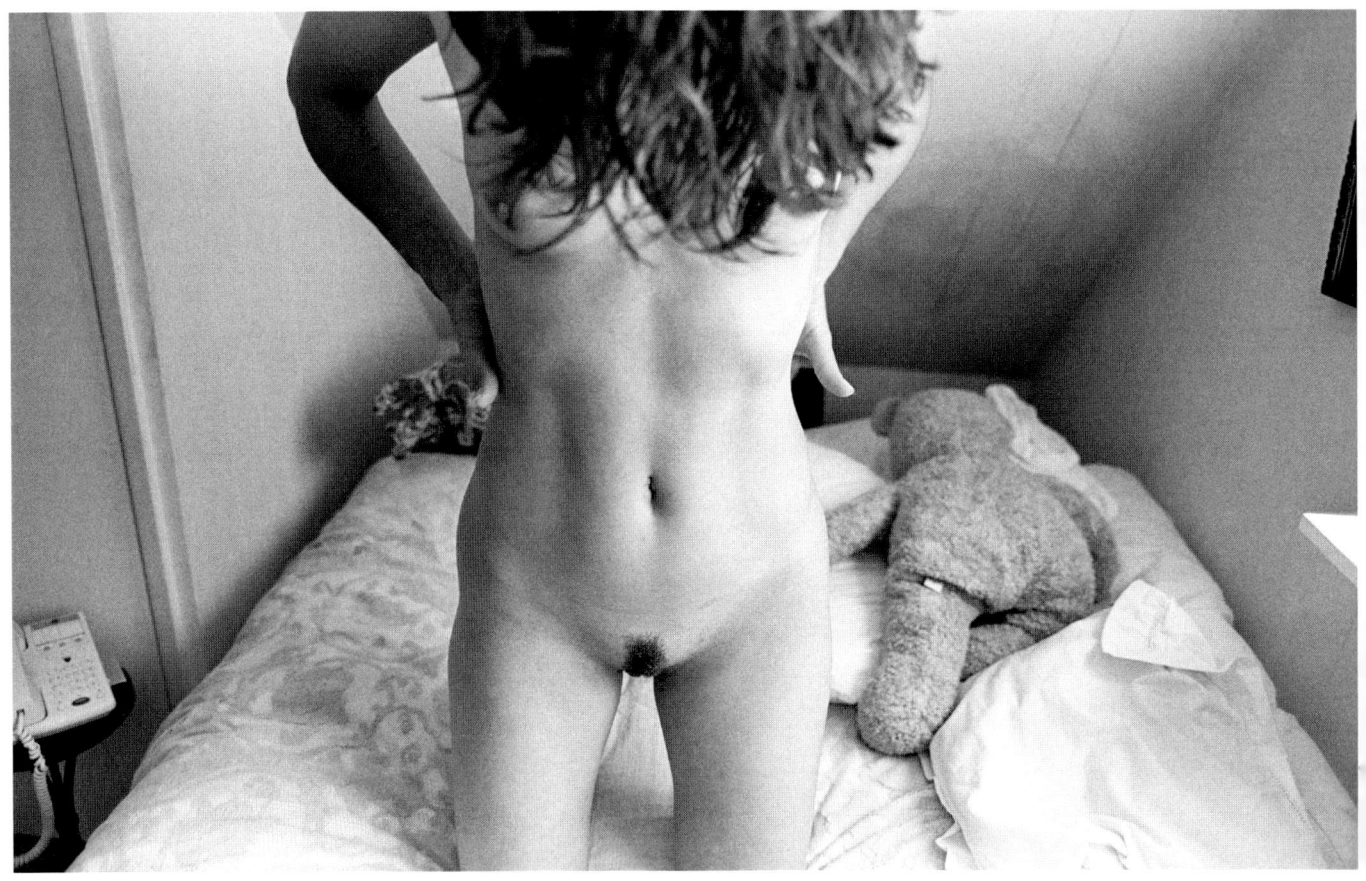

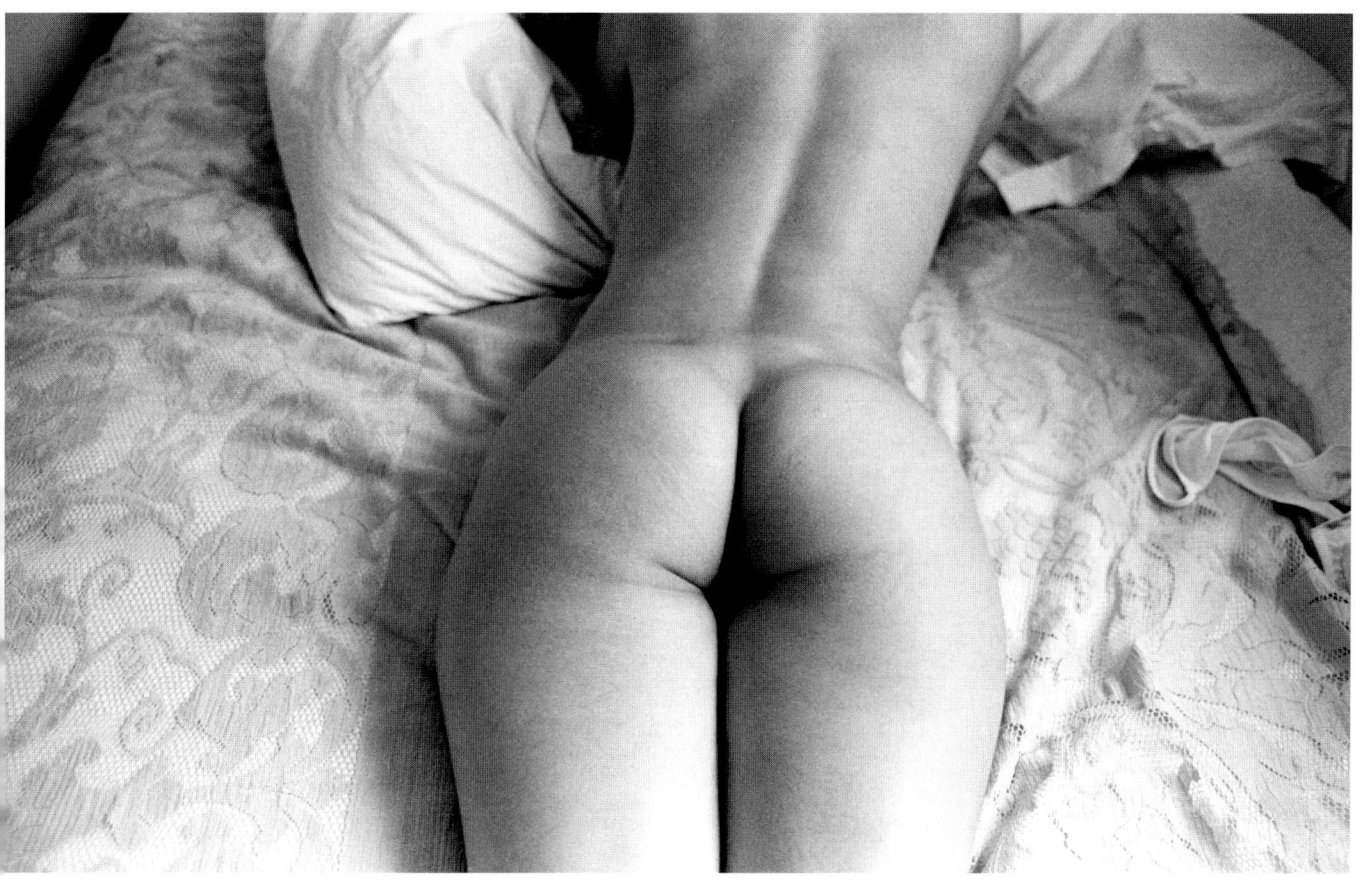

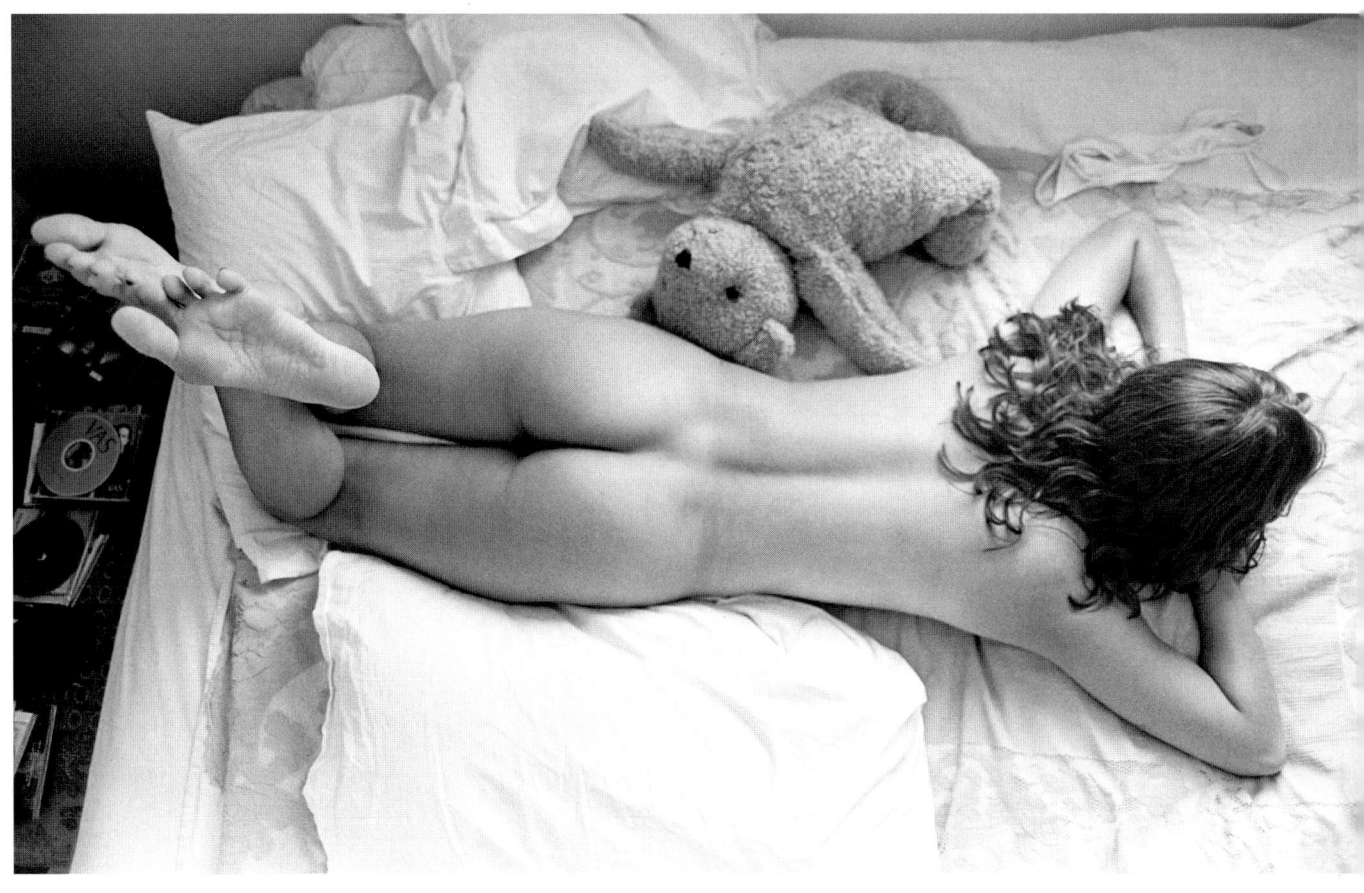

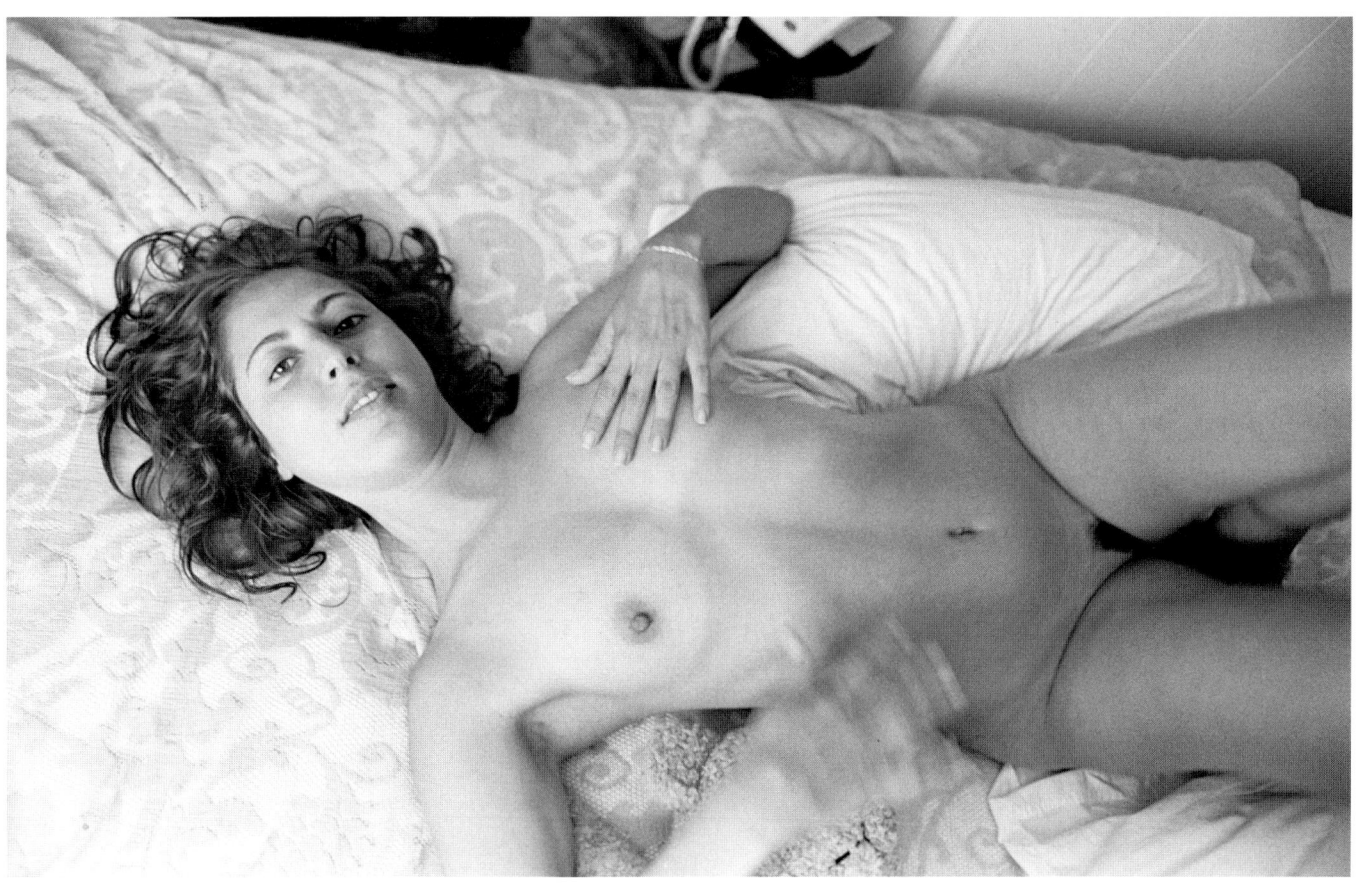

Christy · I met Christy through my friend Skye. She's Puerto Rican and Italian. Everything about Christy was beautiful: her face, smile, hands, body and feet. We shot in her Manhattan apartment, then on her roof, where she wrapped herself in an Italian crocheted bedspread, making nearby office workers very happy. Christy now studies homeopathic medicine.

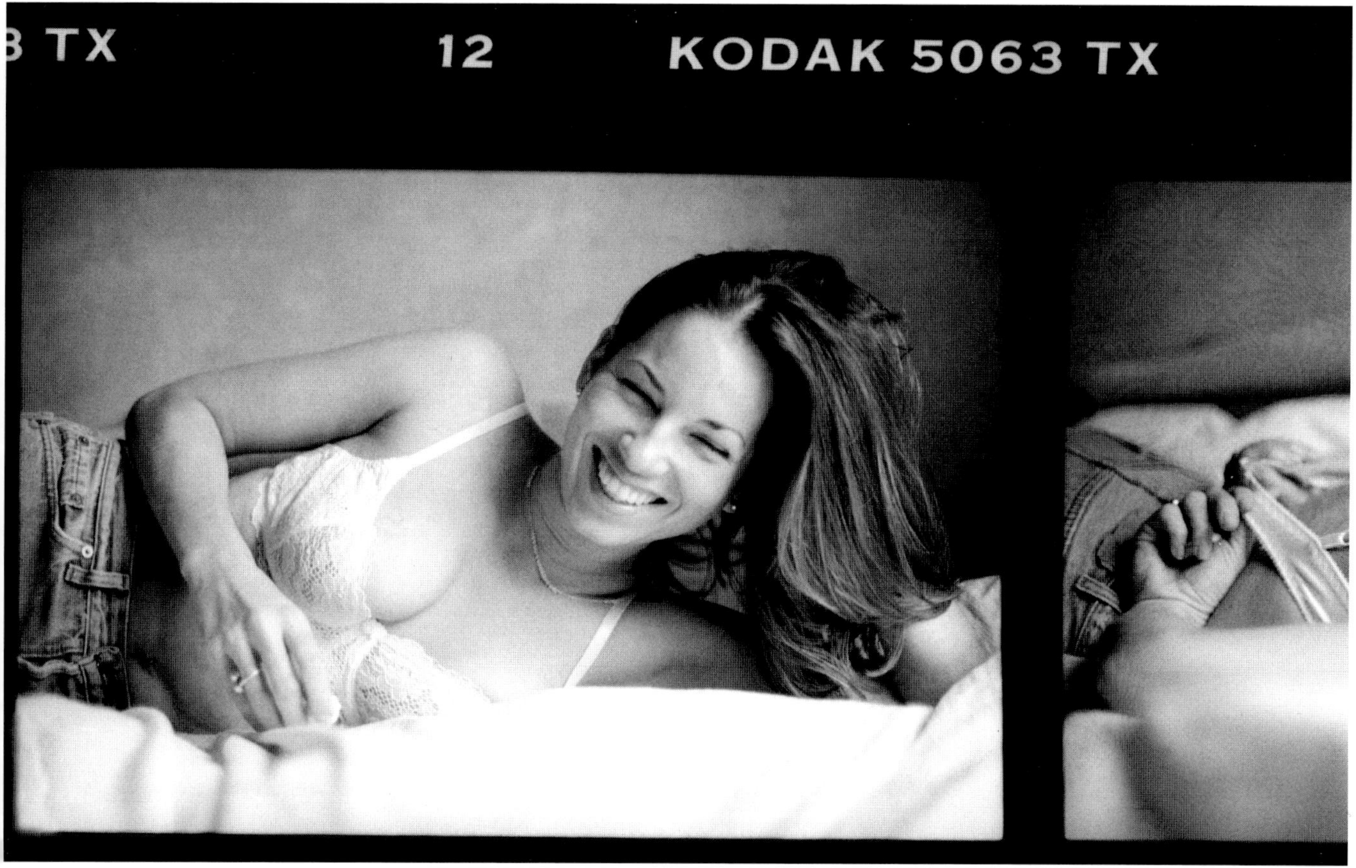

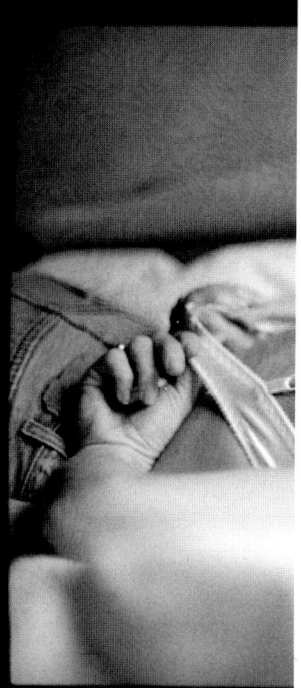

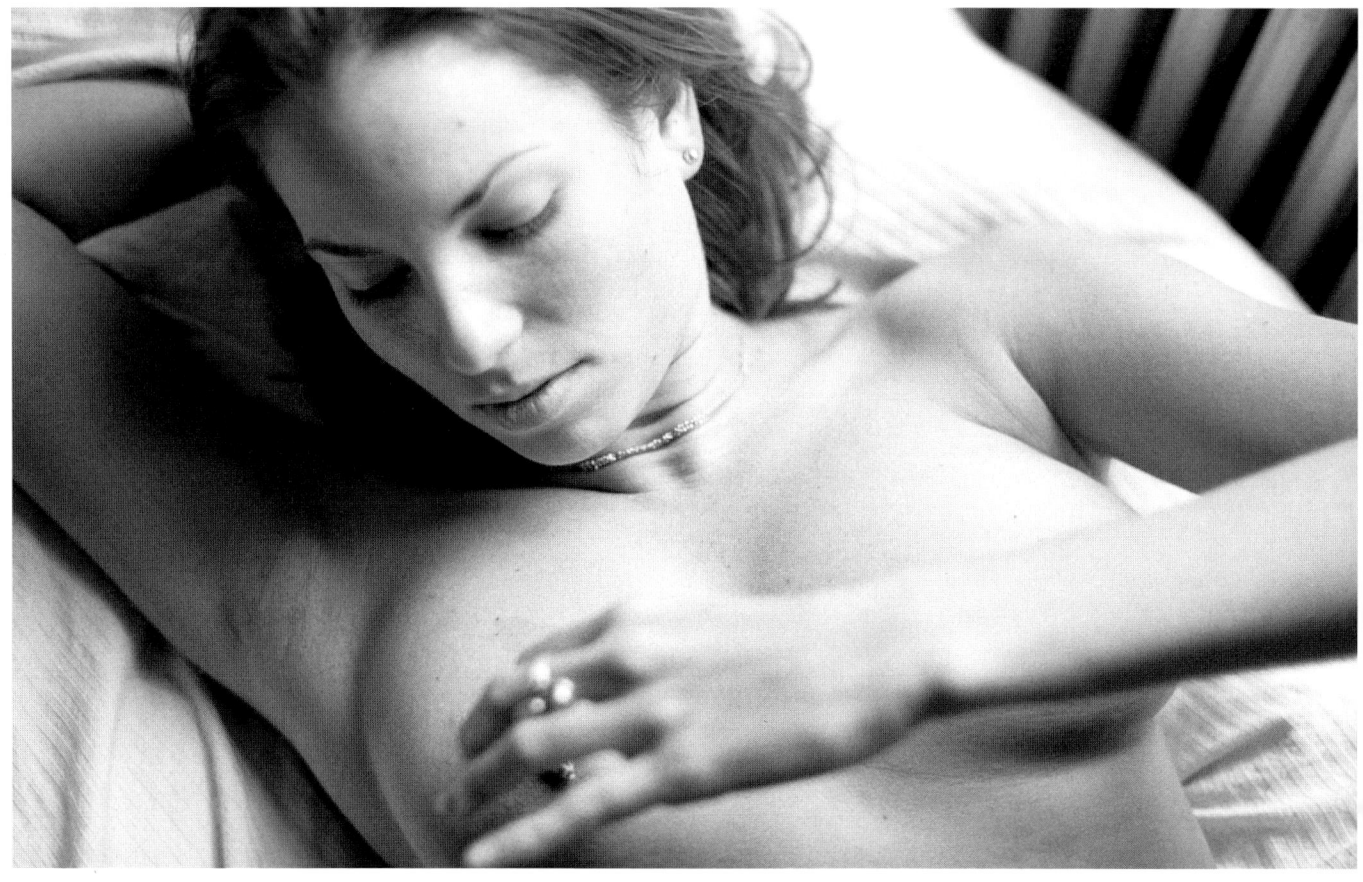

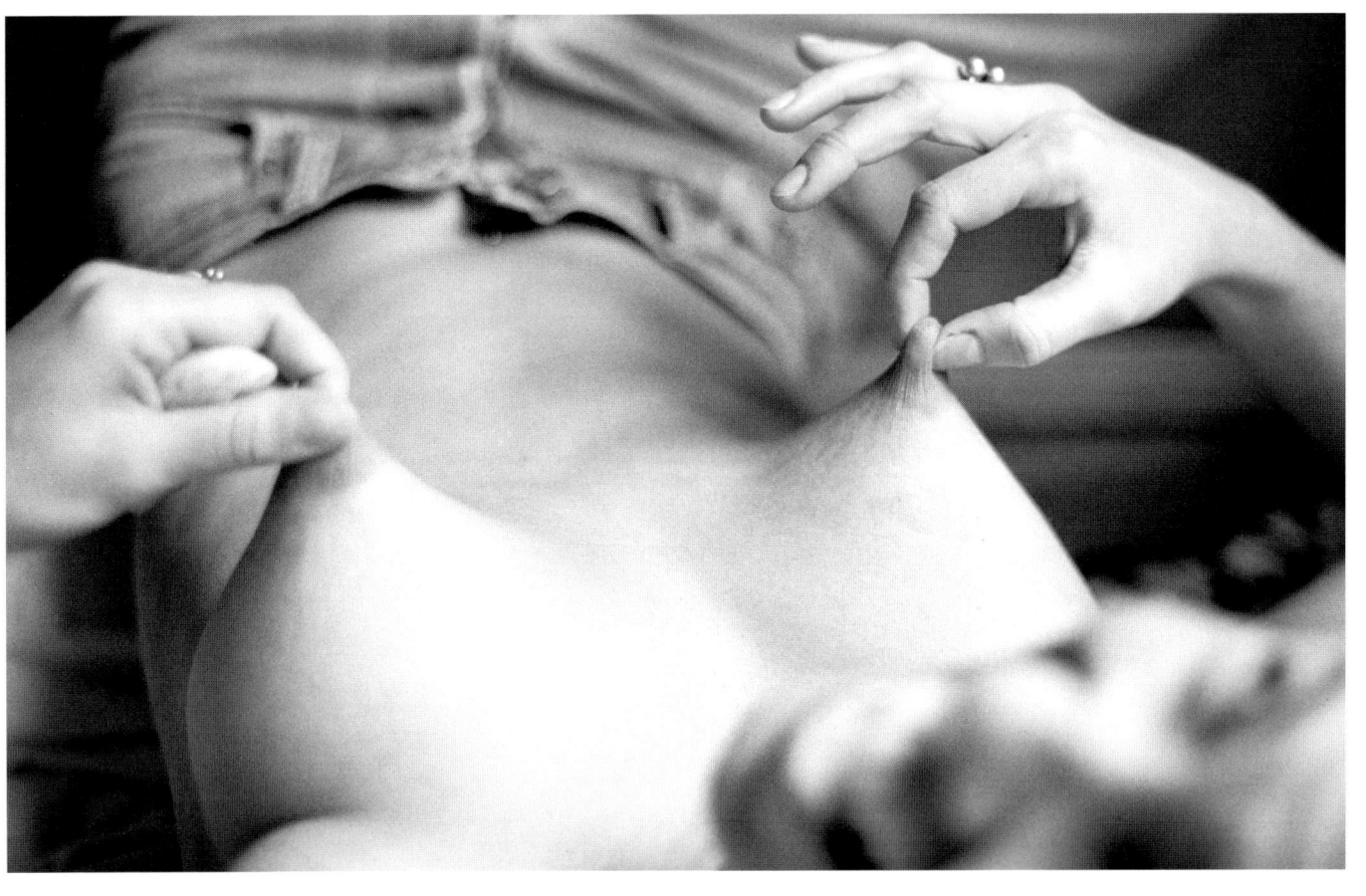

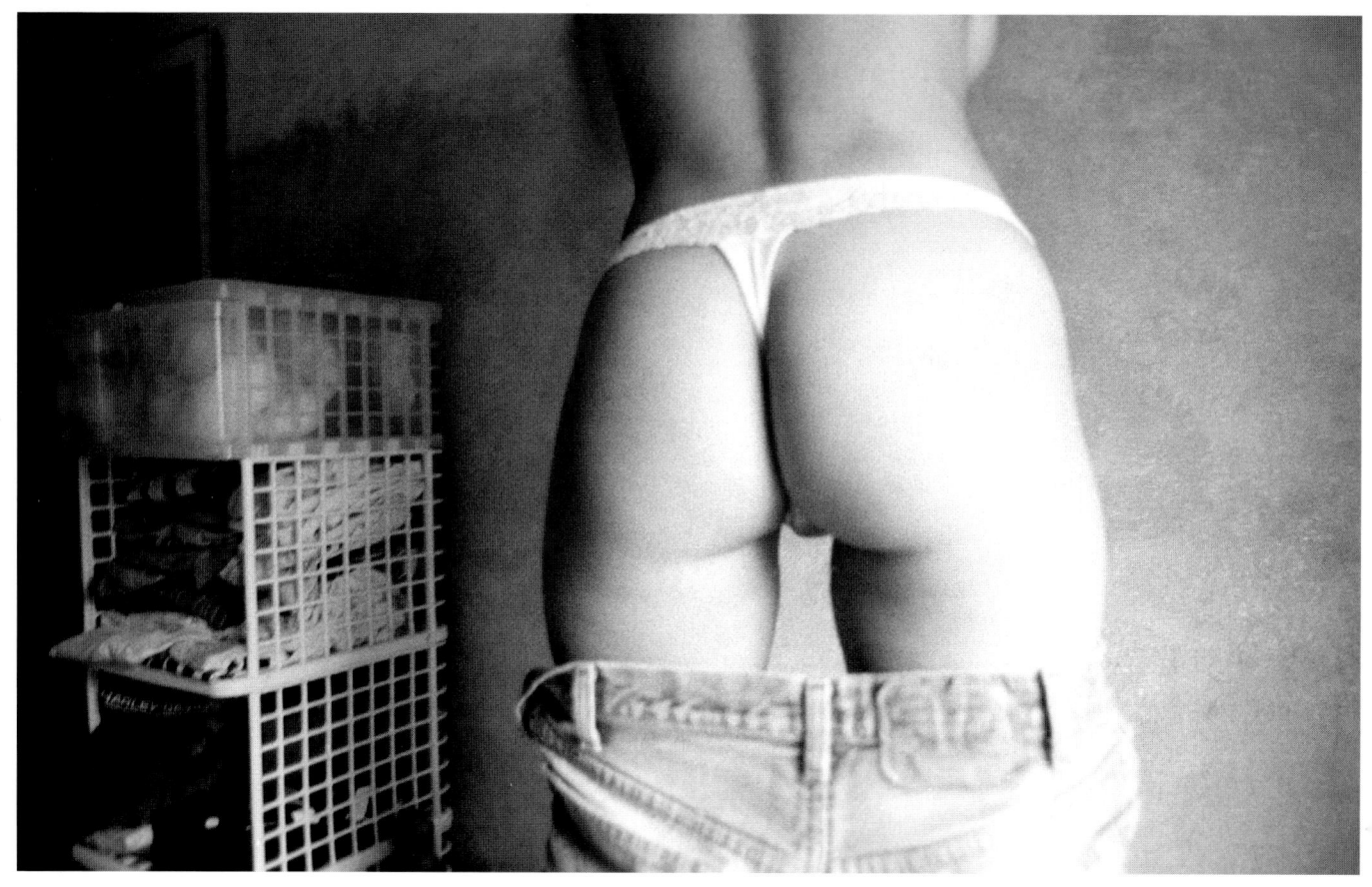

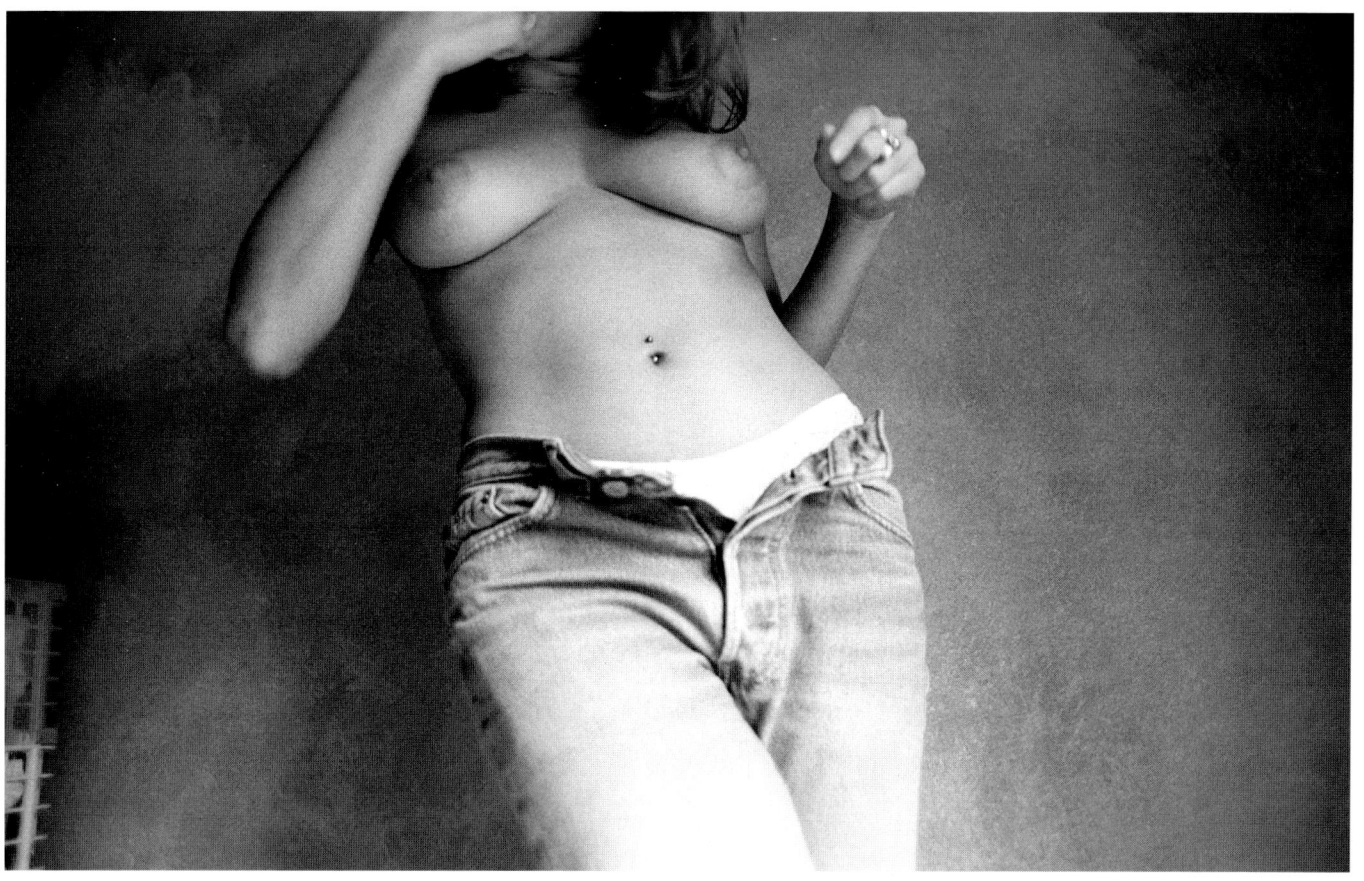

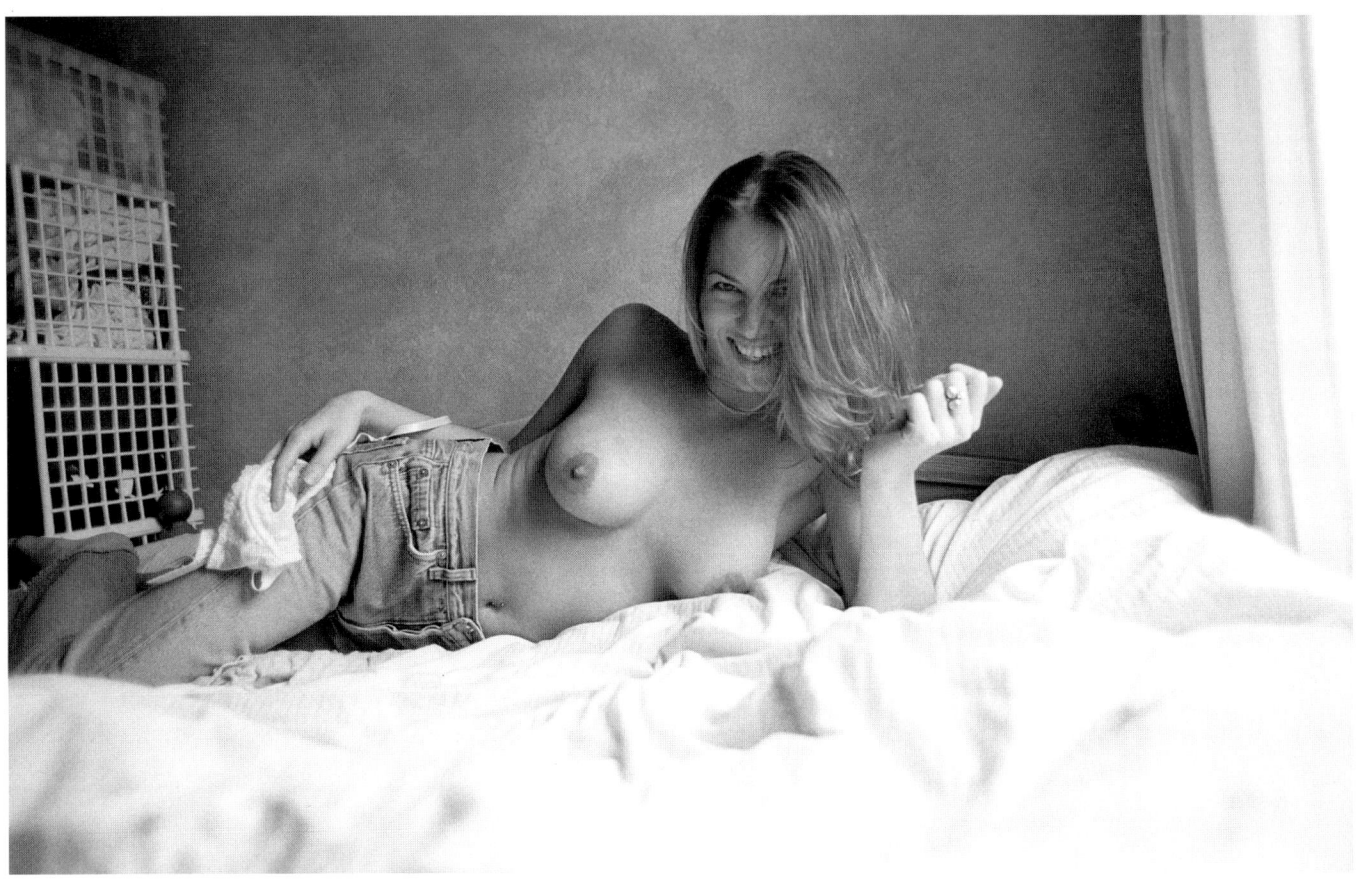

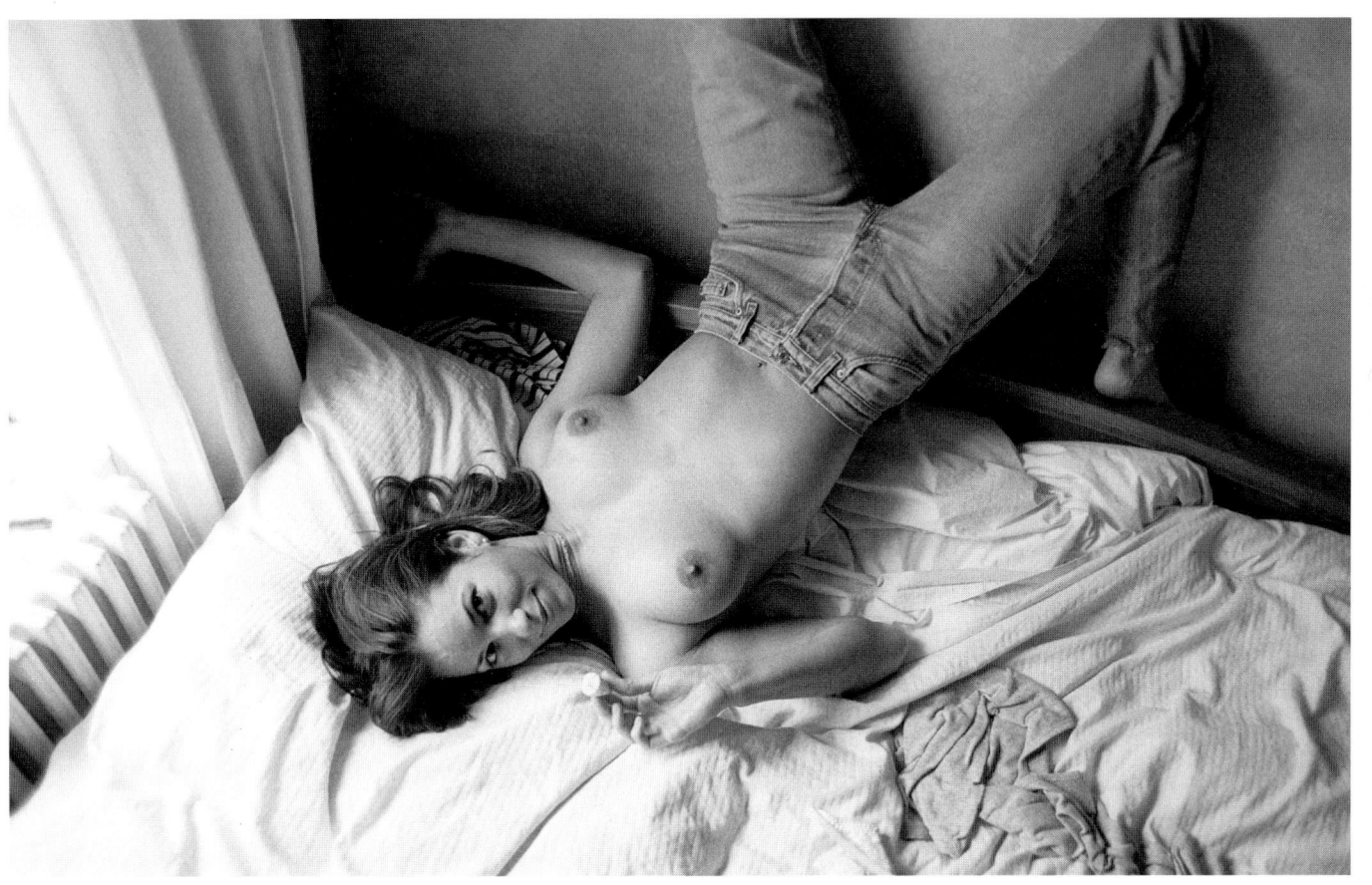

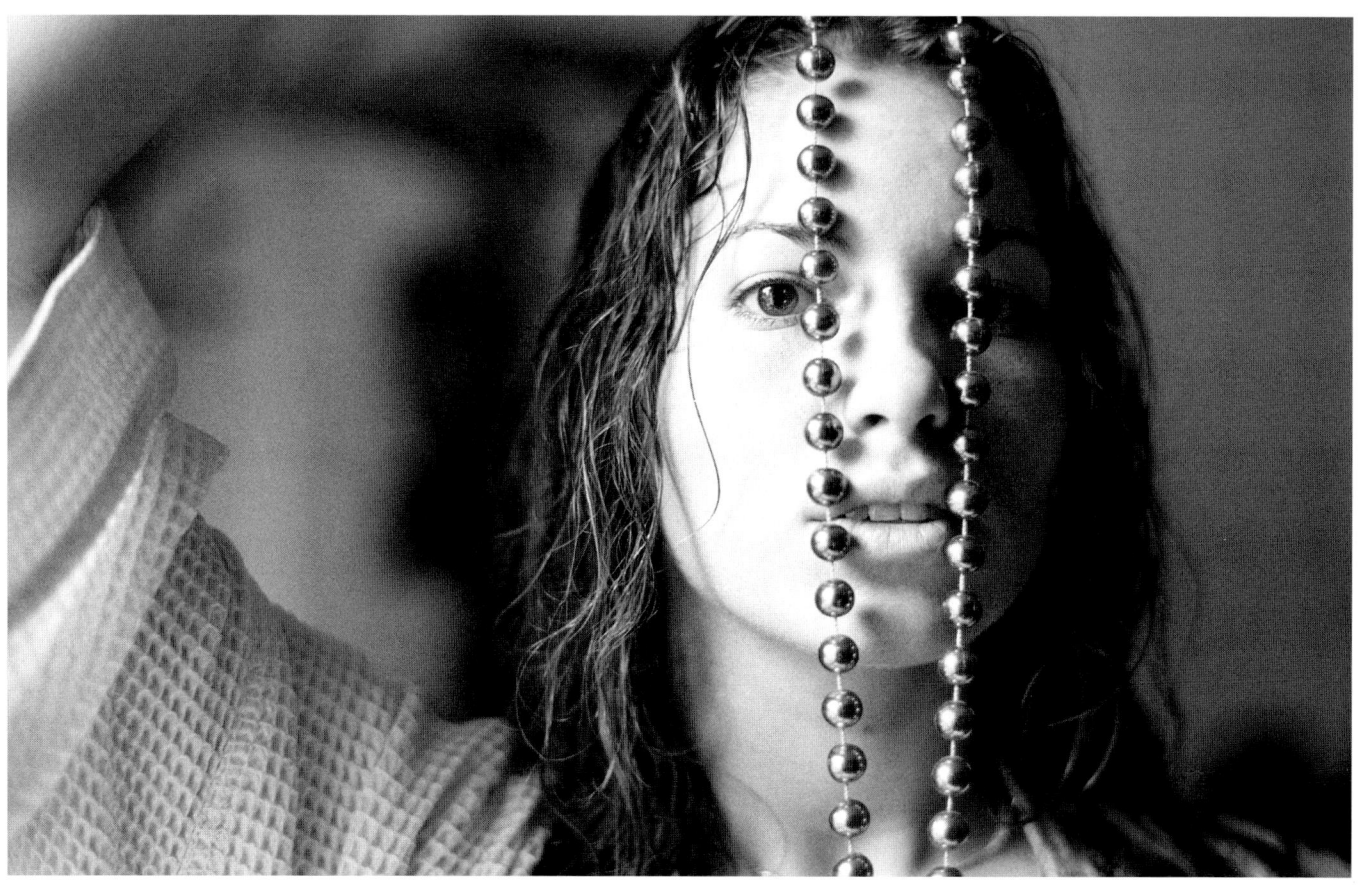

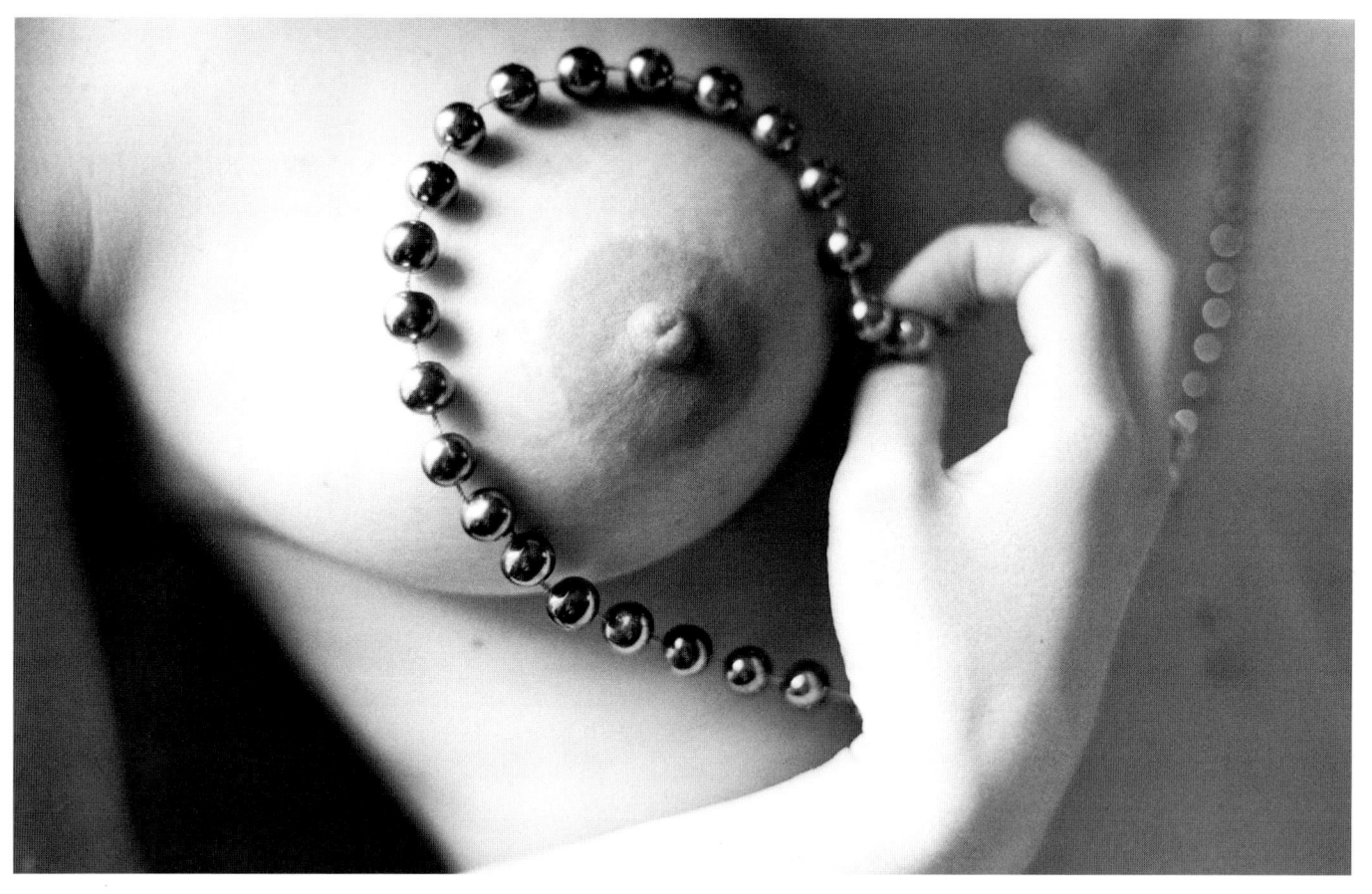

Cynthia · I met Cynthia through another artist. She's a graphic designer who lives with her sister and 3 cats in Brooklyn. When I arrived at her apartment, she was eating sushi for breakfast. Cynthia was shy at first, laughed a lot, and imitated characters from "Saturday Night Live." She thought that her cat "Milo" photographed better than she did.

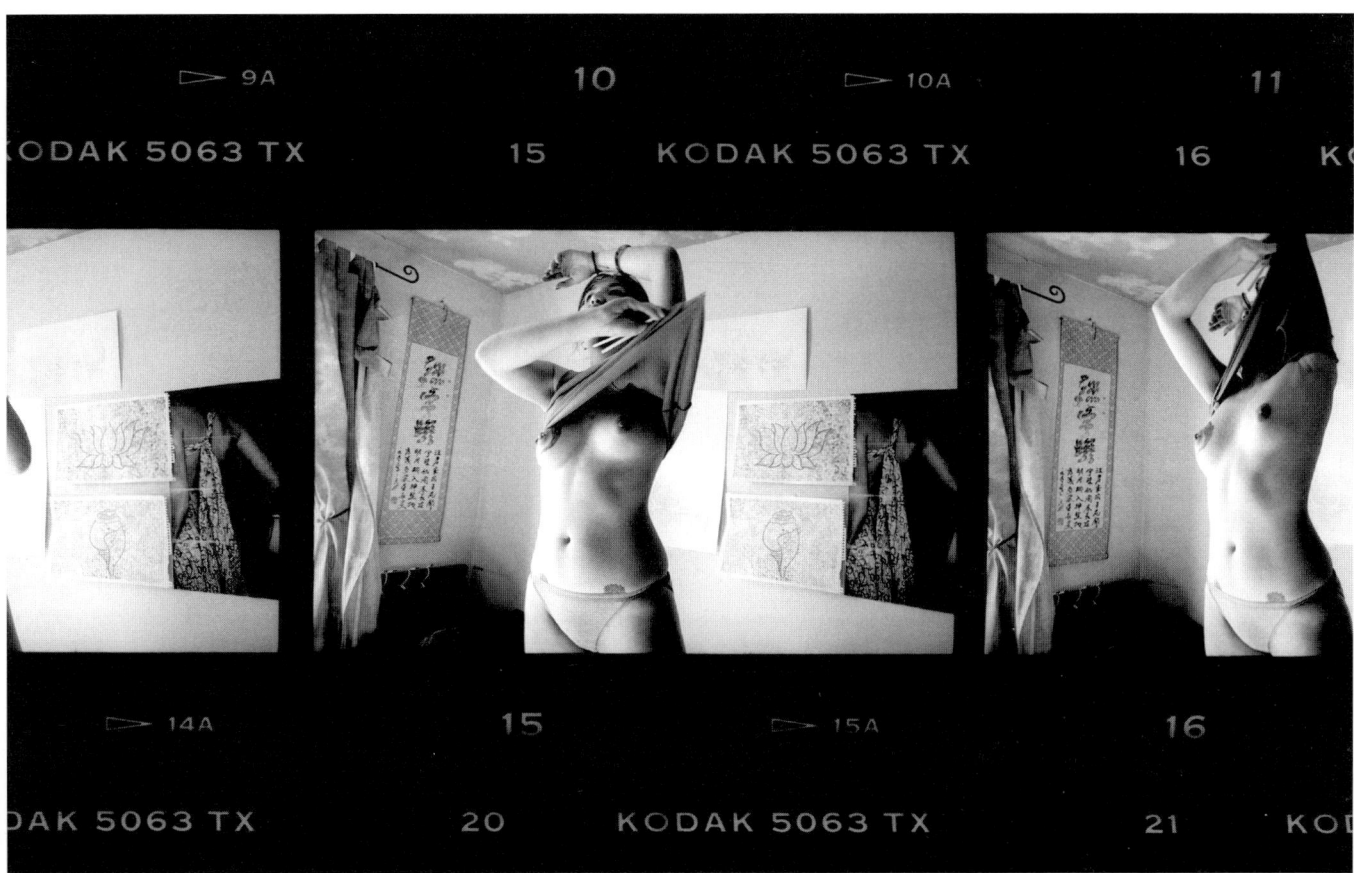

95

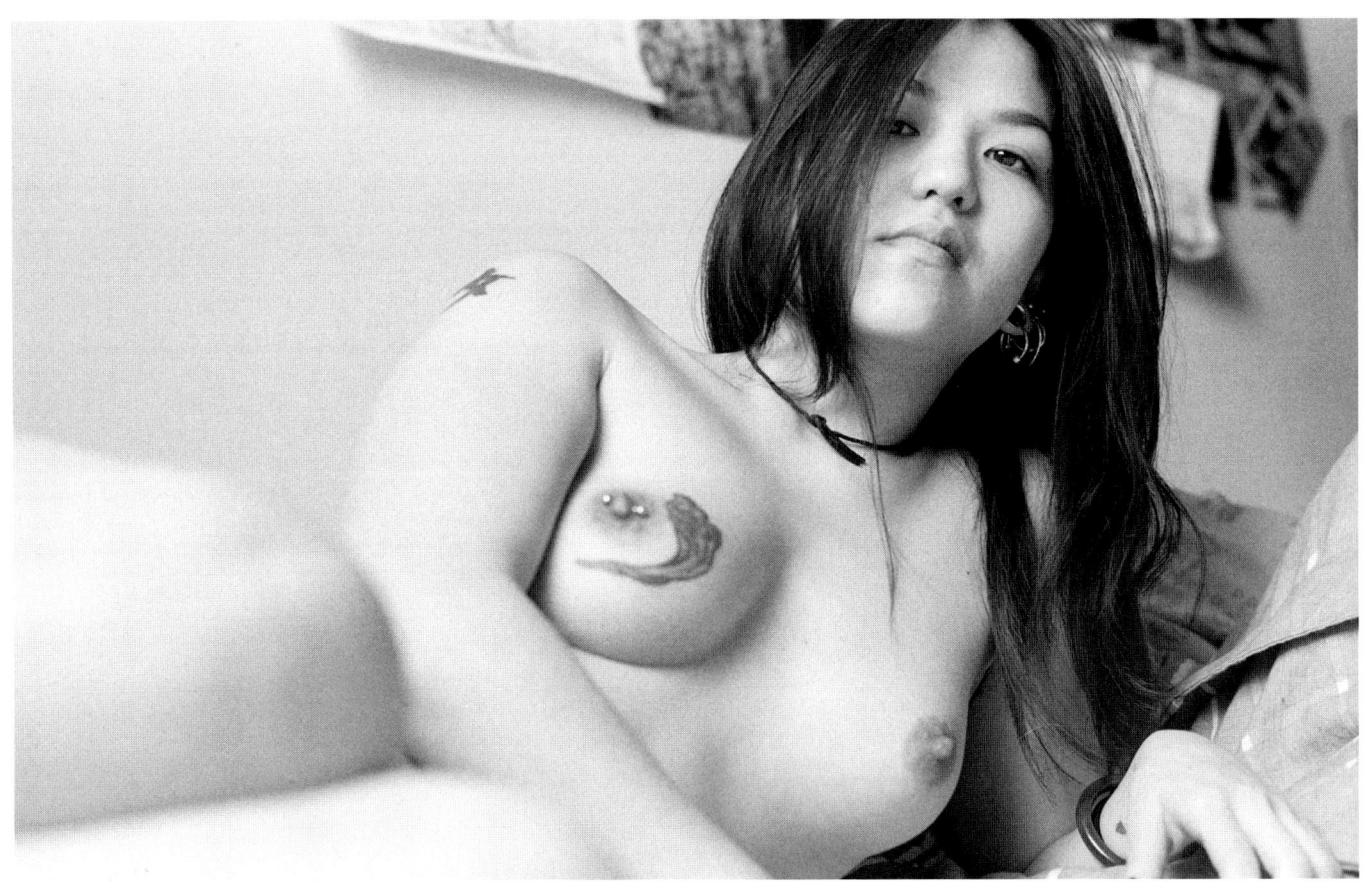

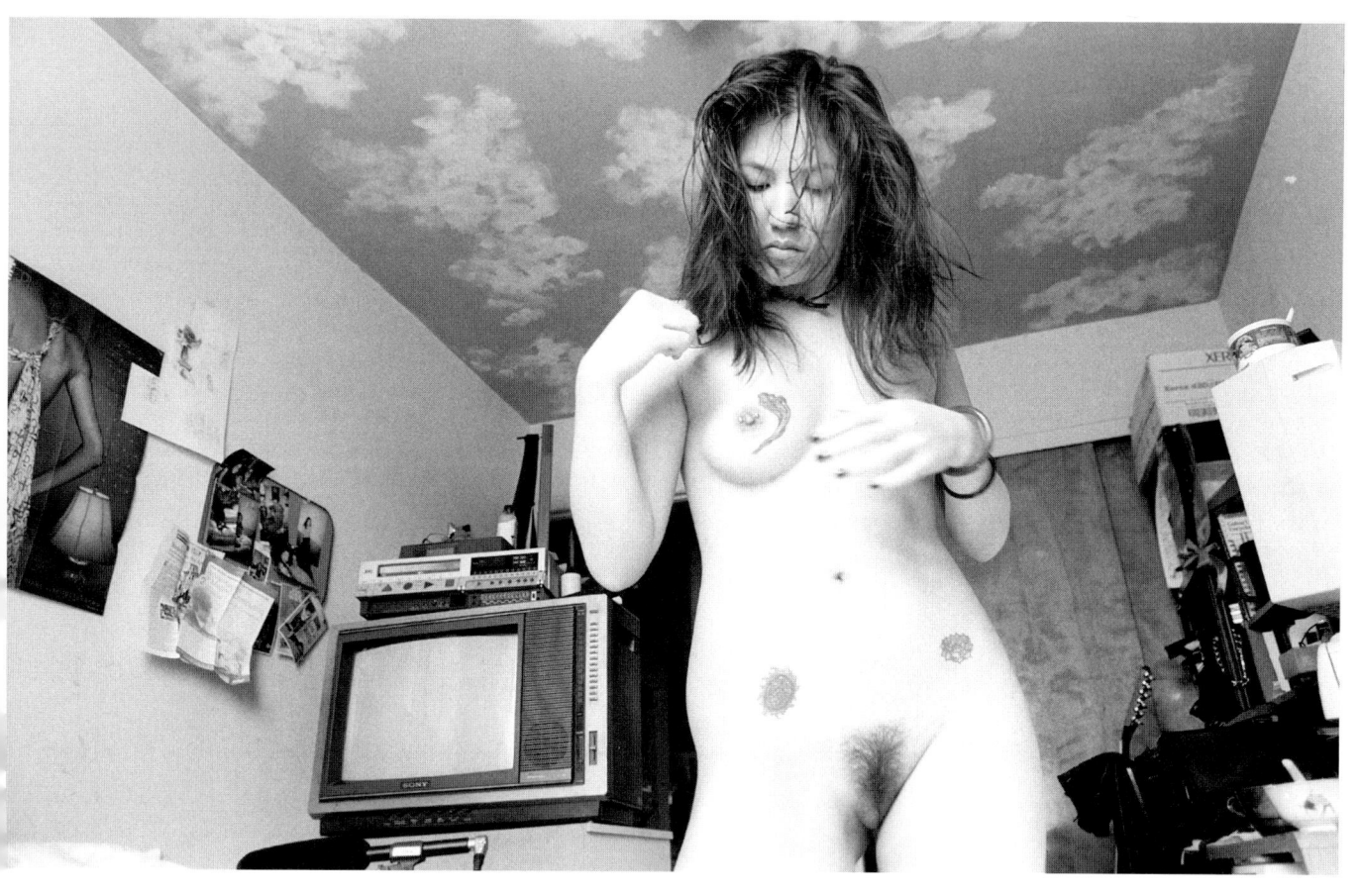

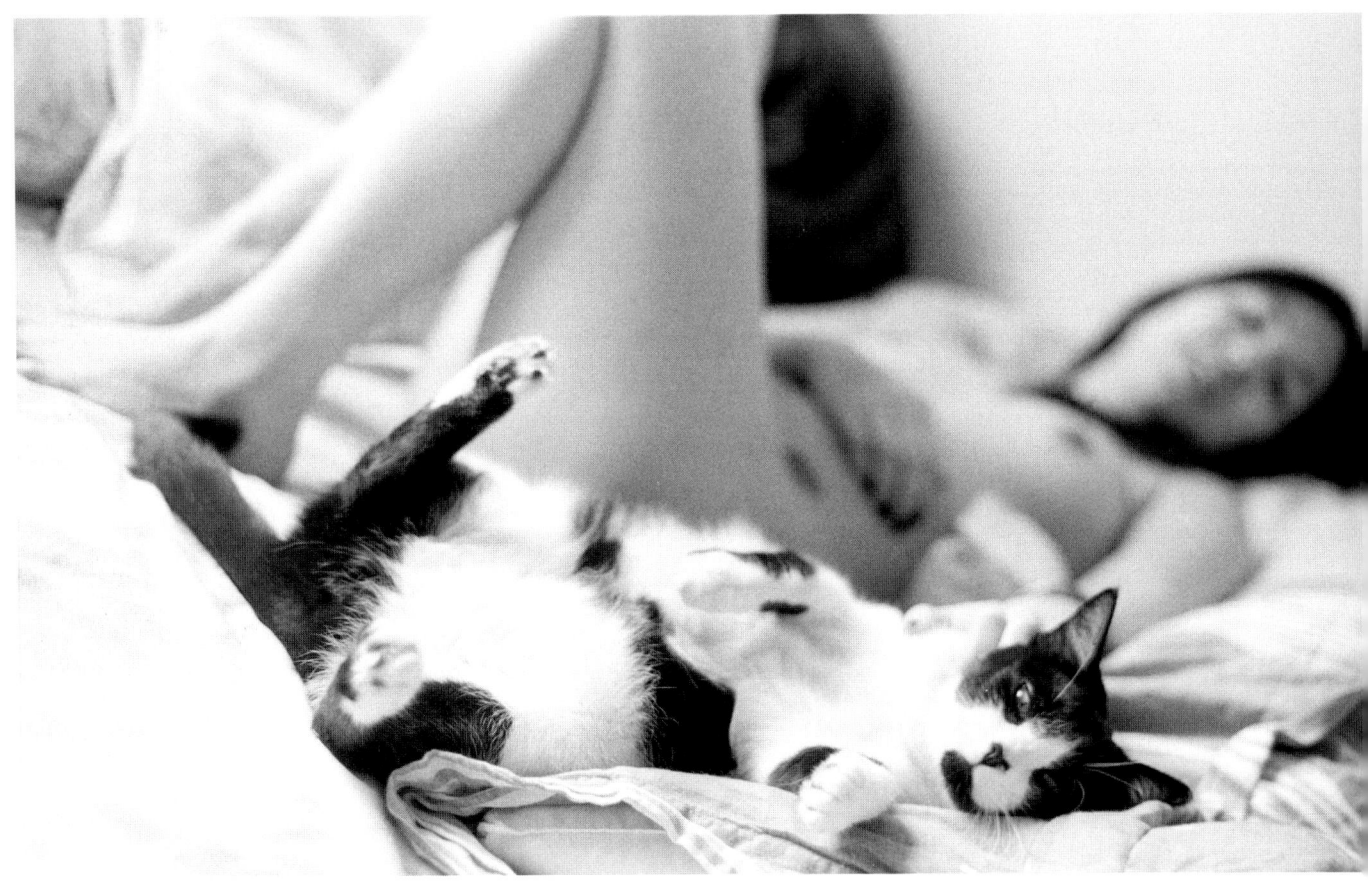

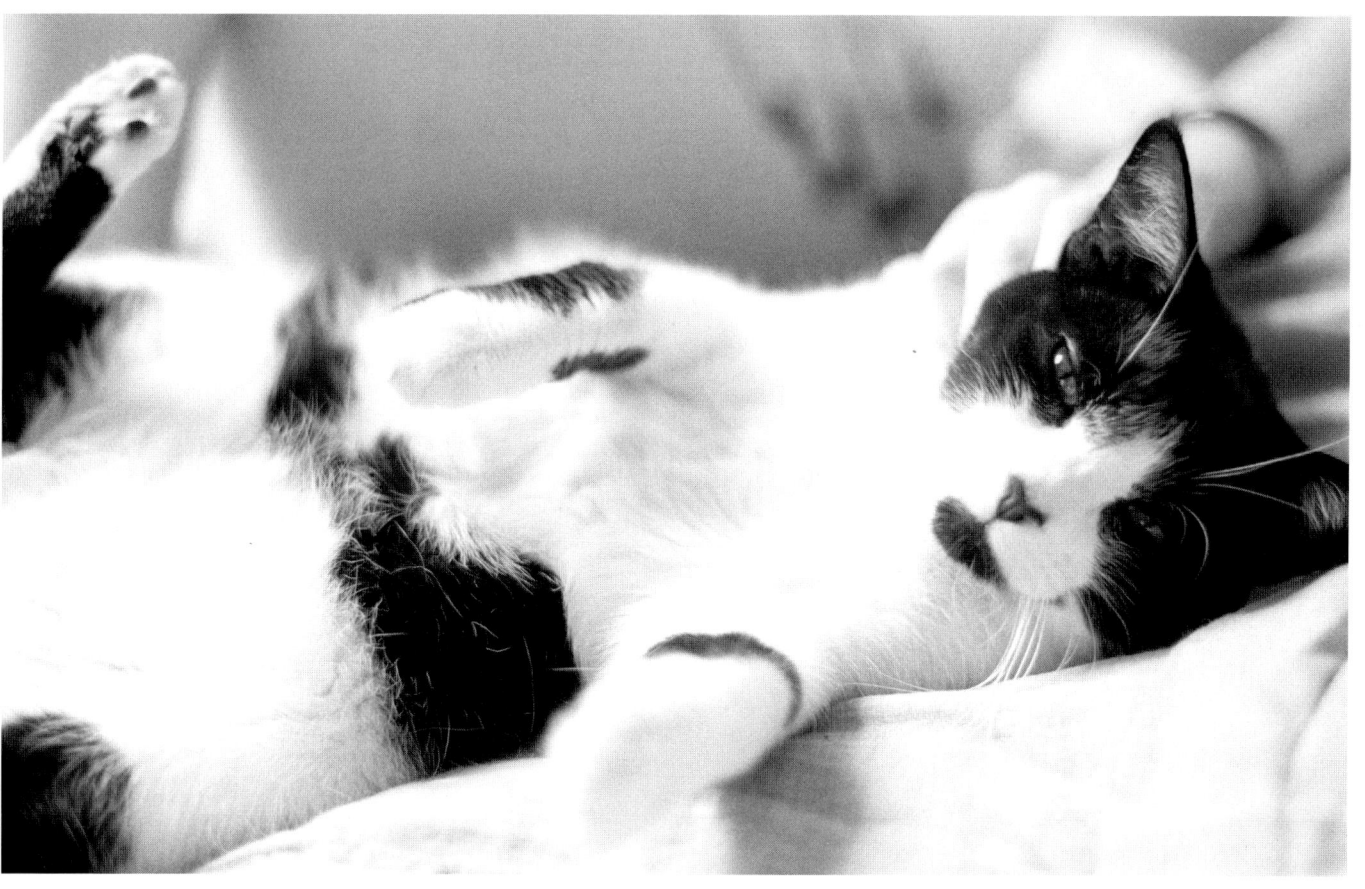

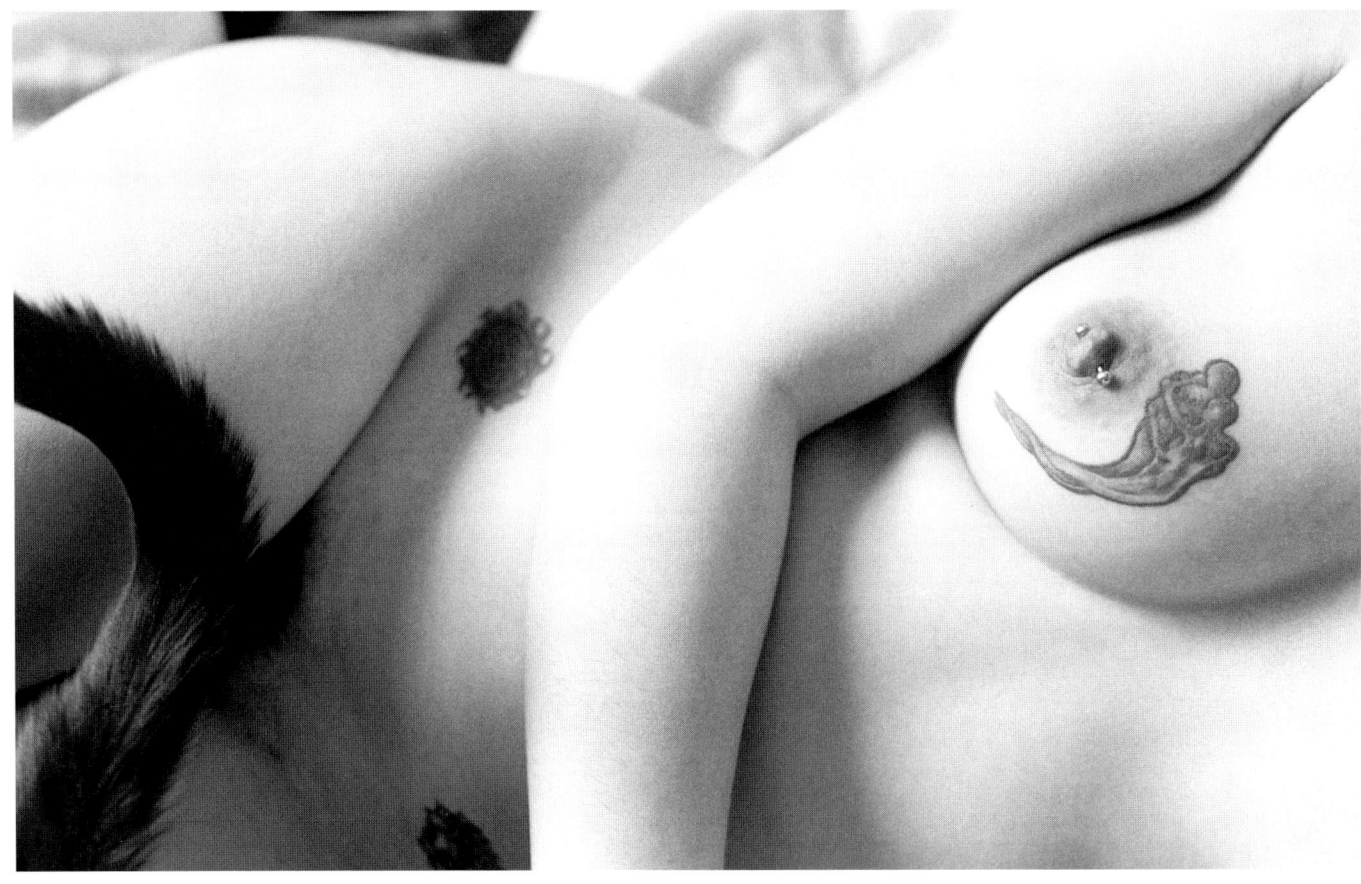

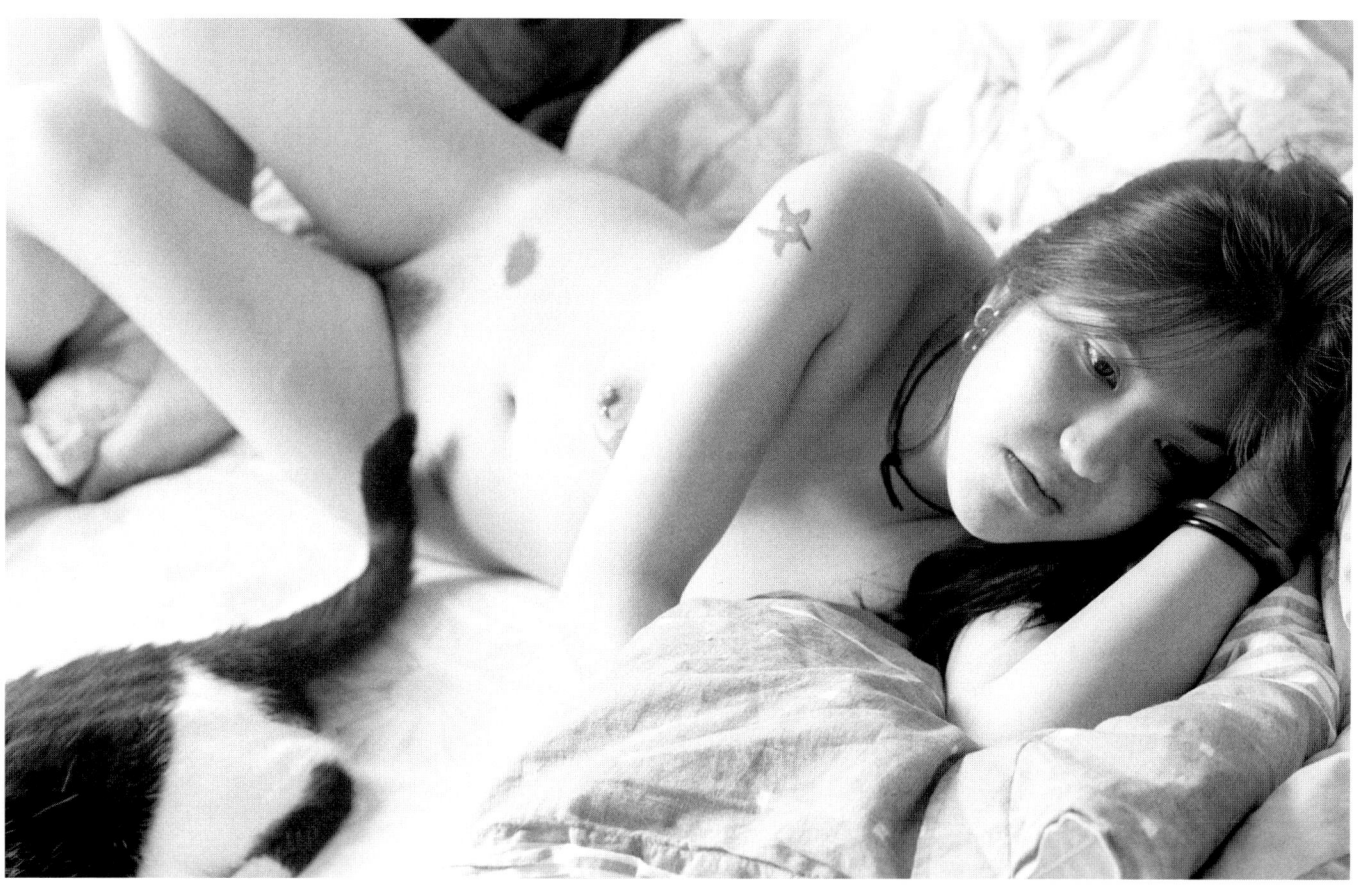

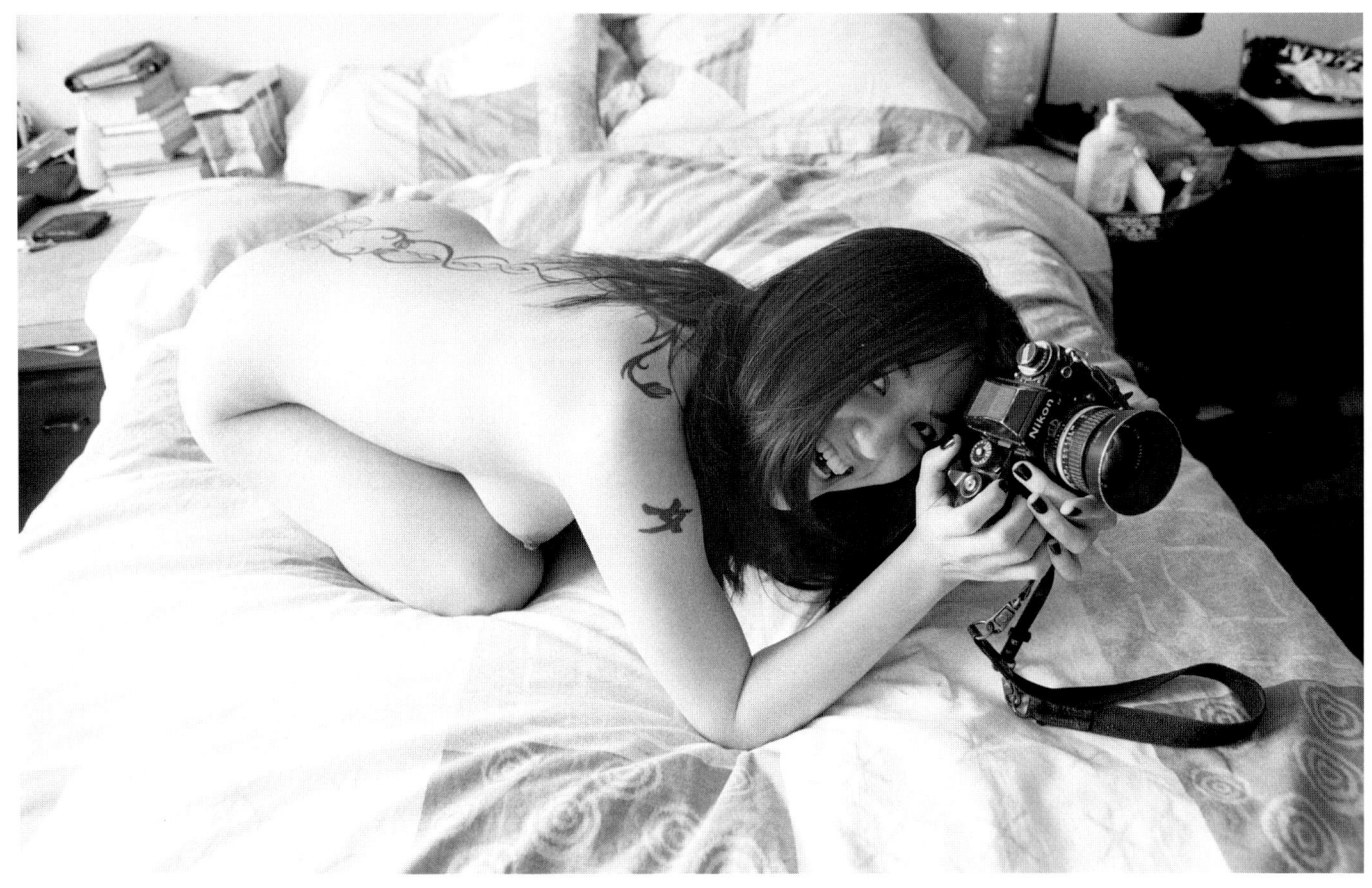

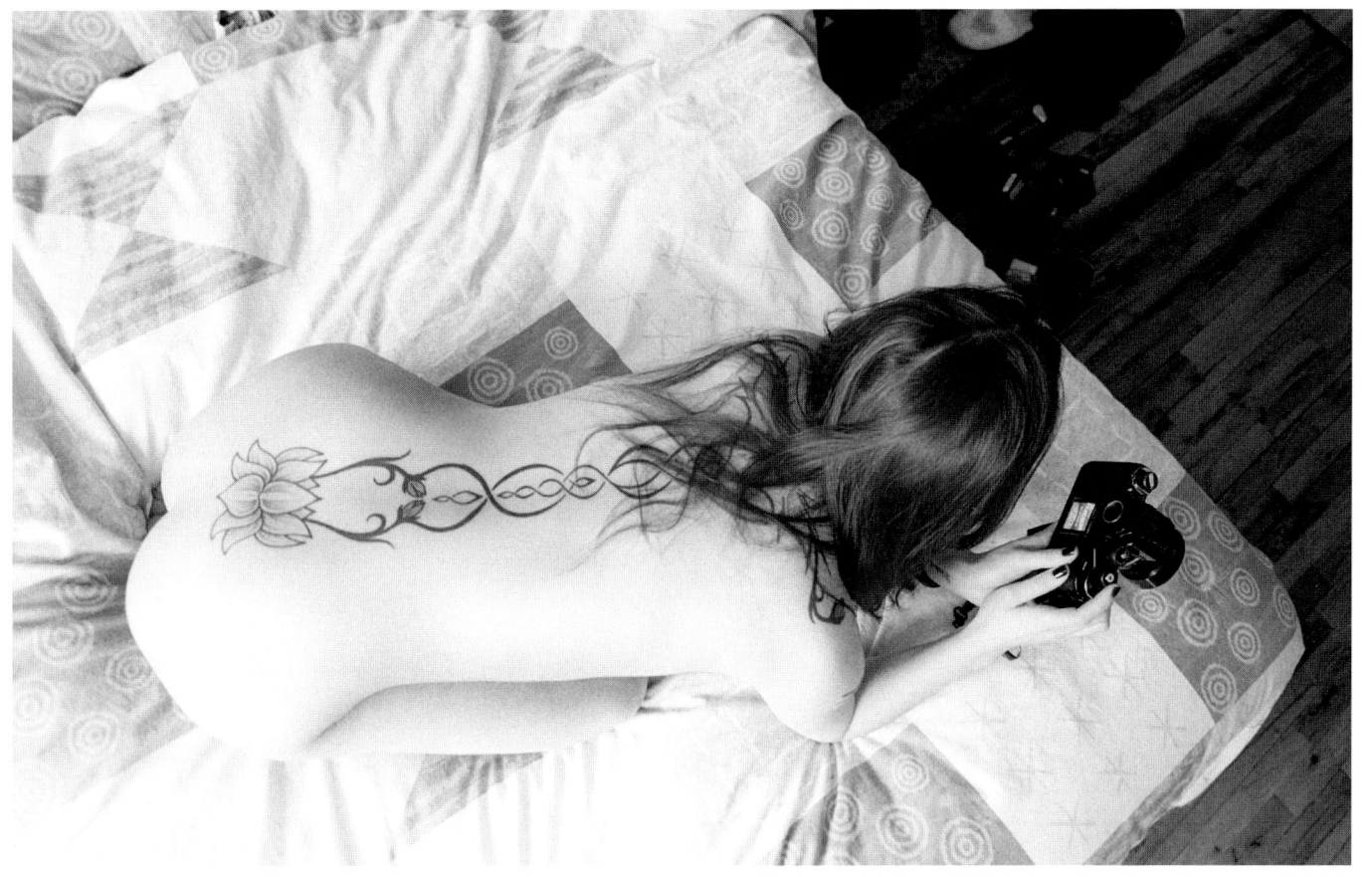

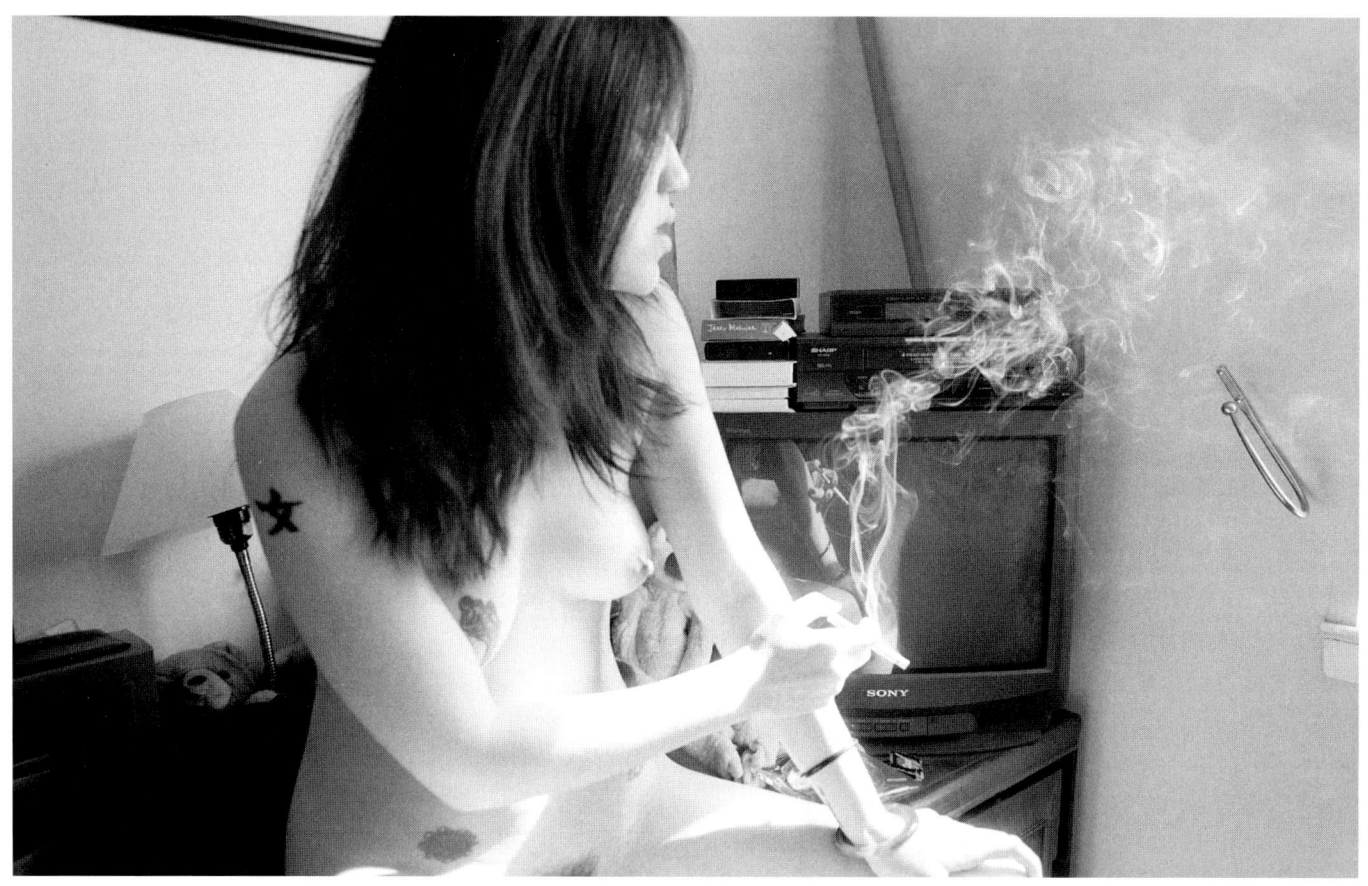

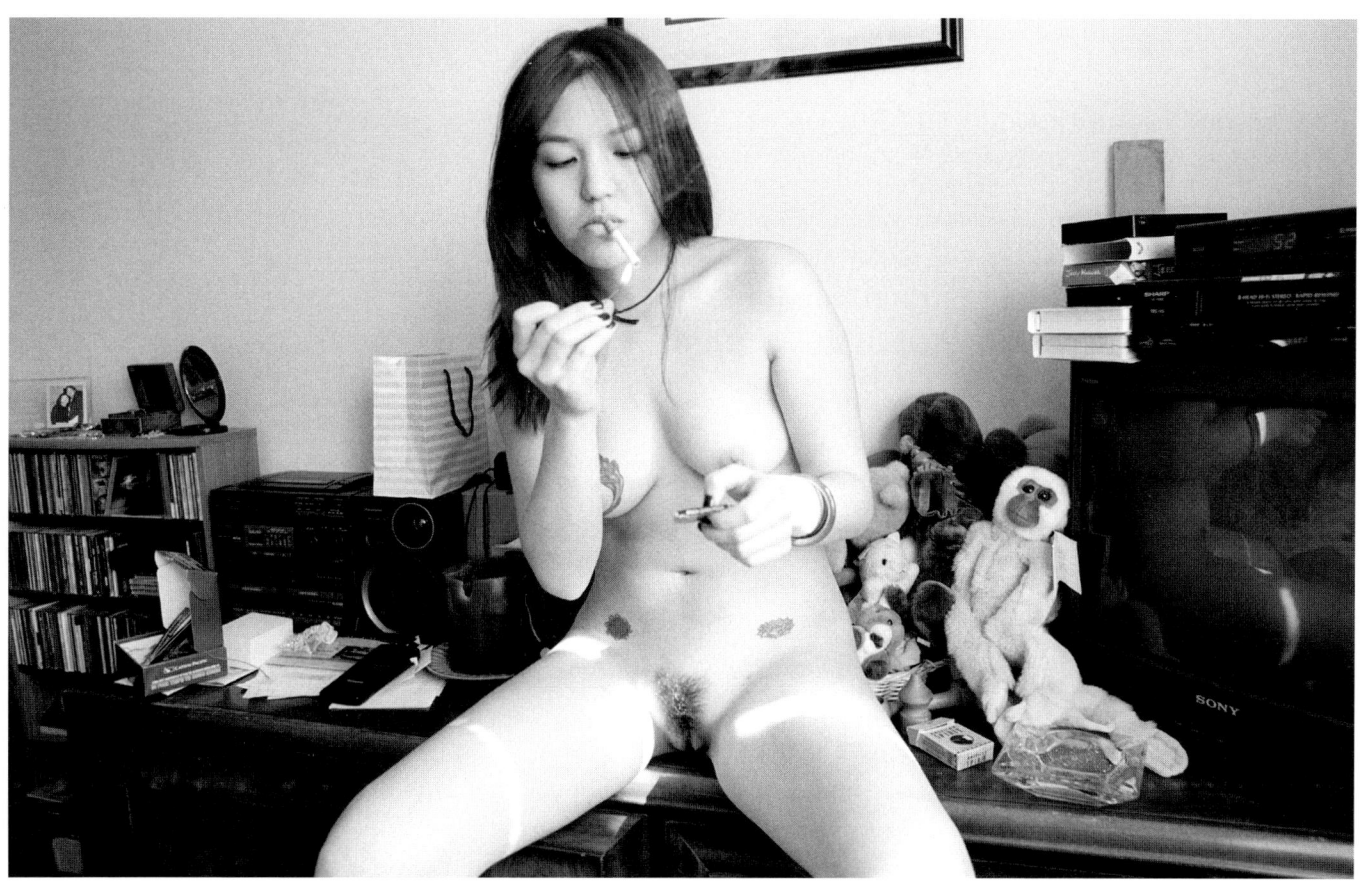

Diana · I met Diana when she was auditioning to be a show host for an internet company. She had big, beautiful eyes, and a really interesting look. I photographed her in her upper east side apartment, by the one big window in her bedroom. Diana is Mexican, and an actress.

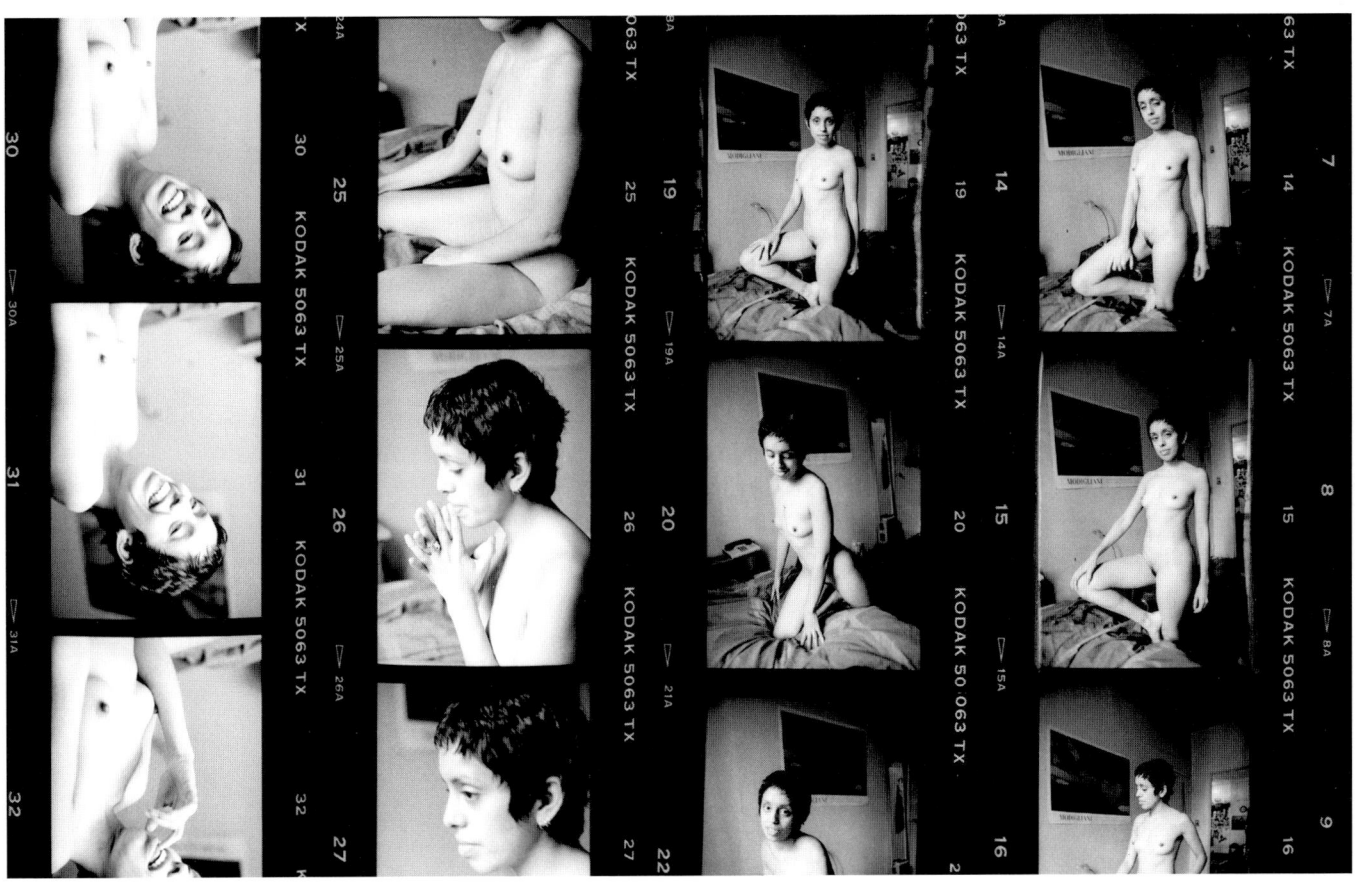

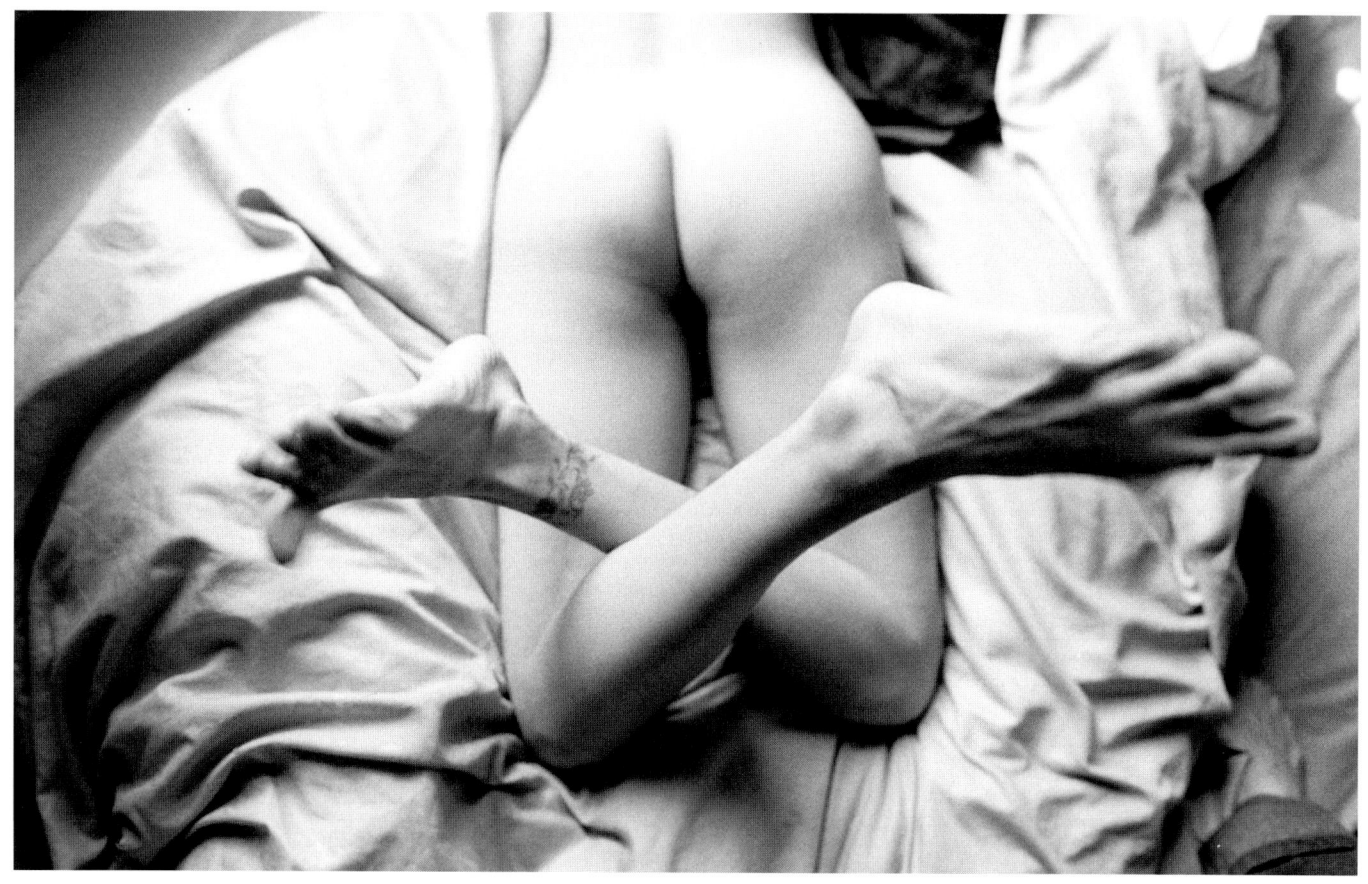

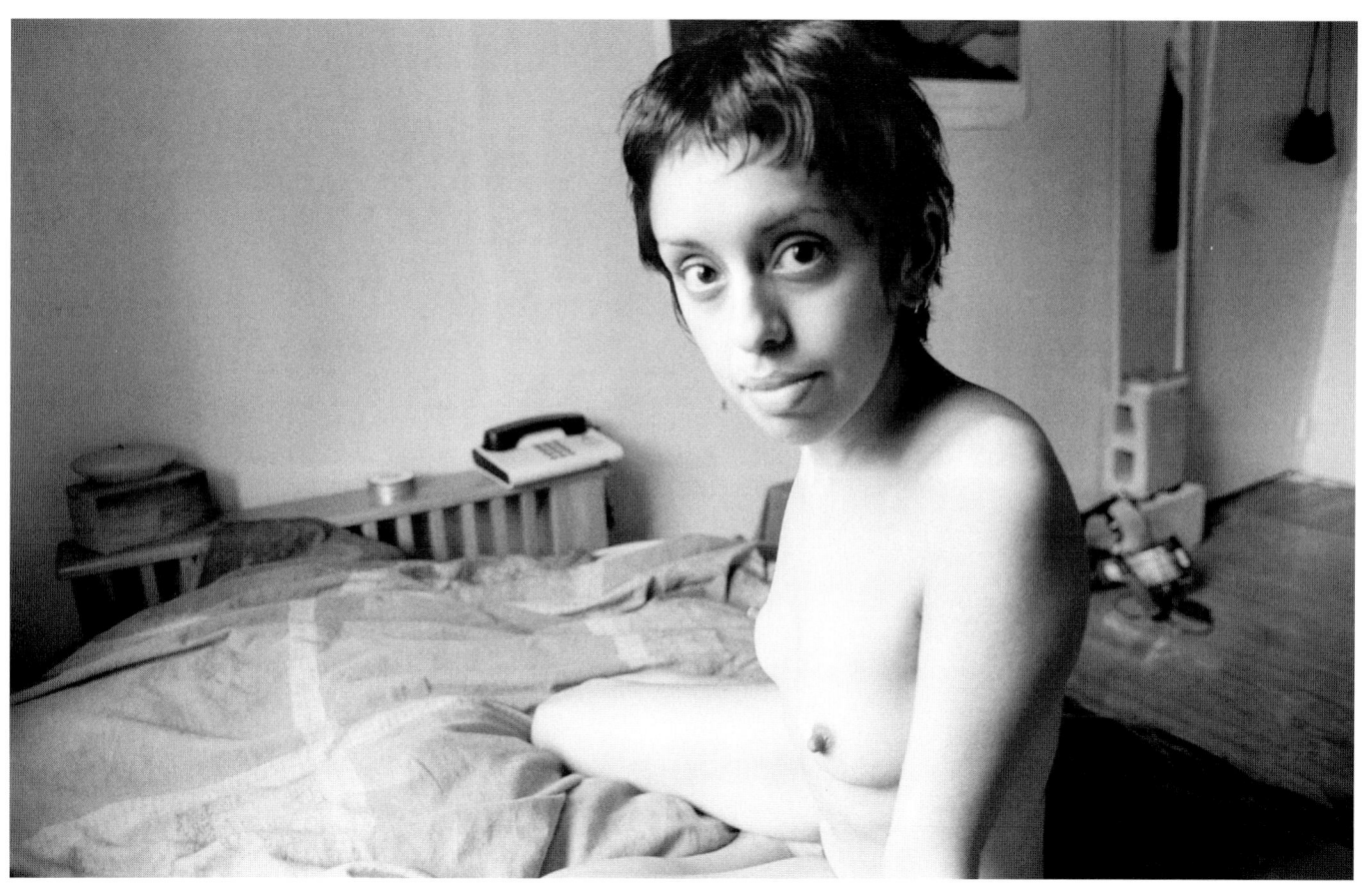

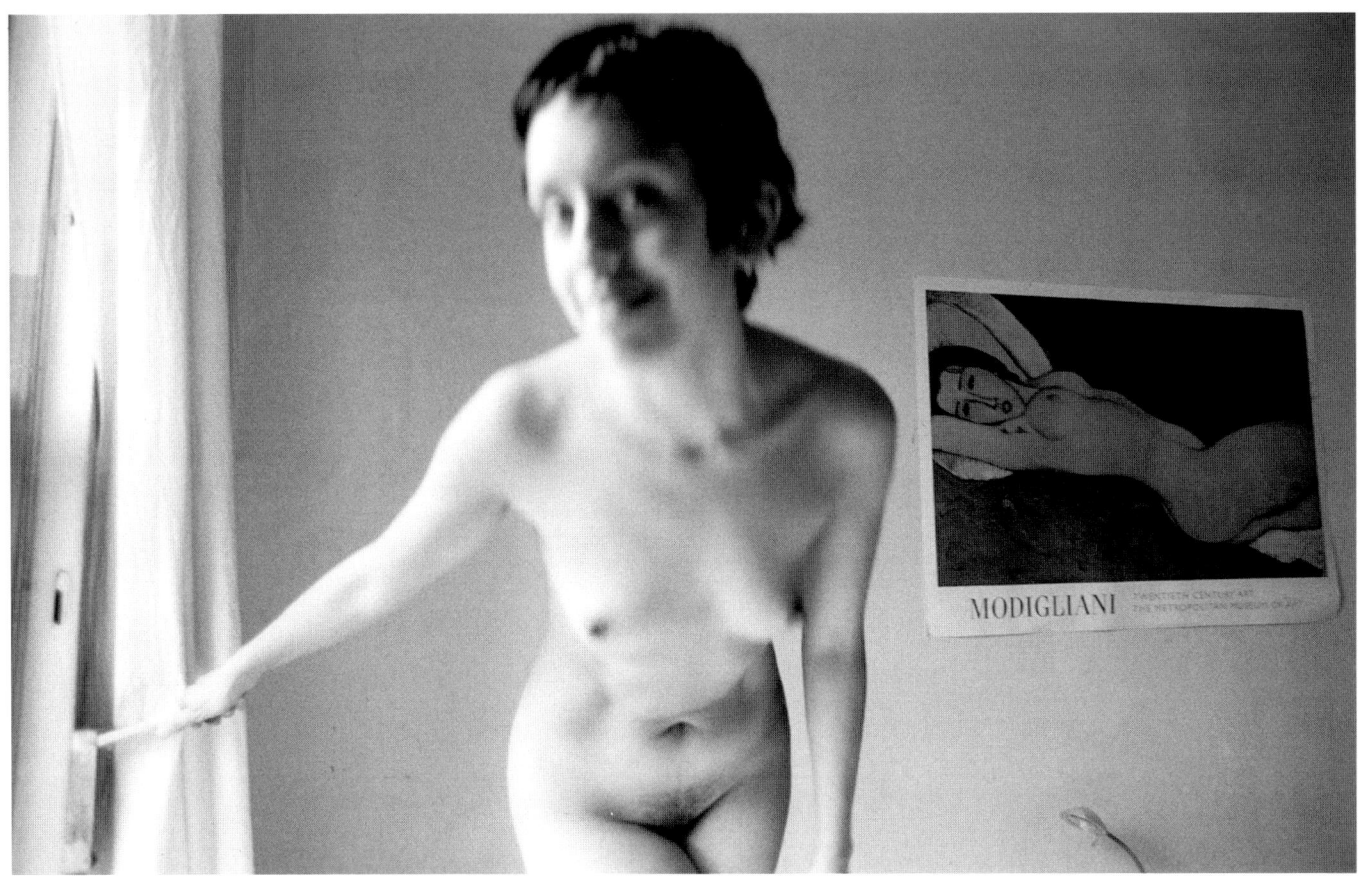

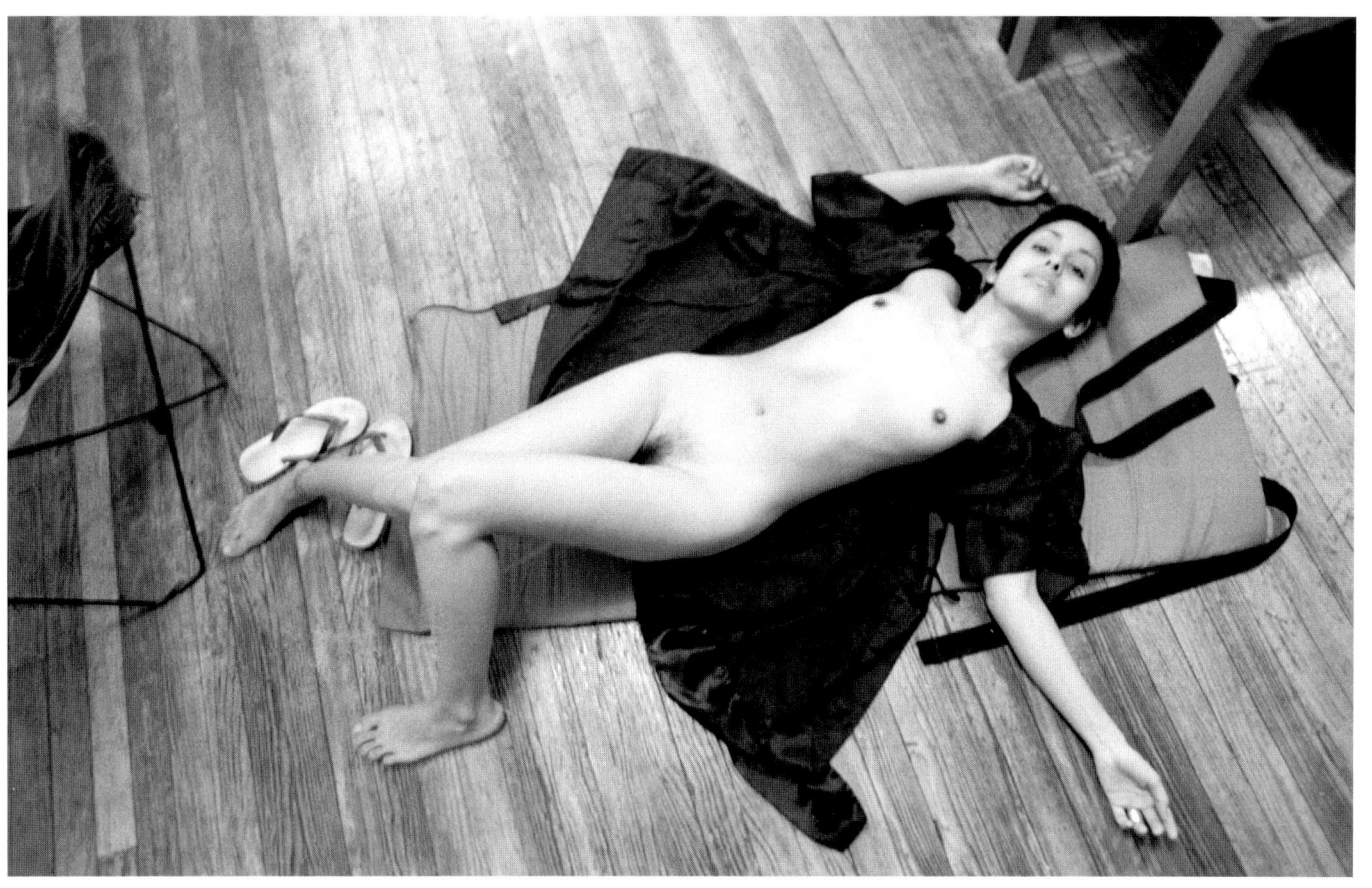

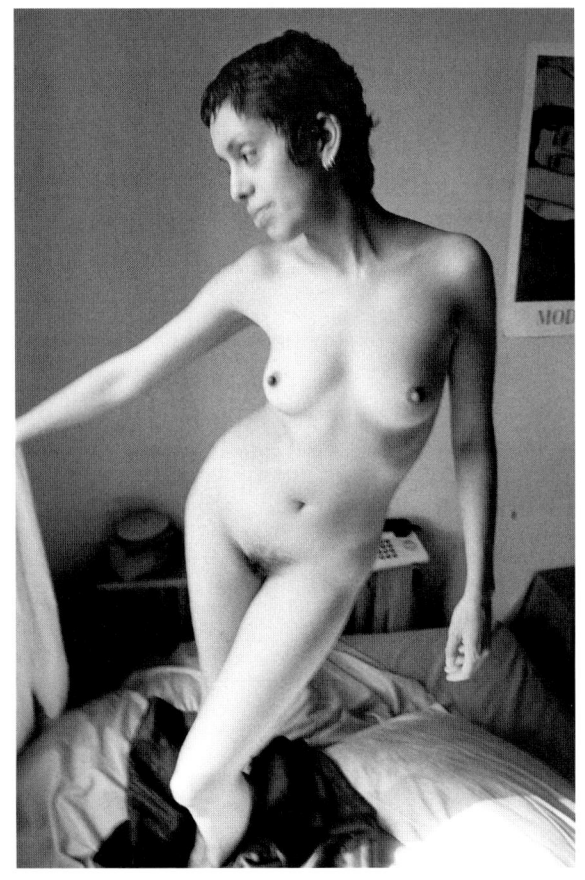
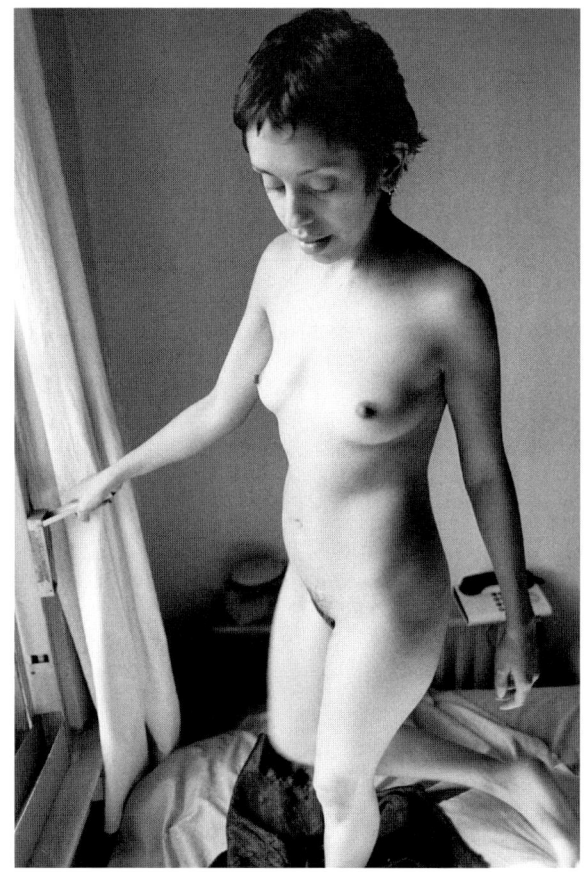

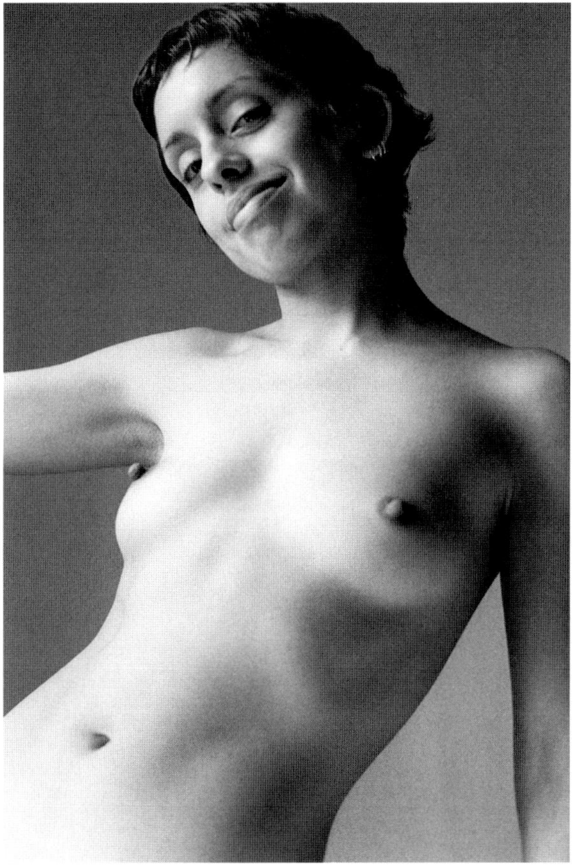

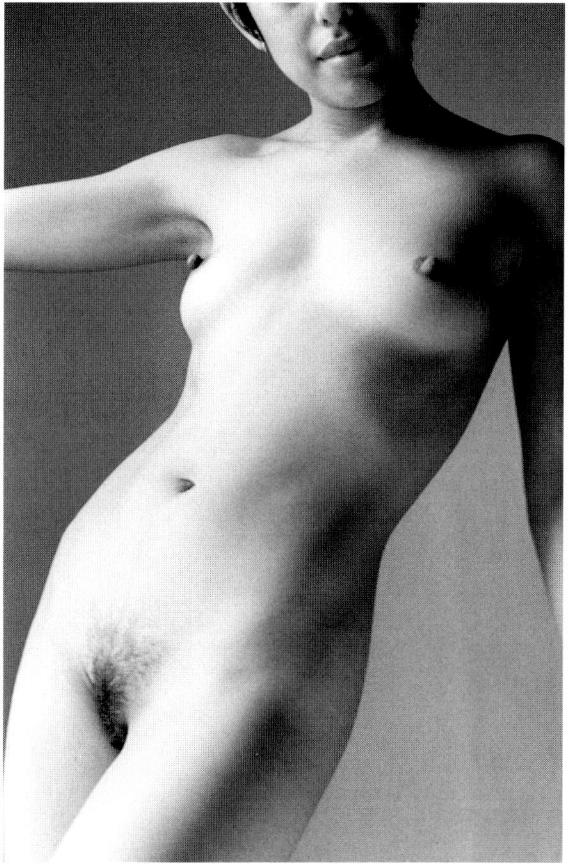

Gabby · I met Gabby in Central Park, while filming on my rollerblades. We quickly became good friends. Gabby, who is from Argentina, told me that she always wanted to do a nude photo shoot, but was too shy. I photographed her in a friend's apartment in the west village. She brought Jack Daniels and I brought smoke. Gabby had one of the cutest asses I've ever seen.

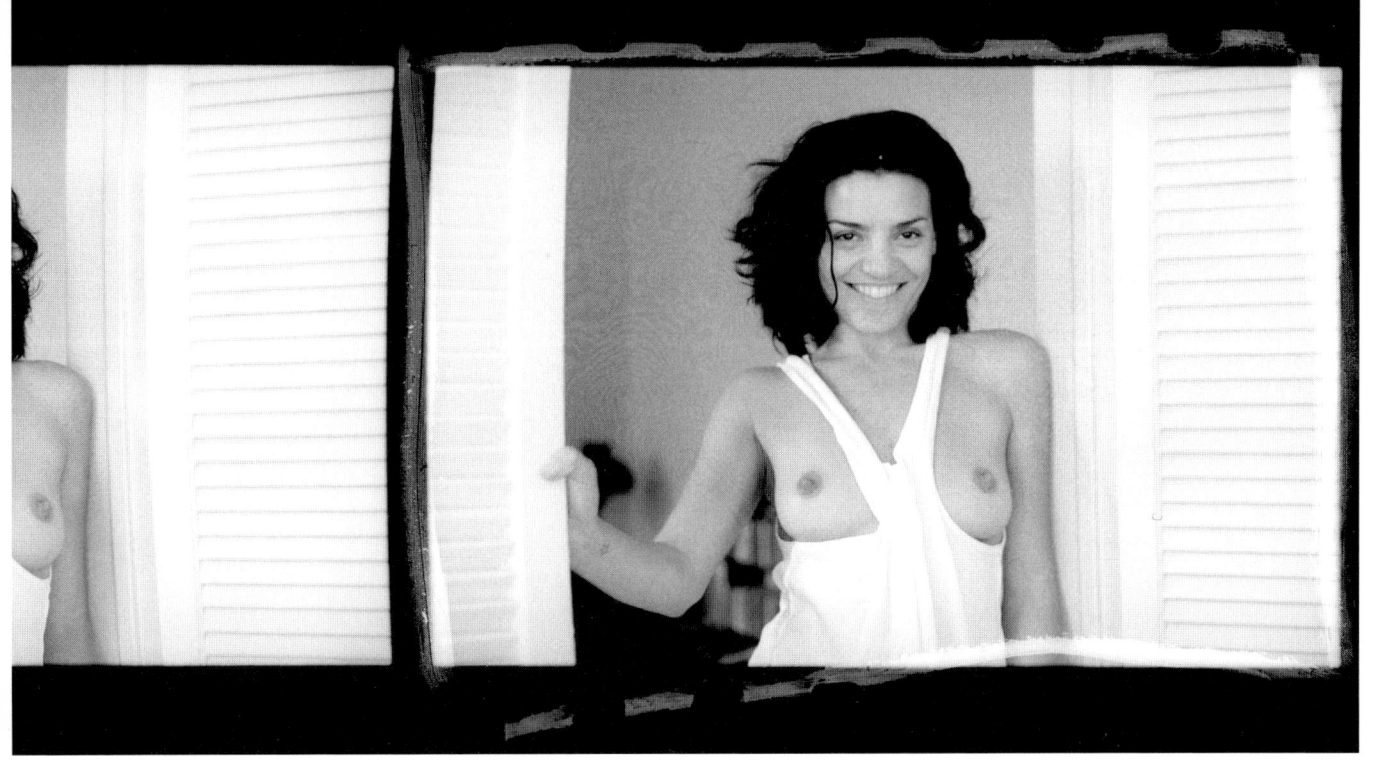

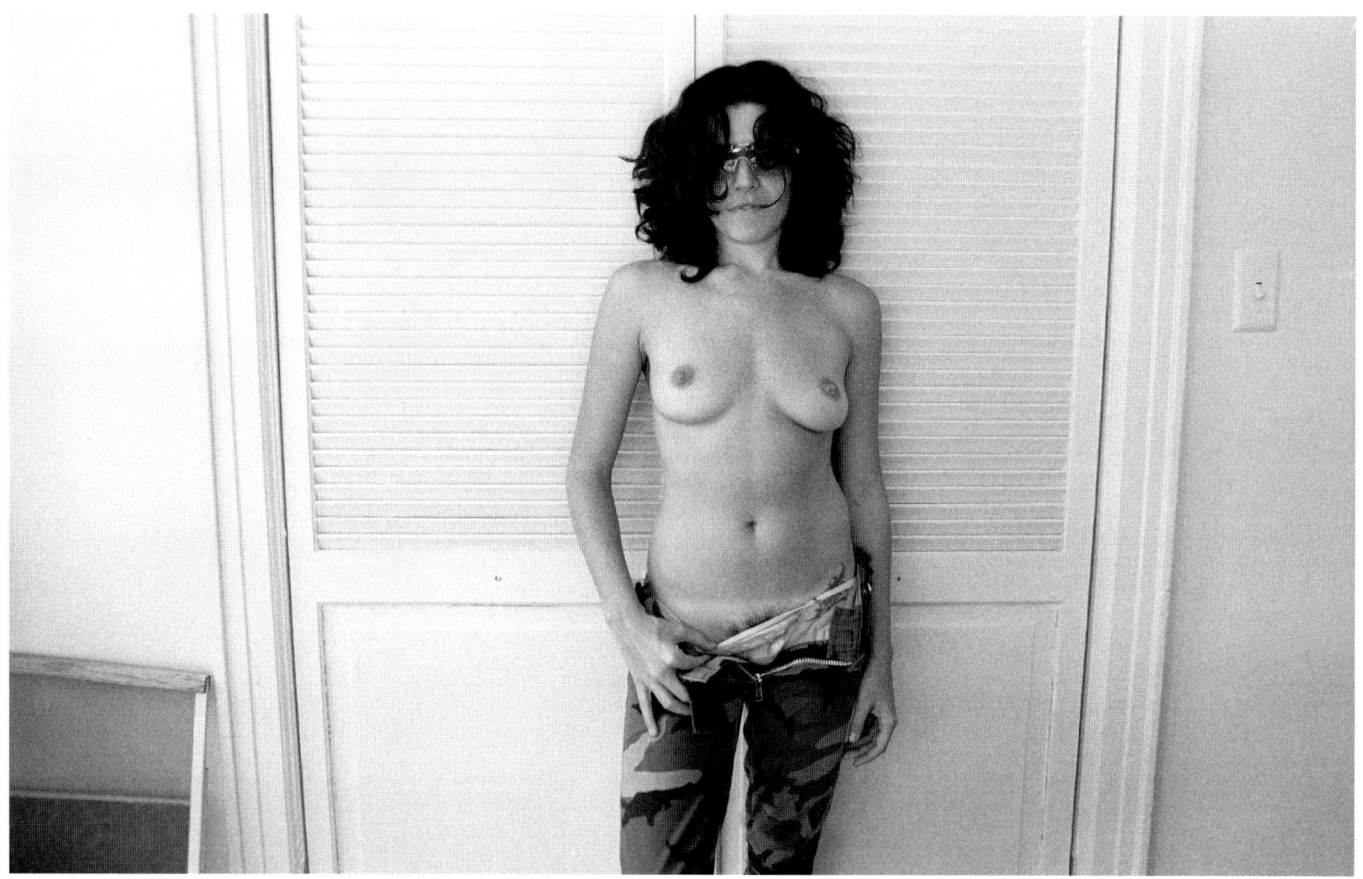

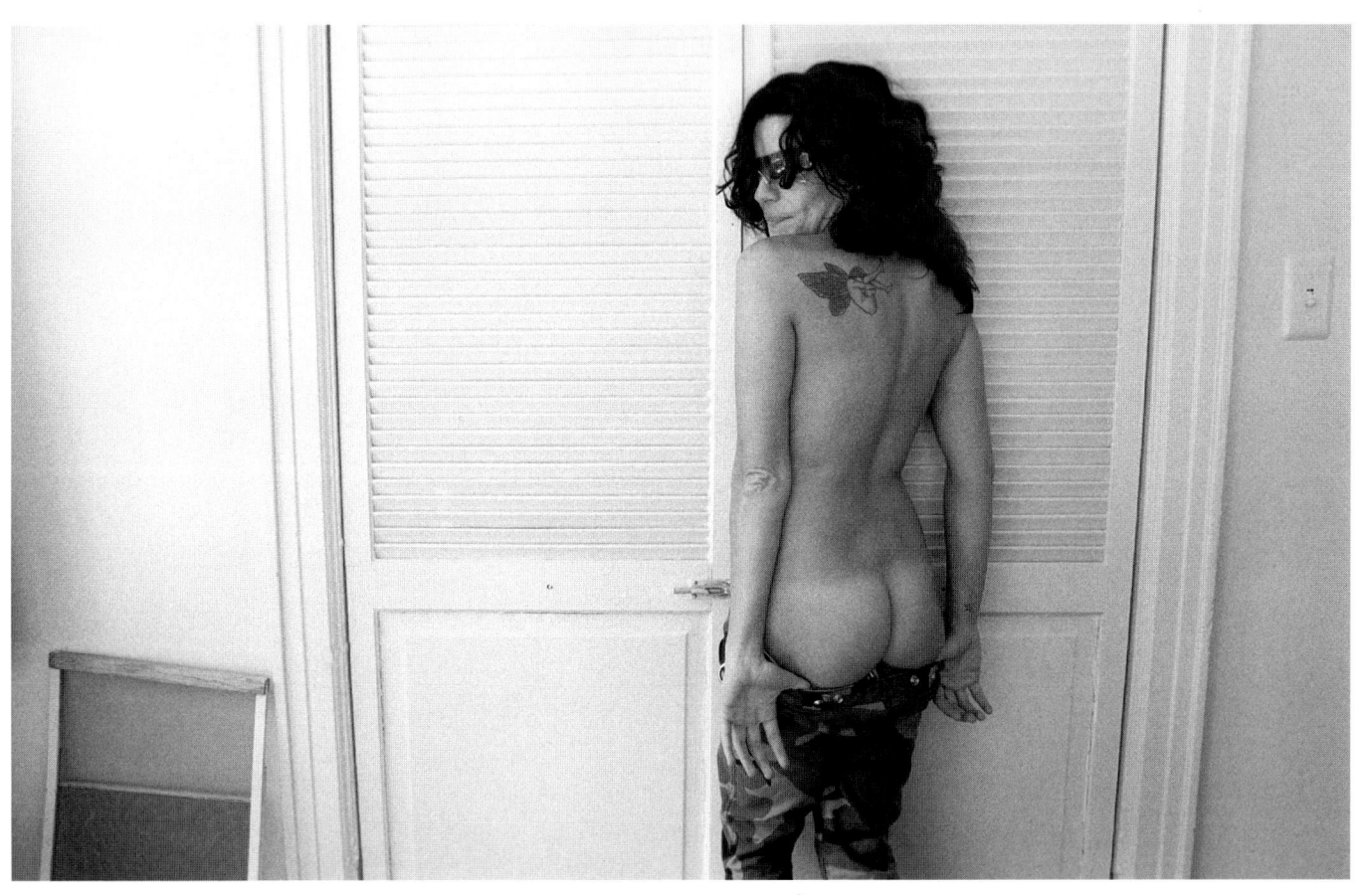

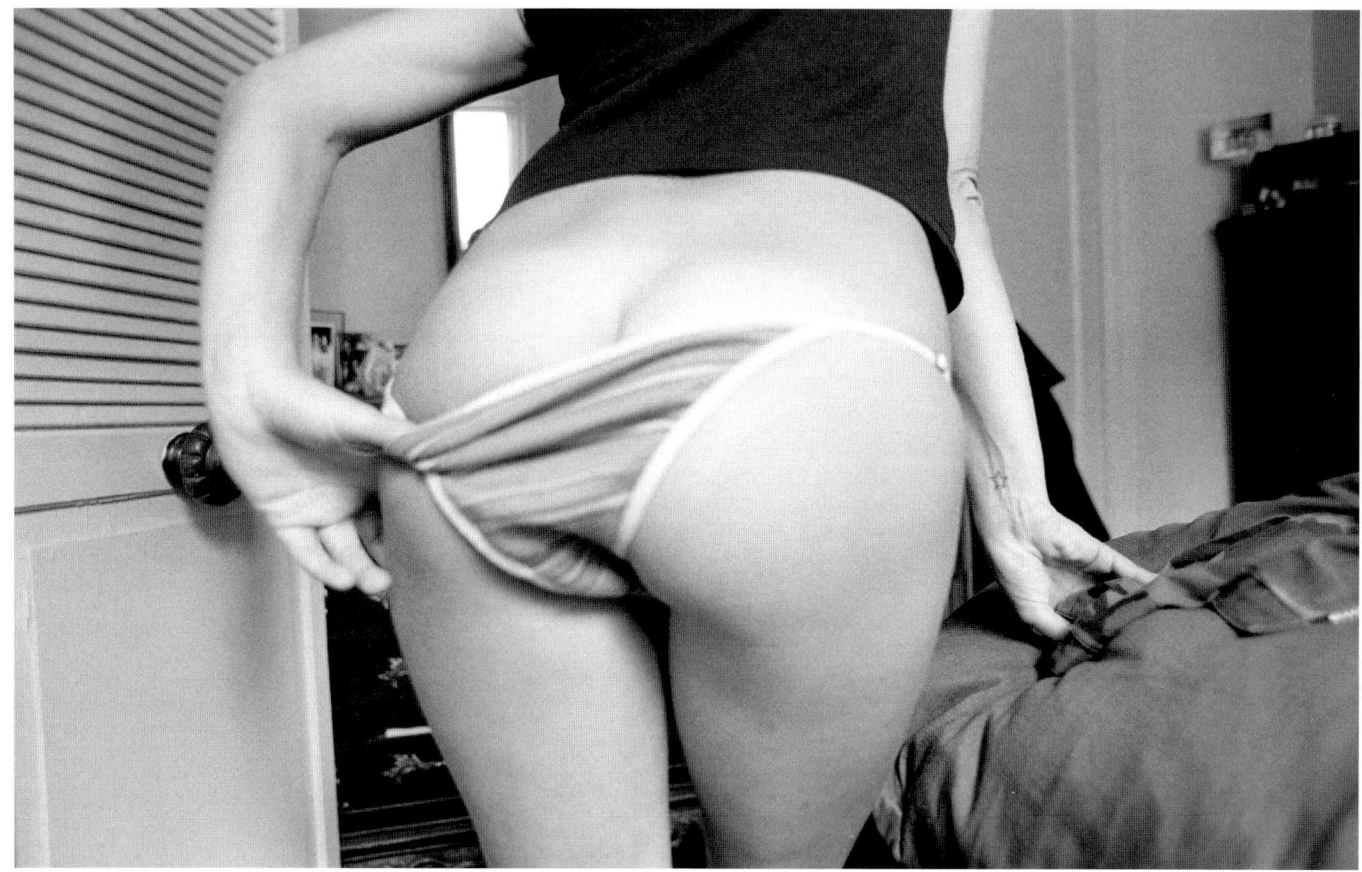

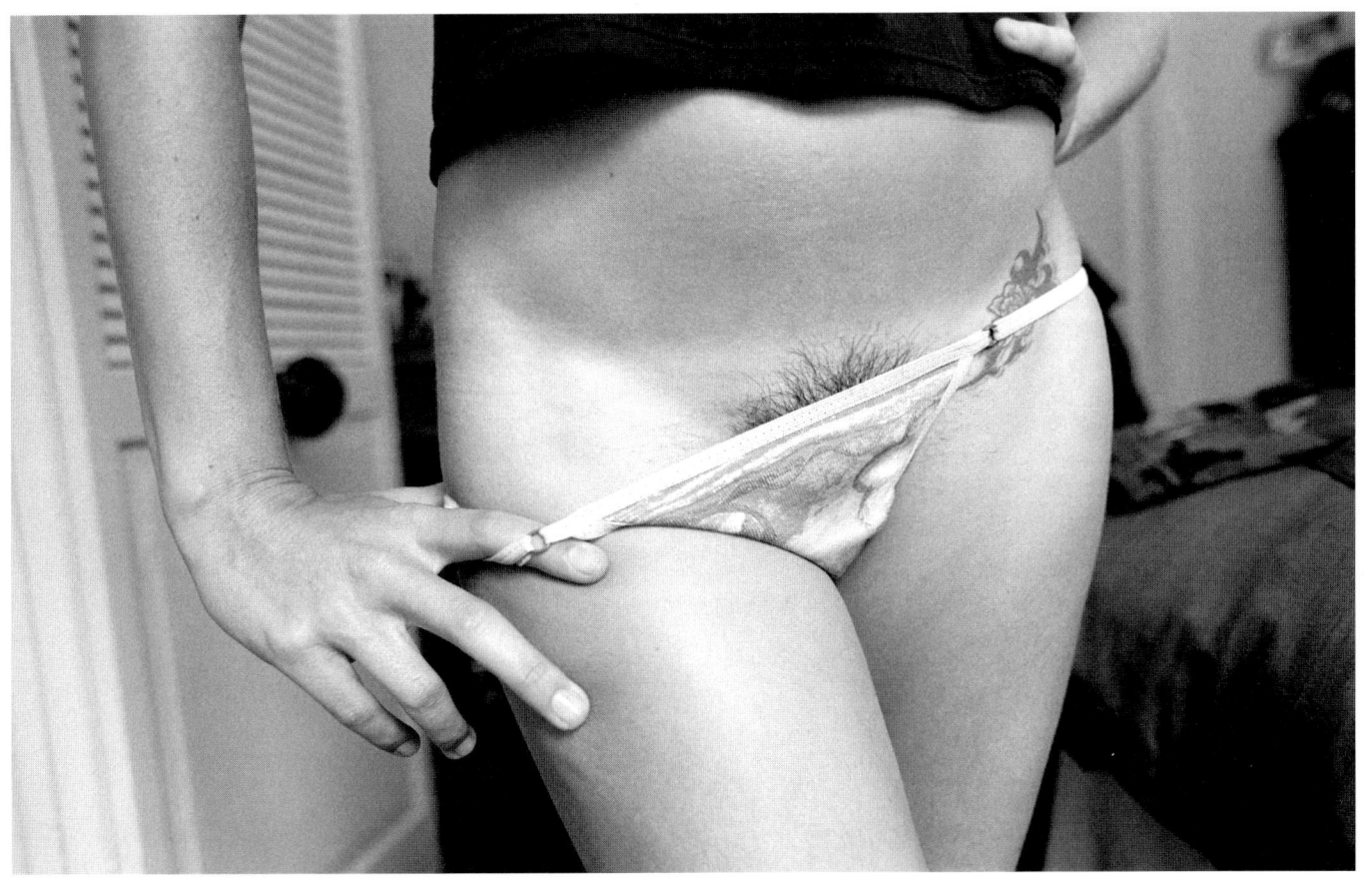

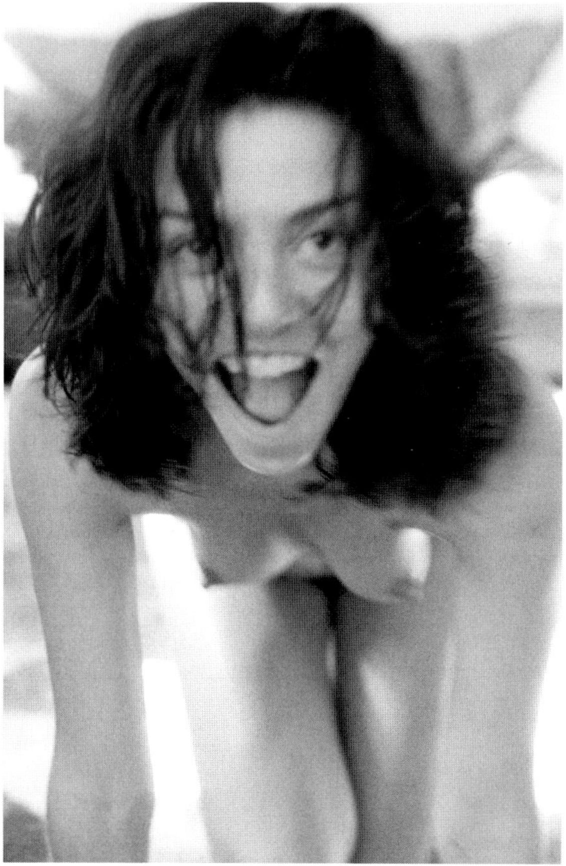

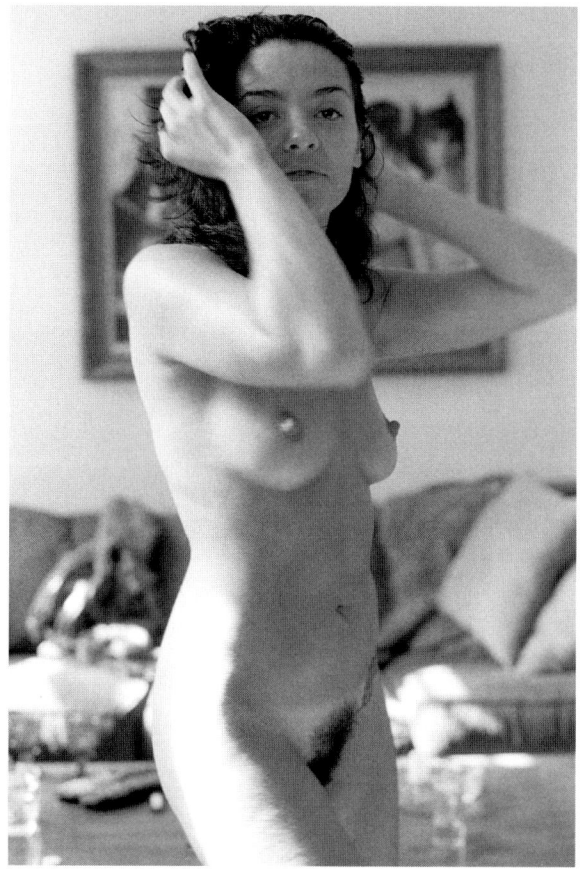

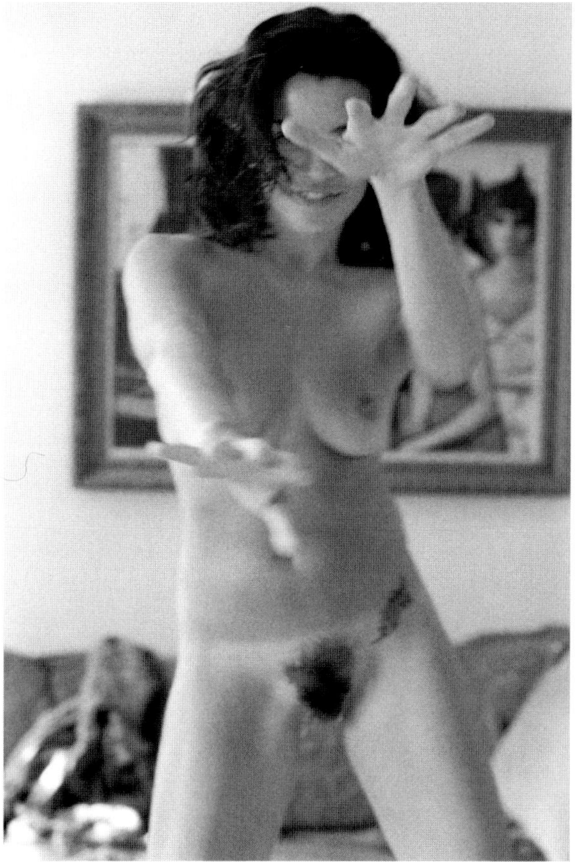

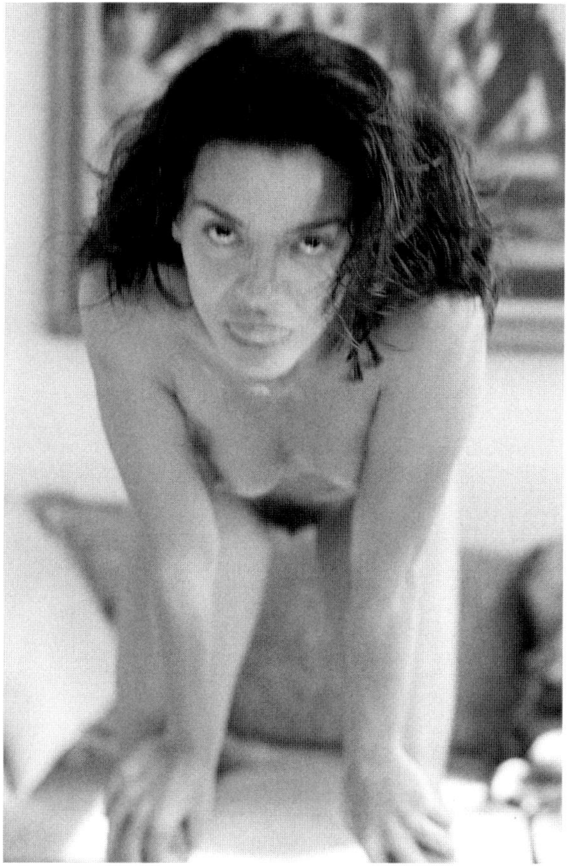

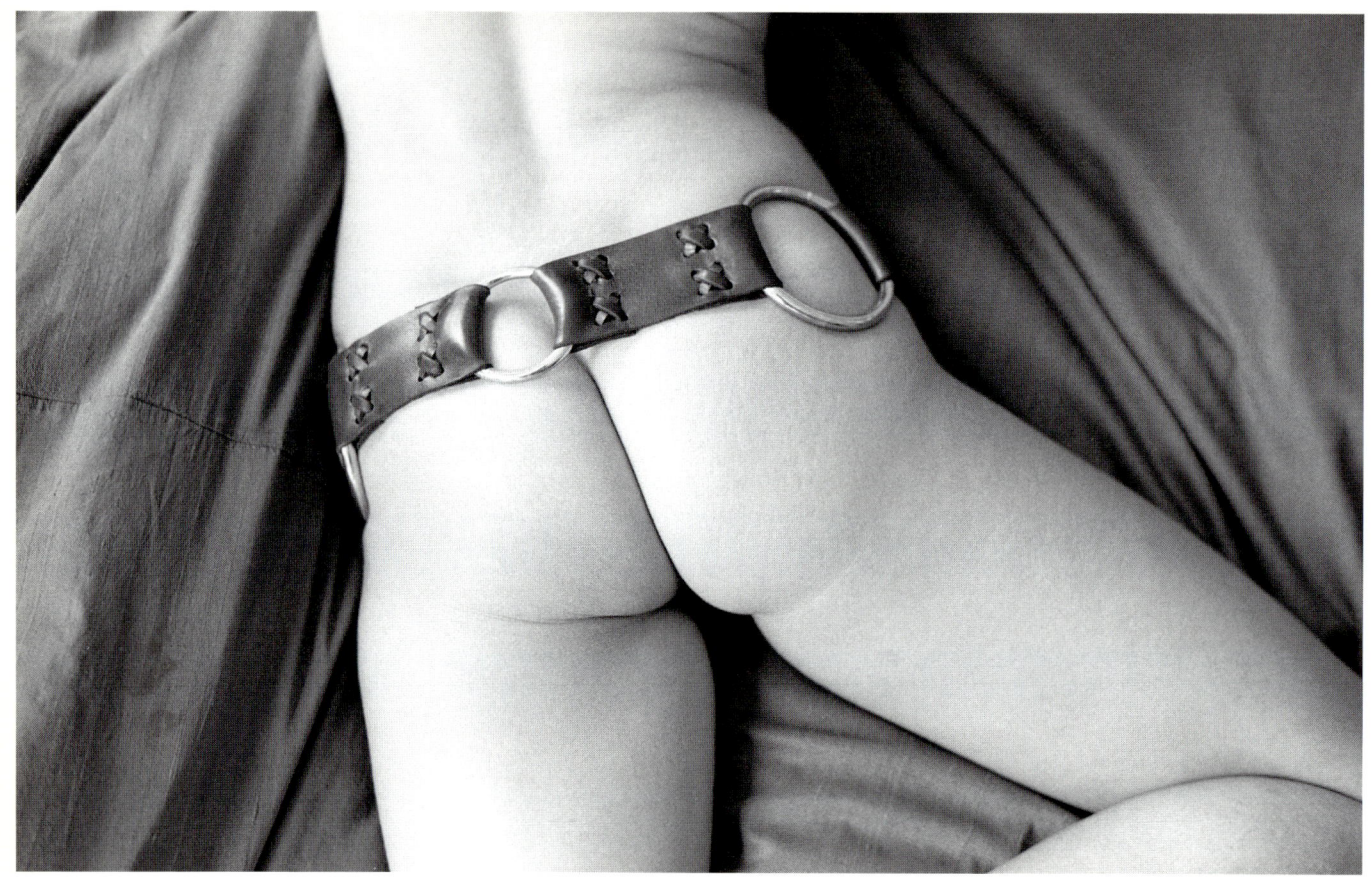

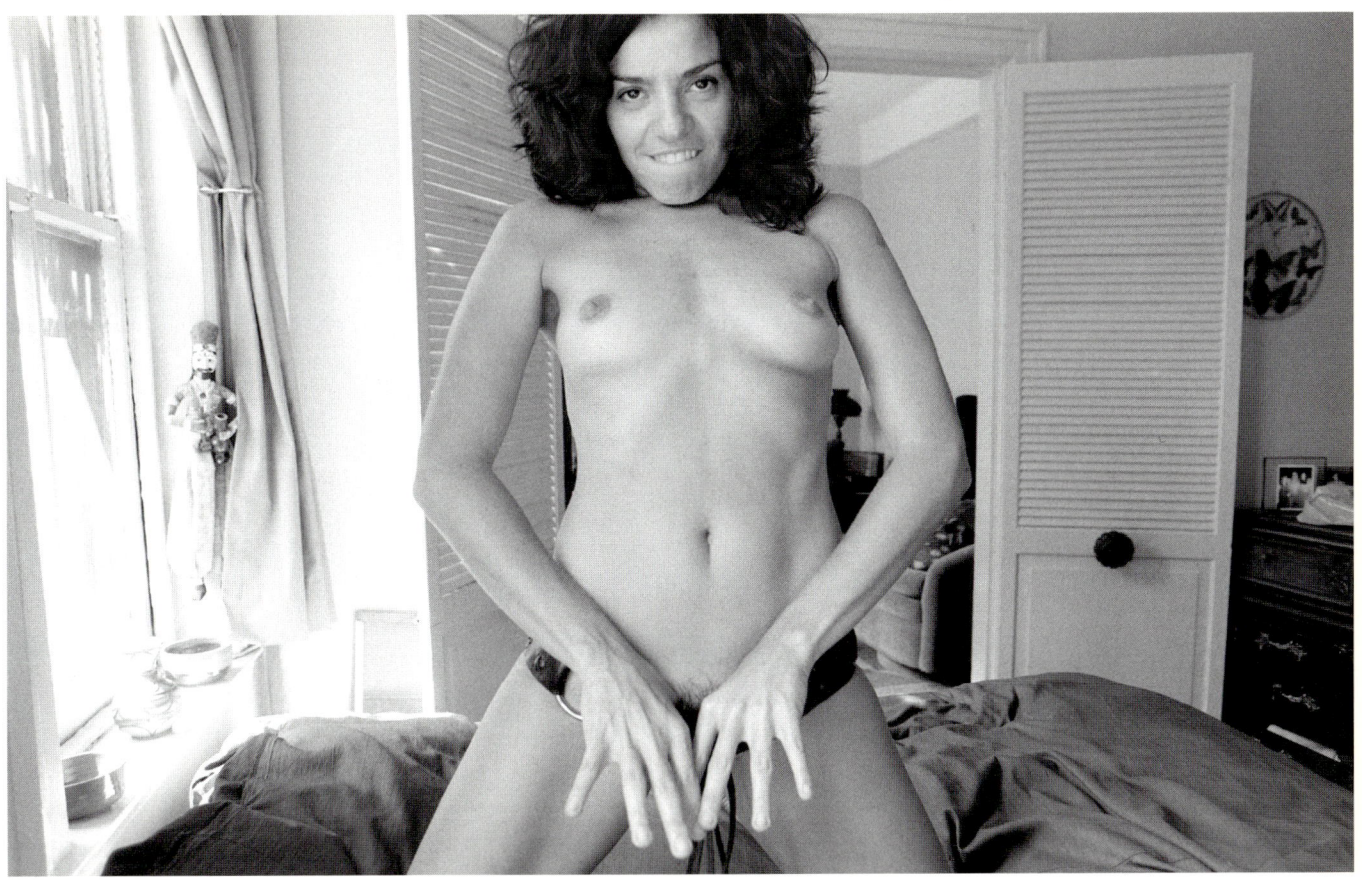

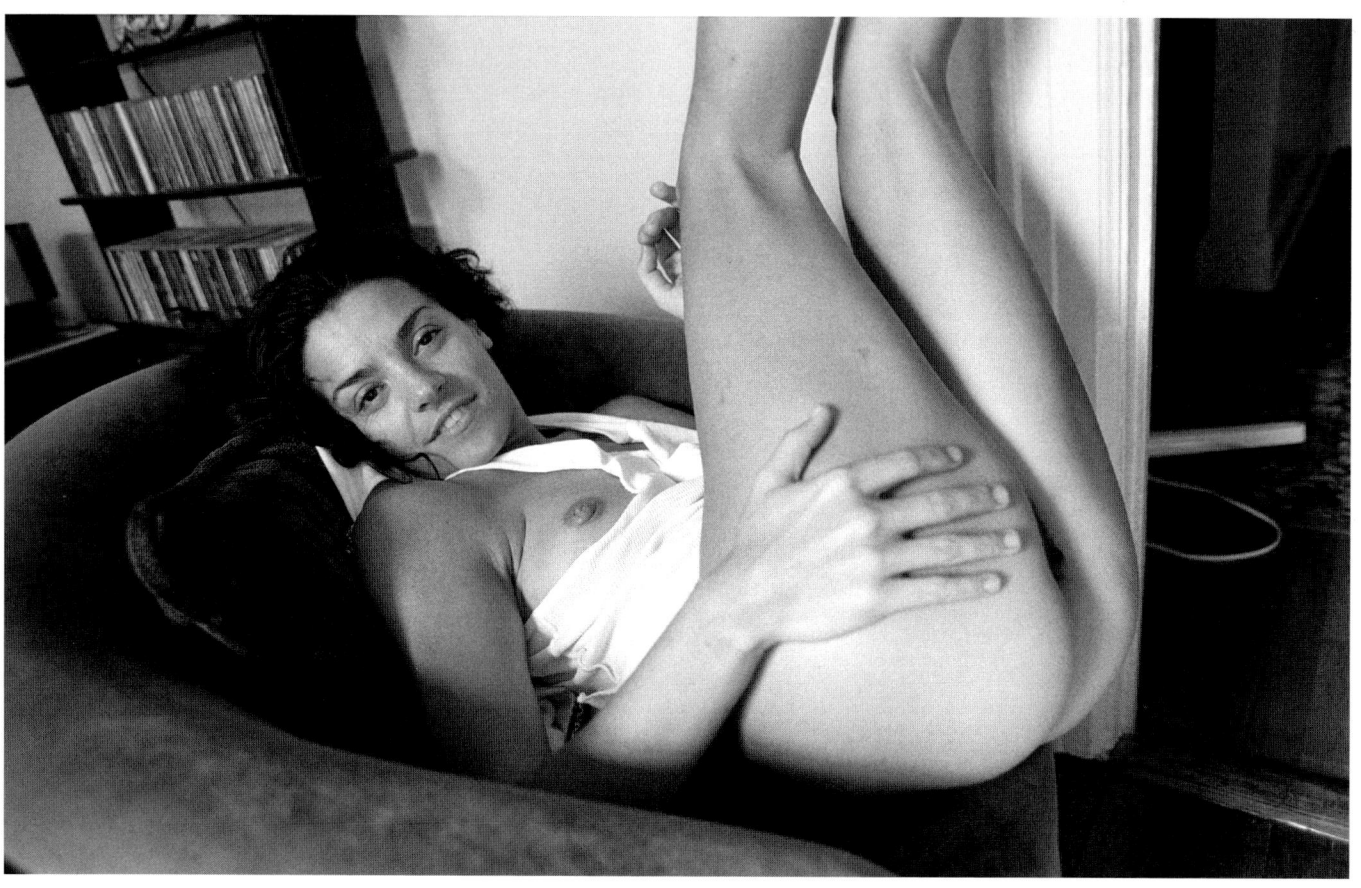

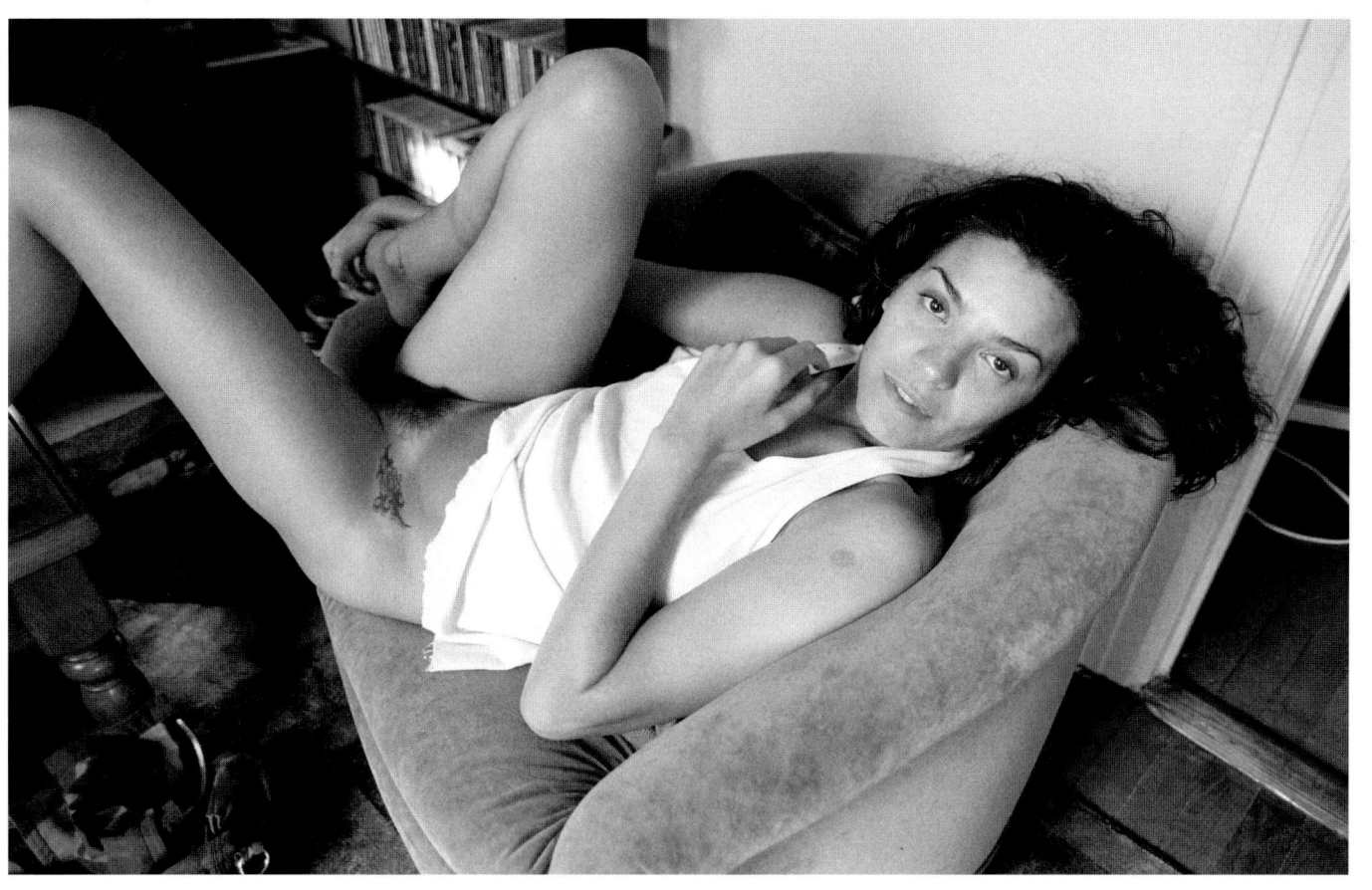

Gabriella · I met Gabriella in a performance space on the lower east side. She was drinking a tall Budweiser, and watching comedy in front of a bar. I photographed her in her mother's large apartment on the upper West Side. It was filled with art and artifacts, and had many huge windows. I tried to make the photos fit the environment.

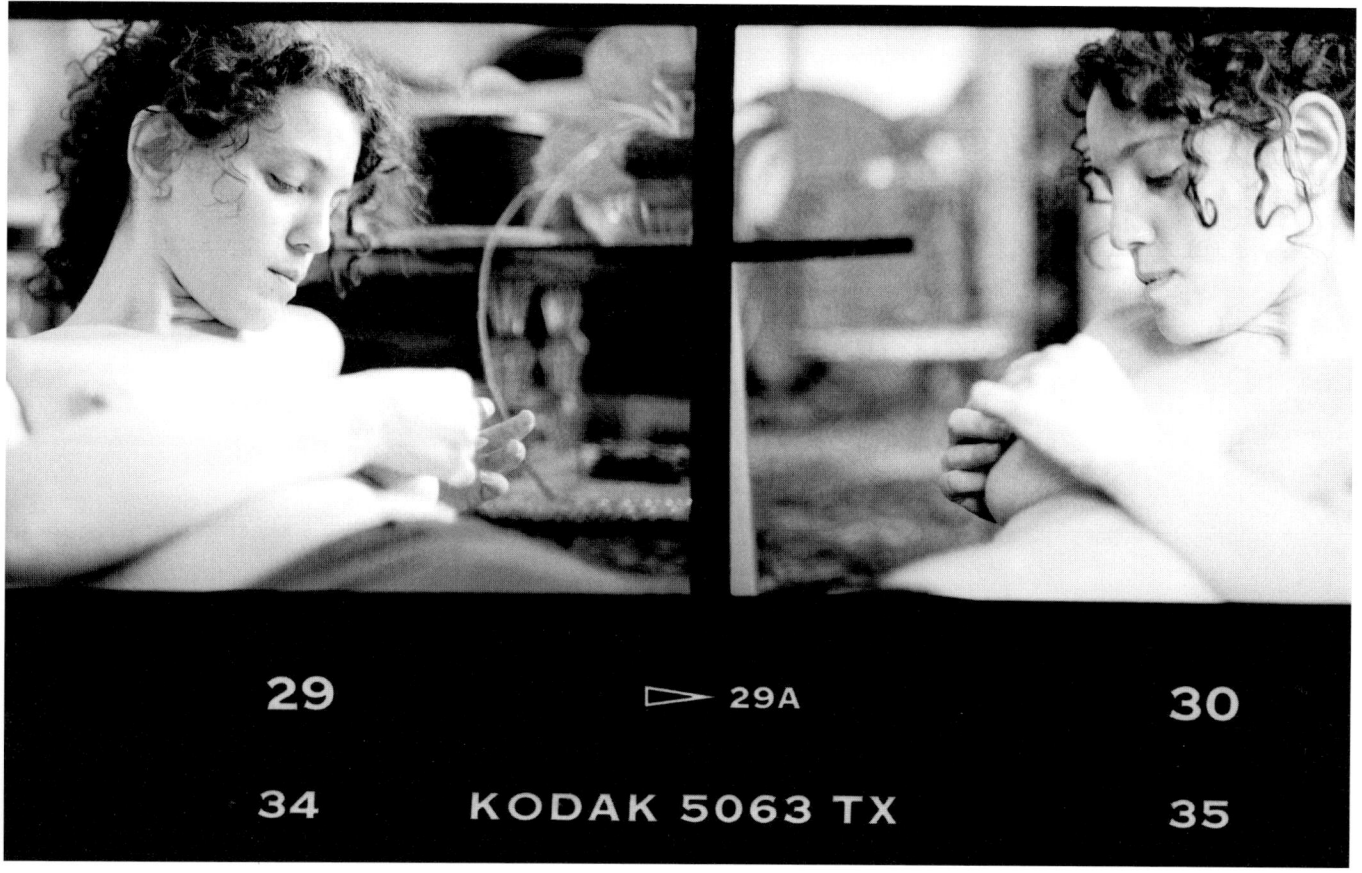

29 ▷ 29A 30

34 KODAK 5063 TX 35

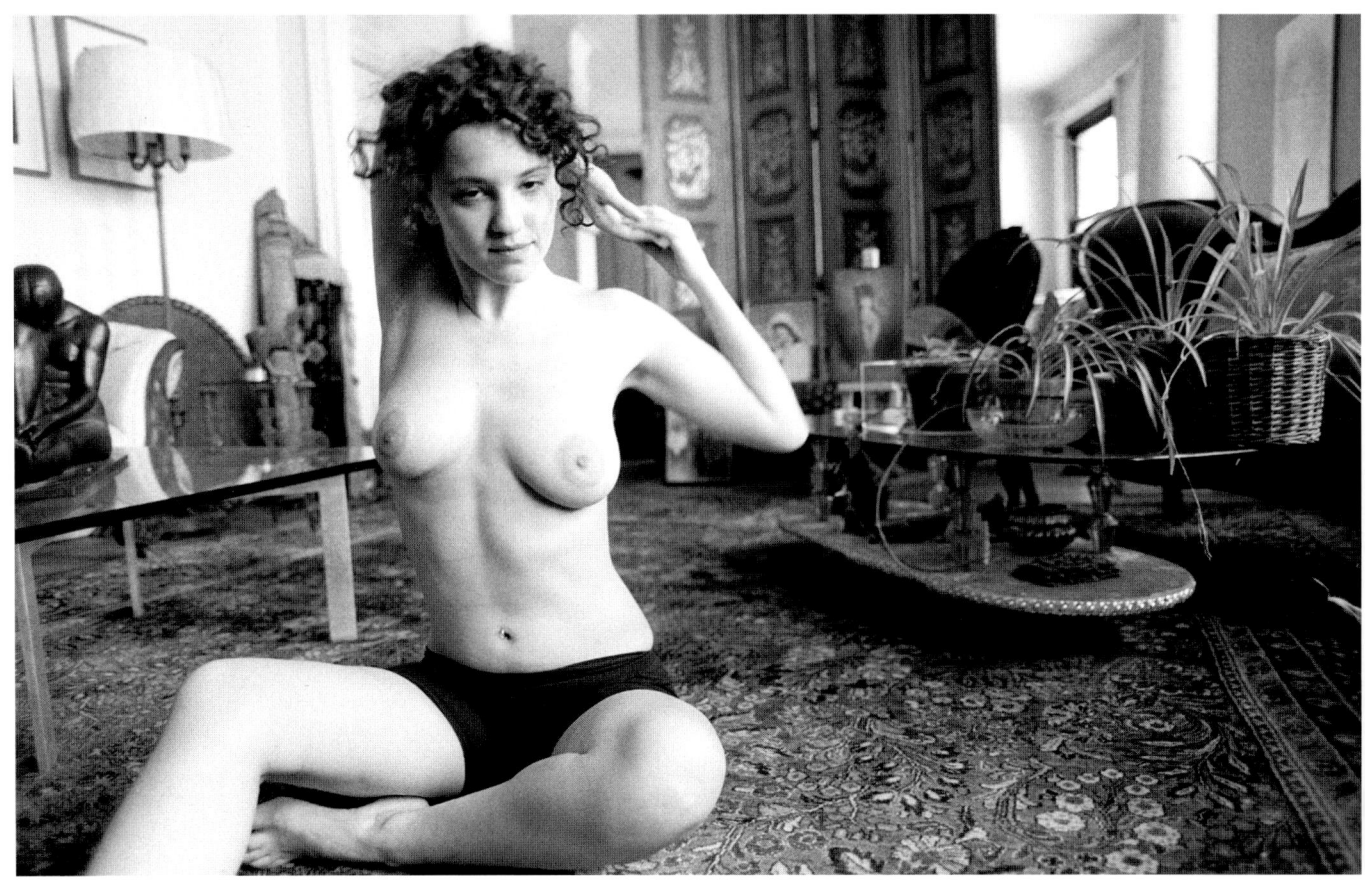

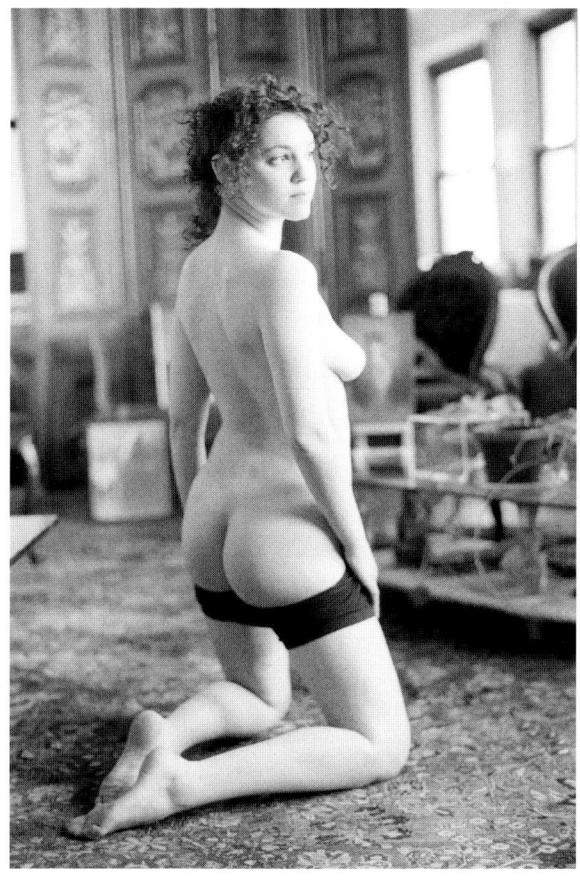 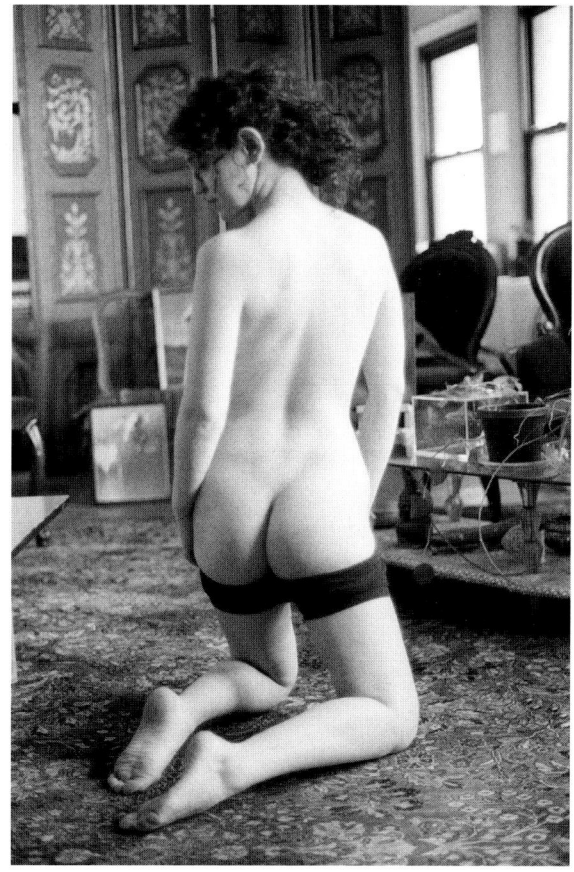

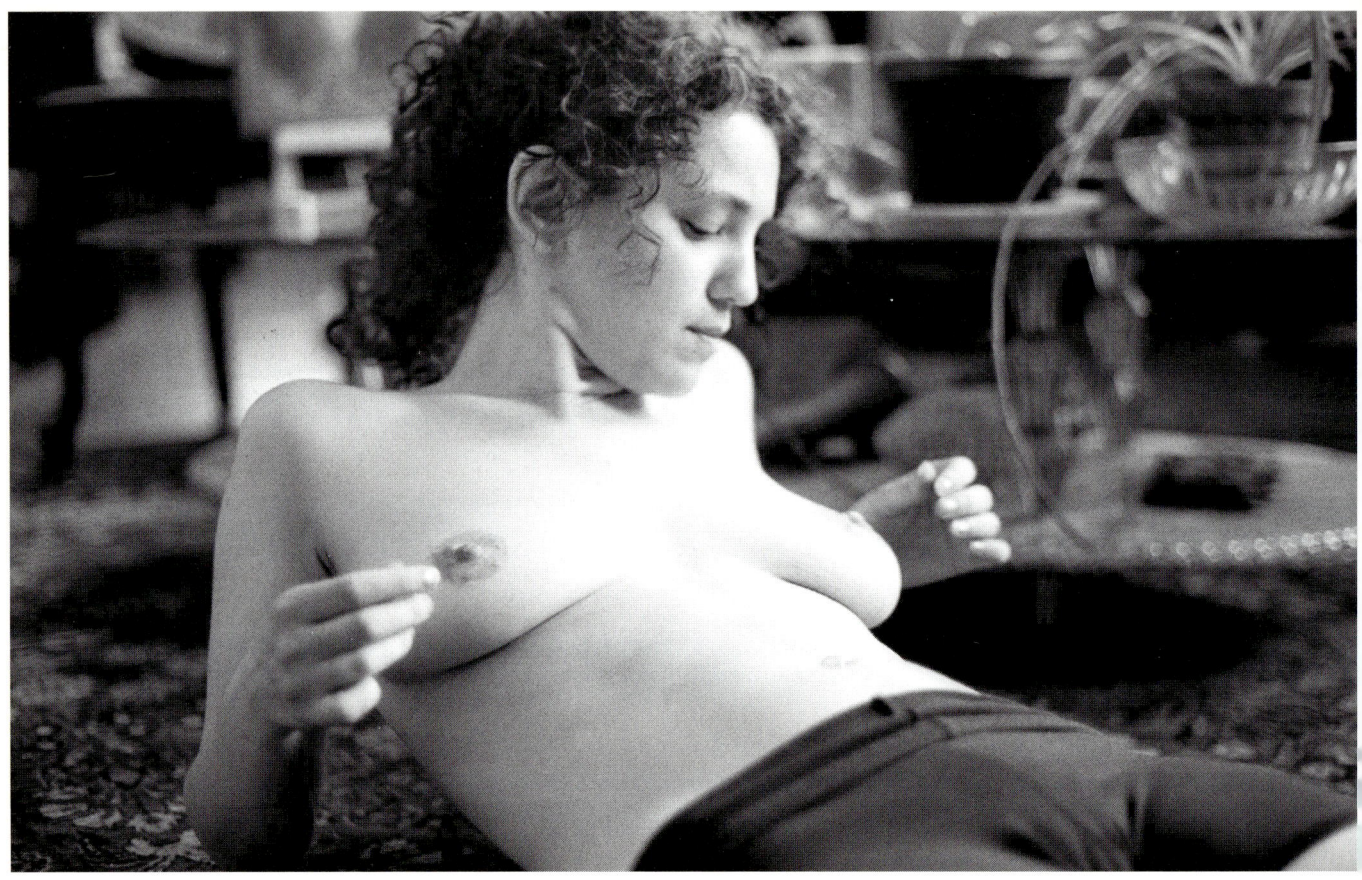

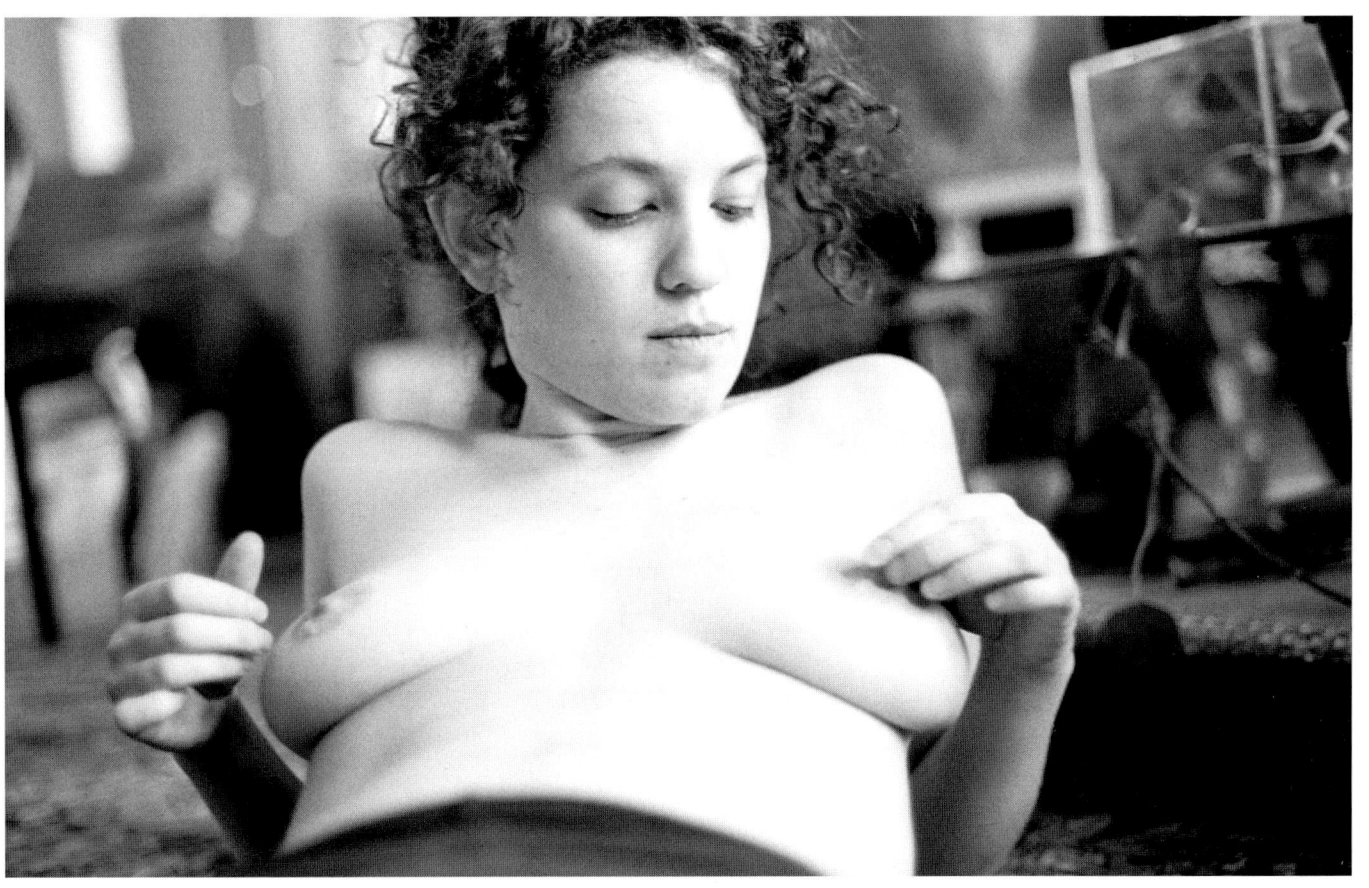

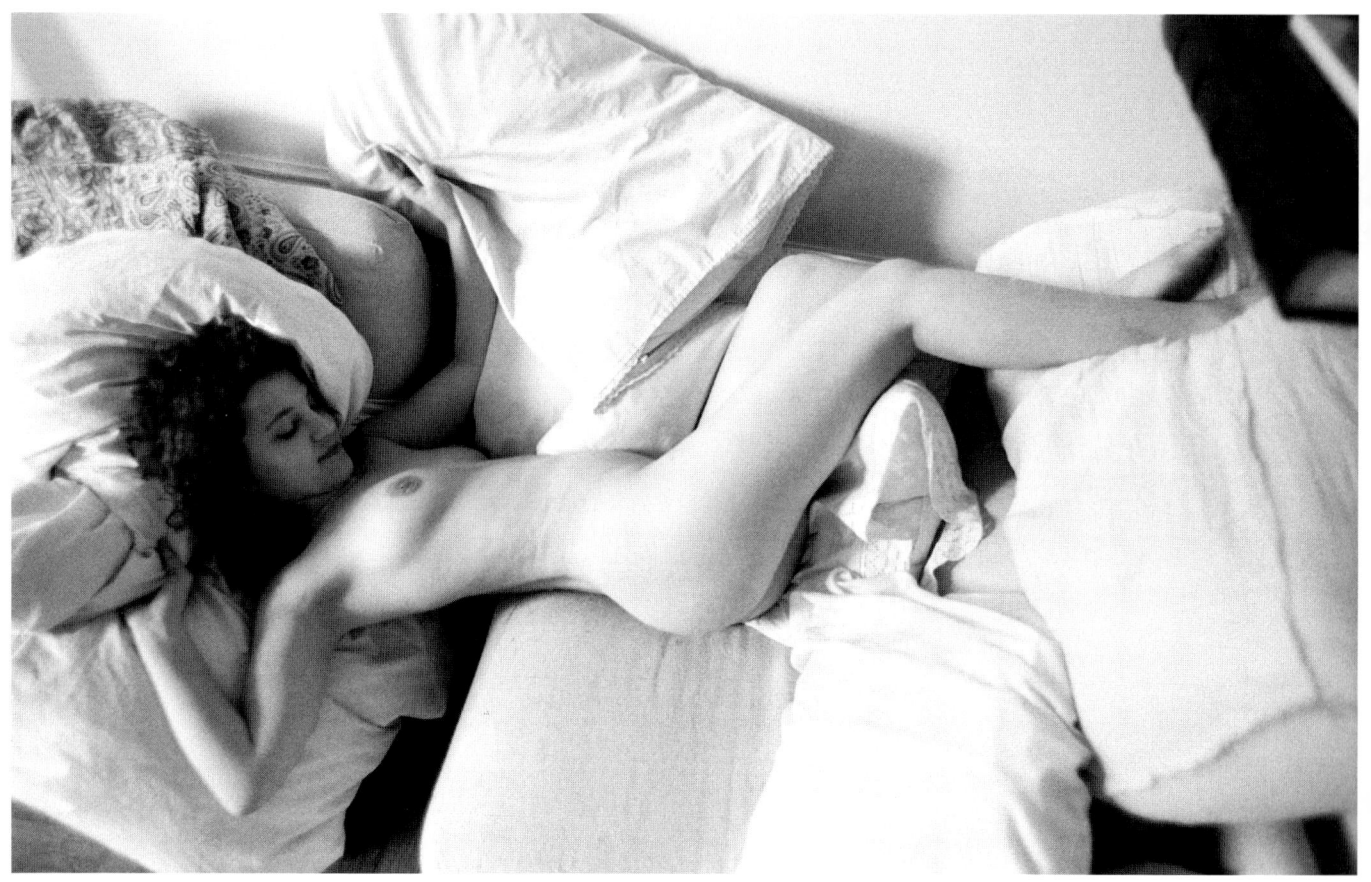

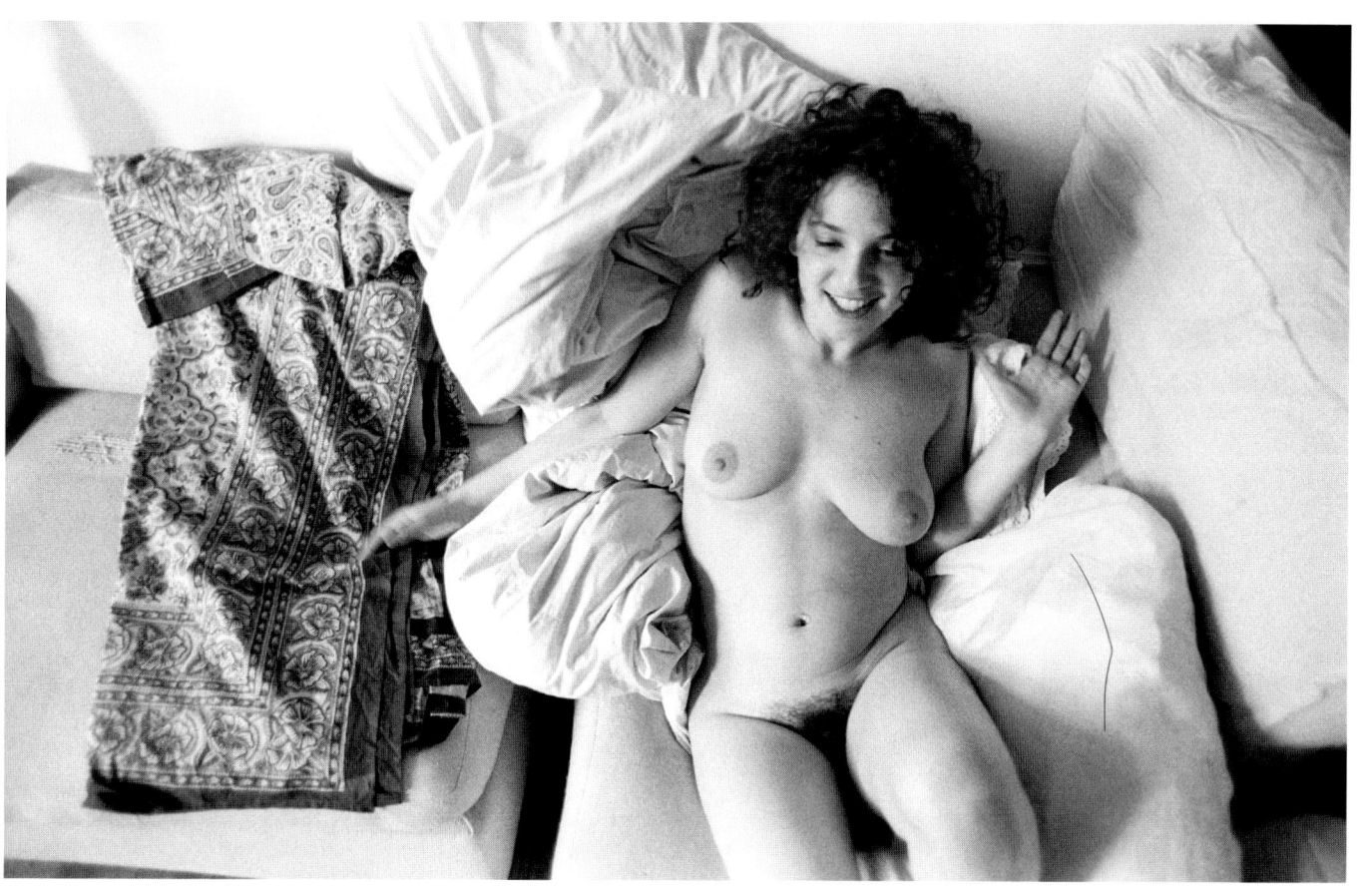

Gaby · I met Gaby on Elizabeth St. on a Wednesday, and photographed her the following Monday morning. I brought over coffee, bagels and milk. Gaby smoked cigarettes, ate cherries, and listened to Charles Mingus. Gaby is a super happy person with a great smile, and we got along very well. Her dog "Lola" hid until the end of the shoot, when she decided to be in pictures.

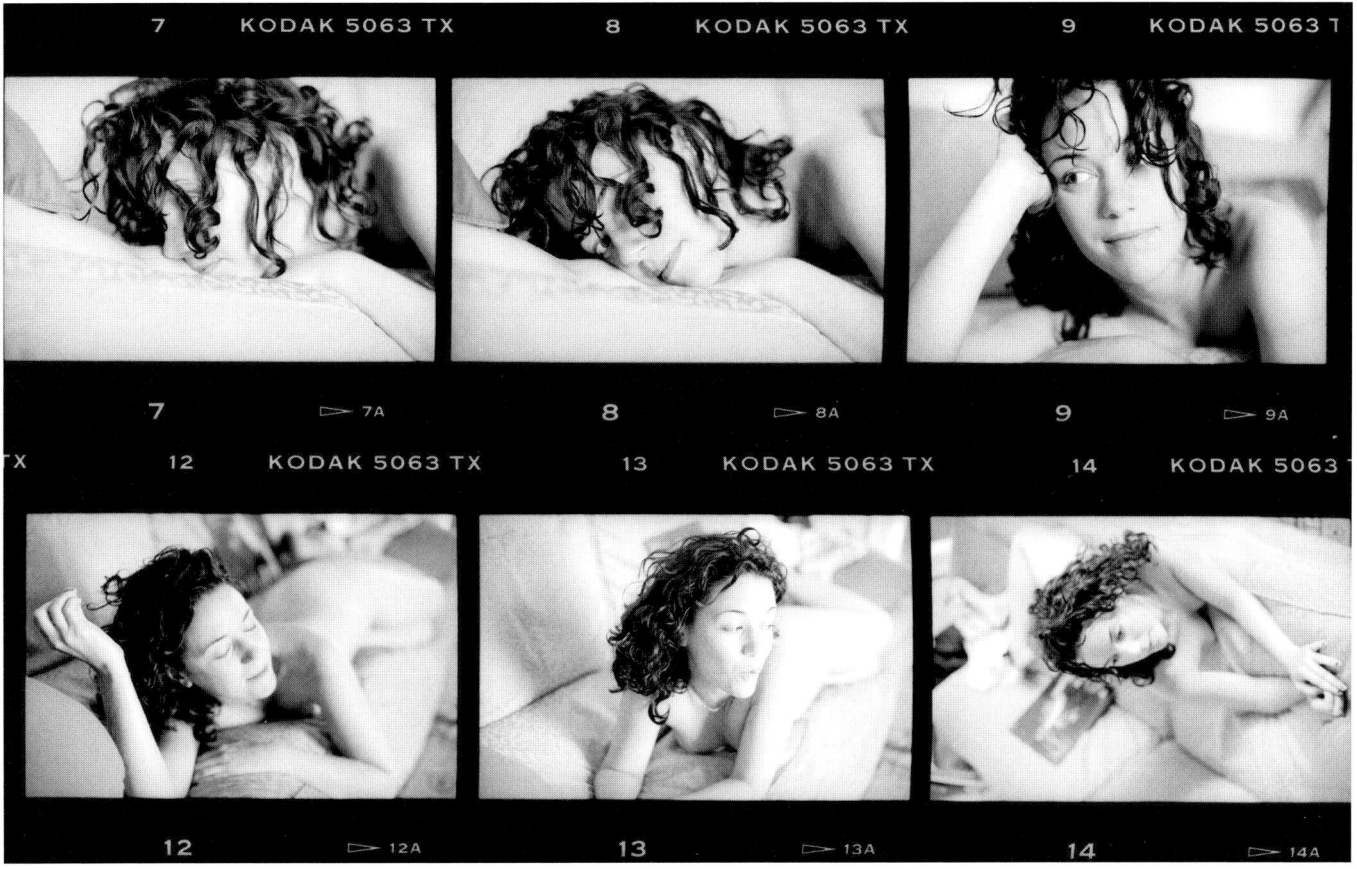

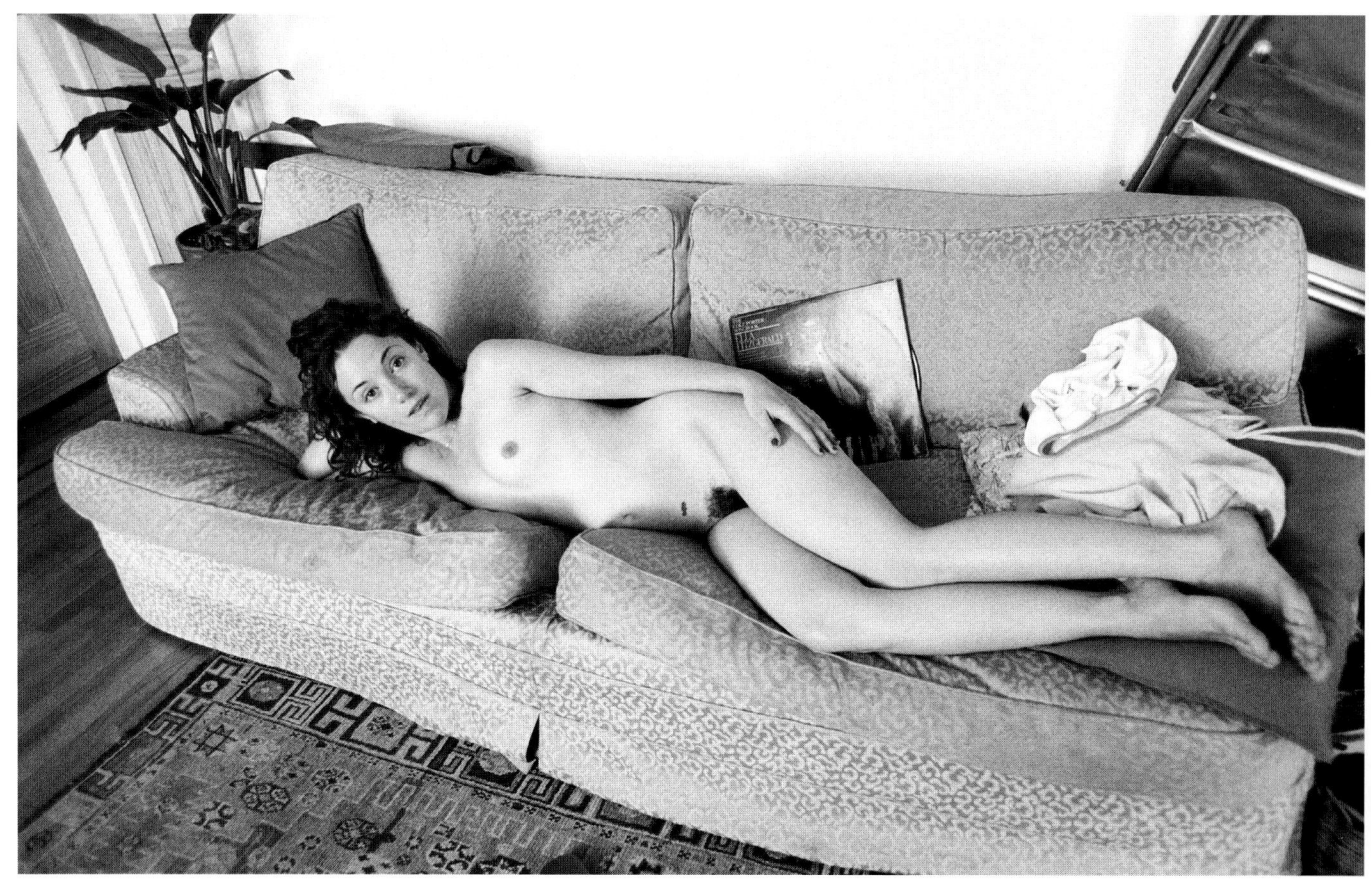

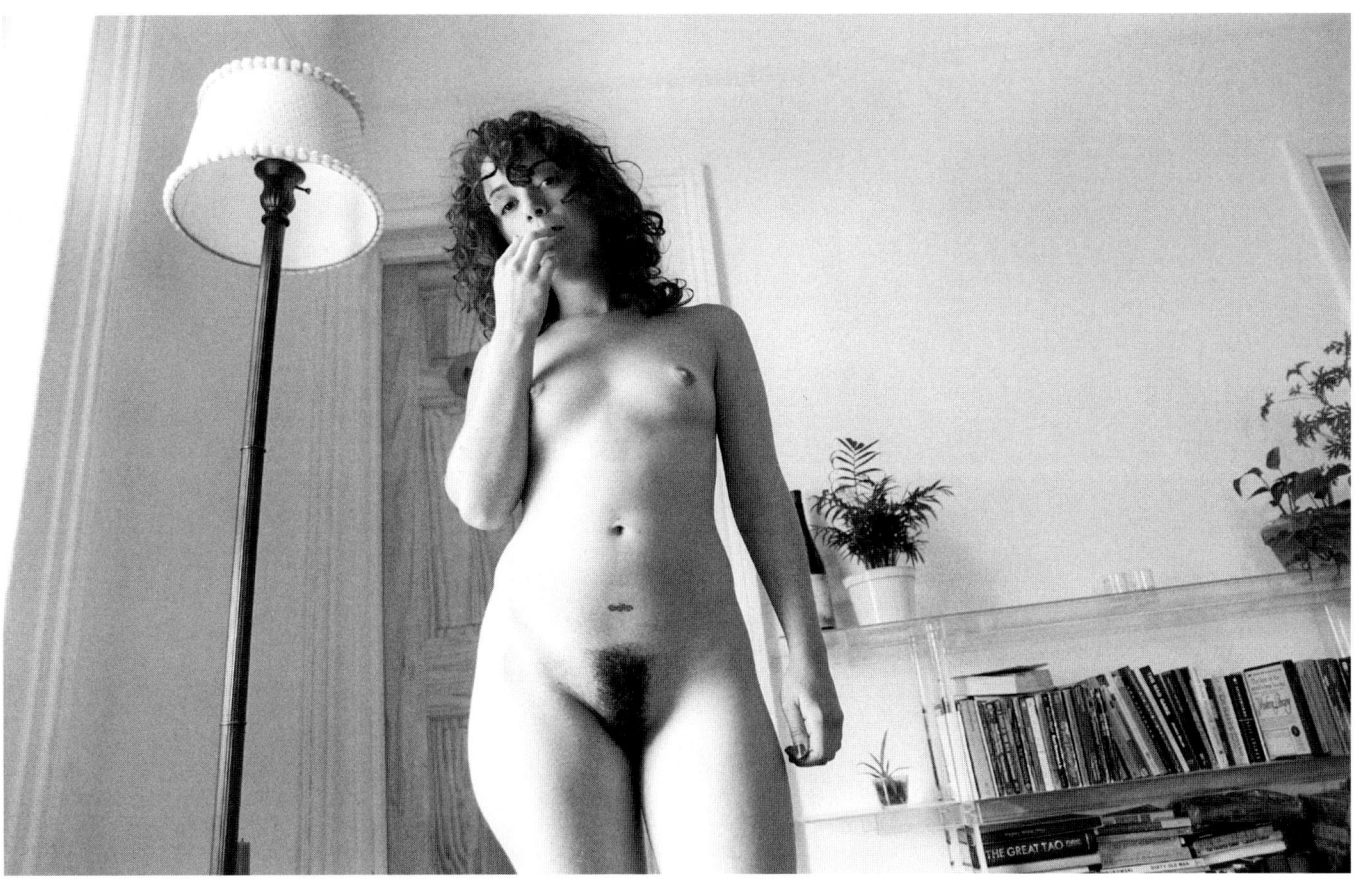

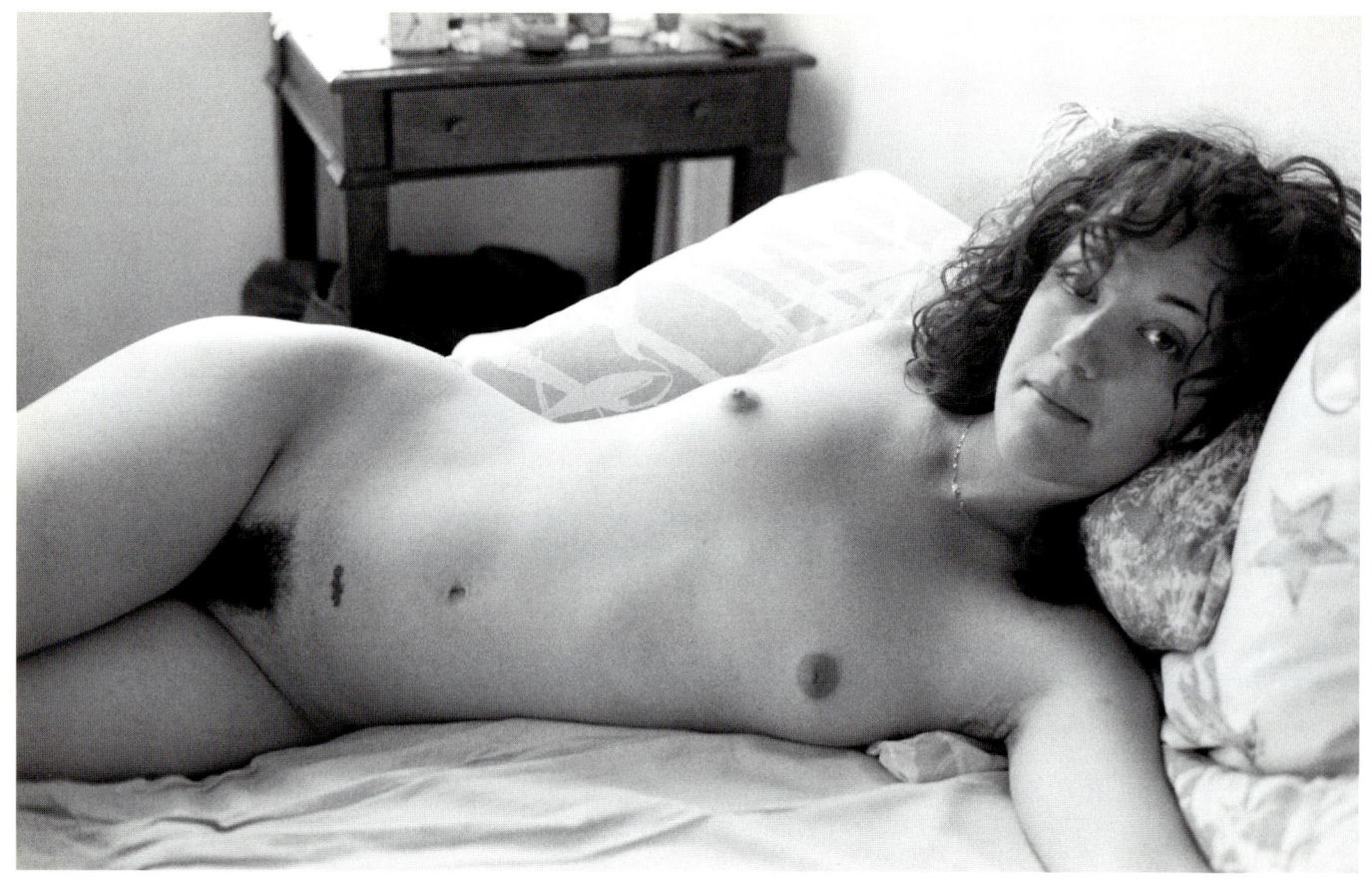

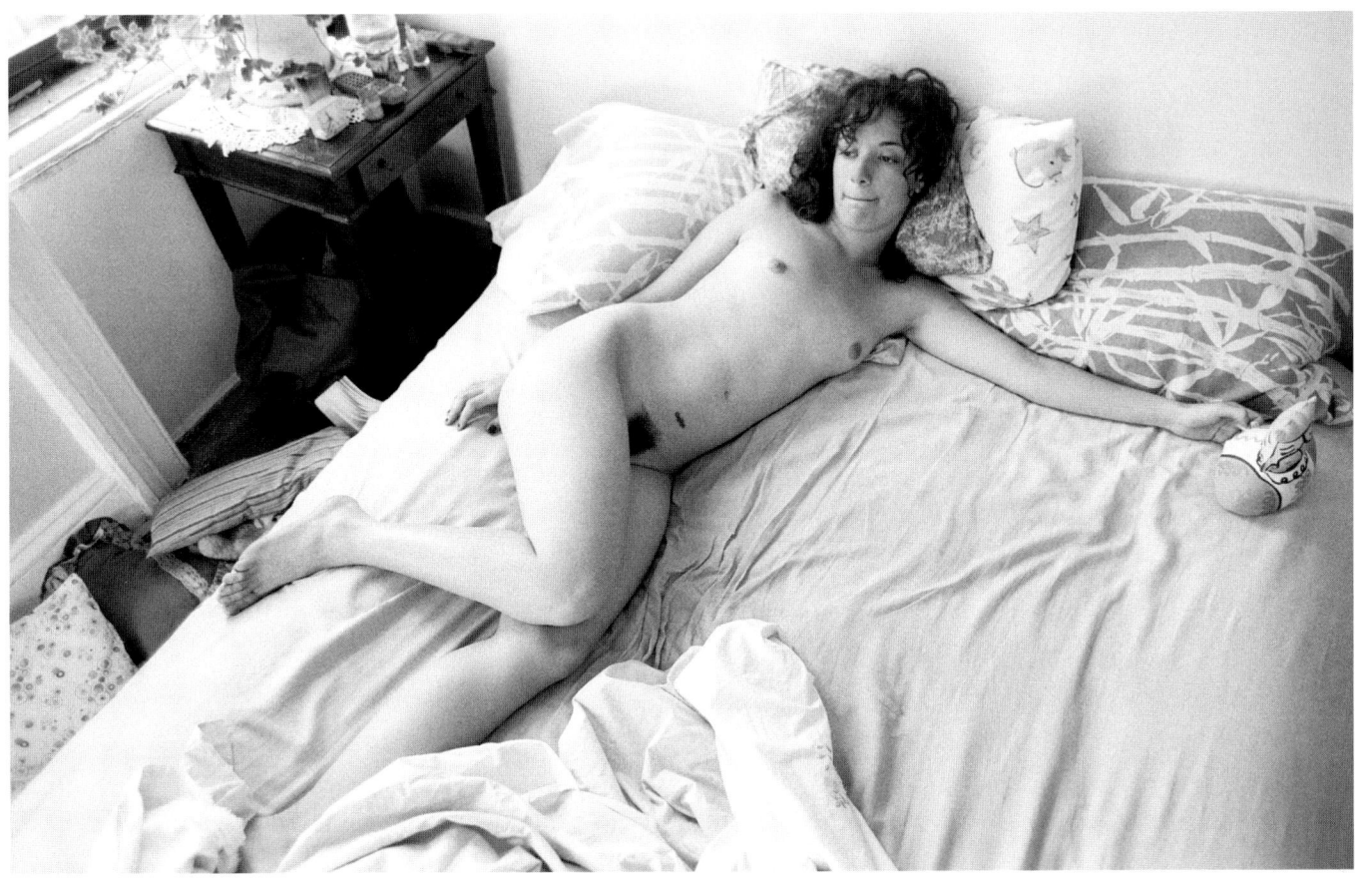

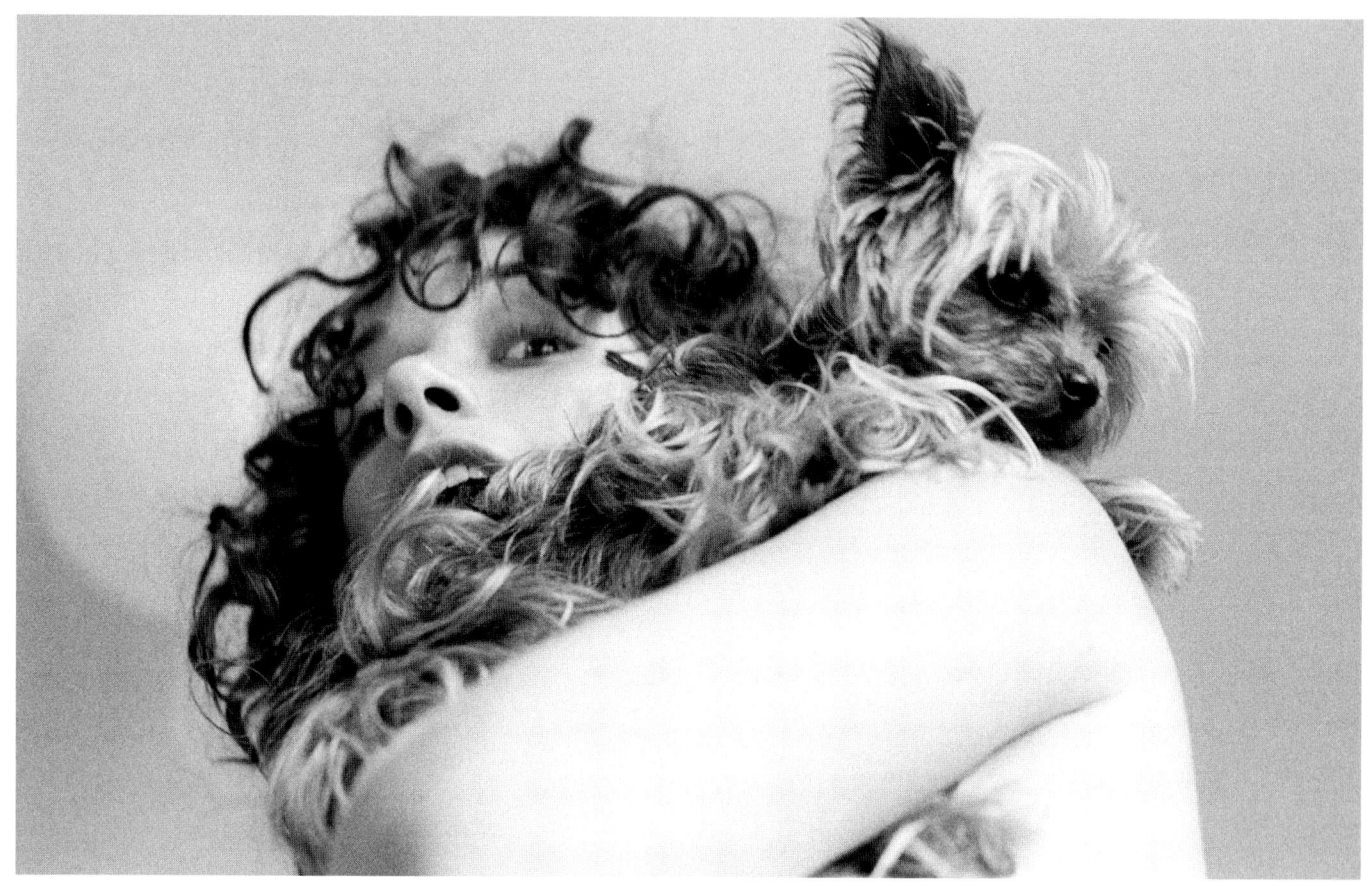

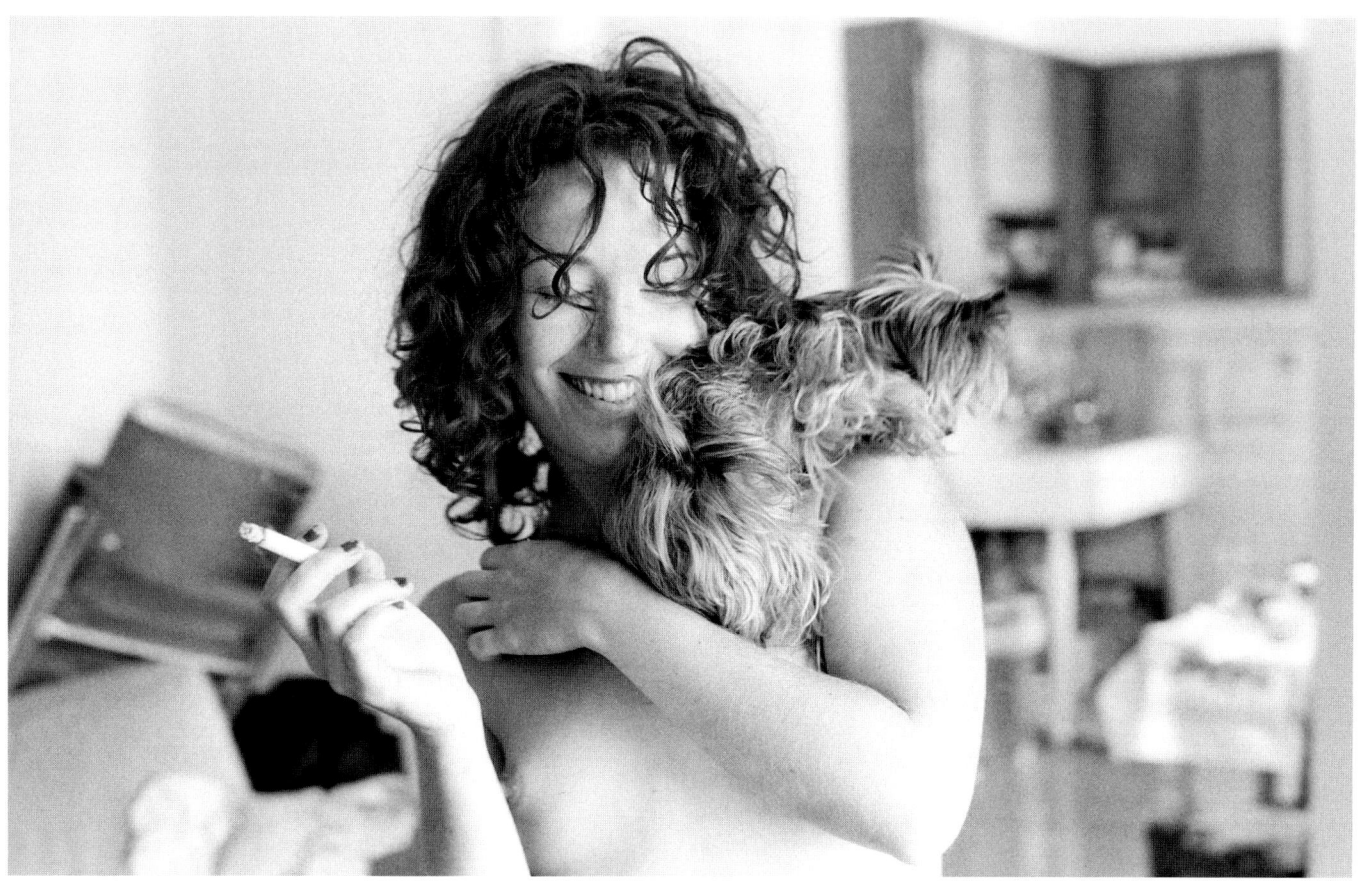

Hil · I met Hil because she was my boss at an internet company. I photographed her twice, in her big Manhattan loft. Hil was like a spiritual, sensual animal, and purred like a cat. It was hard to take a bad picture of her. Hil is half Chinese and half Jewish. People always ask me about that when they see her photos.

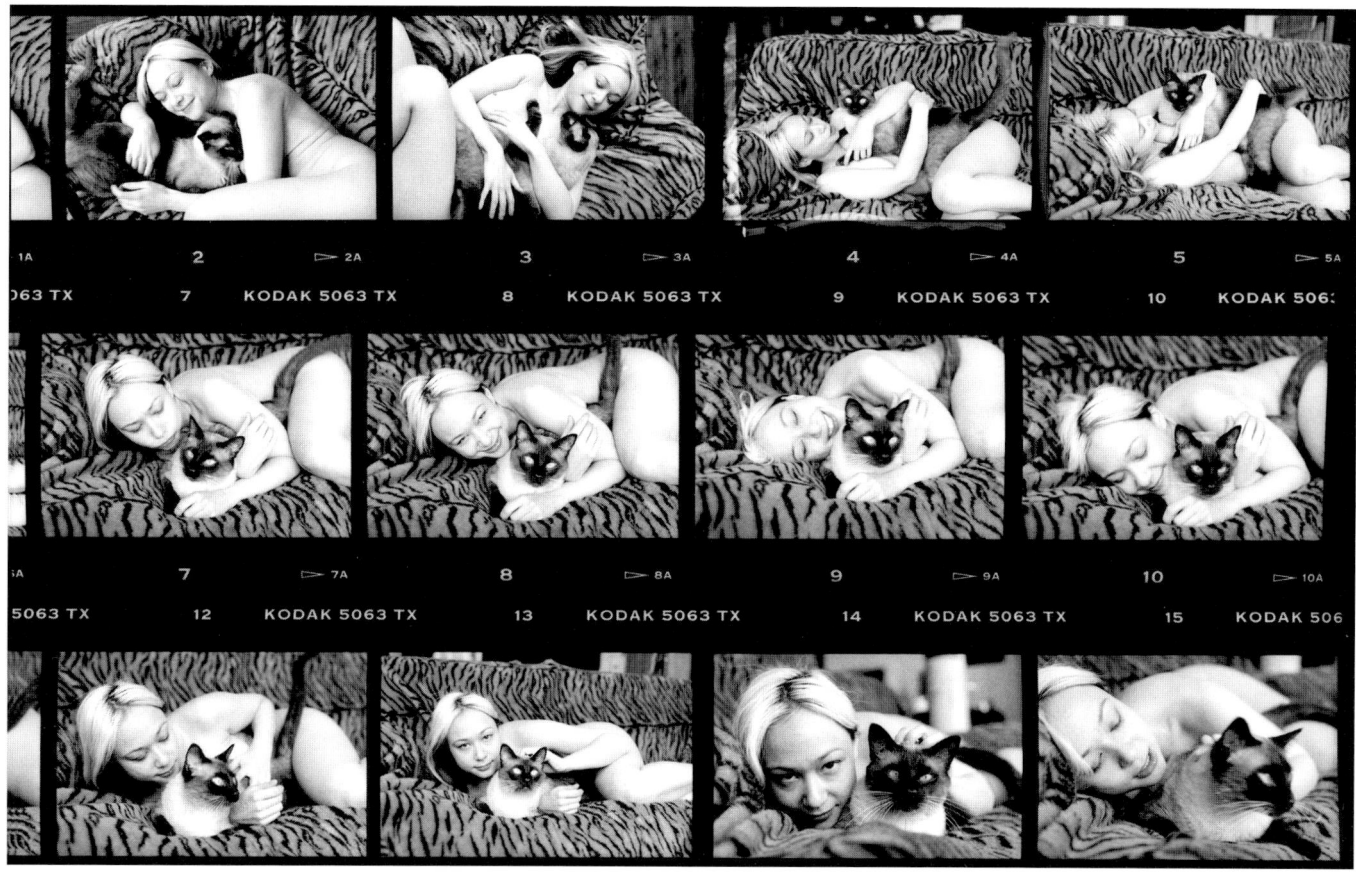

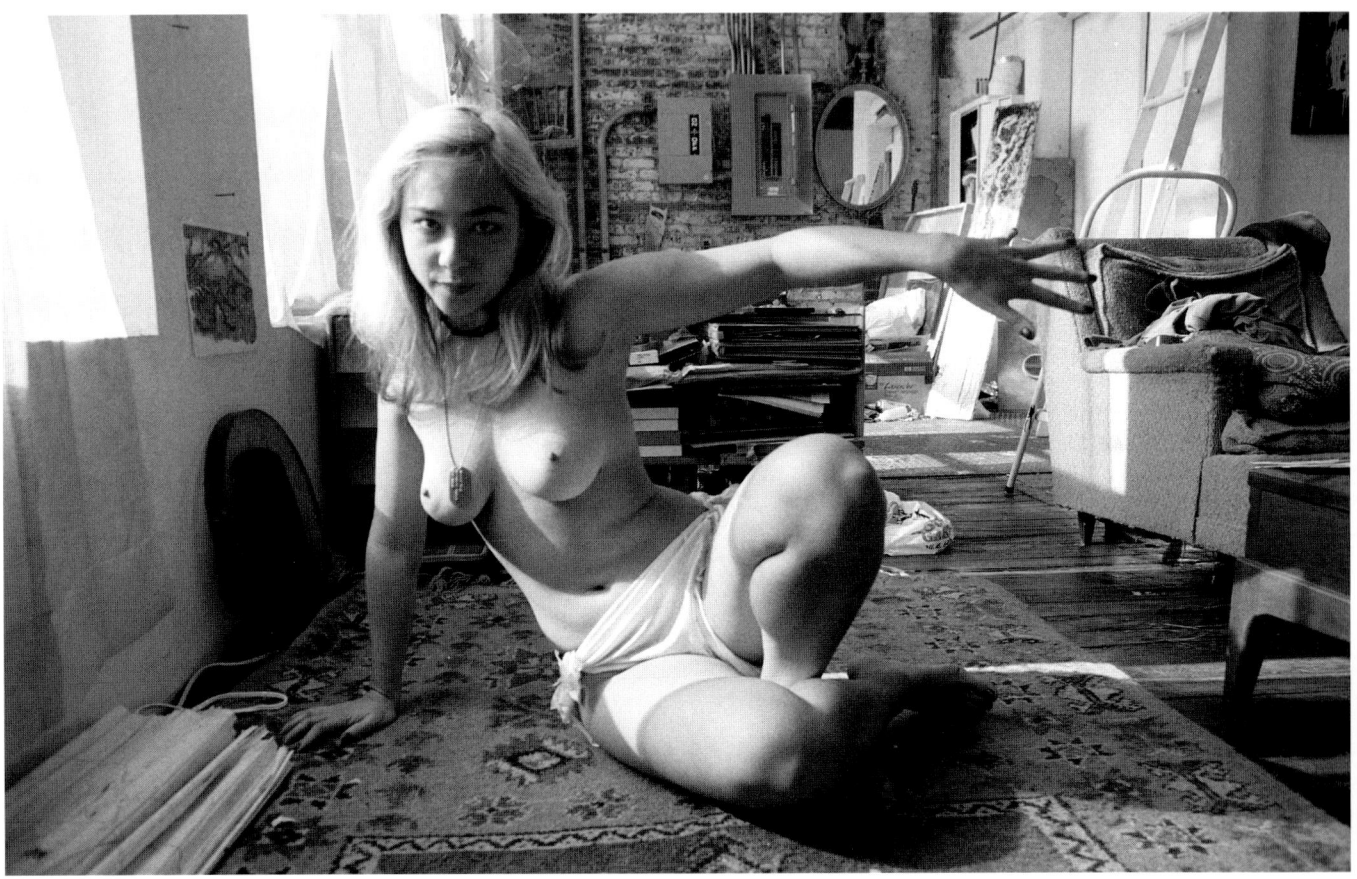

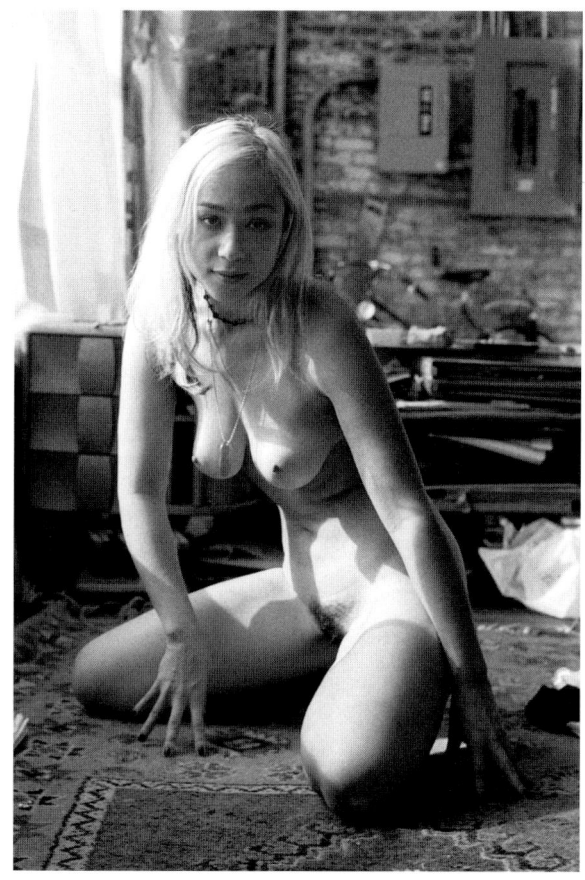

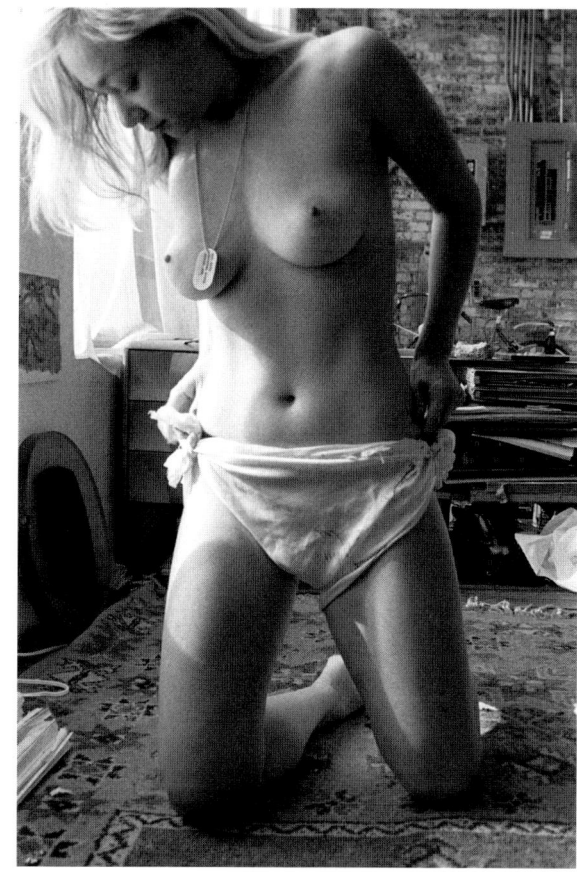

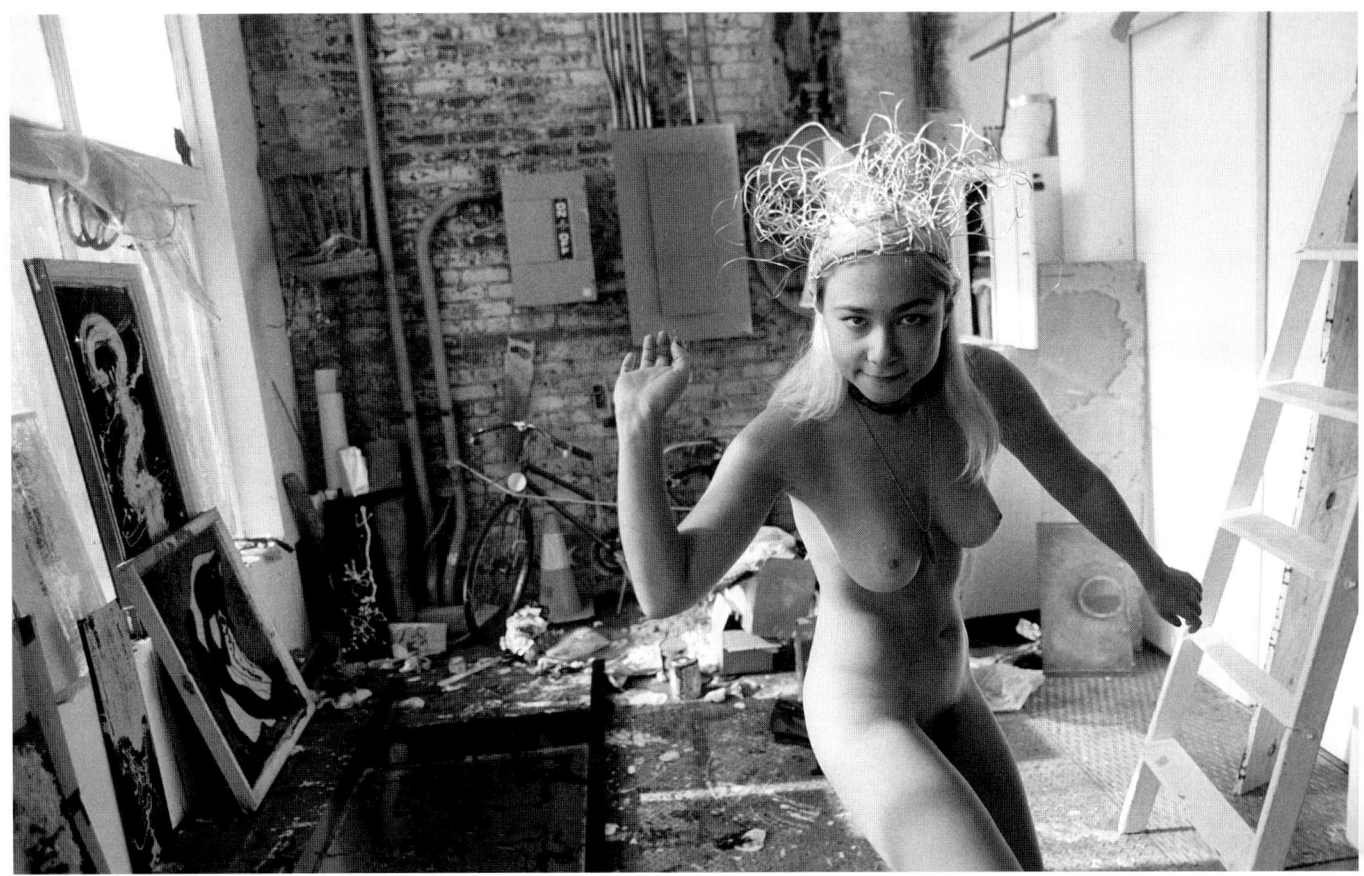

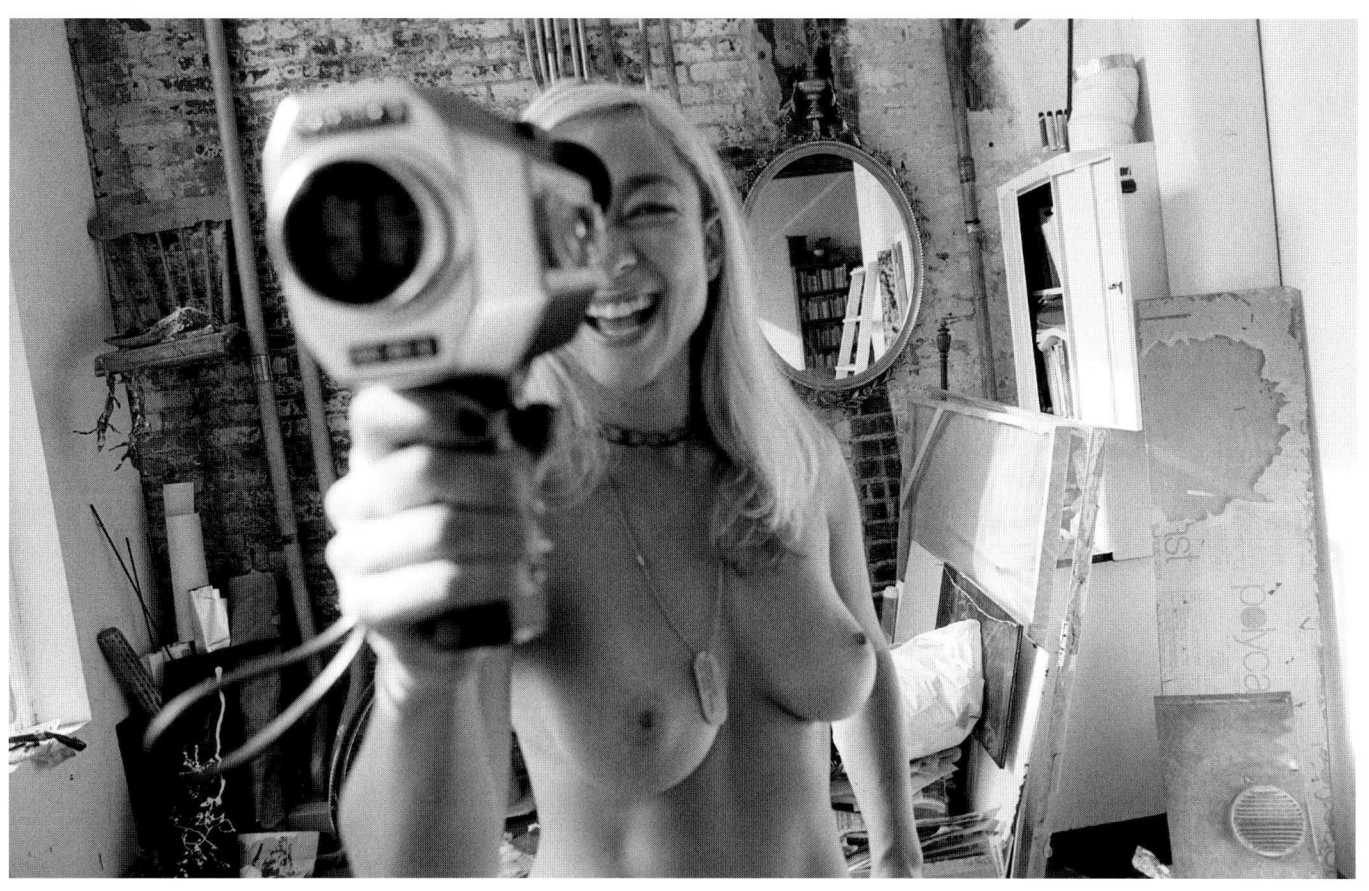

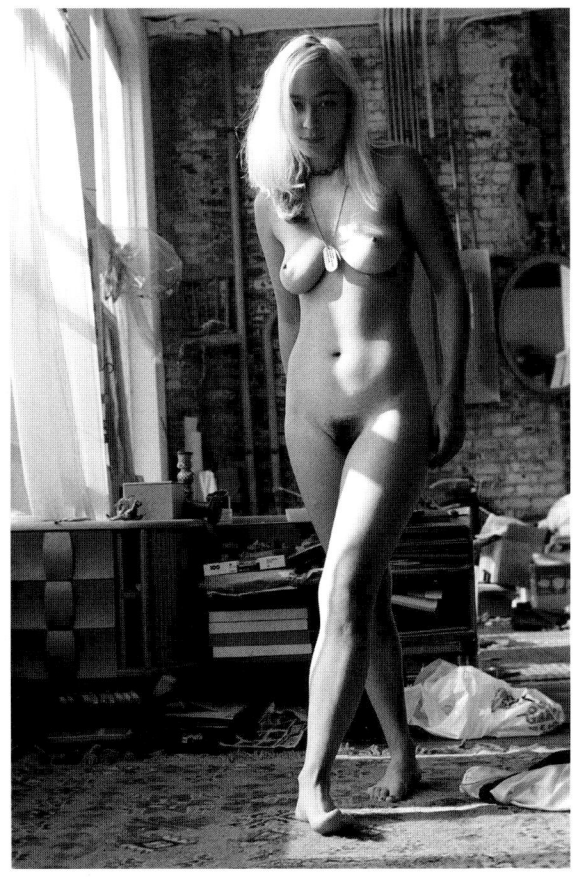
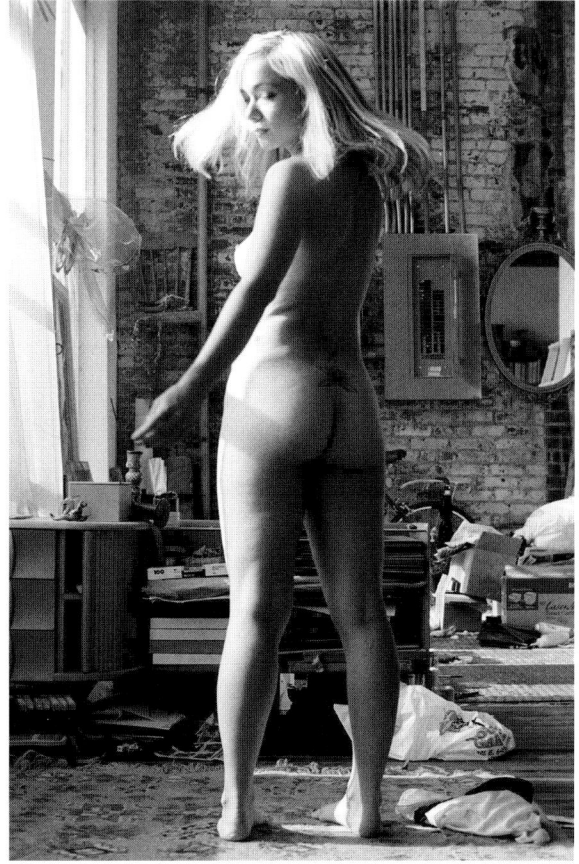

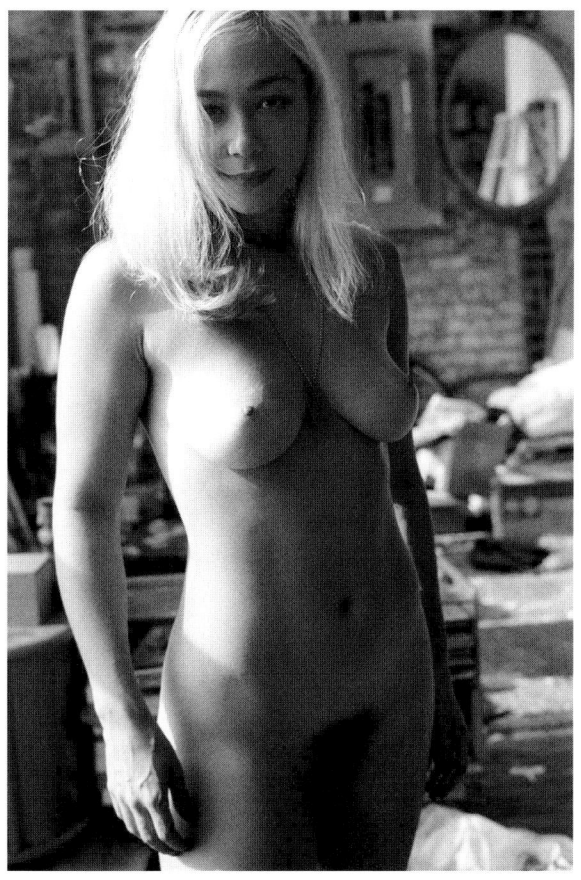
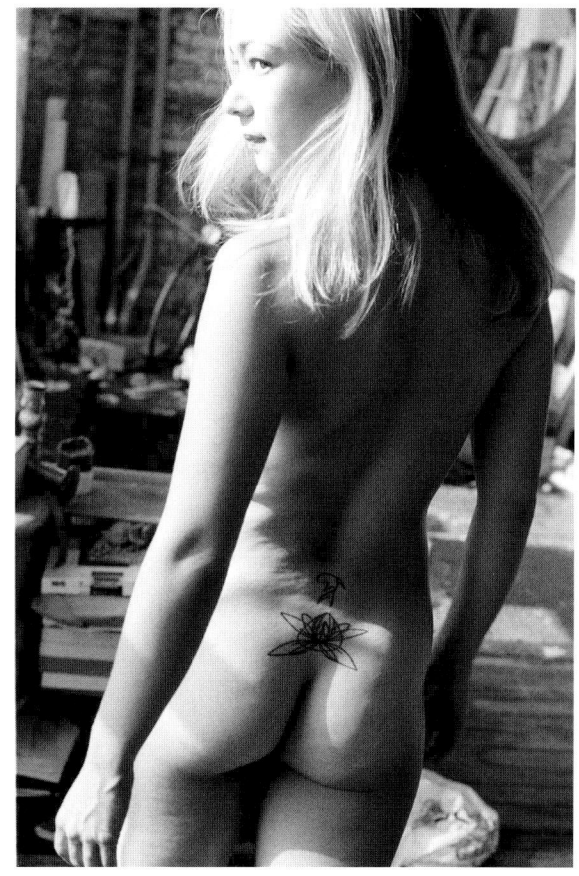

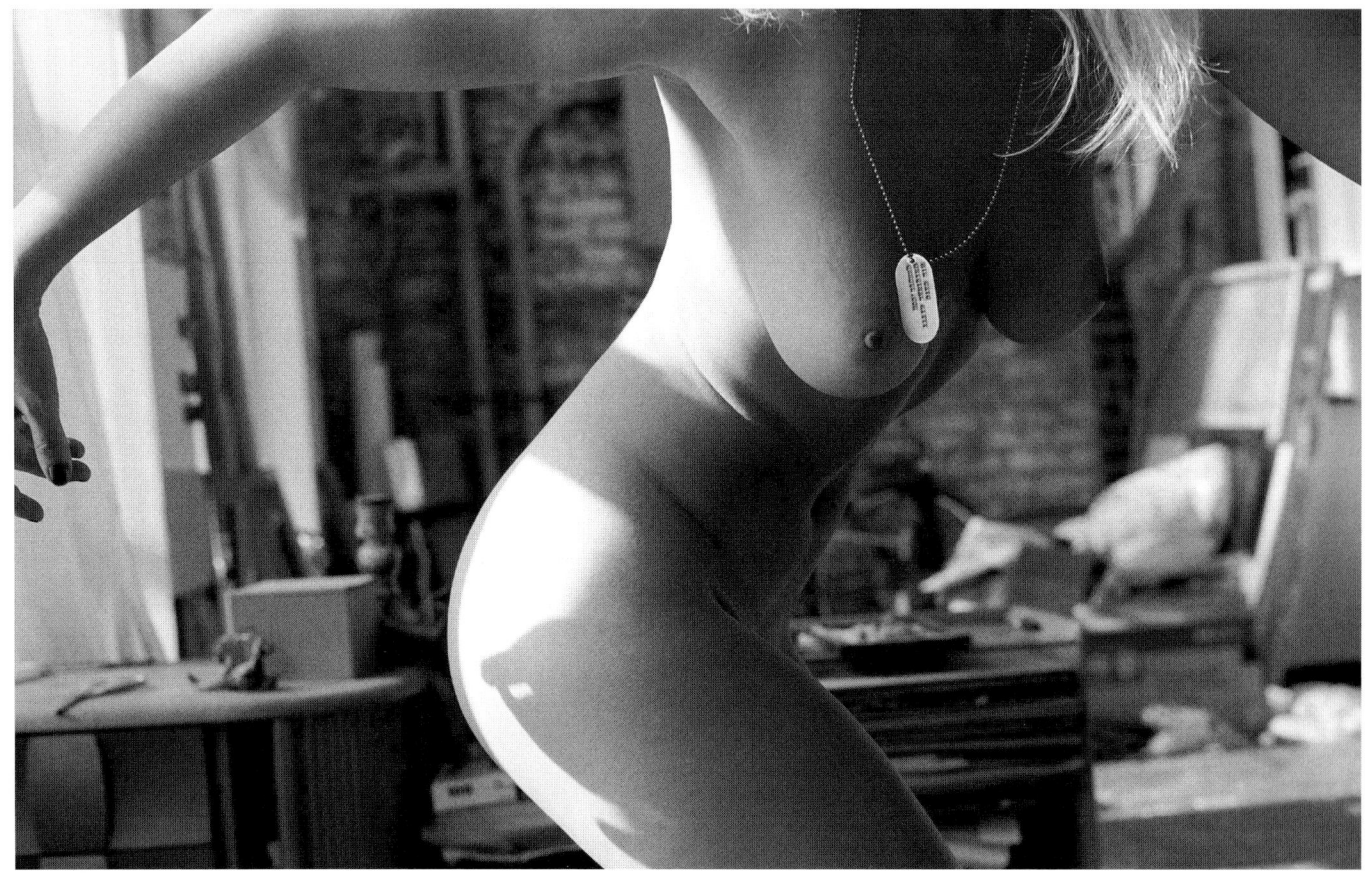

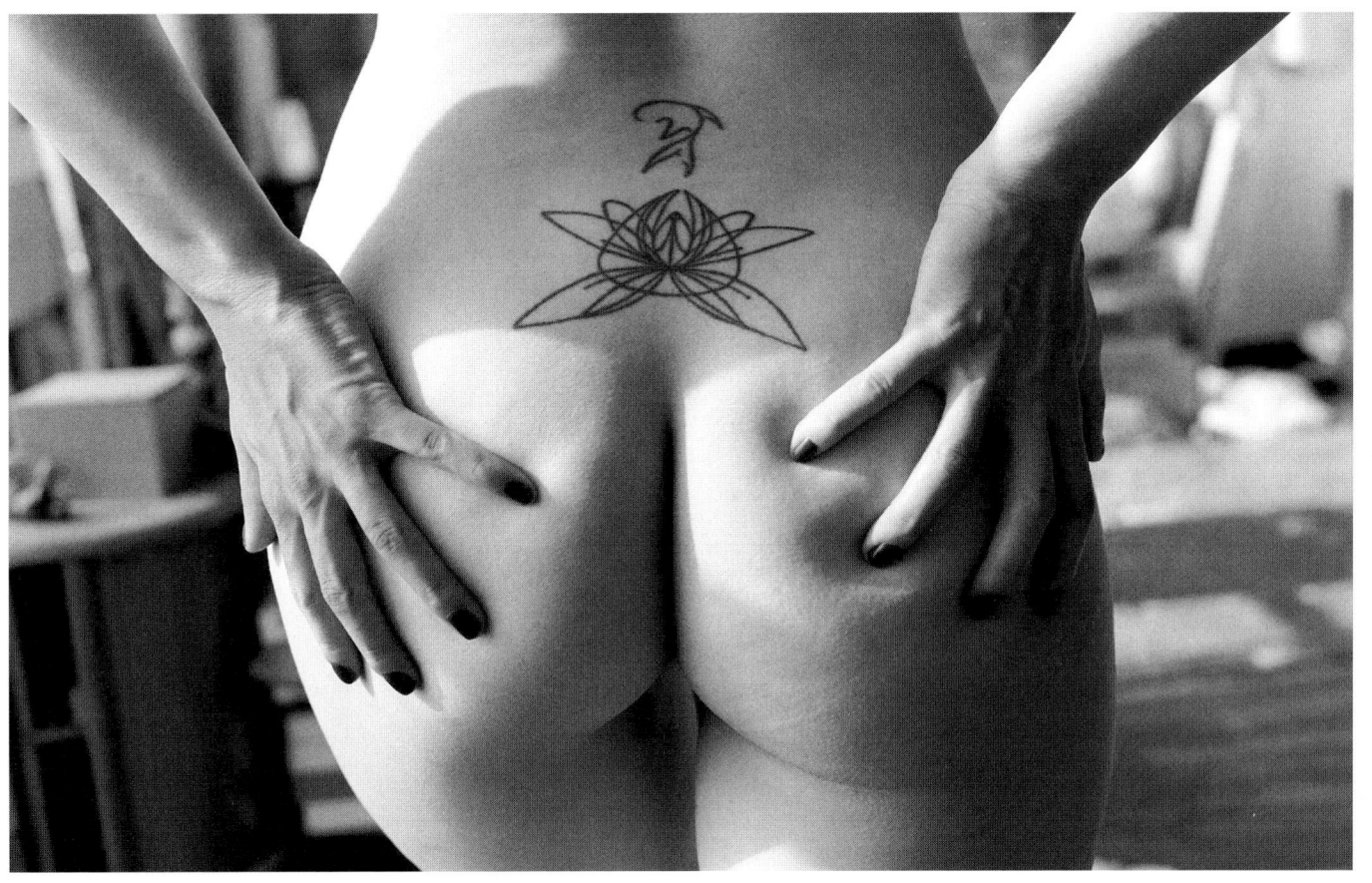

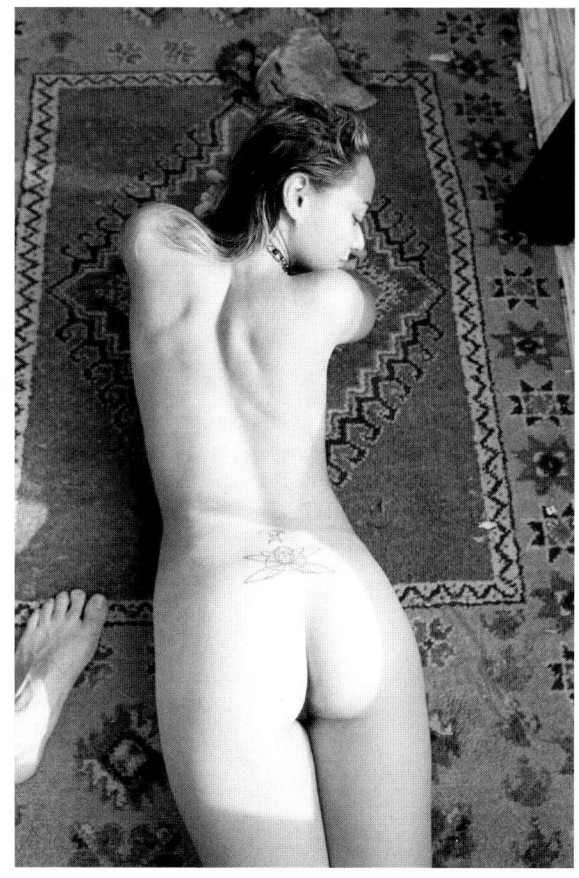
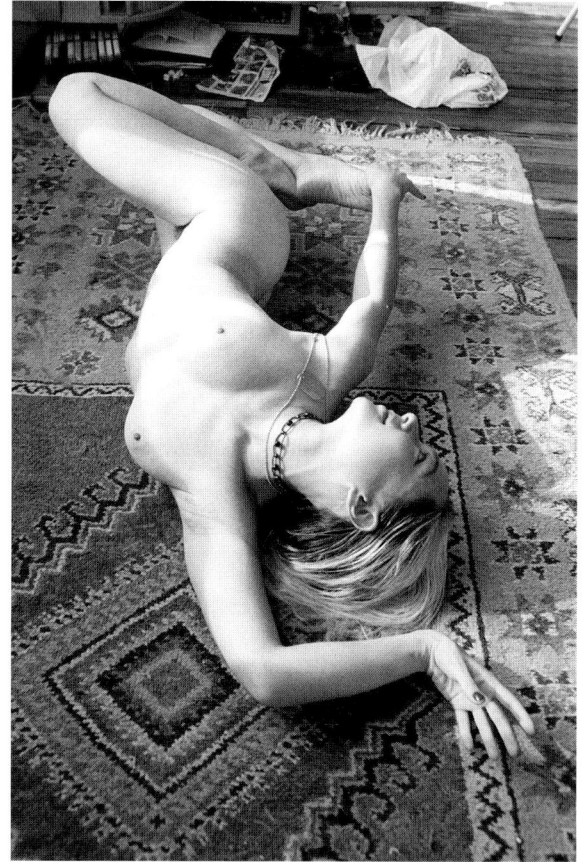

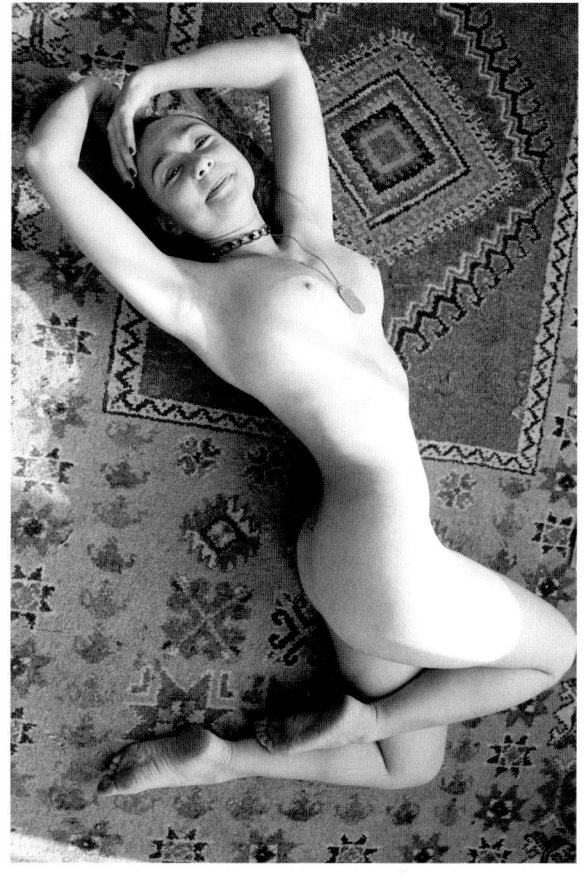
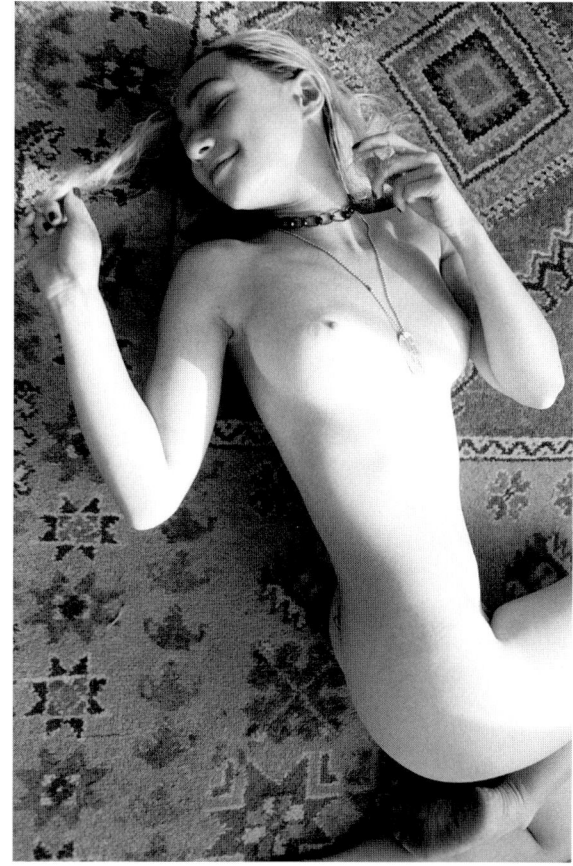

Jaiko · I met Jaiko somewhere in the streets of New York. She was pretty voluptuous for a Japanese woman. We shot in her east village apartment, while a German TV crew filmed us. Jaiko had worked with several other art photographers, so I just tried to make sure she had fun. I liked her egg shaped clock too.

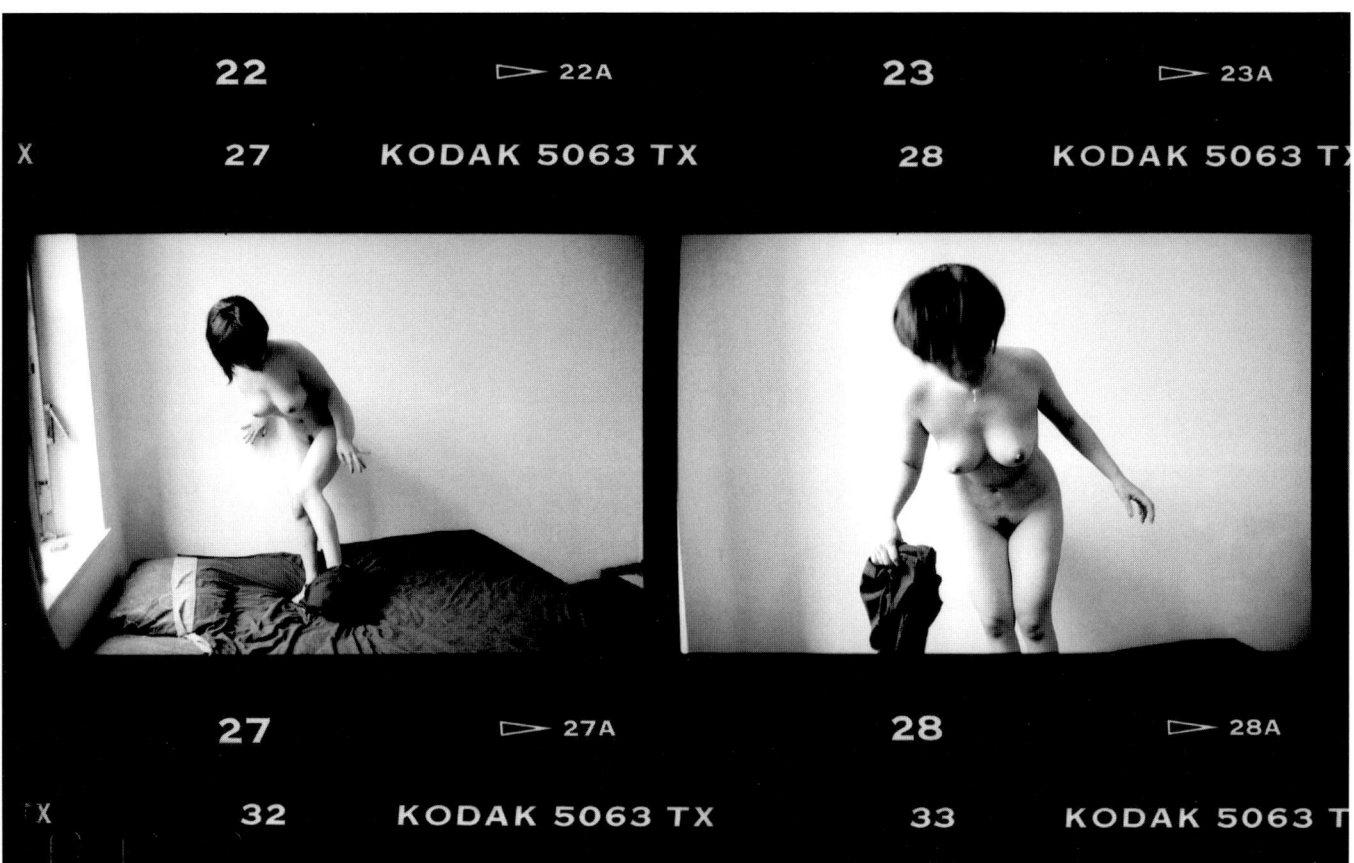

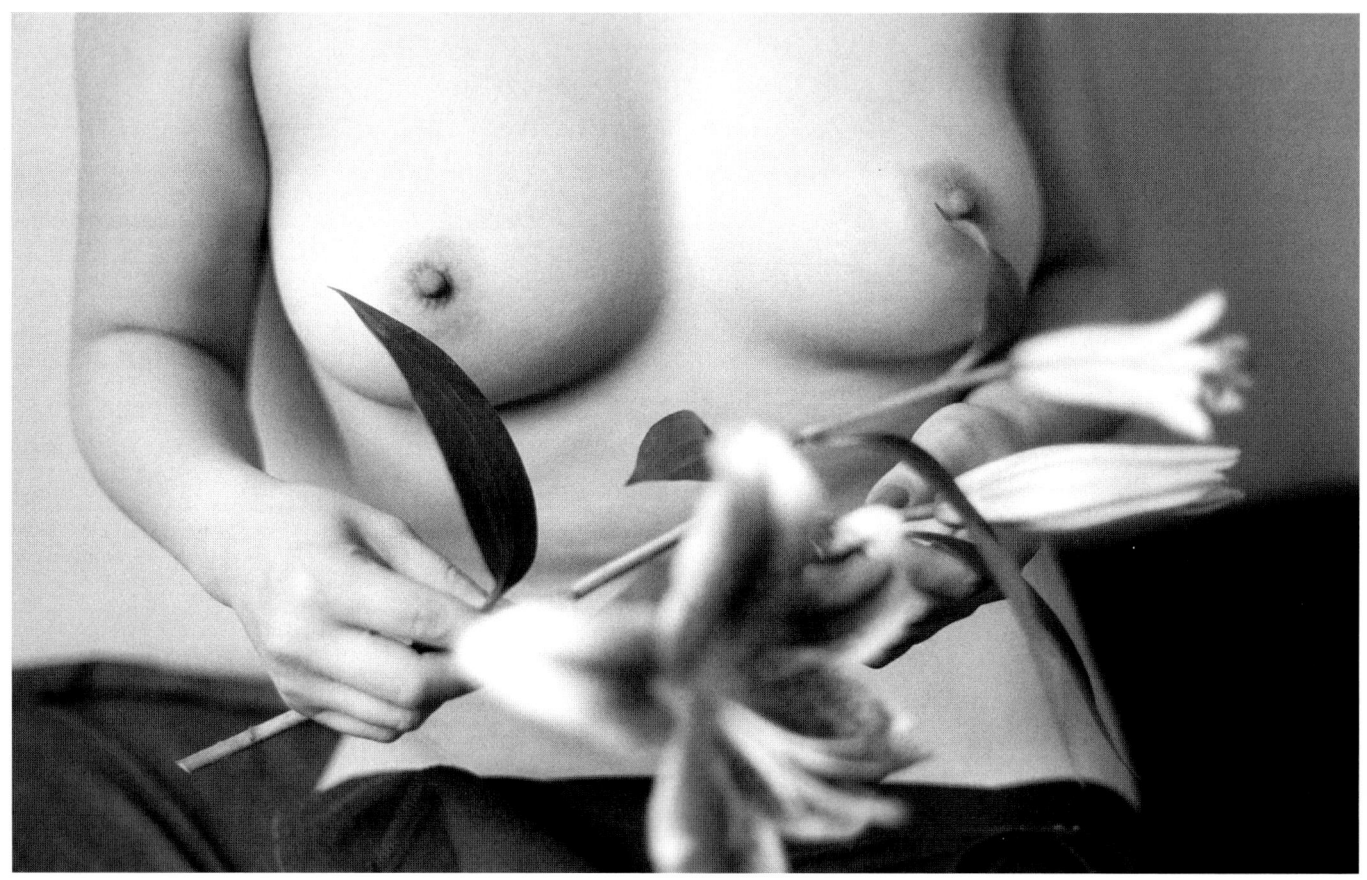

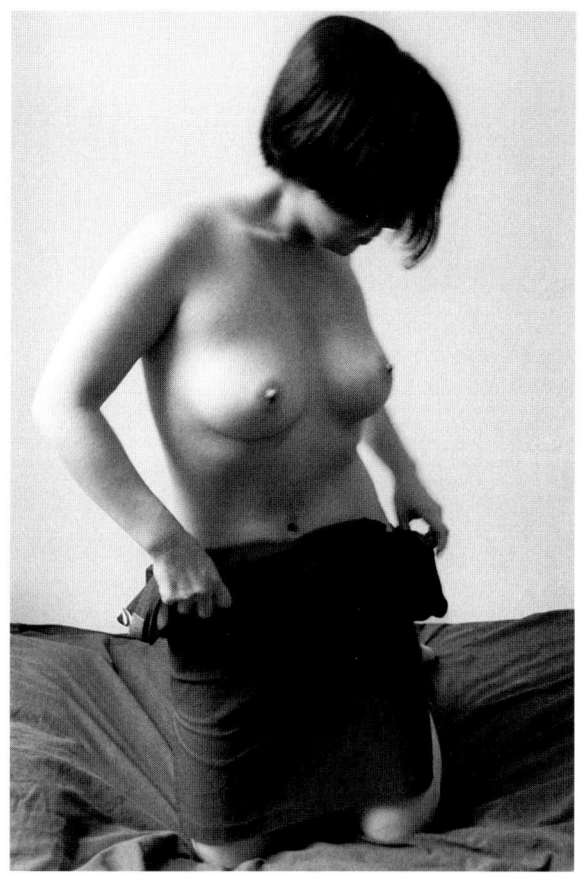

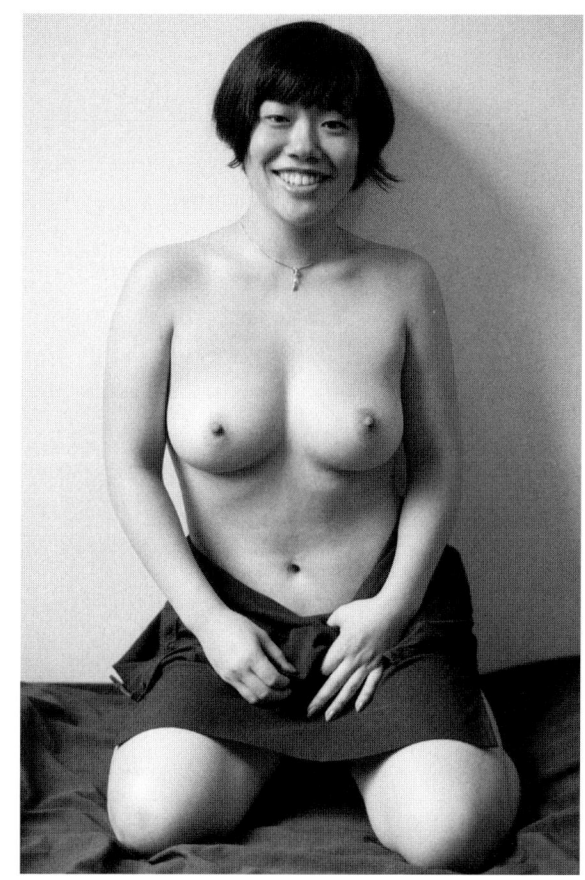

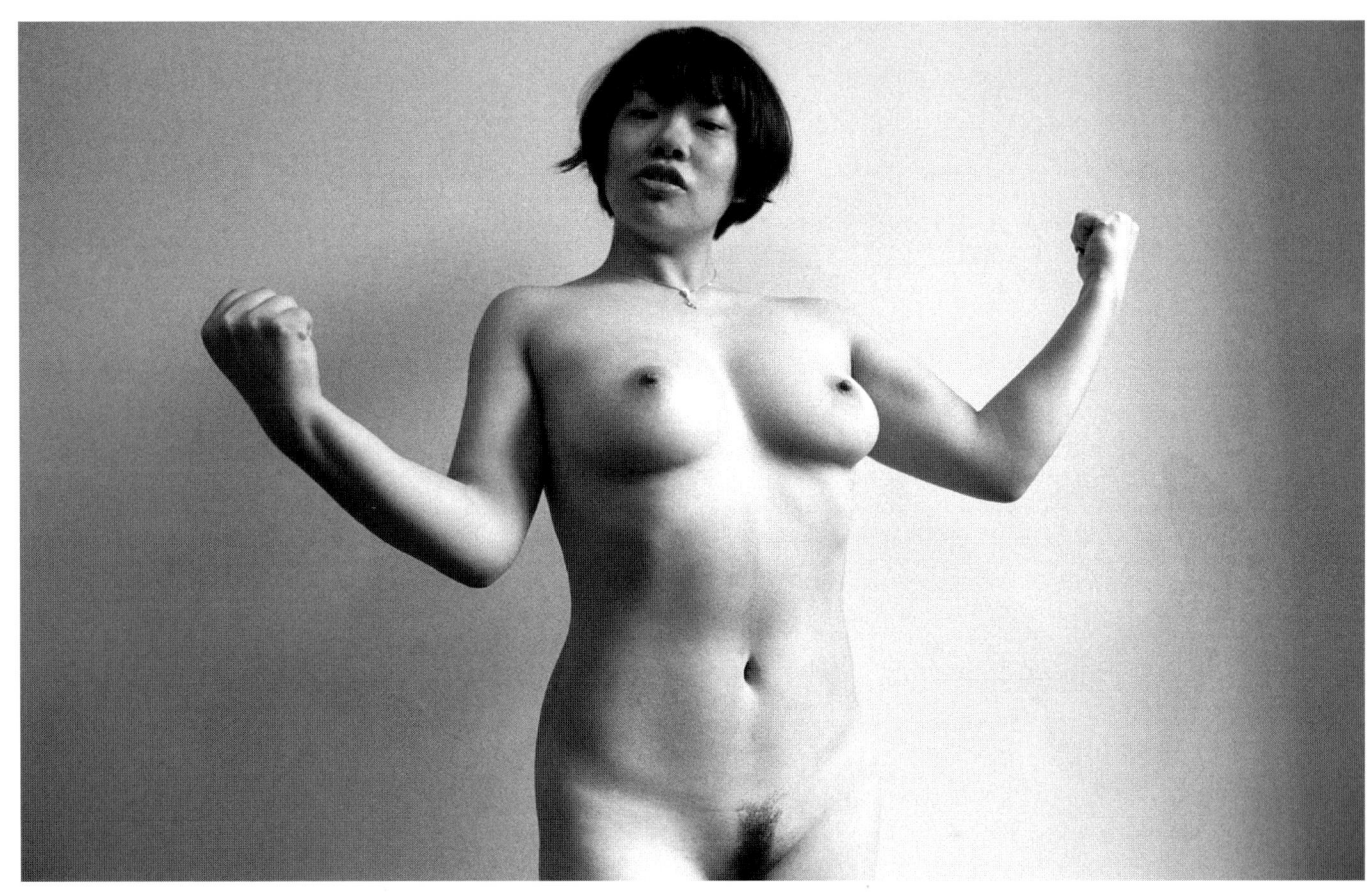

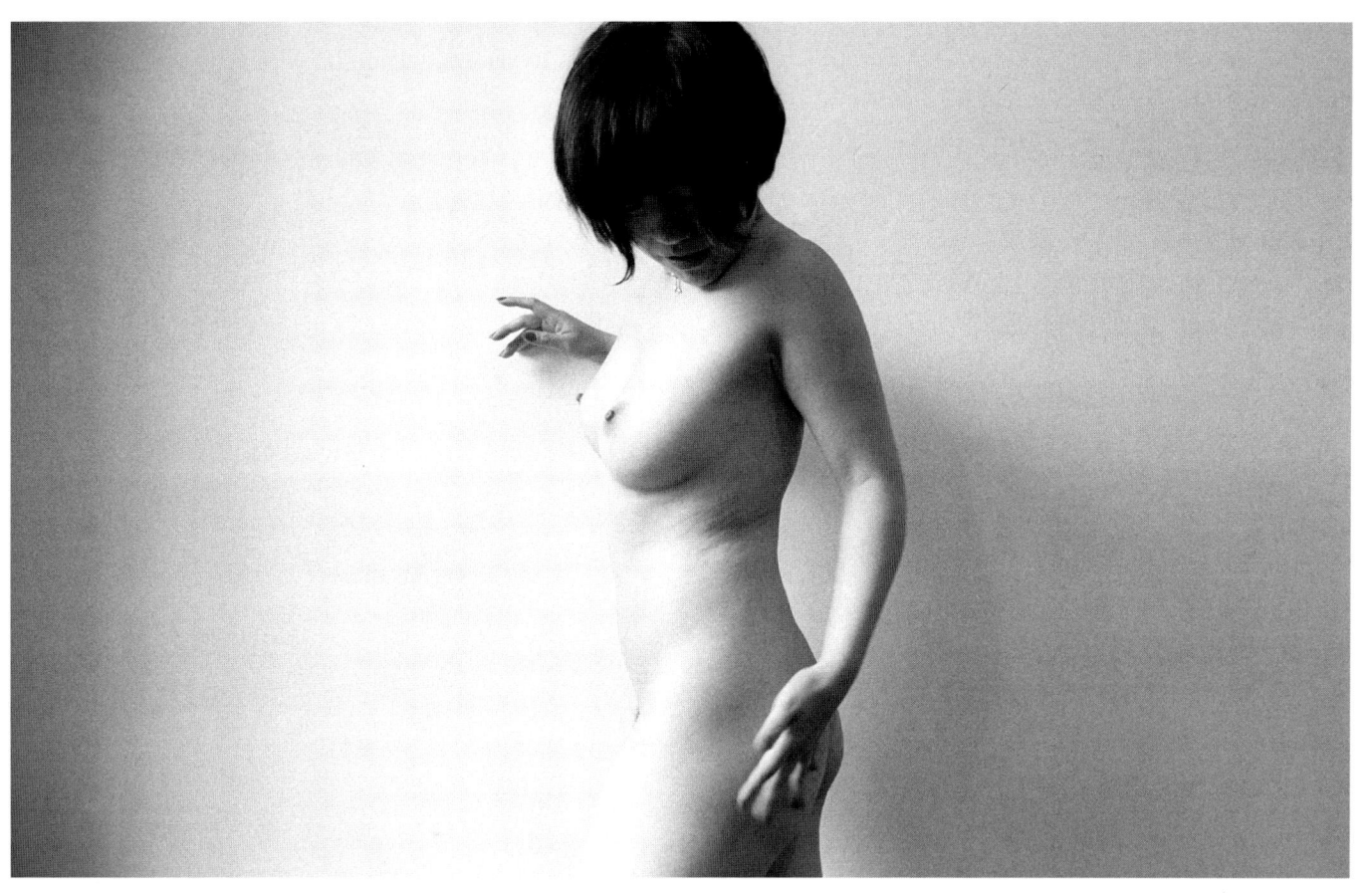

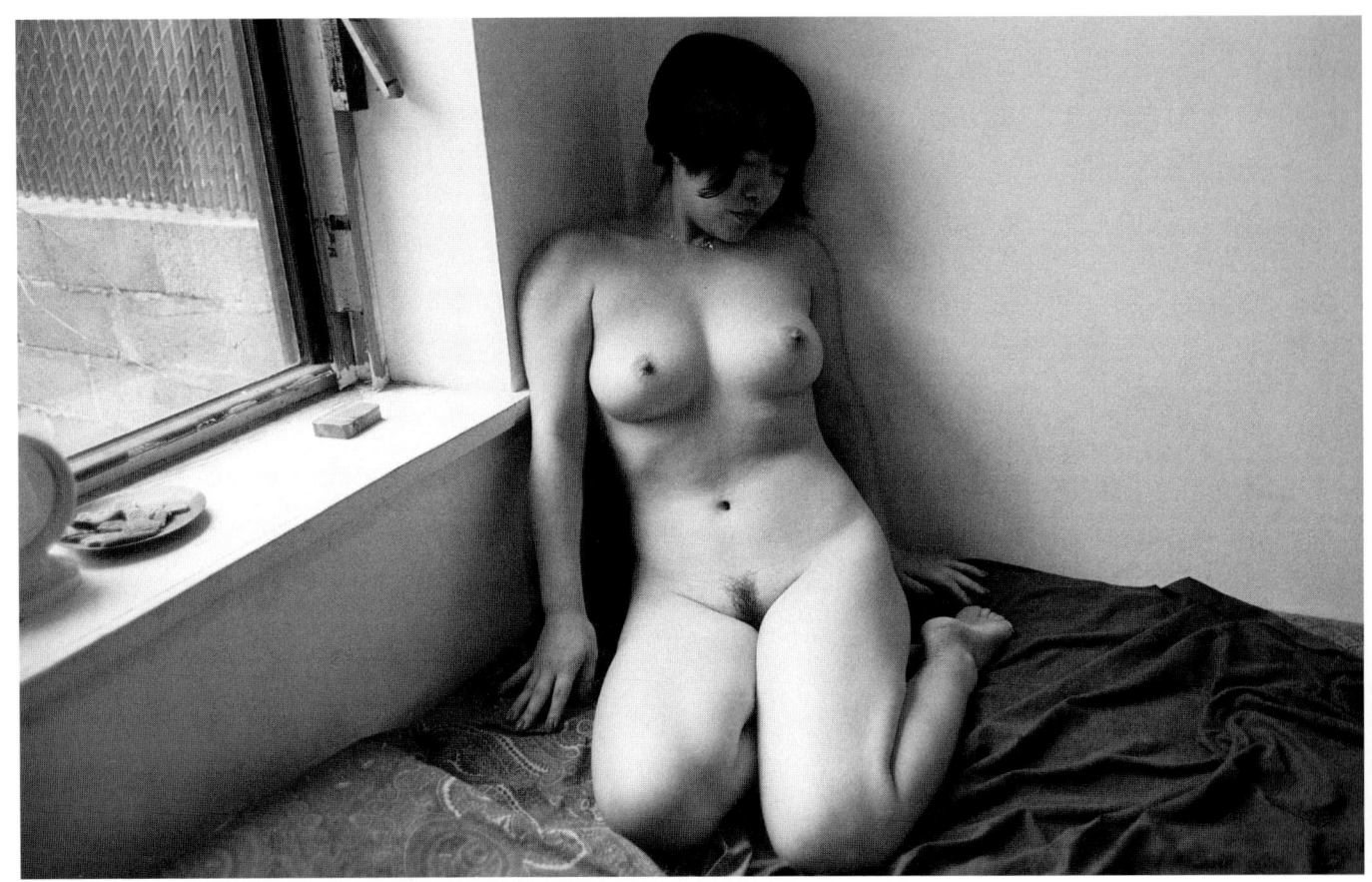

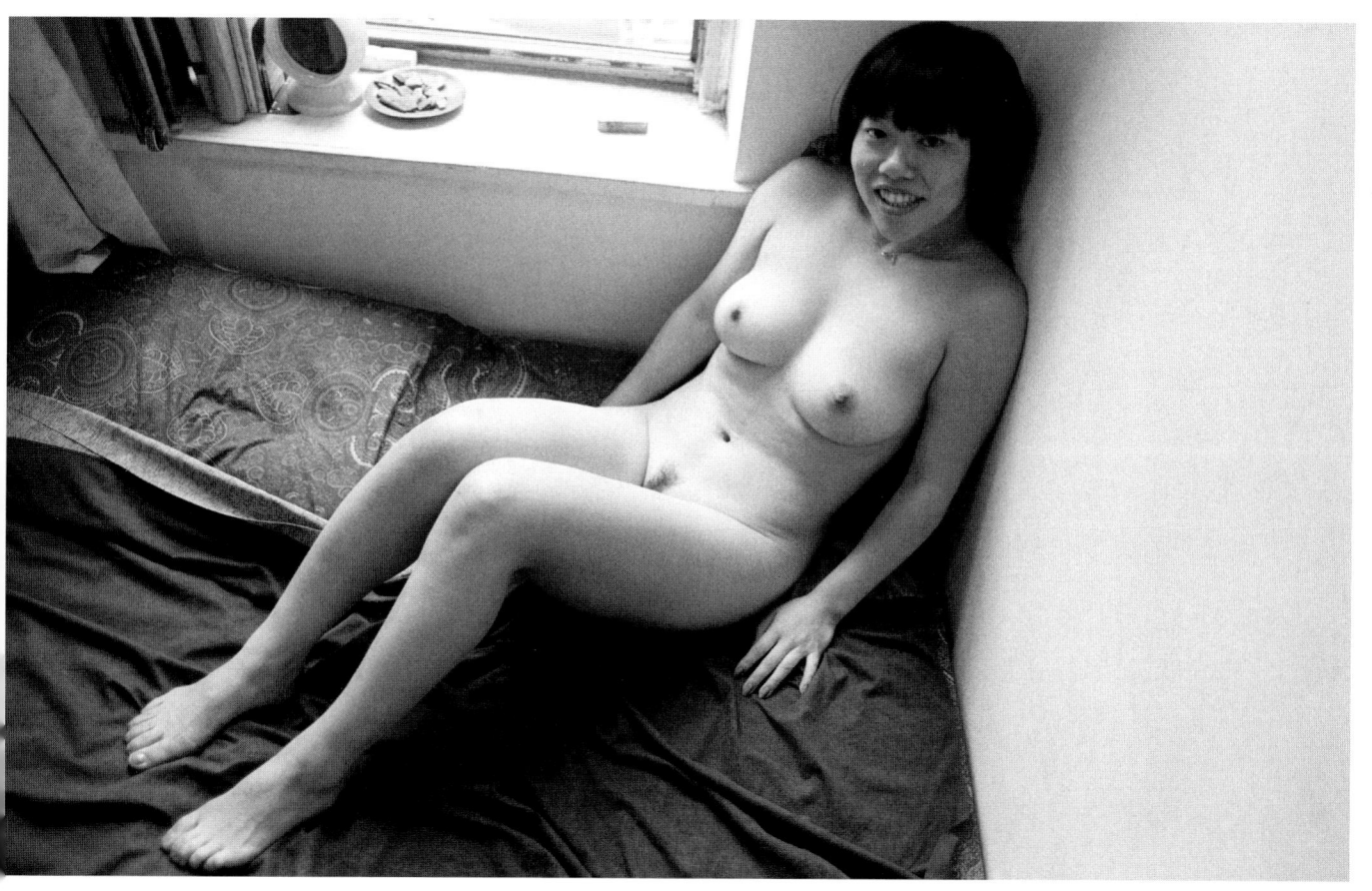

Lady Jane · I met and photographed Lady Jane during the Millennium. She was a burlesque dancer, and produced her own show. She had a dog named "Doodles" that never left our side. Jane had many tattoos, giggled a lot, and danced for me in the living room.

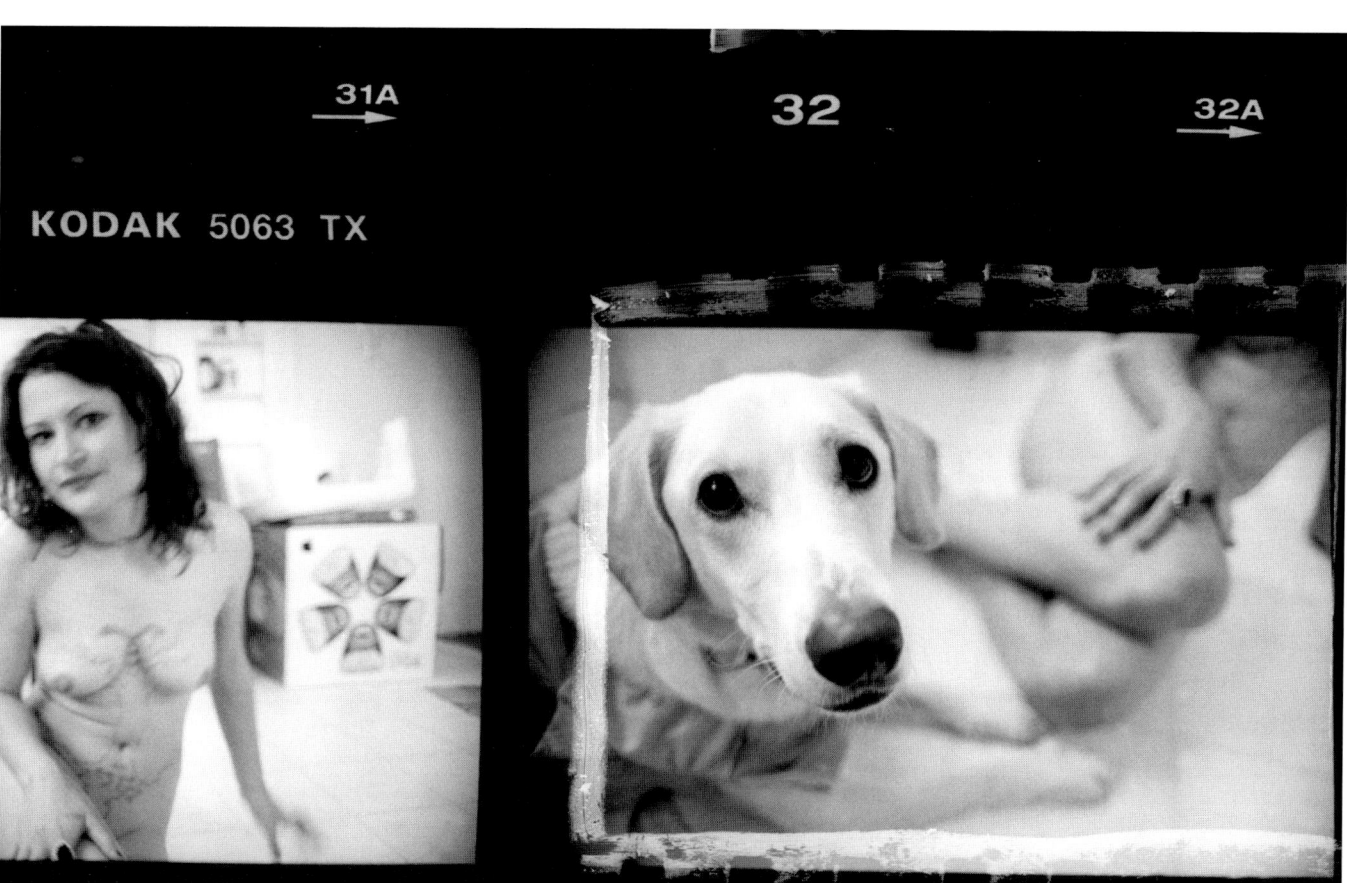

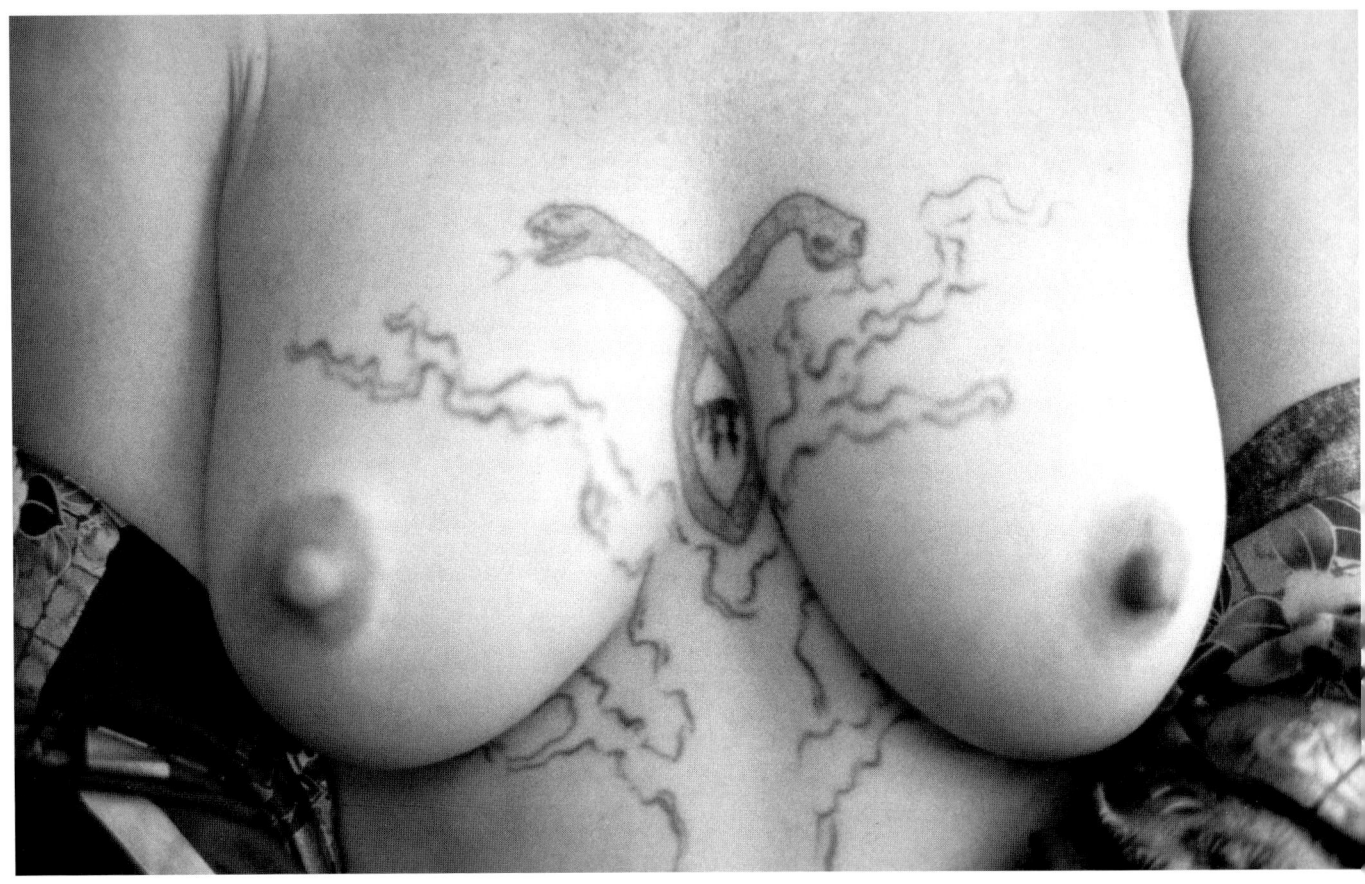

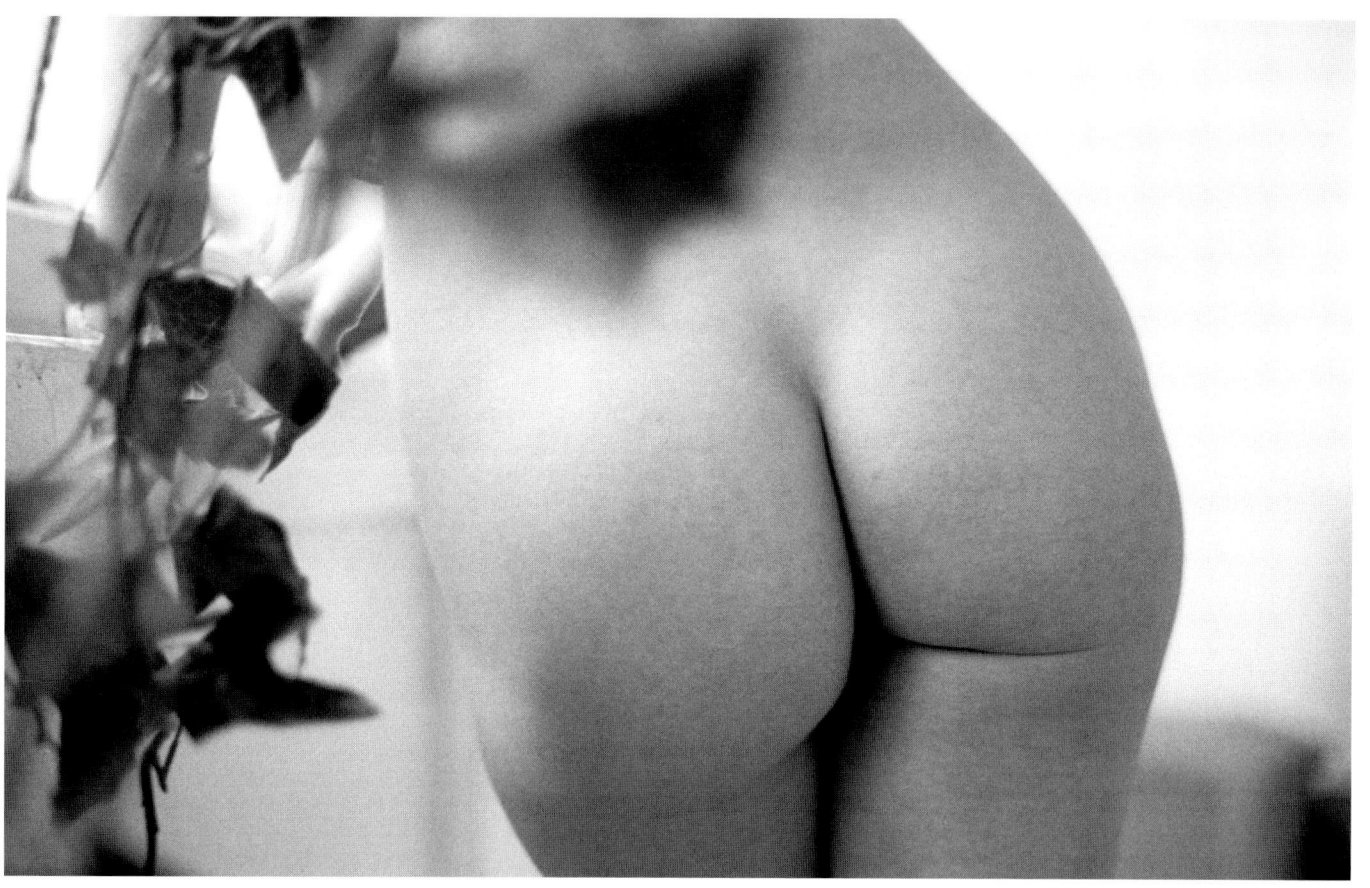

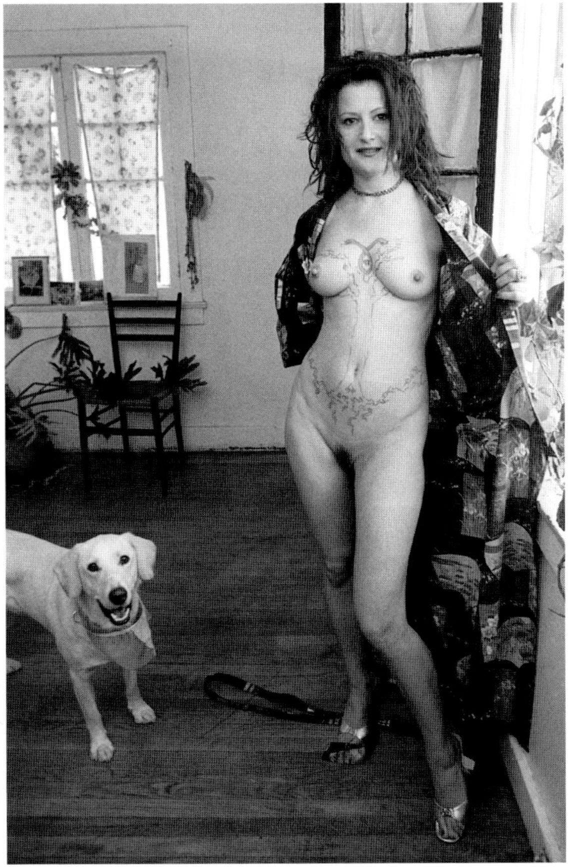

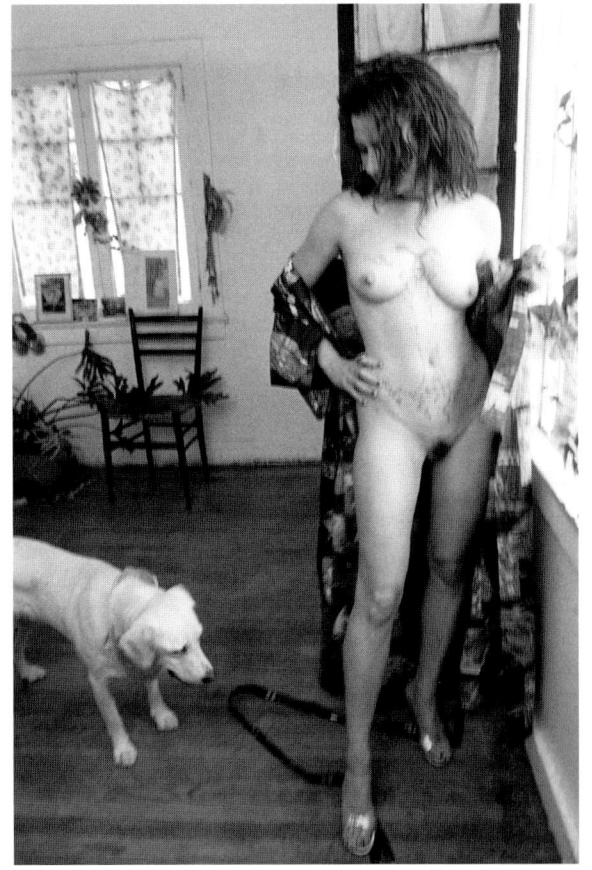

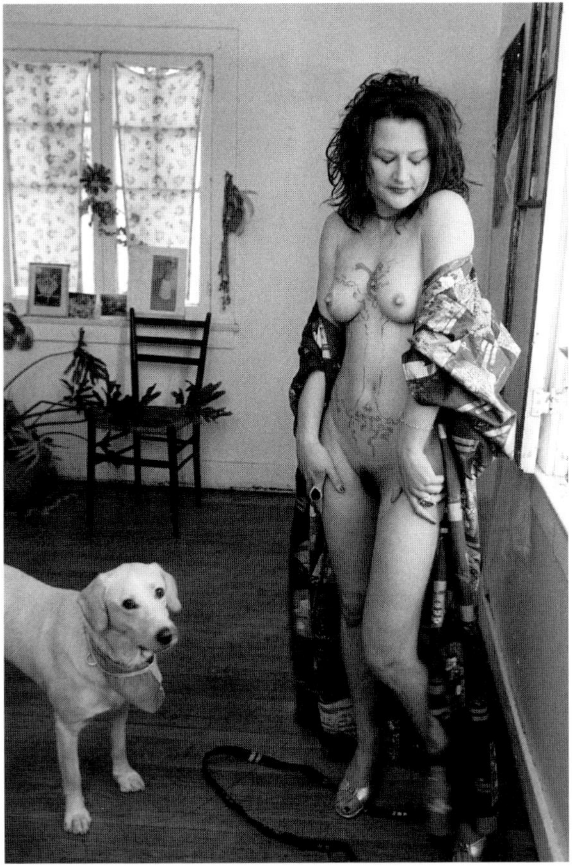

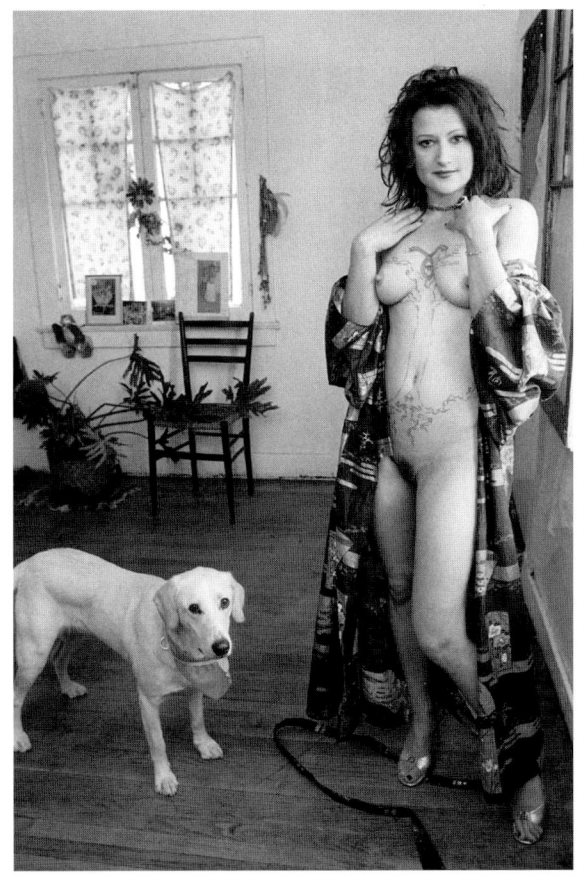

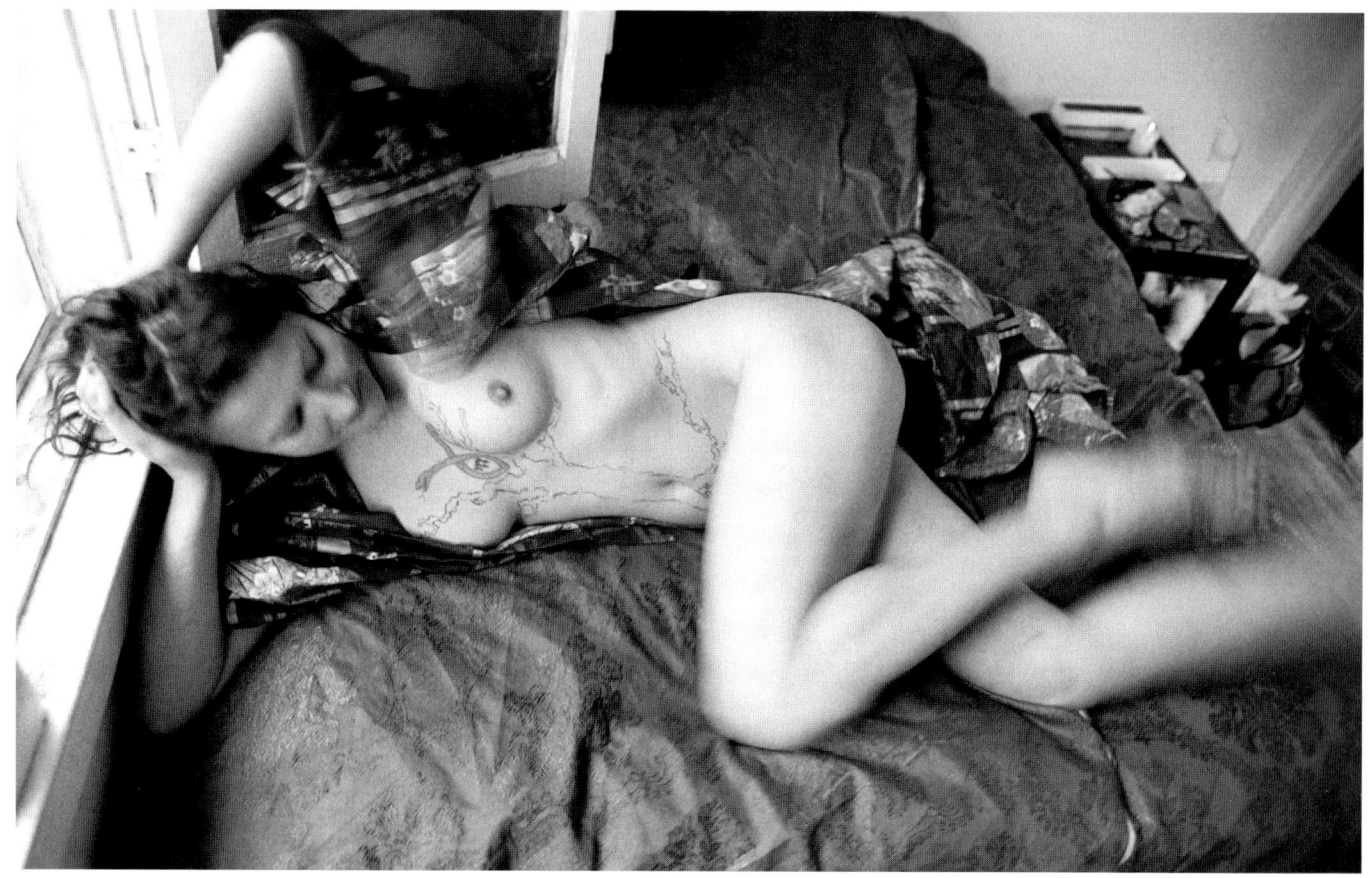

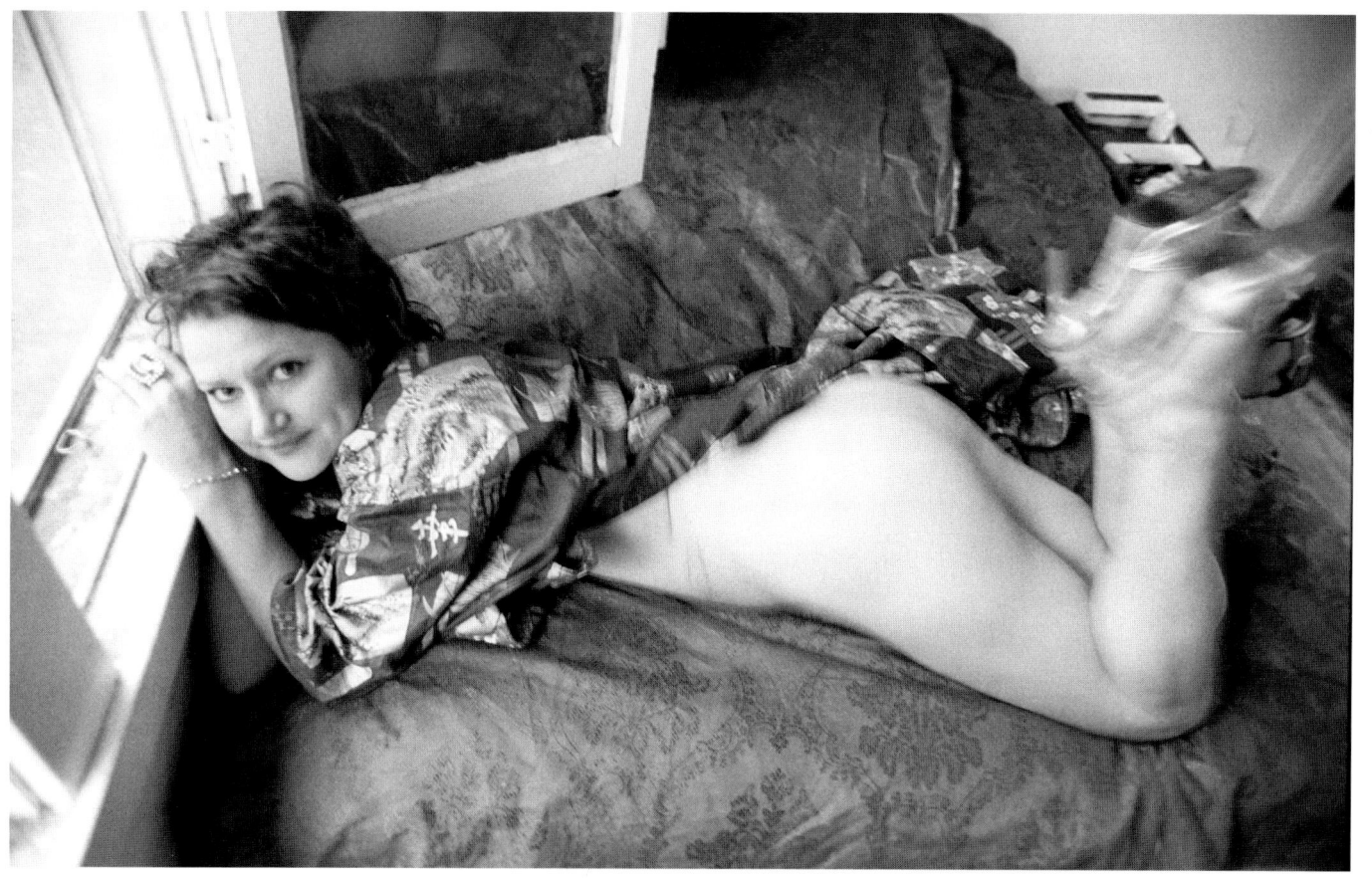

Jen · I first met Jen at a magazine party in New York. We also hung out at the "Burning Man" festival in Nevada. Jen lived in the east village with another Jen, and had a huge kitchen with a black and white tiled floor. She ate pomegranate seeds, drank water and smoked with me. Jen is very talkative, good with words and loves Jewish men.

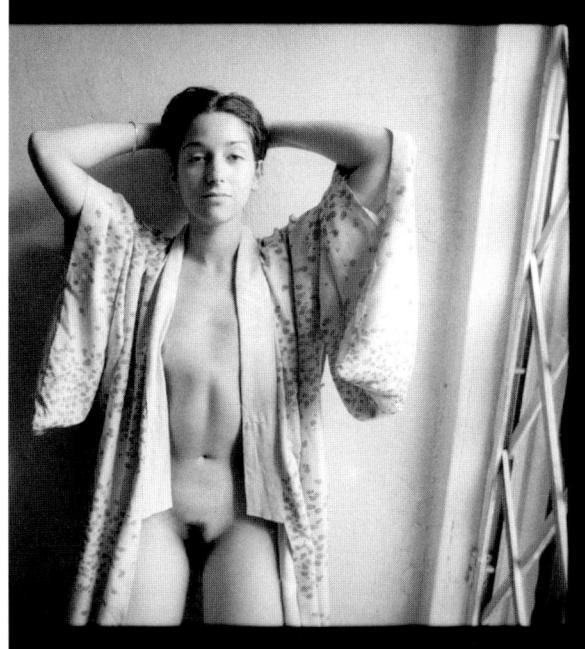
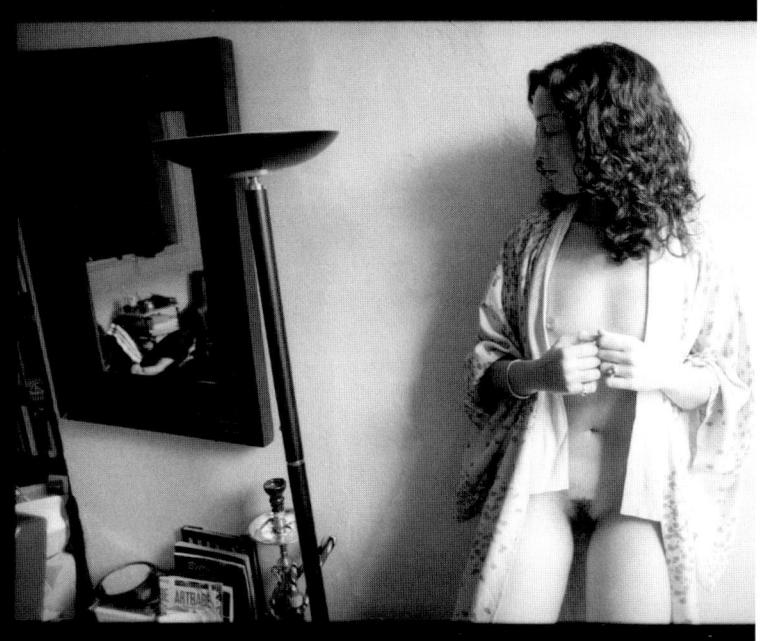

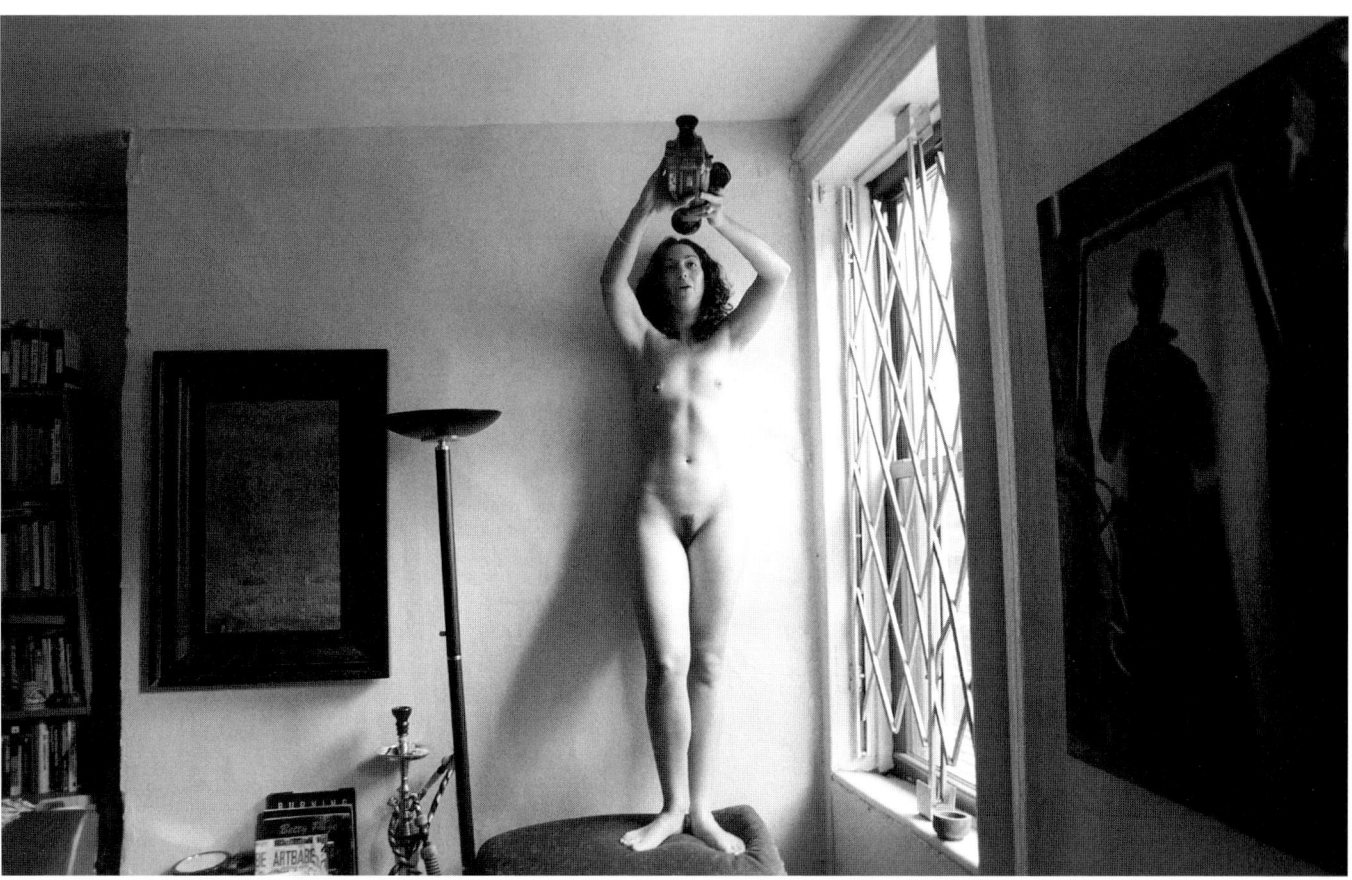

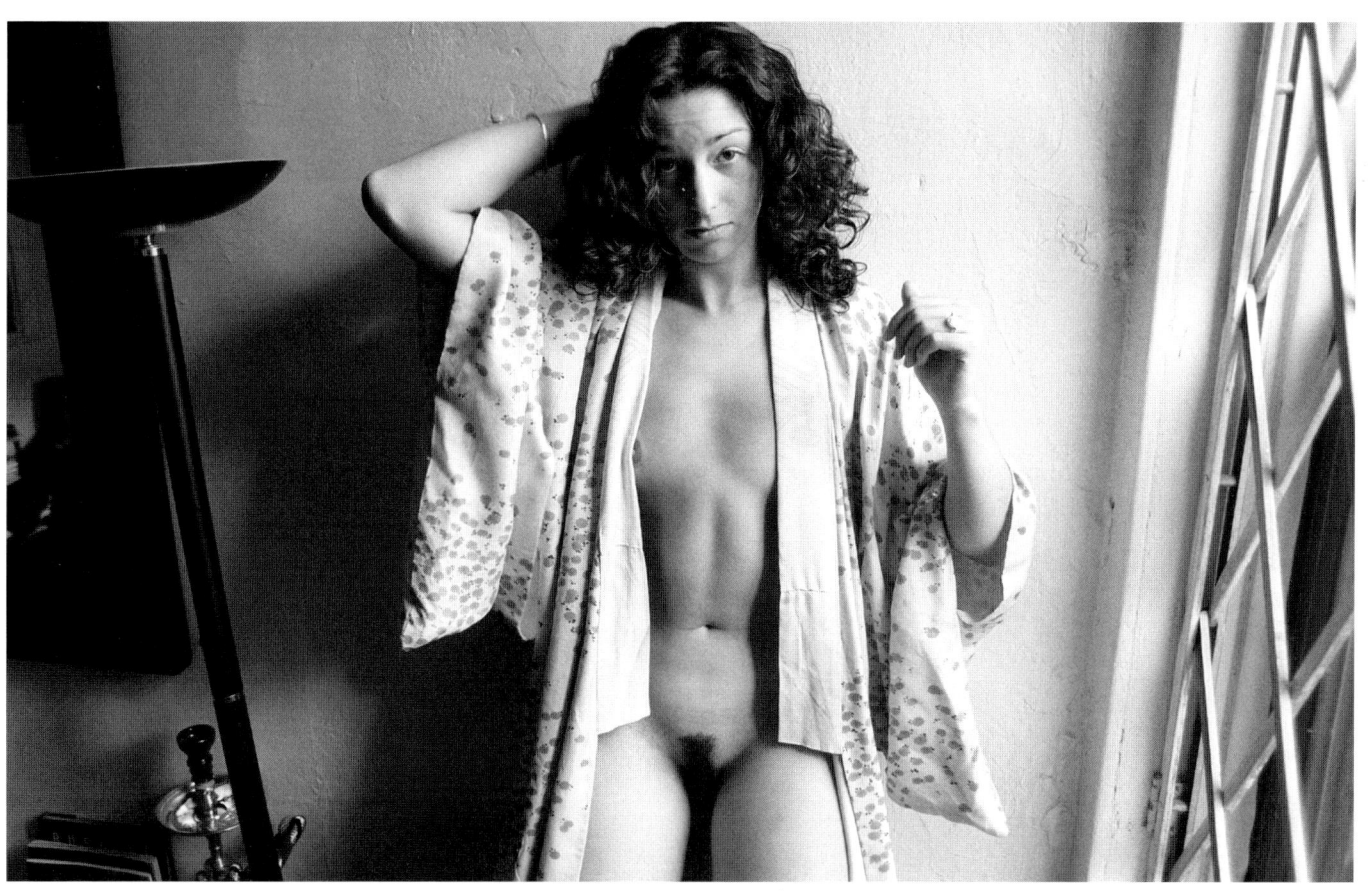

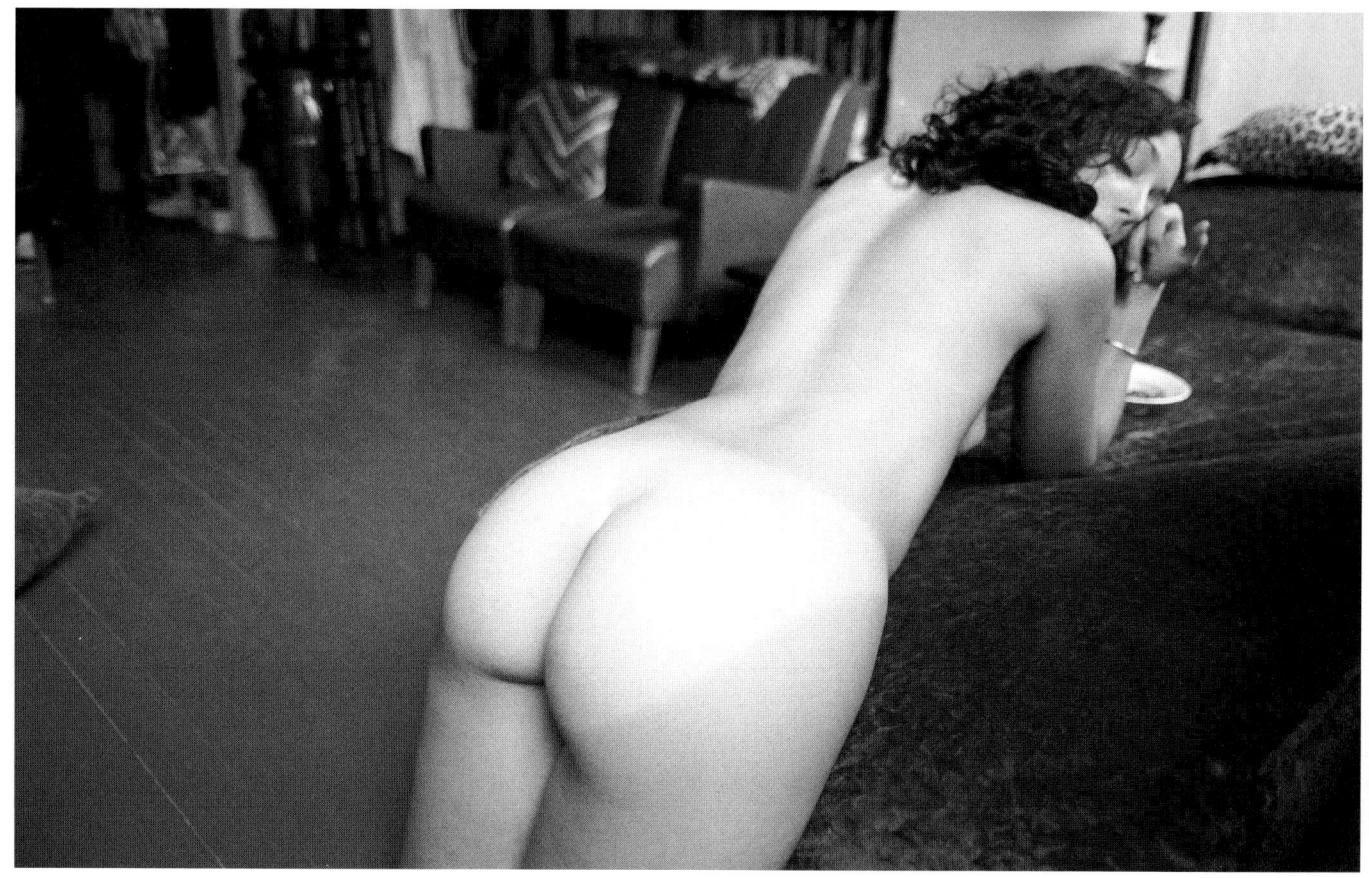

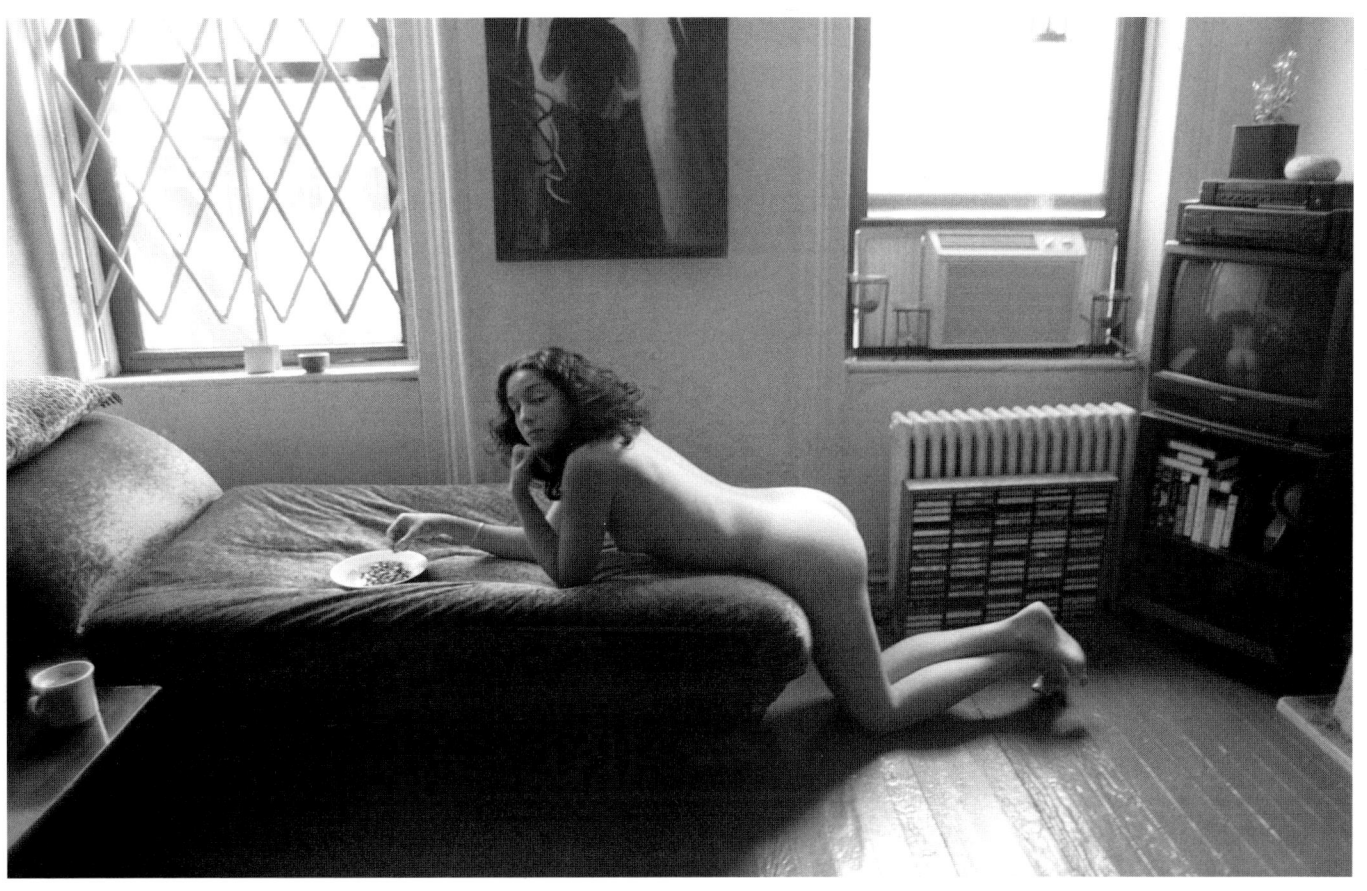

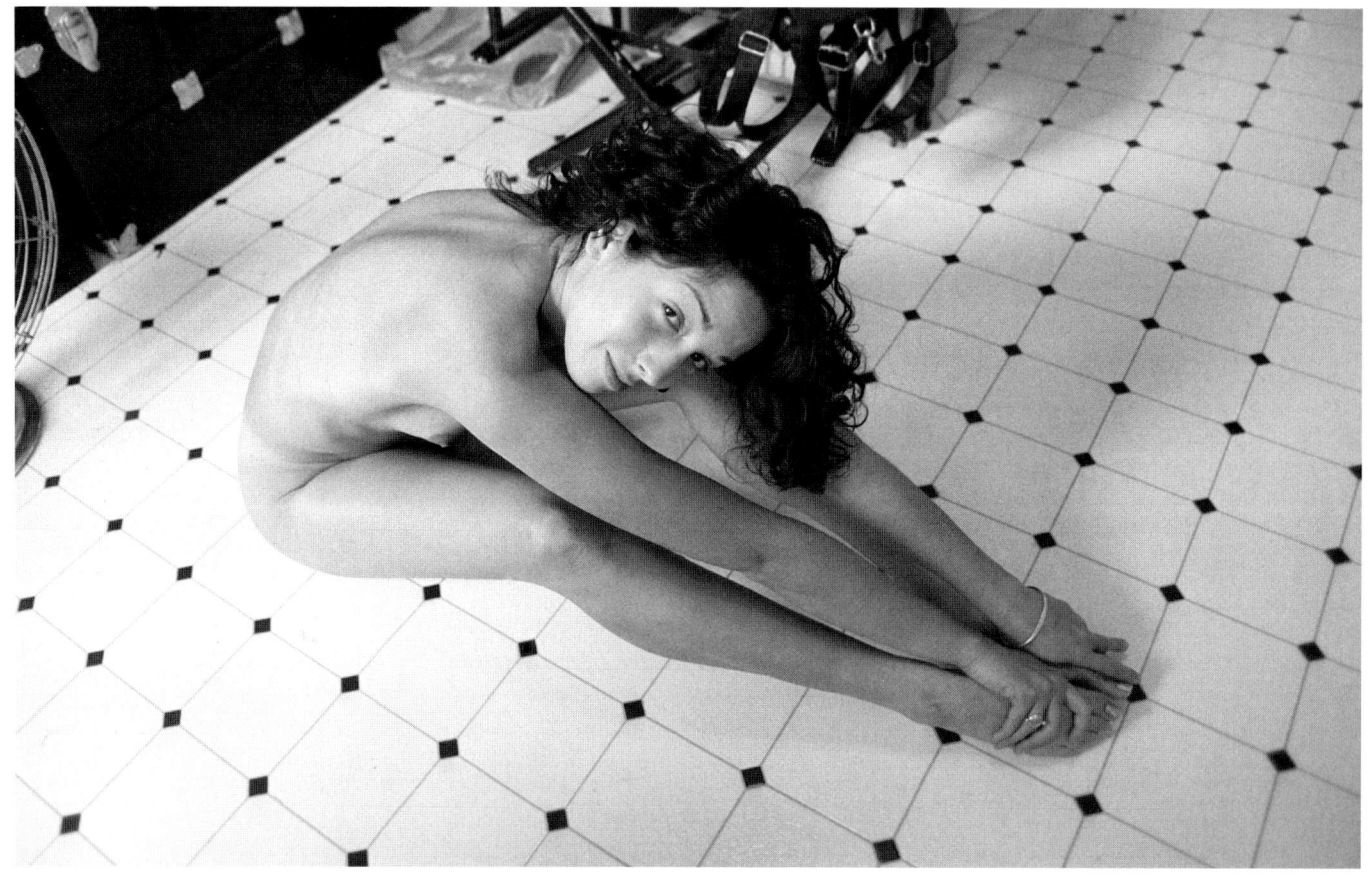

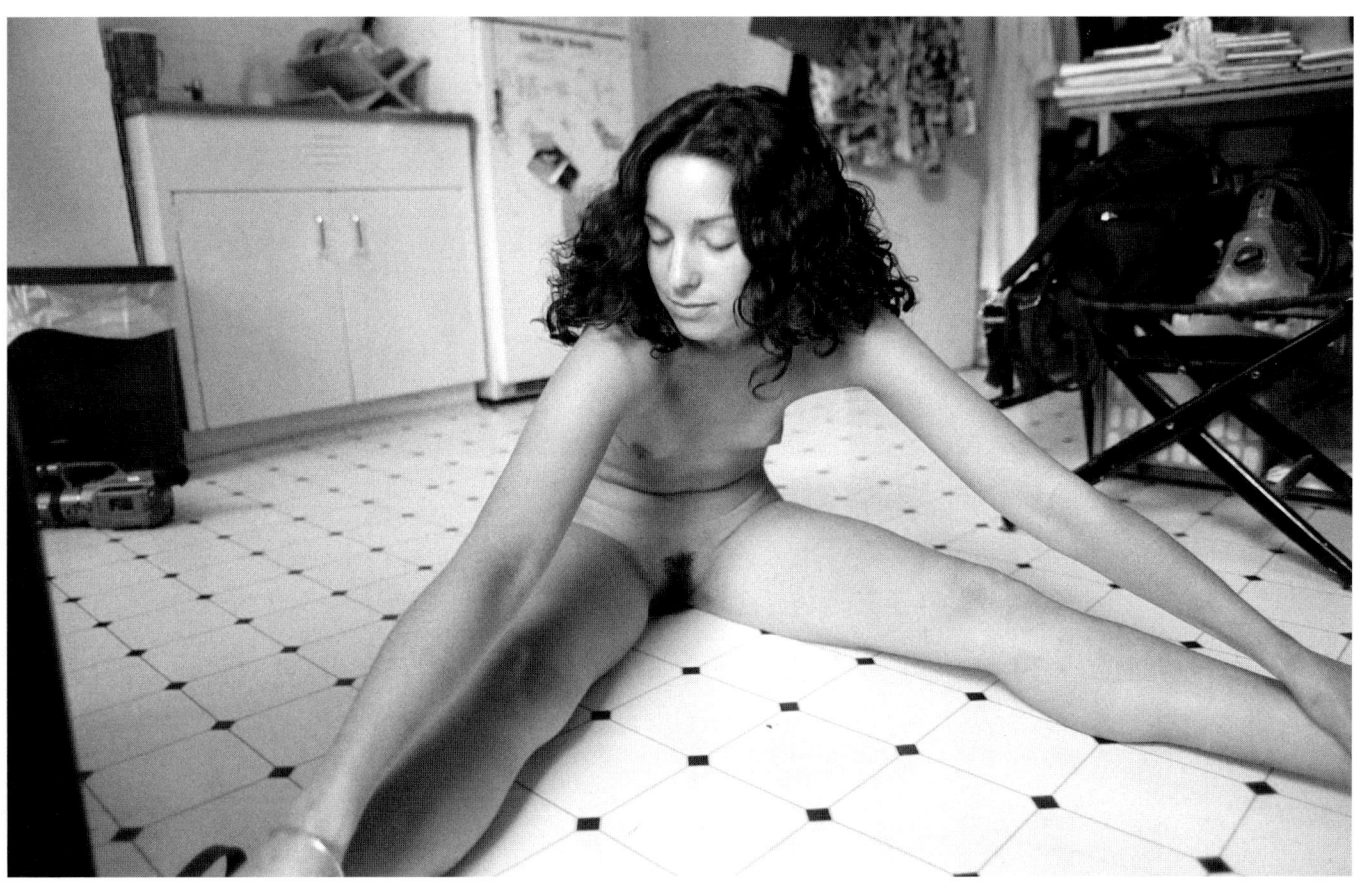

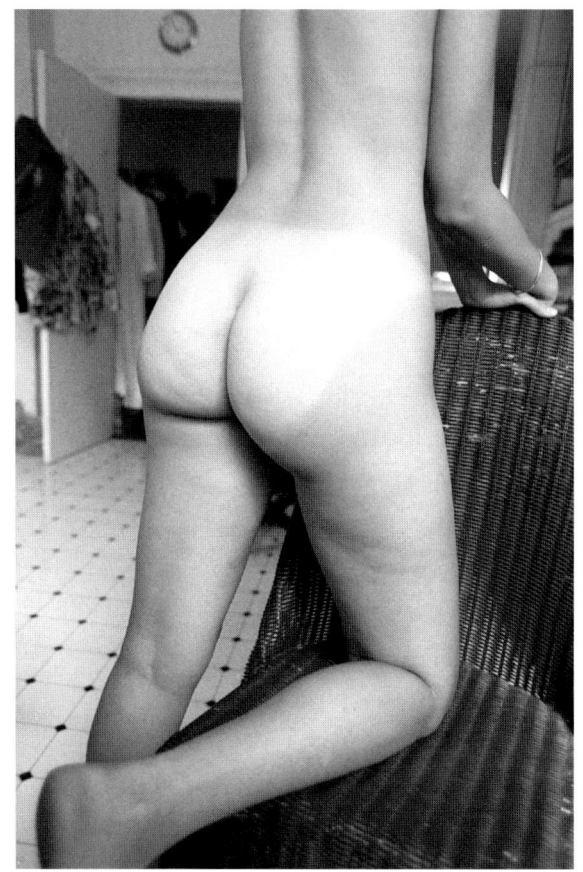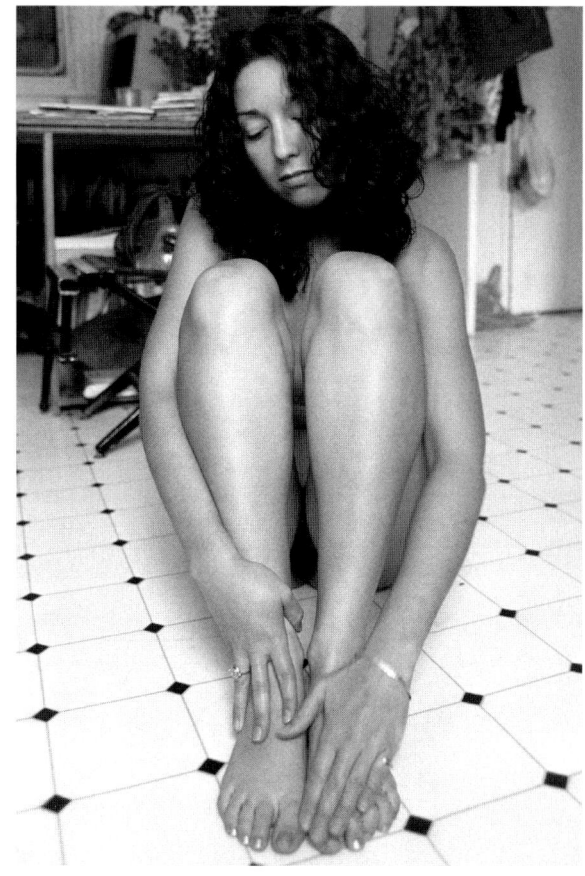

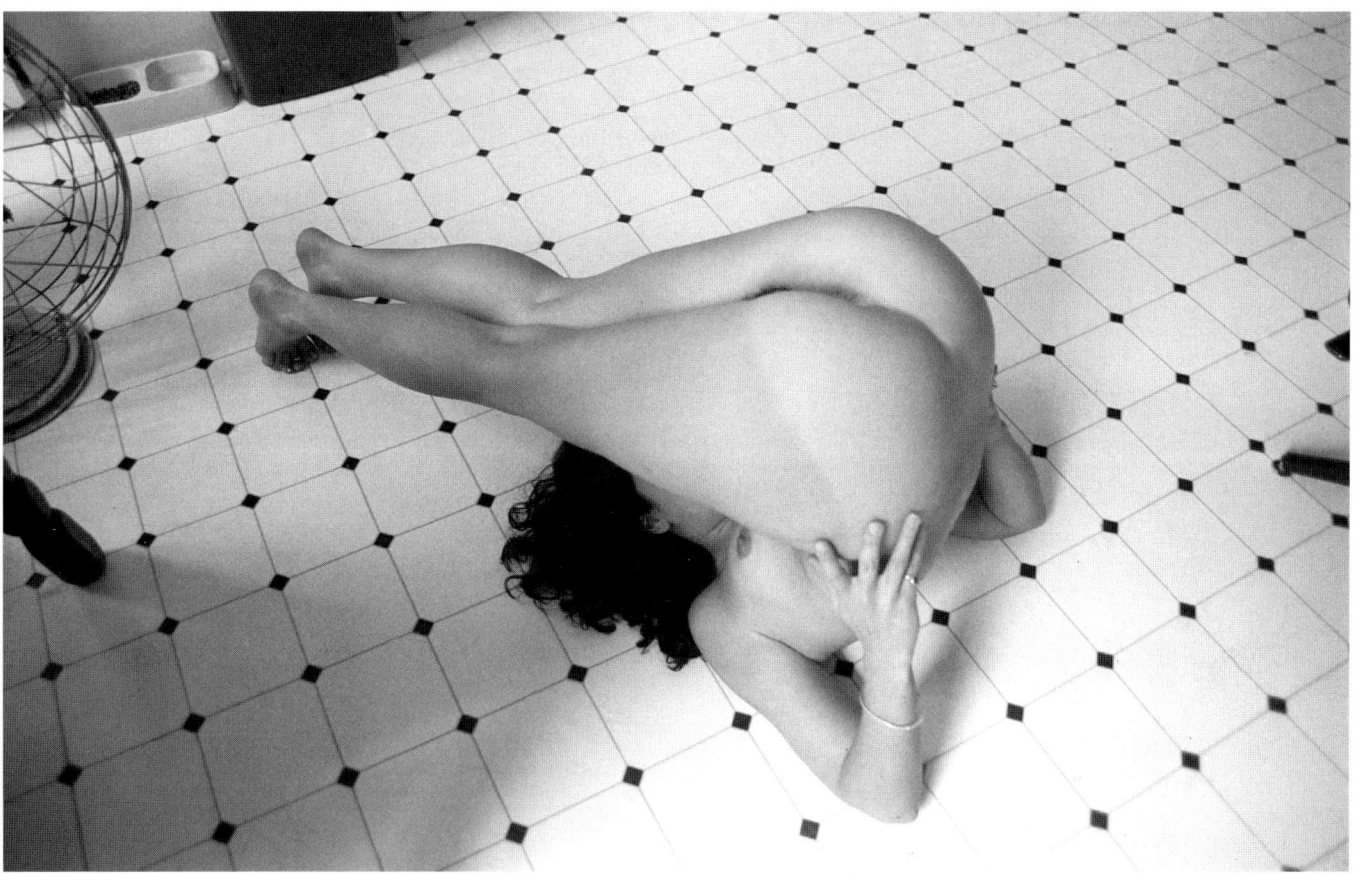

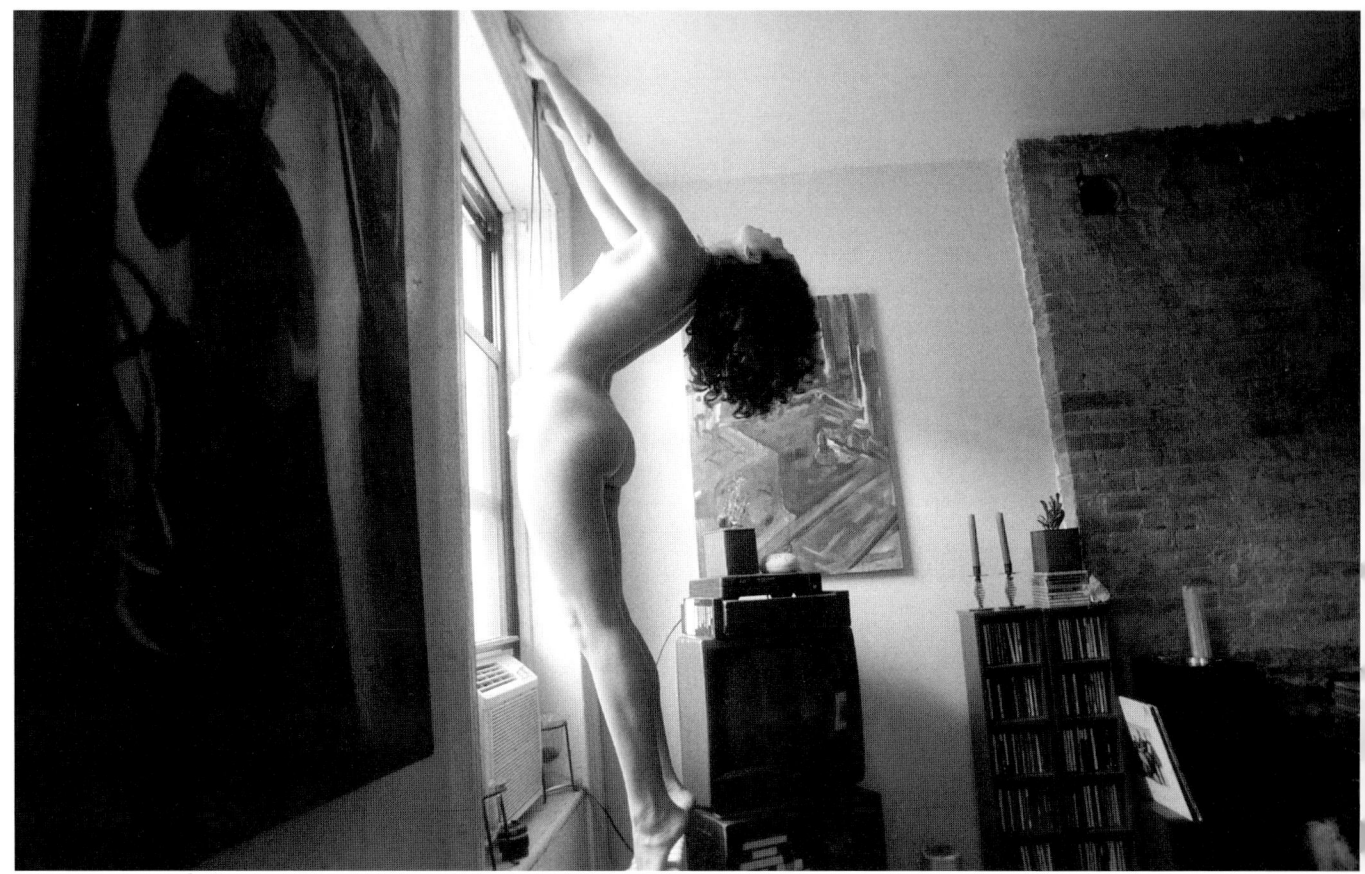

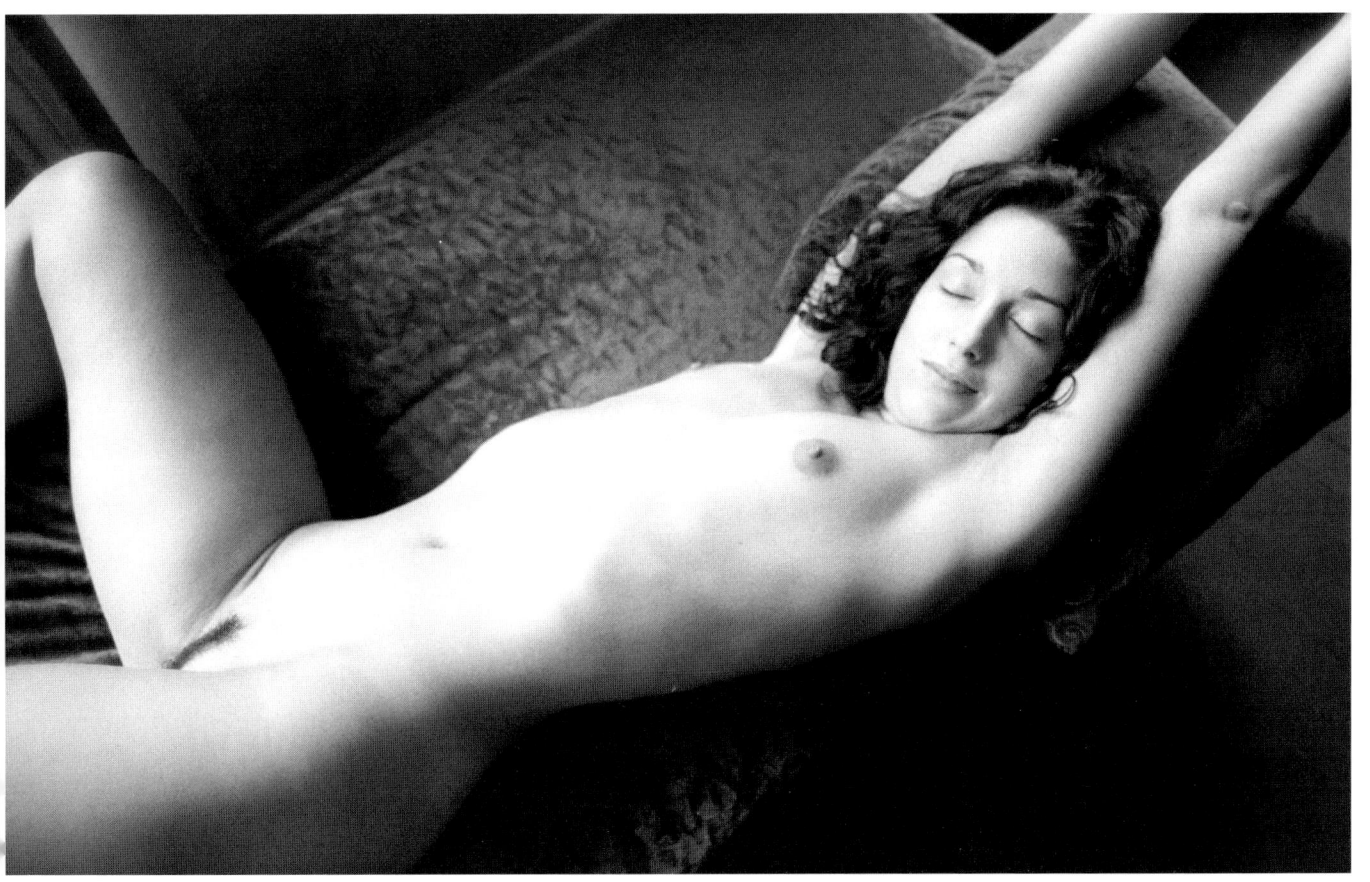

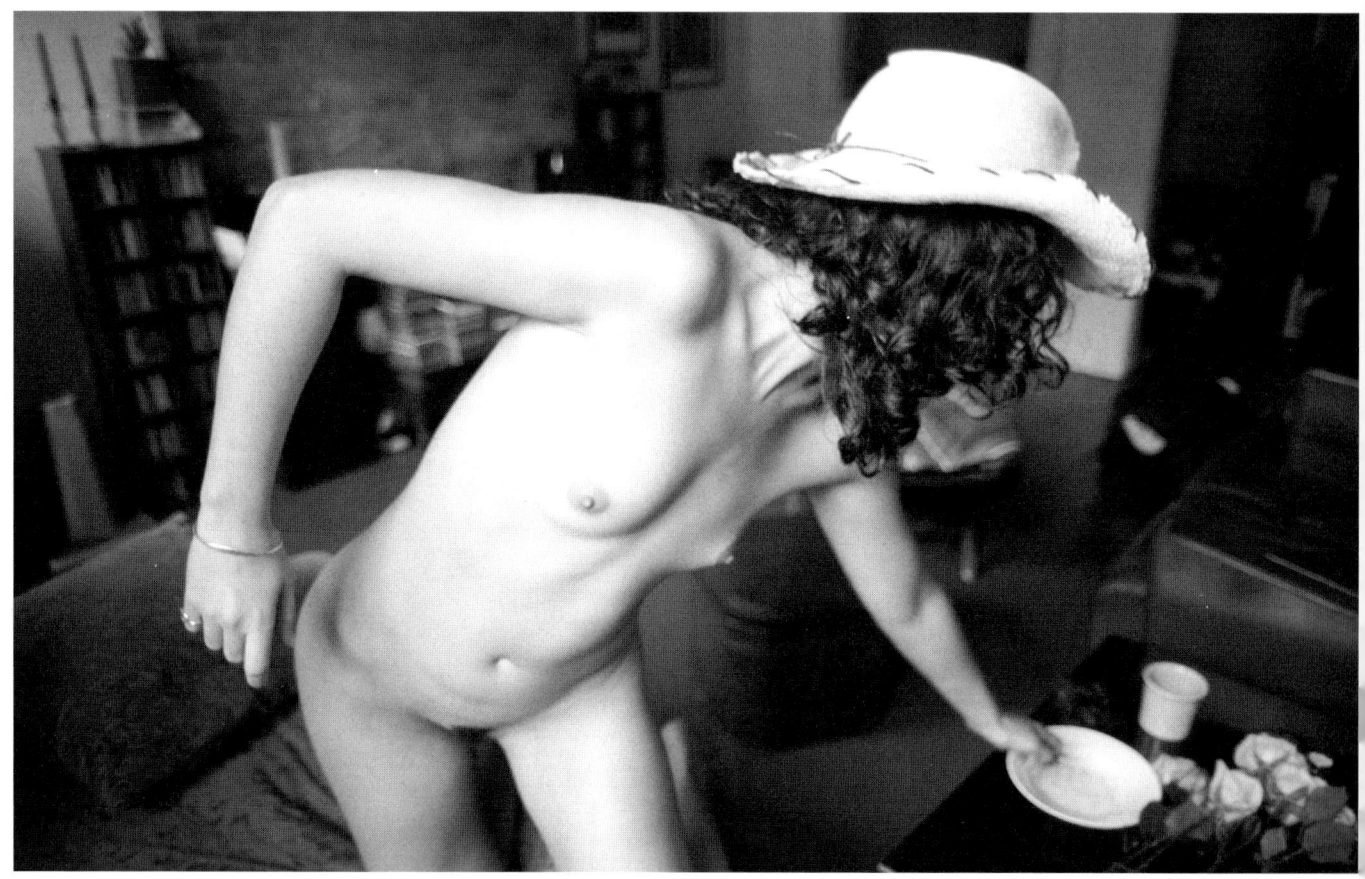

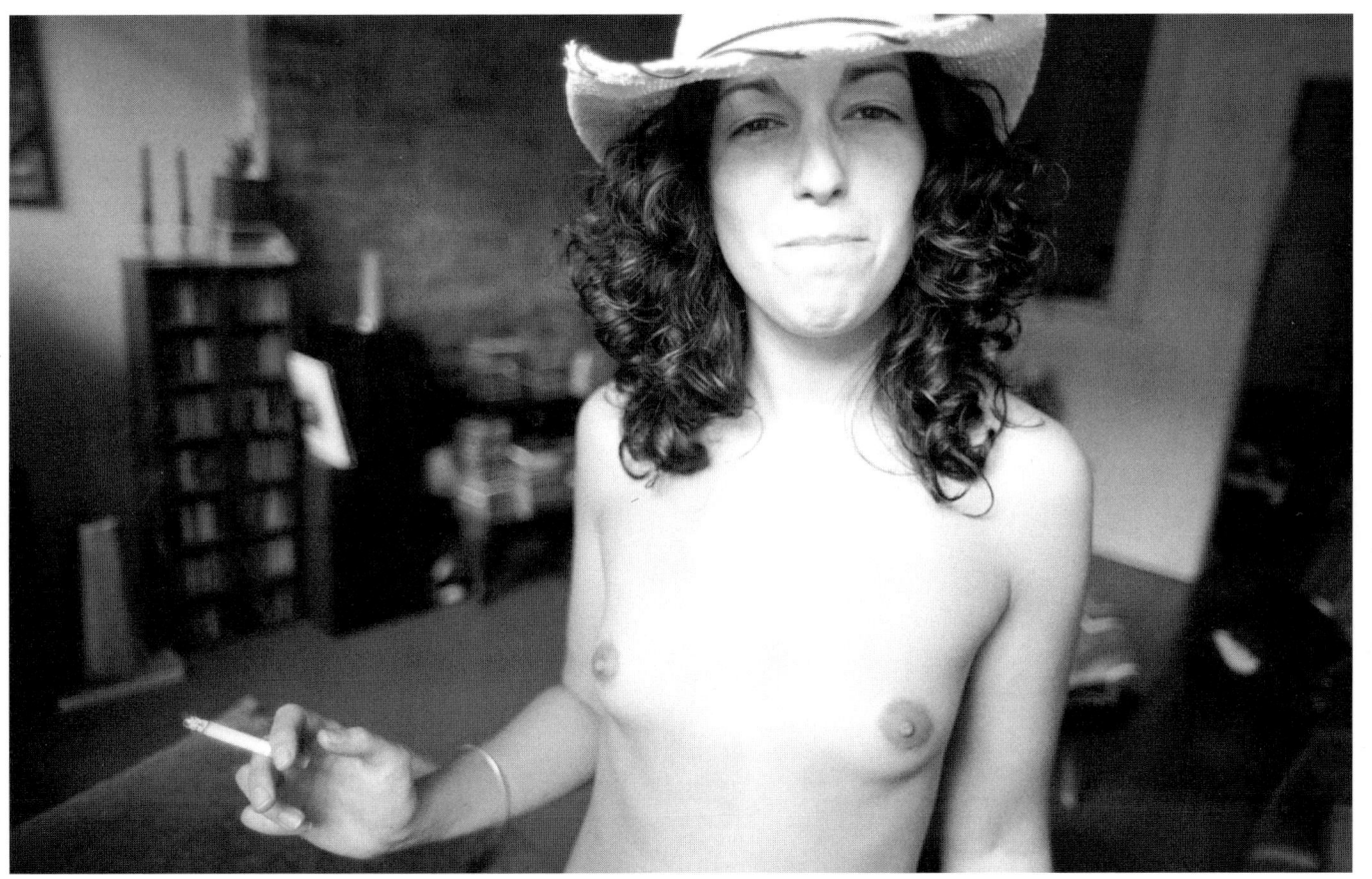

Juju · Juju was the roommate of a close friend of mine. She's an actress and singer, from Brazil. I photographed her in her Manhattan apartment, with her cat "Blue." Juju was a romantic, soft spoken woman, who danced some ballet to Spanish Music, and drank Coca-Cola from a 2 liter bottle.

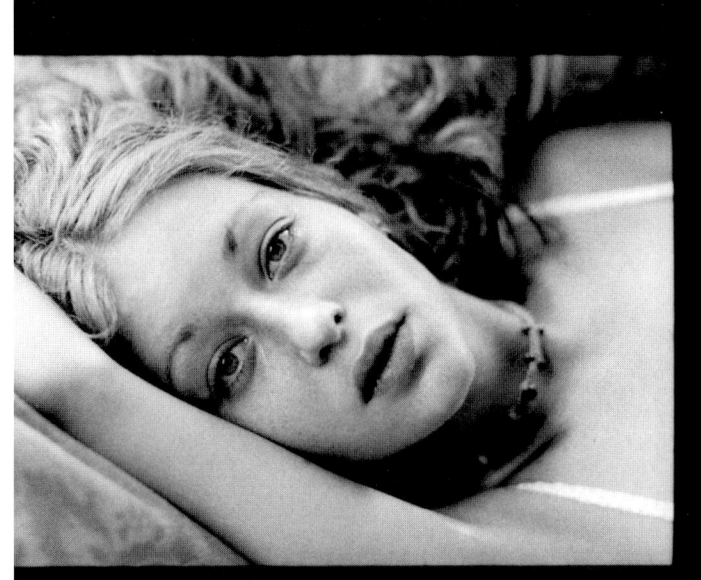
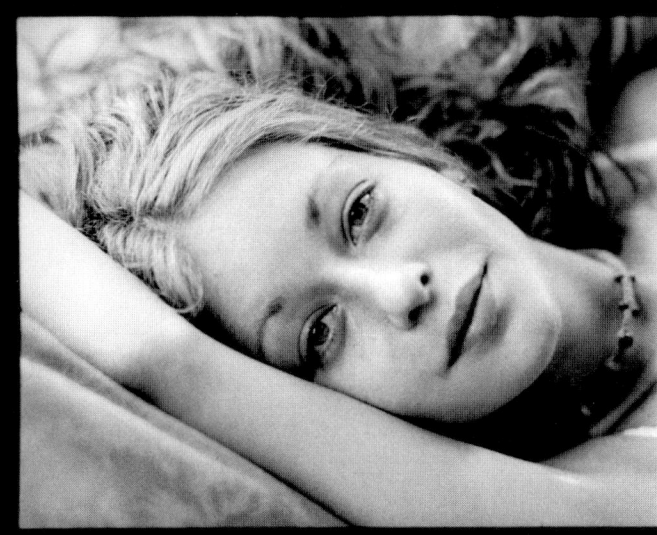

4 ▷ 4A 5

063 TX 9 KODAK 5063 TX 10

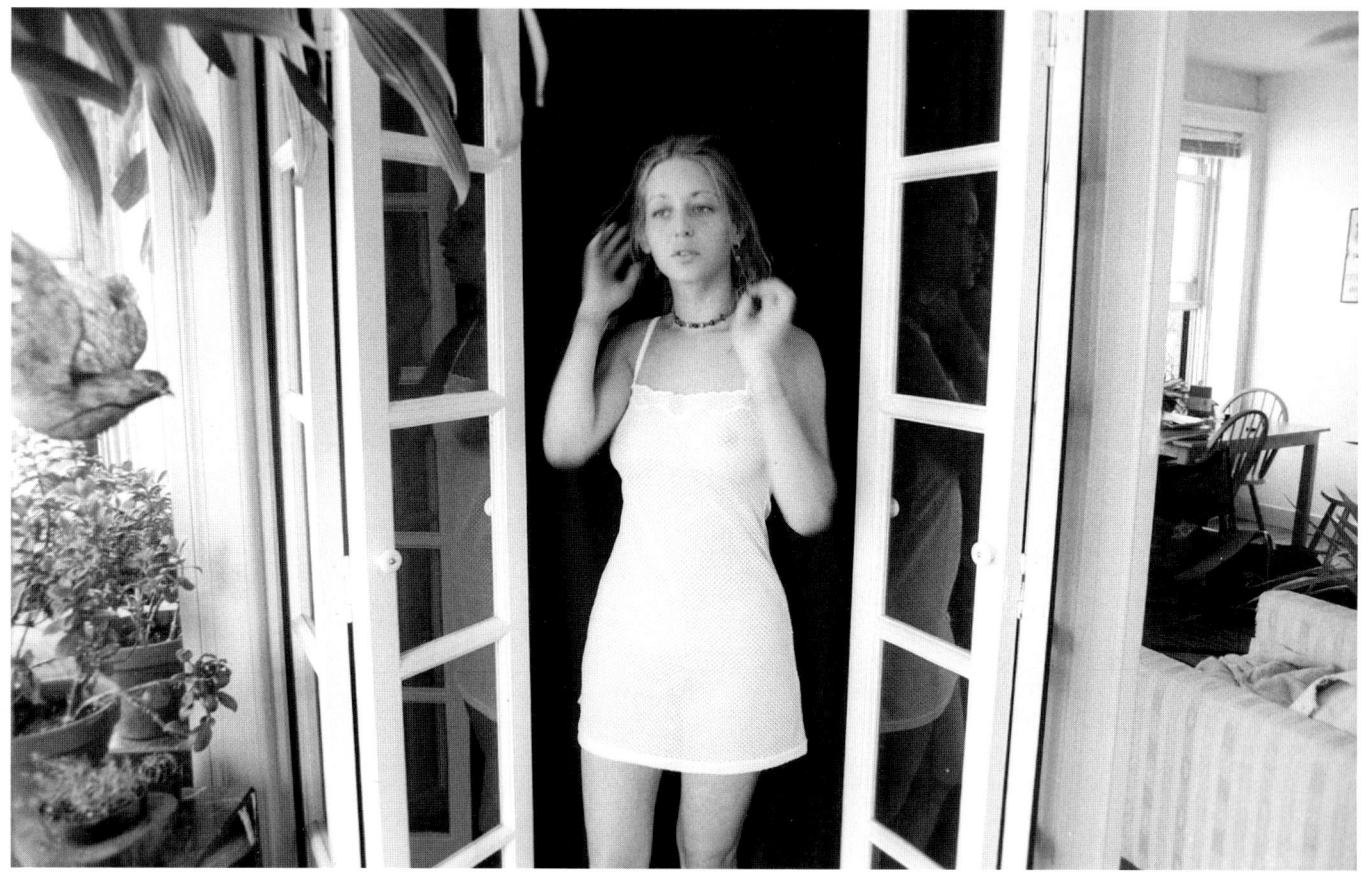

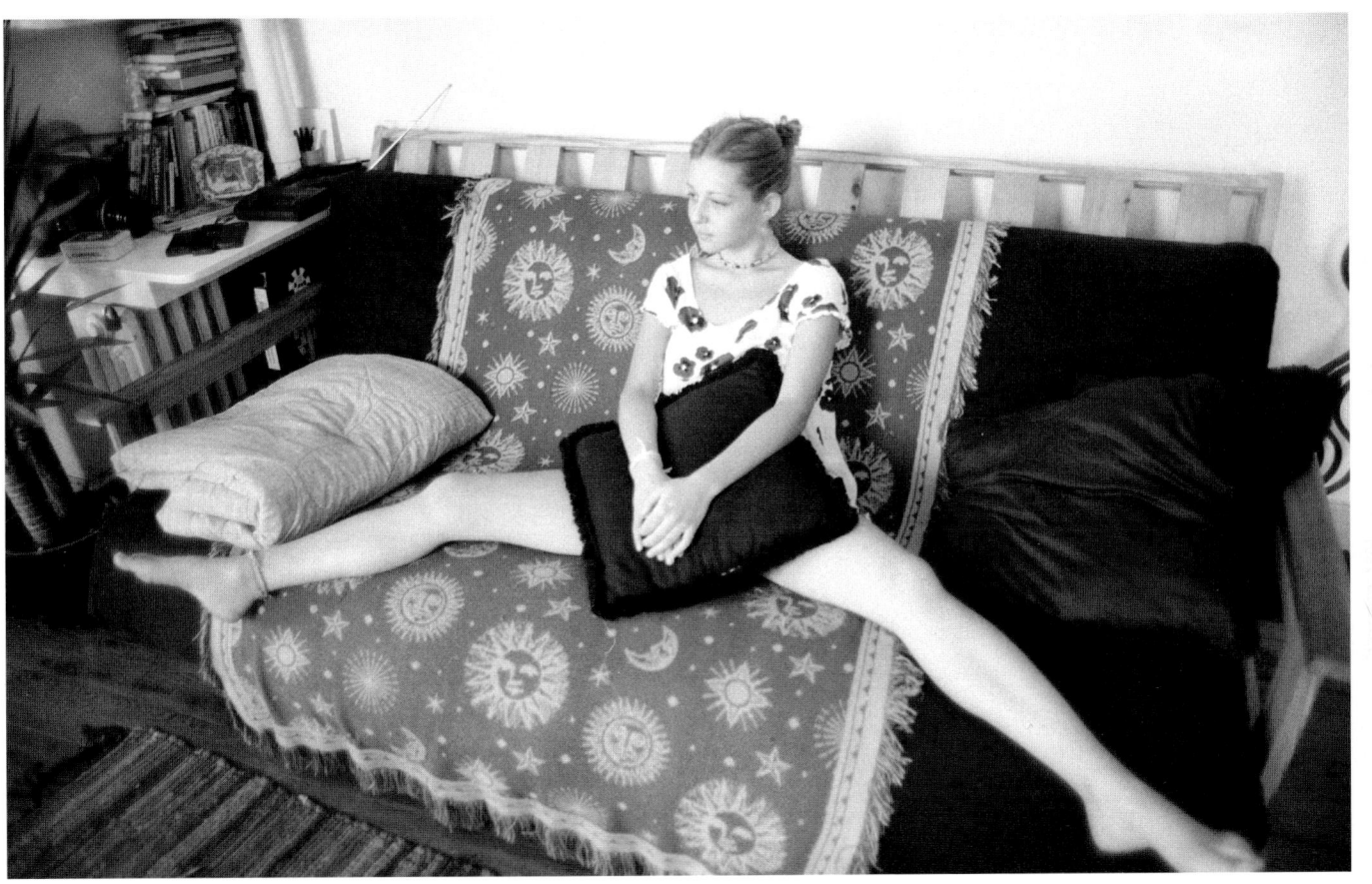

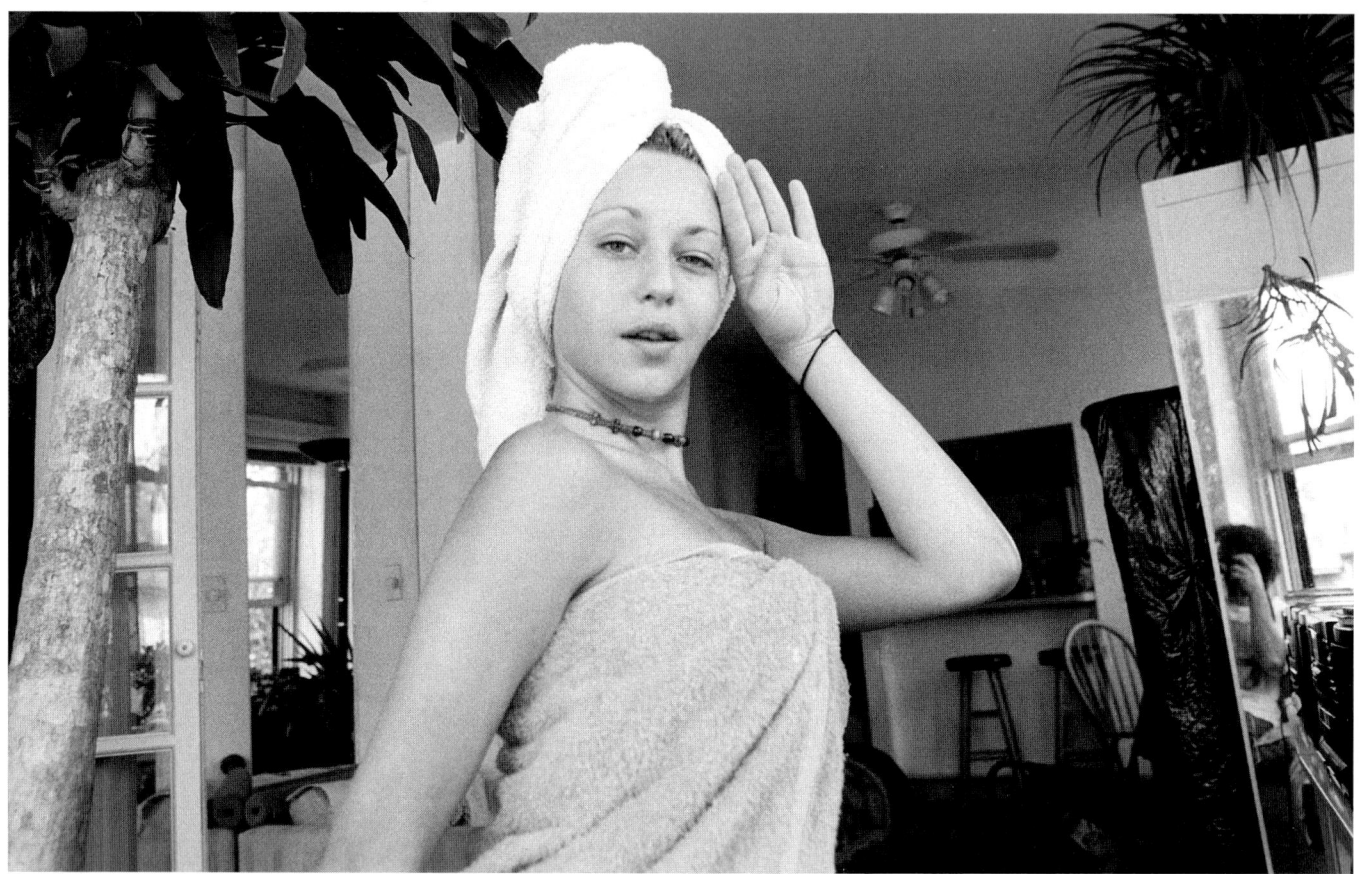

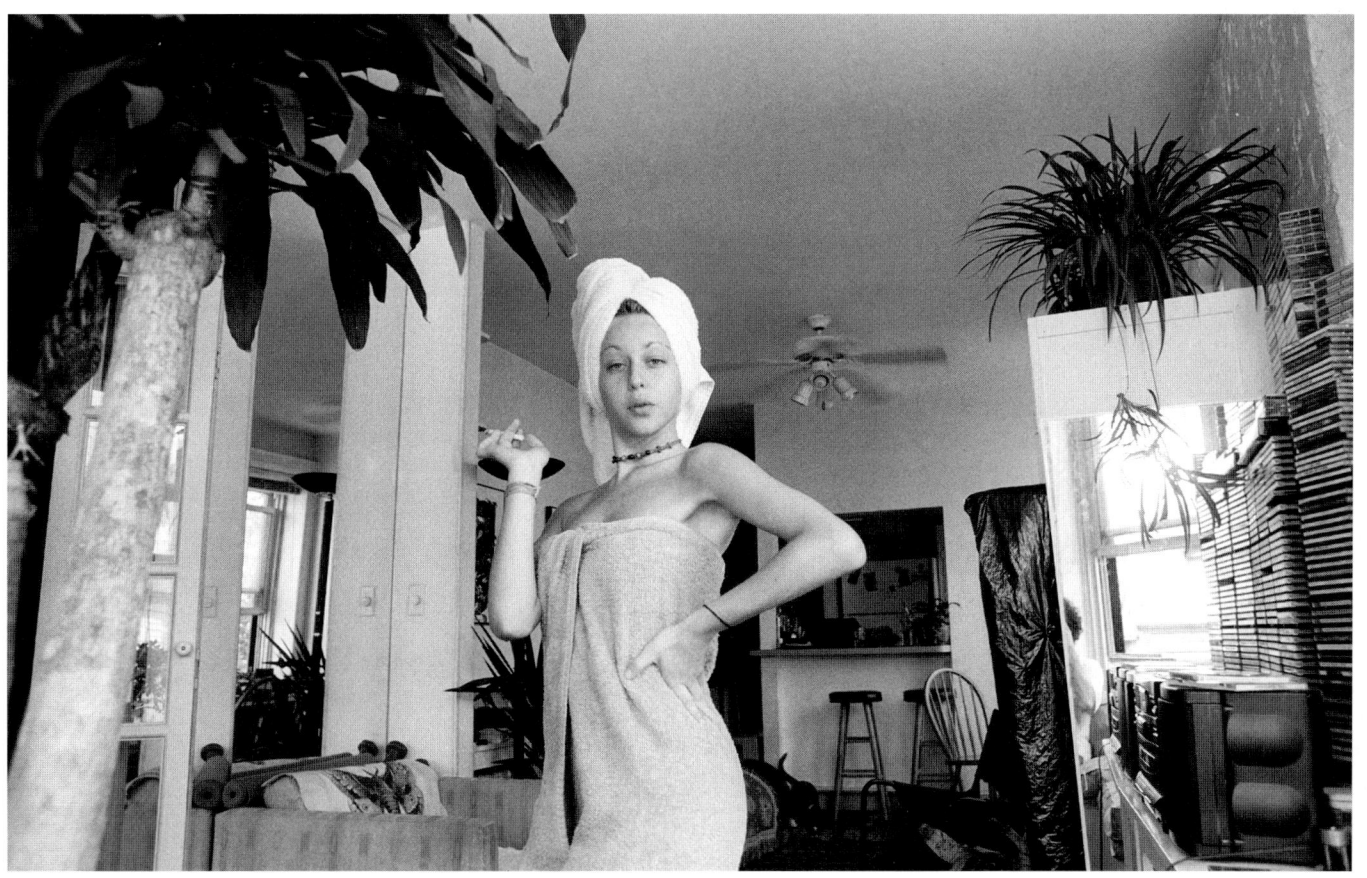

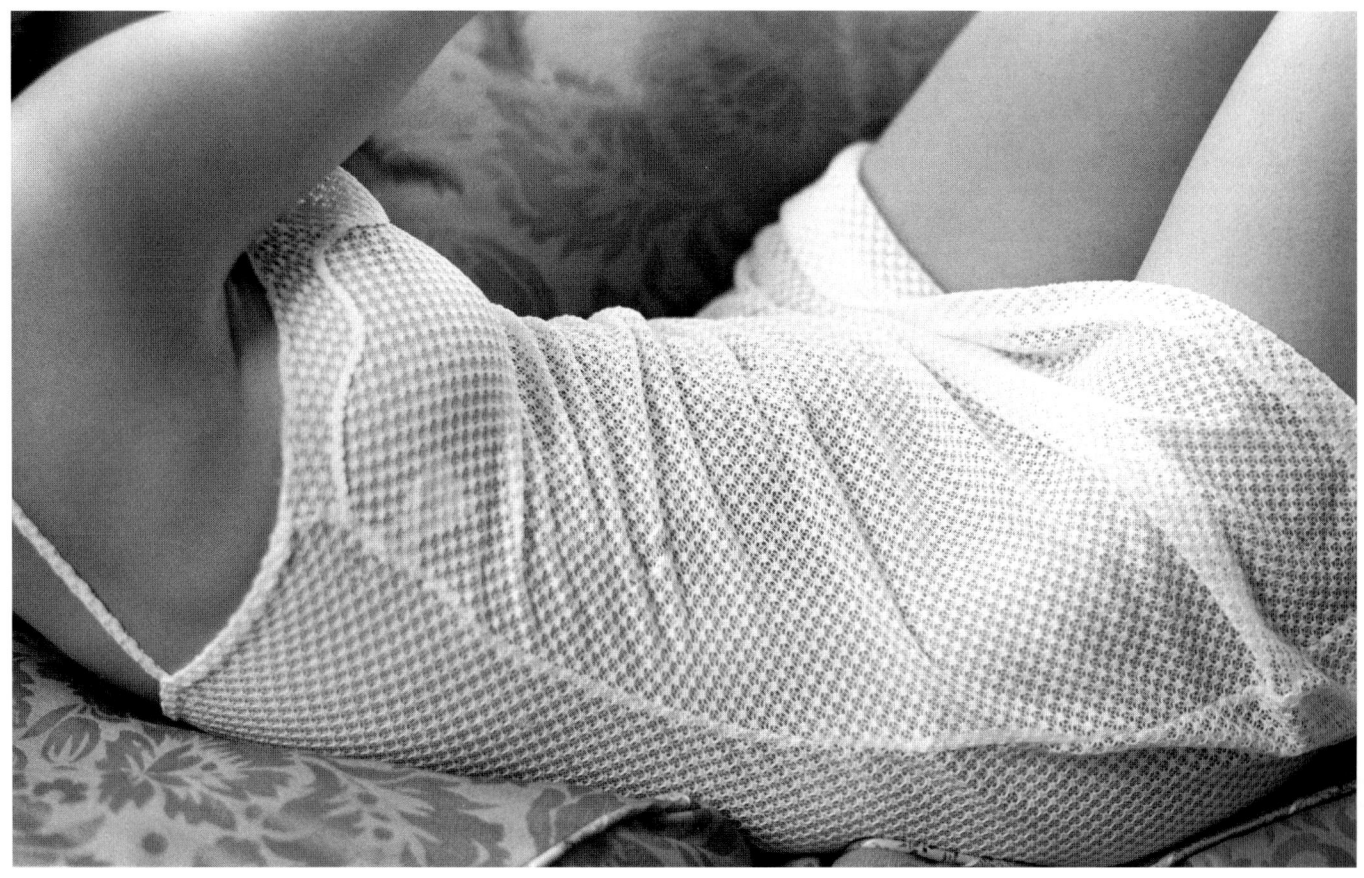

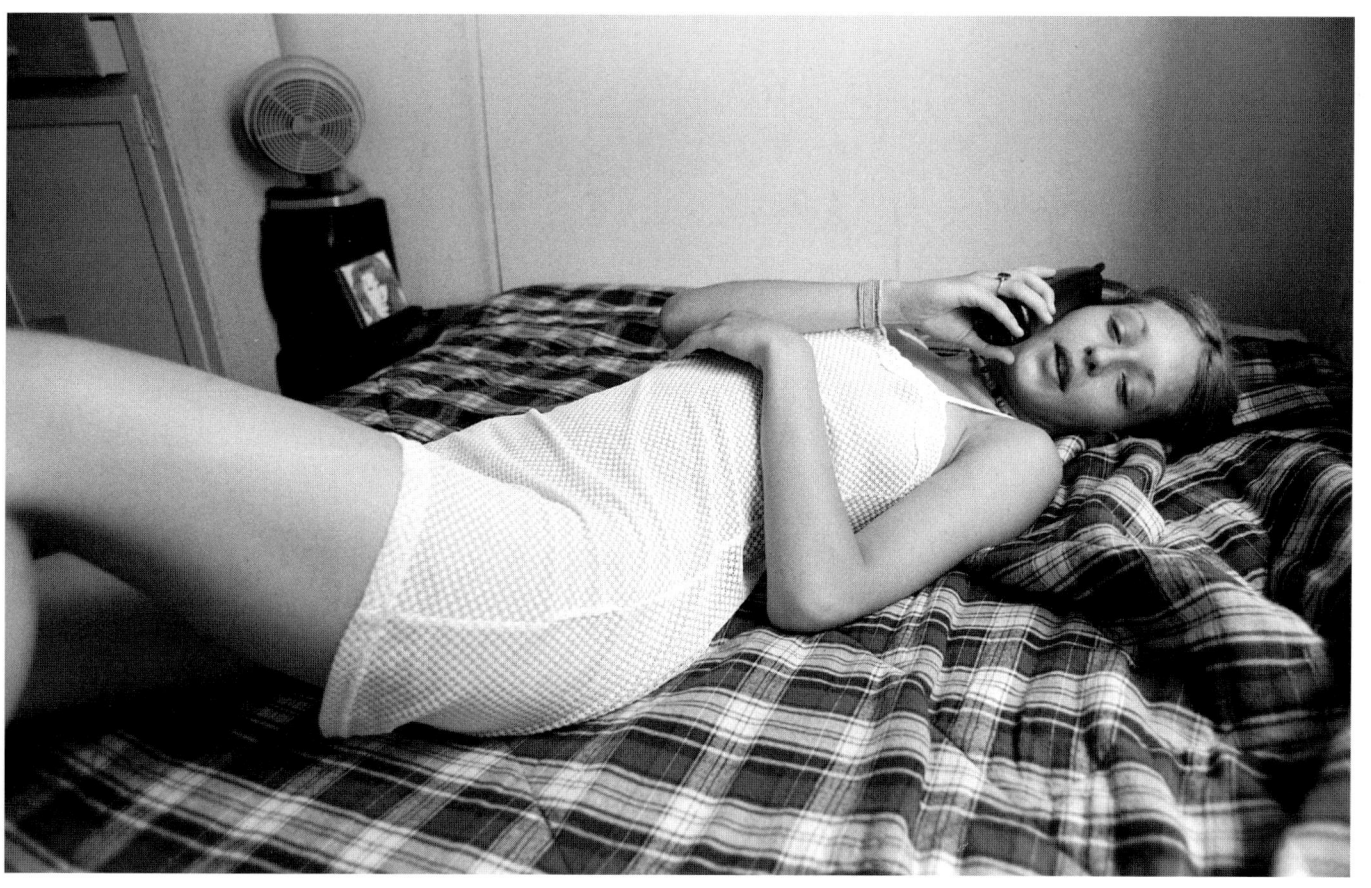

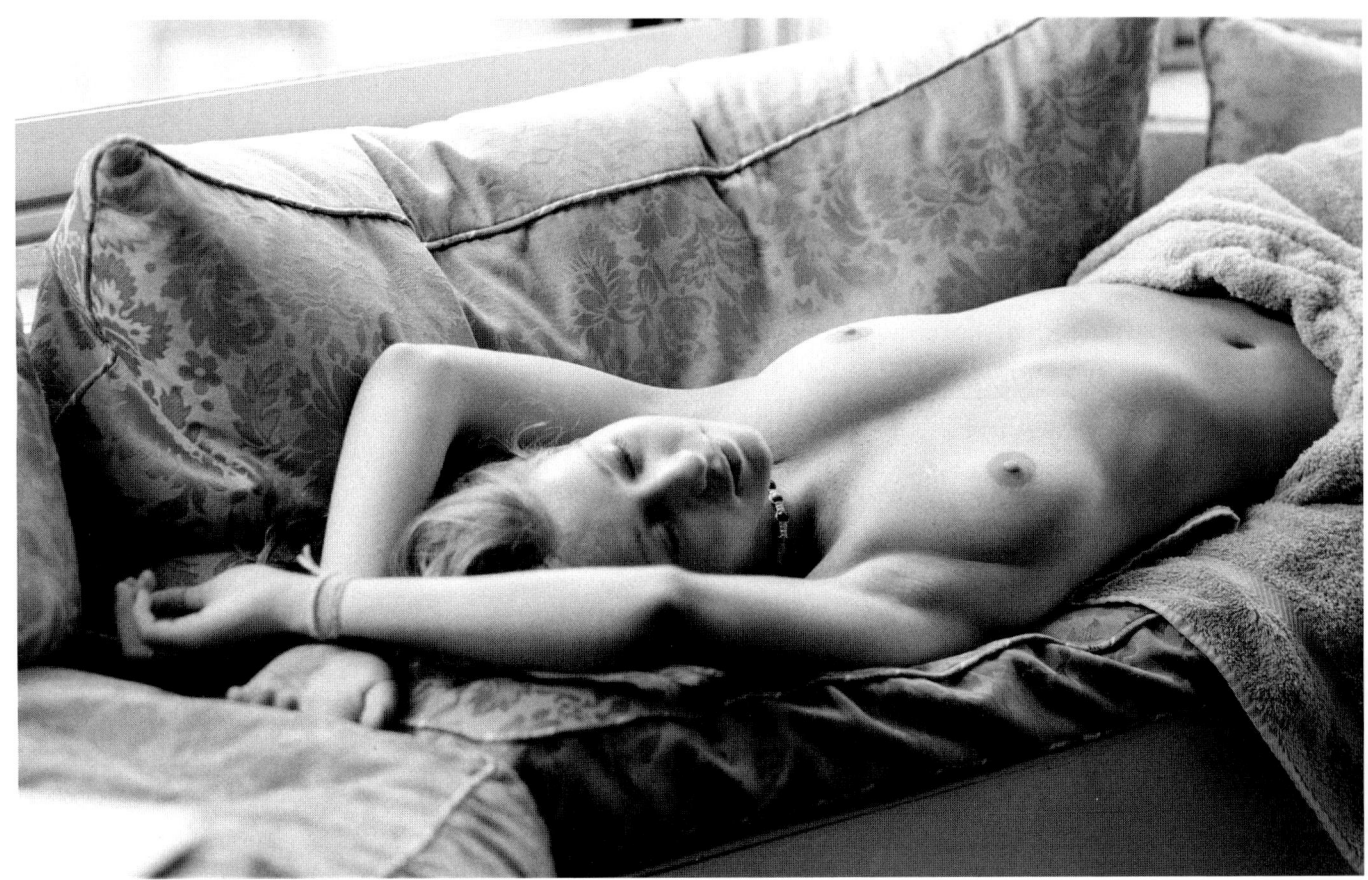

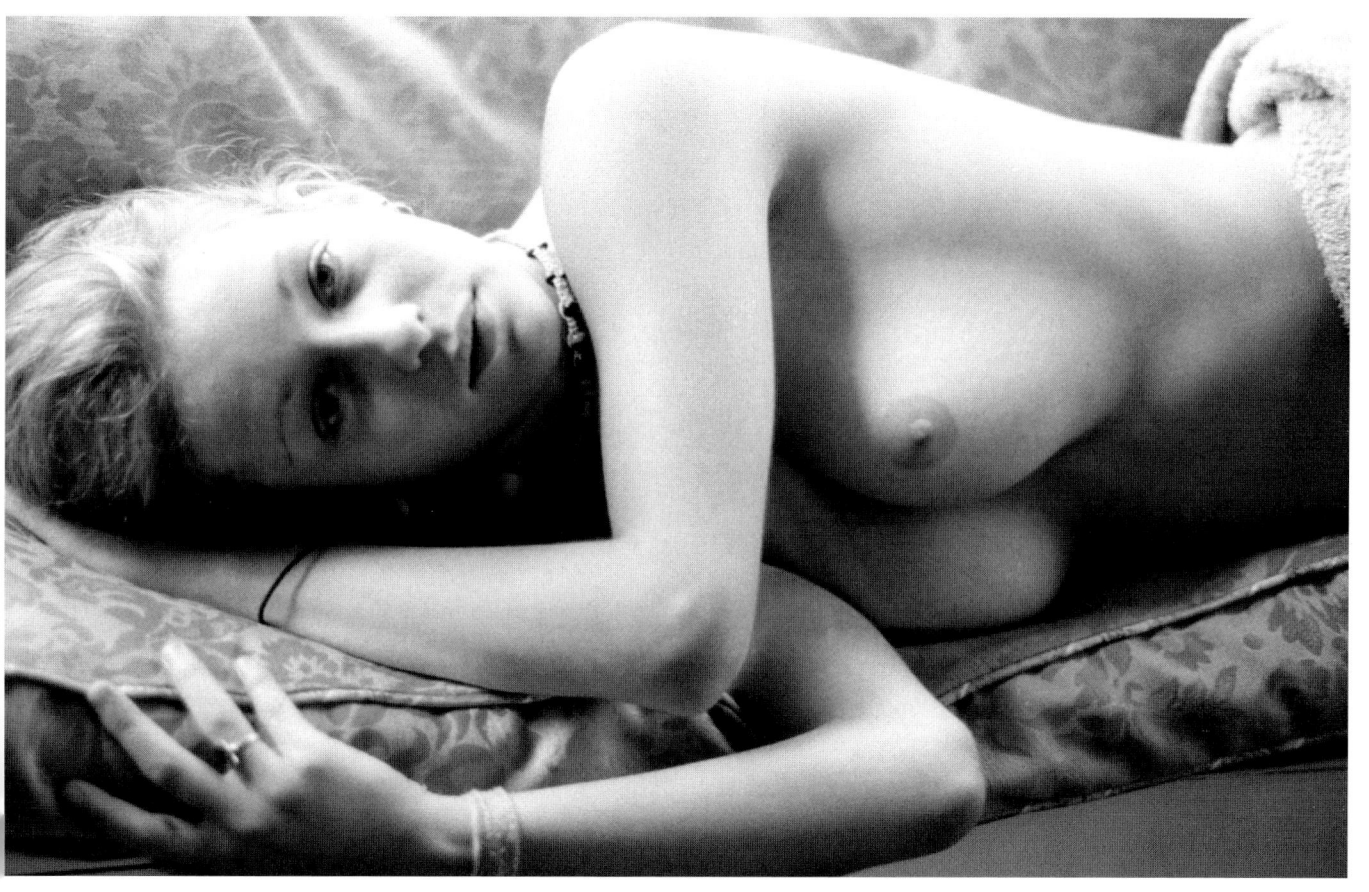

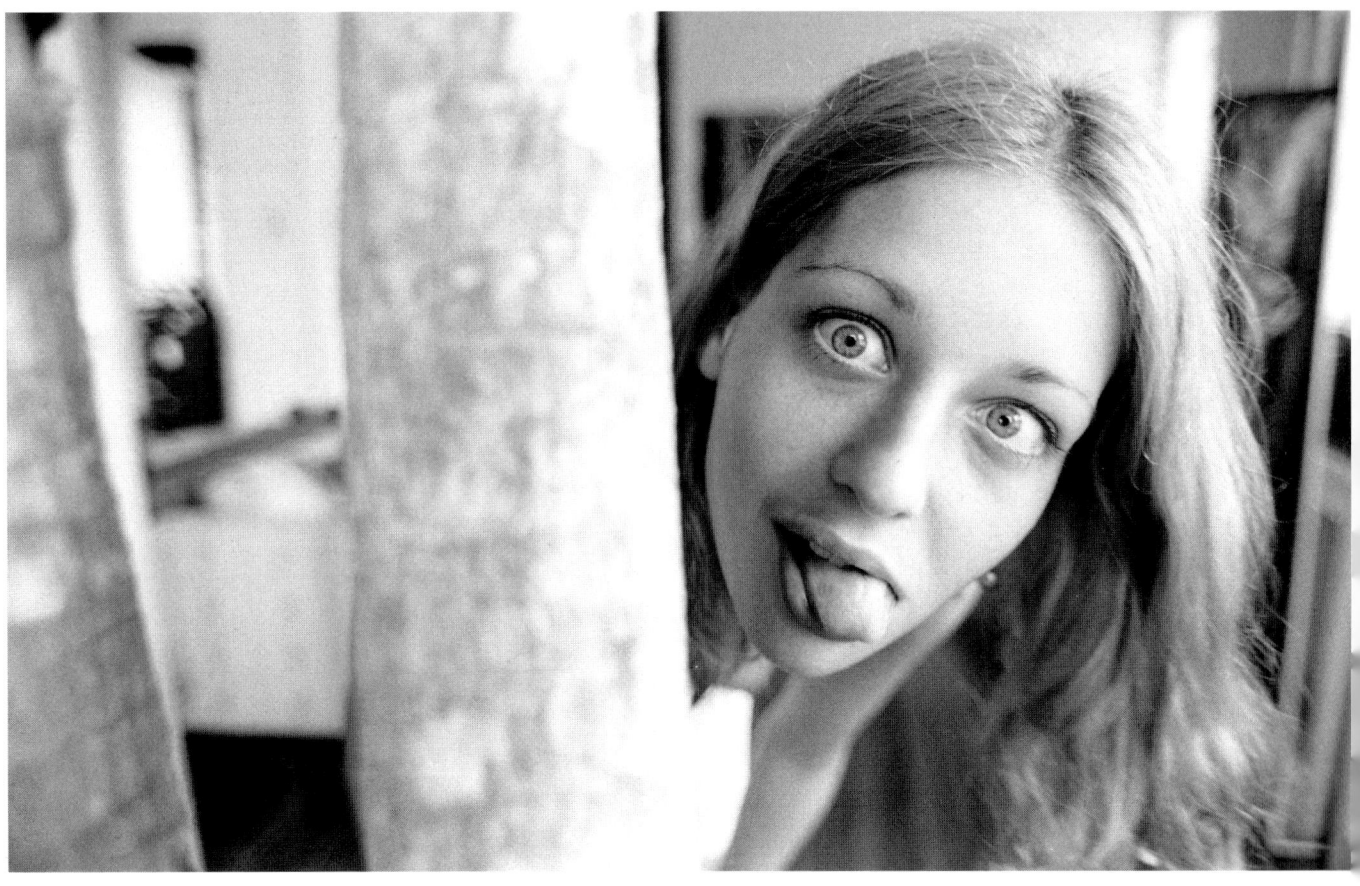

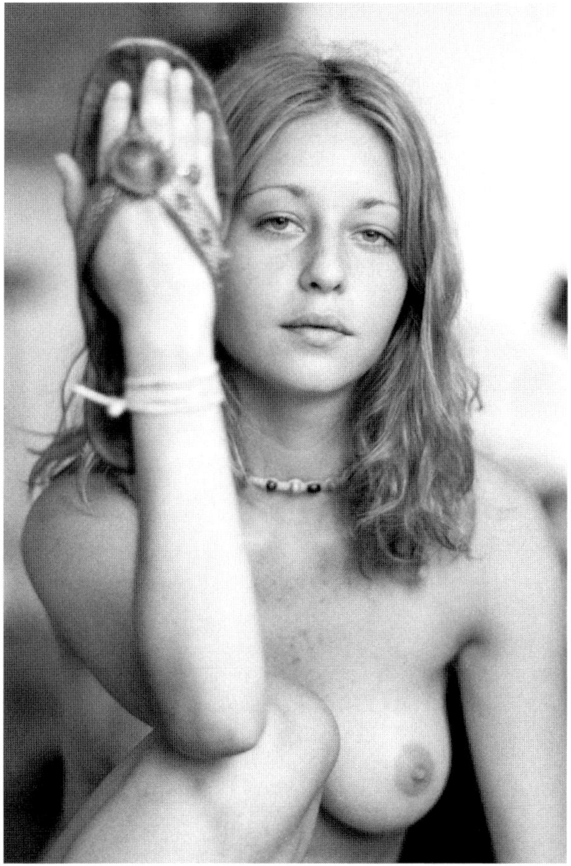

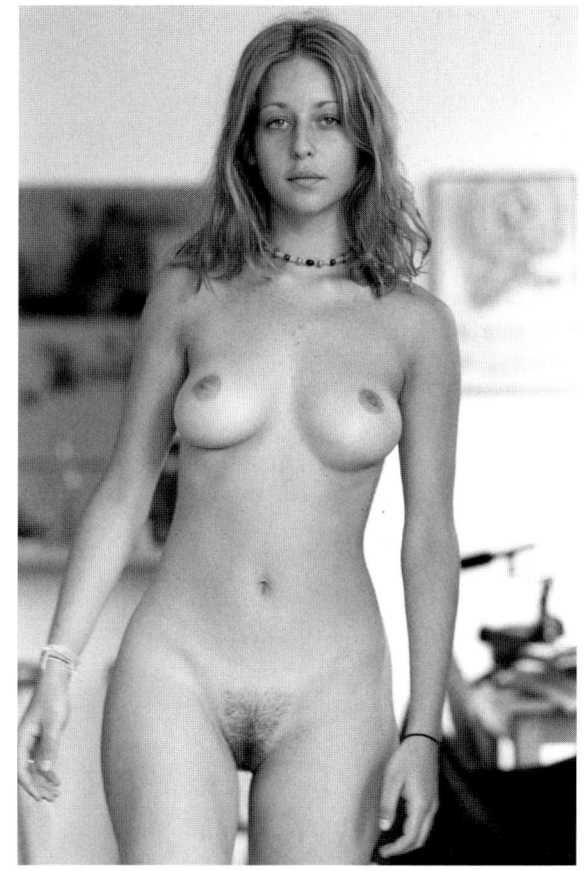

Julia · I used to work with Julia at an Internet company. She's half Chinese and half Austrian. I photographed her in every room of my newly renovated apartment, which made me very happy. Julia is a vegan, with freckles on her back in the shape of a foreign land.

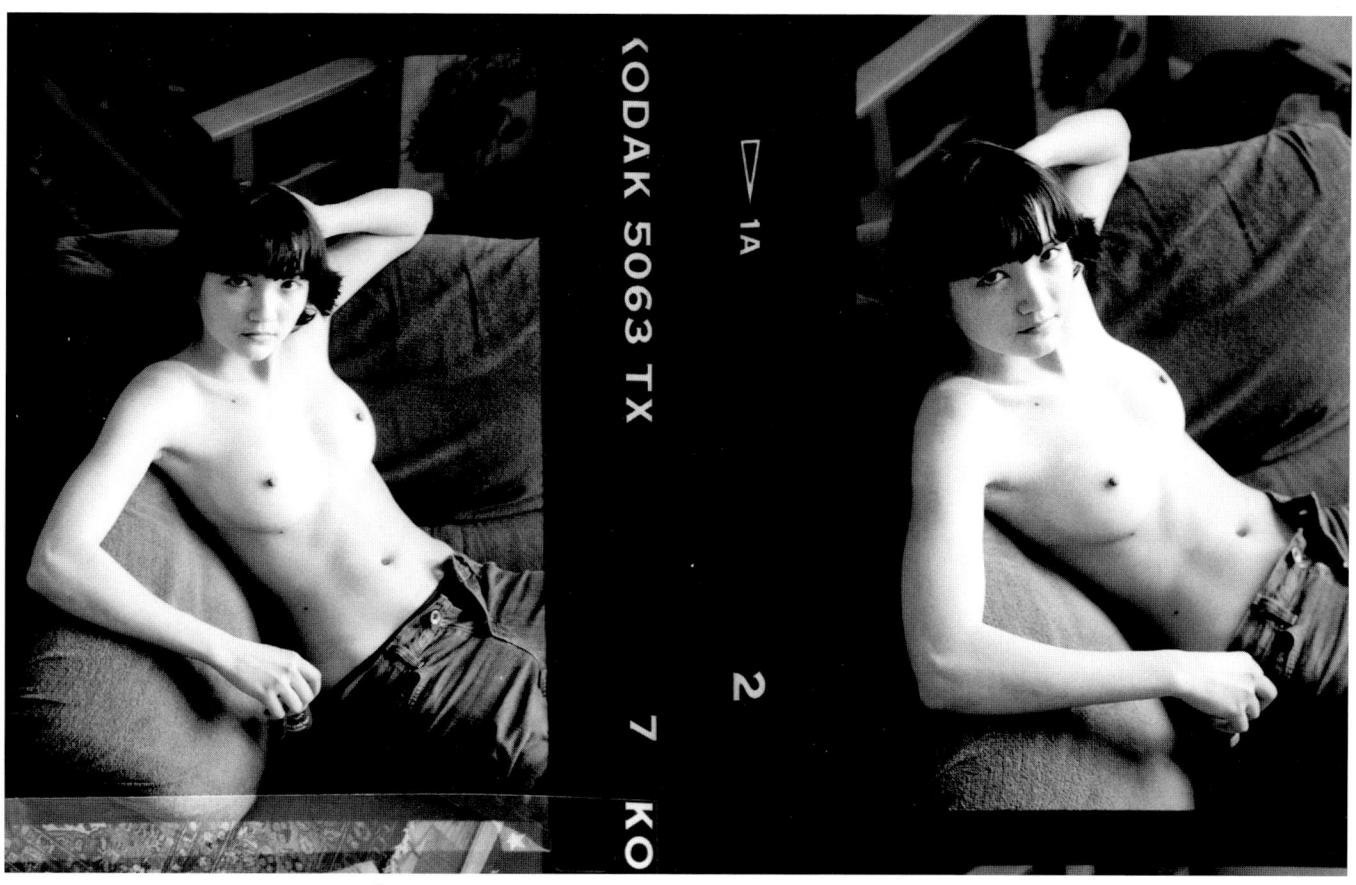

KODAK 5063 TX

1A

2

7

KO

197

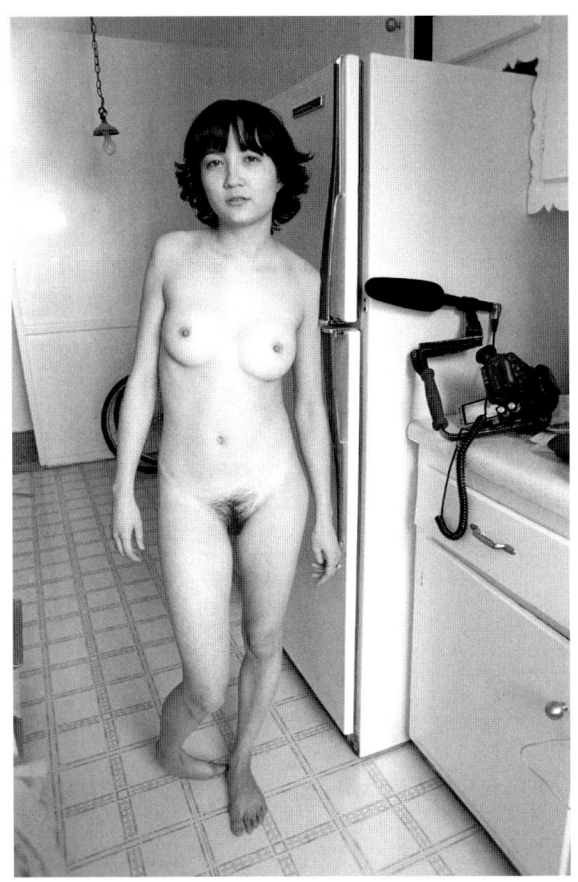
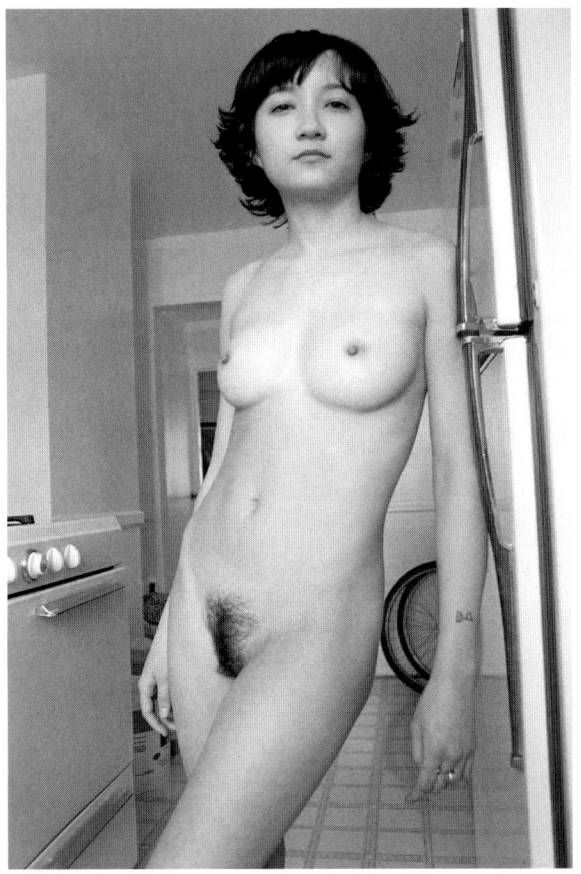

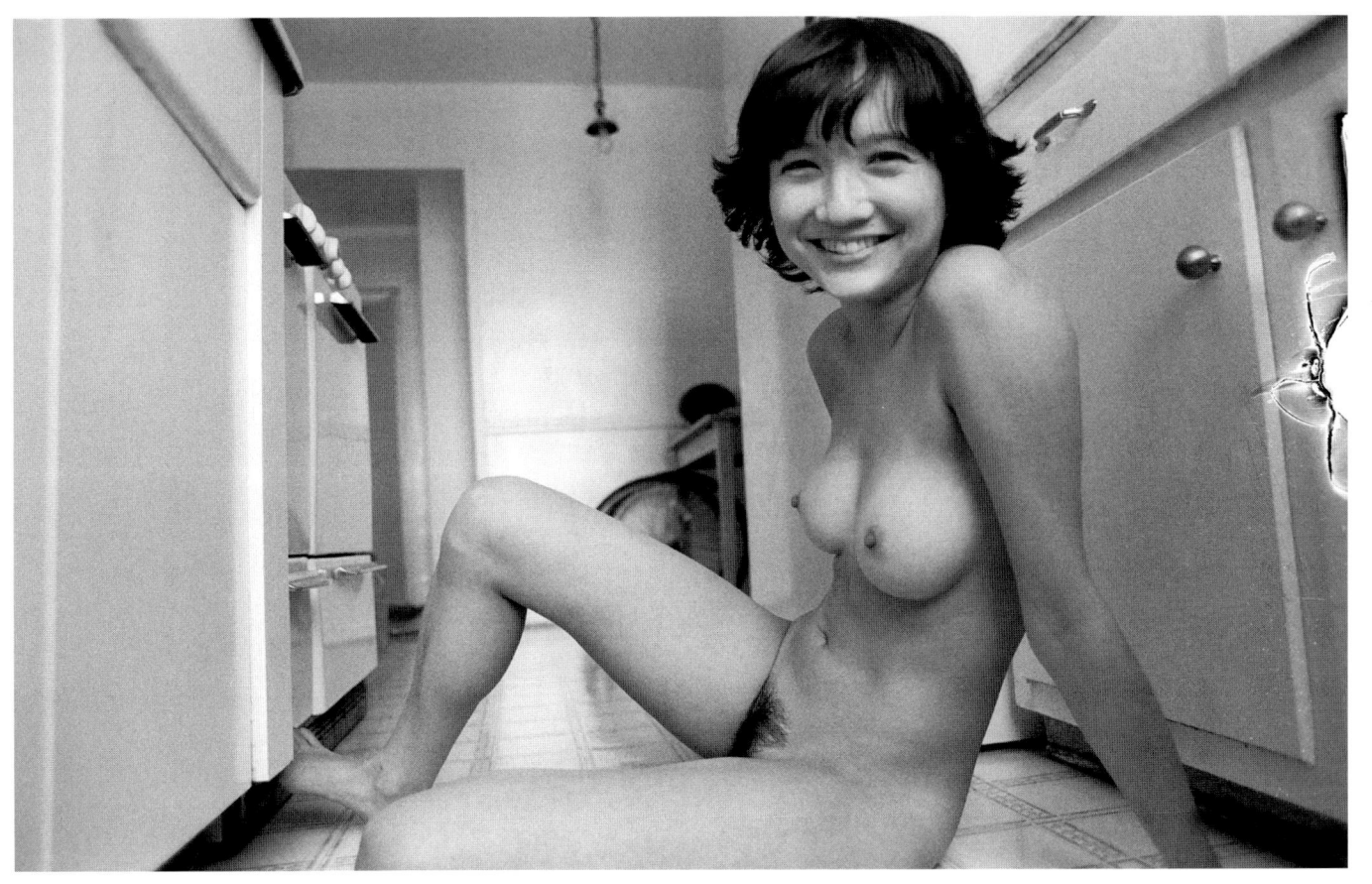

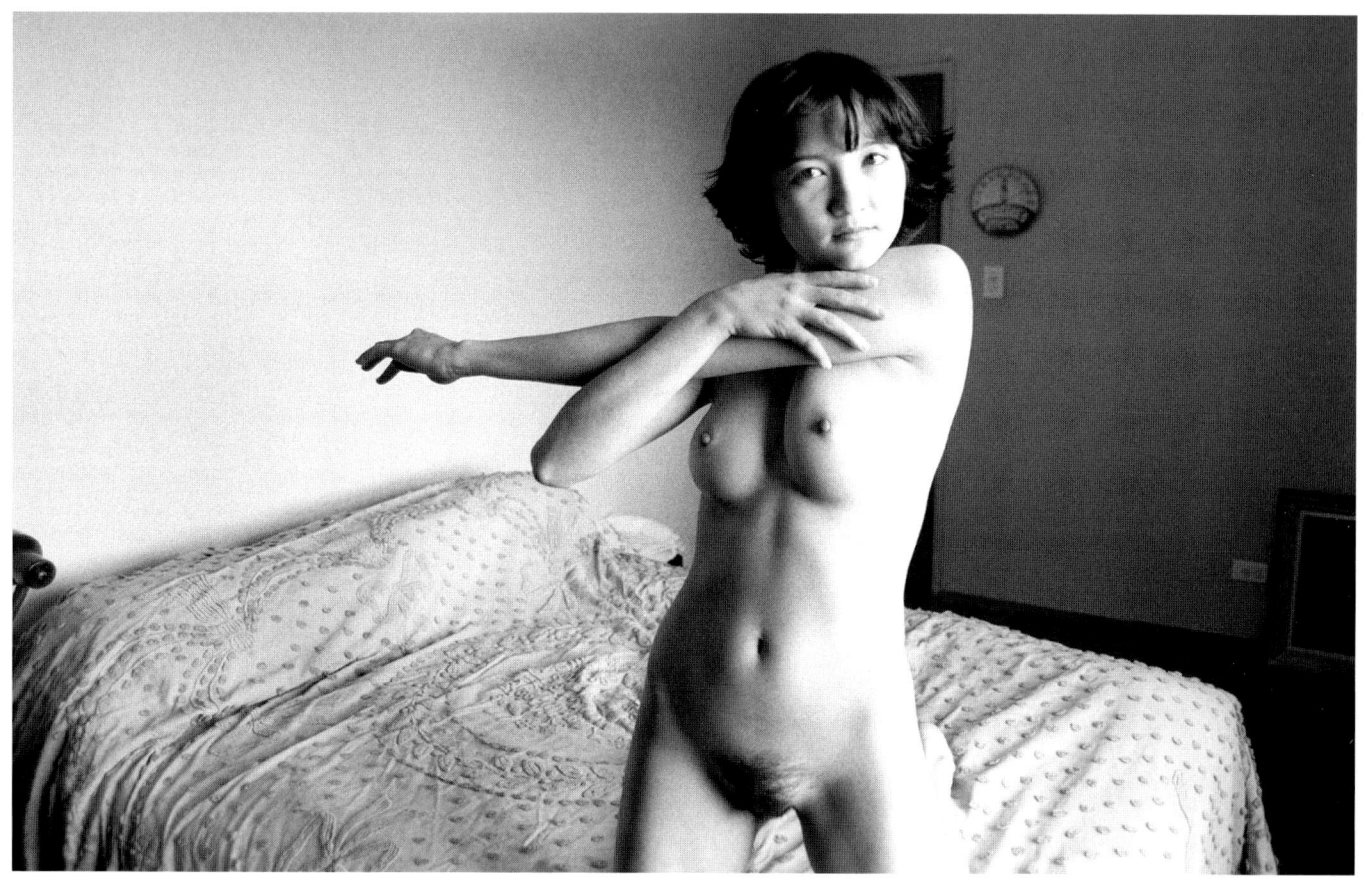

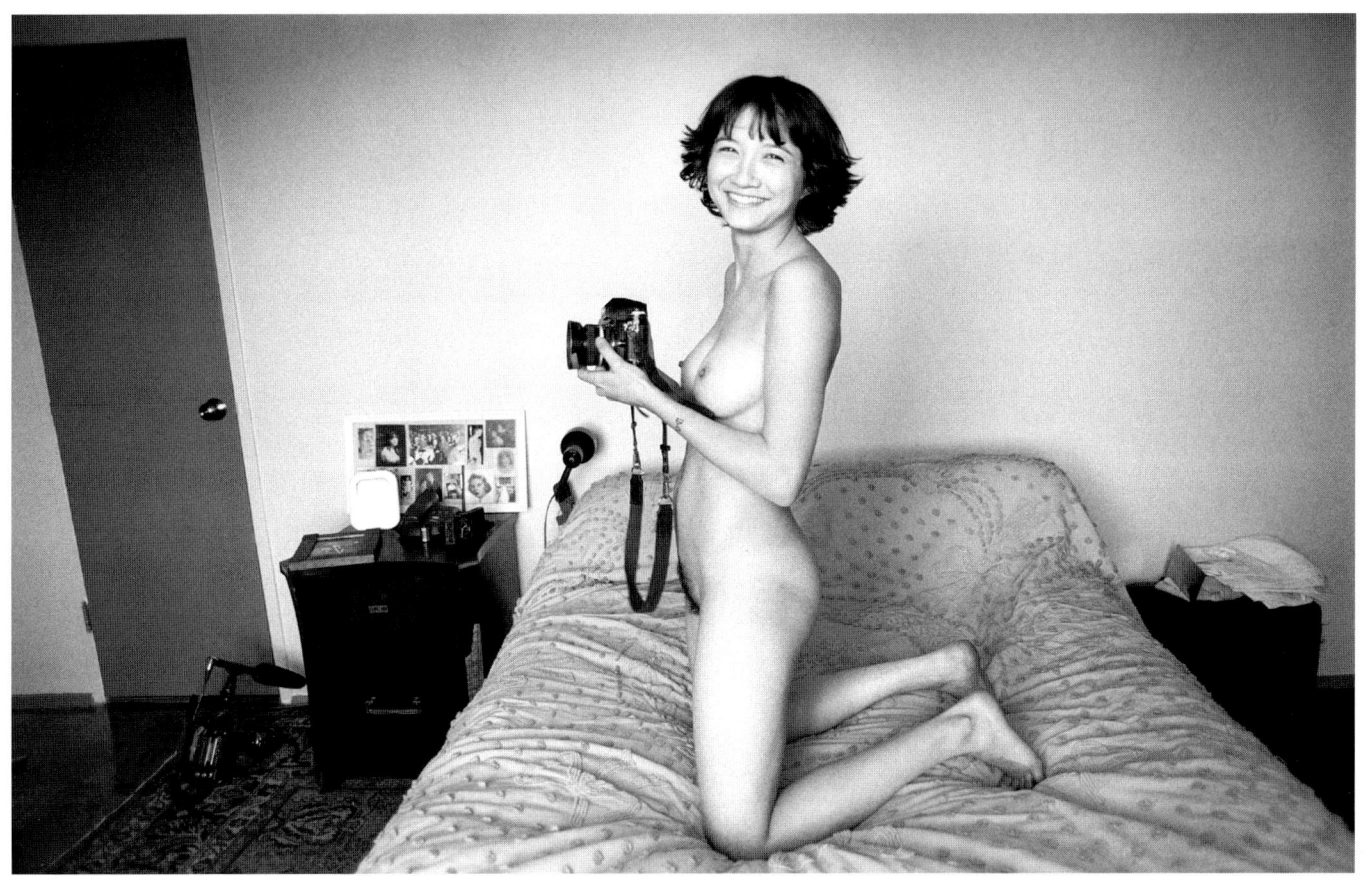

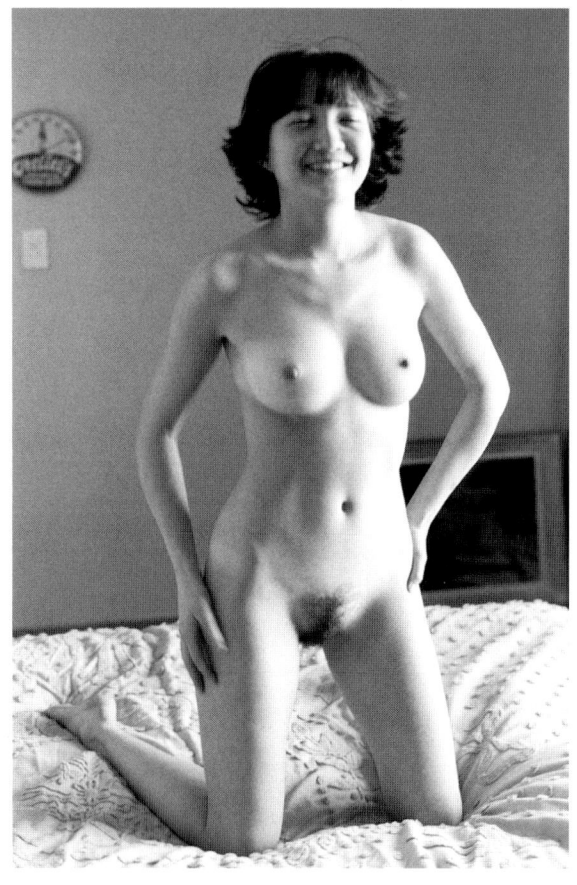
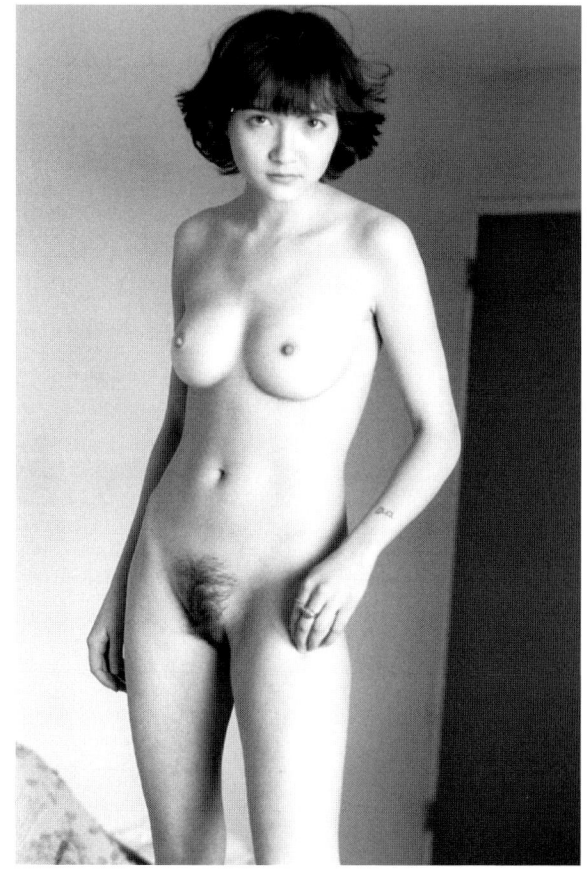

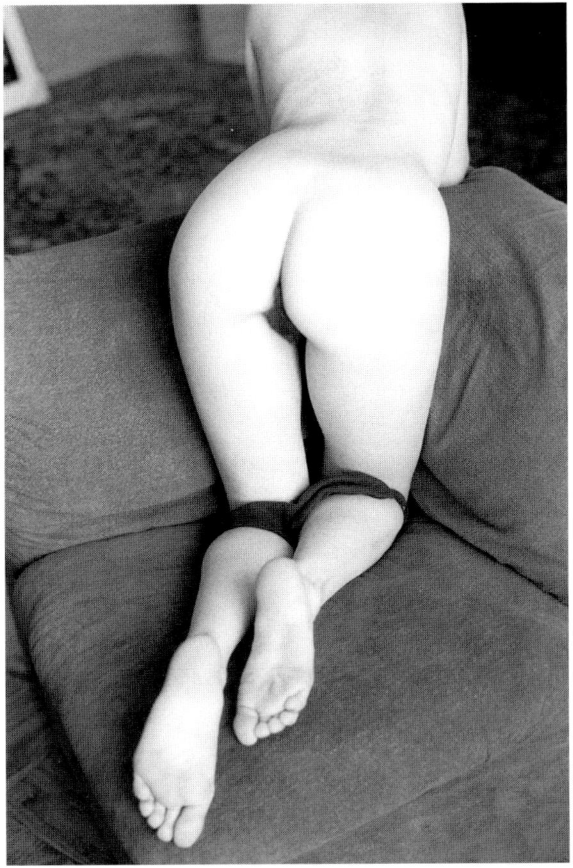

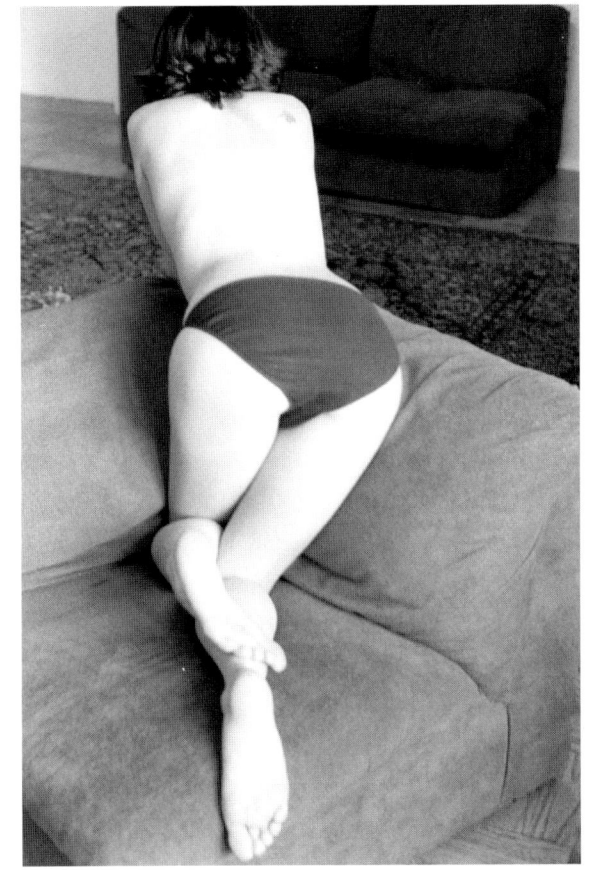

Julie · I met Julie in a media law office. We shot in her Brooklyn apartment a few weeks later. She had two roommates, but asked them to leave for a few hours. We ate bagels with cream cheese, drank Bloody Mary's, and smoked a little. I tried to get Julie's hair really wet and messy, but she preferred not too.

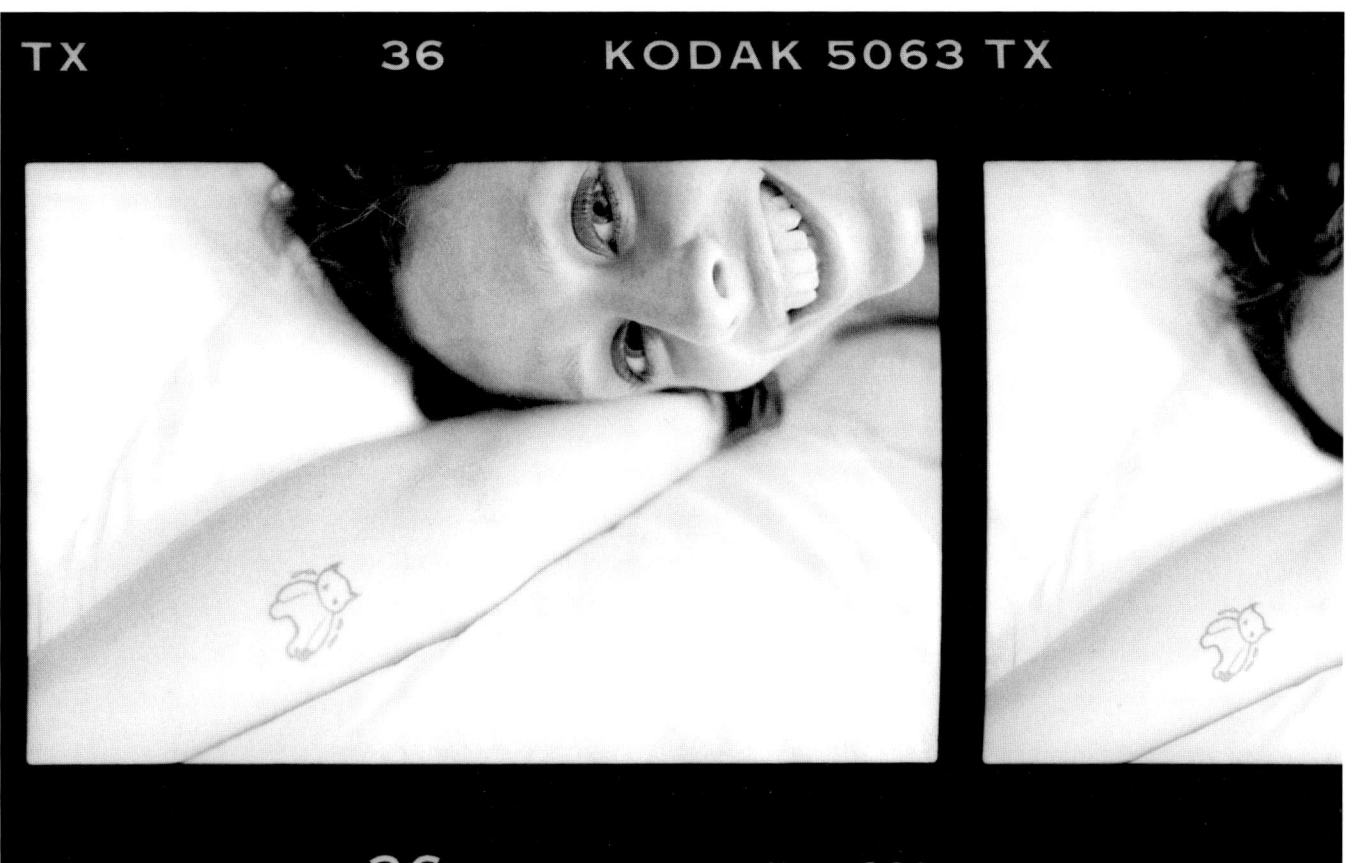

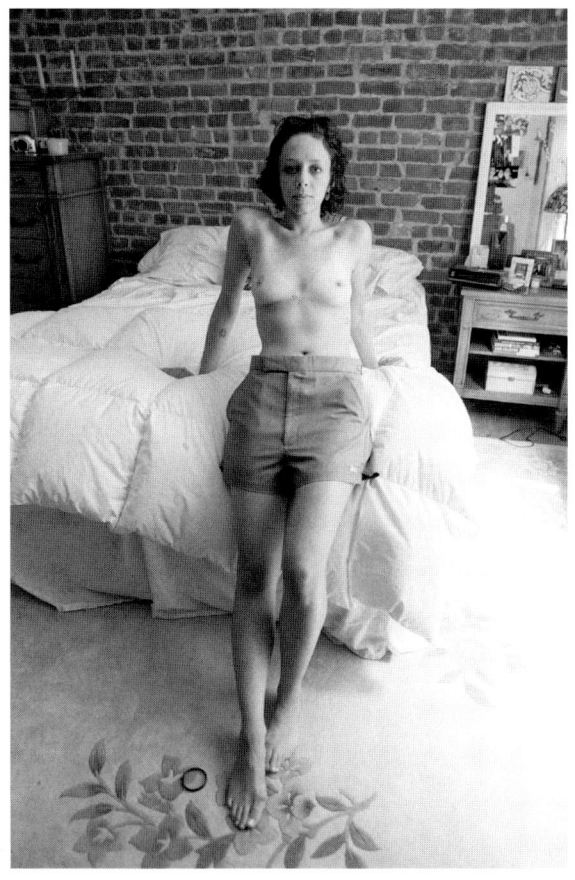
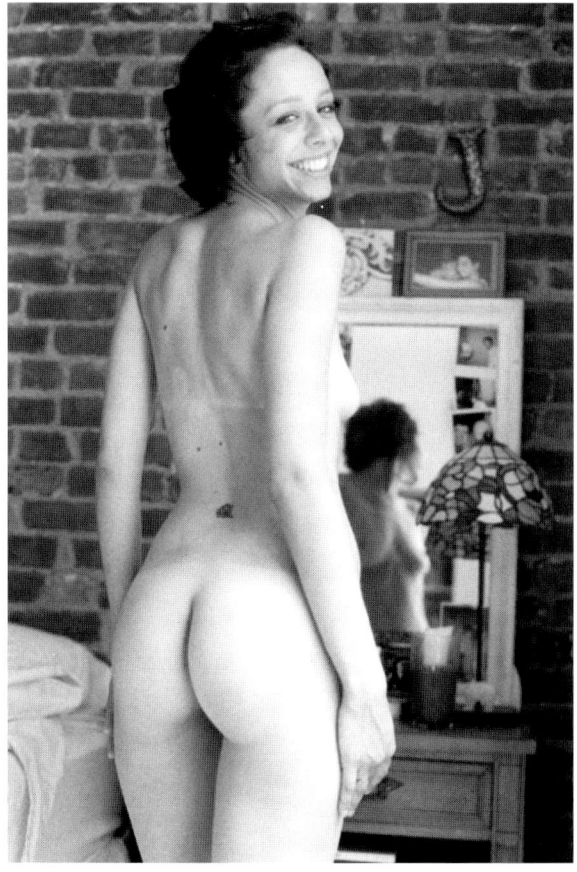

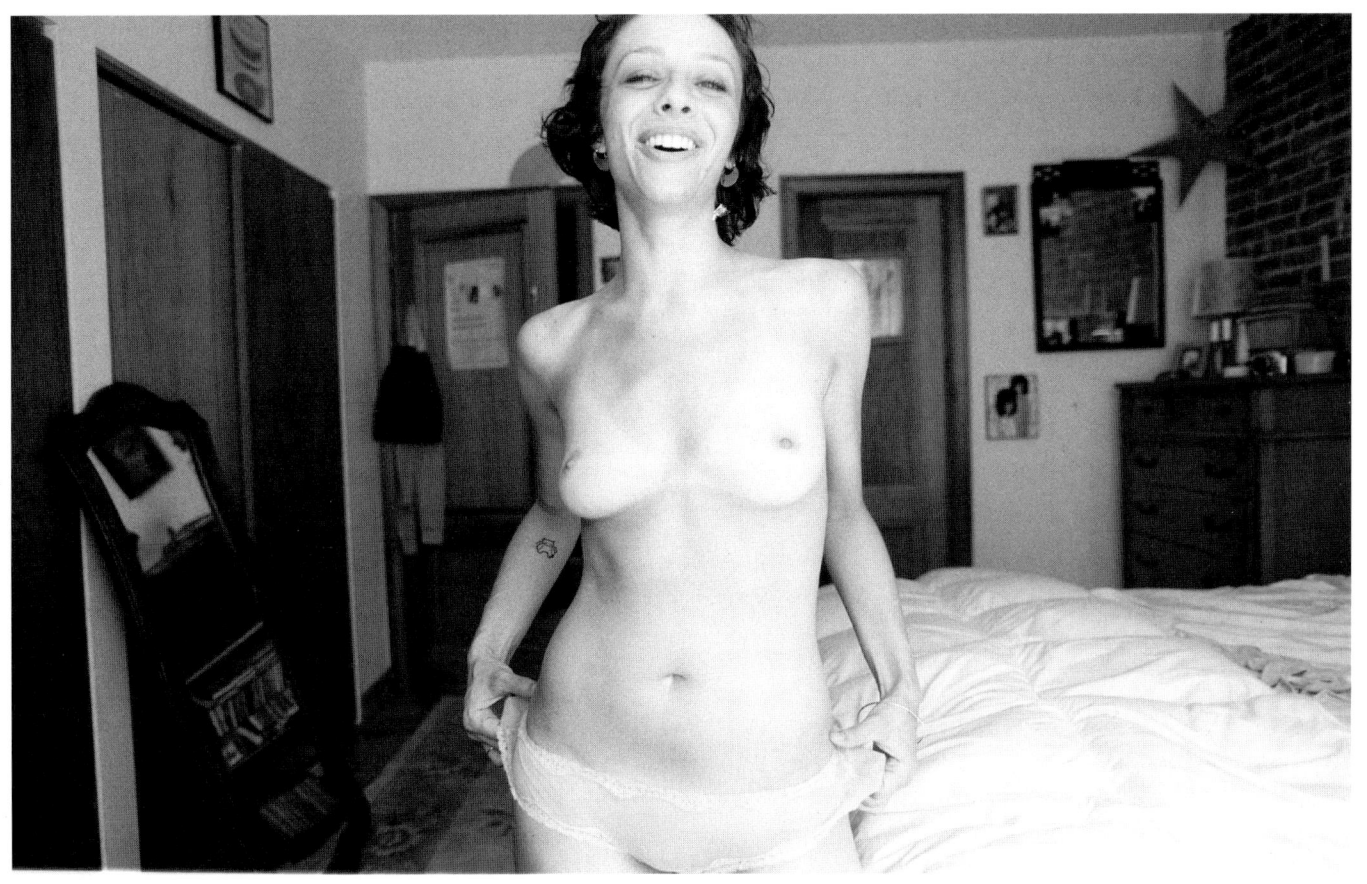

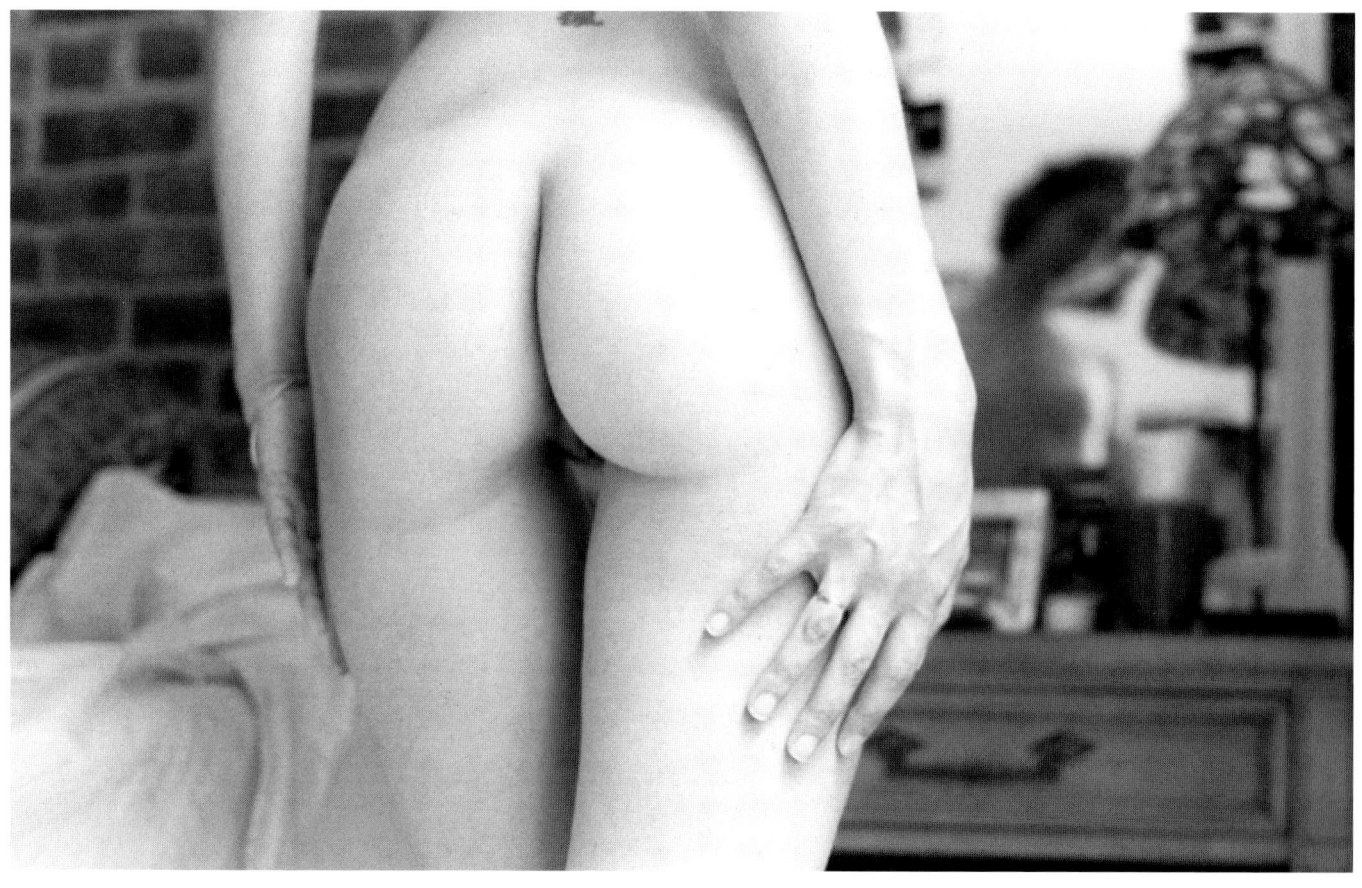

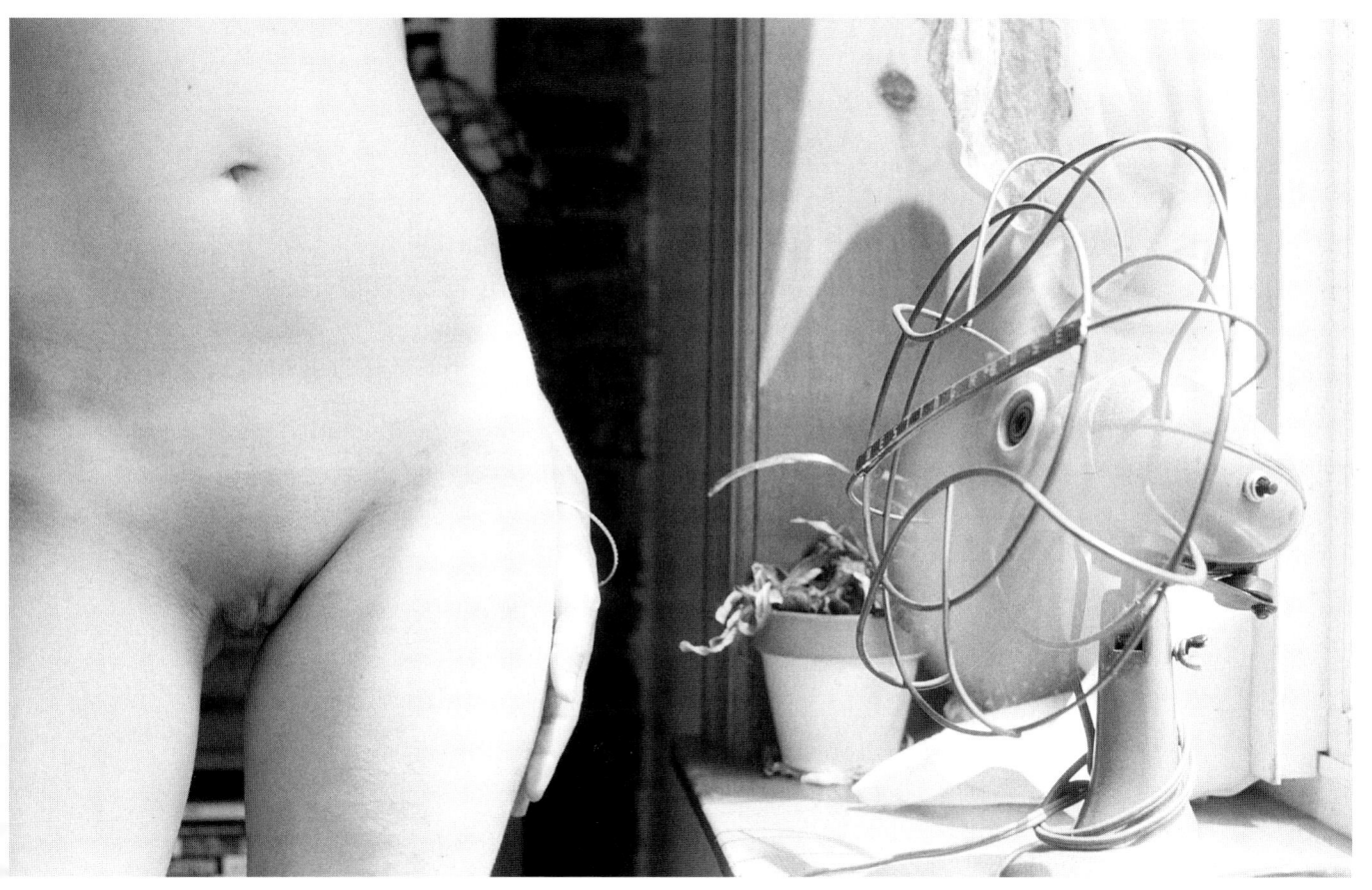

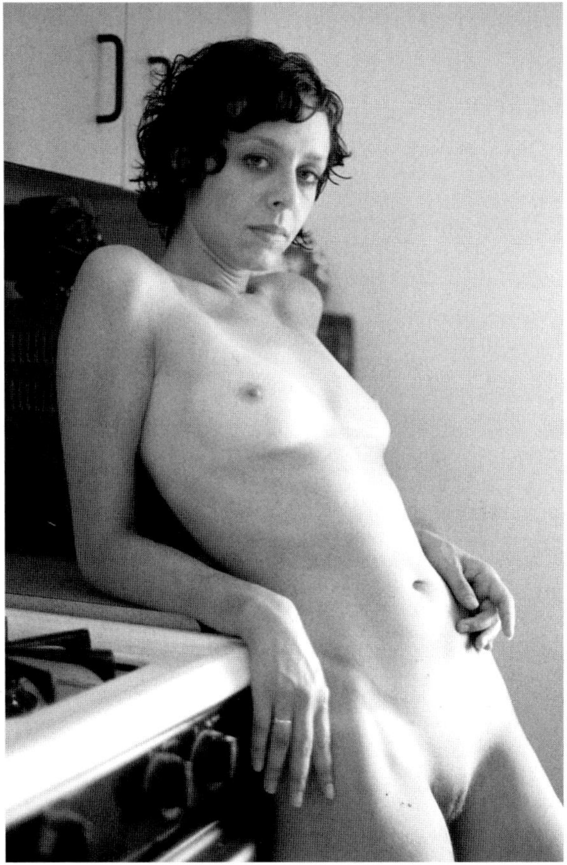

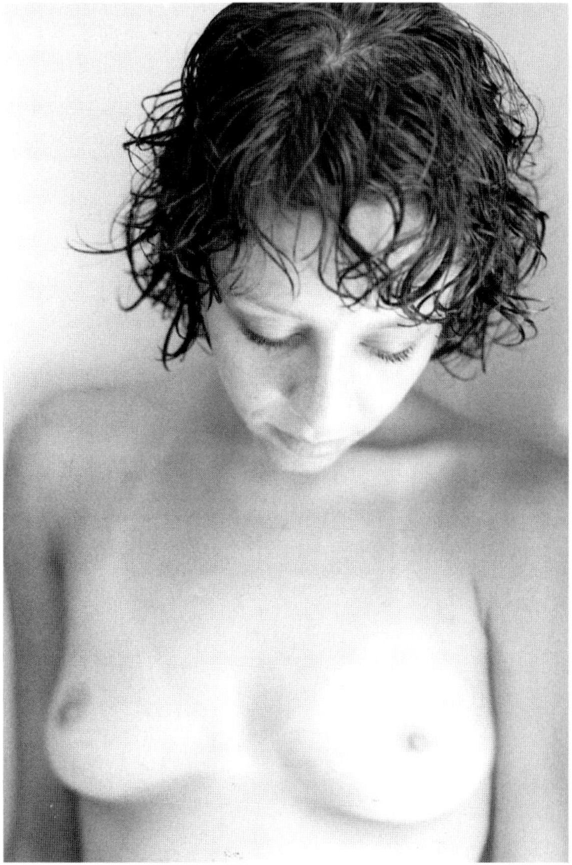

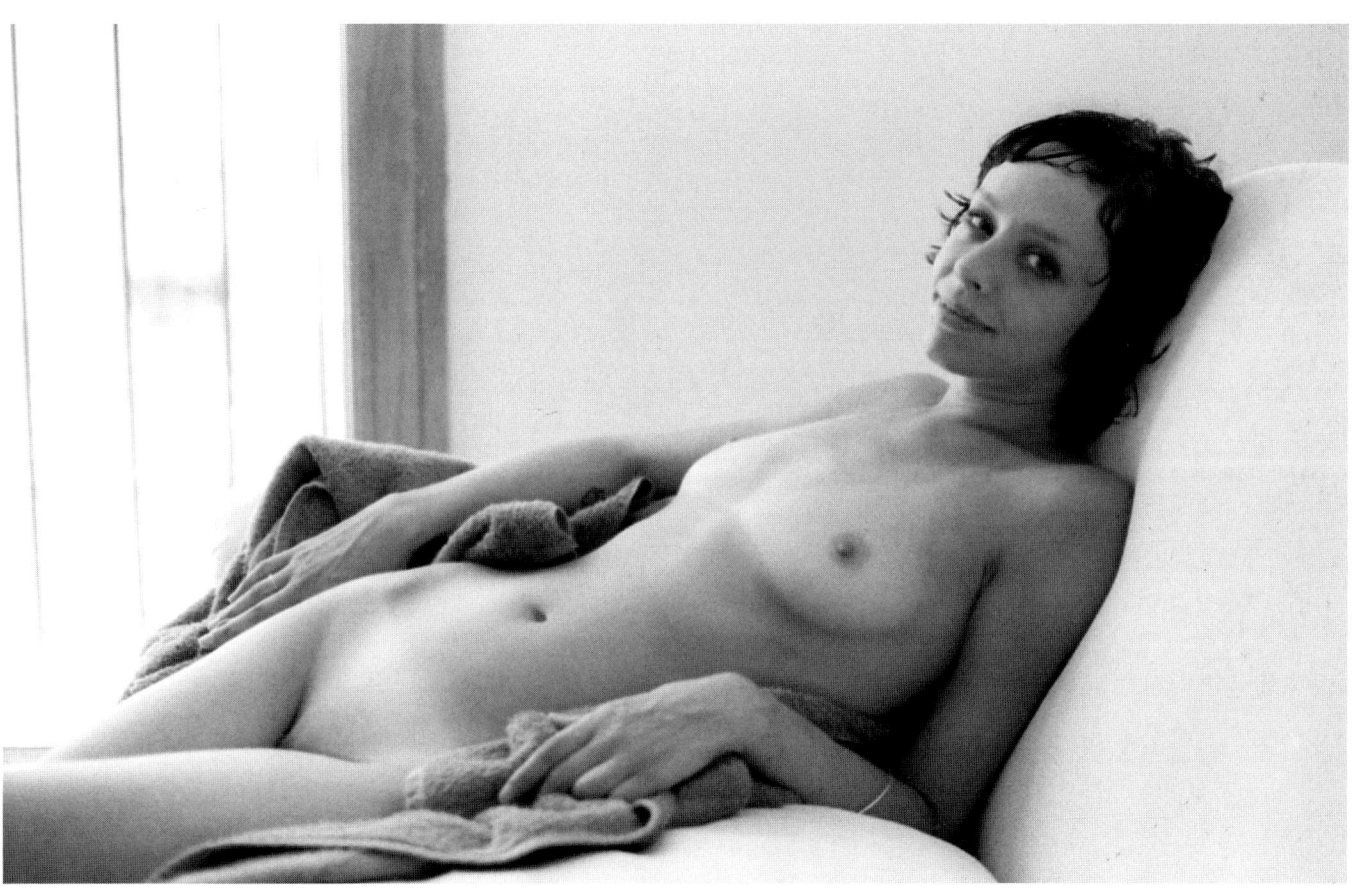

Kaiama · Kaiama emailed me after seeing my photos, and asked if I would like to photograph her. She told me she was a former dancer who taught French, who's background was Bahamian. I said yes. I photographed Kaiama and her cat "Charlie", in her beautiful apartment on Riverside drive. Kaiama was elegant, sophisticated, and had great posture.

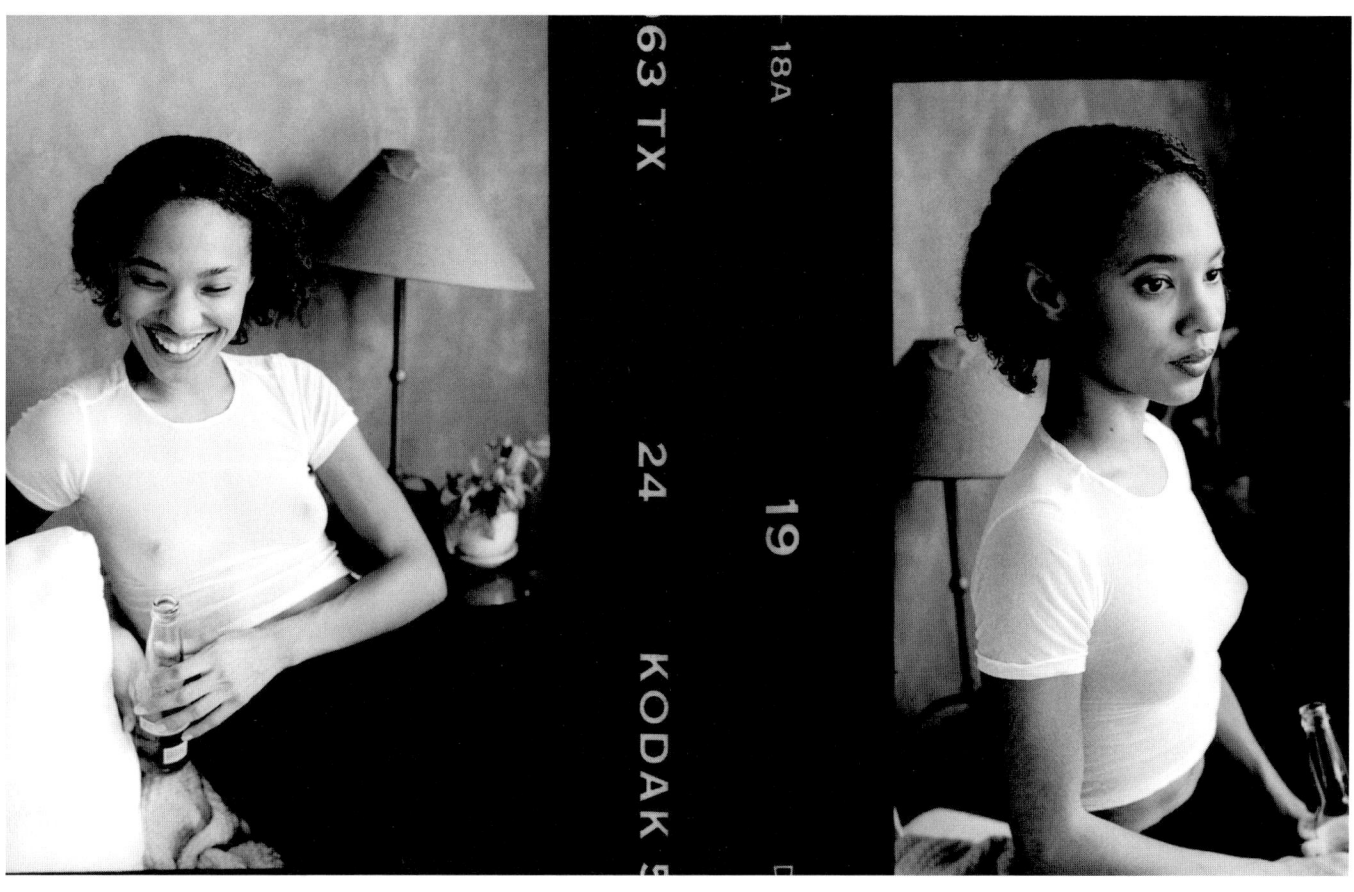

63 TX 18A 24 19 KODAK

213

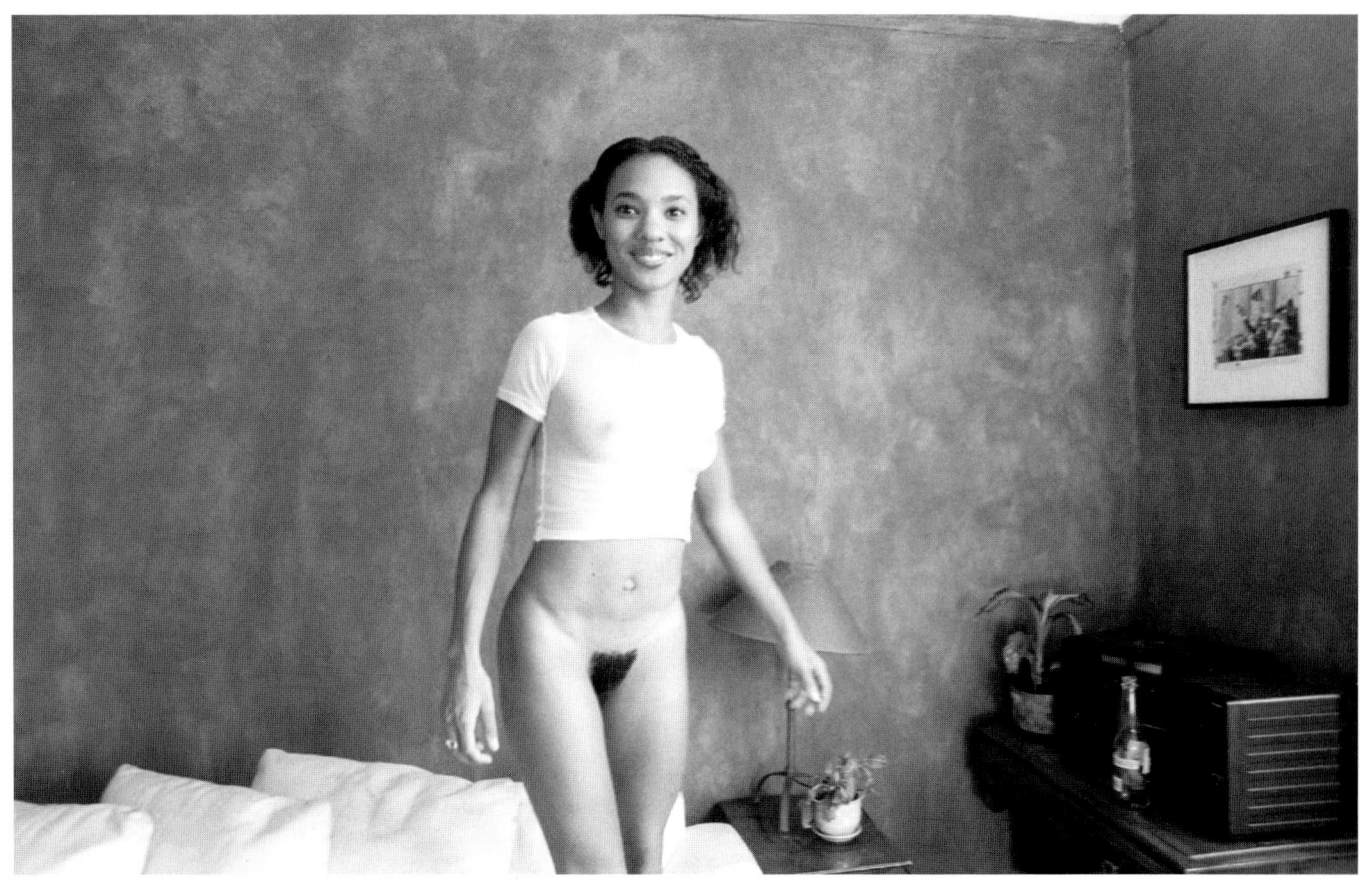

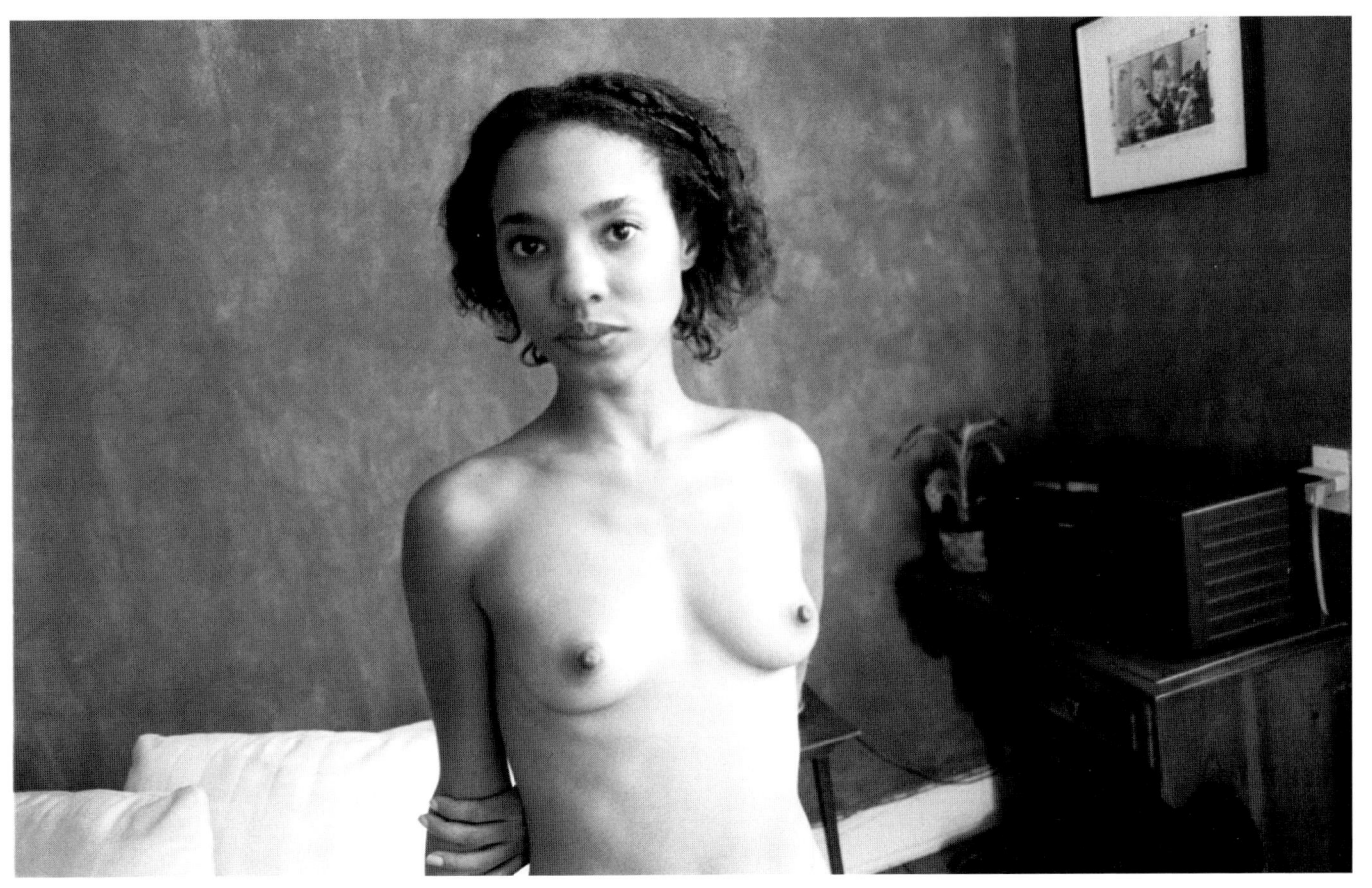

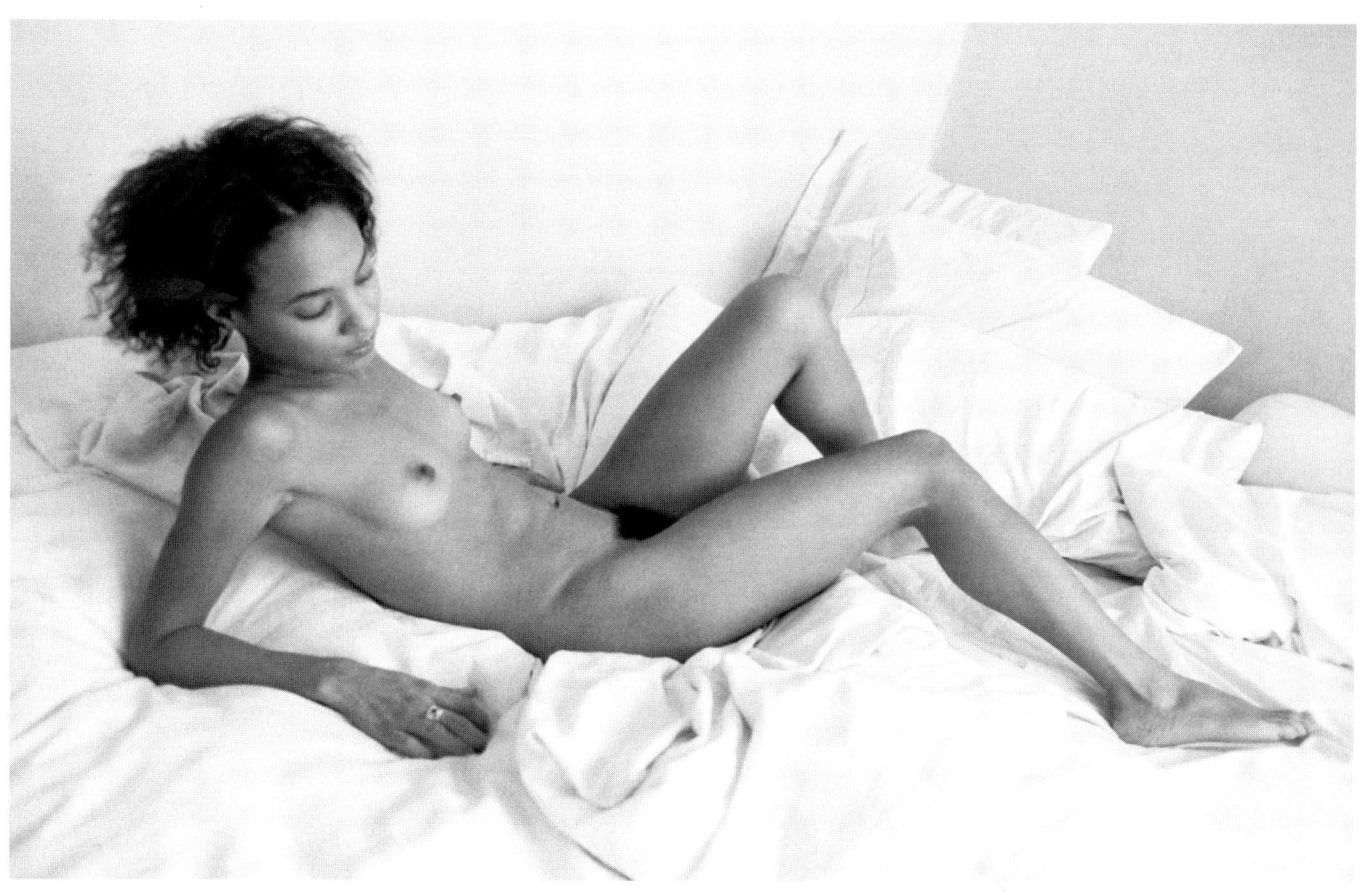

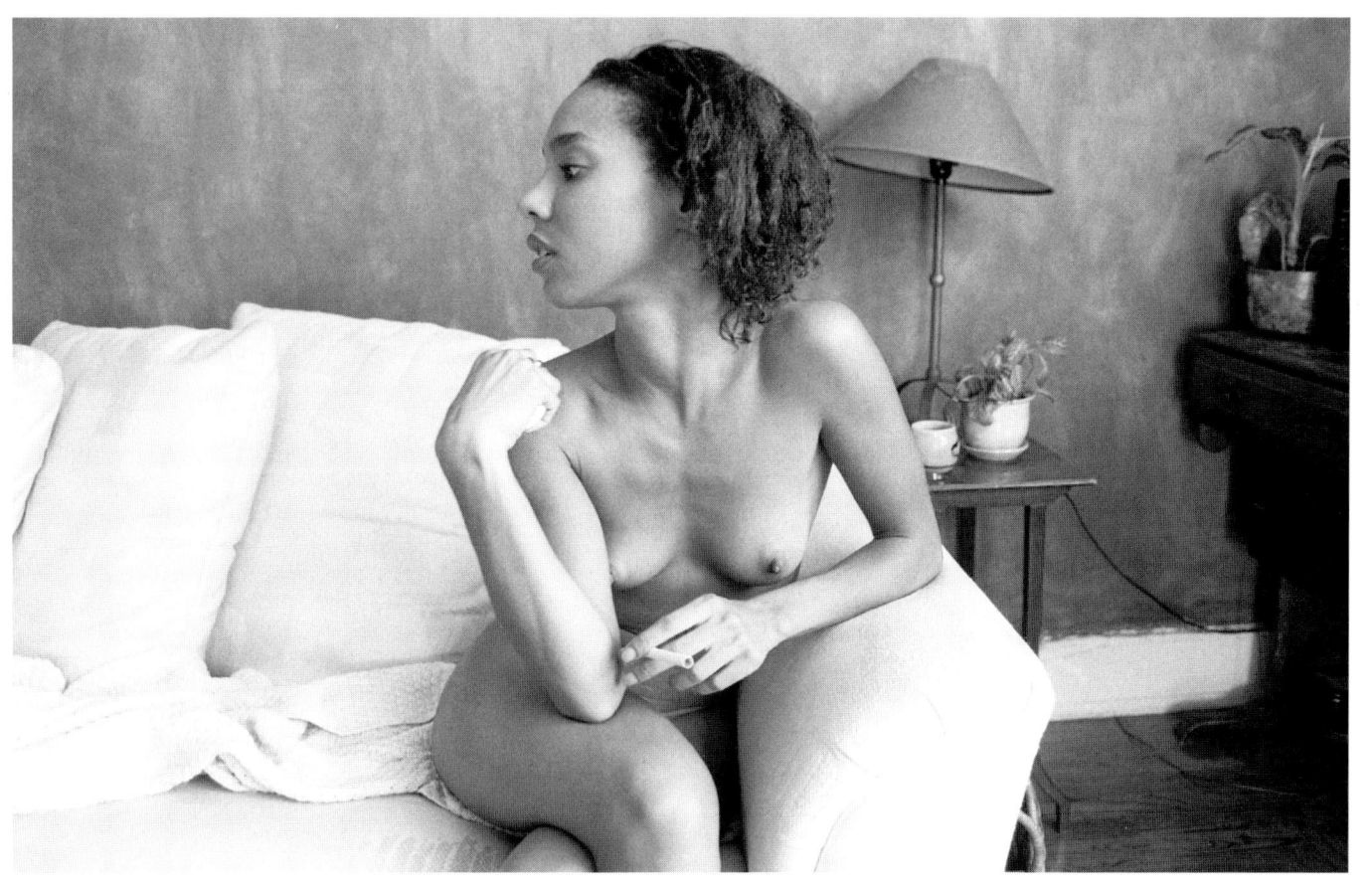

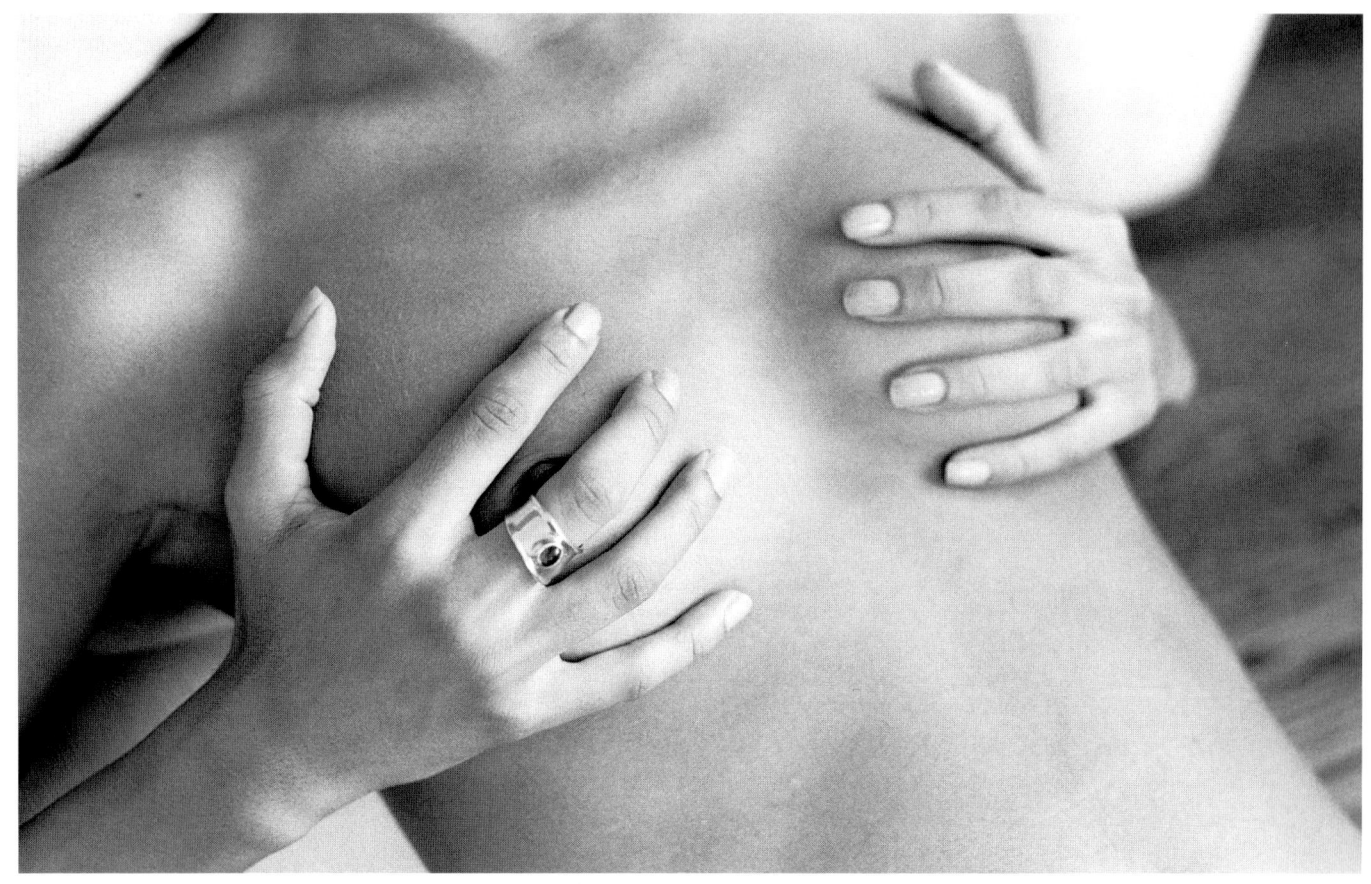

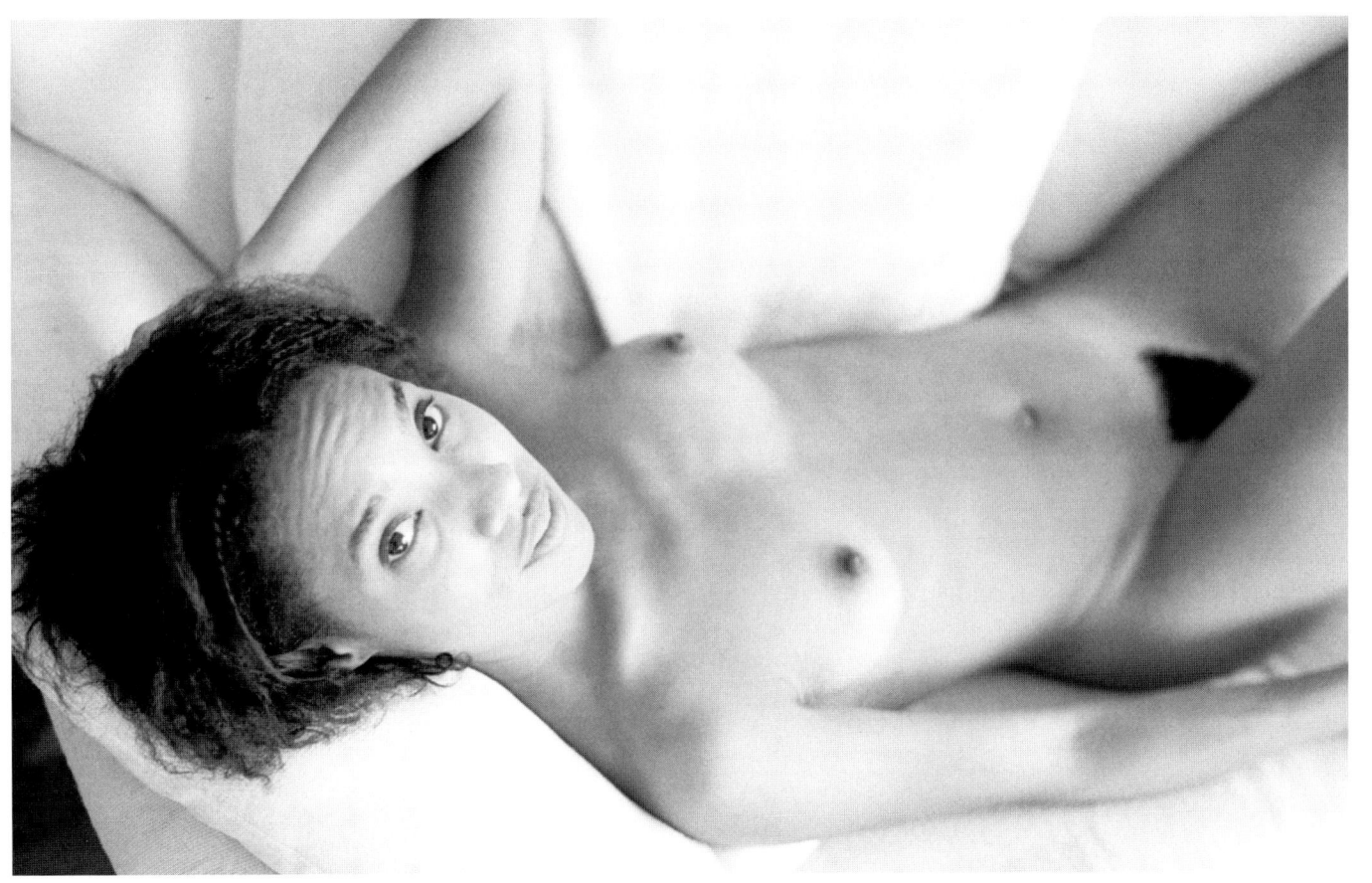

Kiliaen · Kiliaen was the girlfriend, of a good friend of mine. She lived in a loft in Tribeca, which had big windows and white, brick walls. Kiliaen was very nervous that garment workers across the street could see her. This made for some fun pictures. Her hat became a prop, as well as a security blanket.

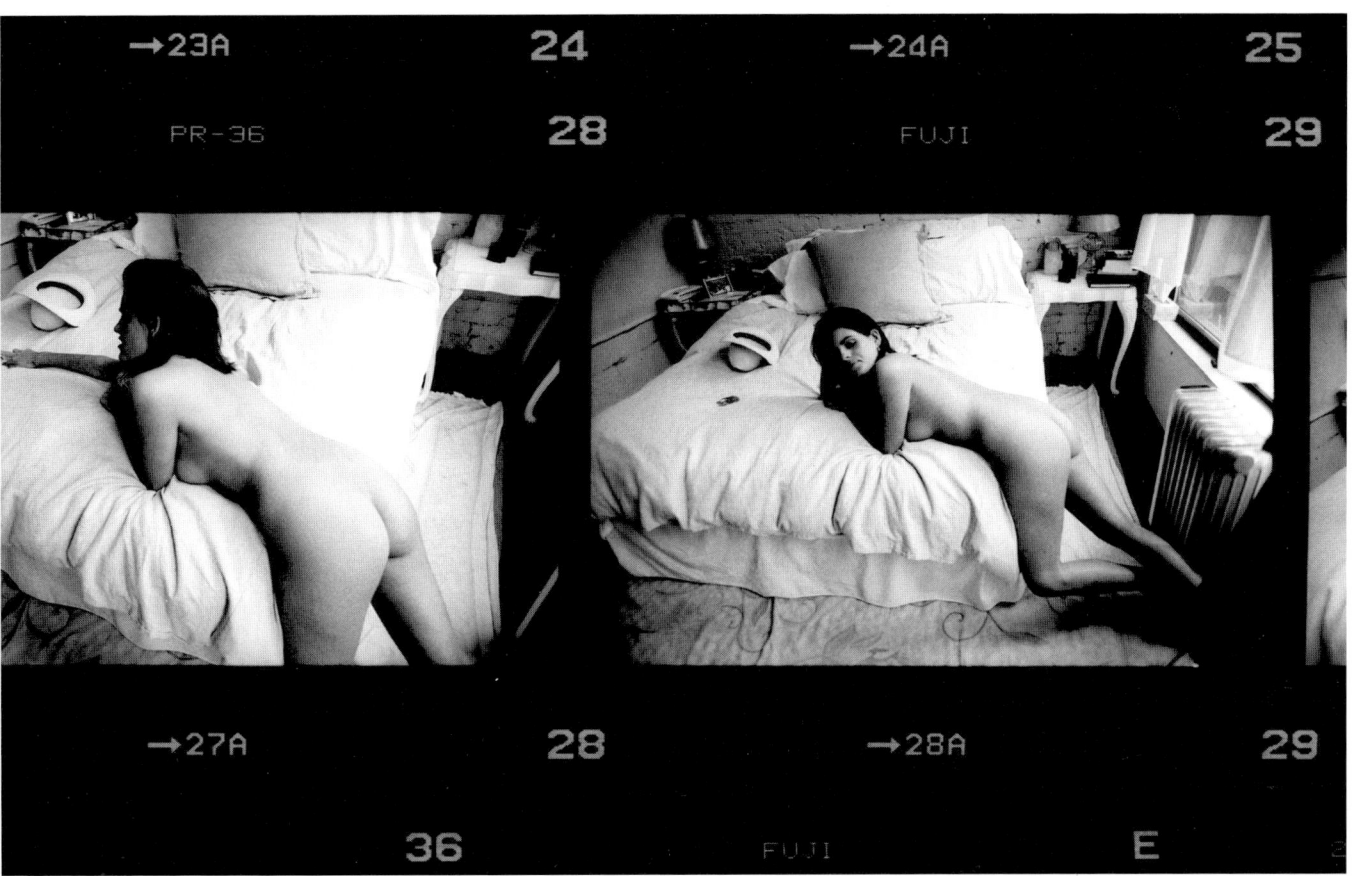

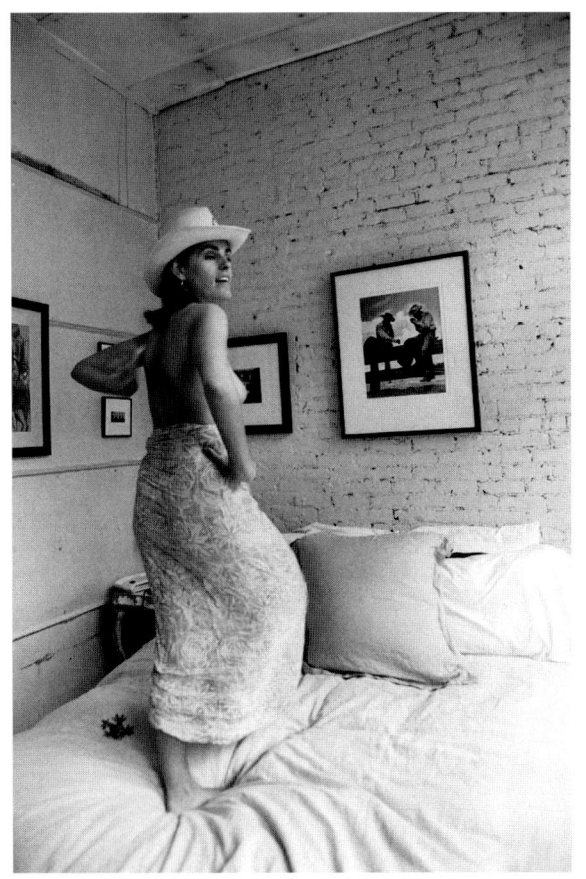
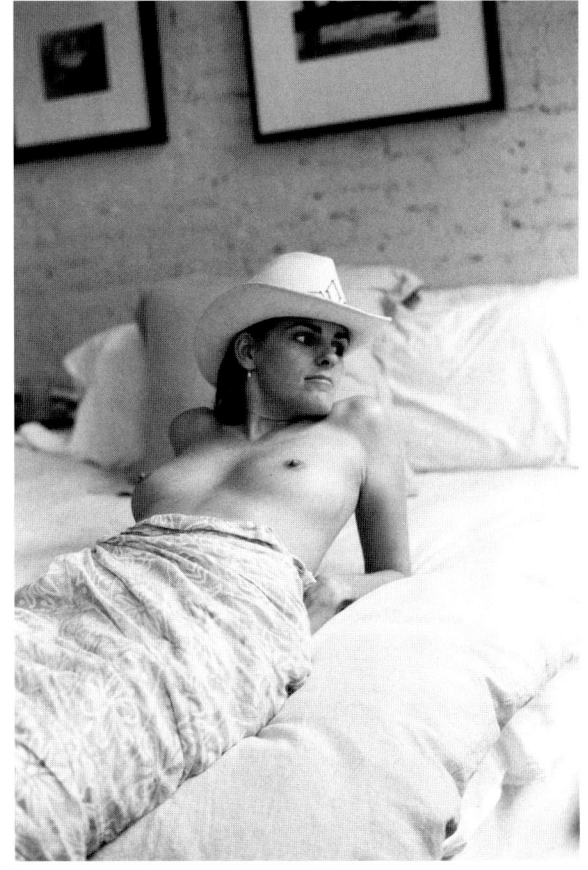

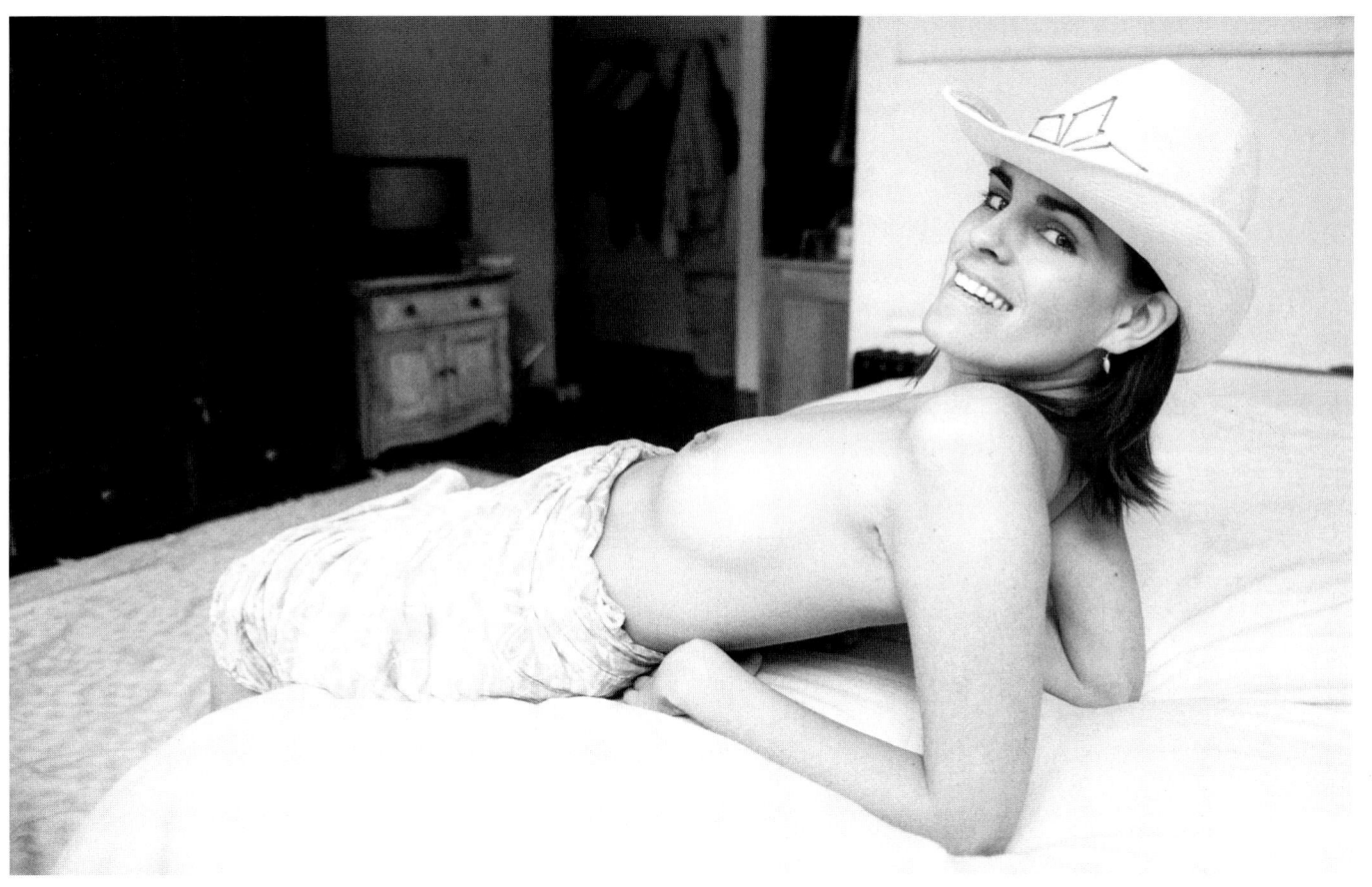

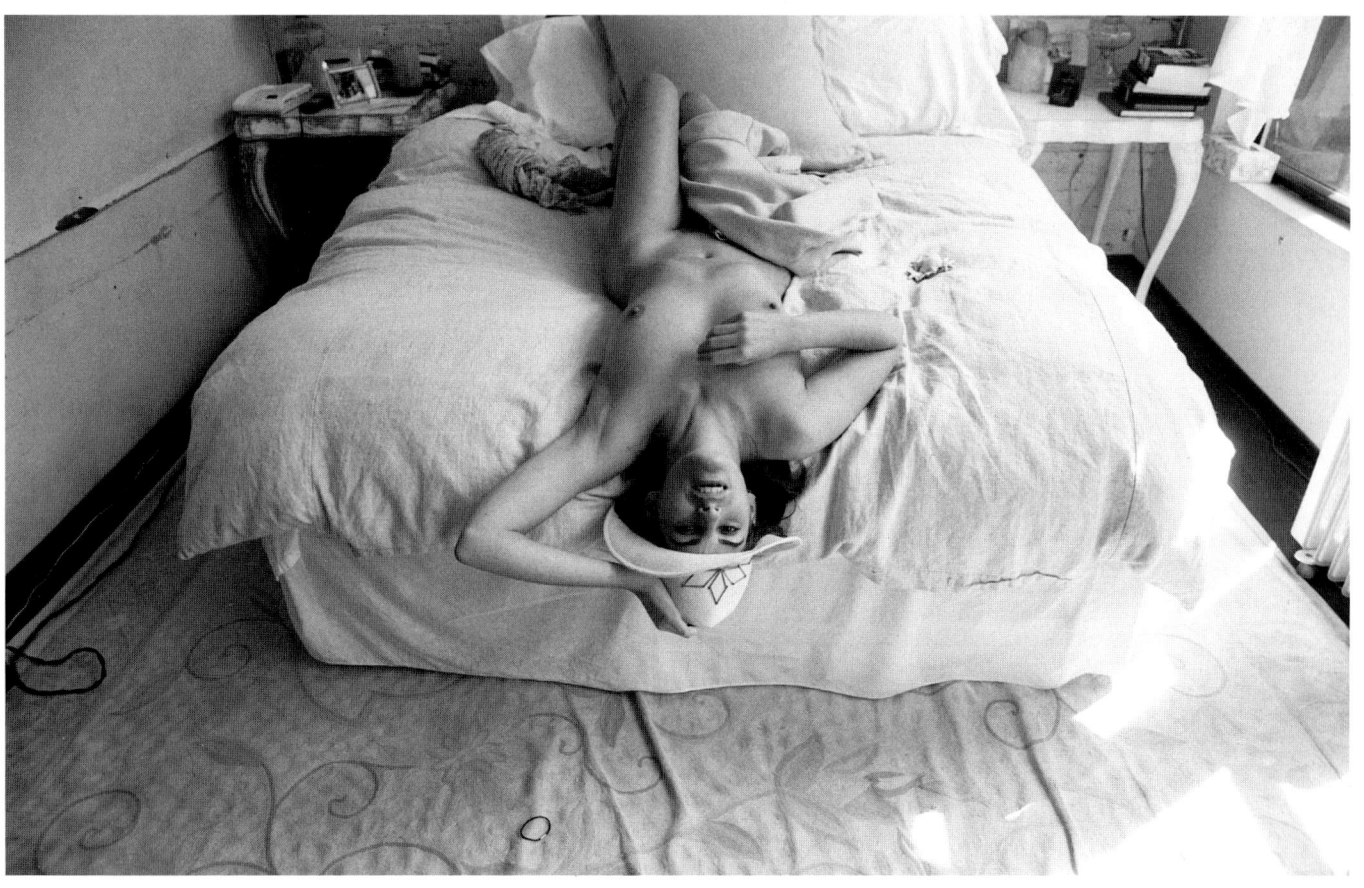

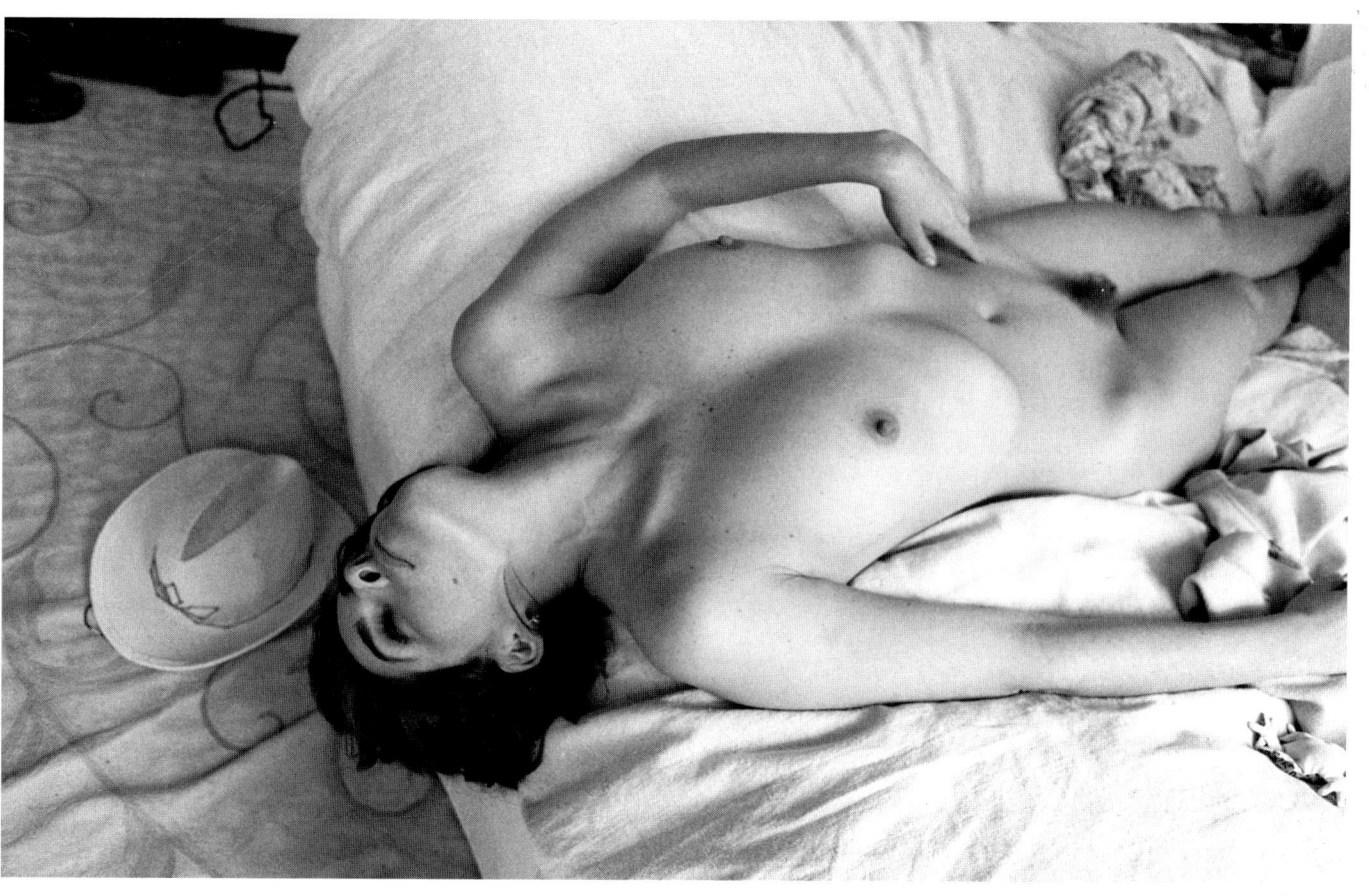

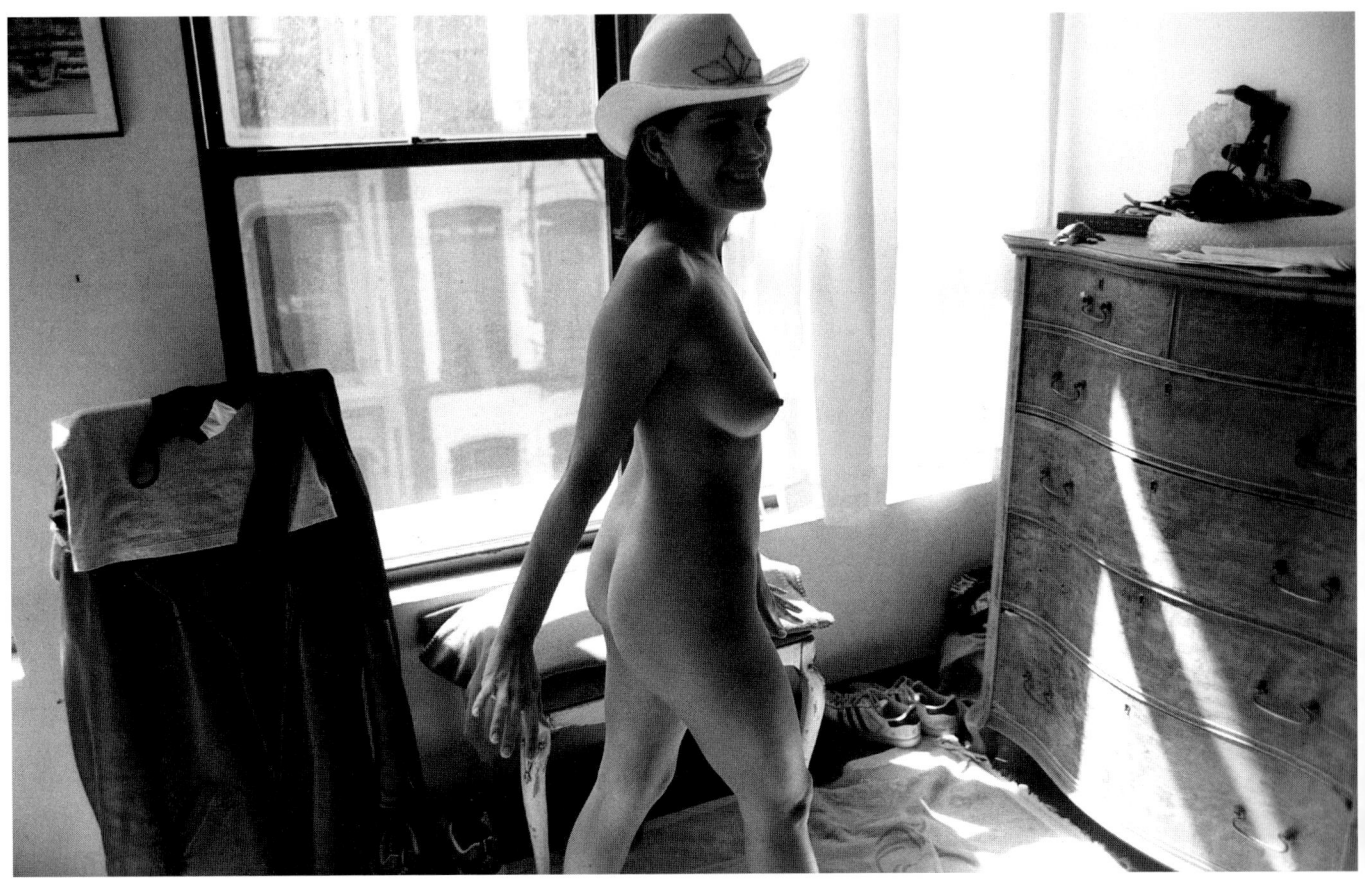

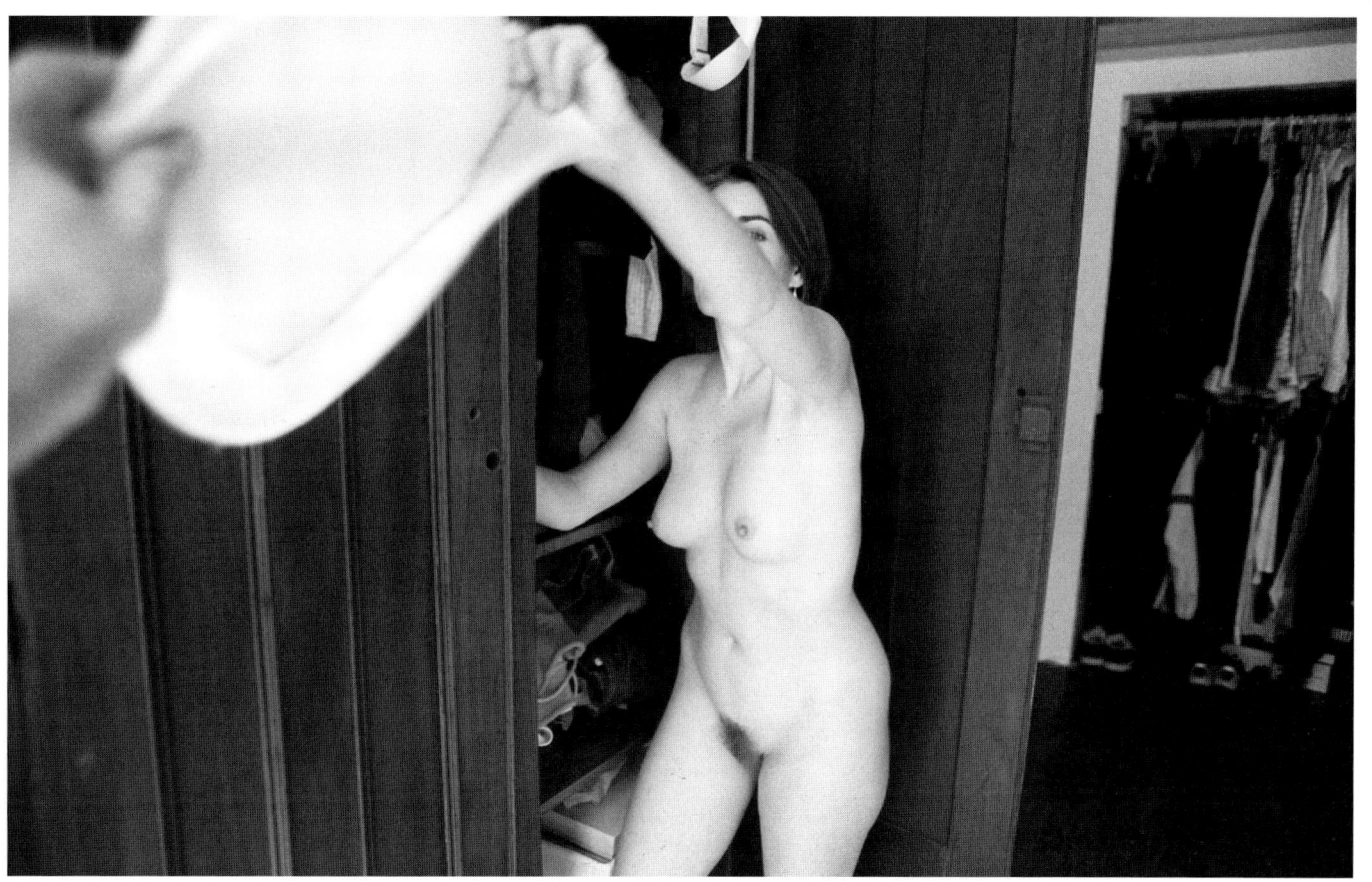

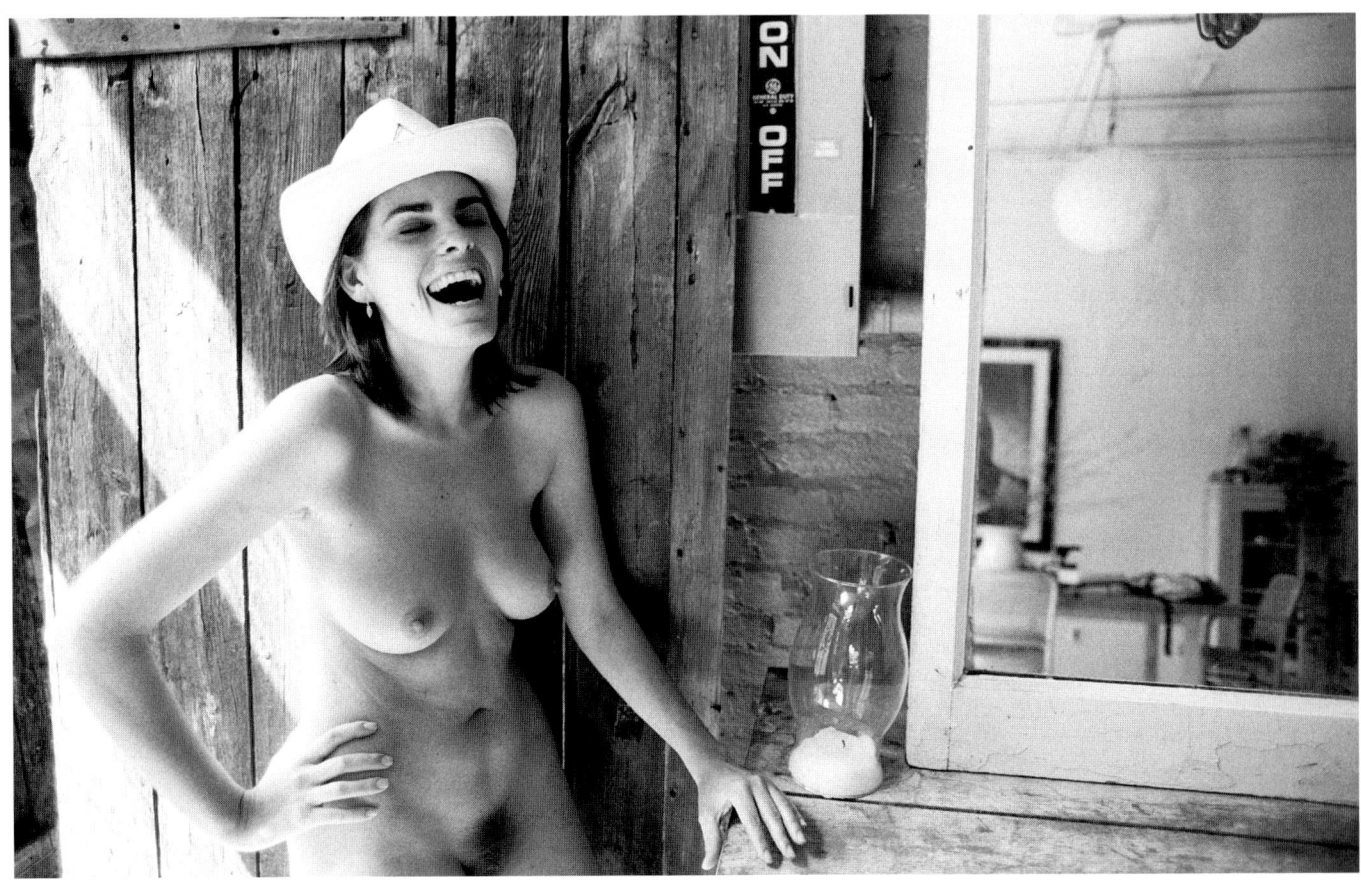

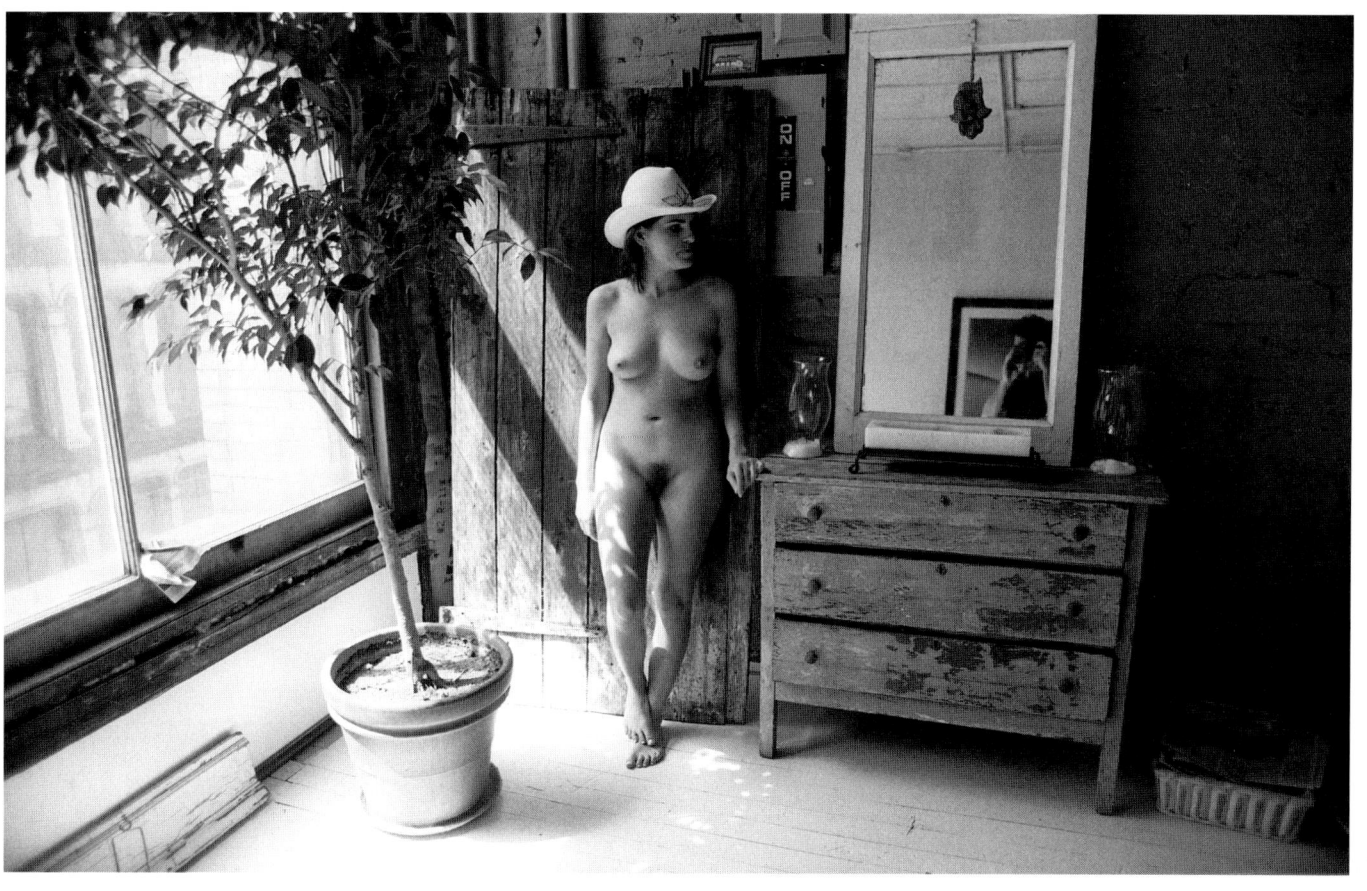

Kilsy · Kilsy has been a friend of mine since I came to New York in 1994. I met her in a Moroccan restaurant in the Village. This was our third shoot. Kilsy is full of energy and creativity. She is a clothing designer, musician, producer, and the ultimate muse. Kilsy lives in a long loft on Broadway, and had really 80's style hair the day we shot.

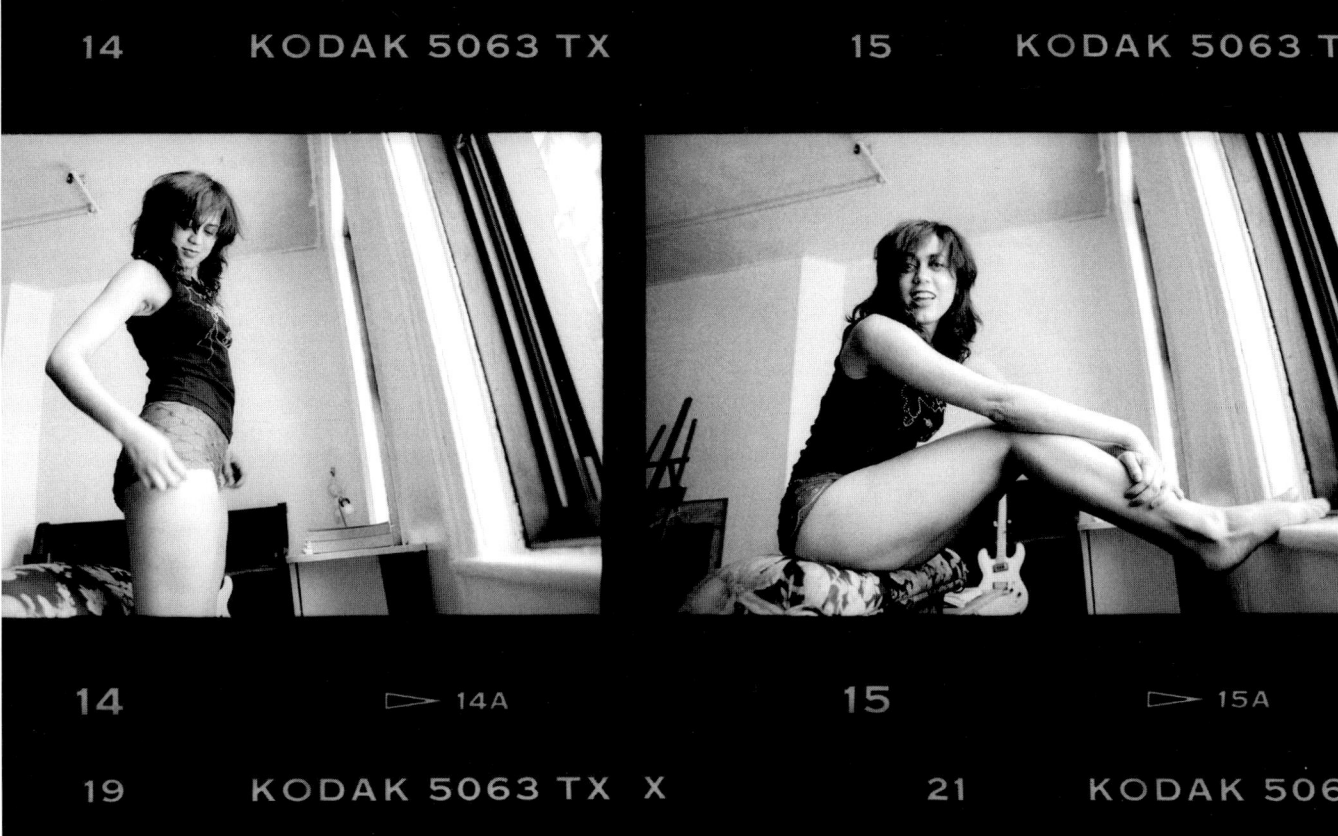

14 KODAK 5063 TX 15 KODAK 5063 T

14 ▷ 14A 15 ▷ 15A

19 KODAK 5063 TX X 21 KODAK 506

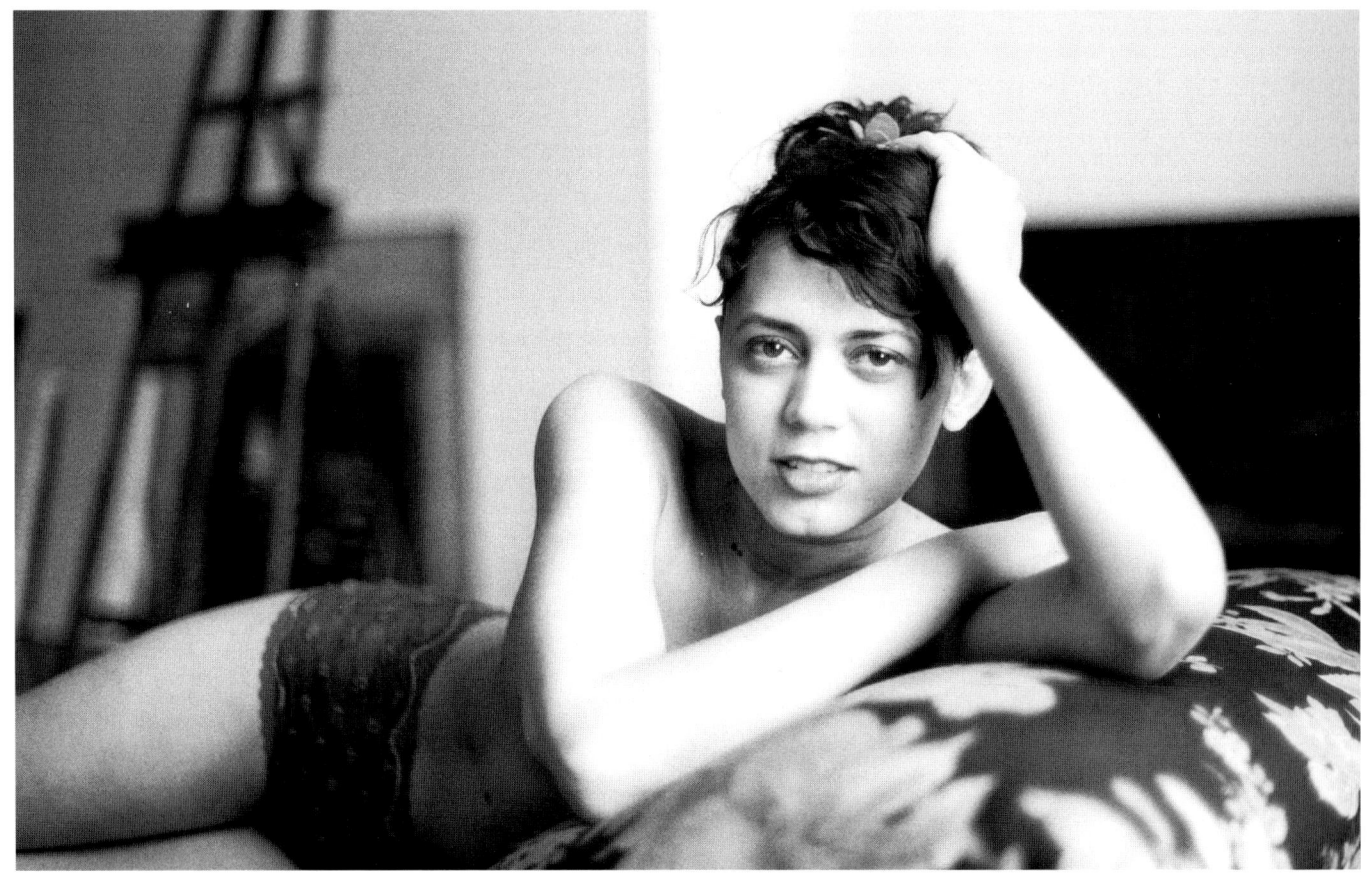

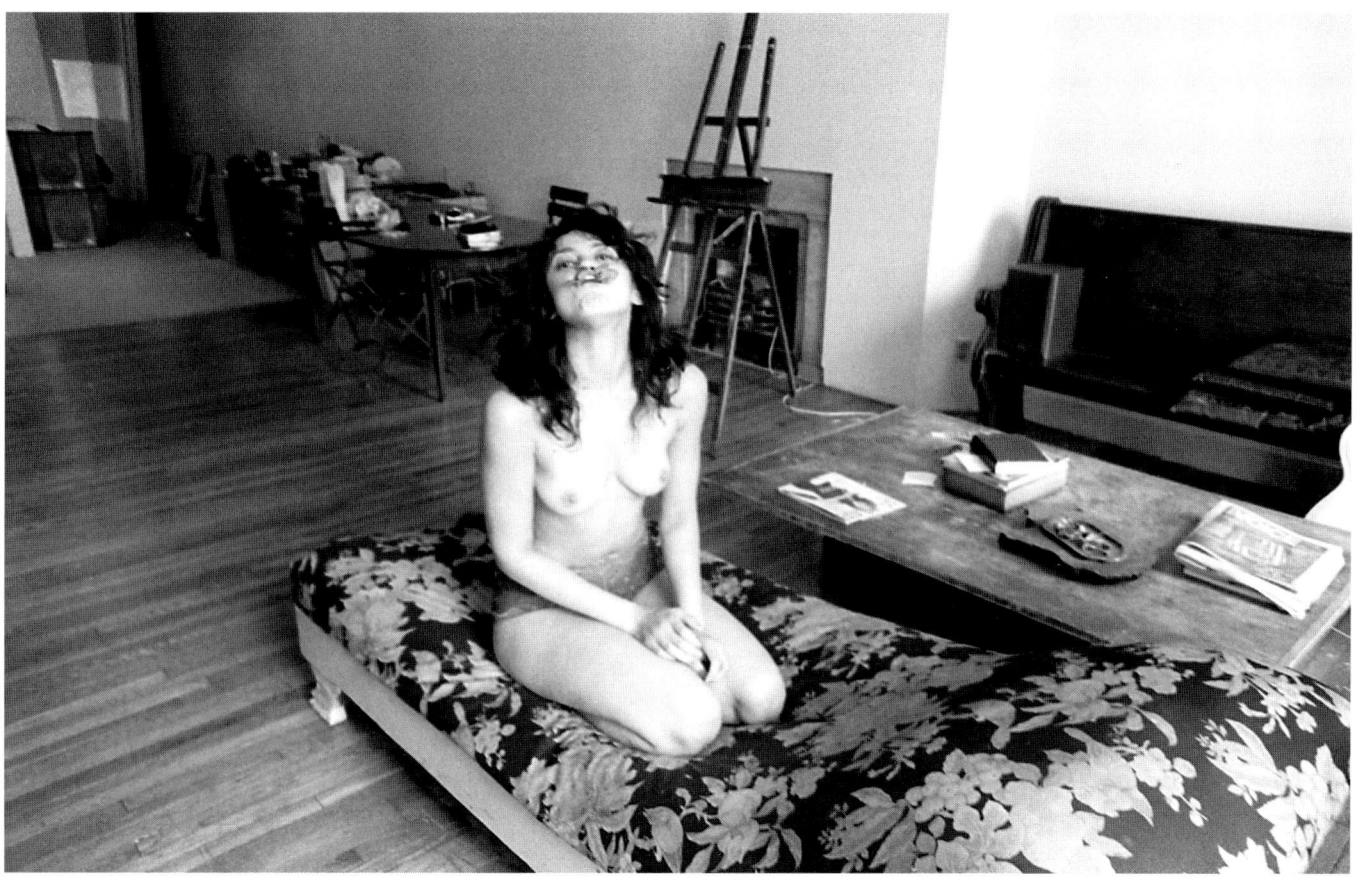

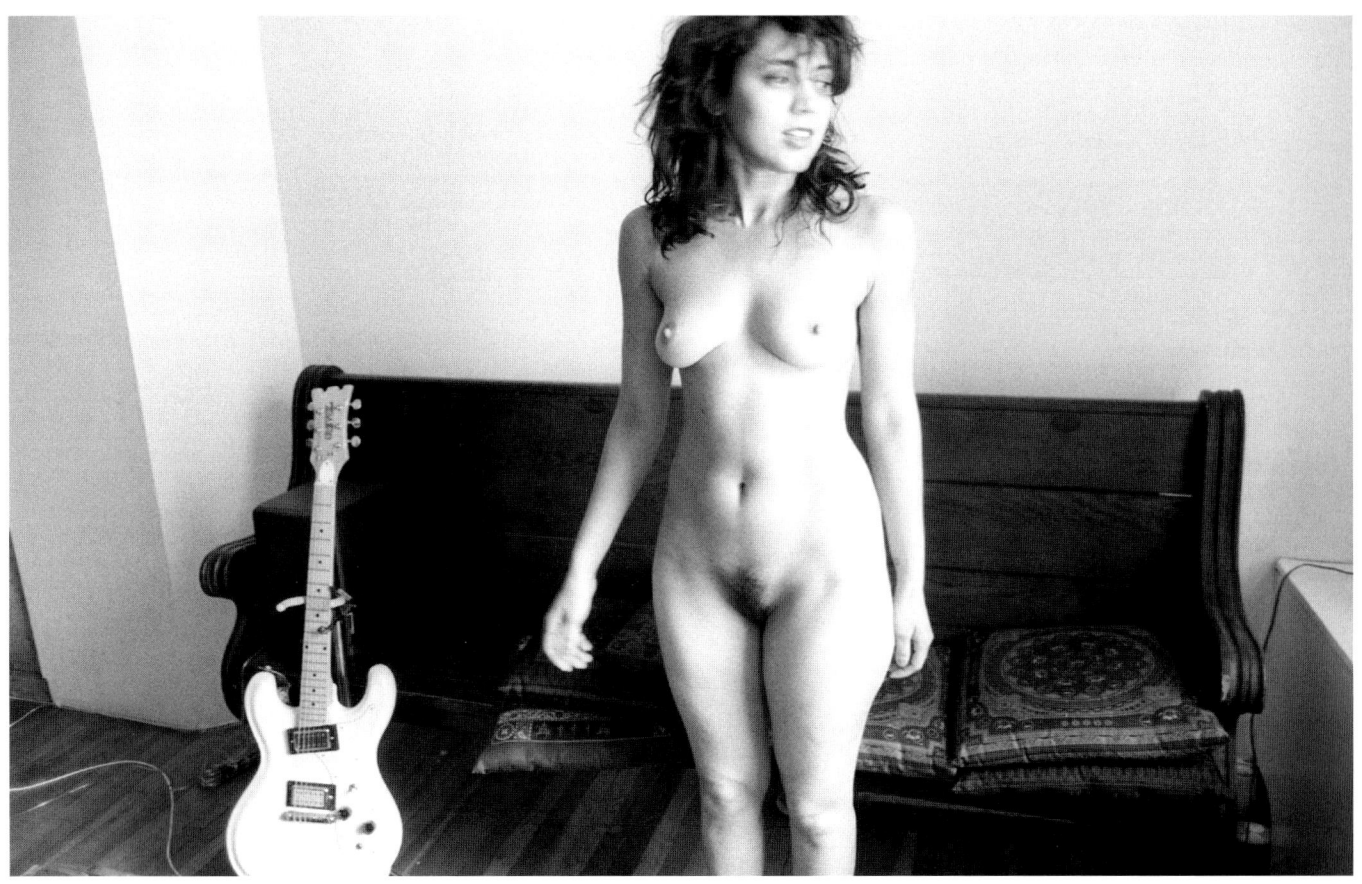

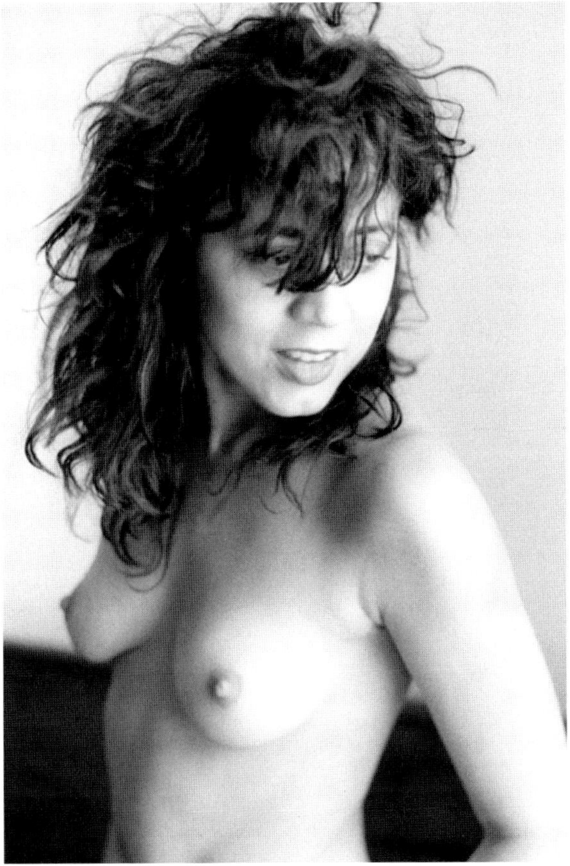

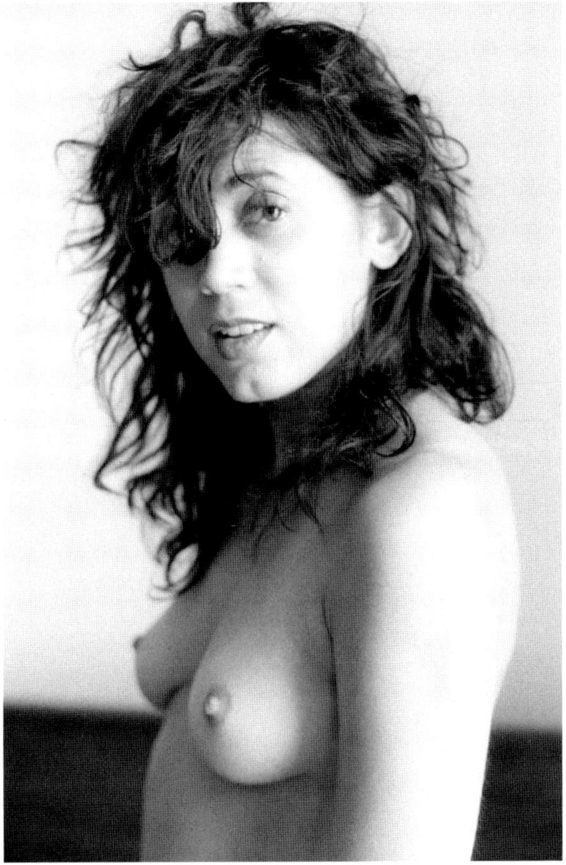

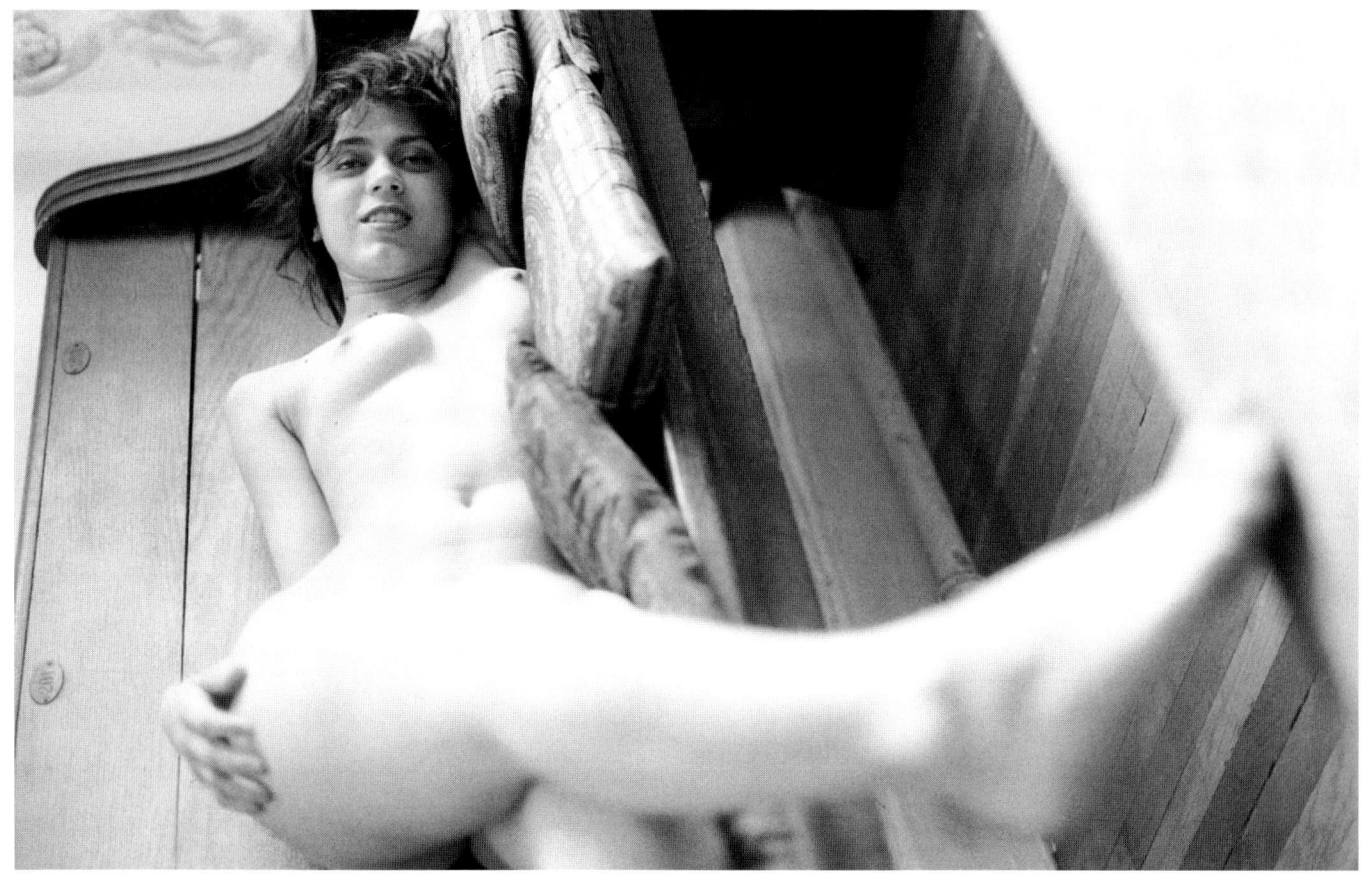

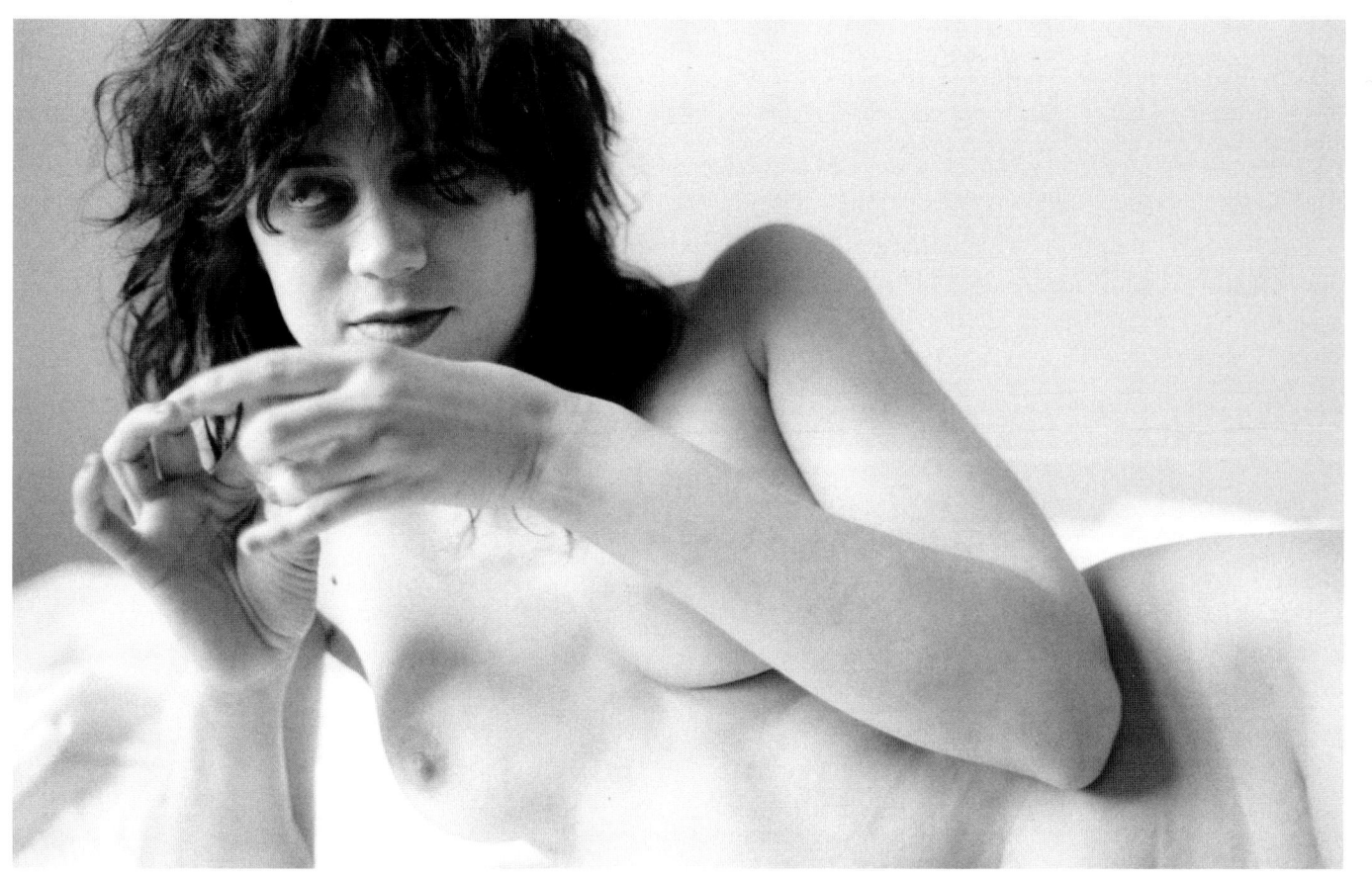

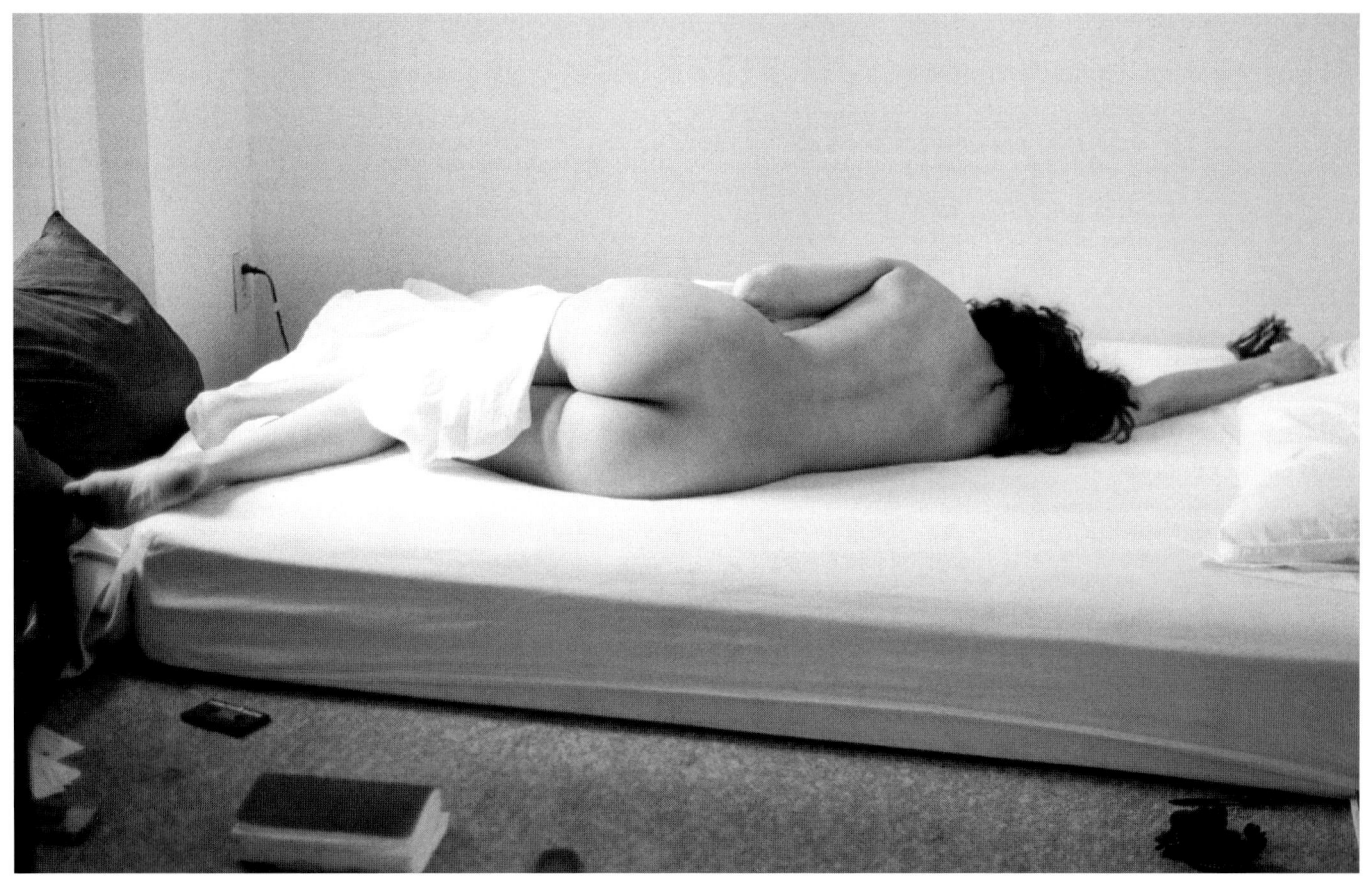

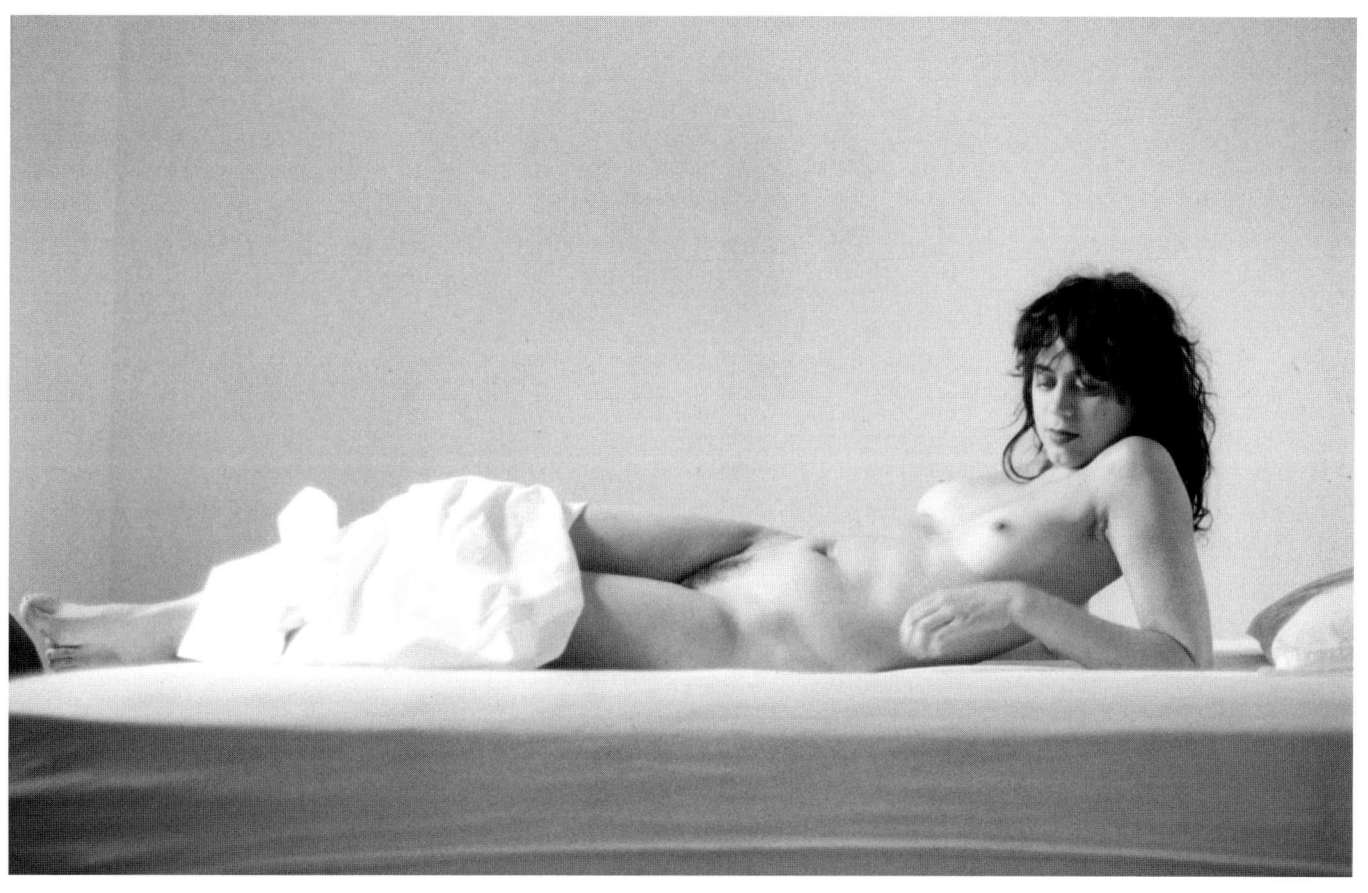

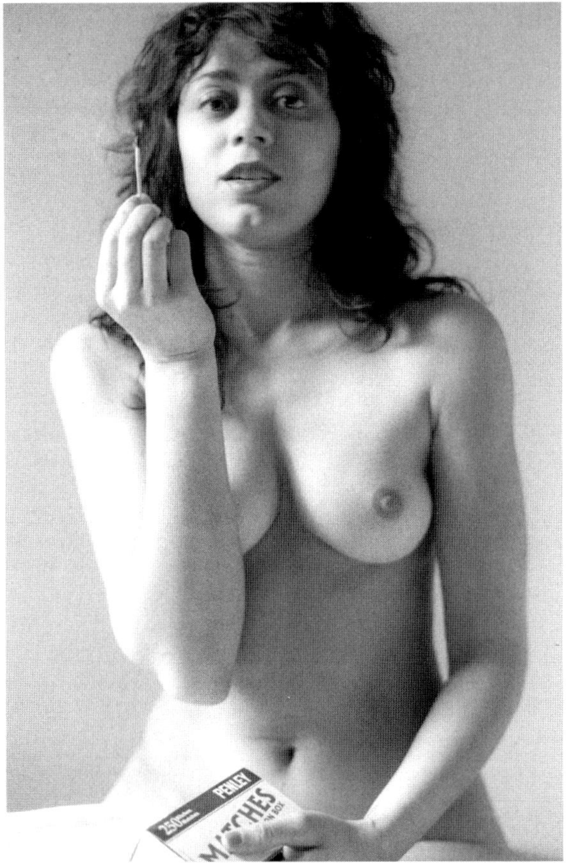
250
PENLEY
MATCHES

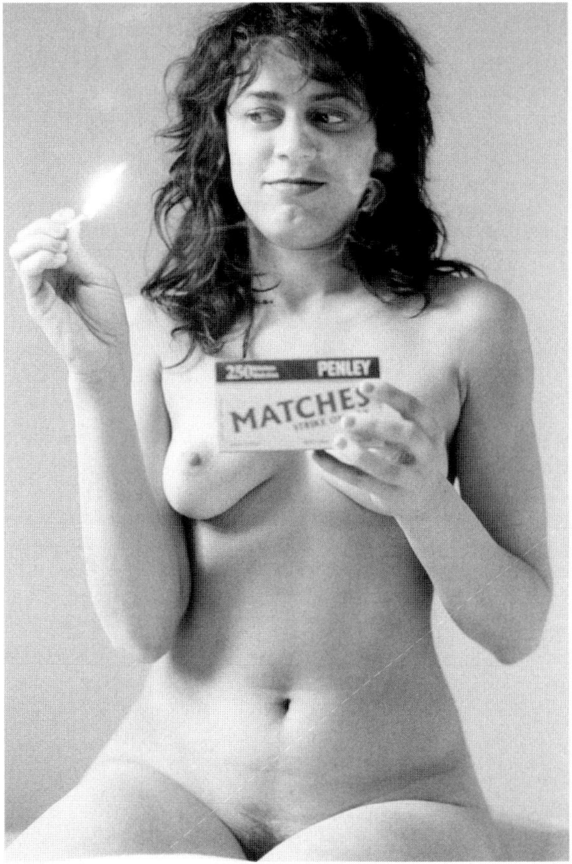
250
PENLEY
MATCHES

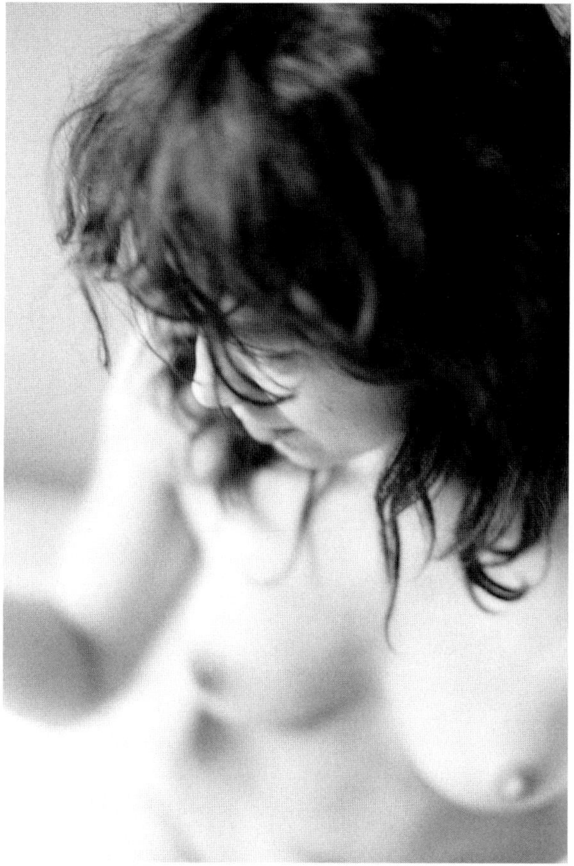

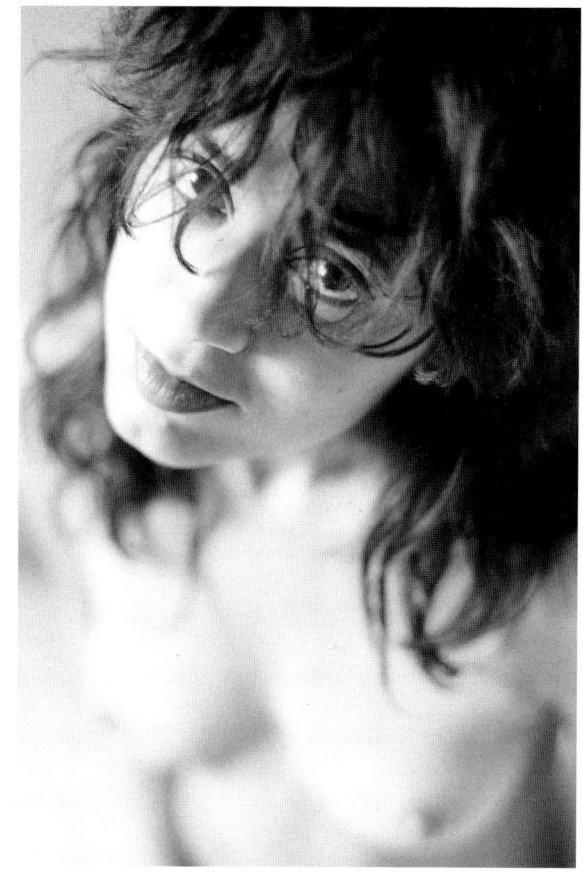

Krystl · Krystl actually saw me before I saw her. She was watching a Godzilla film on tv, and then flipped to a Manhattan cable show that I did, which showed my videos and photographs of people nude. She was hooked and wanted to pose.. Krystl loves red currant scented candles, yoga in Brooklyn, rice pudding and anything pink and sparkling.

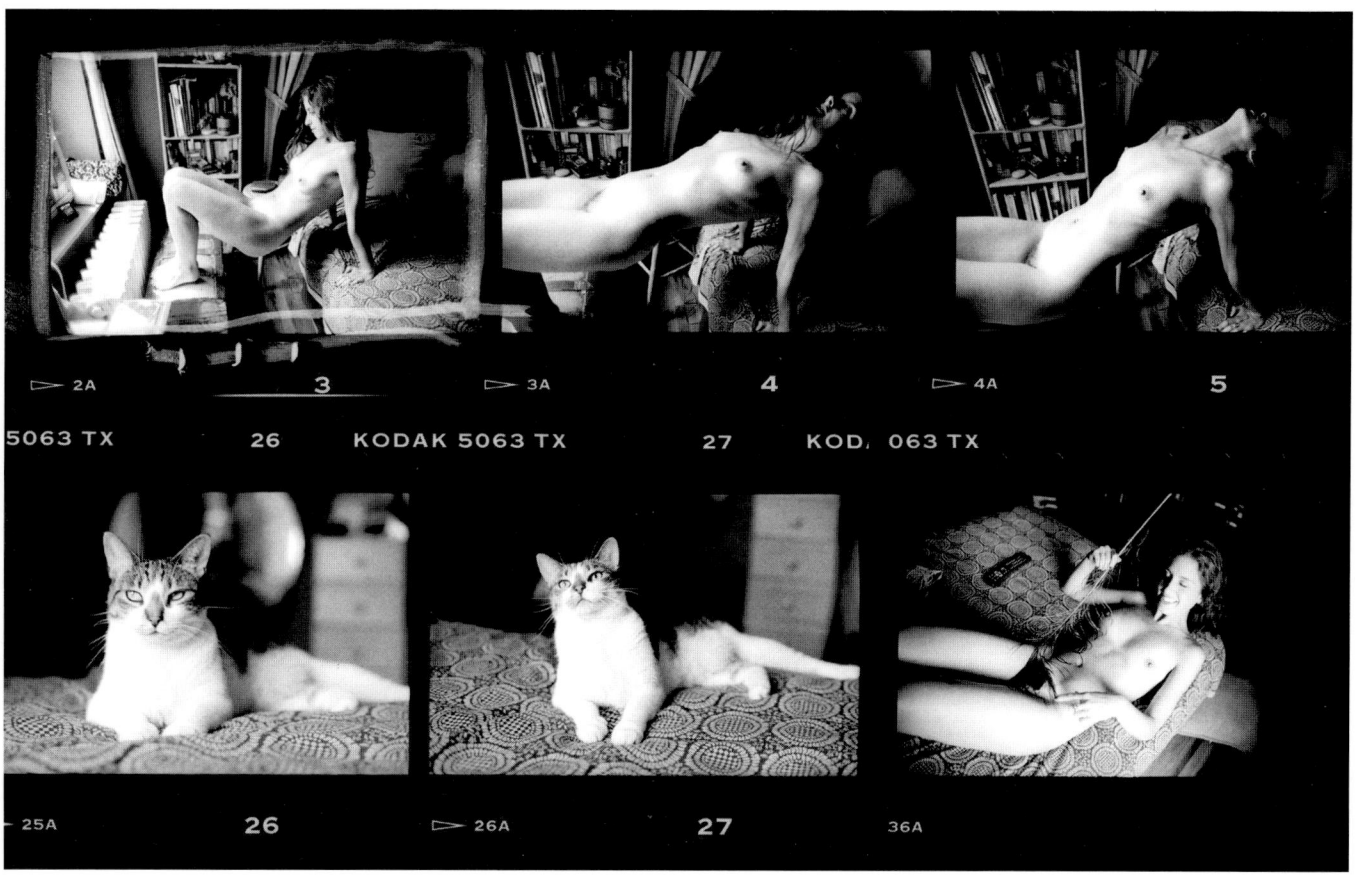

2A   3   3A   4   4A   5

5063 TX   26   KODAK 5063 TX   27   KOD. 063 TX

25A   26   26A   27   36A

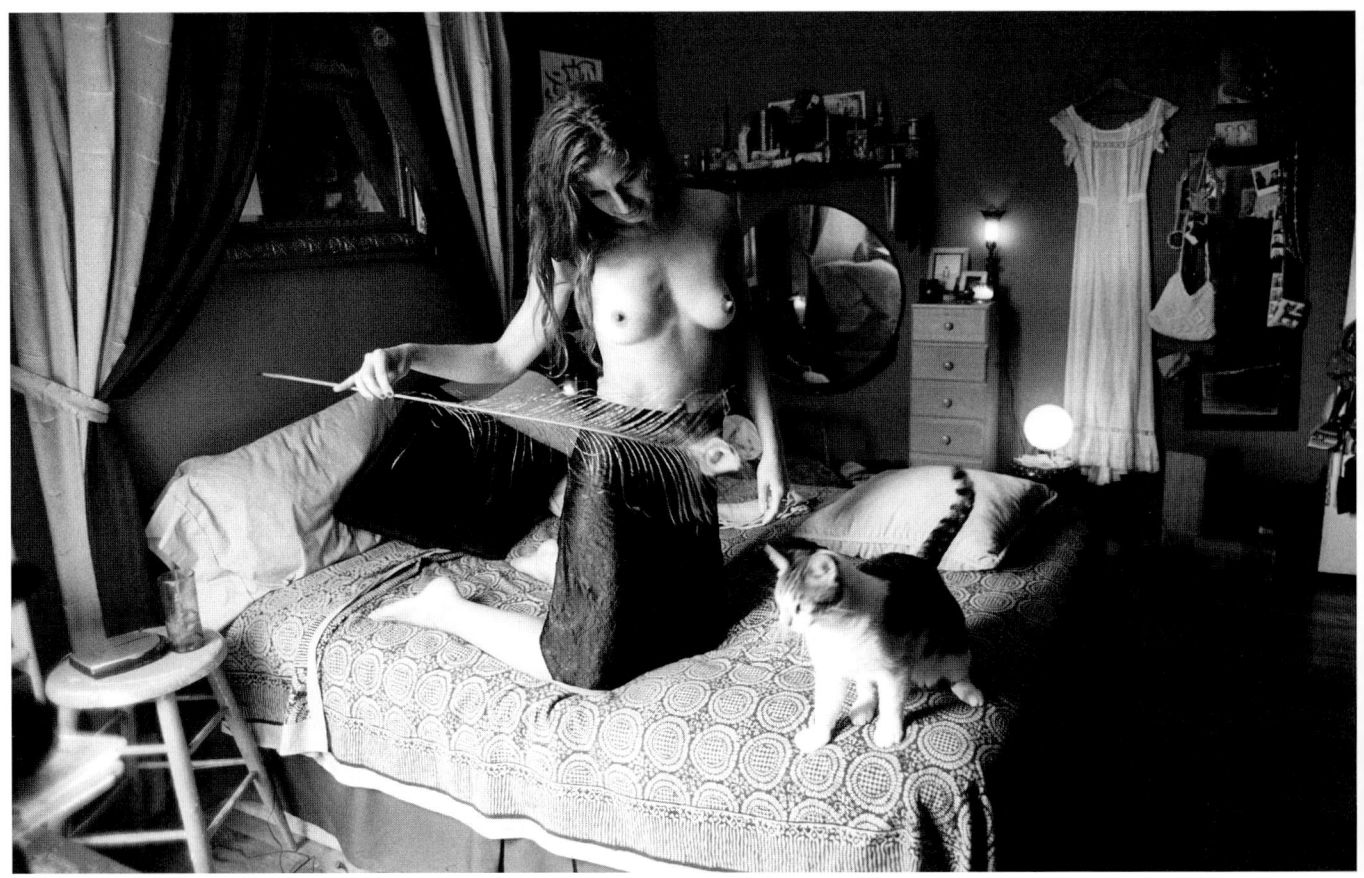

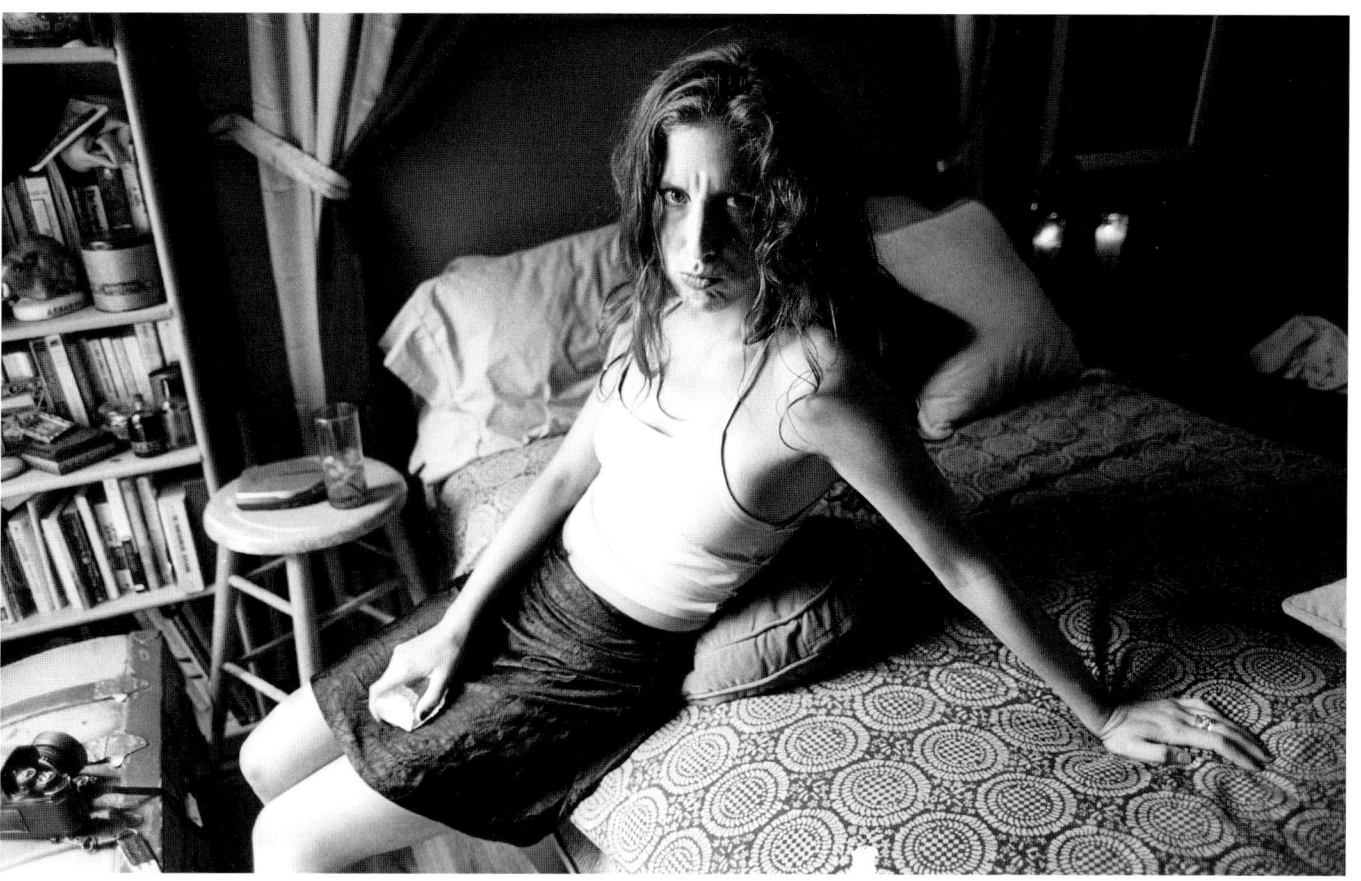

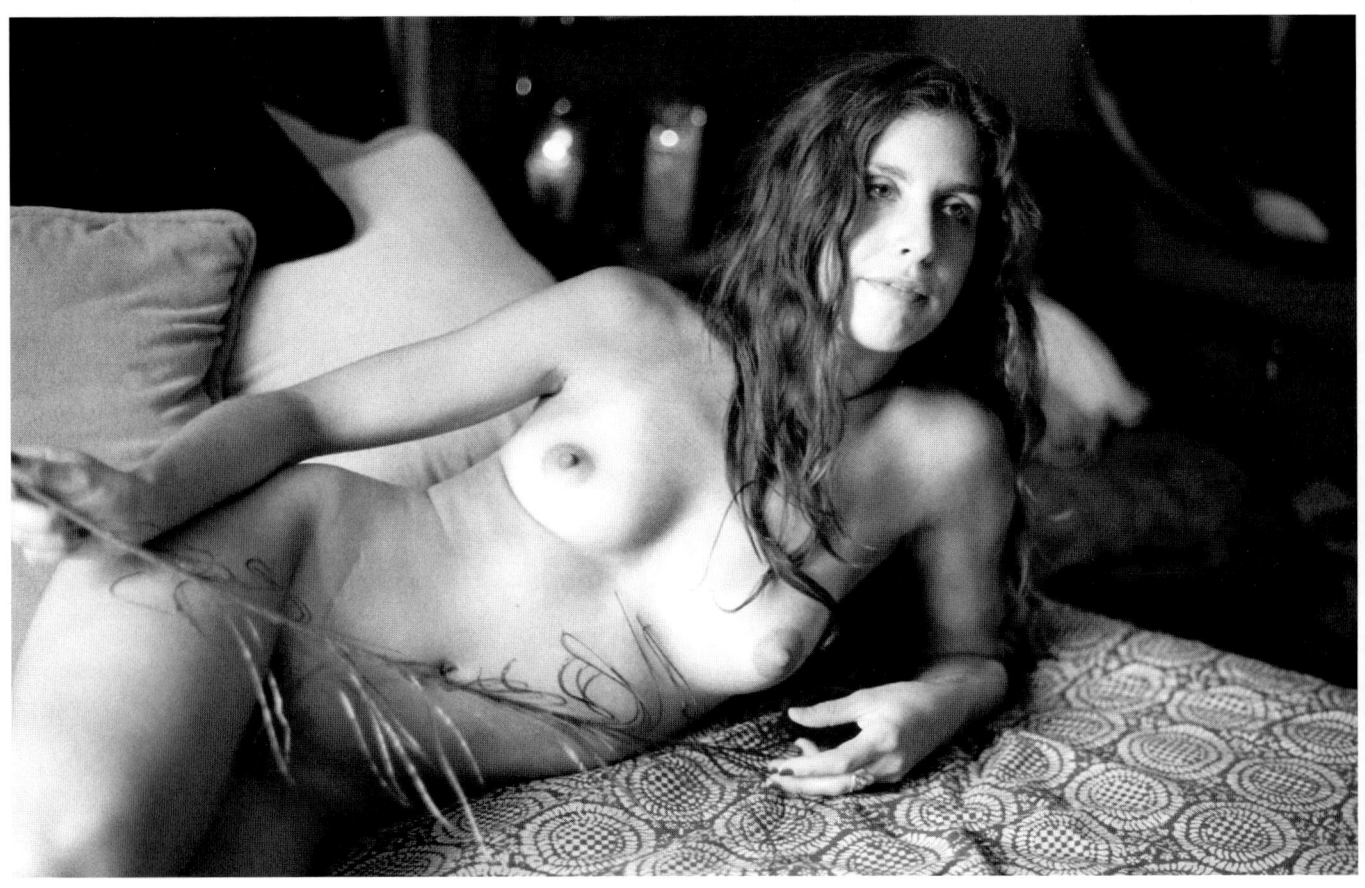

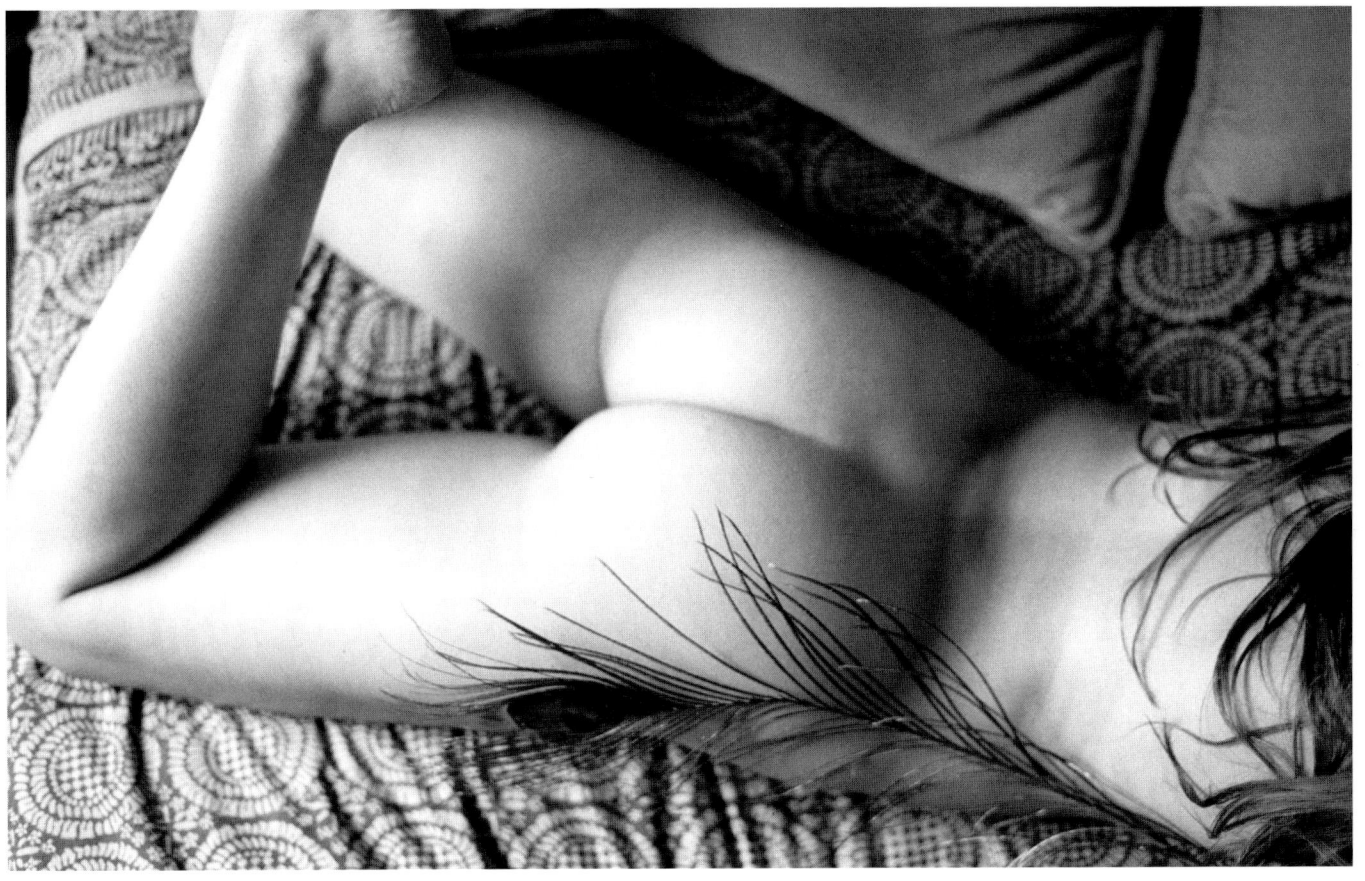

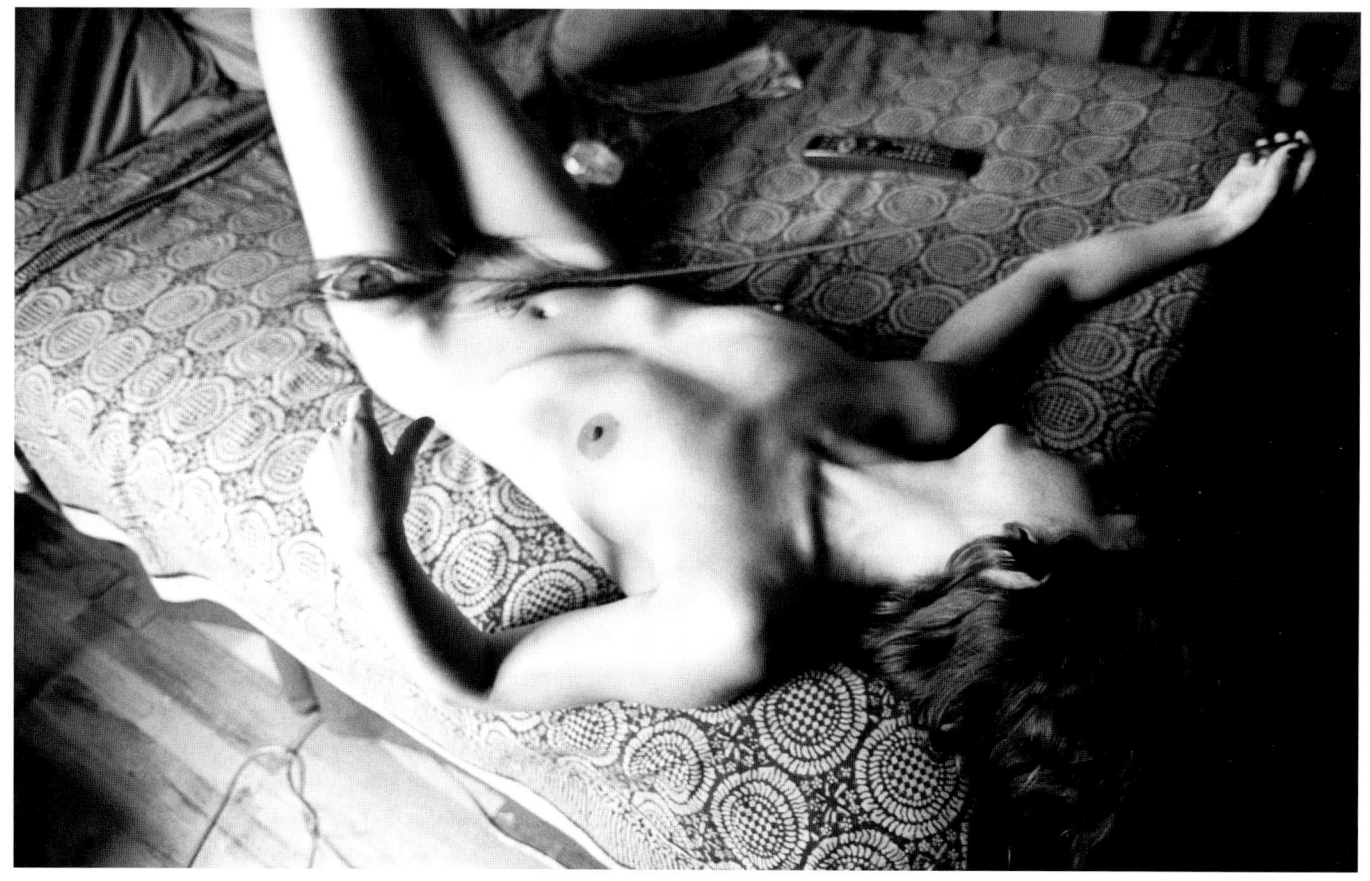

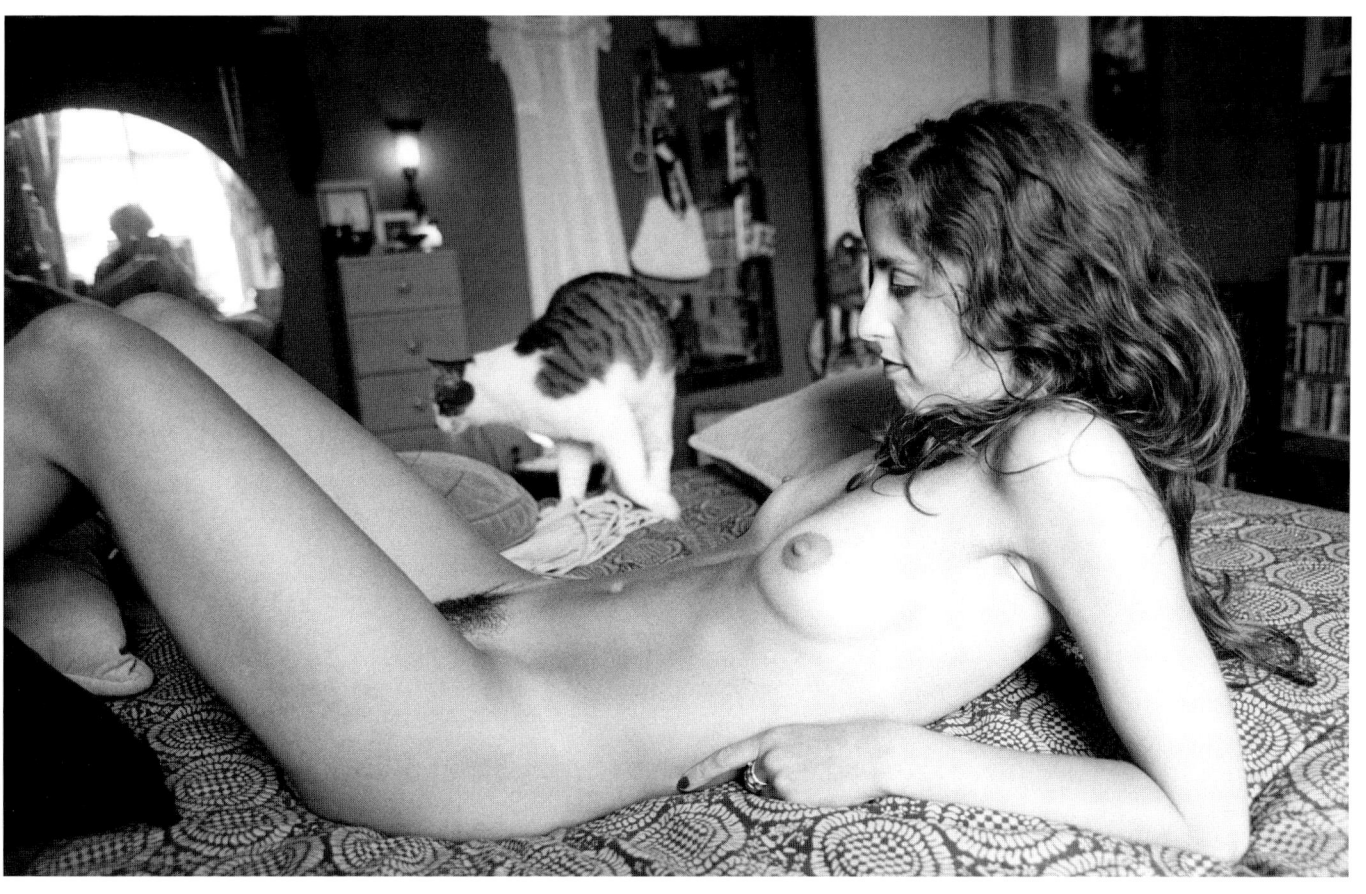

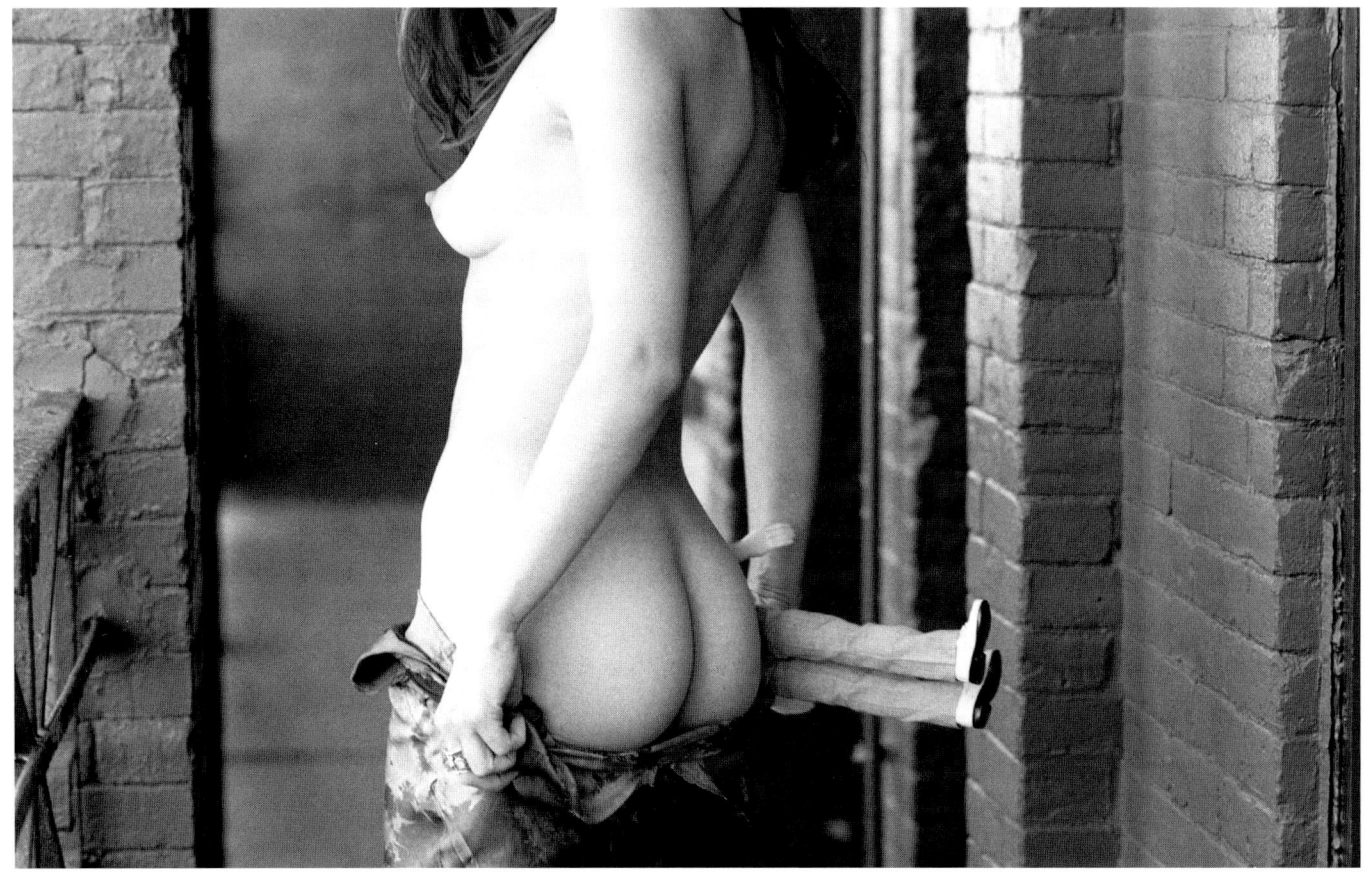

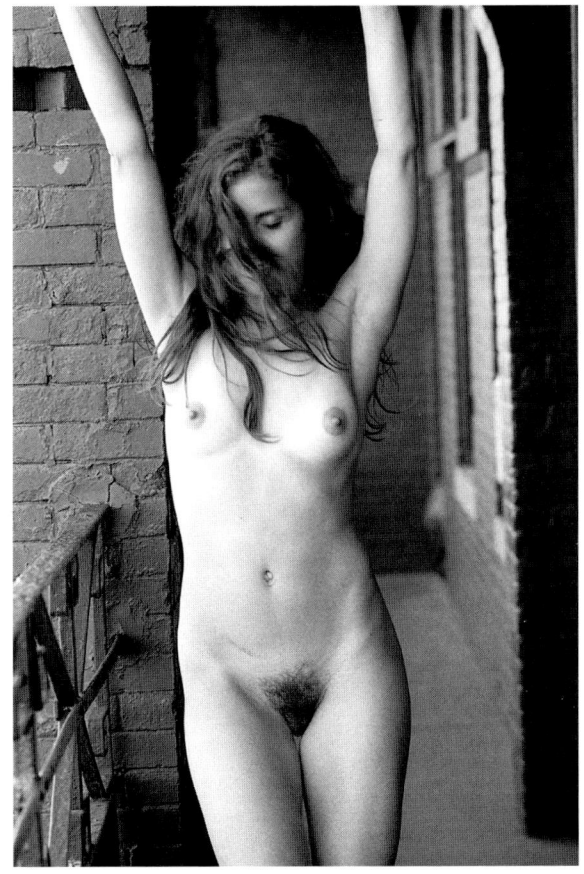
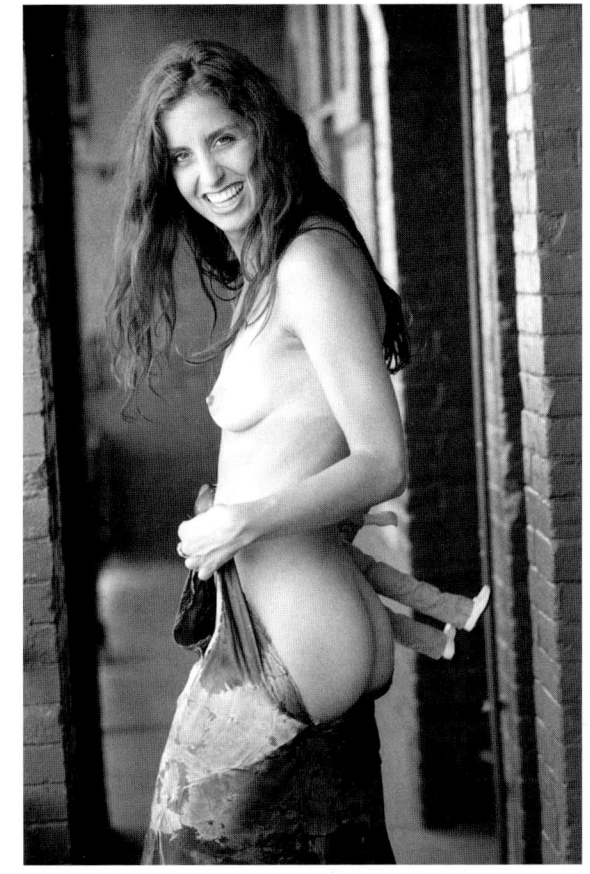

Marianne · I've know Marianne longer than anyone else in this book. I used to photograph her when she modeled in Philadelphia in the early 90's. Marianne and I have a special connection, and always seem to find each other. She loves red wine and beautiful mirrors. Marianne is a practicing Buddhist, has a baby, and frequently travels to France and India.

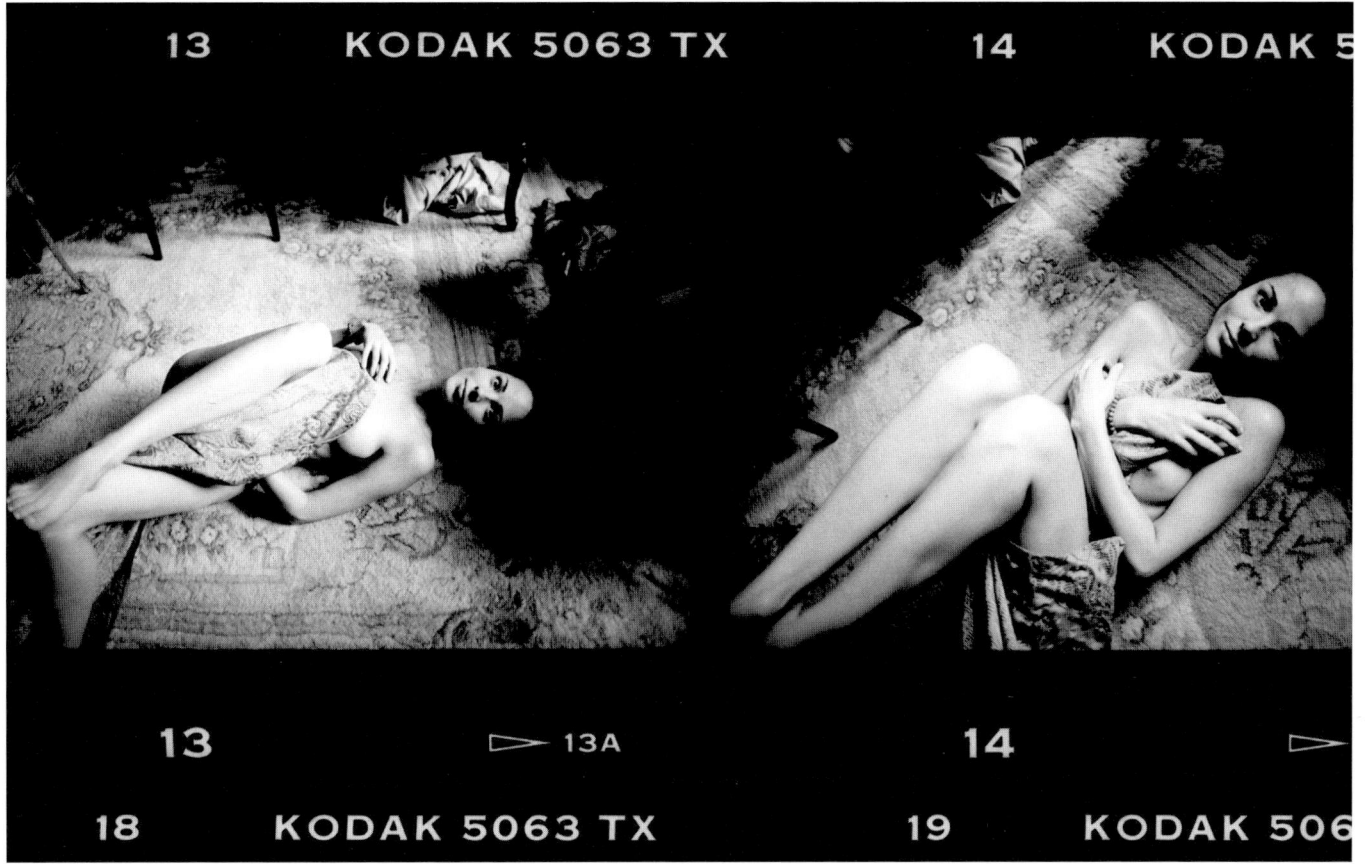

13   KODAK 5063 TX   14   KODAK 5

13   ▷ 13A   14   ▷

18   KODAK 5063 TX   19   KODAK 506

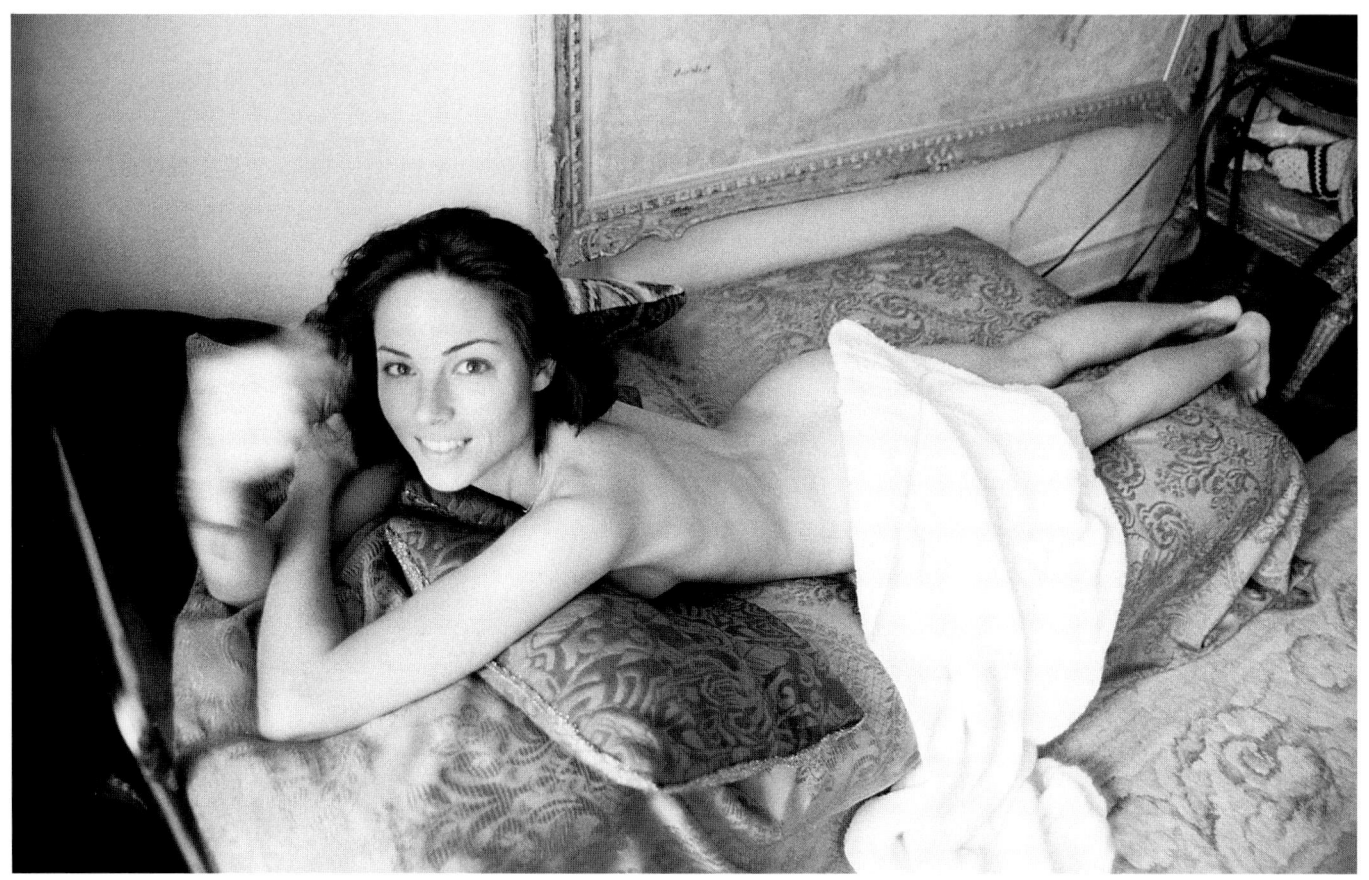

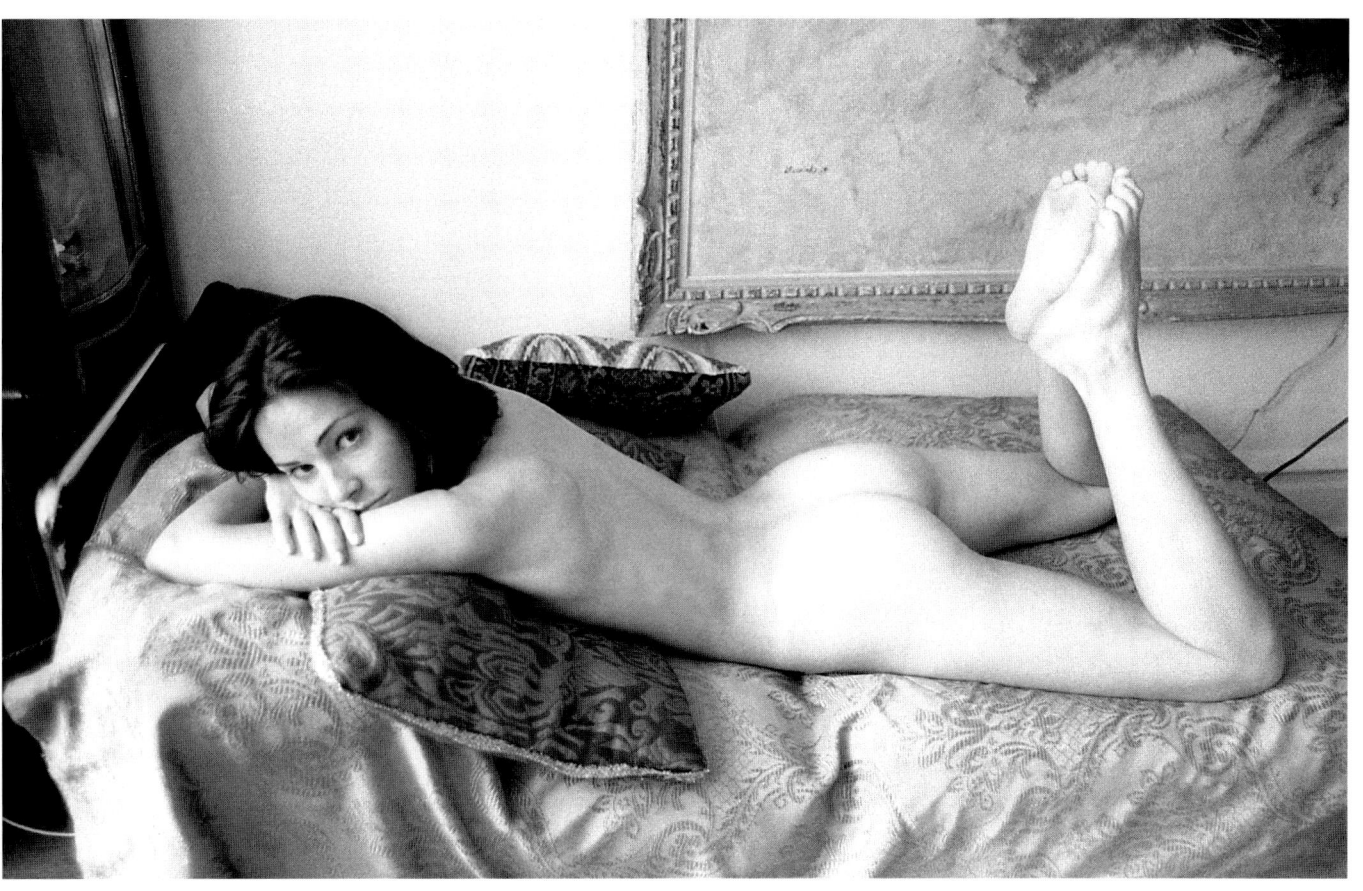

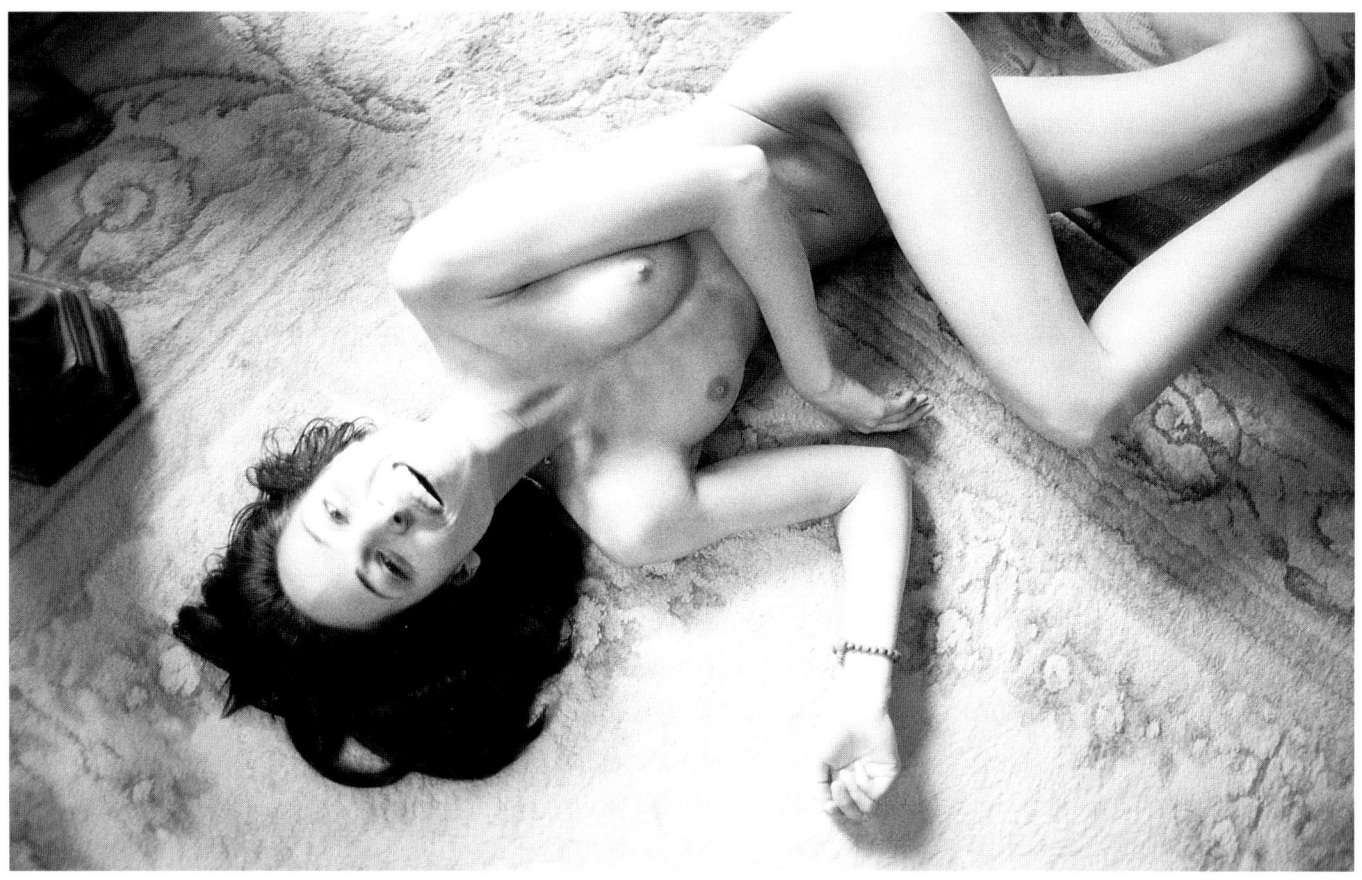

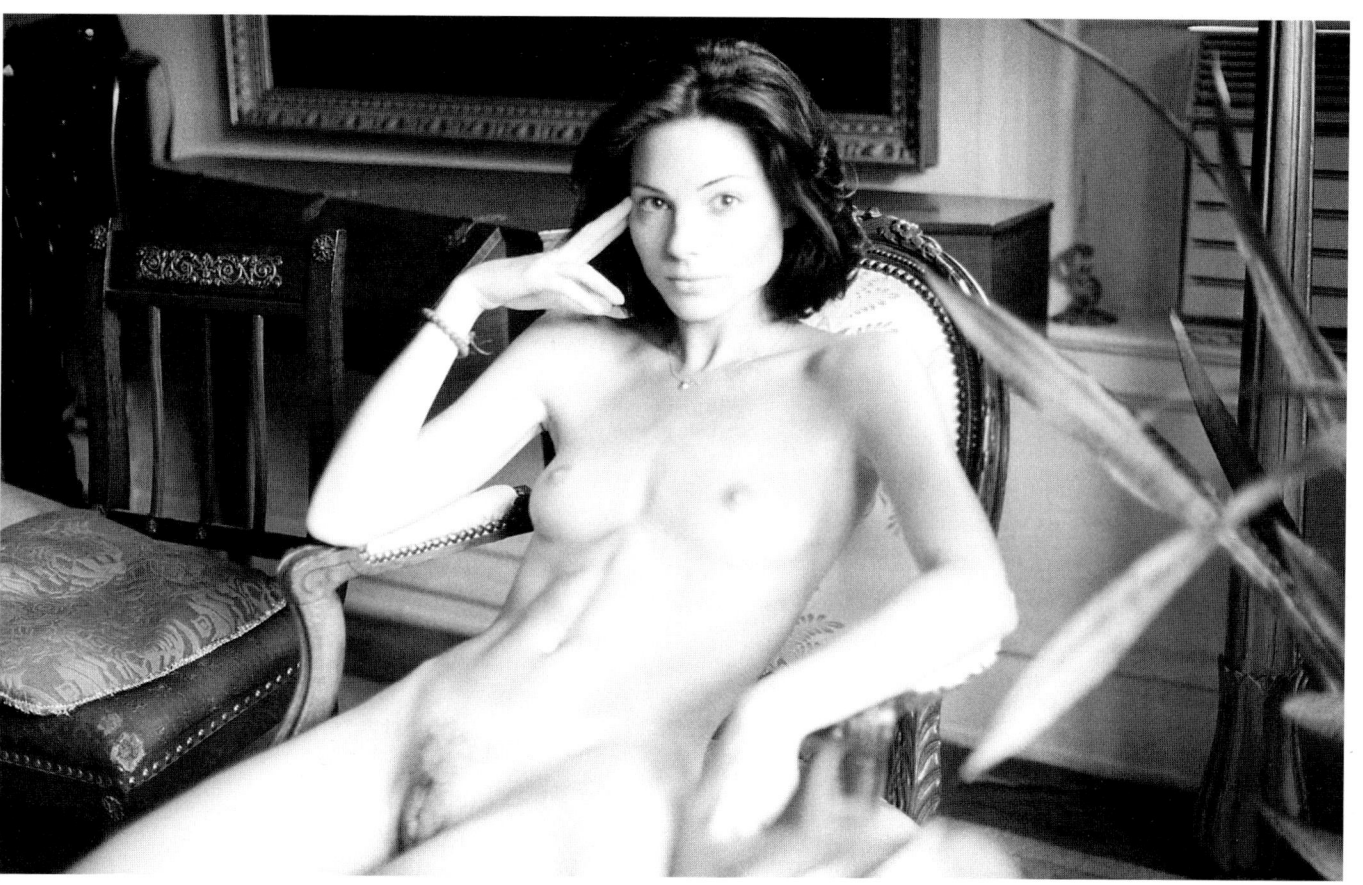

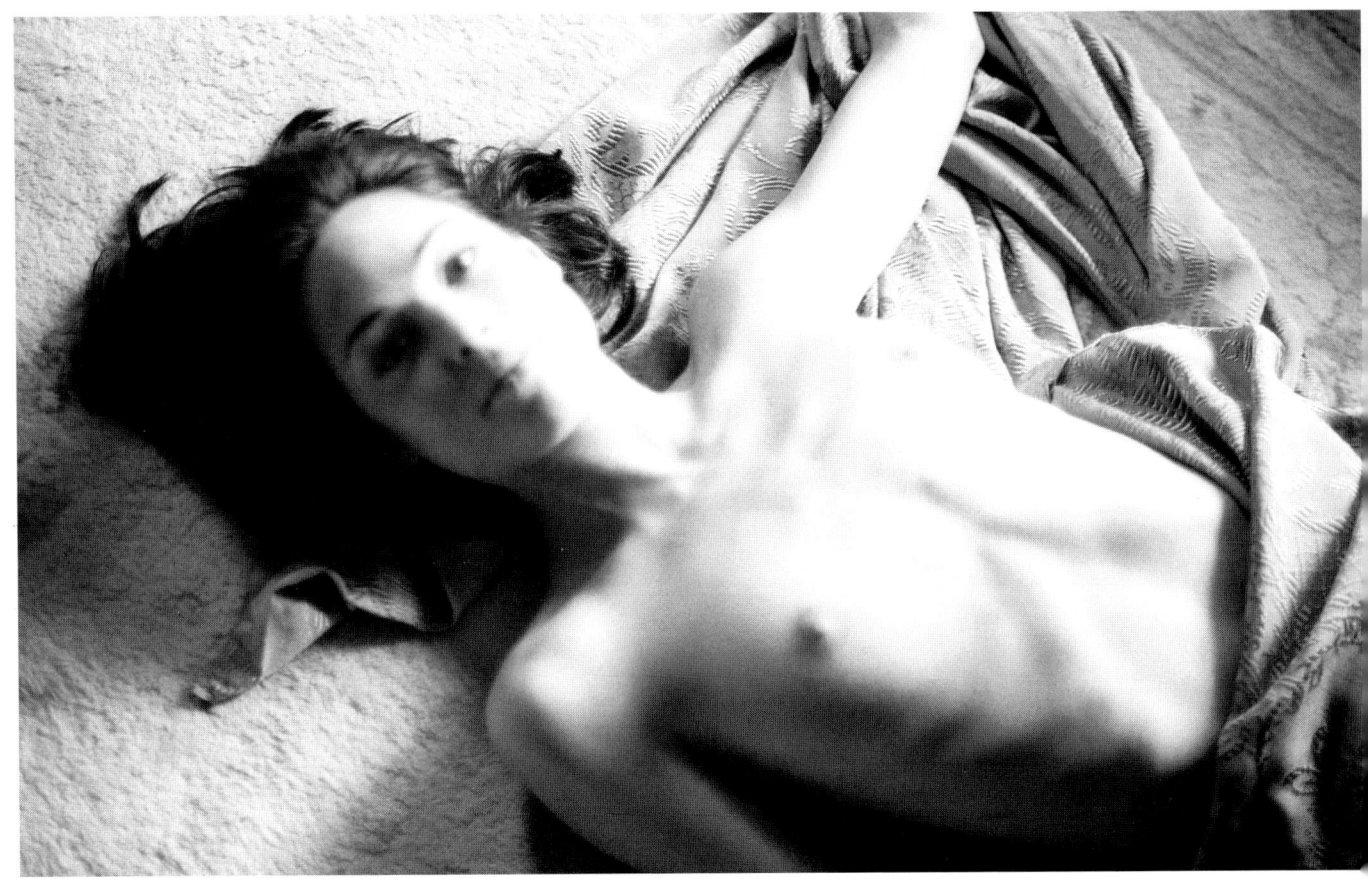

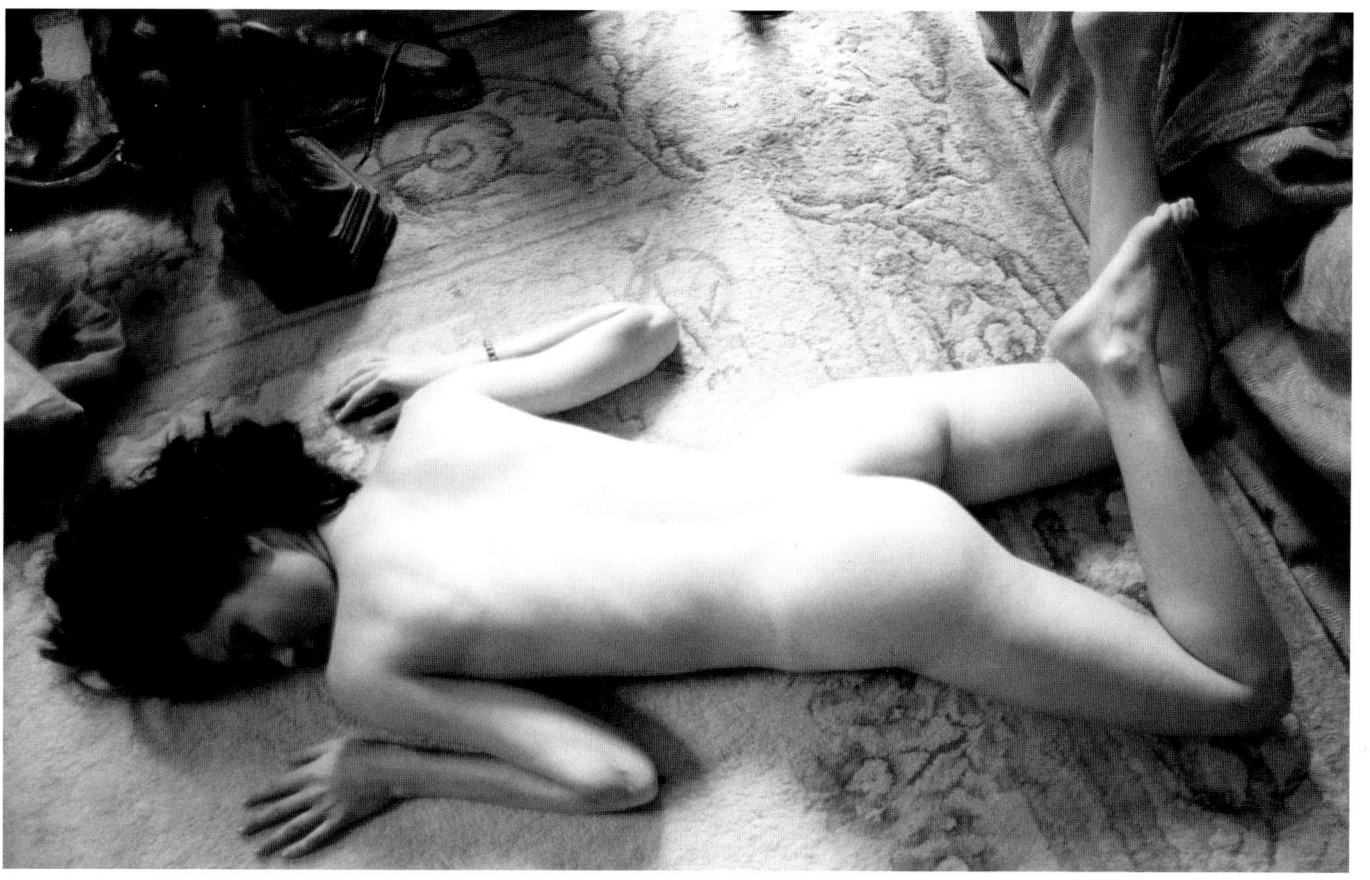

Maya · I met Maya in a bar called "Max Fish" on the lower east side of New York. She's a writer and theatre director, and currently lives in all over the U.S.A. Maya talked on the phone and rolled around a lot while I photographed her.   She has an astonishing vocabulary and one of the highest IQs I've ever encountered.

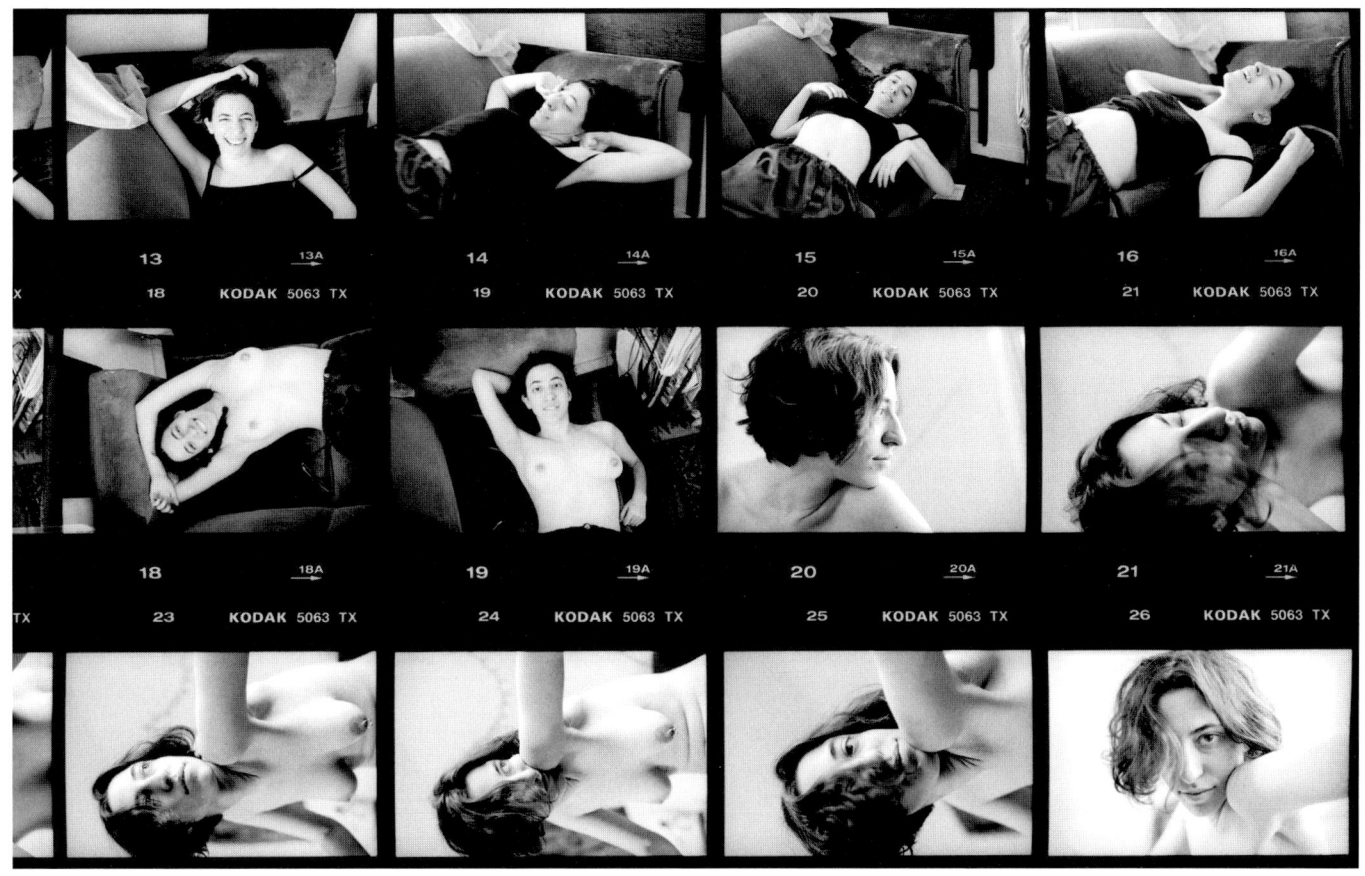

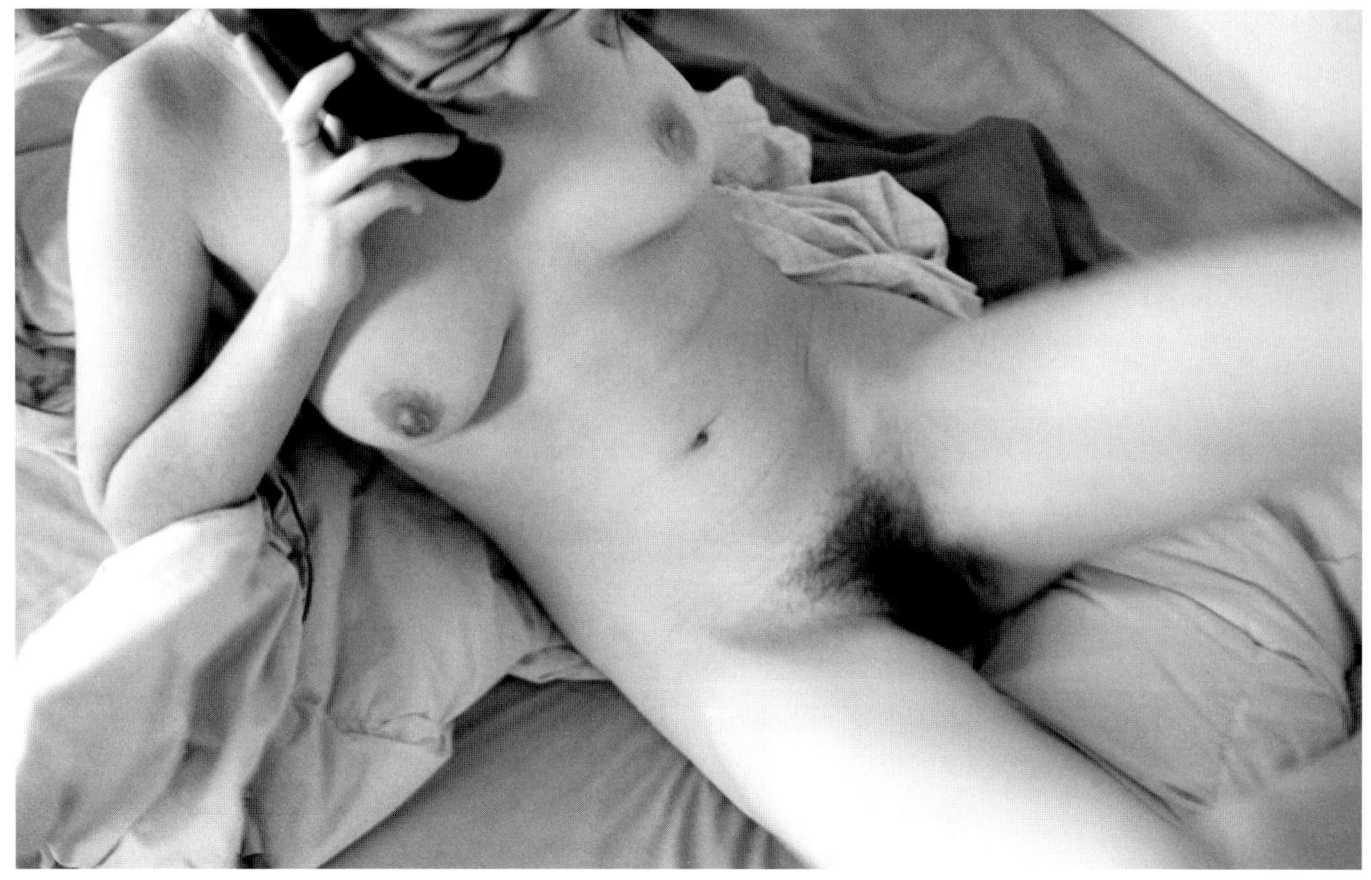

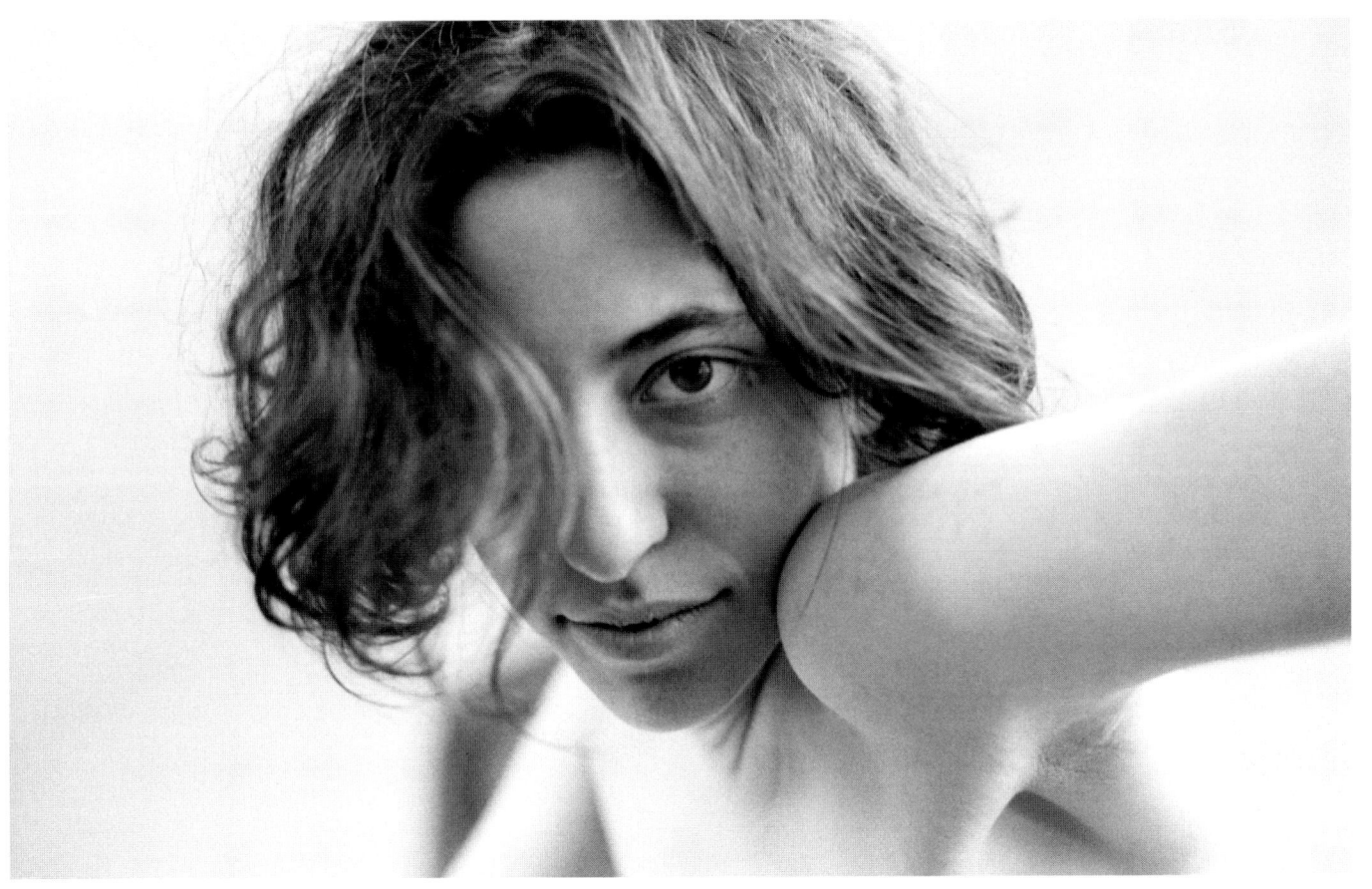

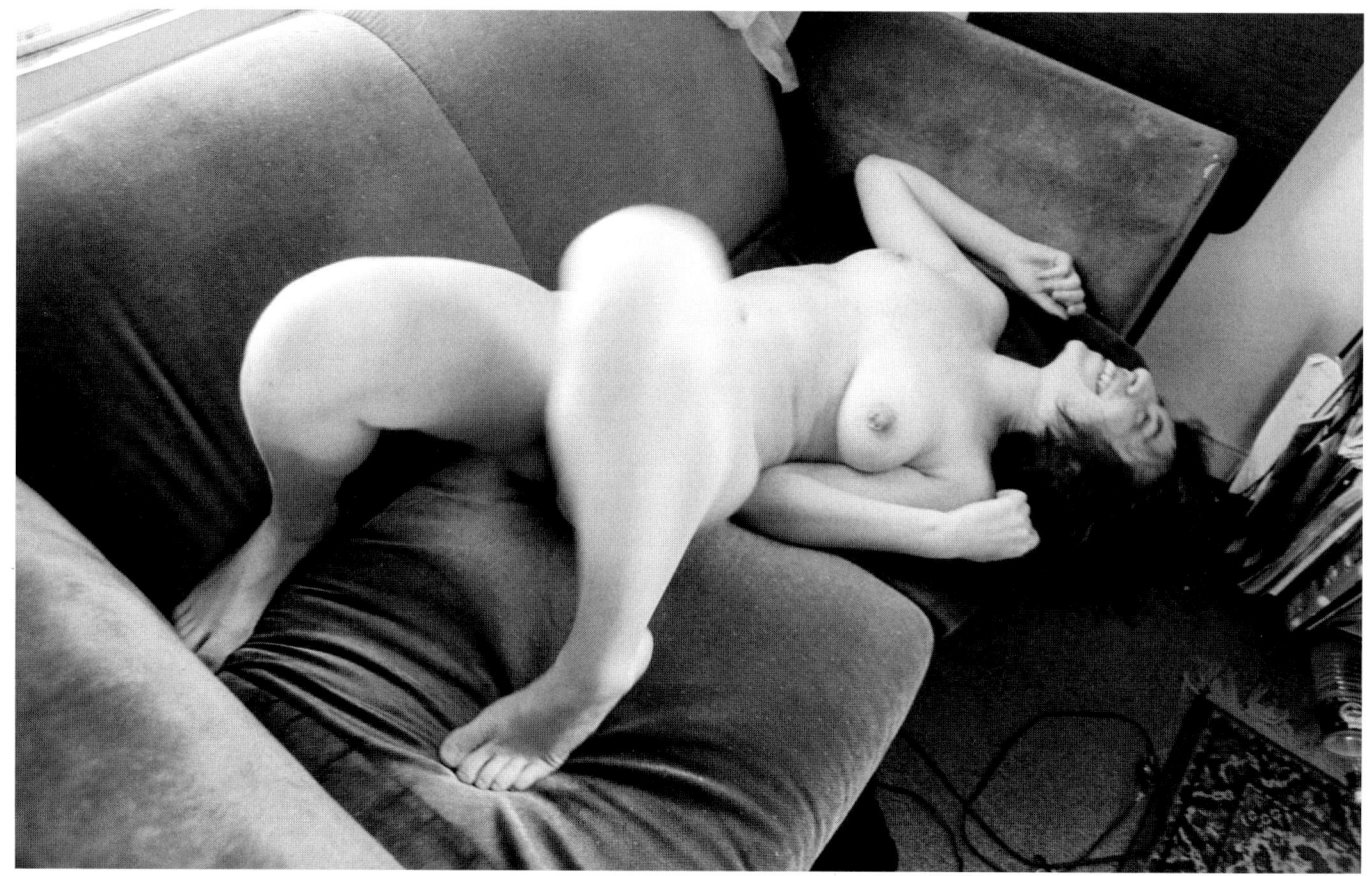

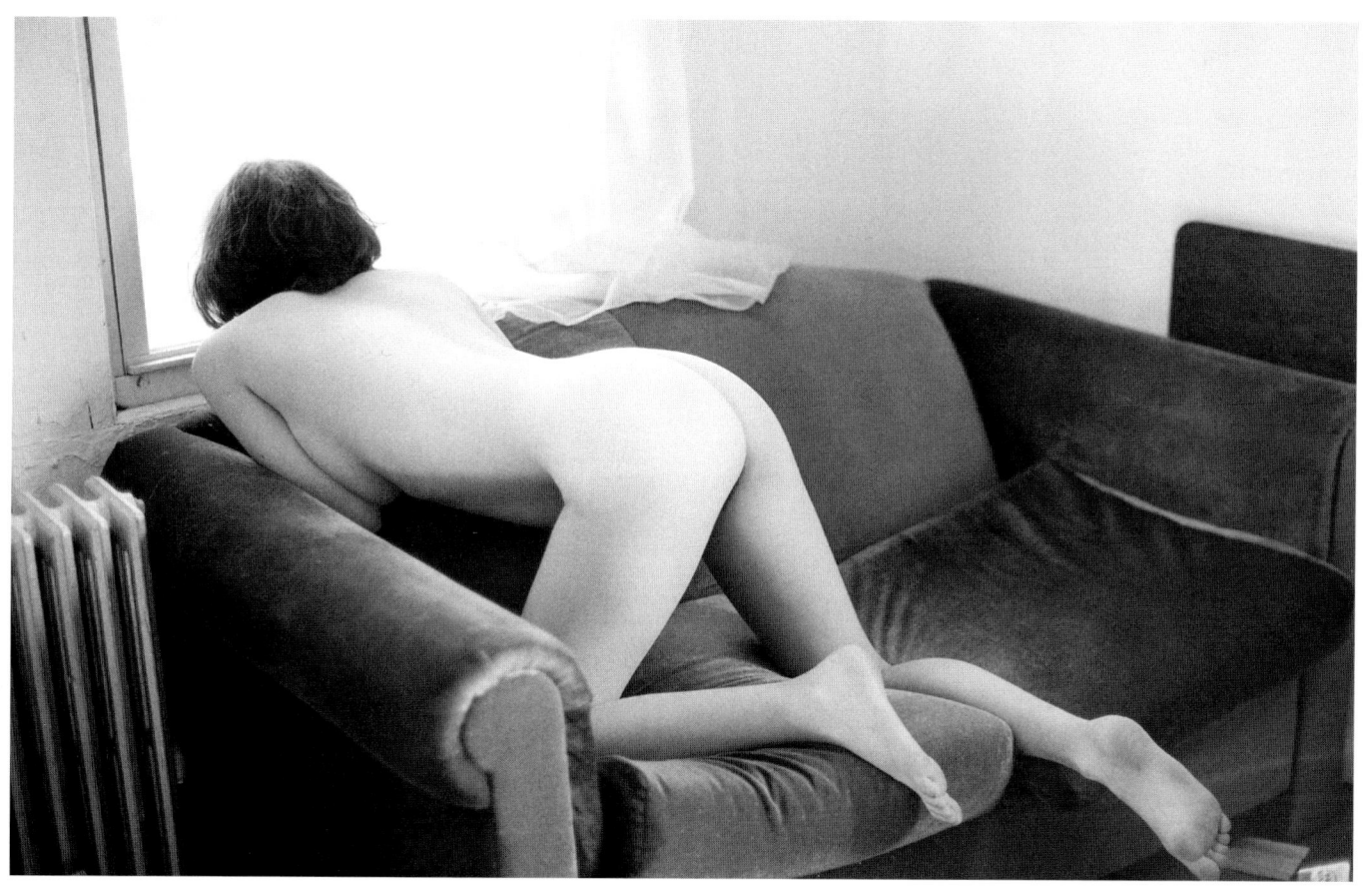

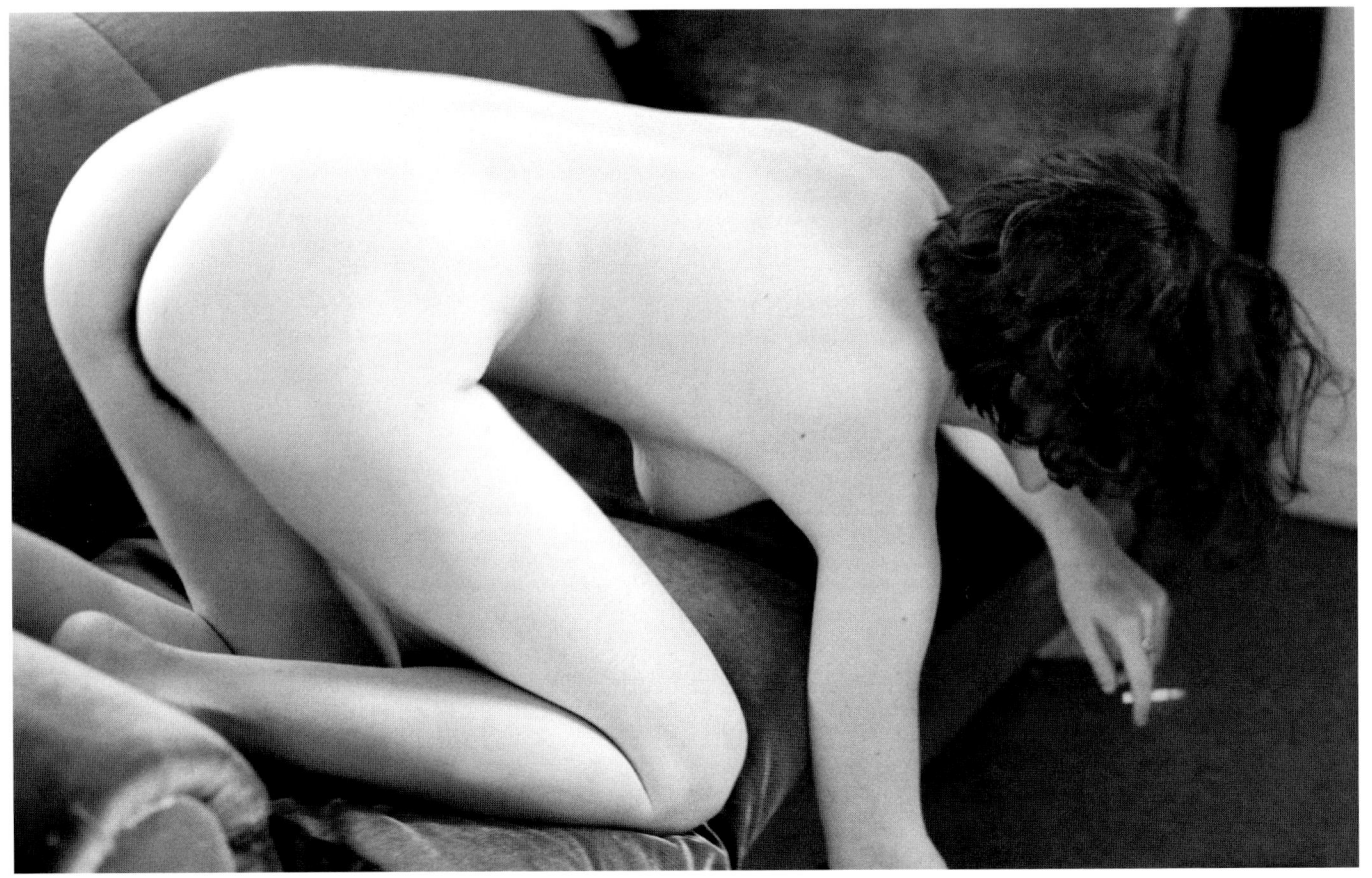

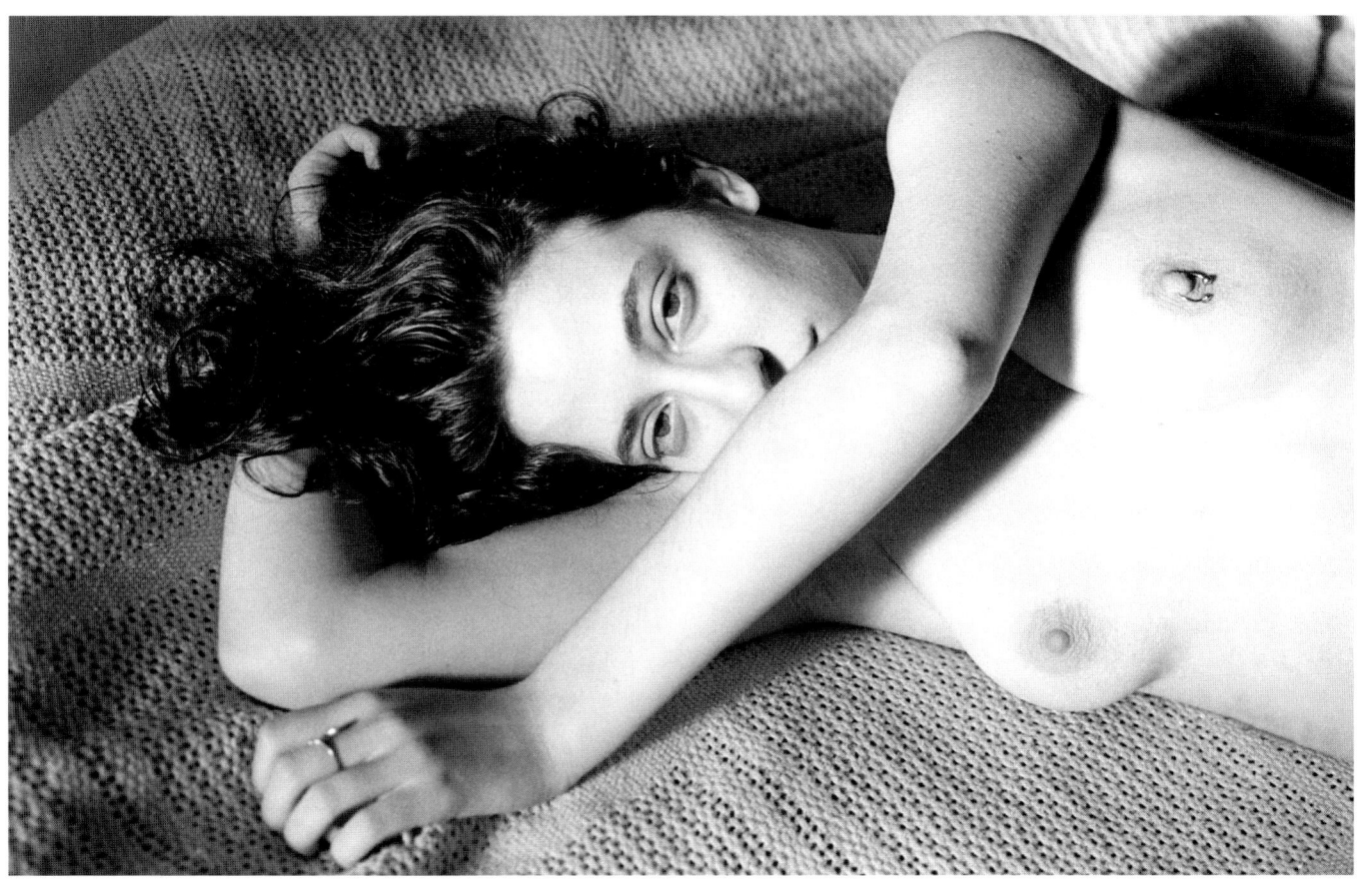

Mei · I met Mei on the Queensboro bridge. I photographed her in her east village apartment, which she shared with three cats and four roommates. Mei and I played upstairs and downstairs and out on her balcony, even though it was March. She has beautiful brown skin and hand rolled her own cigarettes.

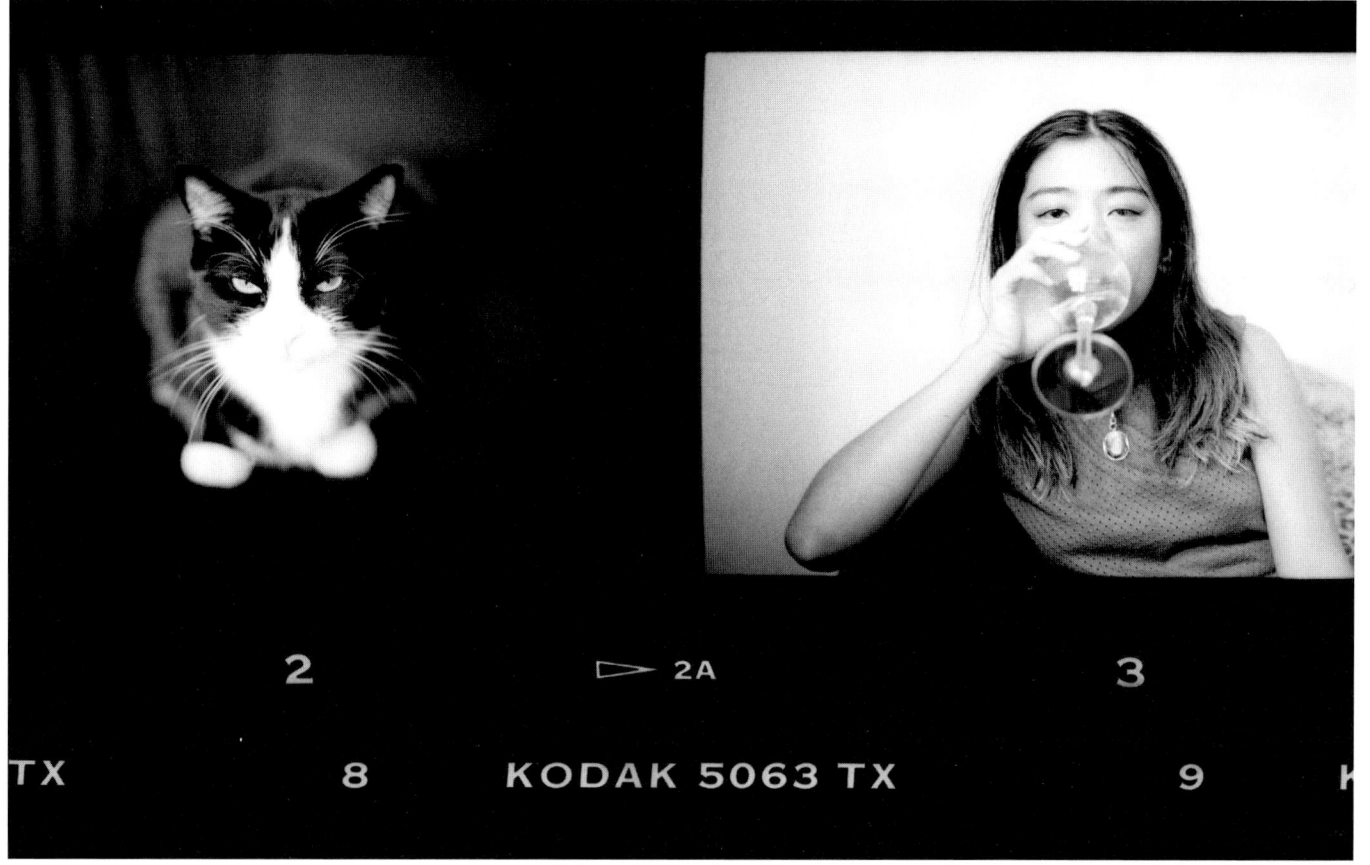

2   ▷ 2A   3

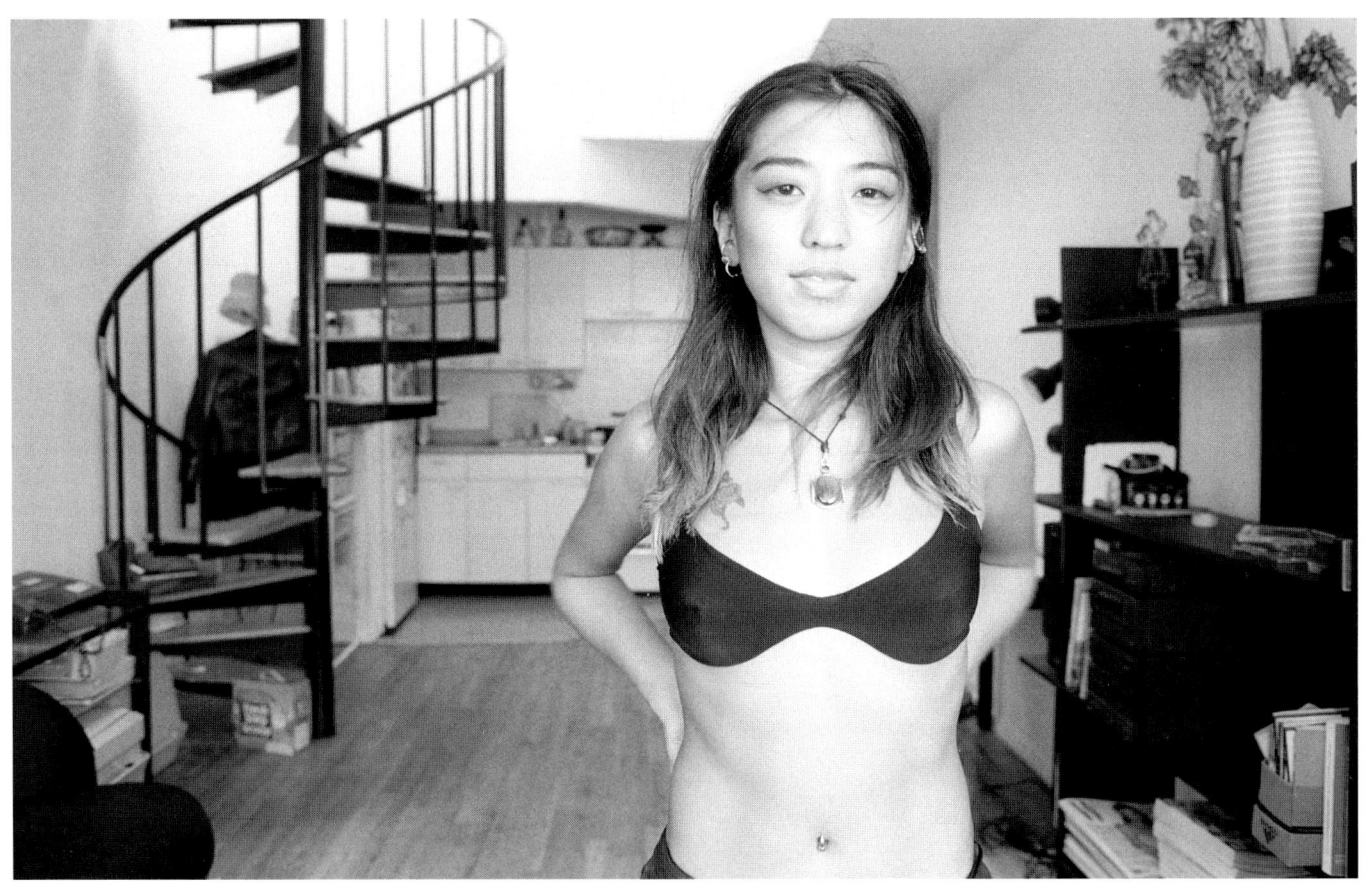

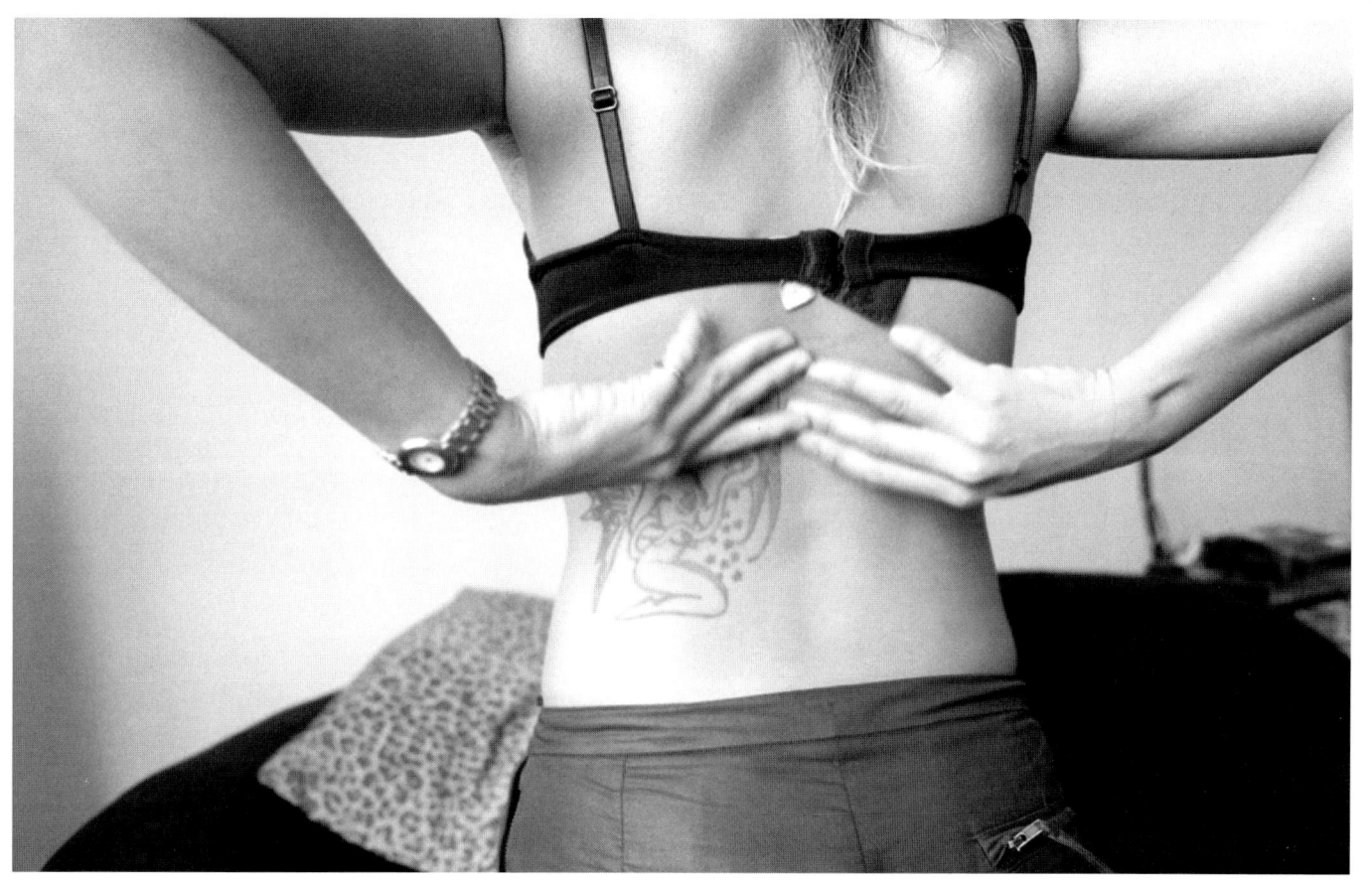

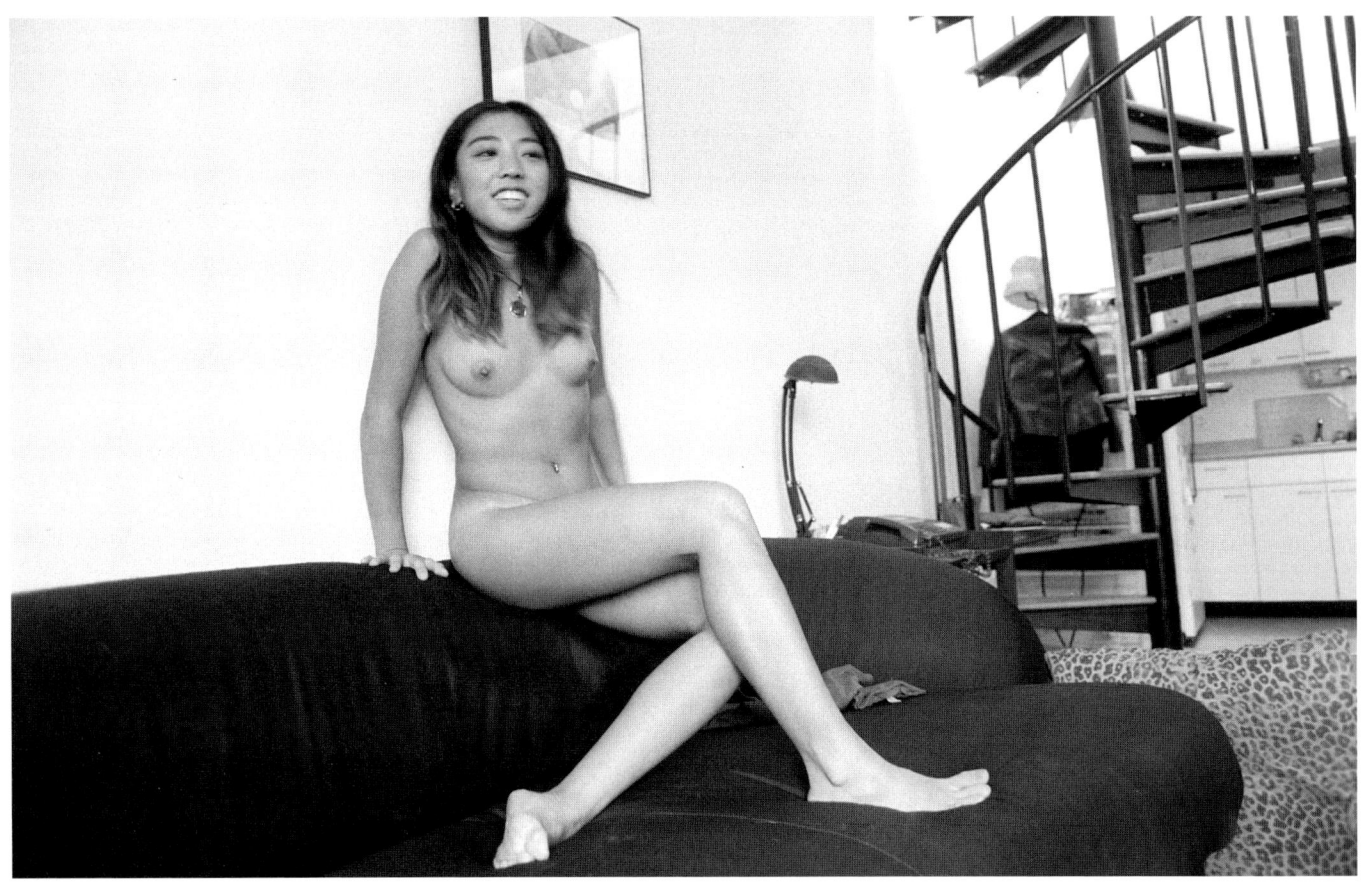

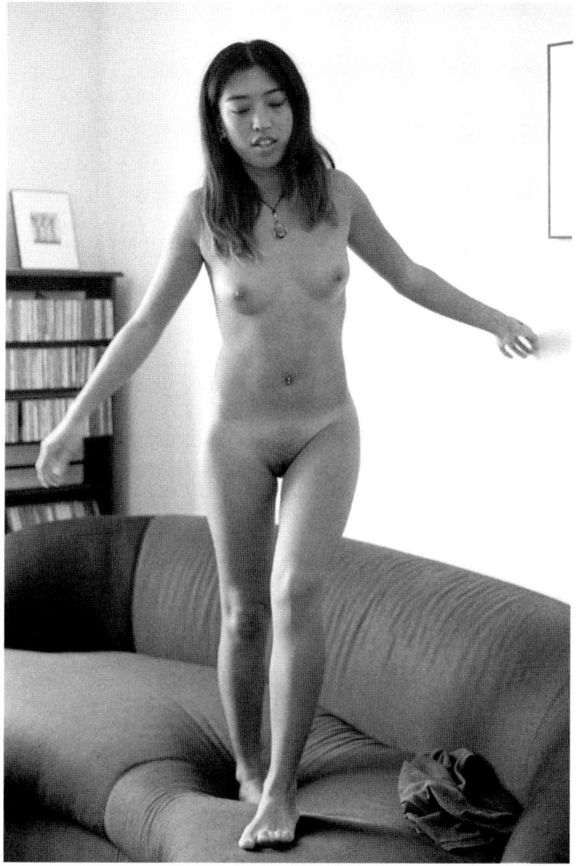

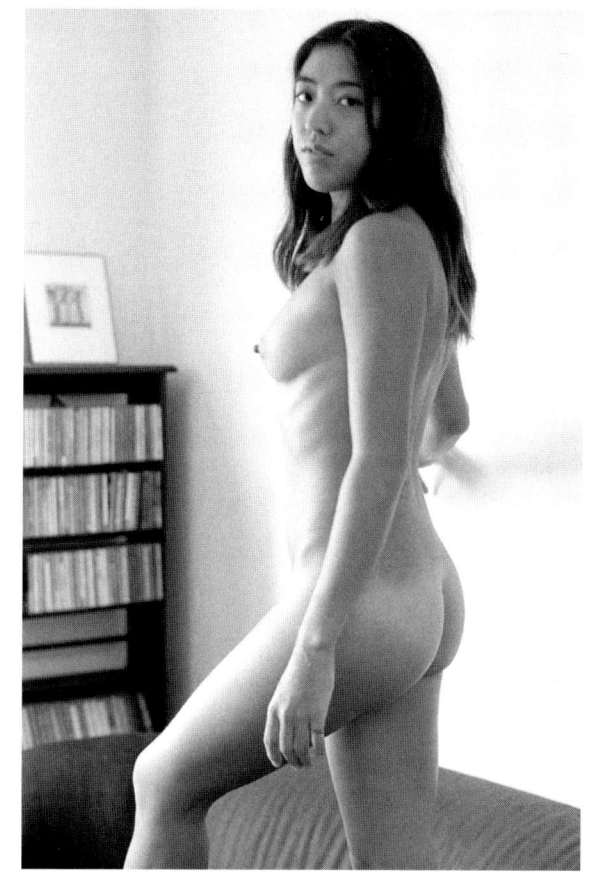

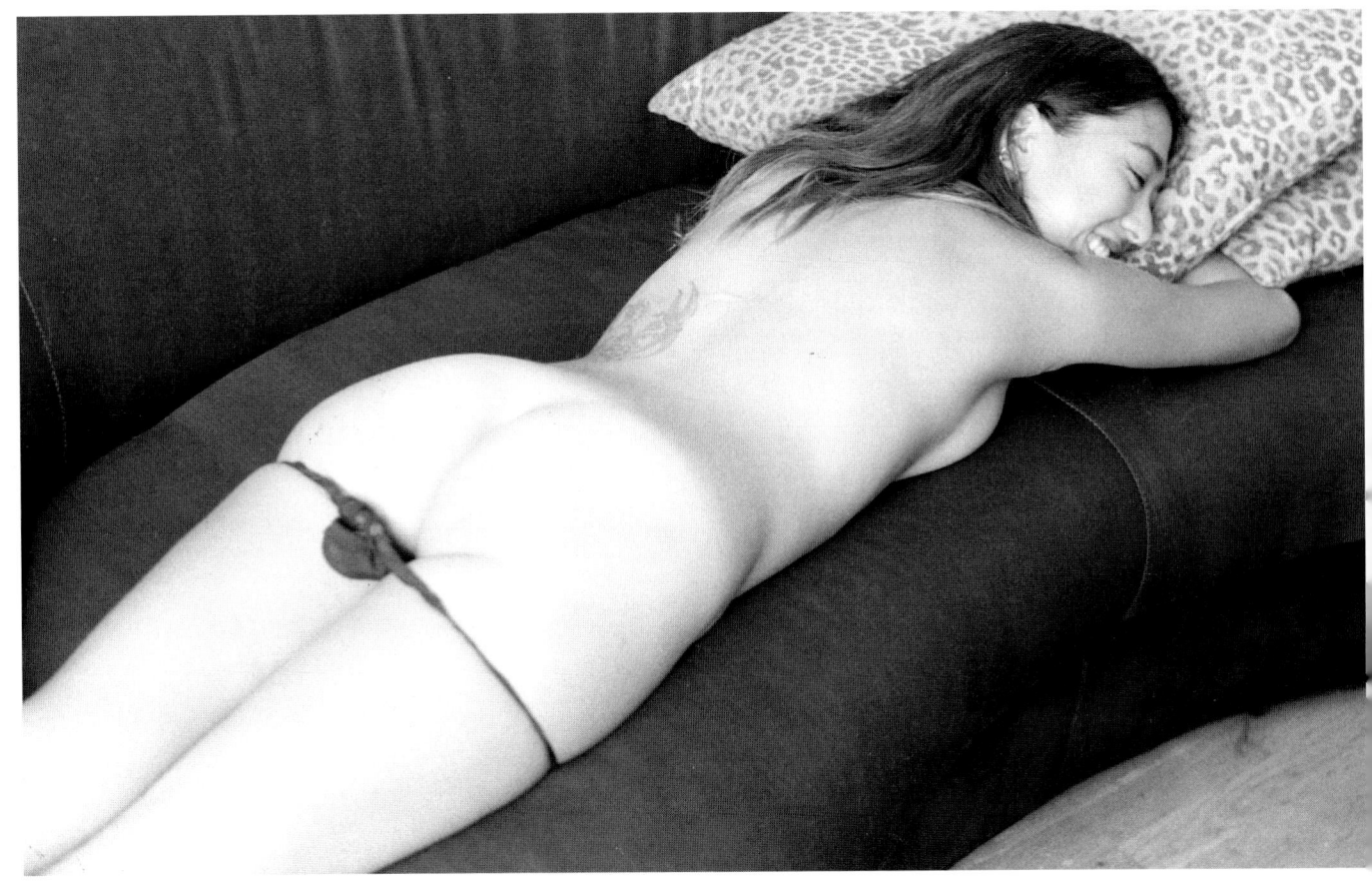

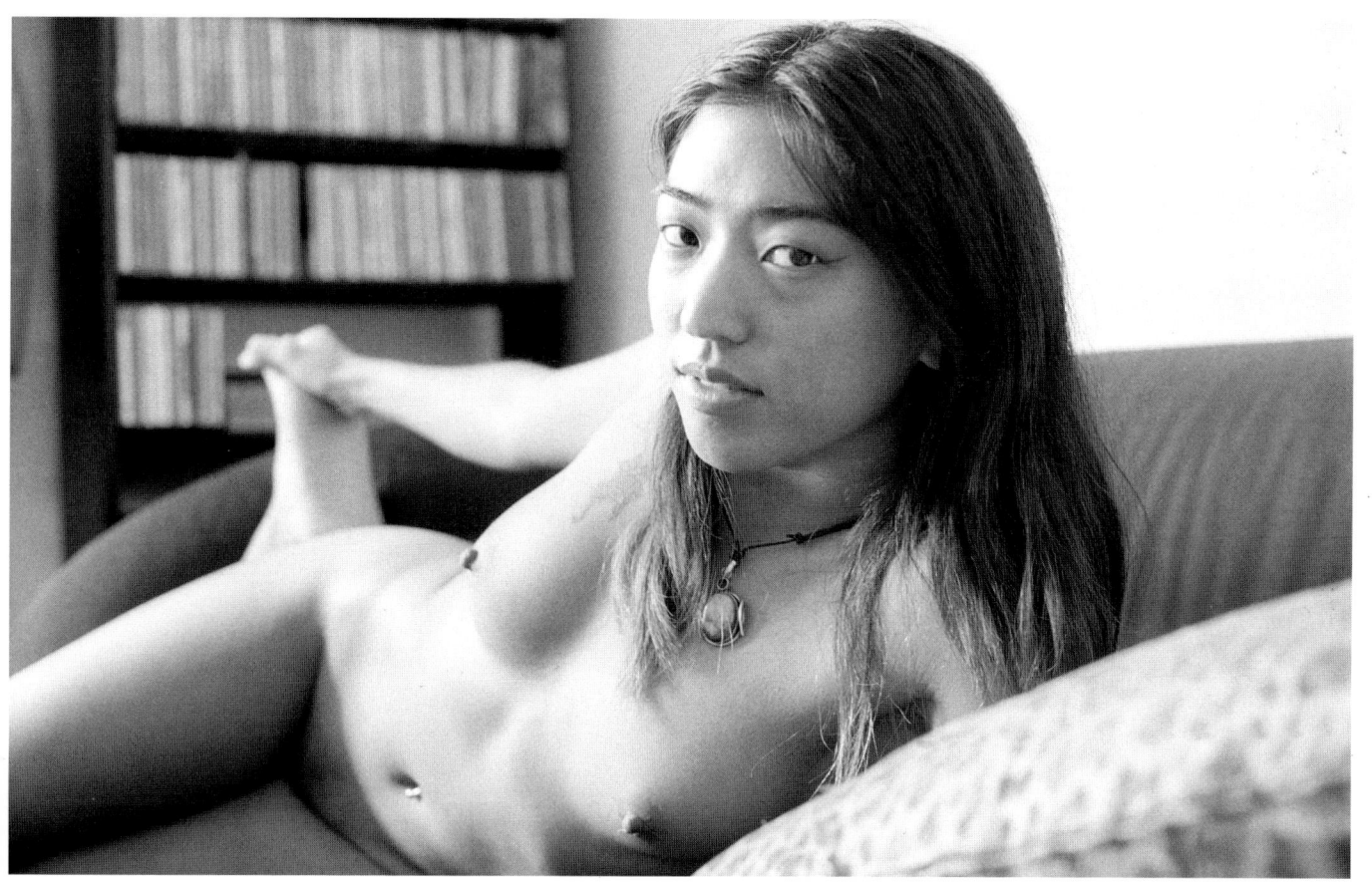

Michal · I met Michal when I was asked to film a play that she was performing in. I fell in love with her hair, and ended up dating her for a few weeks. I photographed her in a friend's apartment in the west village. Michal was kind and considerate, with a very warm heart. She currently lives in Israel with a husband and child.

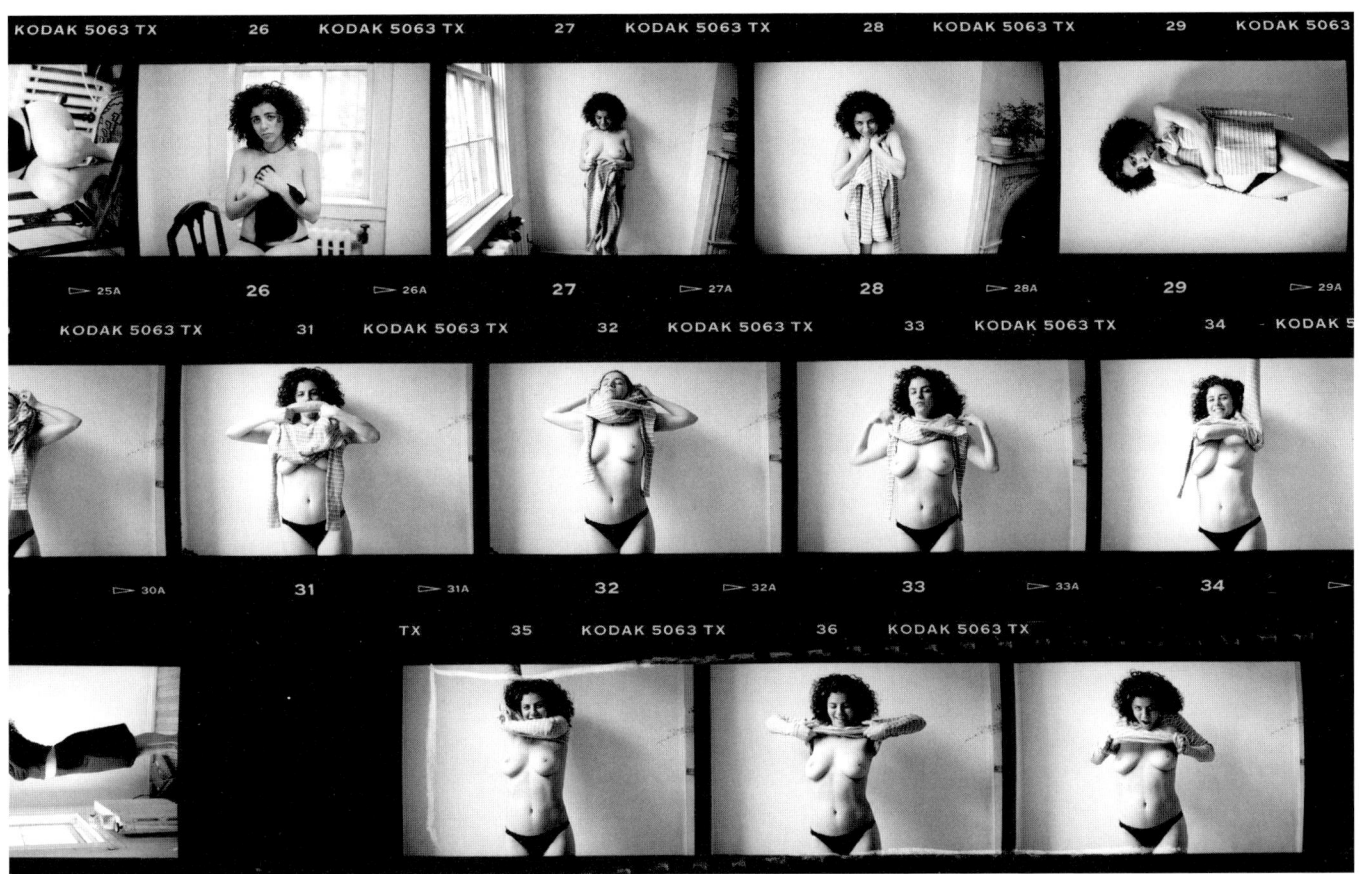

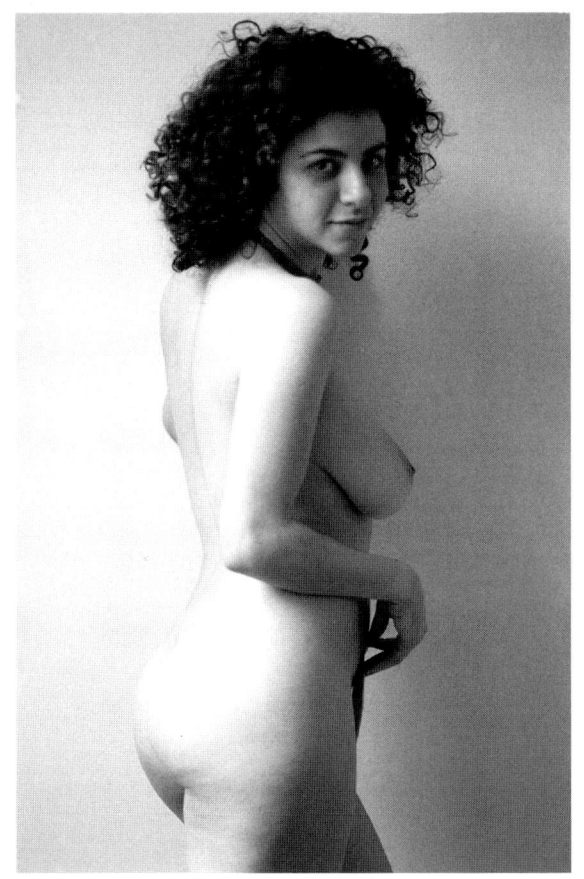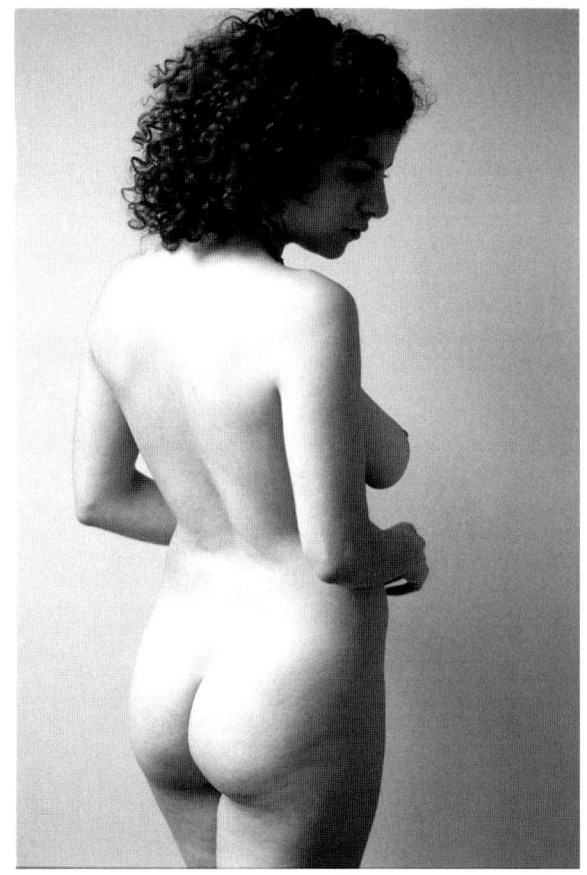

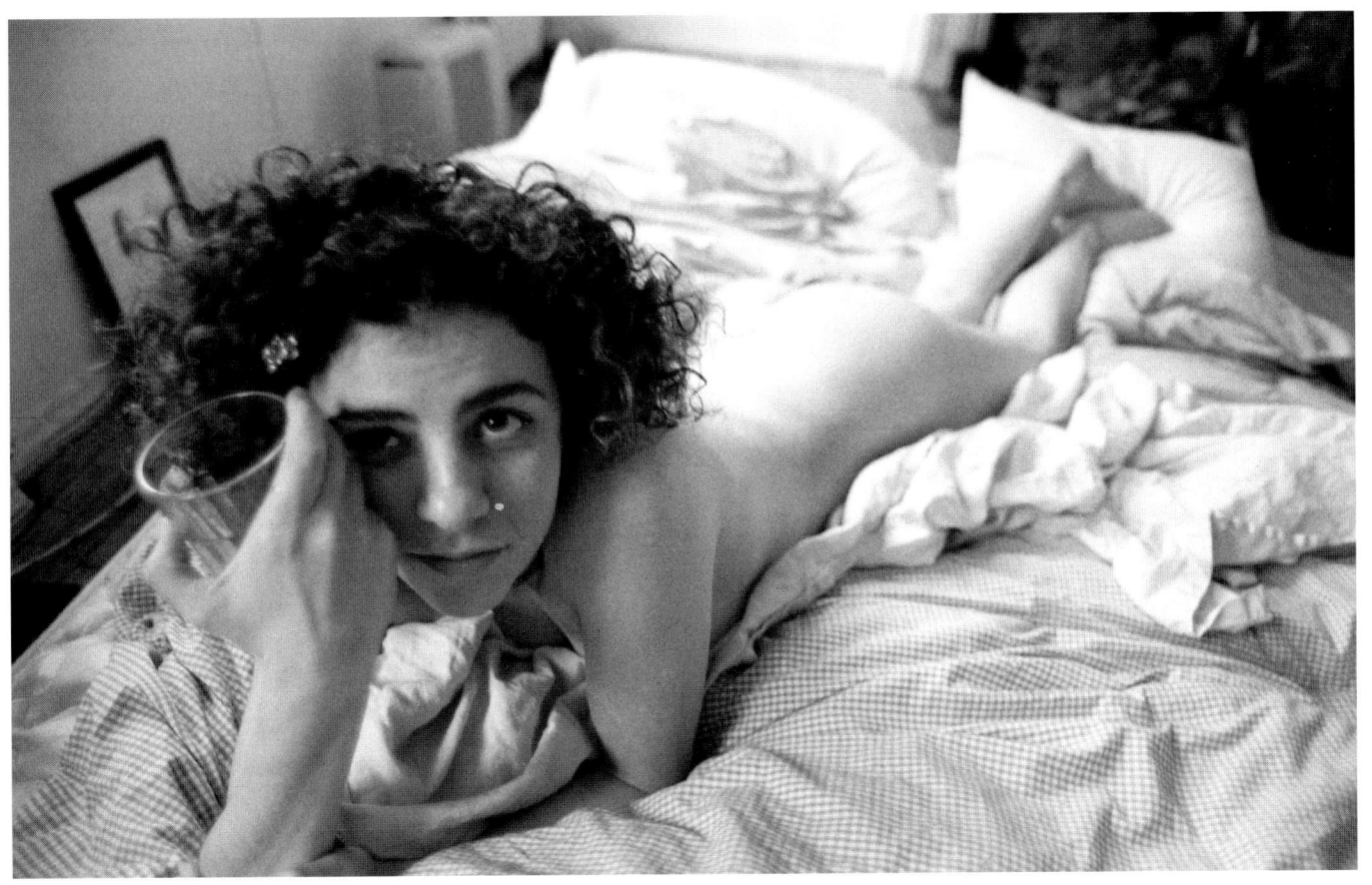

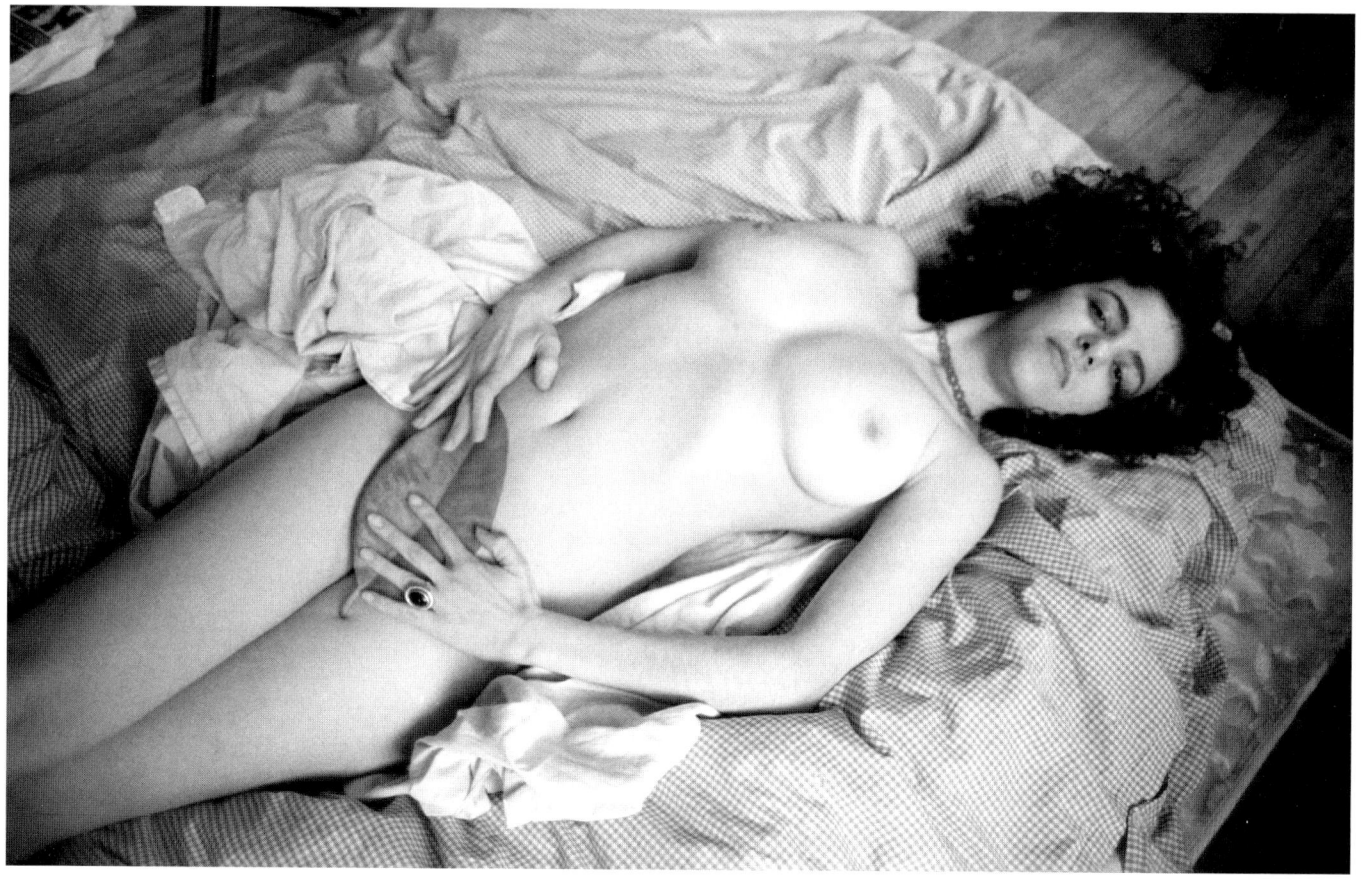

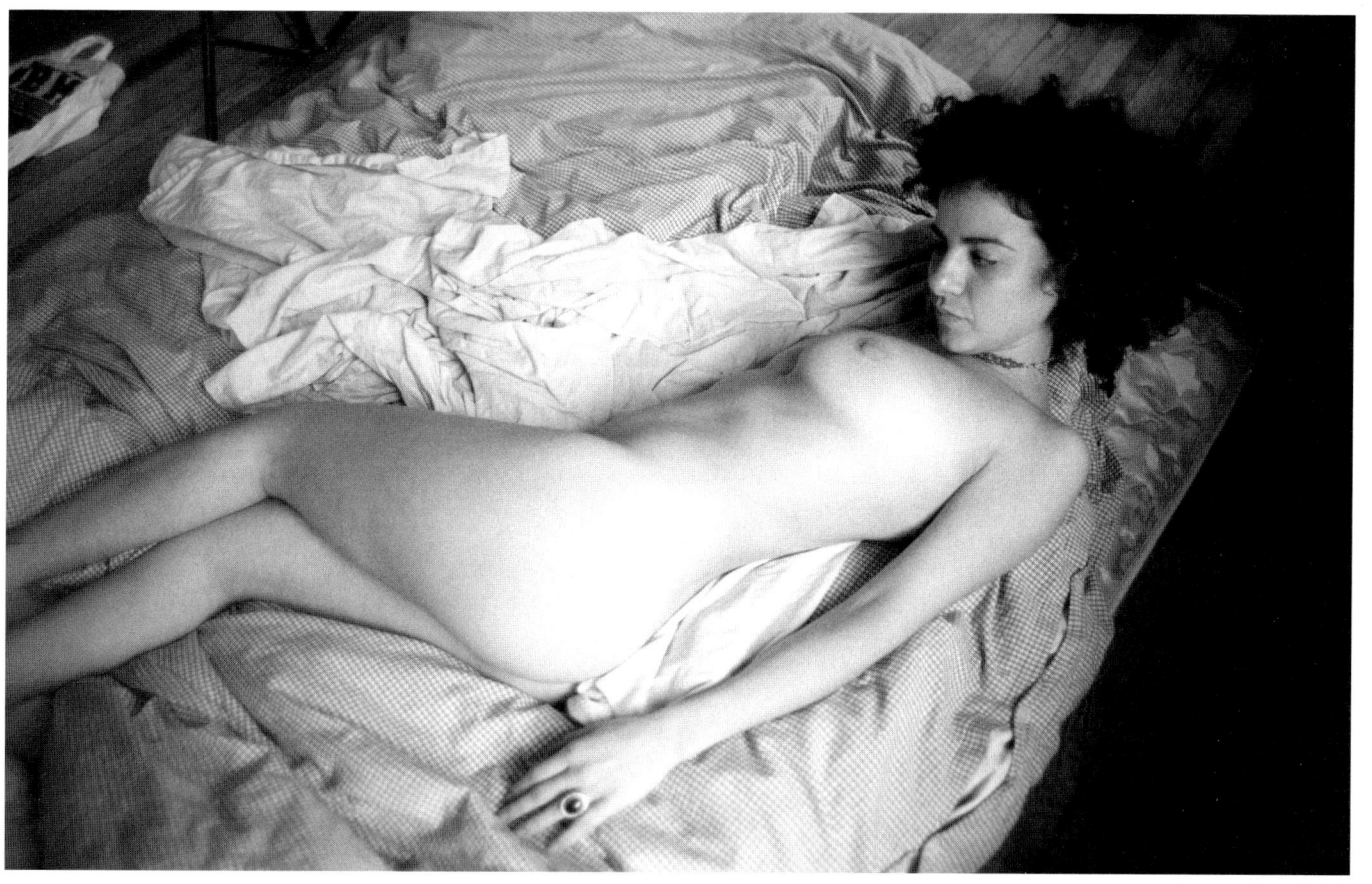

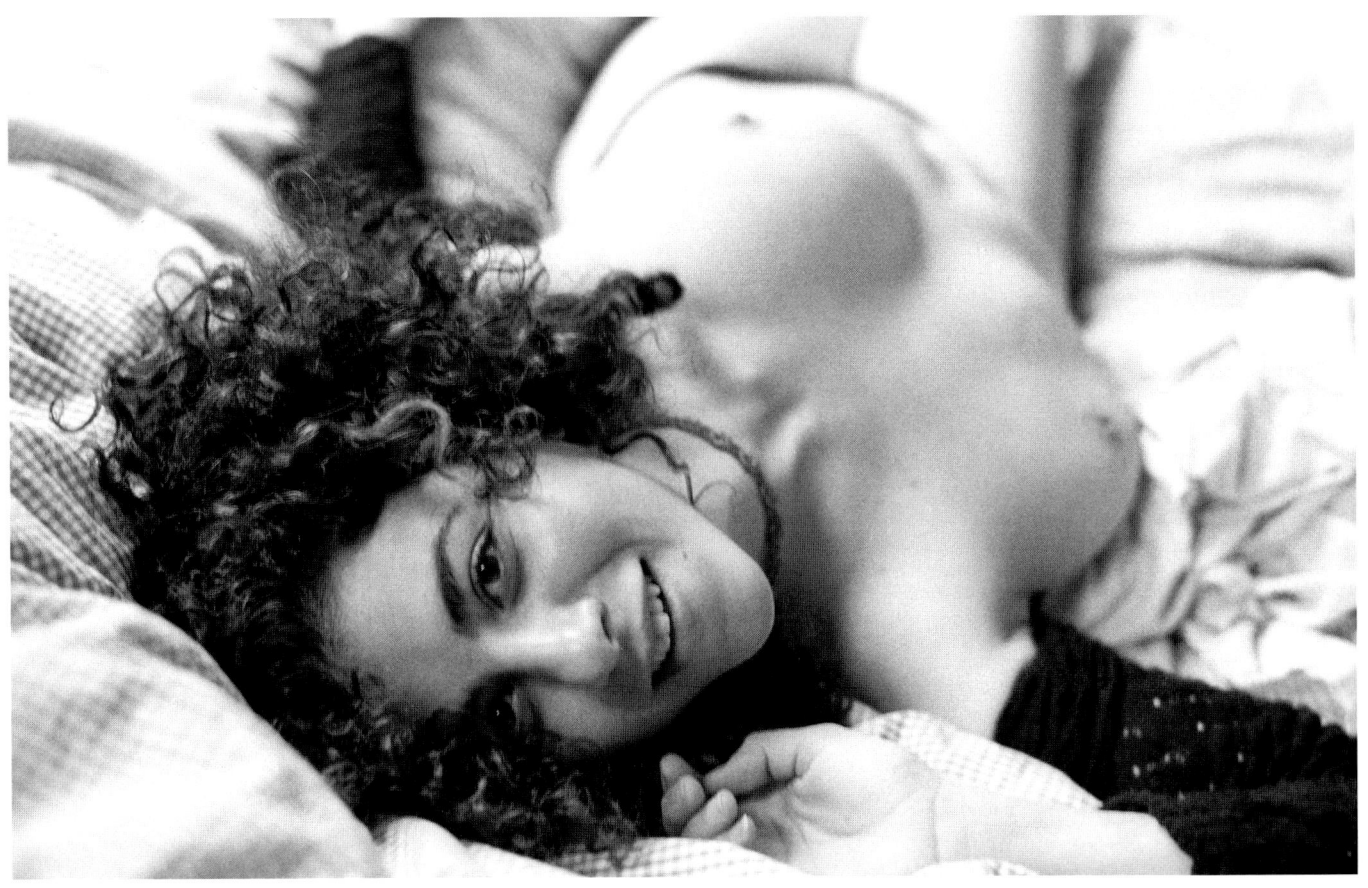

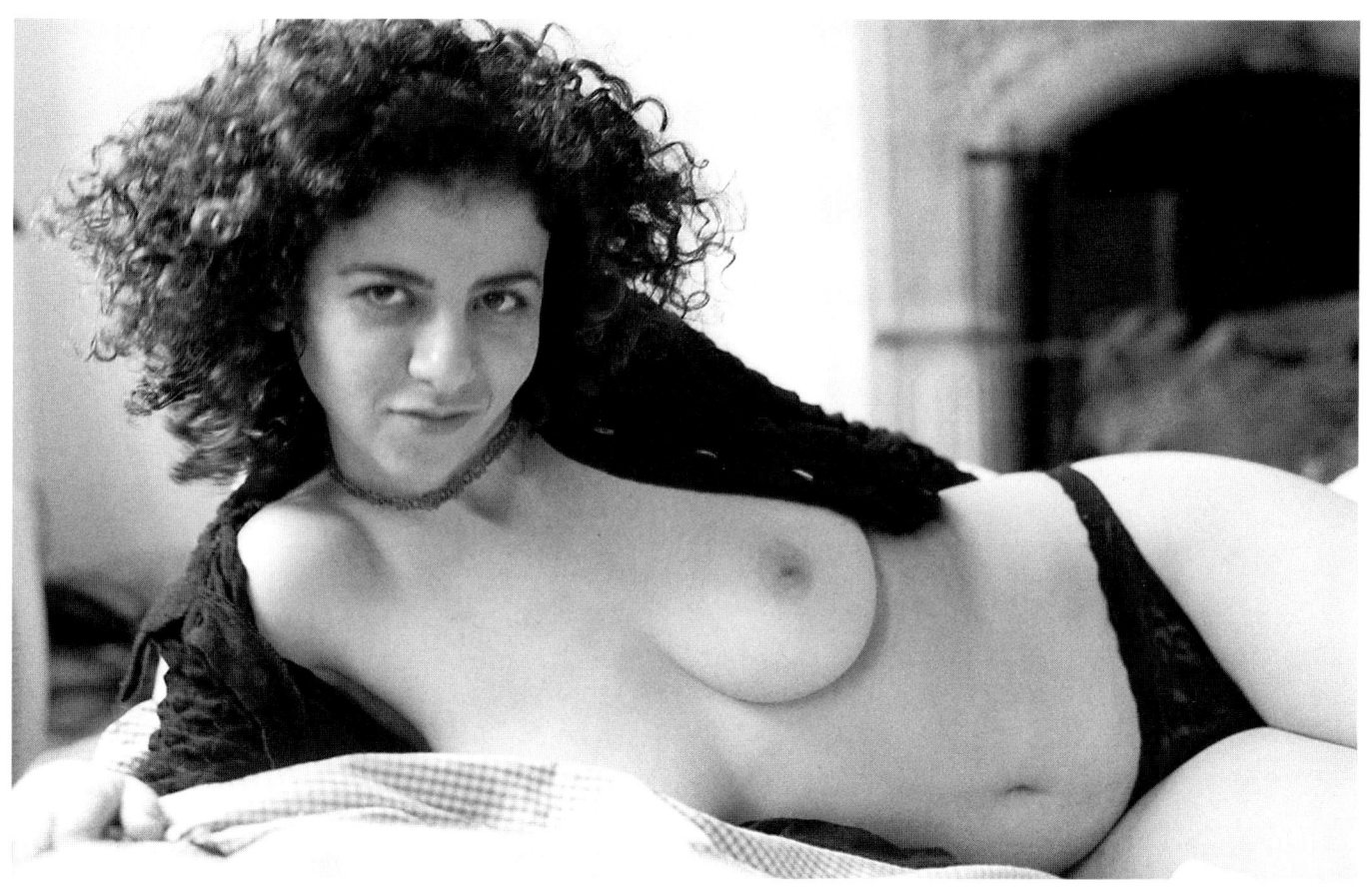

Ruby · I met Ruby on Broadway in SOHO. She had a strong, playful personality, with a bit of sarcasm. I photographed her in her mother's Harlem apartment where she grew up. Ruby had great curly hair, was very expressive, and told me she was happy to be a muse for an artist. I liked that.

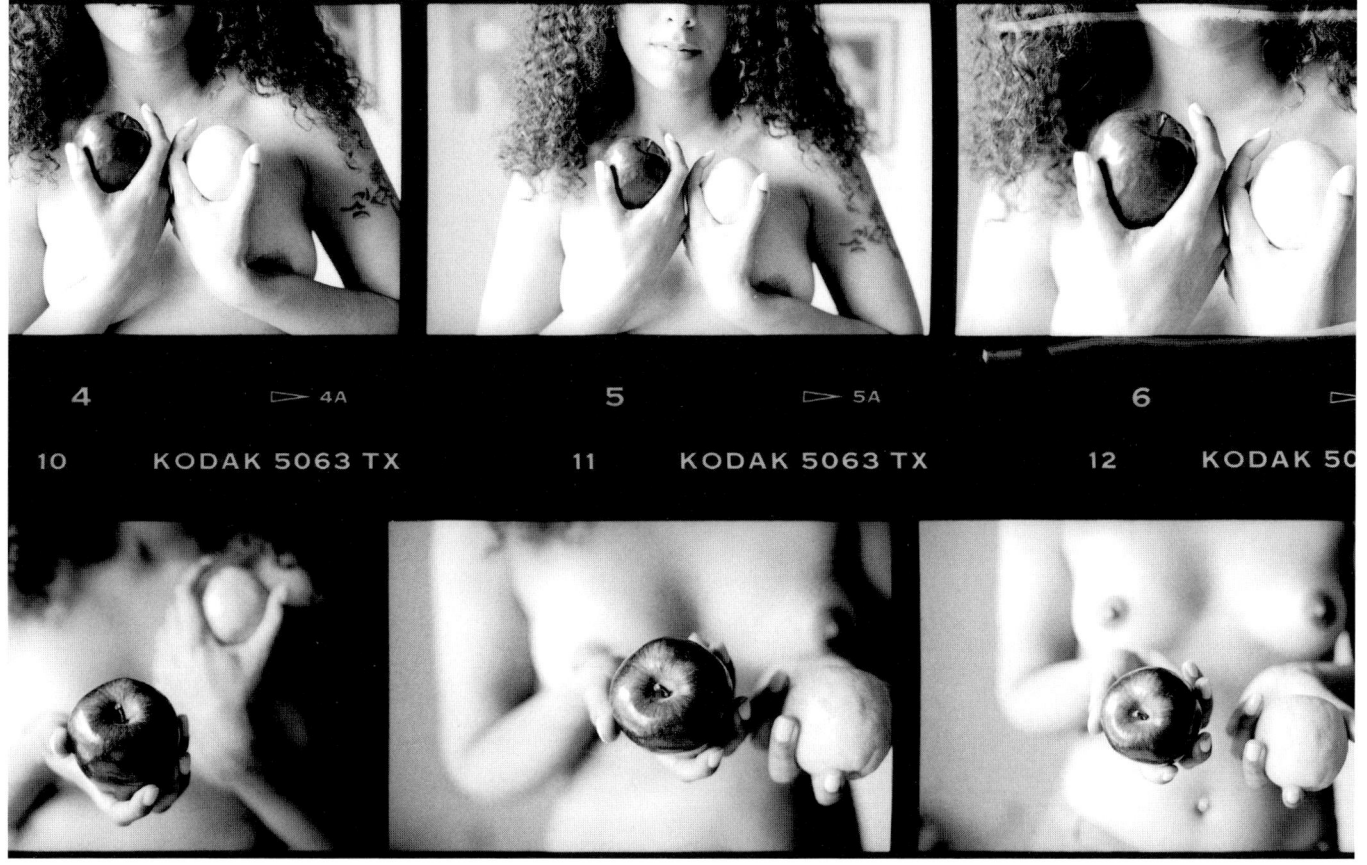

KODAK 5063 TX

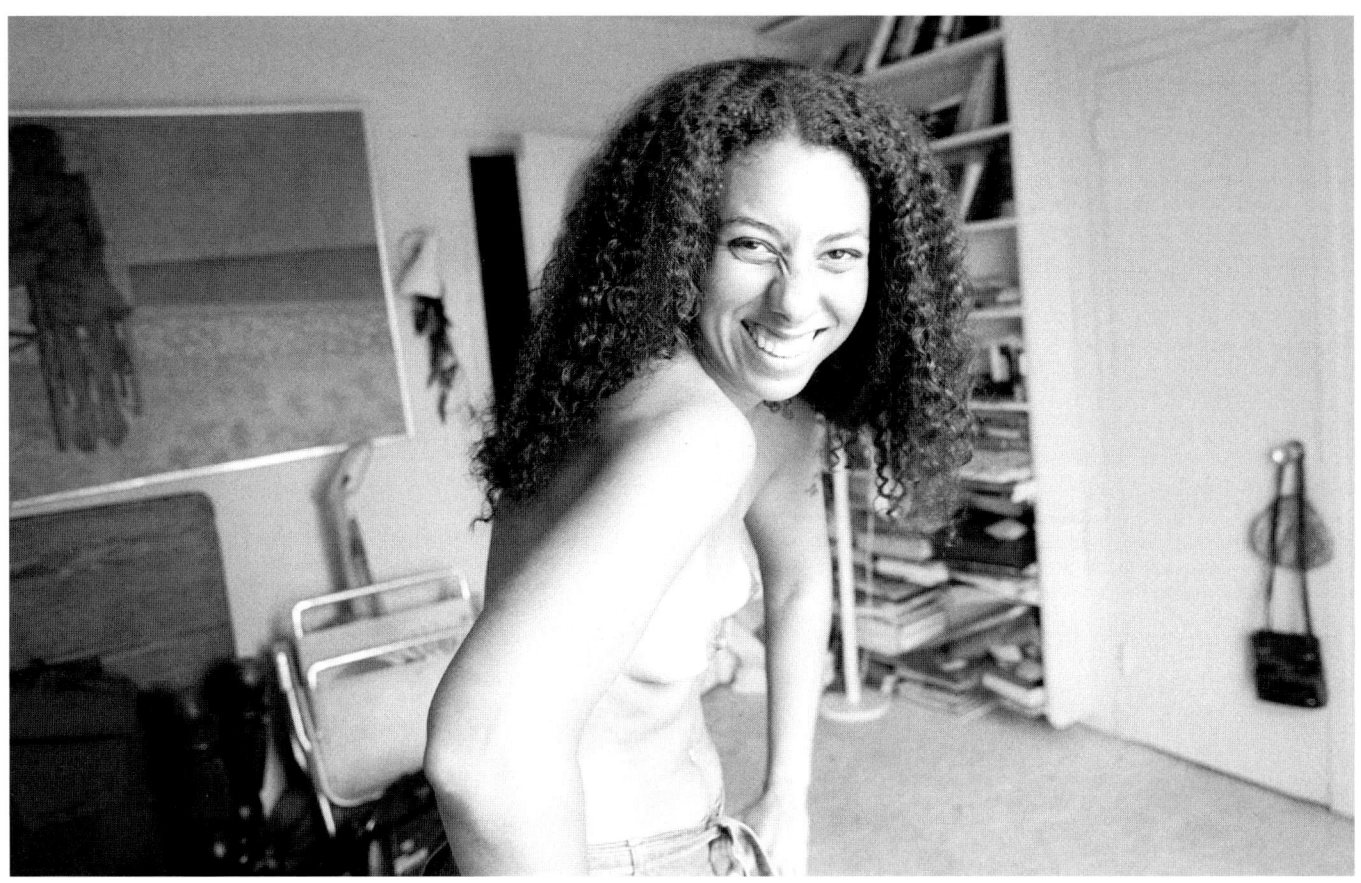

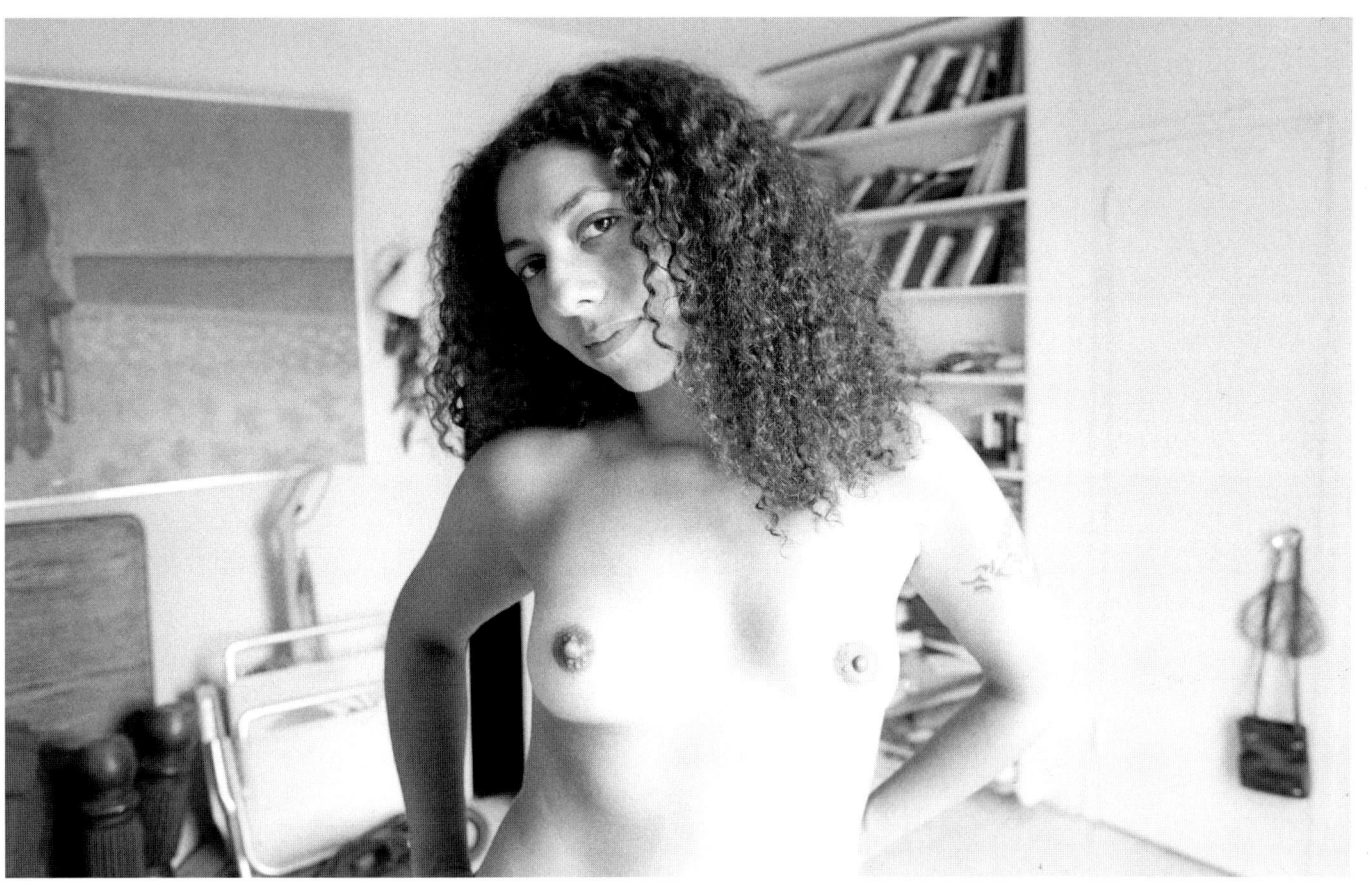

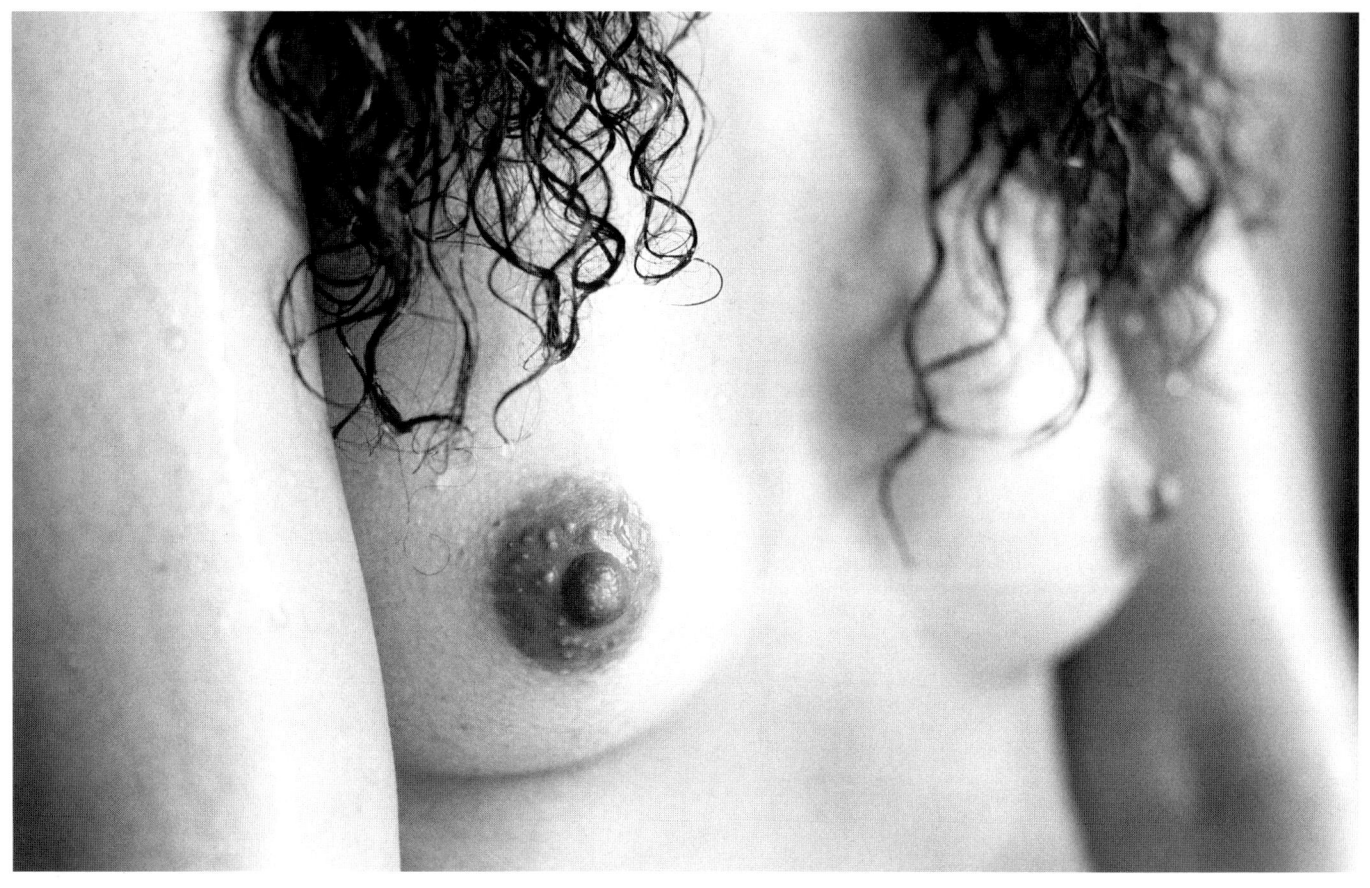

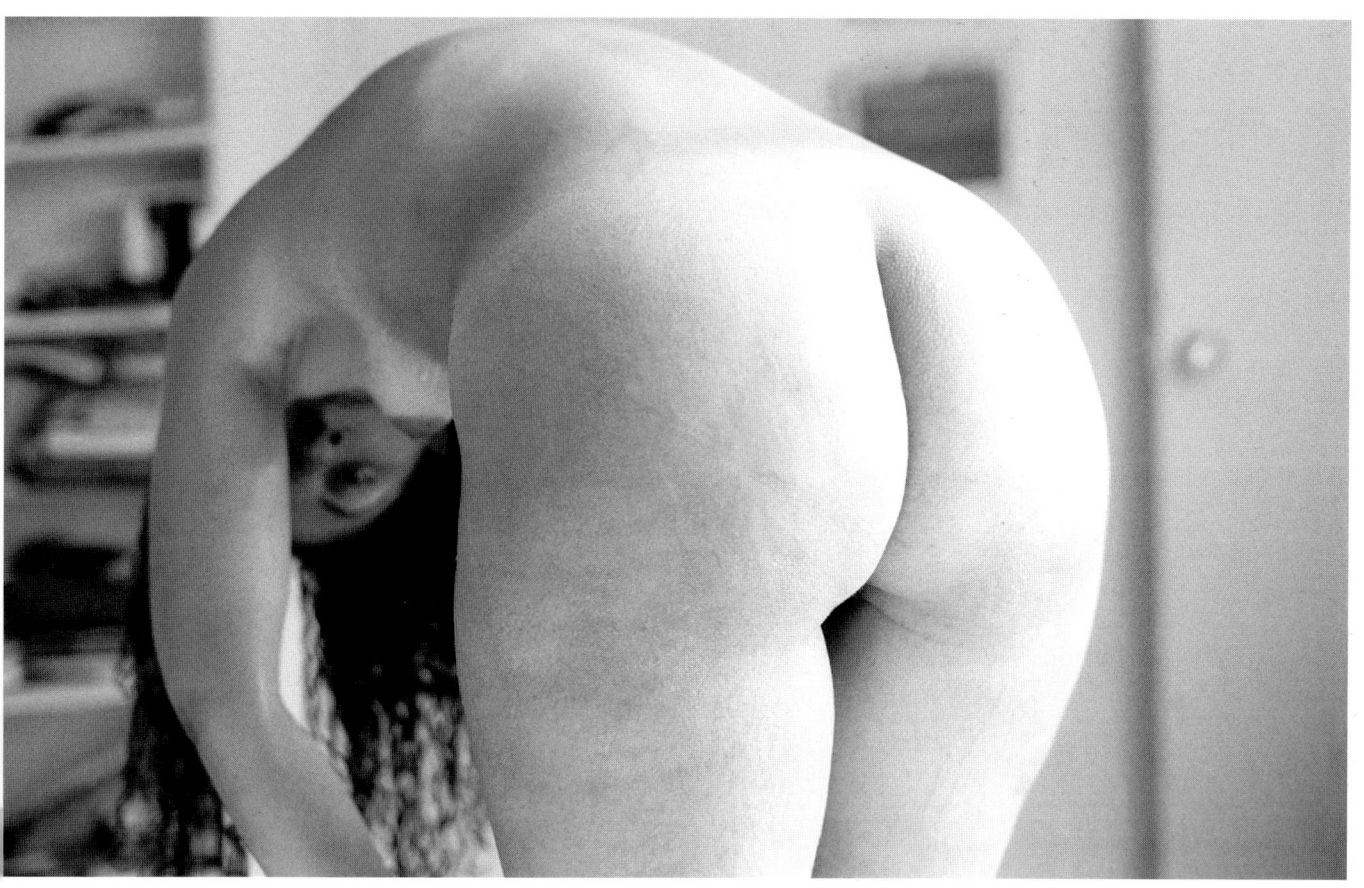

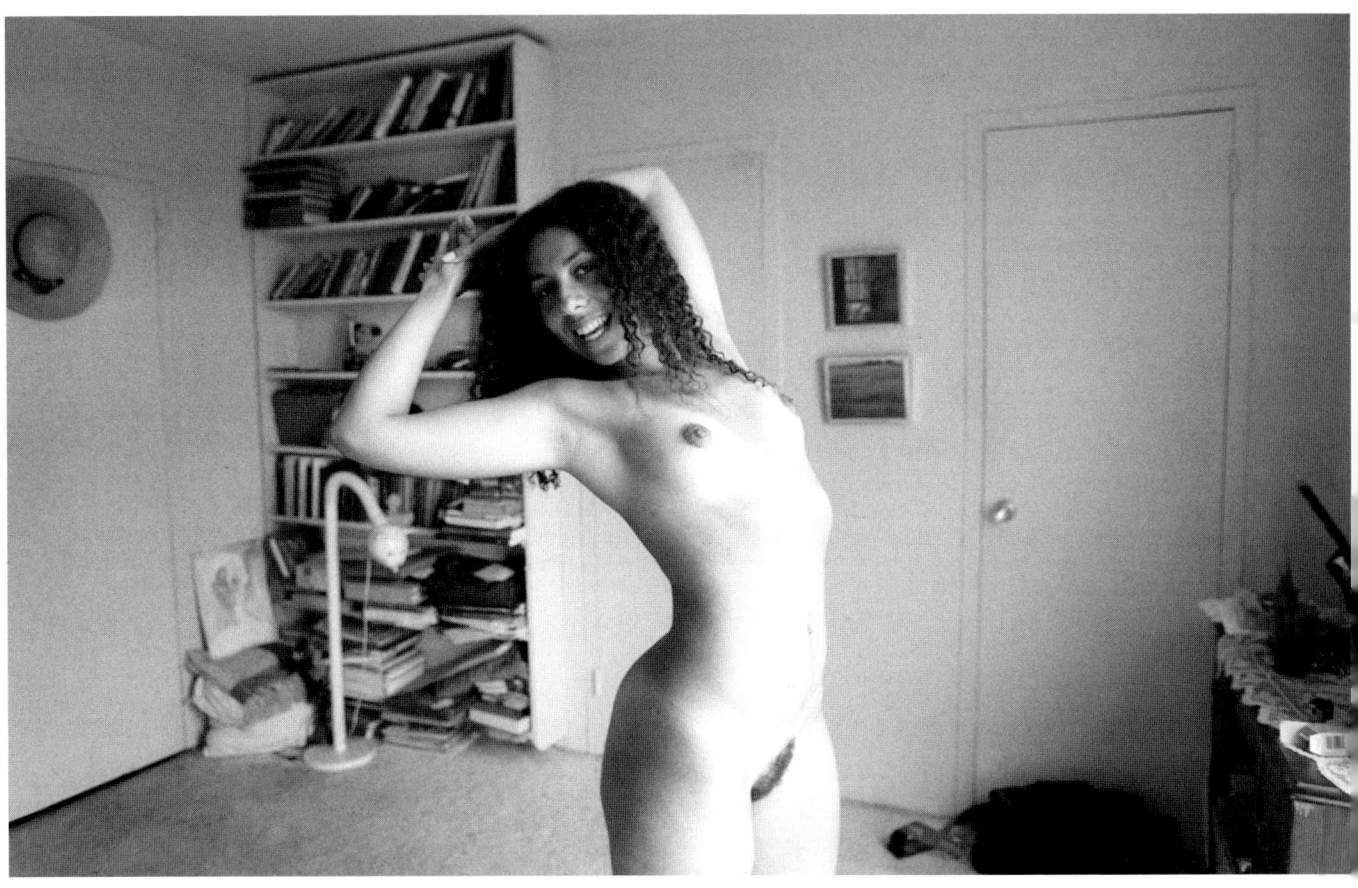

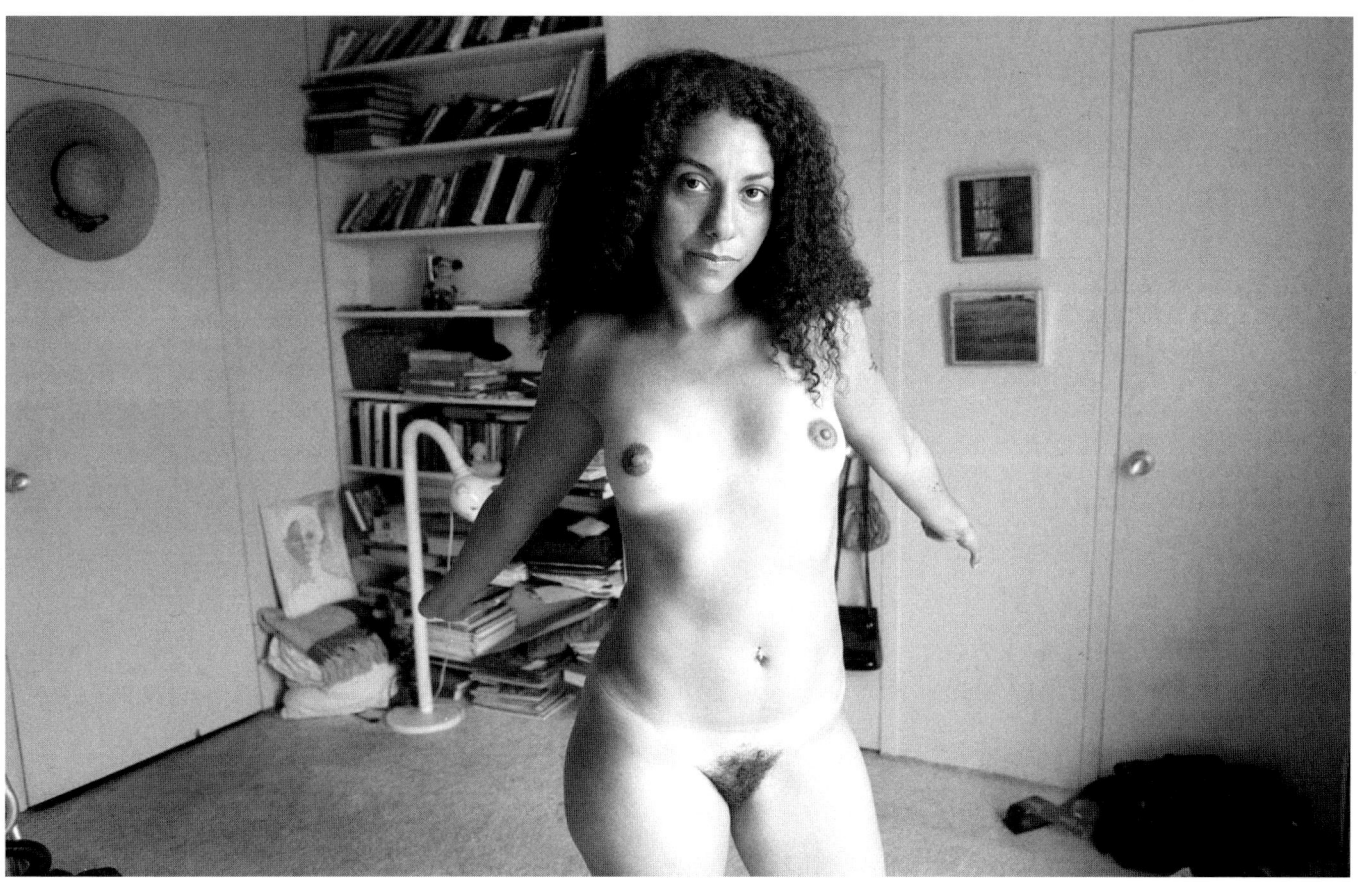

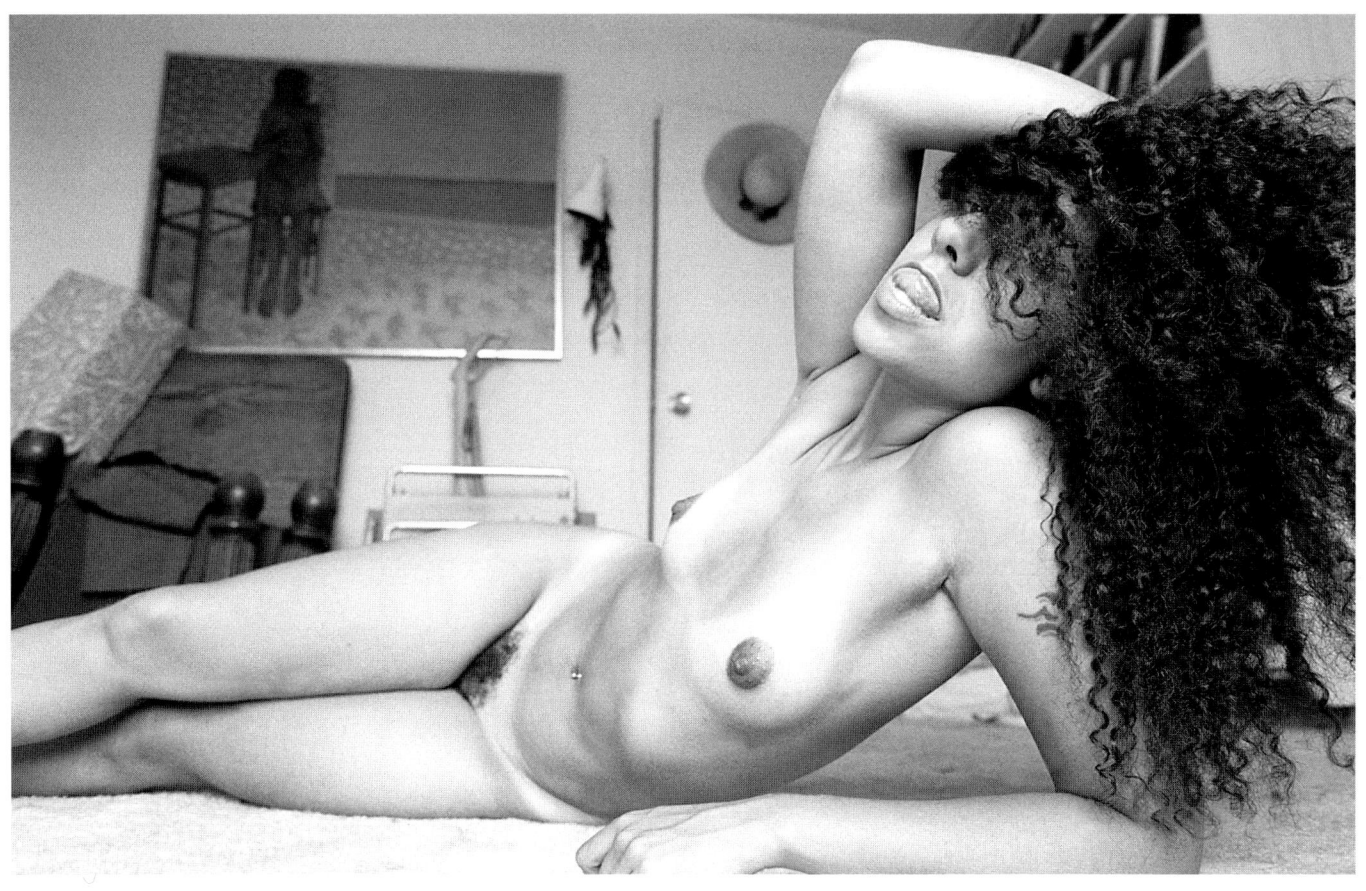

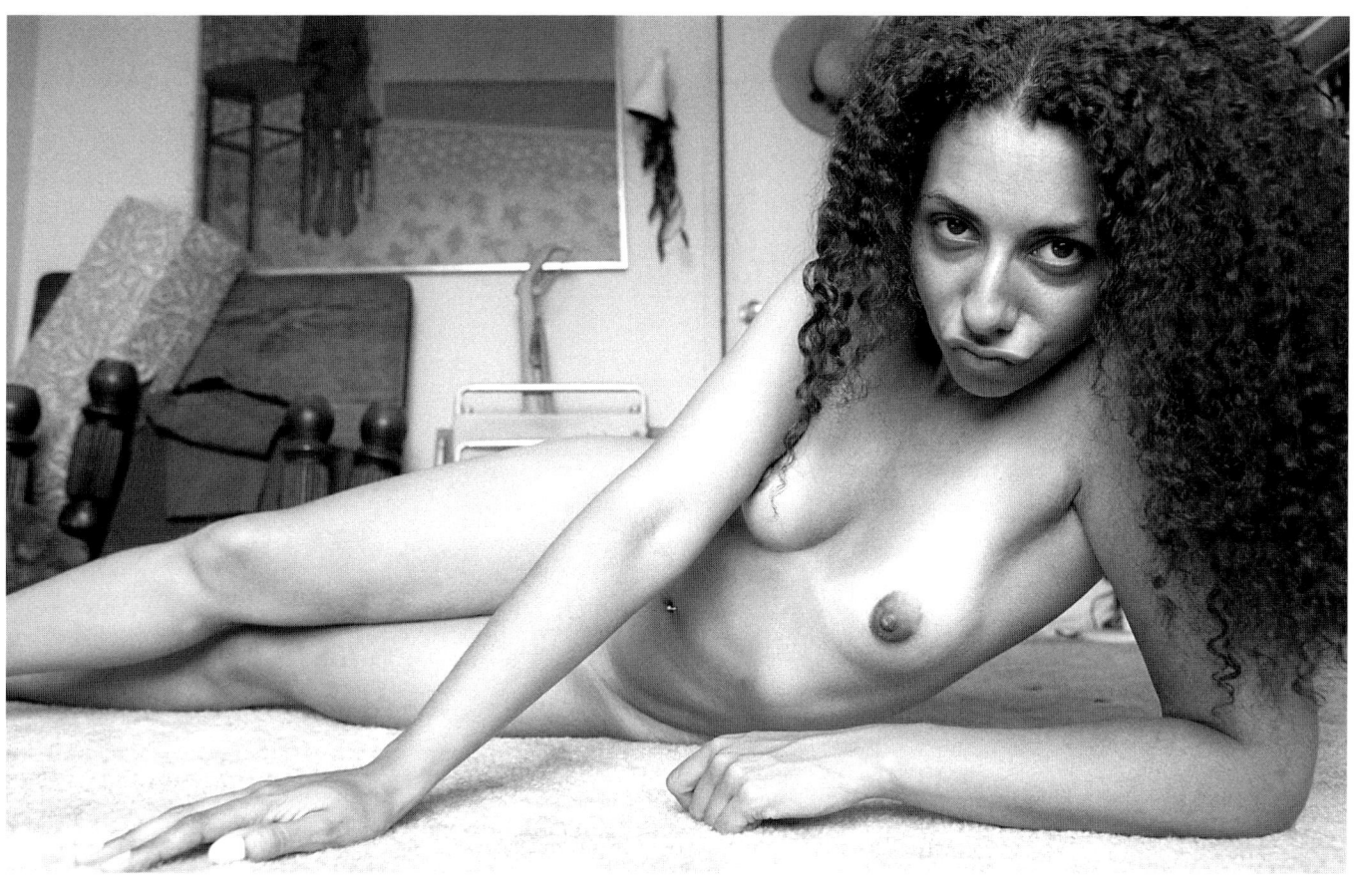

Sara · I met Sara after a cabaret show one night. She was a friend of the cast. I photographed Sara at her boyfriend's apartment on the lower east side. She was naked when I arrived. Photographing Sara was like shooting a pin up model; she moved in great twists and turns and exaggerated movements. The light was also nice.

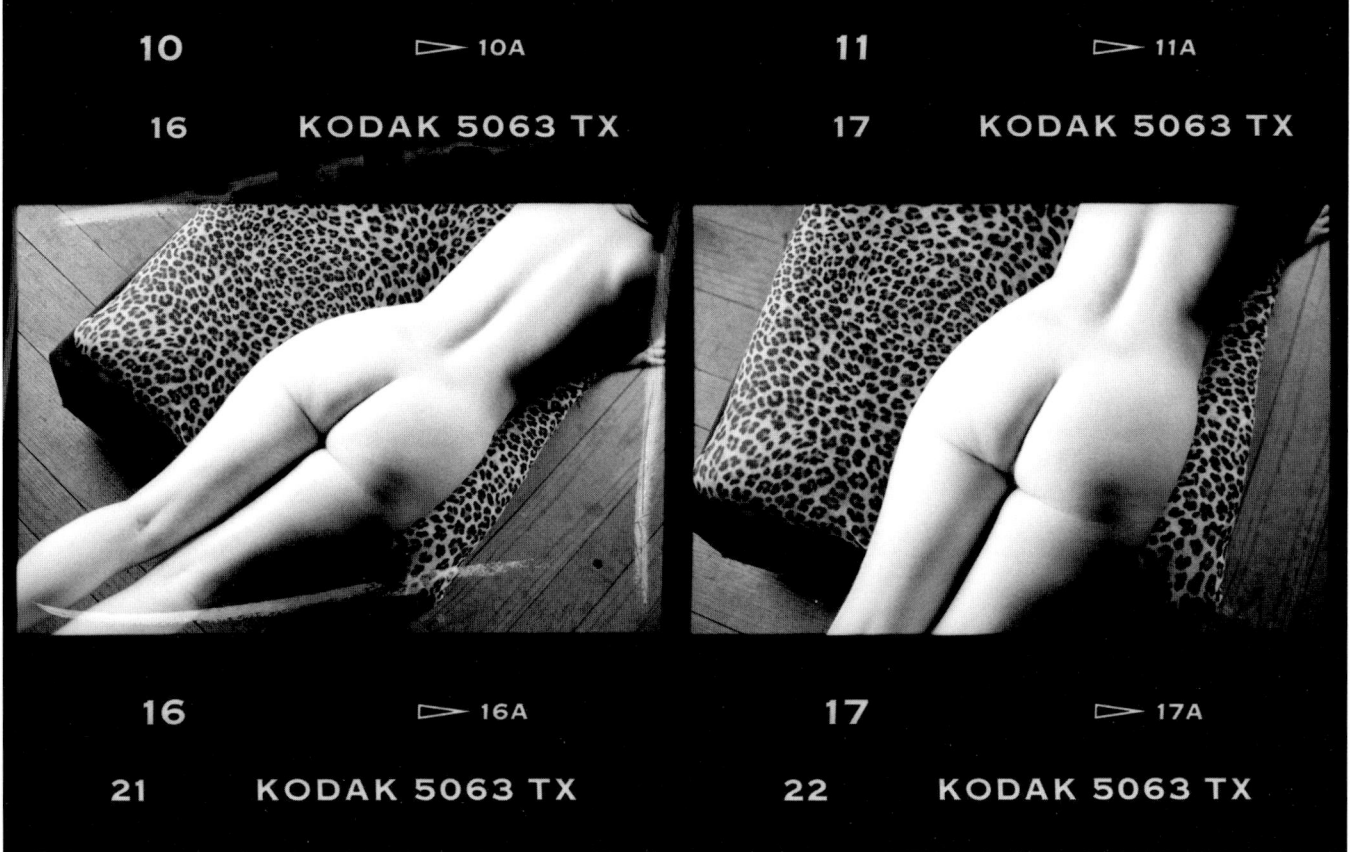

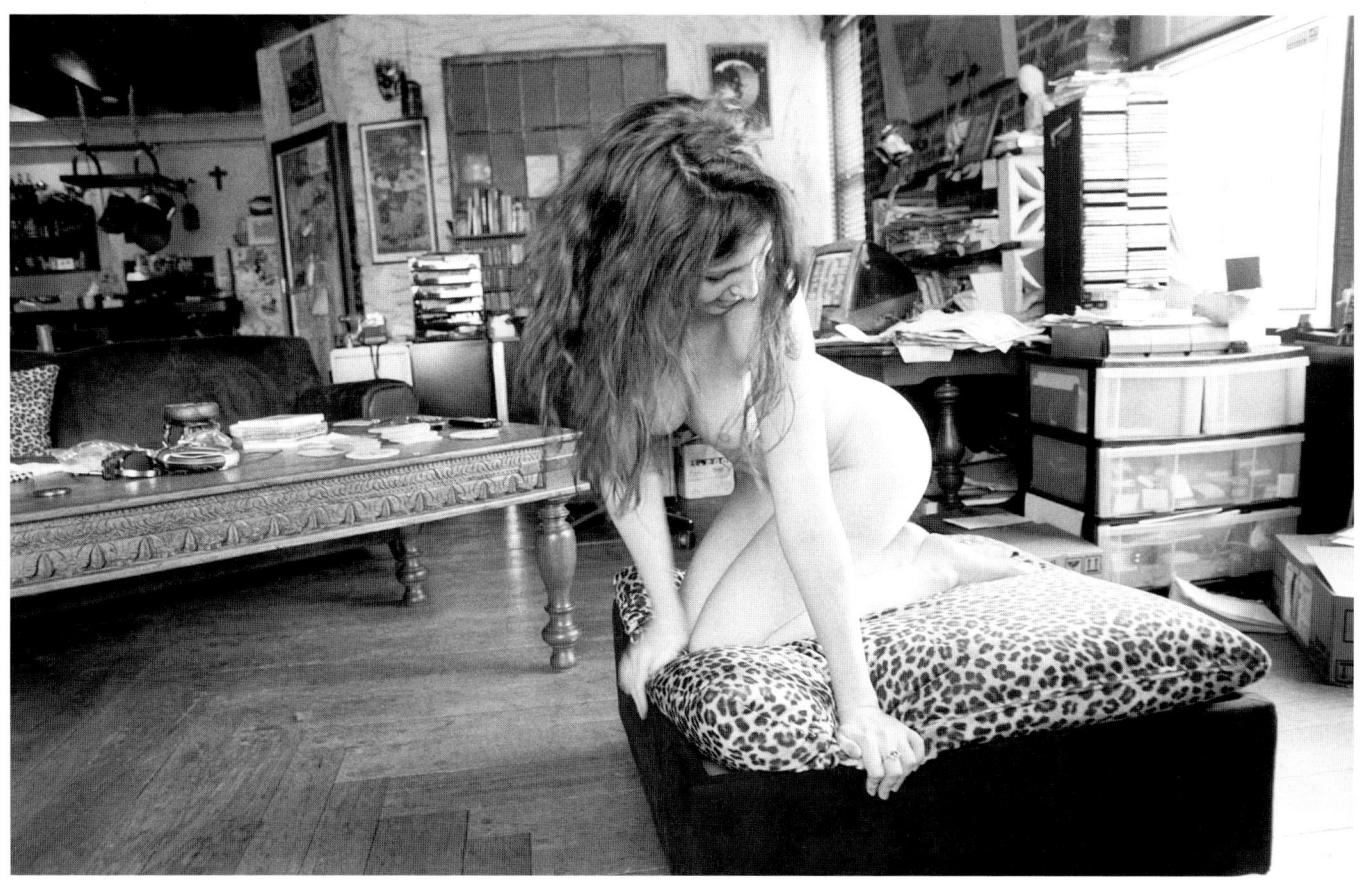

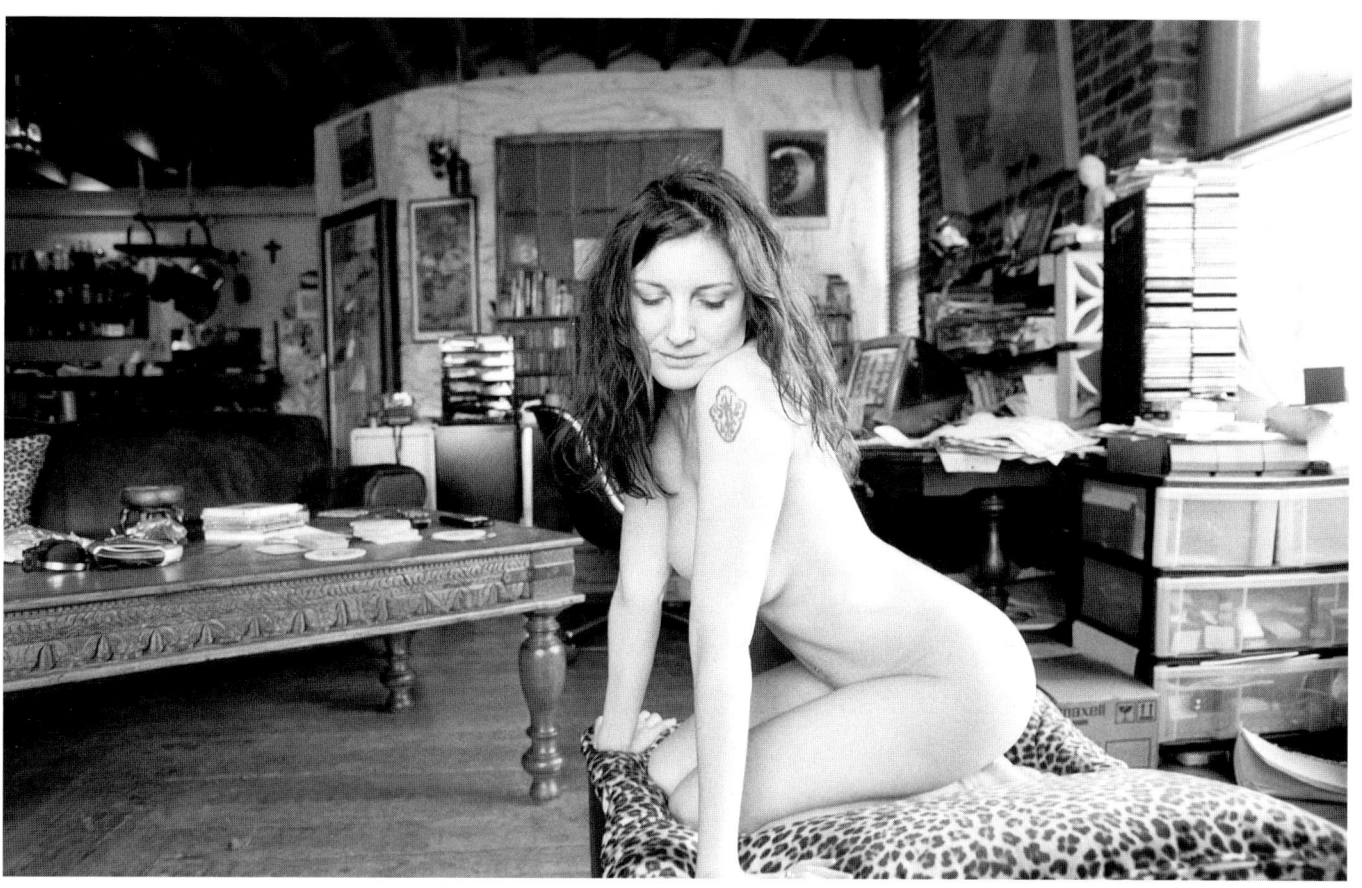

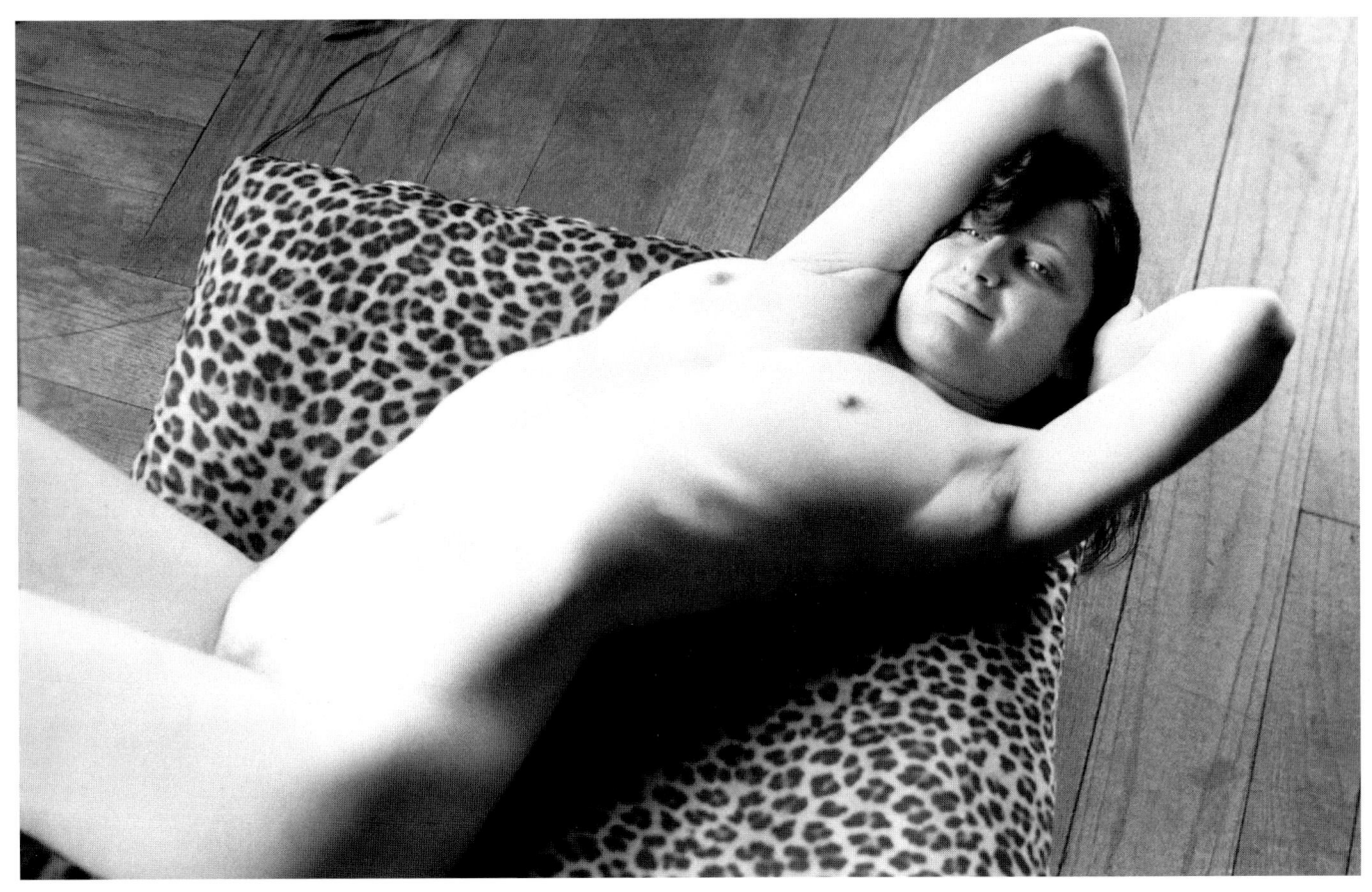

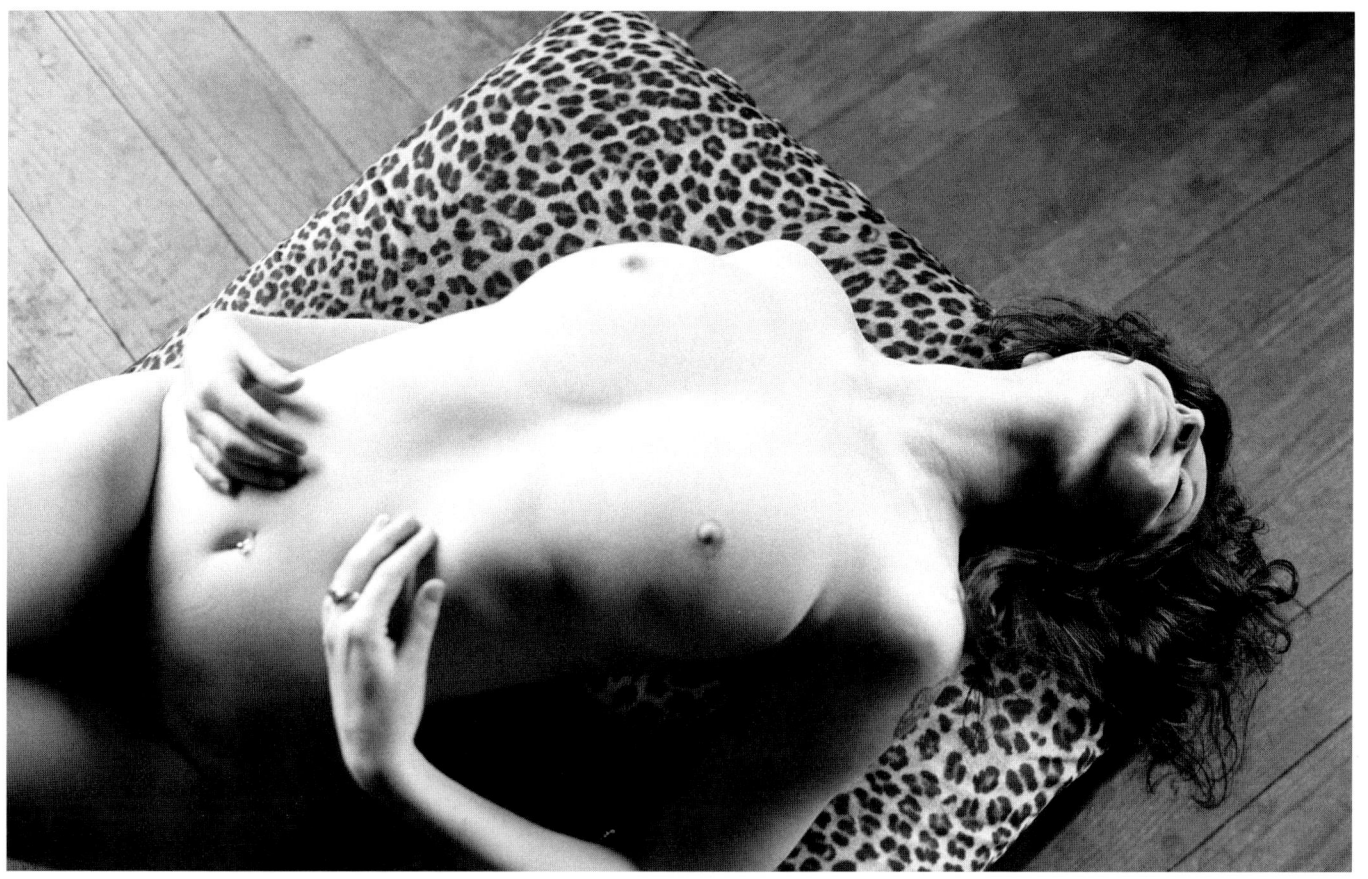

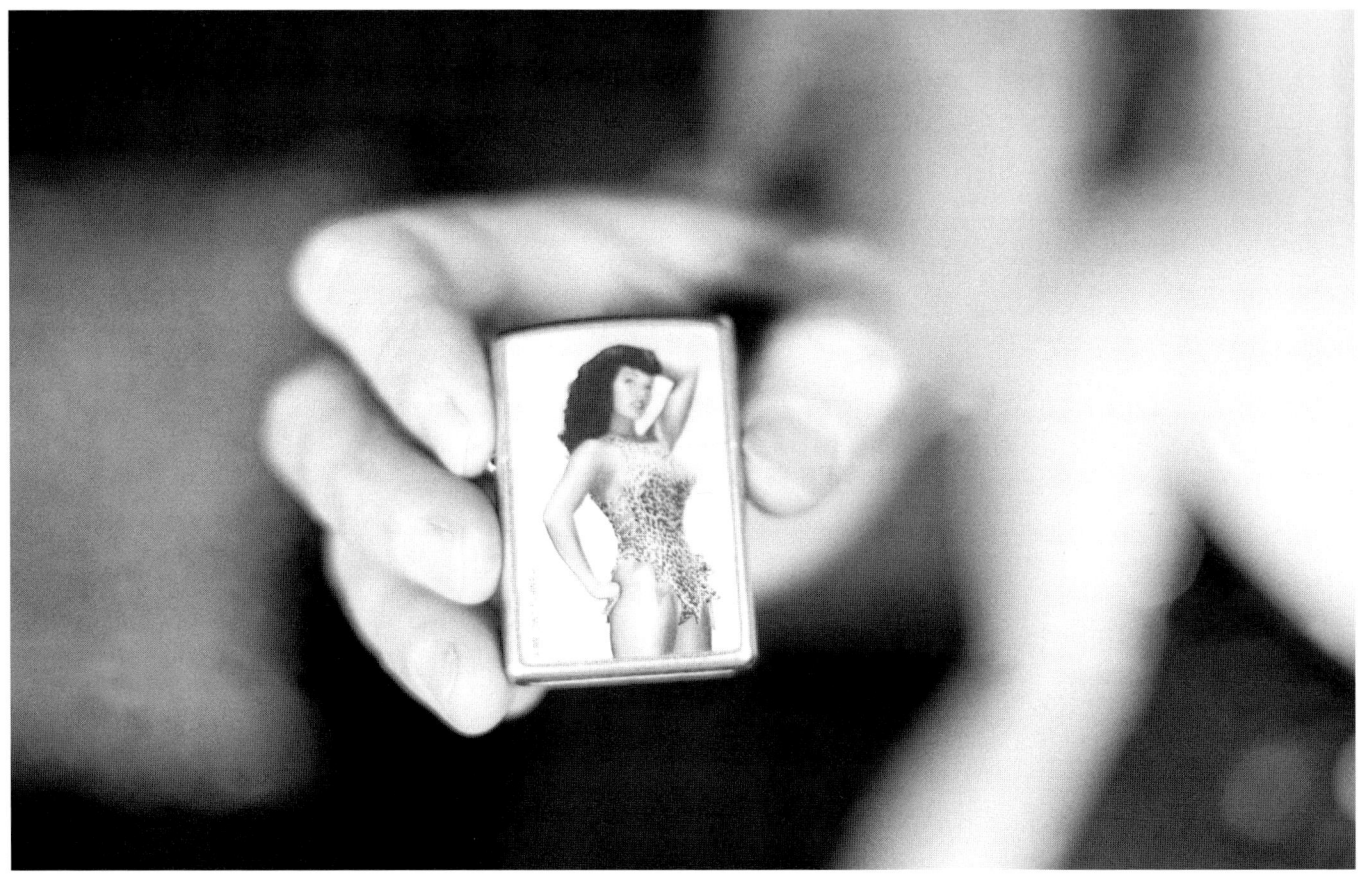

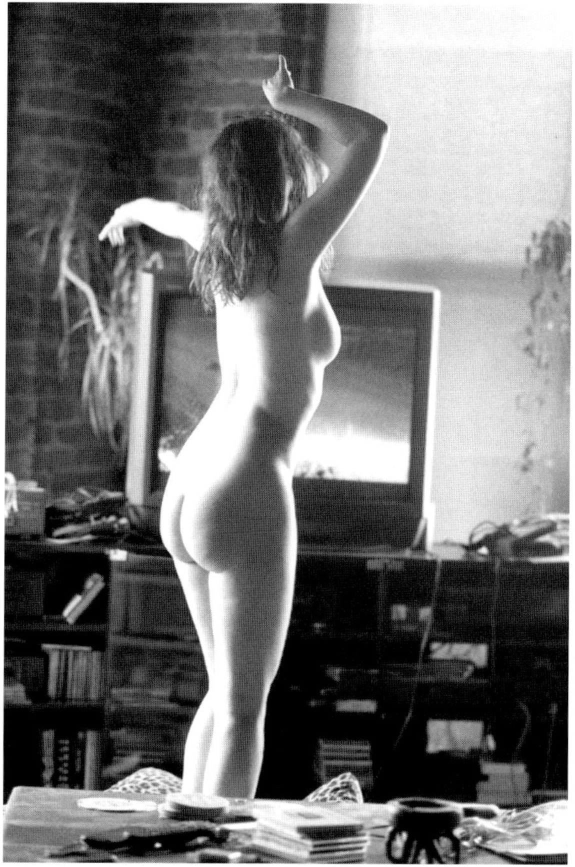

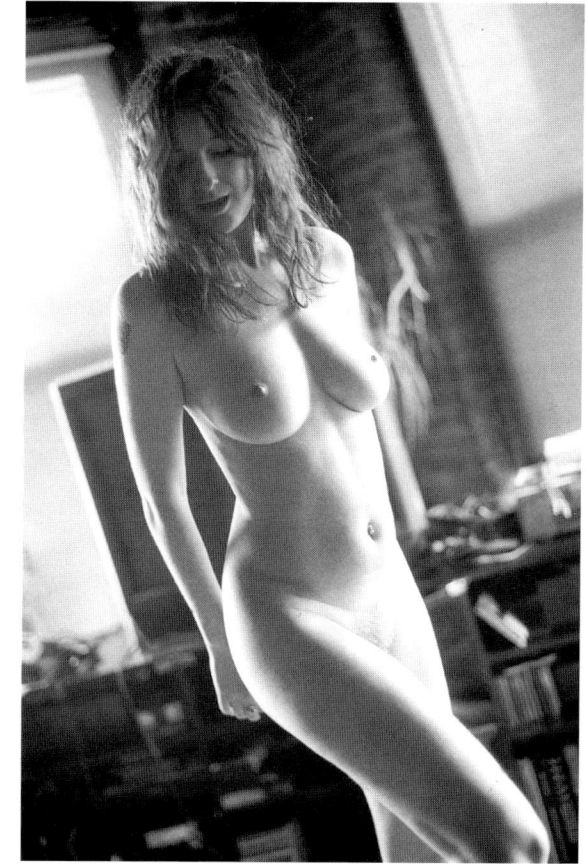

Tamara · I met Tamara in New Paltz, NY, in a huge field of green grass. She was a little shy, but very sweet. I photographed her in my apartment when she came to the city. Tamara loves fruit, and ate four apples during our shoot. She is studying art history and wants to become an artist.

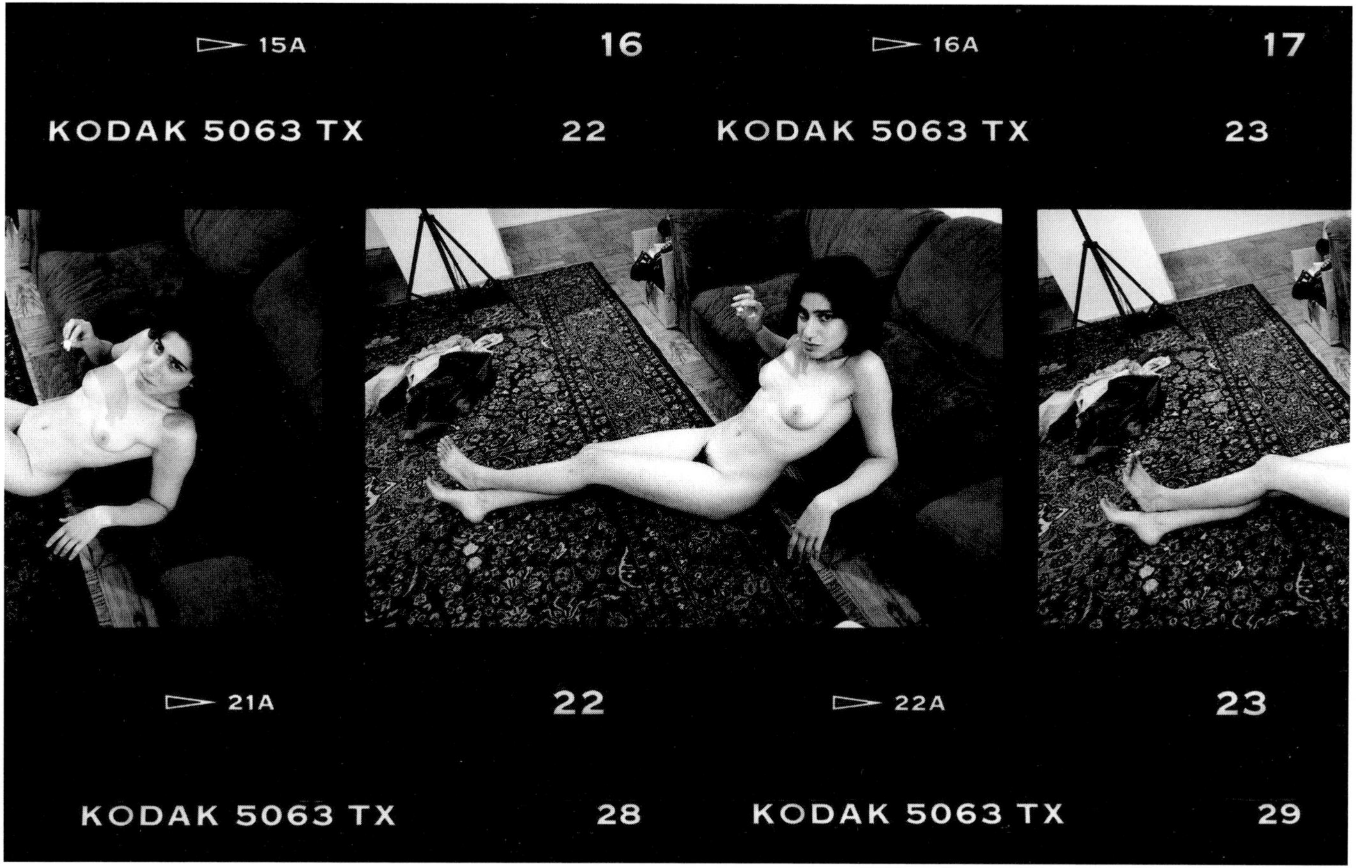
15A
16
16A
17
KODAK 5063 TX
22
KODAK 5063 TX
23
21A
22
22A
23
KODAK 5063 TX
28
KODAK 5063 TX
29

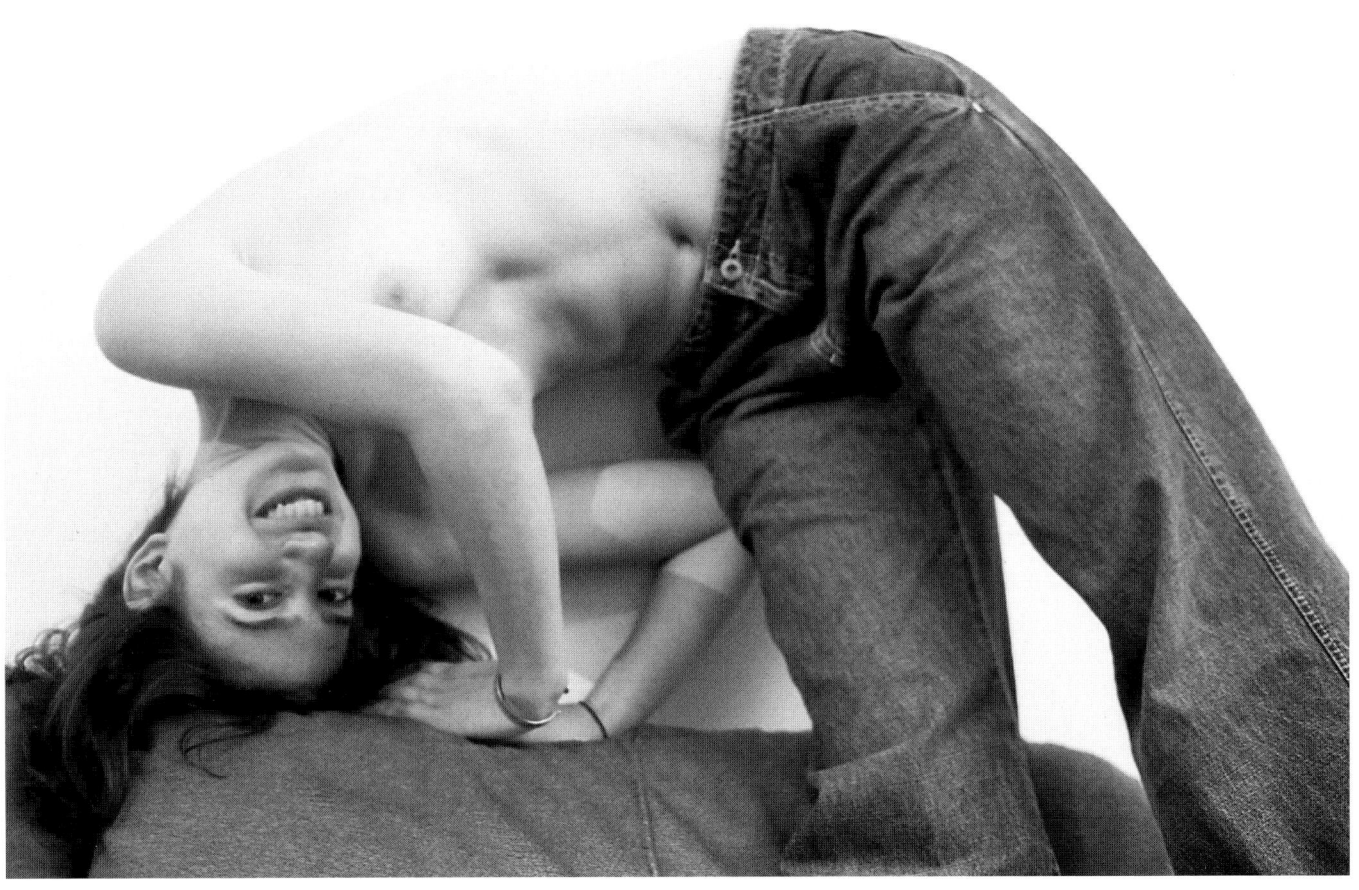

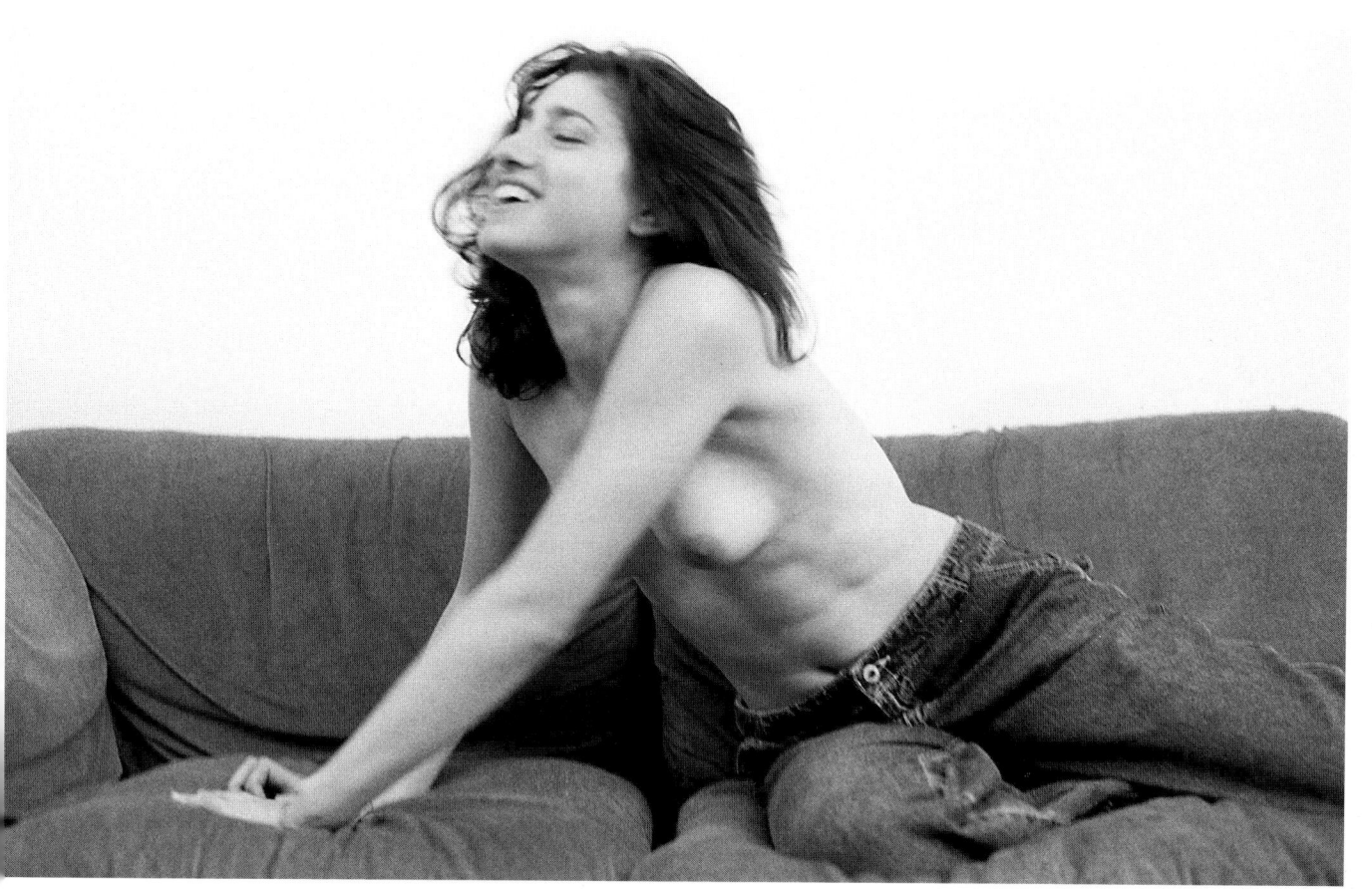

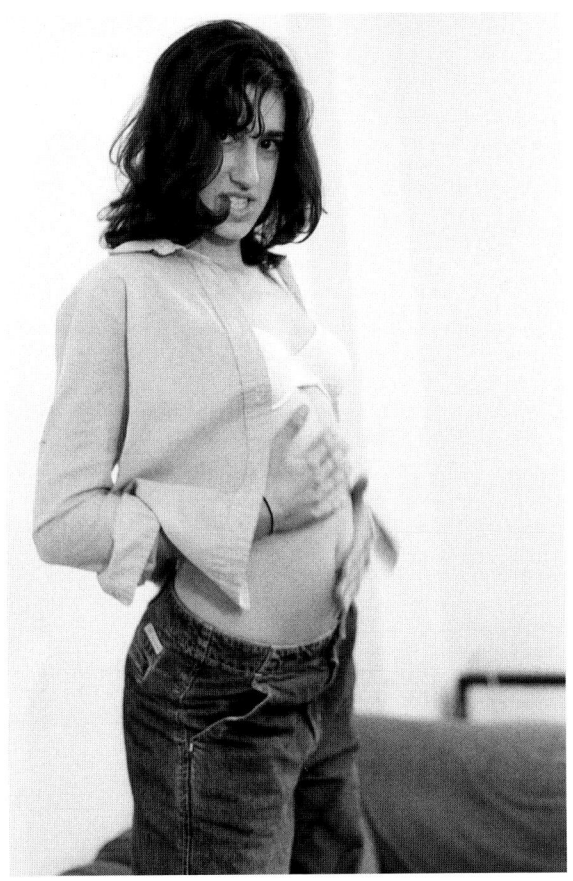

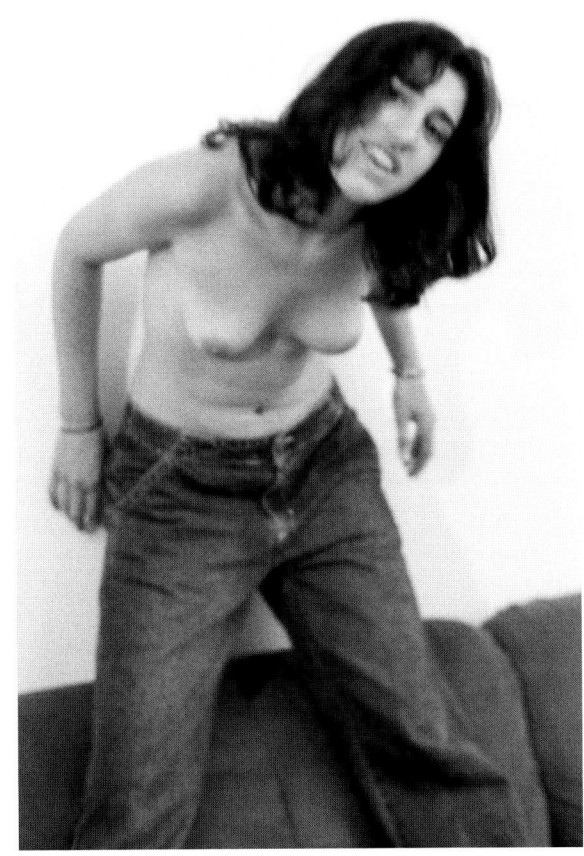

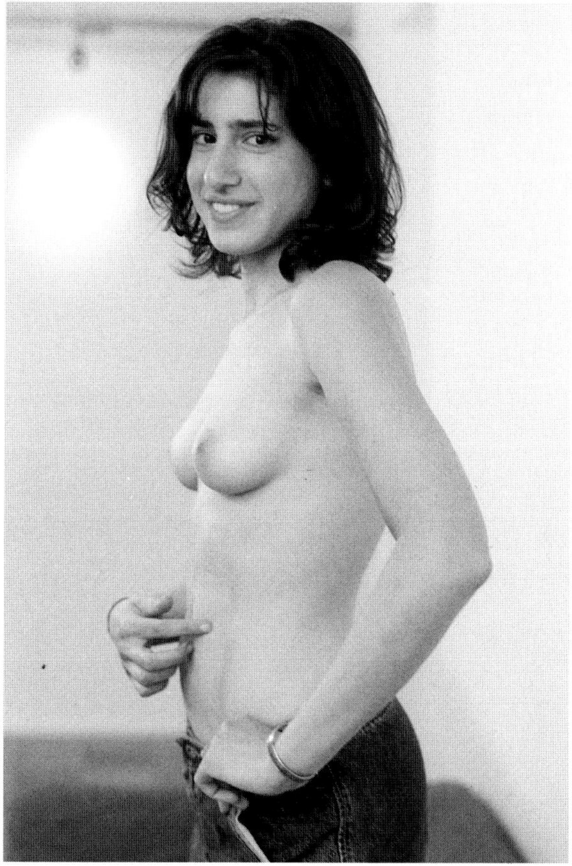

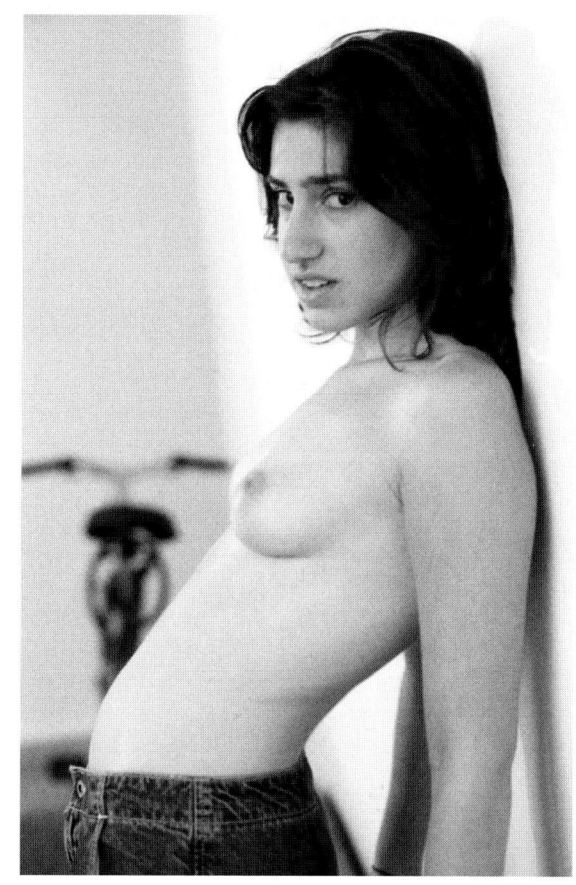

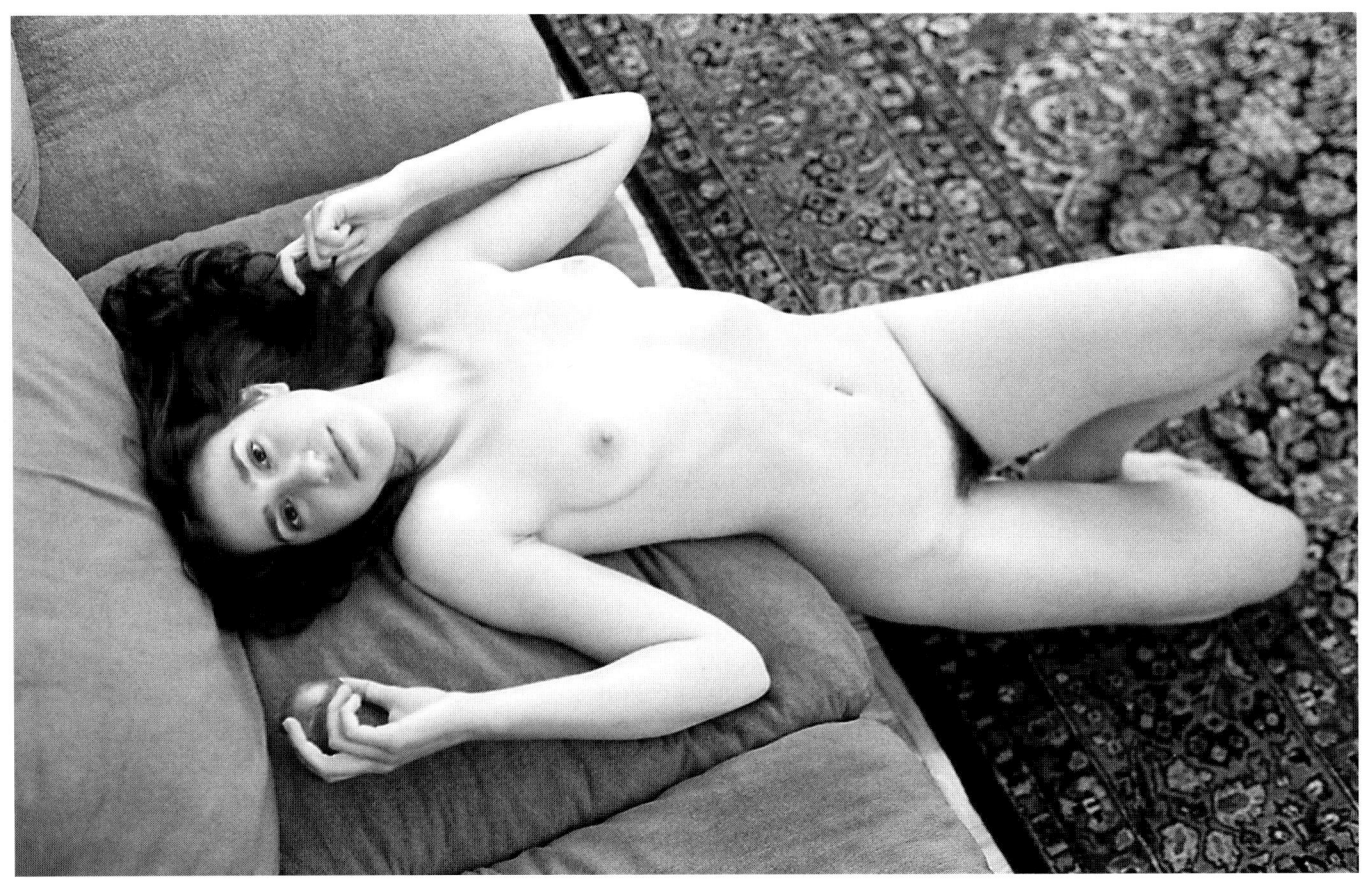

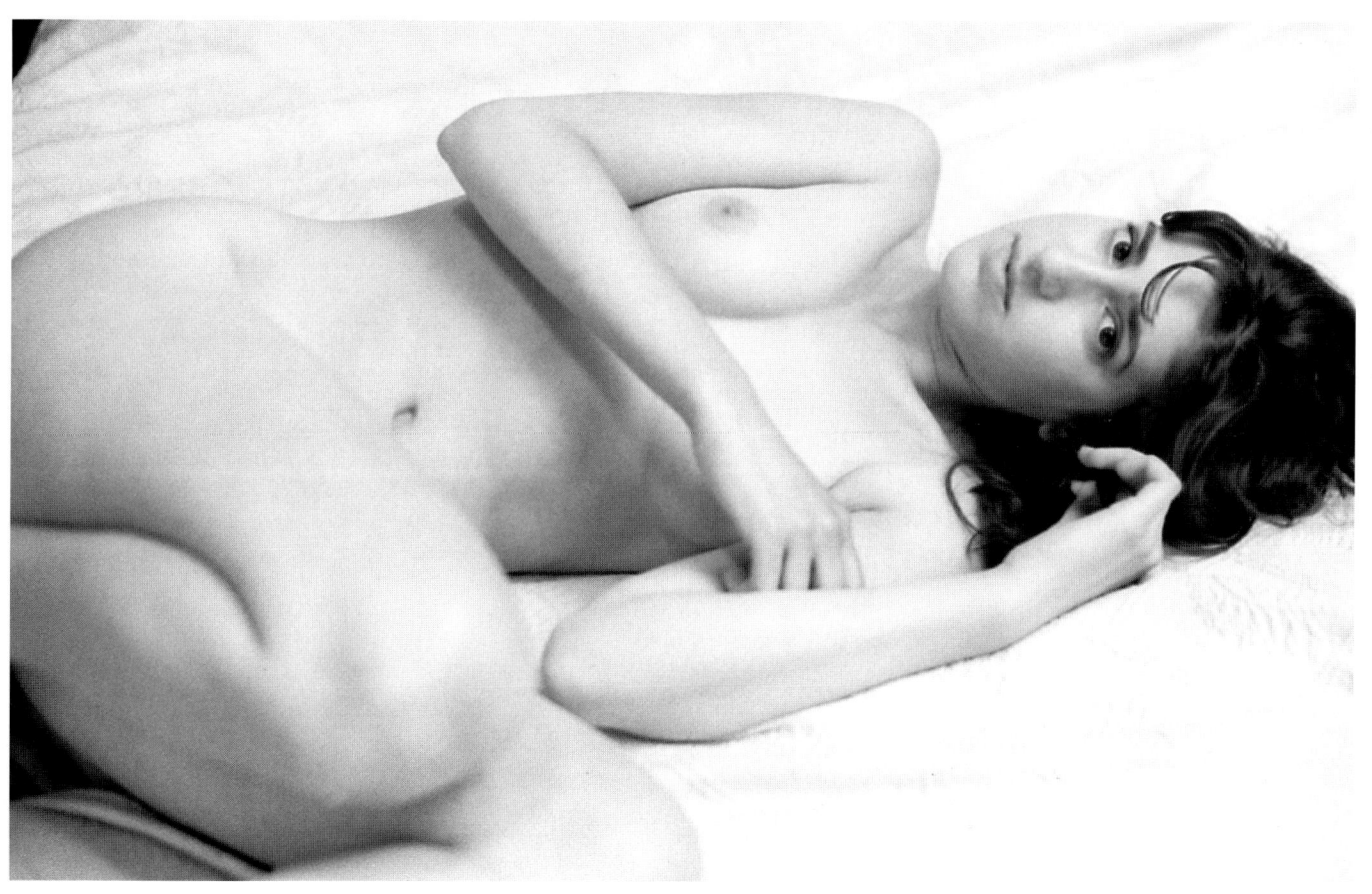

Theresa · I met Theresa at a magazine party, when she was drunk on blue cosmopolitans. I photographed her a few months later in her Brooklyn apartment. Therese told me "I'm just a Vietnamese girl from Kentucky who designs hip-hop clothing." She also smoked cigars, loved art, and said she owned a set of Jackson Pollock "Ultraman" dolls. She had a high voice, laughed a lot, and took pictures of me as well.

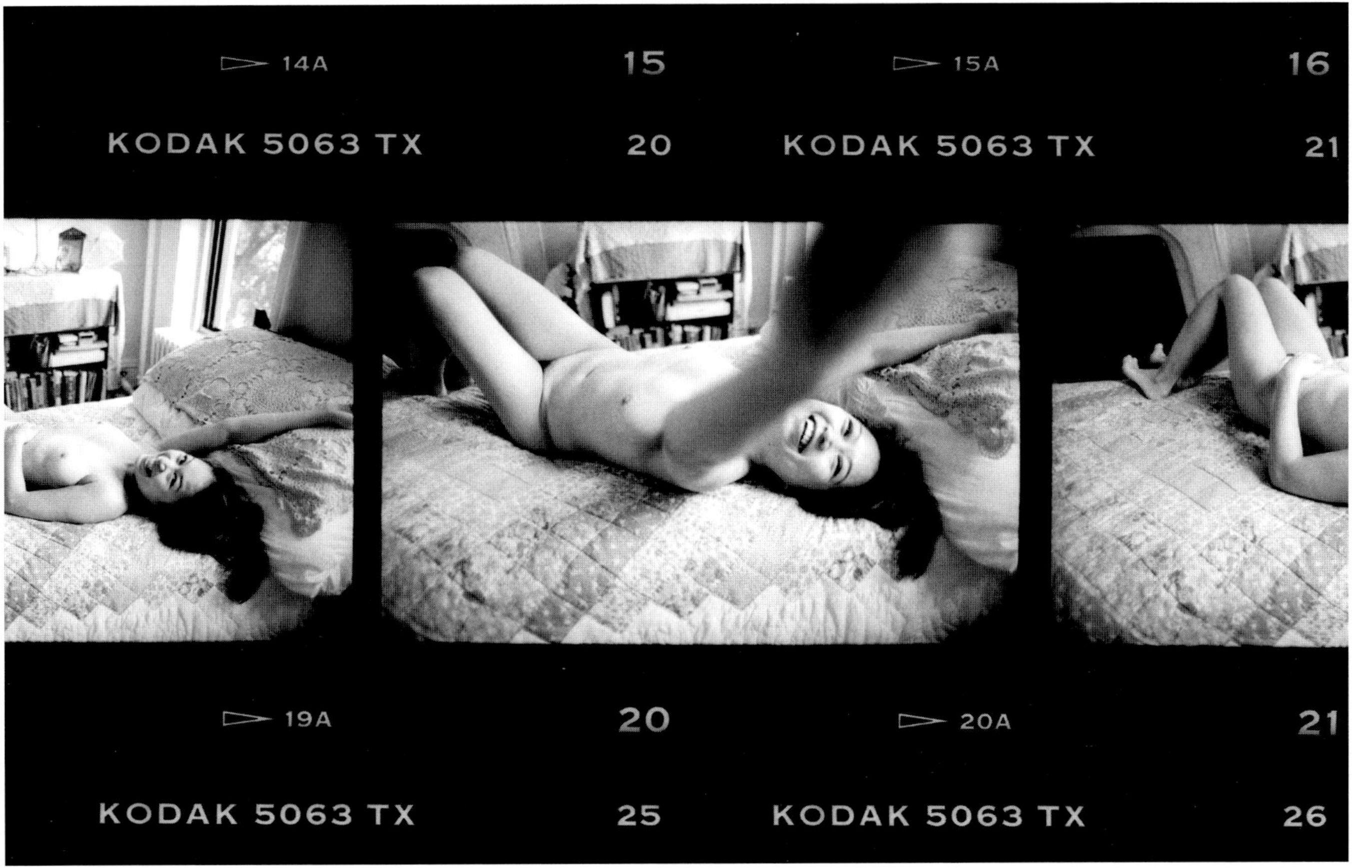
14A
15
15A
16
KODAK 5063 TX
20
KODAK 5063 TX
21
19A
20
20A
21
KODAK 5063 TX
25
KODAK 5063 TX
26

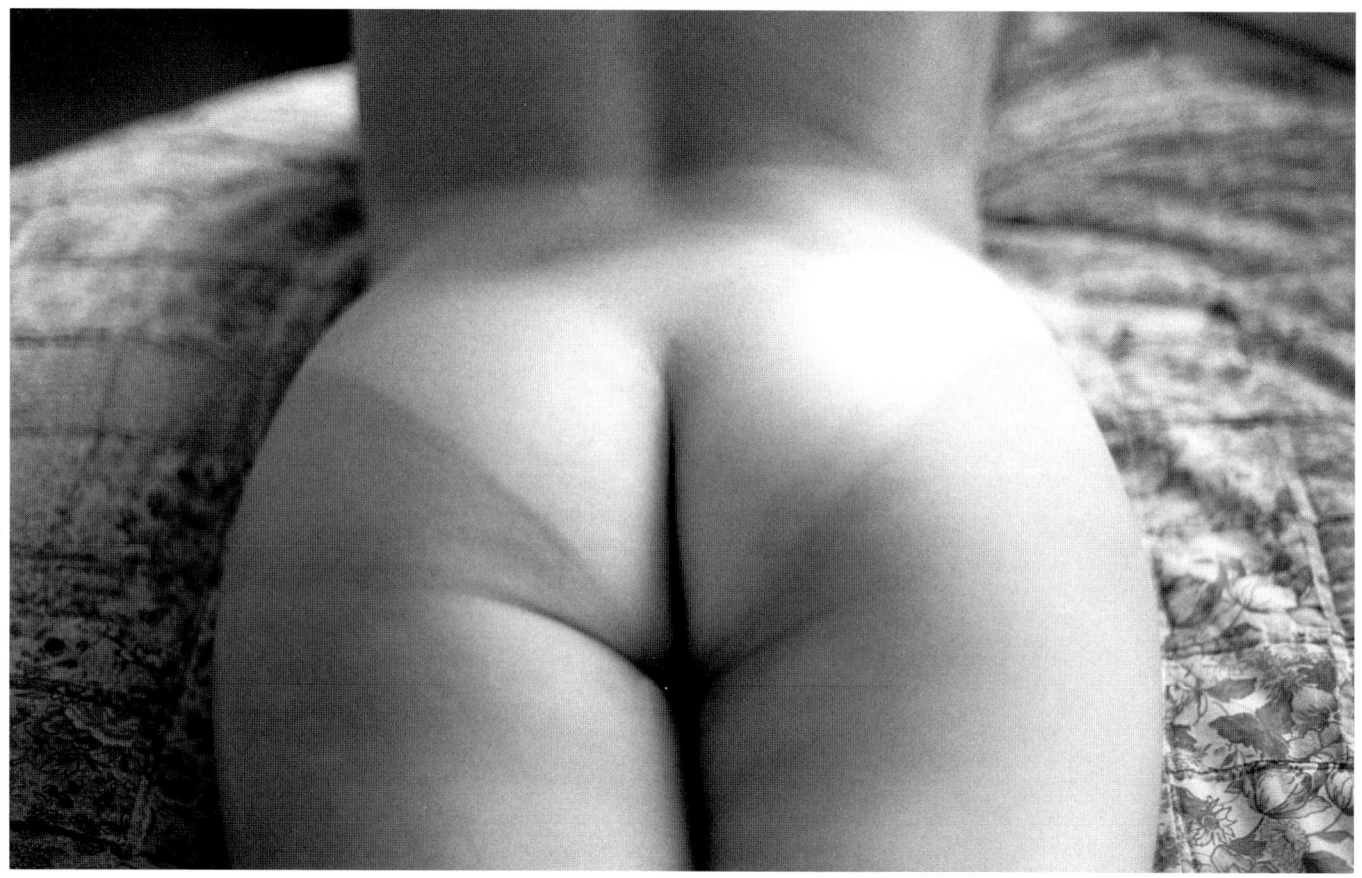

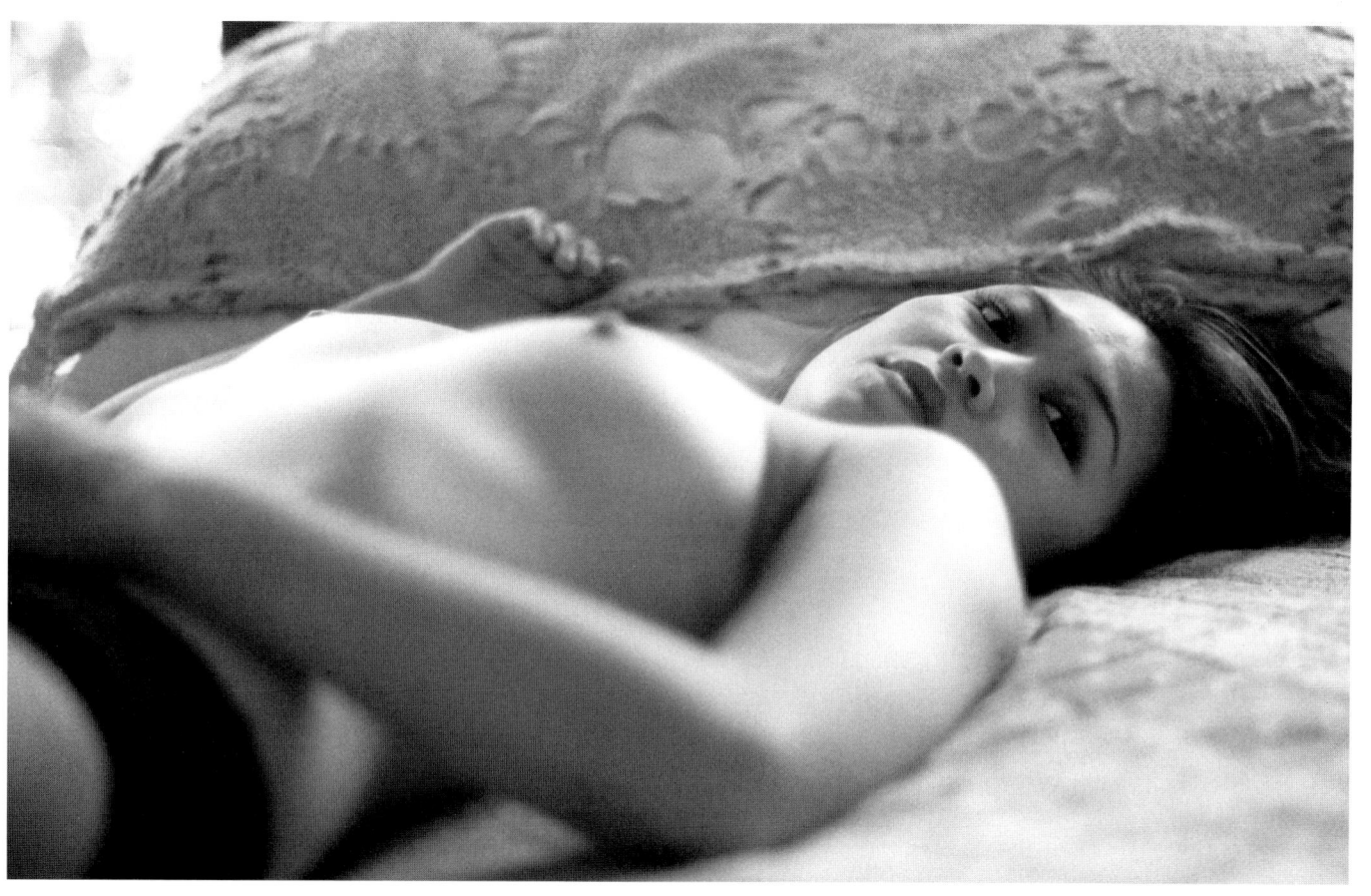

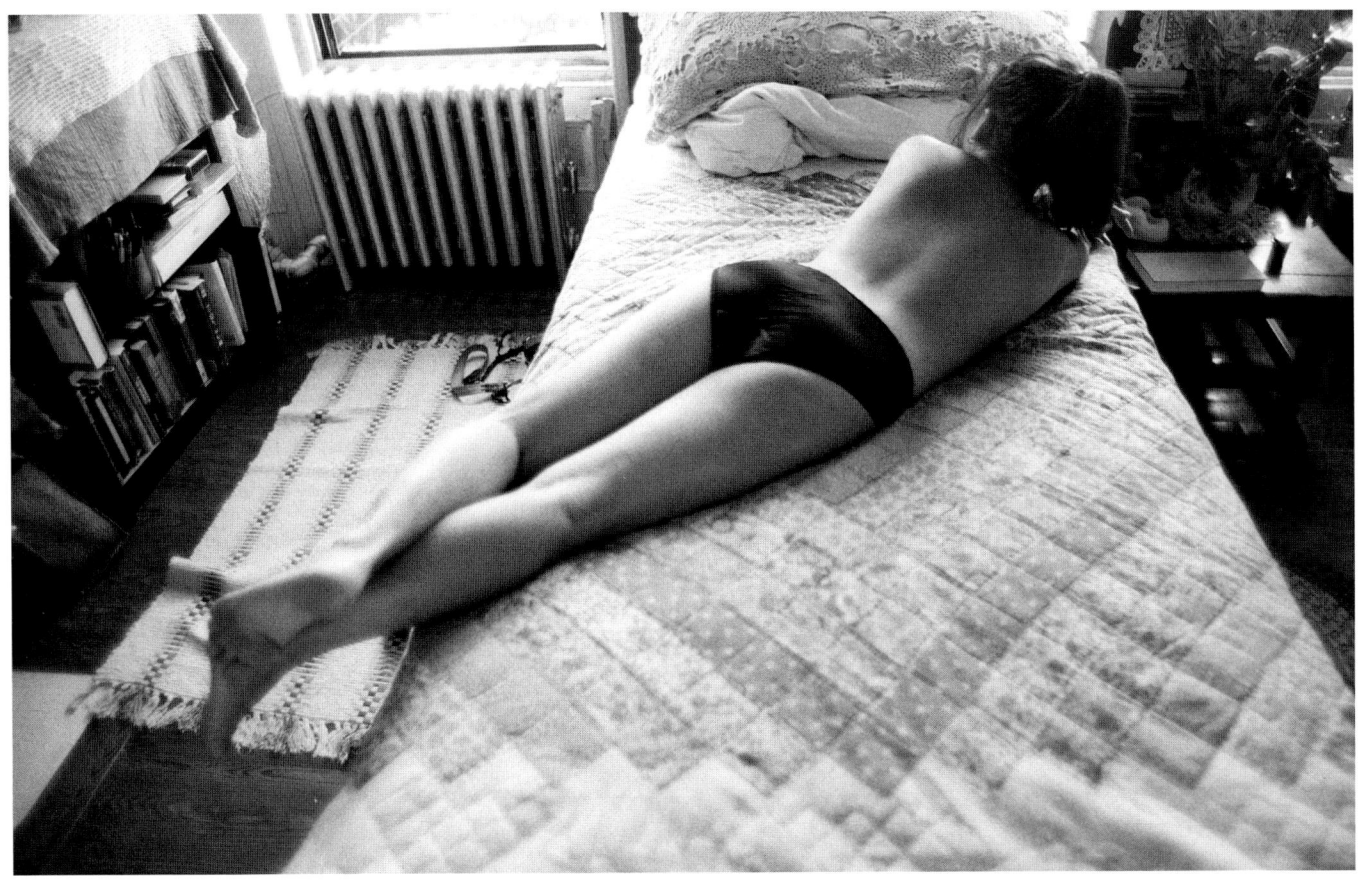

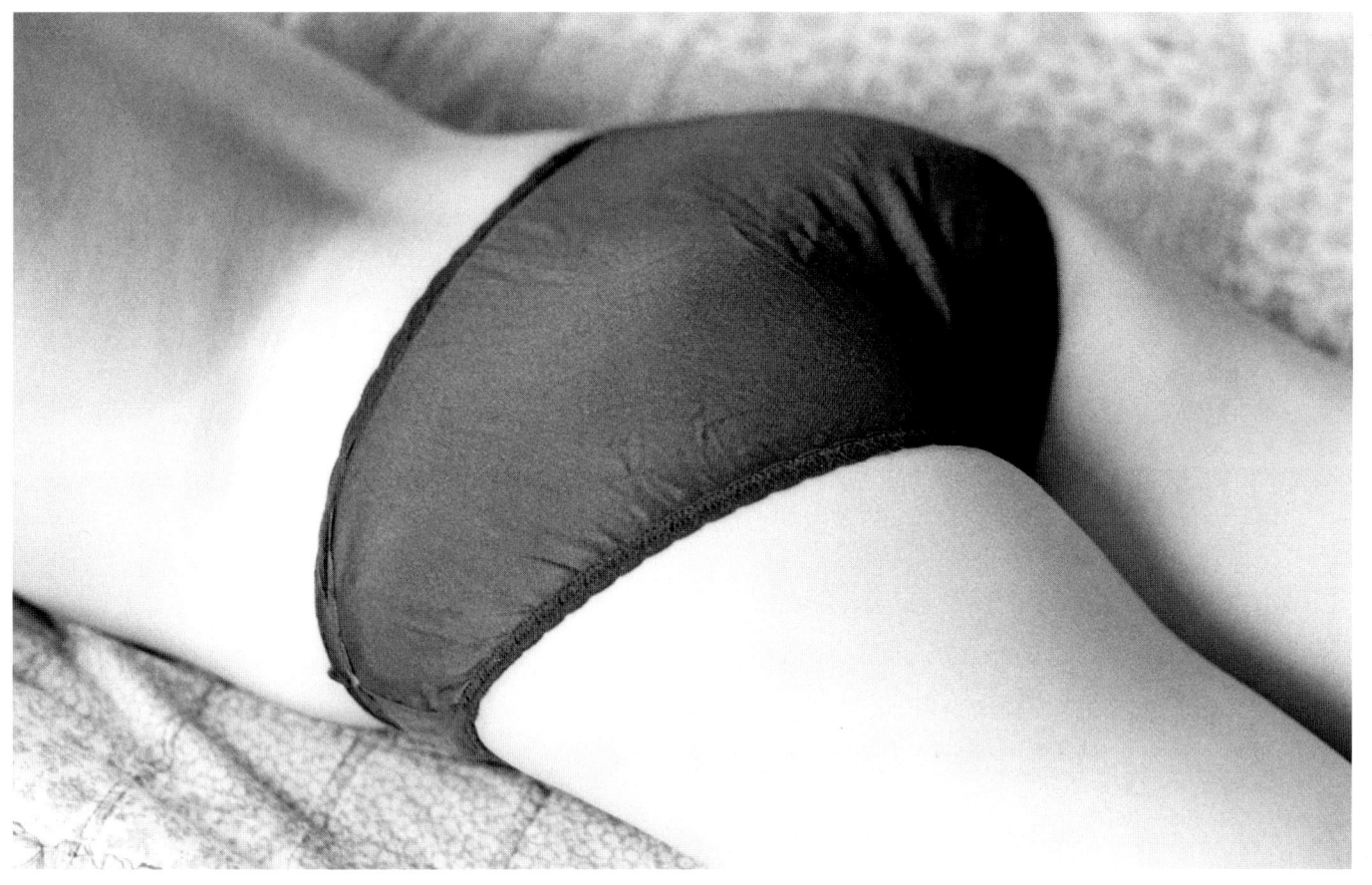

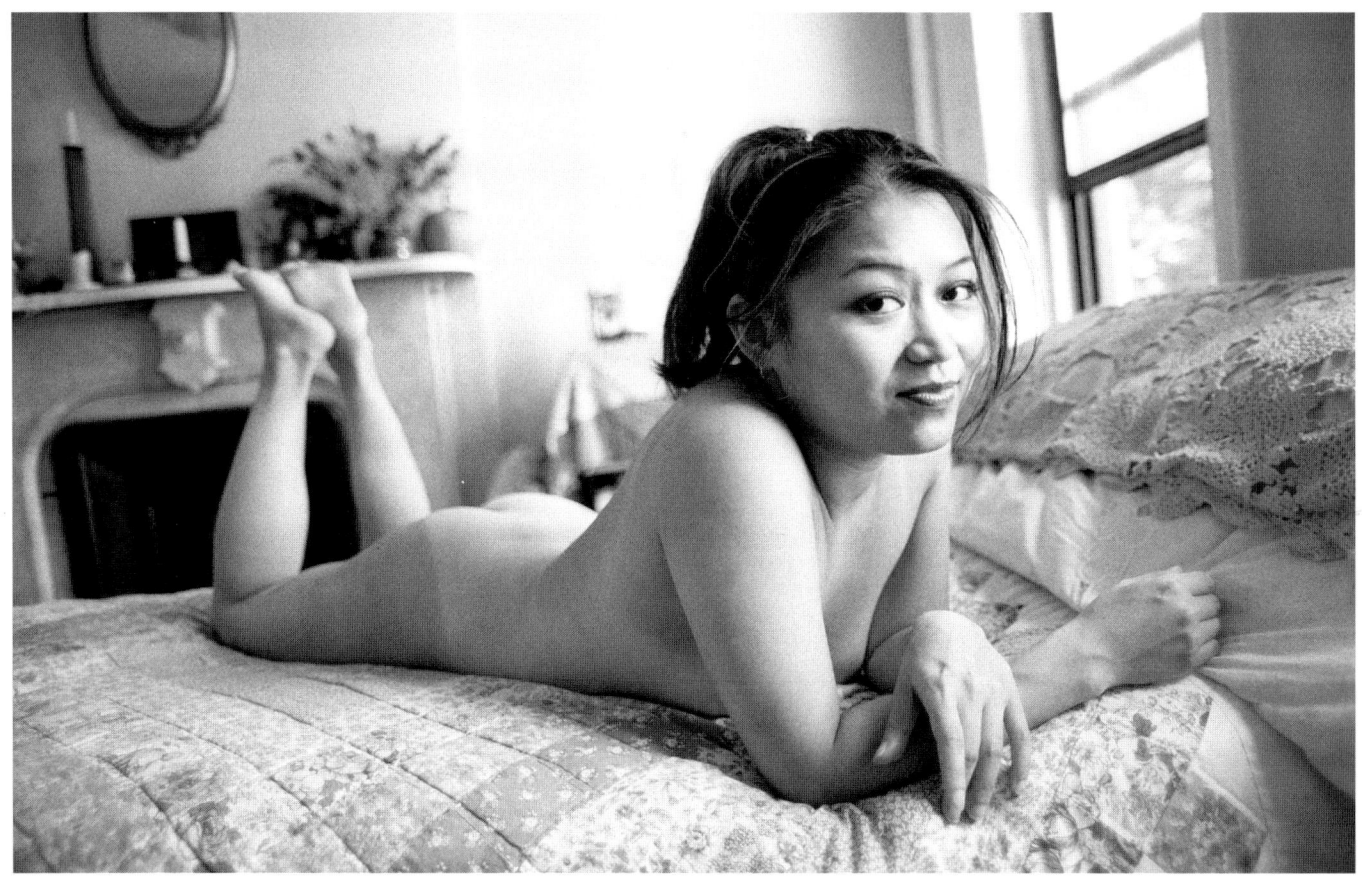

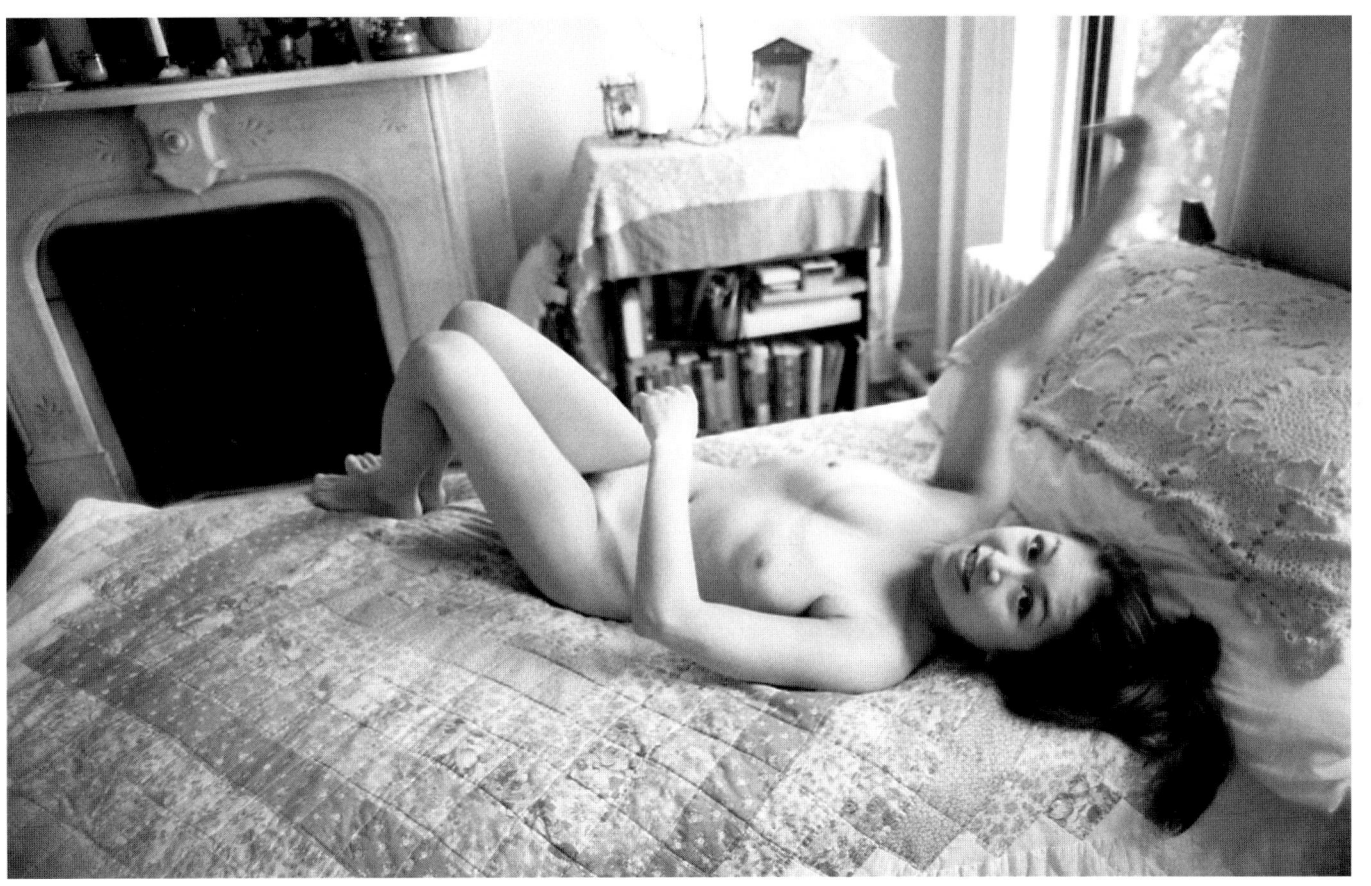

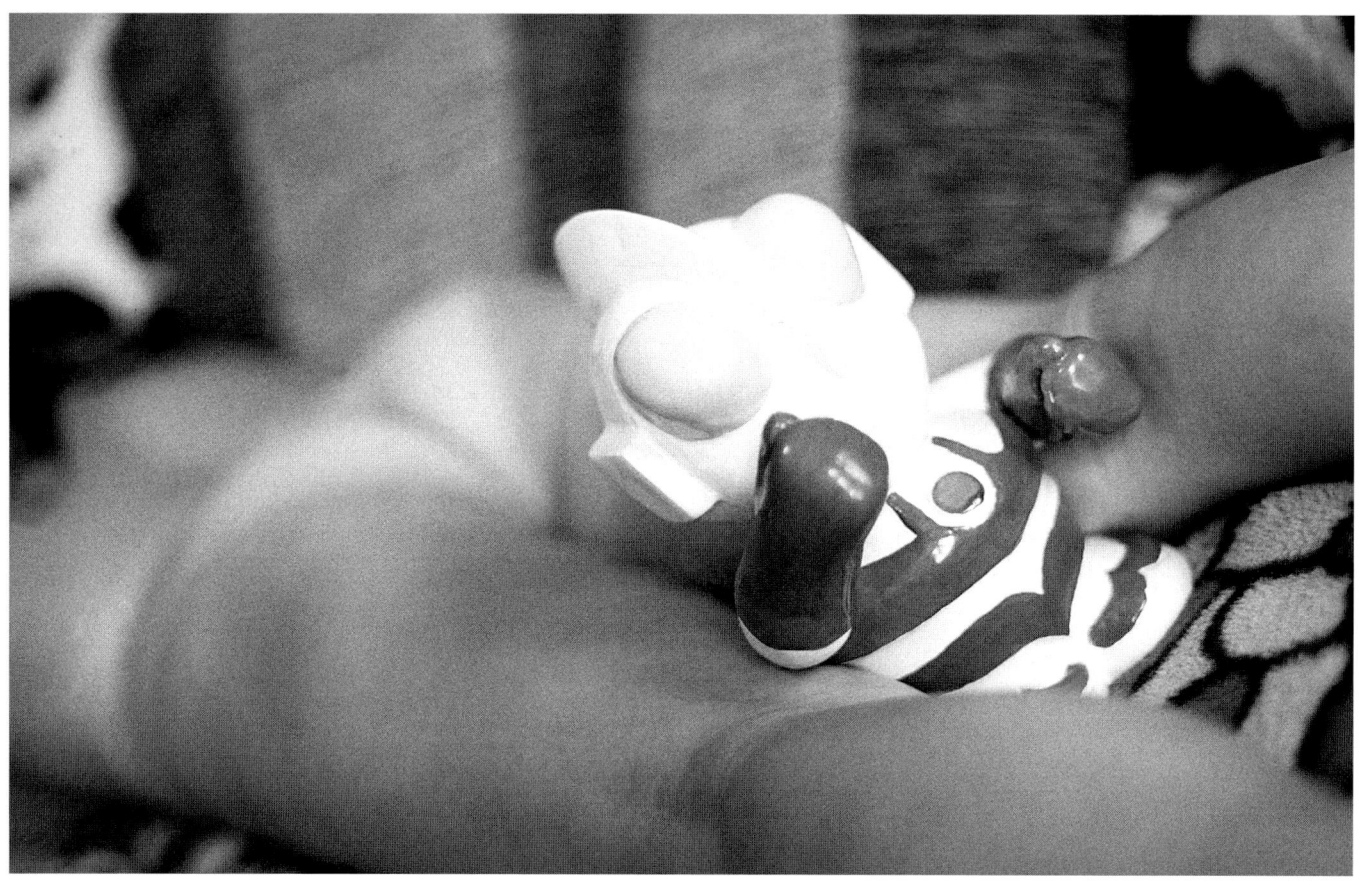

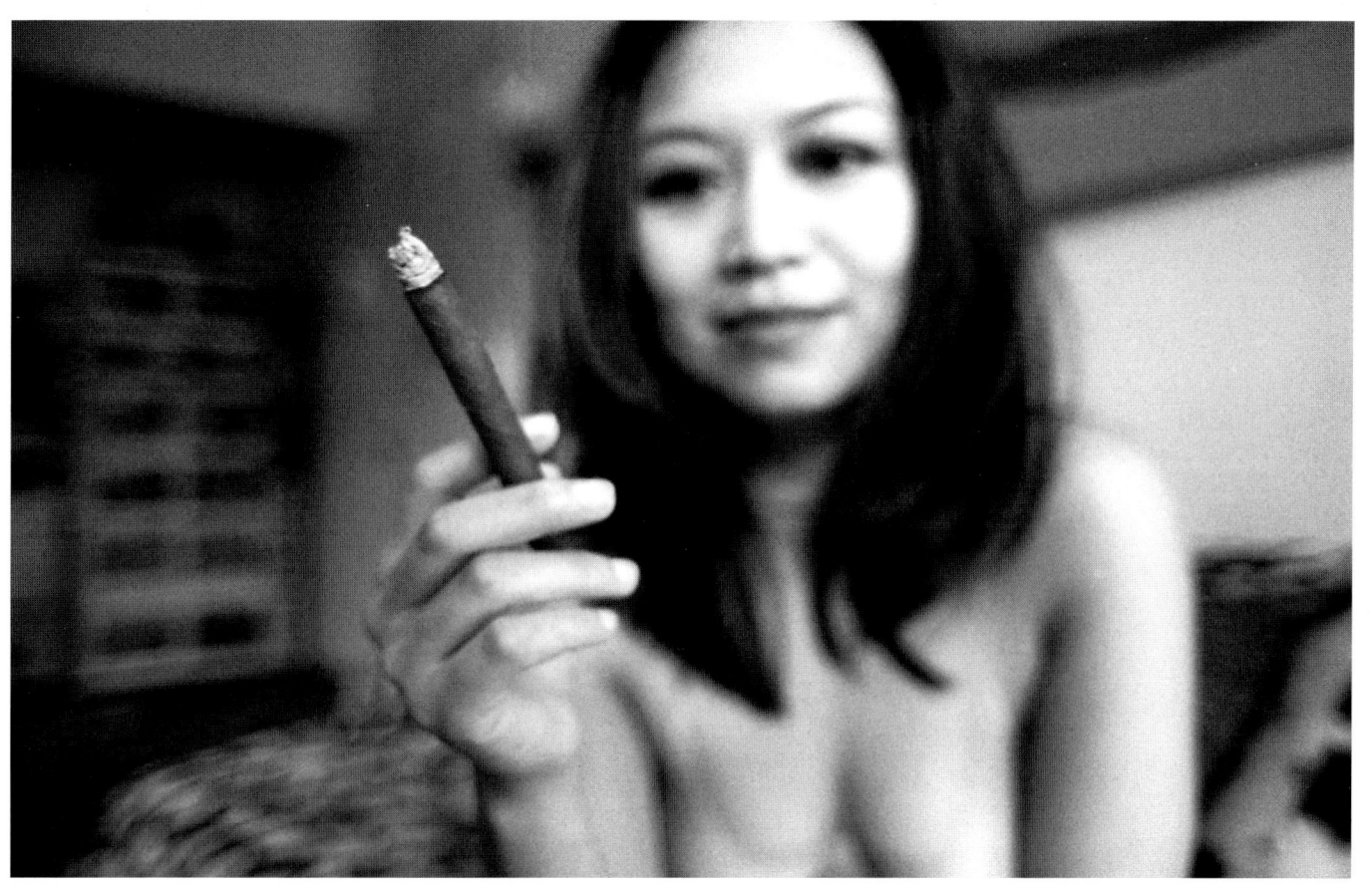

Thuc · I met Thuc many times in and around New York City. She was always playing the trumpet with various bands, promoting causes or protesting outdated laws. I photographed her in her east village apartment, which she shared with two men. I liked Thuc's nose, and how limber she was. Later she rearranged her apt at my suggestion.

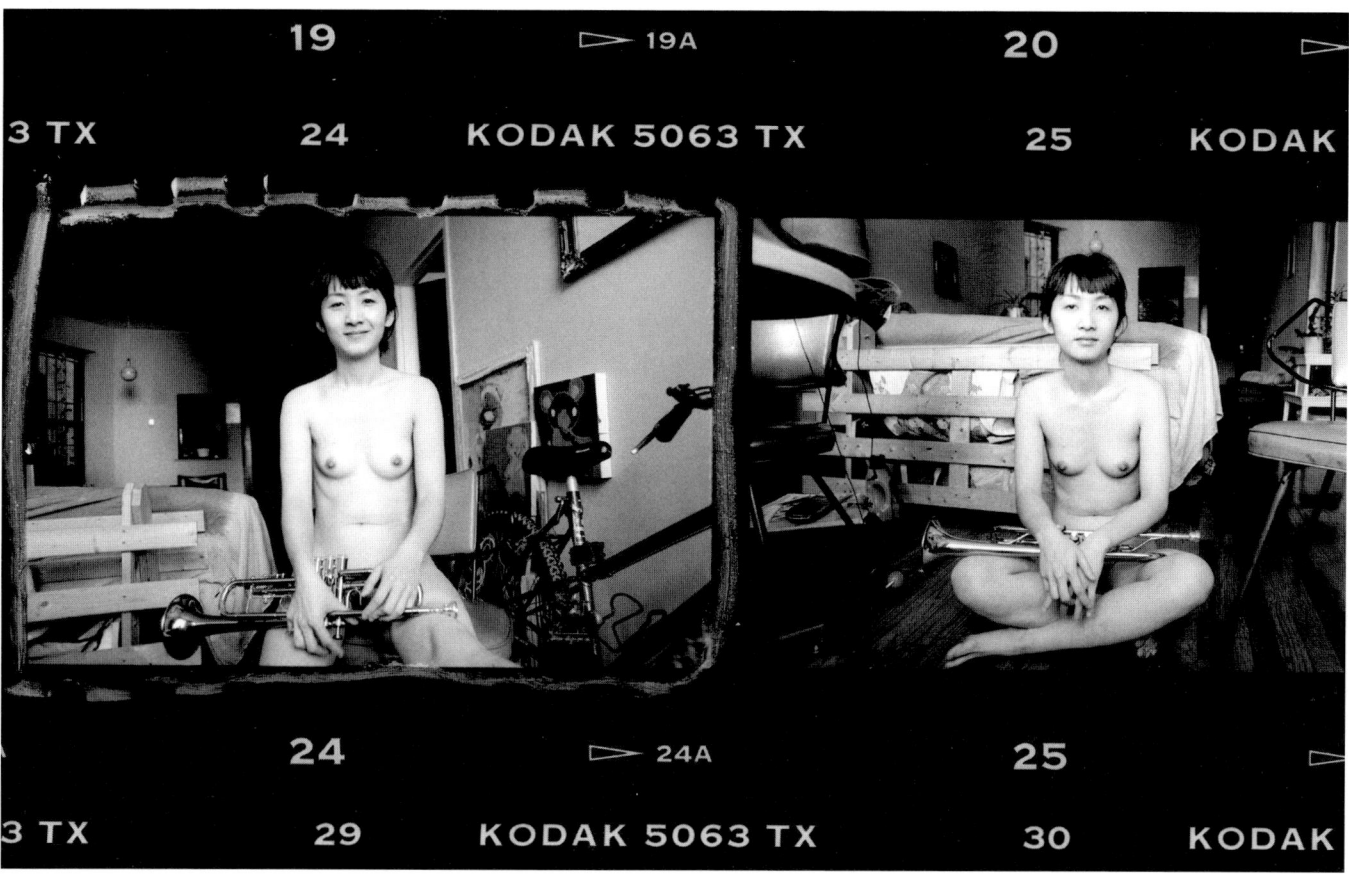

321

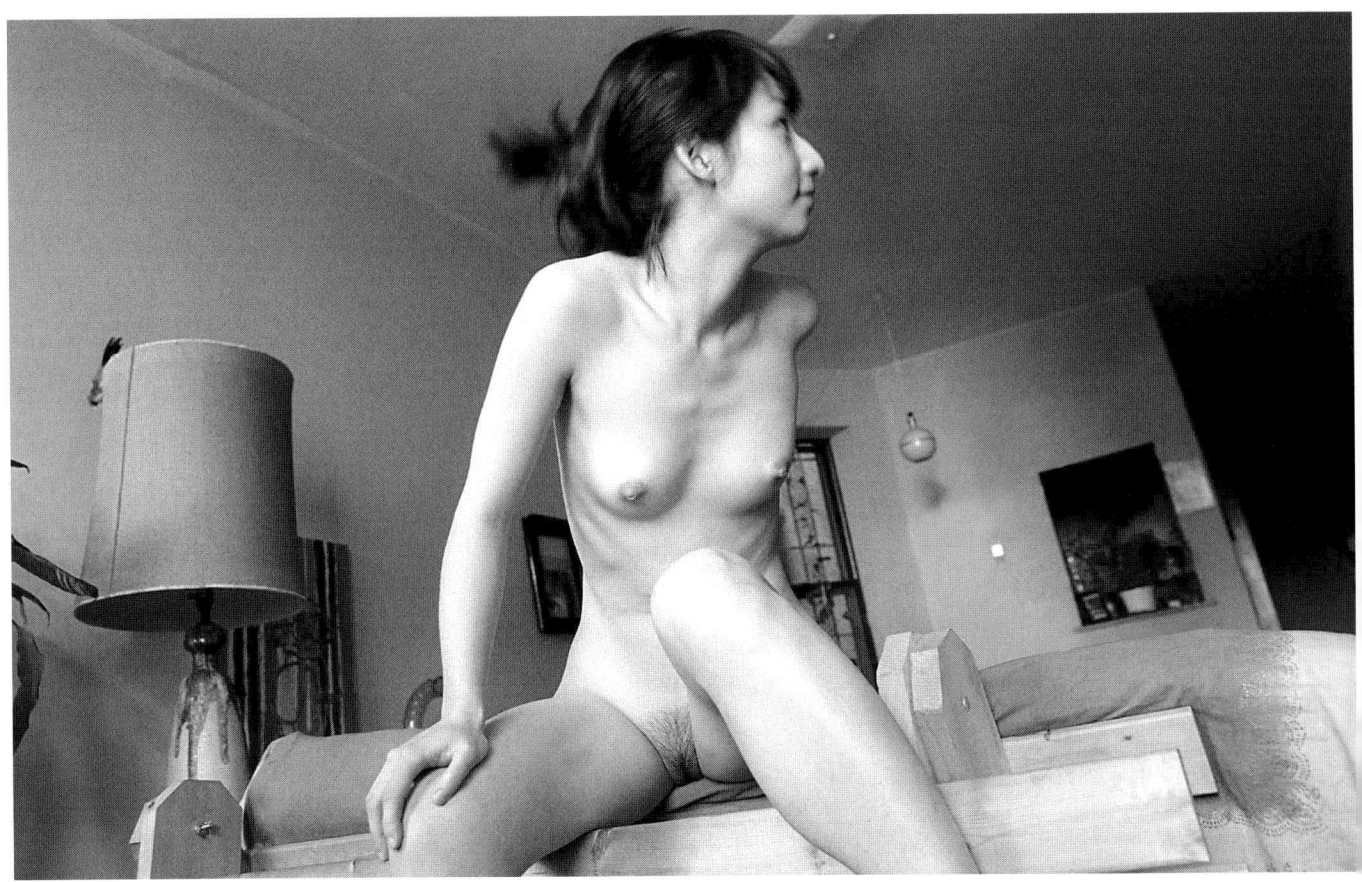

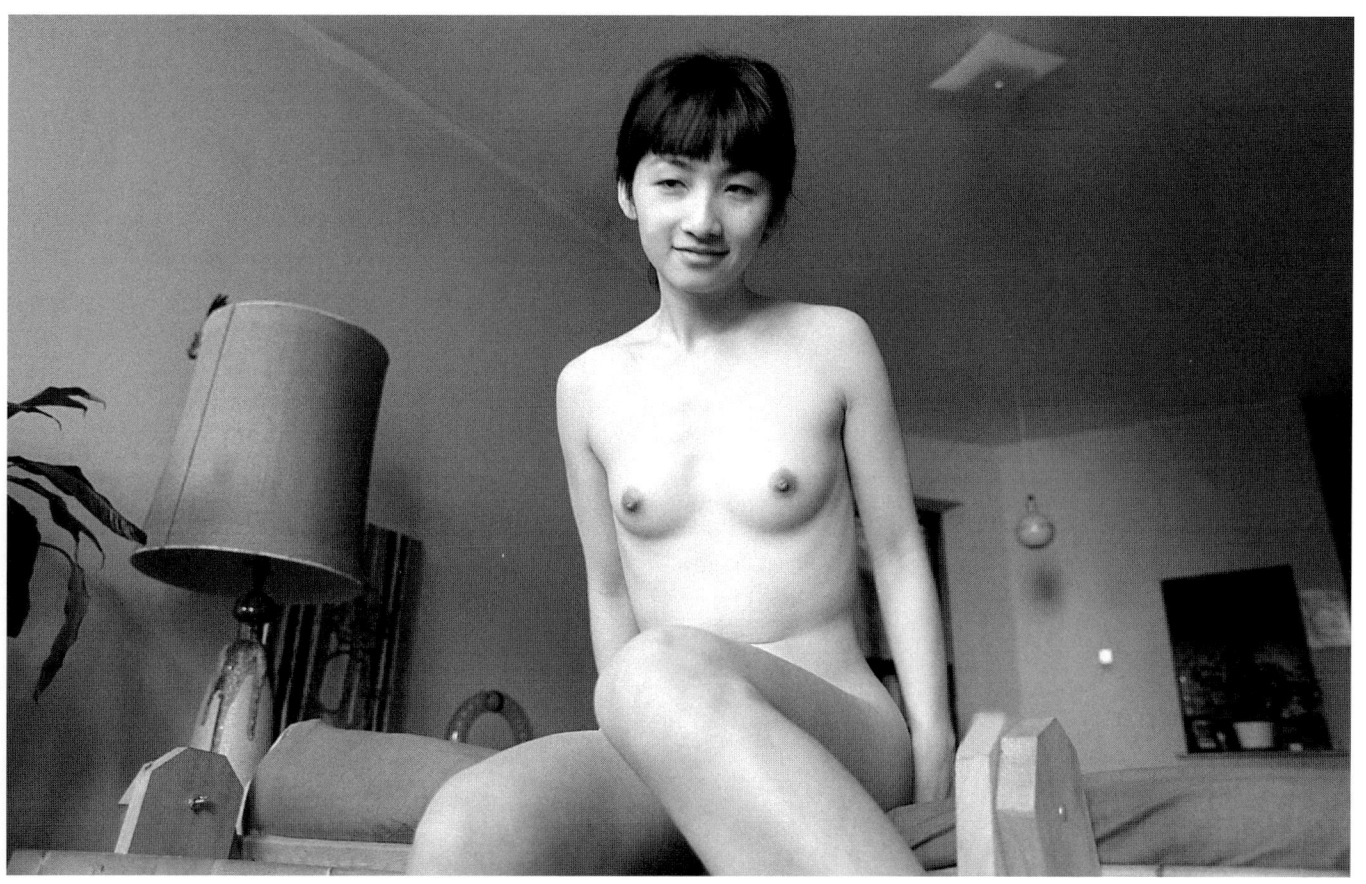

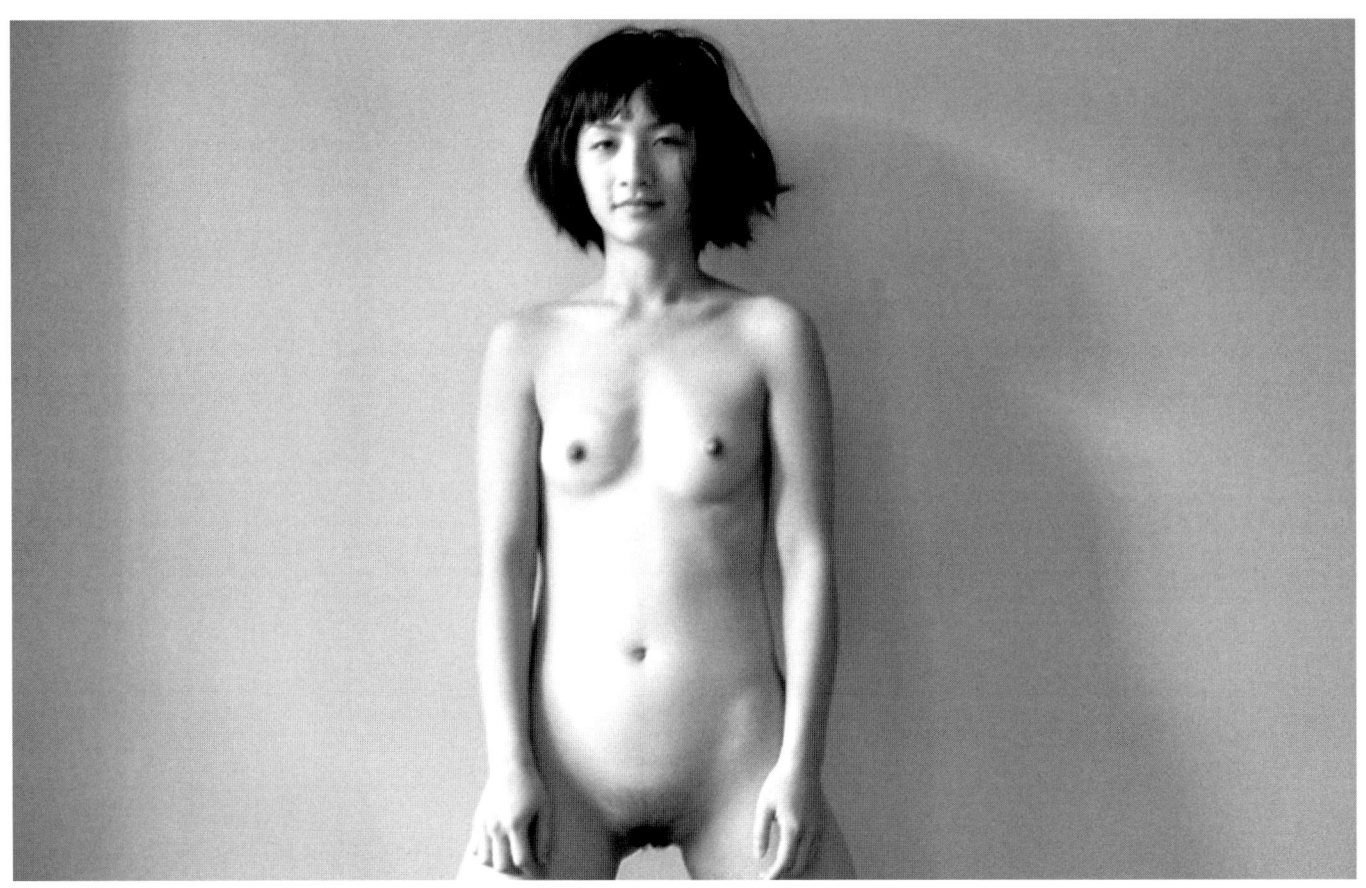

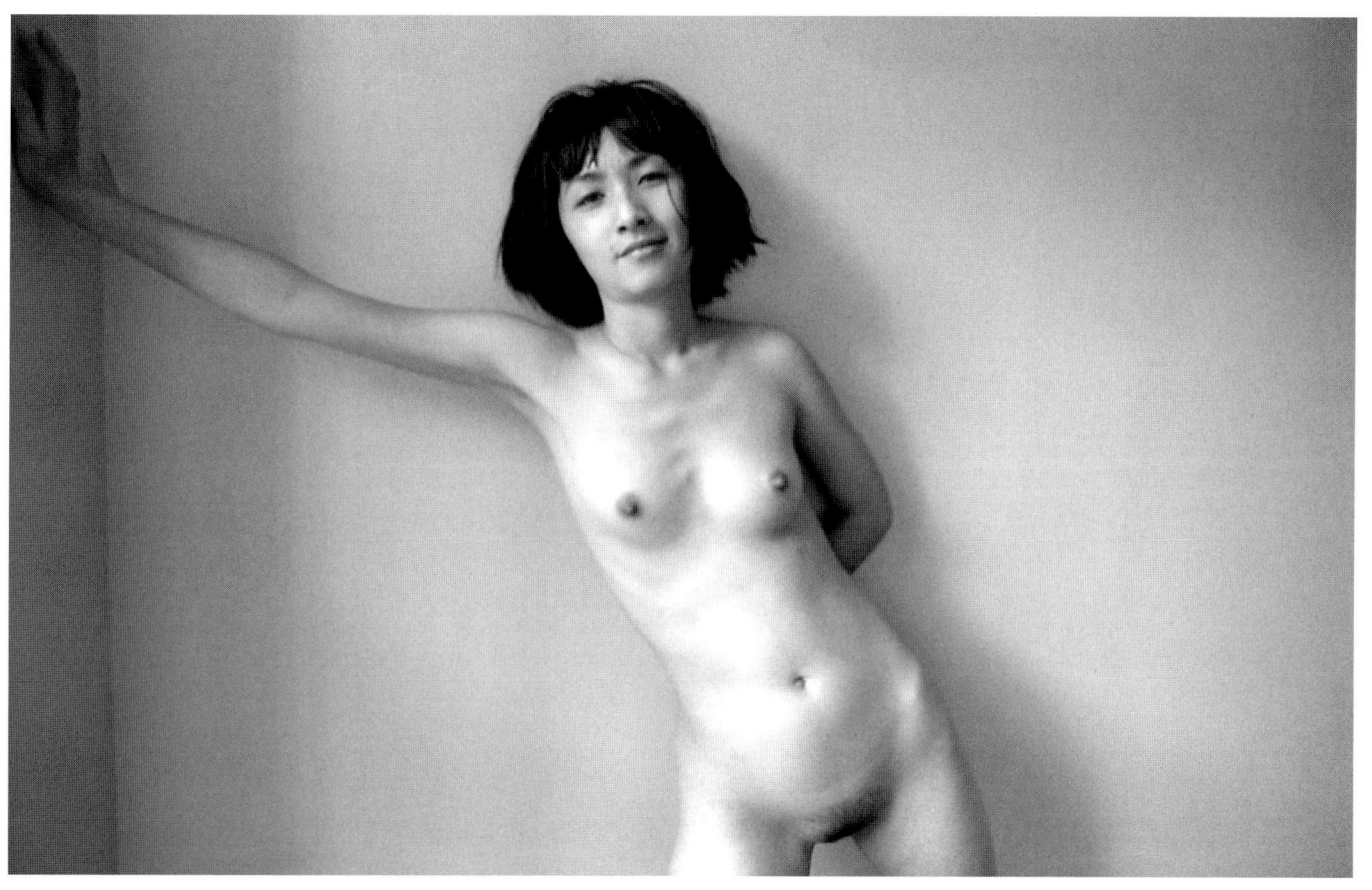

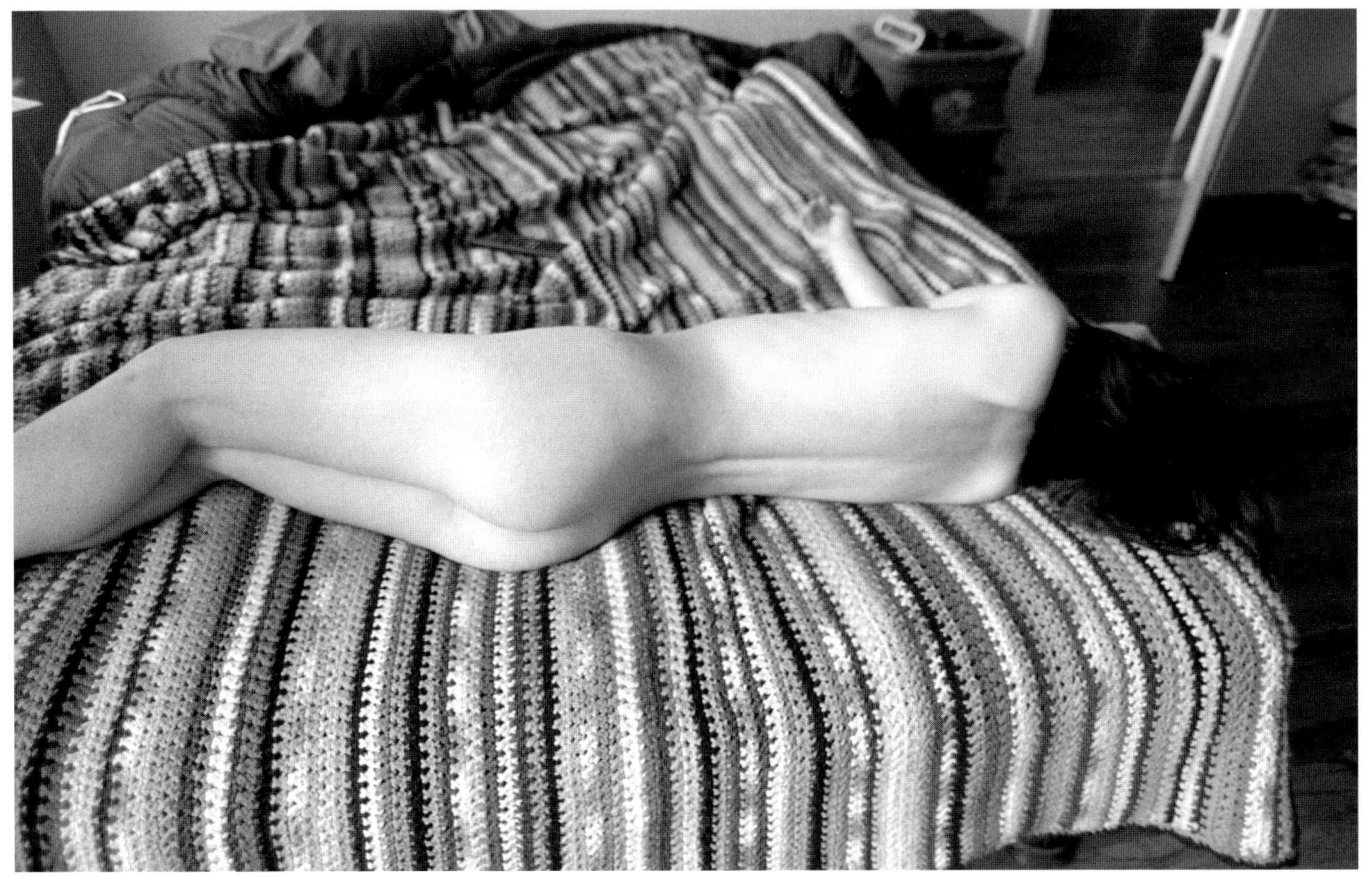

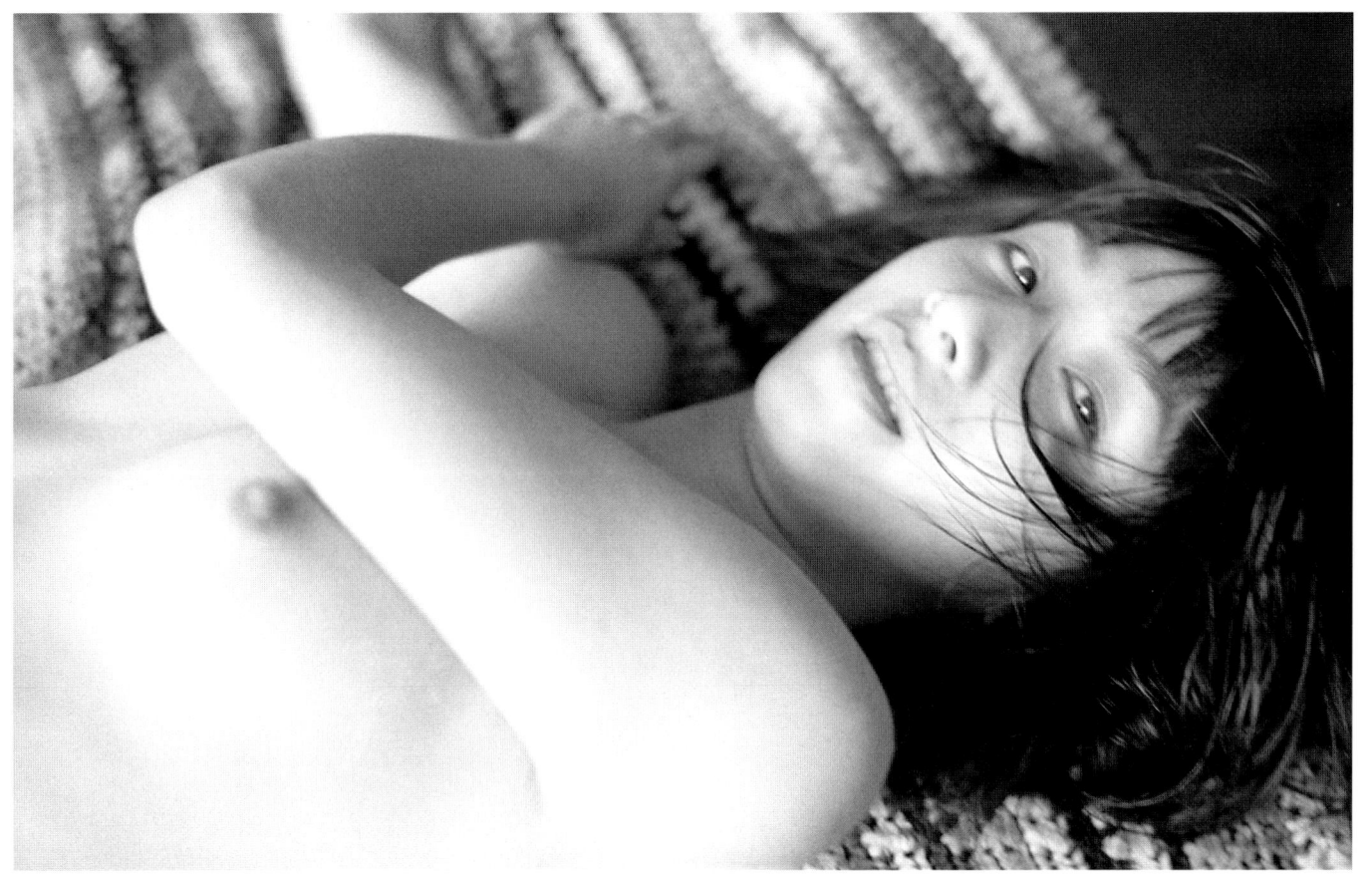

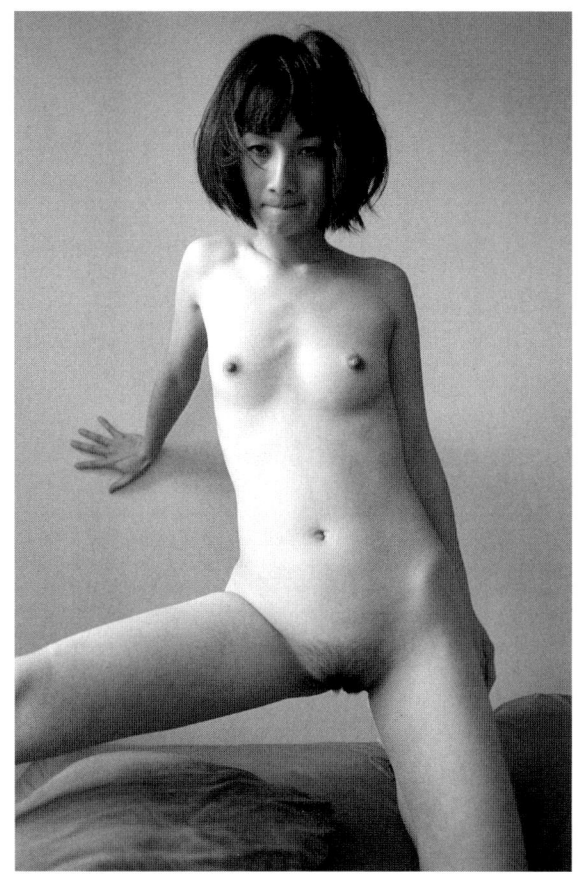
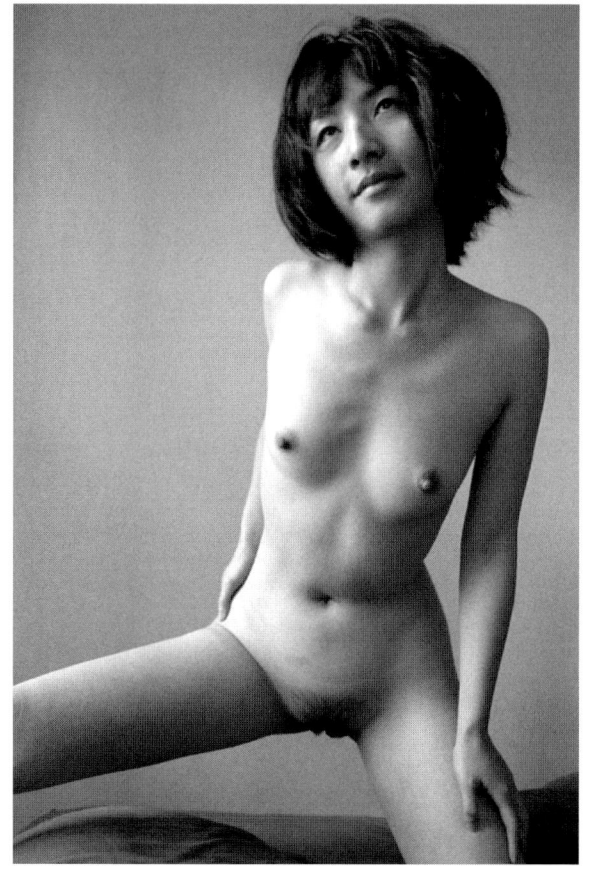

328

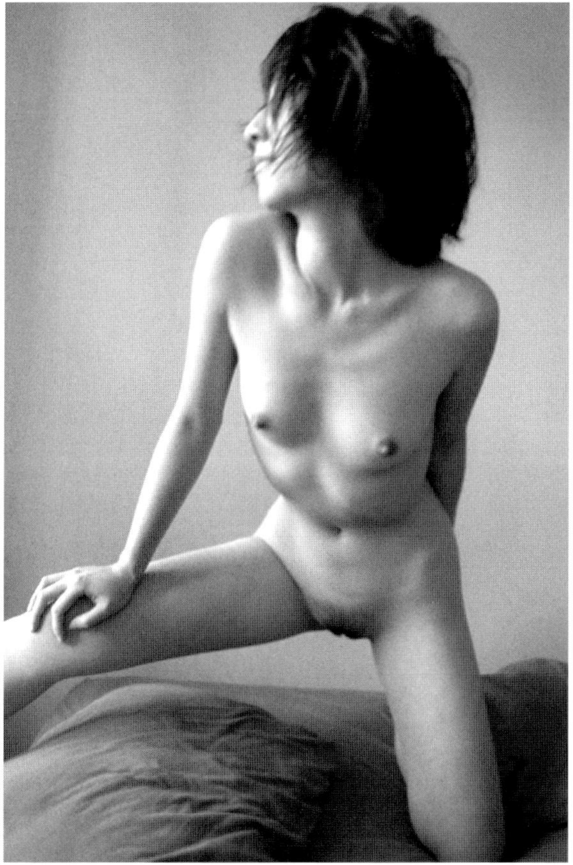

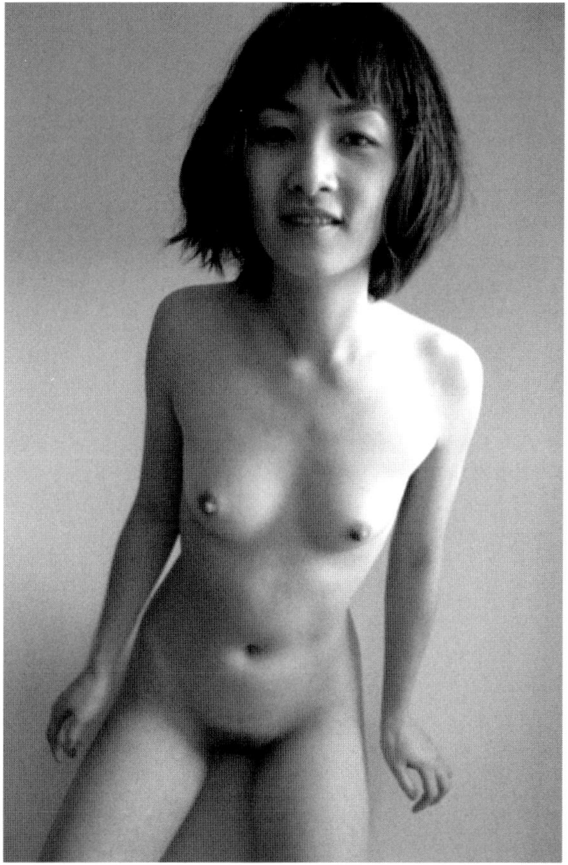

Veronica · I photographed Veronica in a beautiful pop art hotel. We went from my room, to the hall bathroom, to the outdoor garden terrace. Veronica didn't speak English, but brought a translator, who took pictures of both of us. Veronica was like a playboy centerfold from the 70's: curvy and natural and happy.

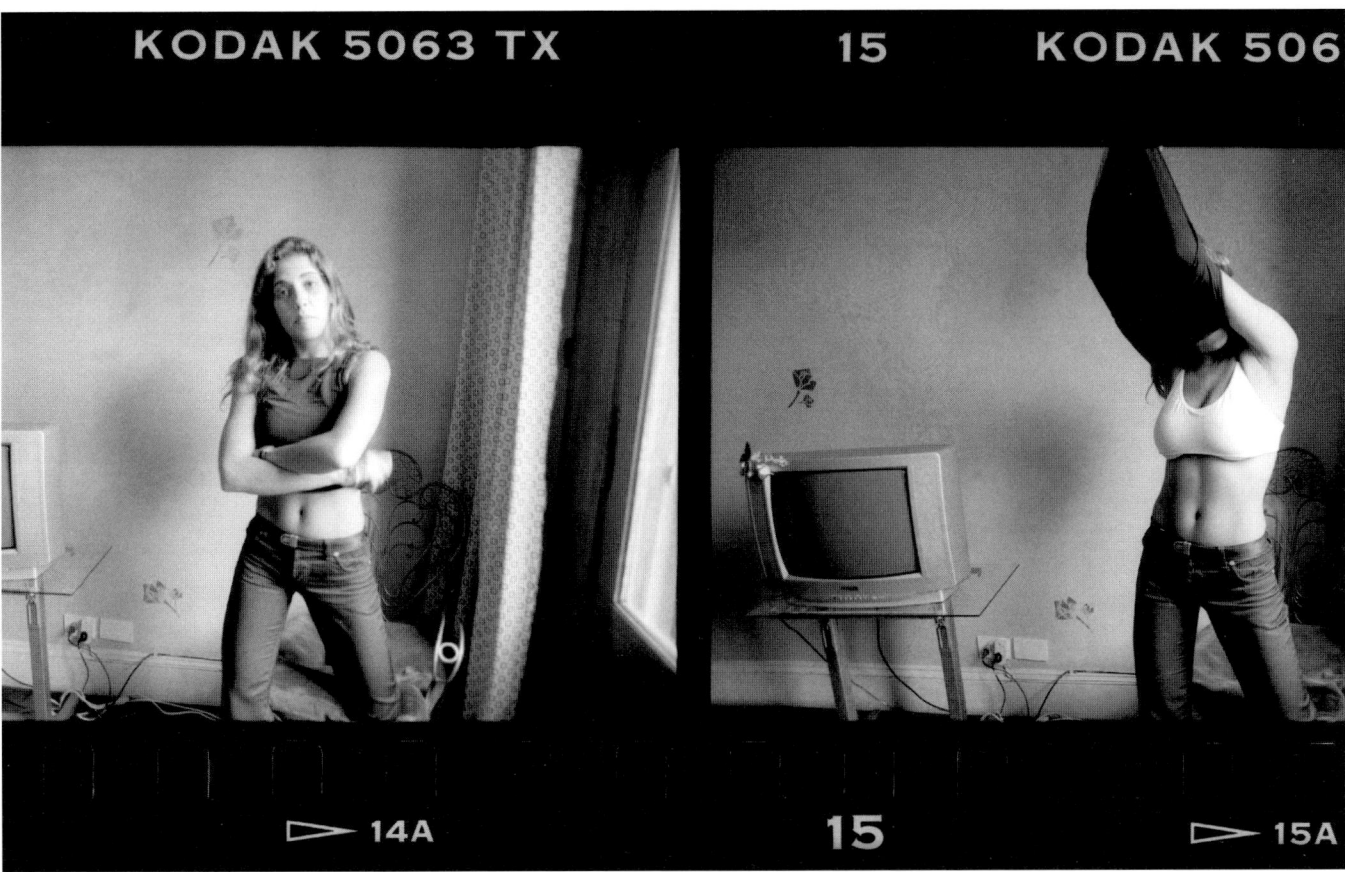

KODAK 5063 TX   15   KODAK 506

▷ 14A   15   ▷ 15A

331

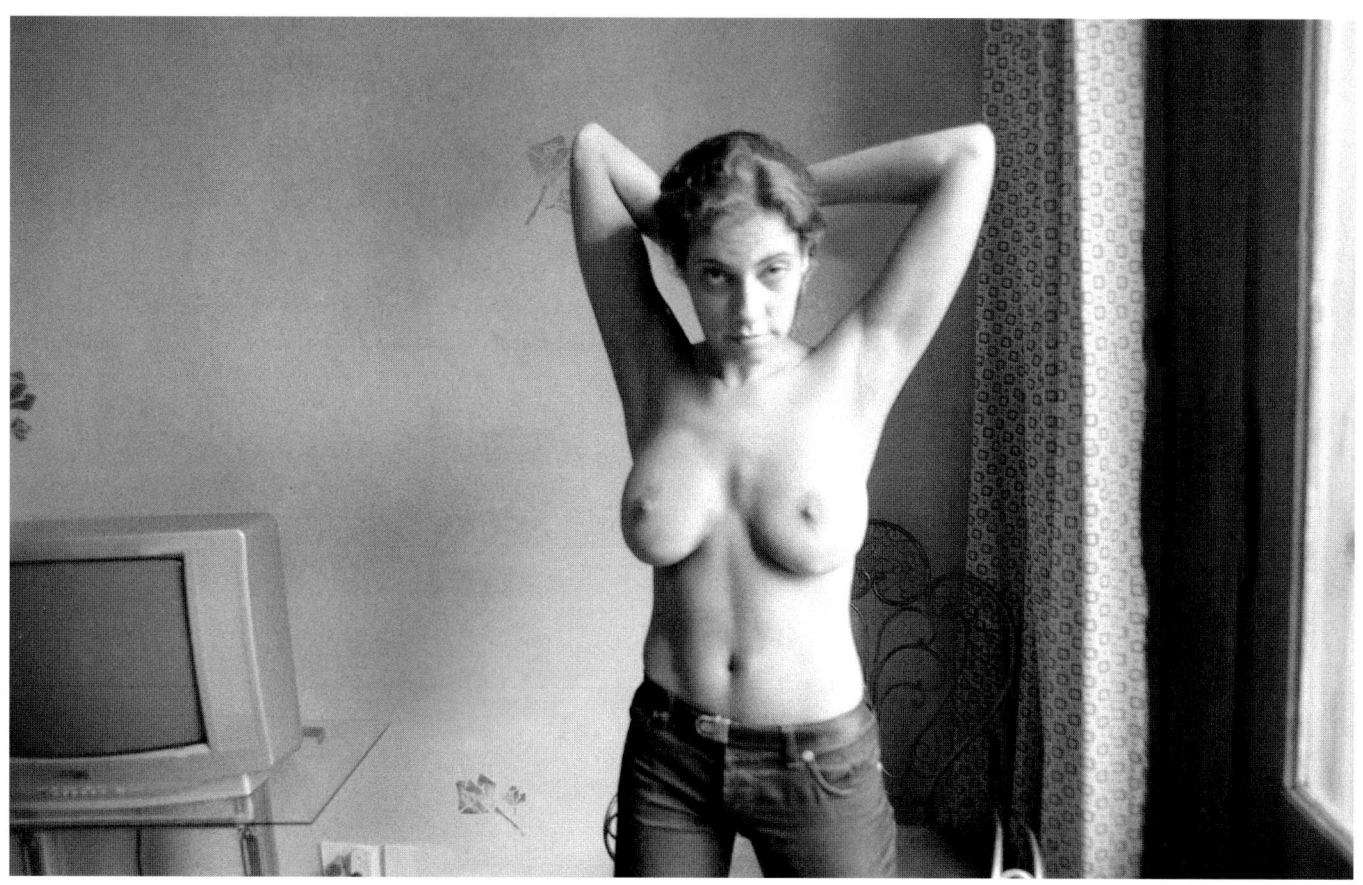

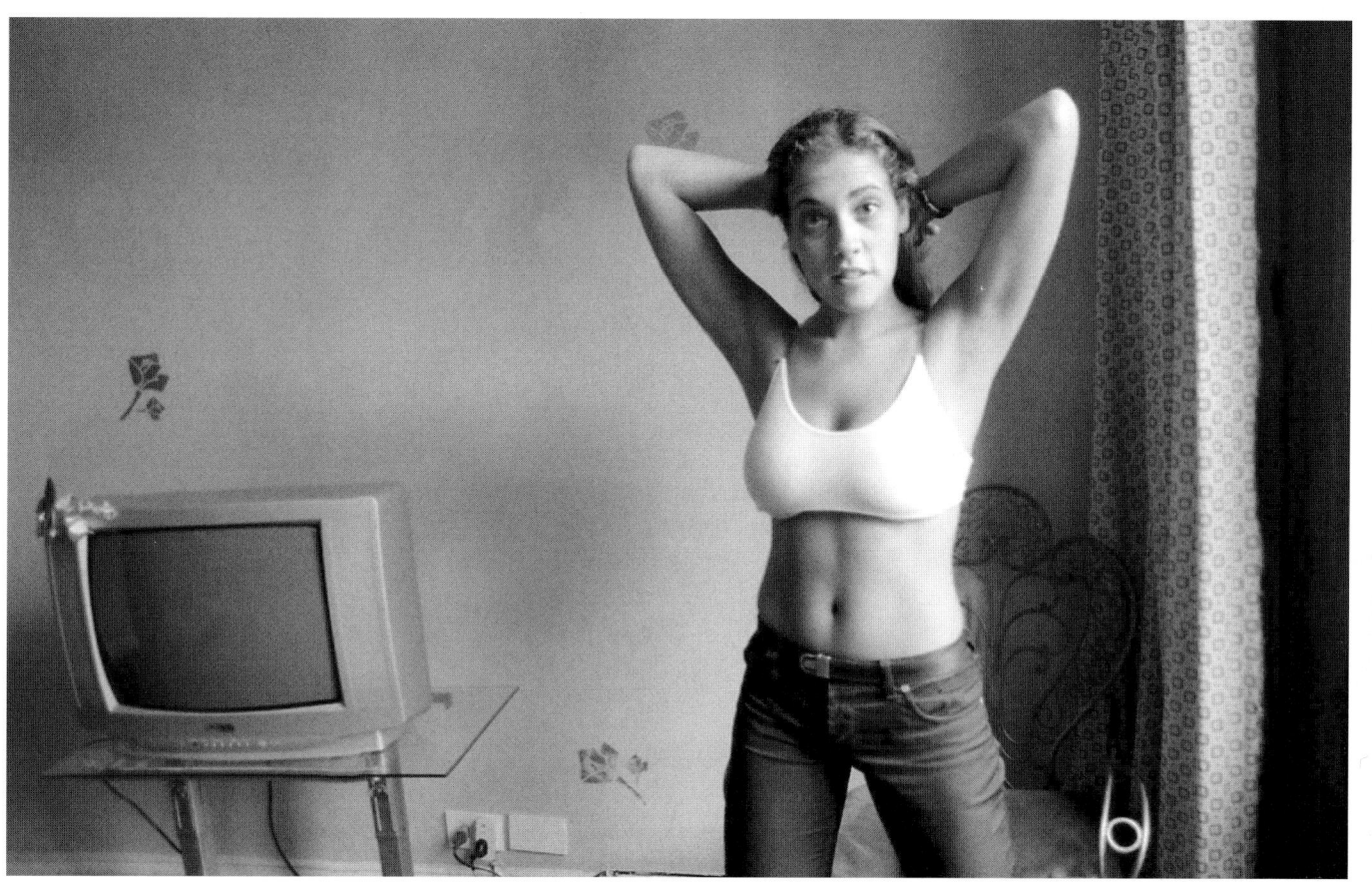

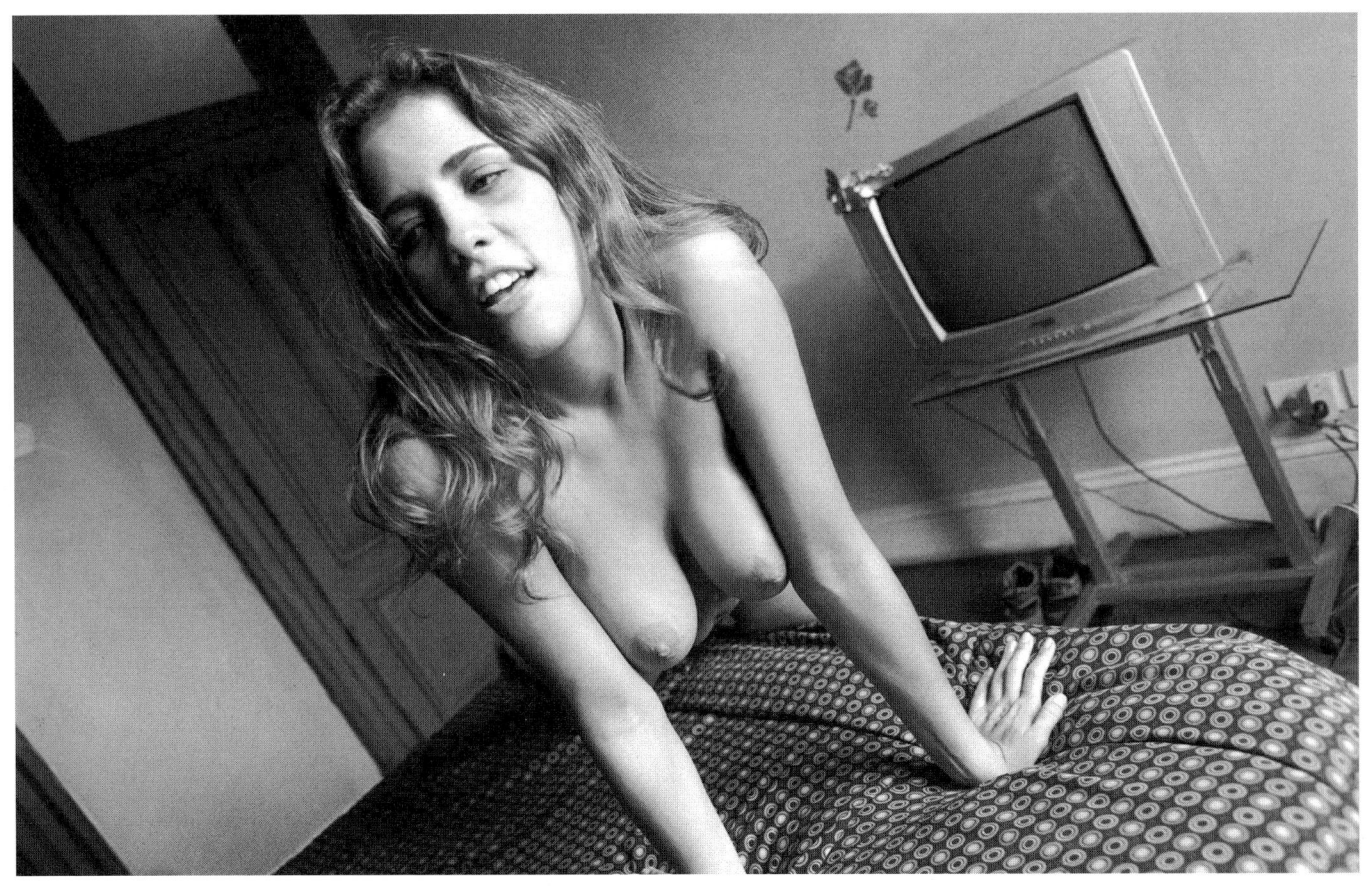

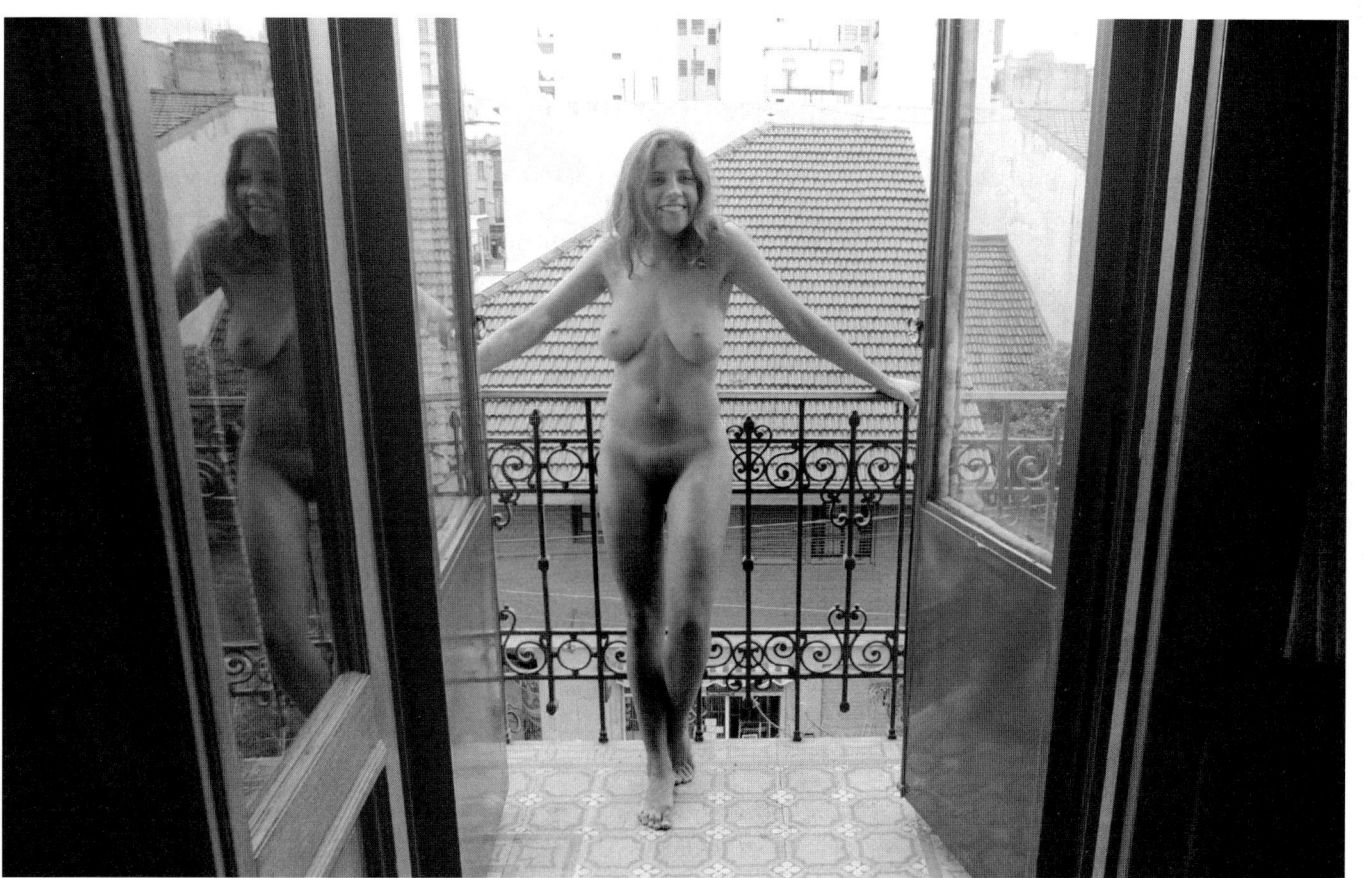

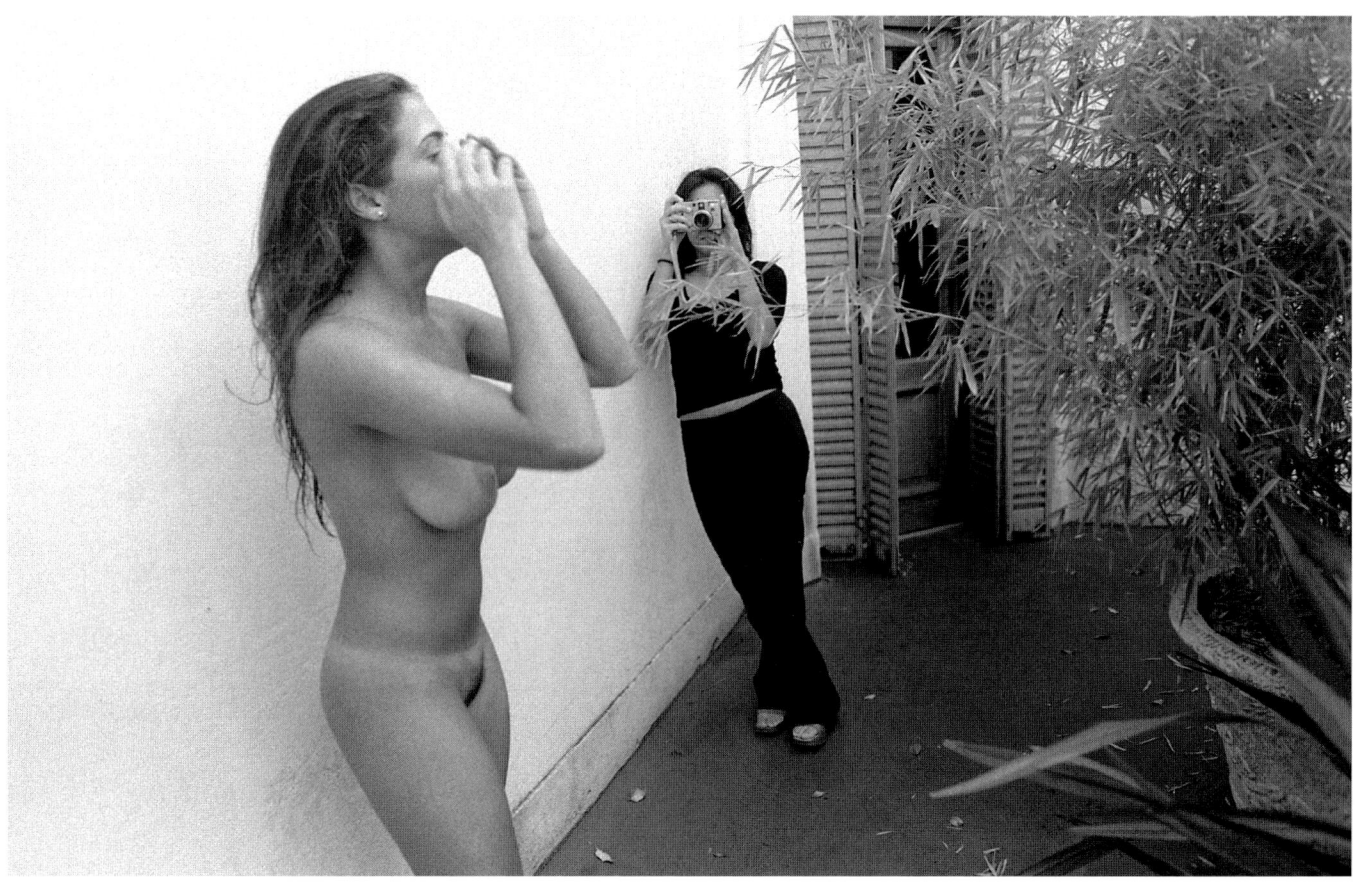

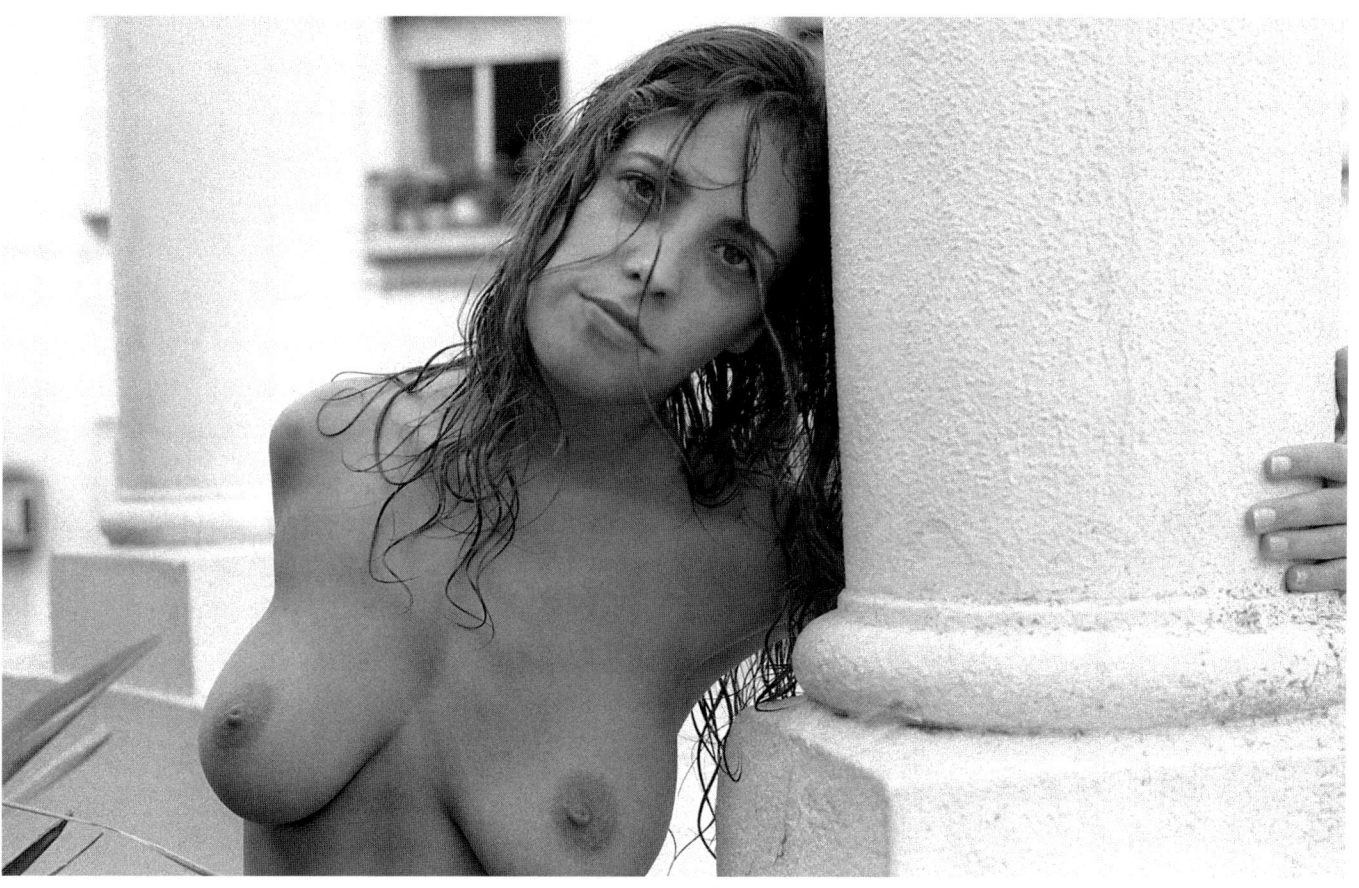

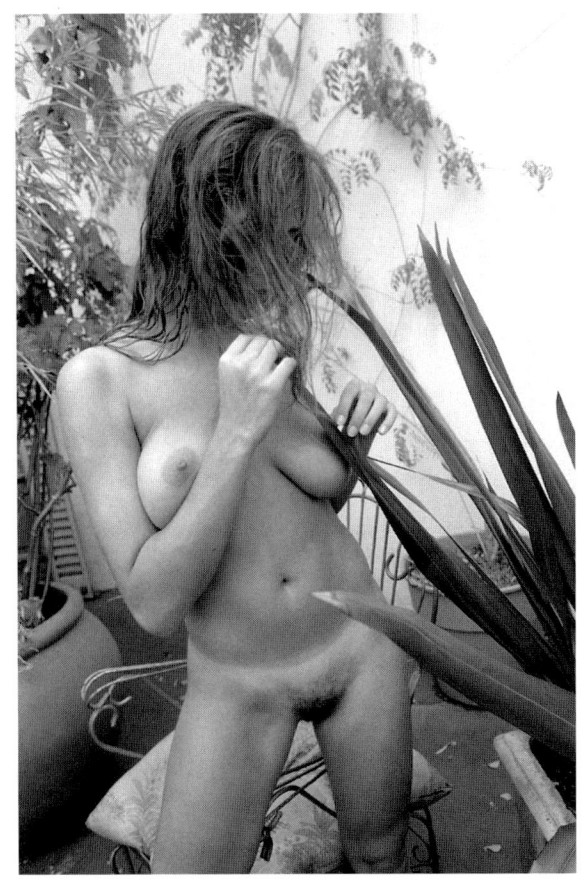
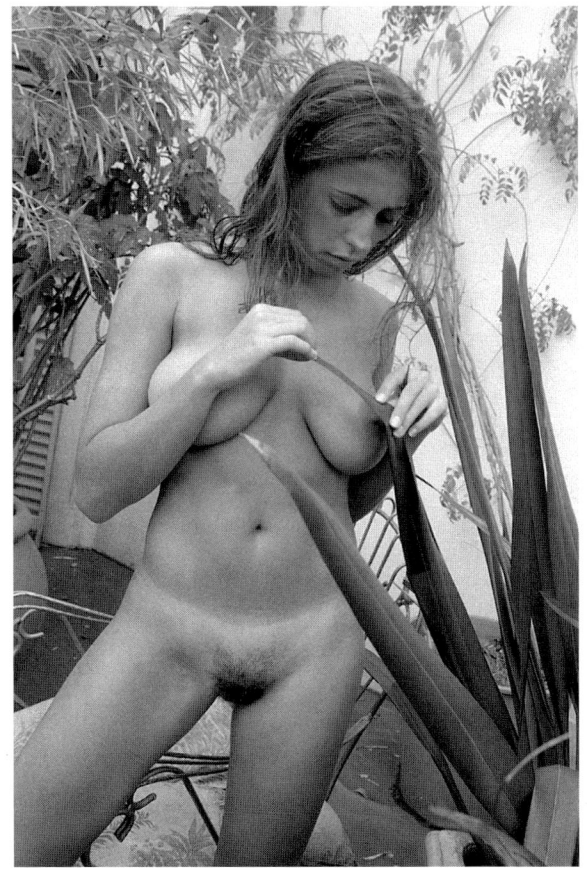

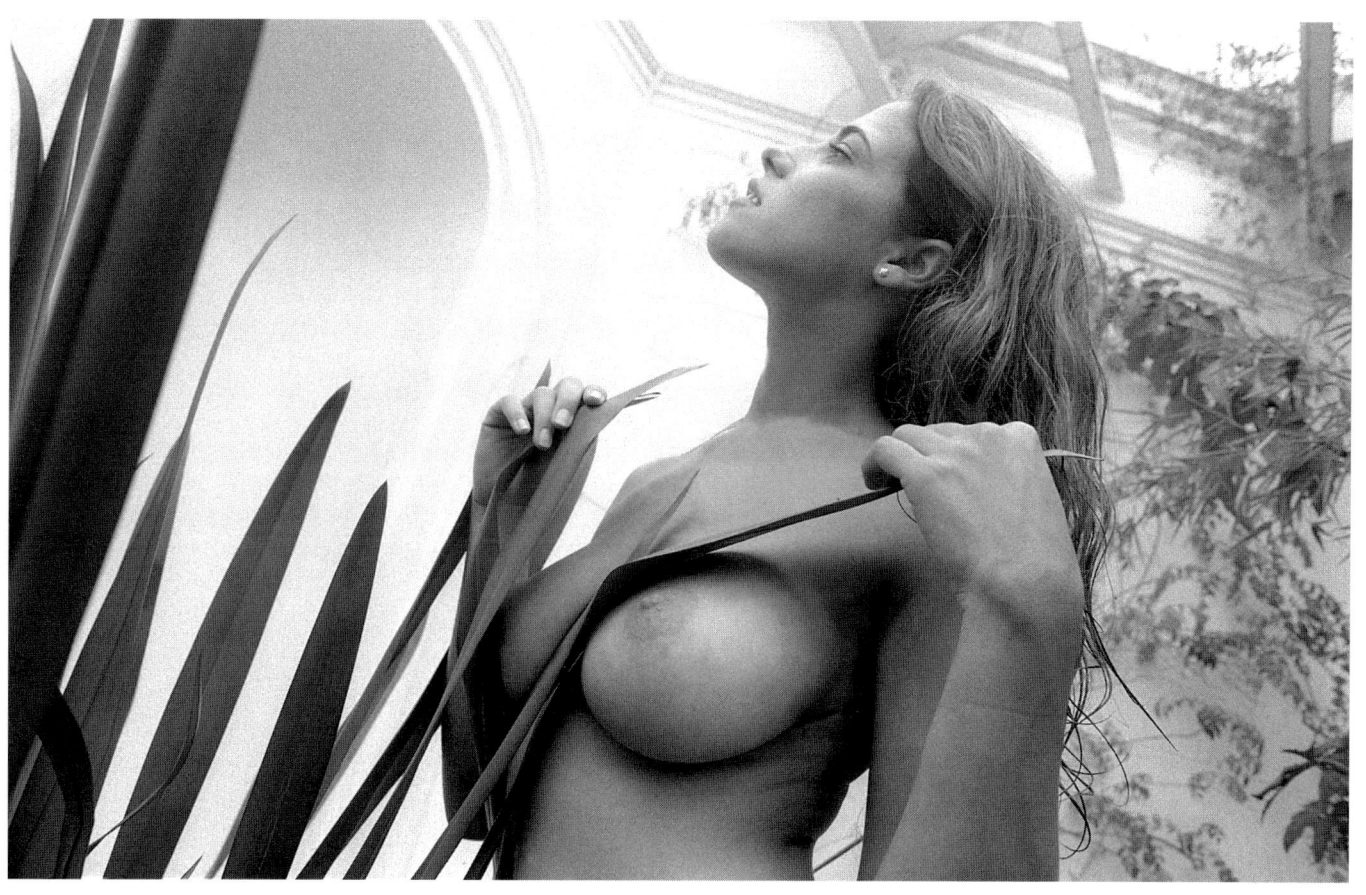

Victoria · I met Victoria in an editing studio, years before taking her picture. I photographed her in her Upper West Side apartment. There was very little daylight, so I kept trying to lure her further out on the fire escape. I think we both had fun with that. Victoria is a singer/songwriter, and has a special inner beauty which came out in the photos.

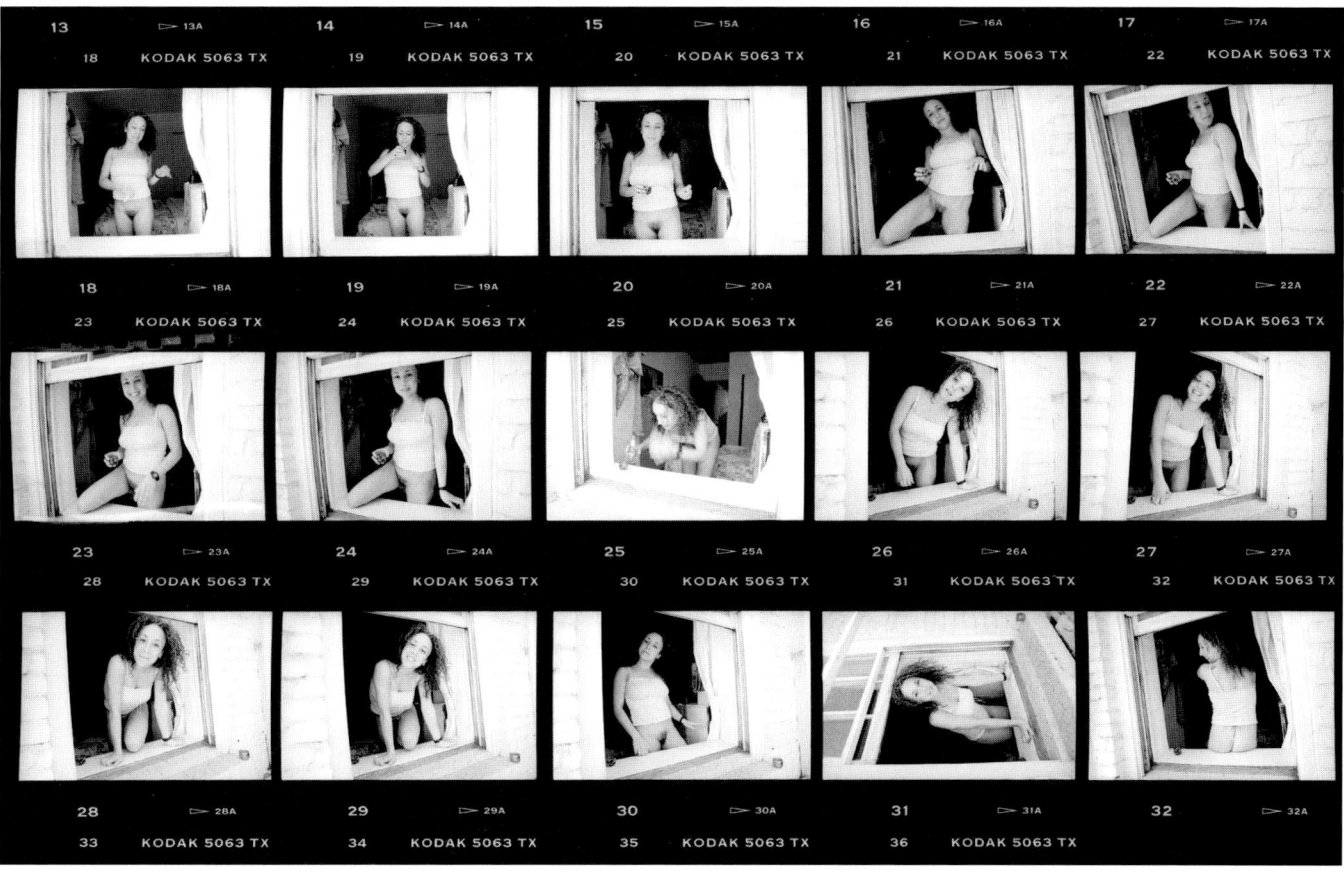

341

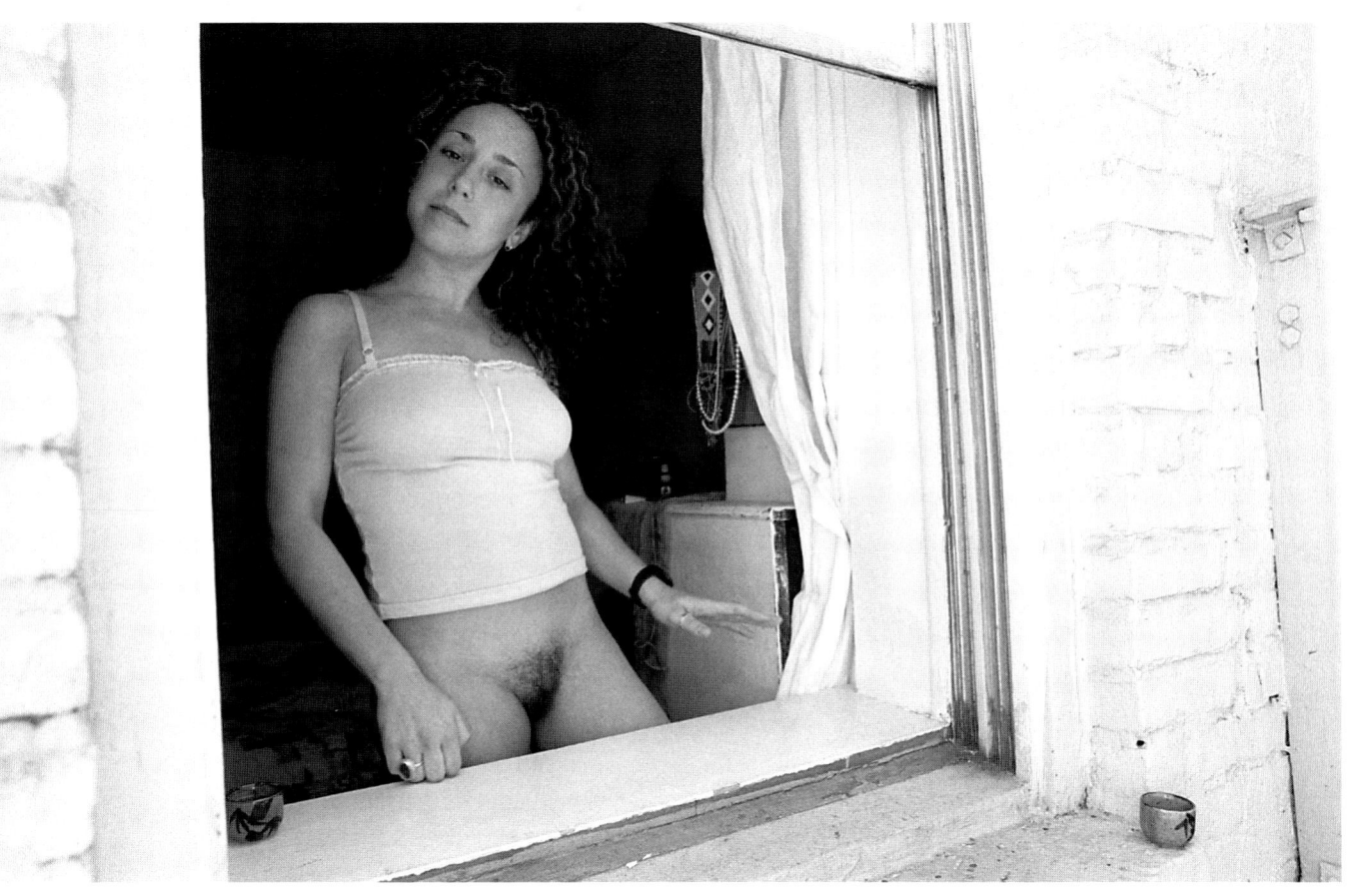

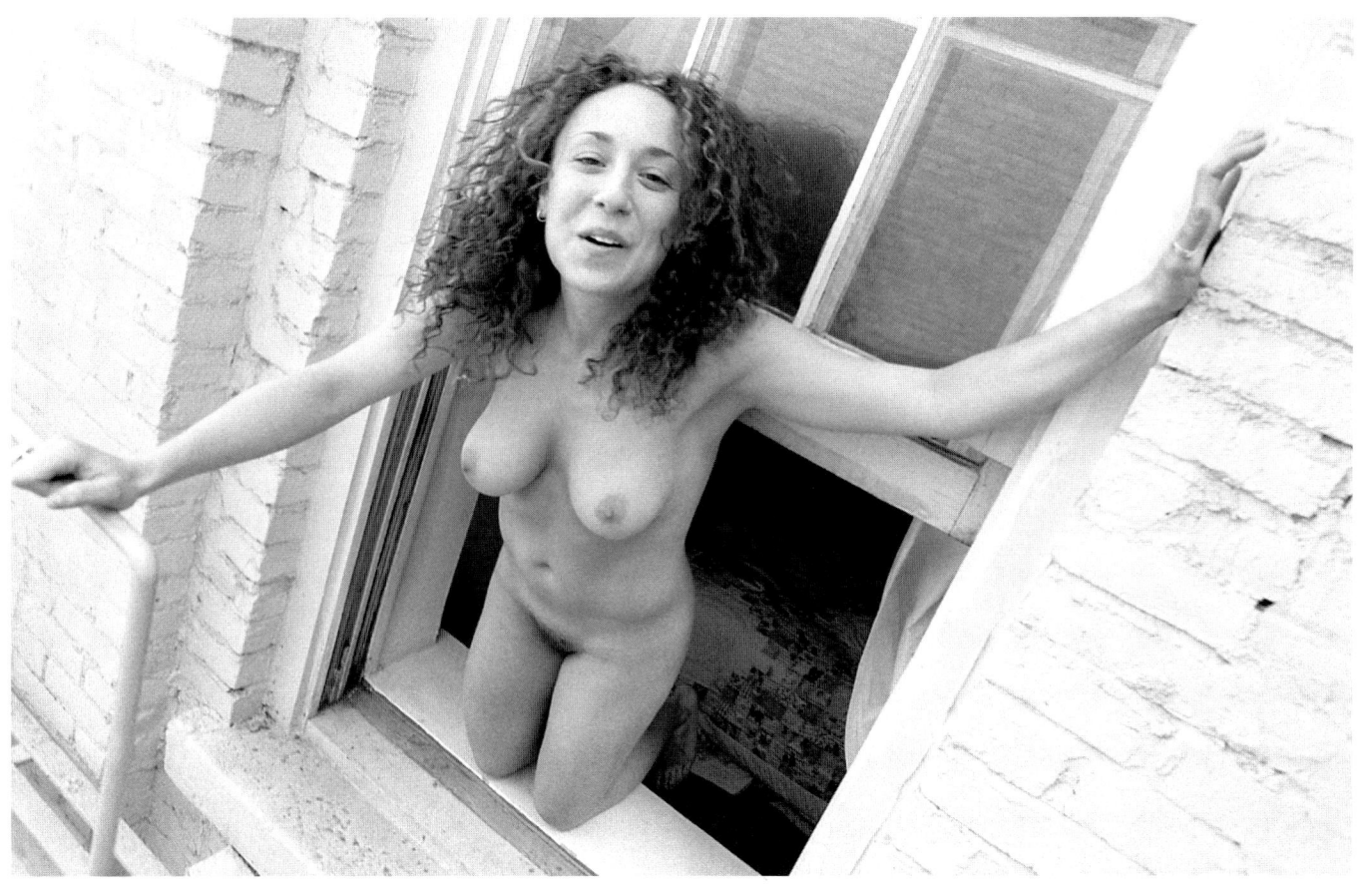

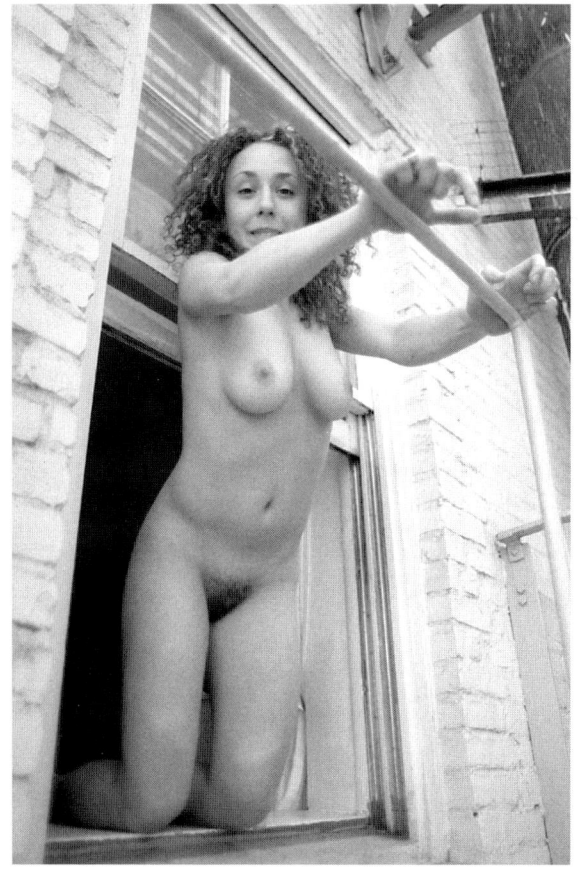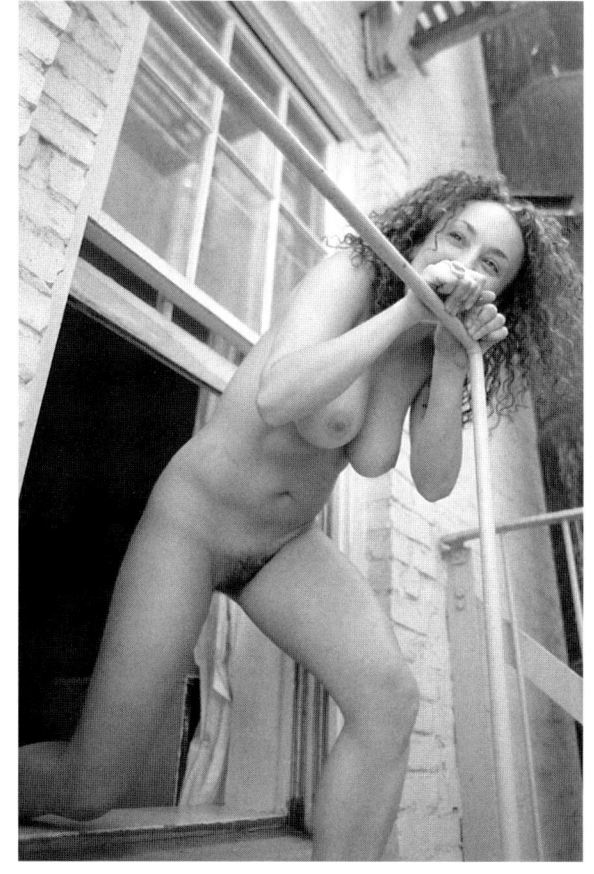

344

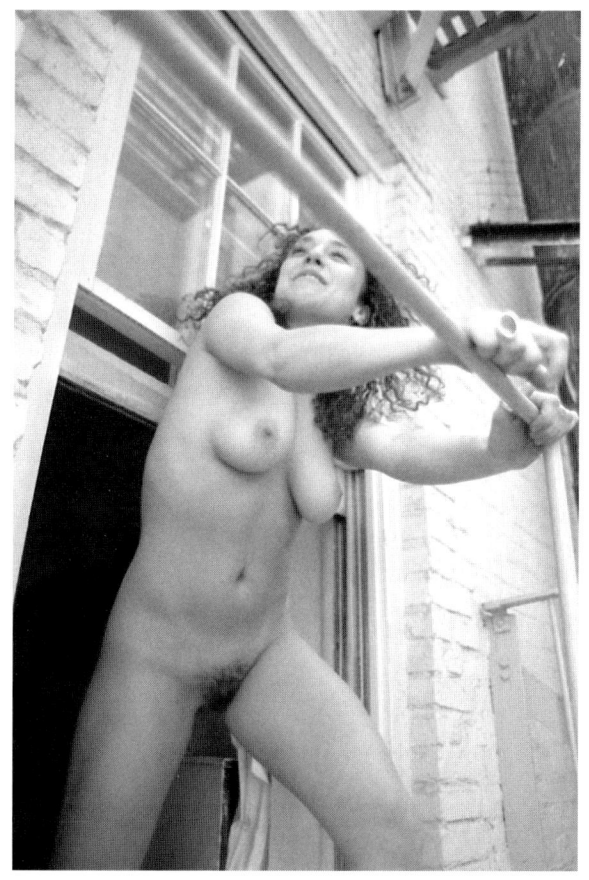
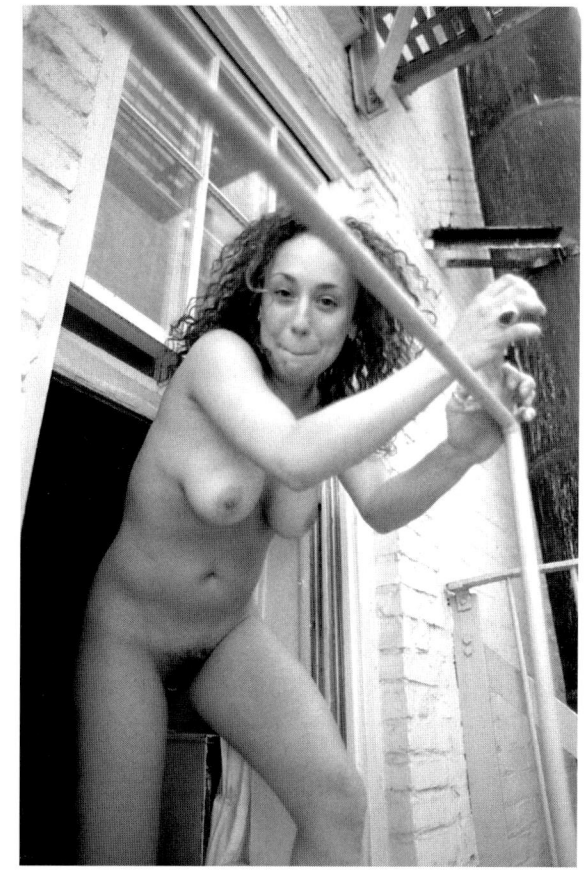

Viva · I met Viva through a friend. She's from Ecuador, and used to go by the alias "Viva Kneivel." I photographed her in her Brooklyn apartment. Viva was previously in fetish films, and danced in clubs and parties around town. Now she's writing, producing, and starring in Spanish soap operas. She knew how to use her body really well, and danced to the "Gypsy Kings" in the kitchen.

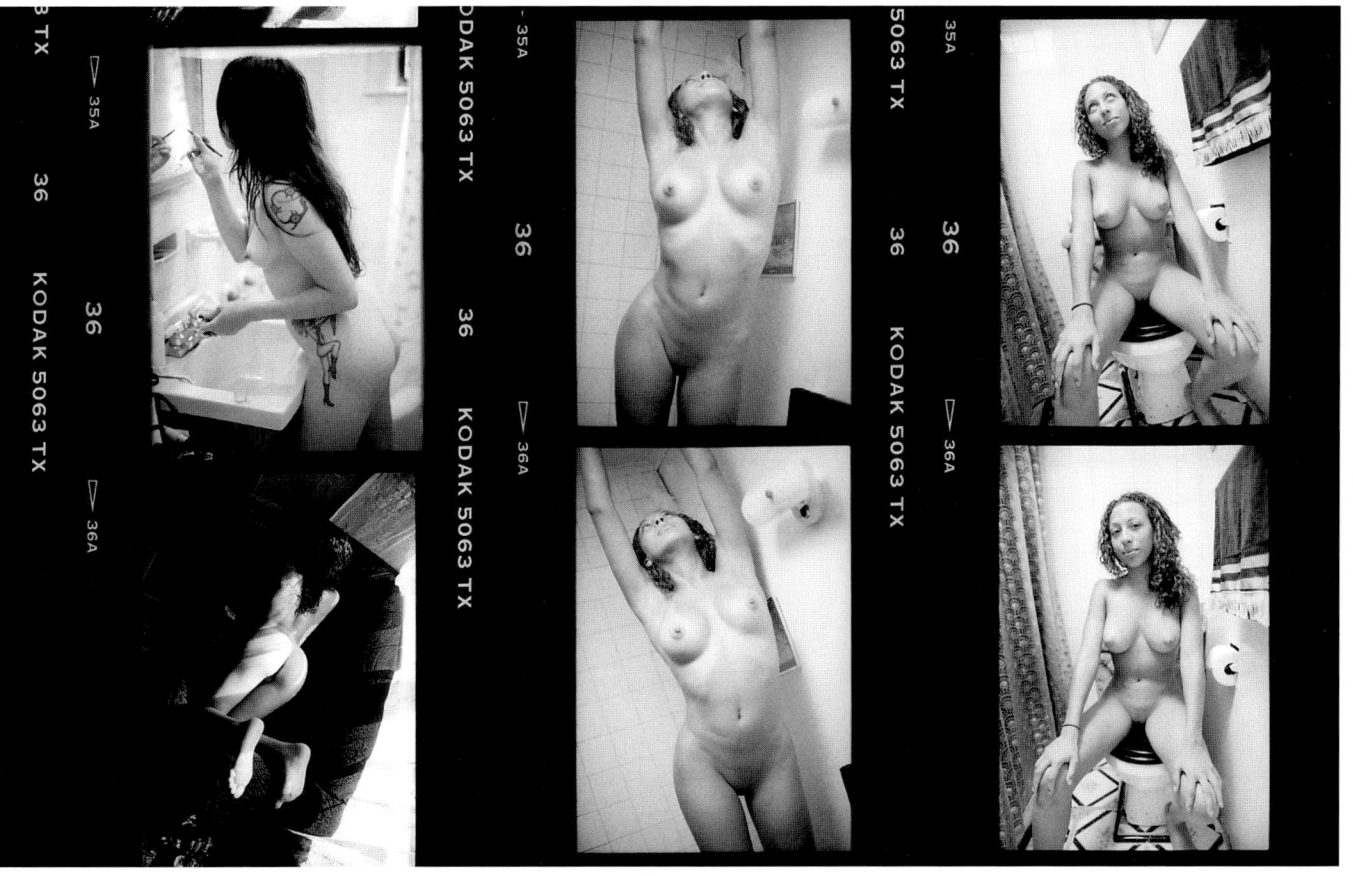

347

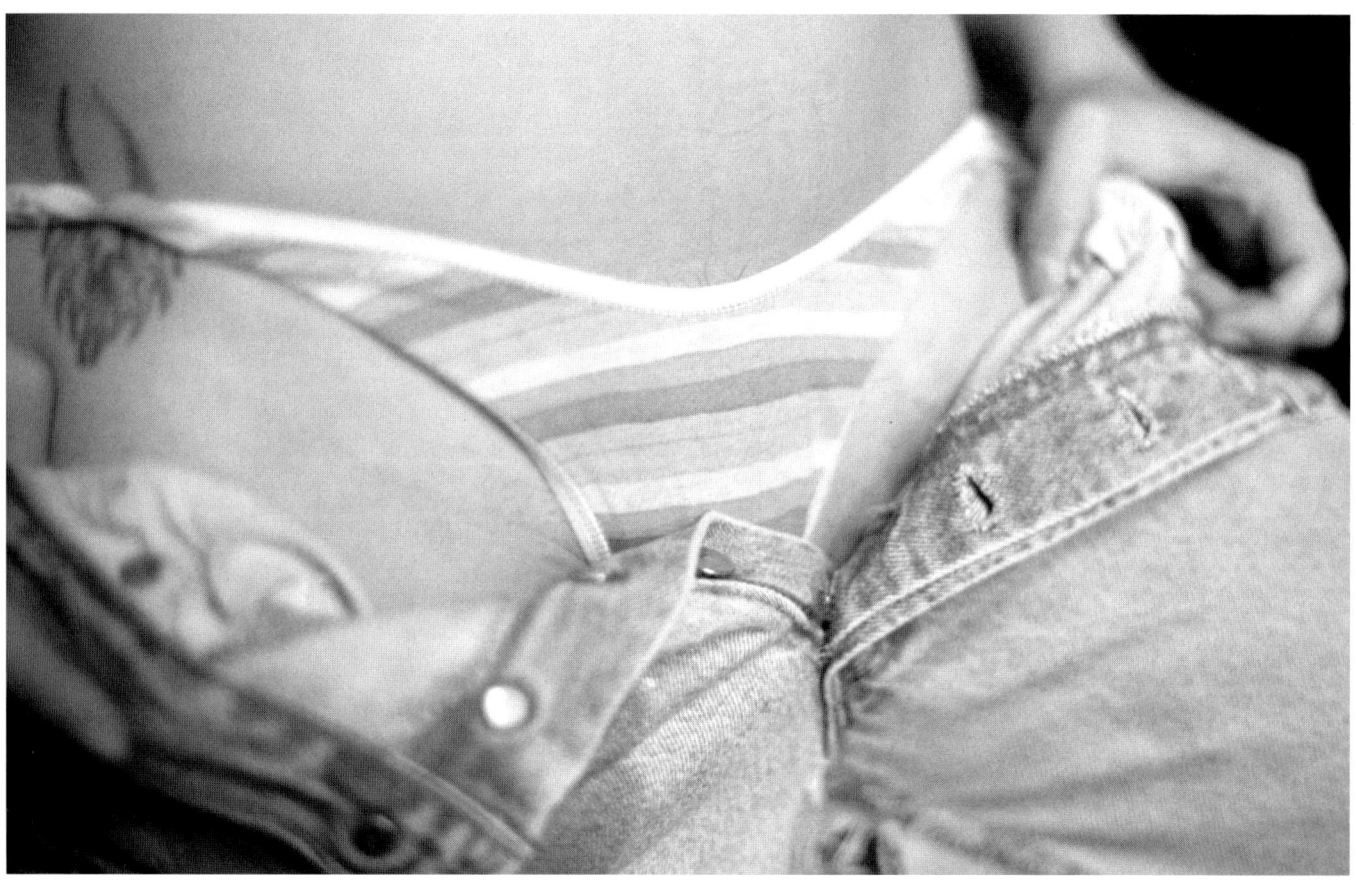

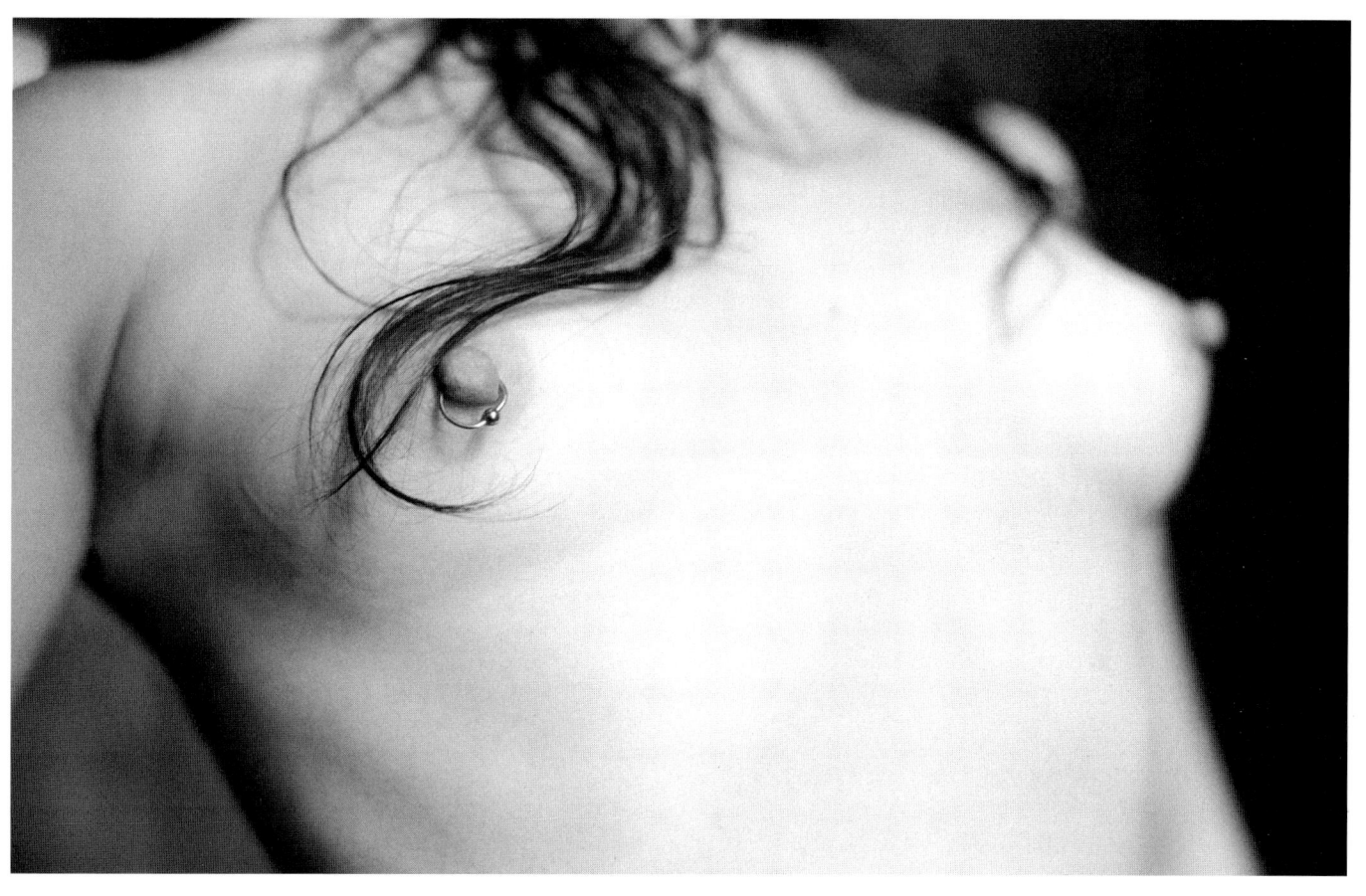

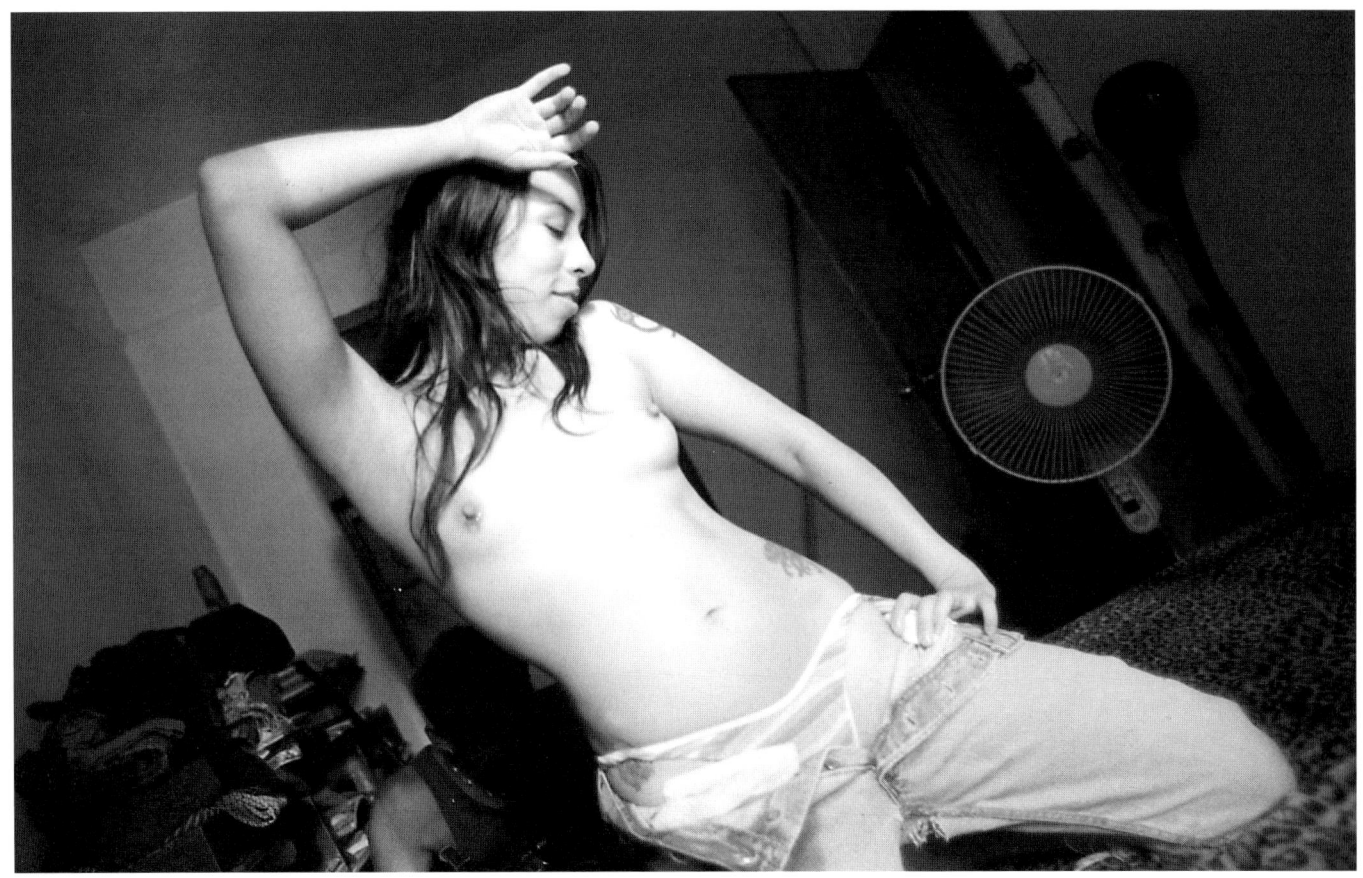

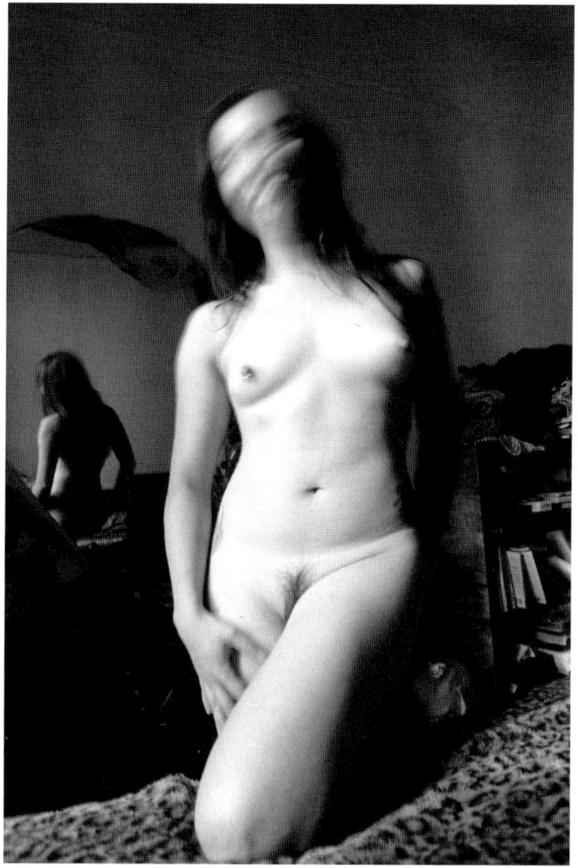

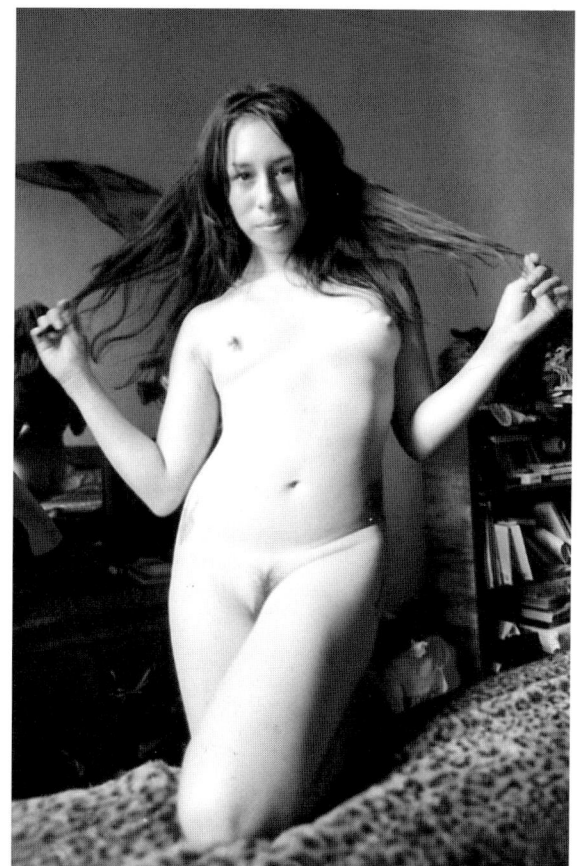

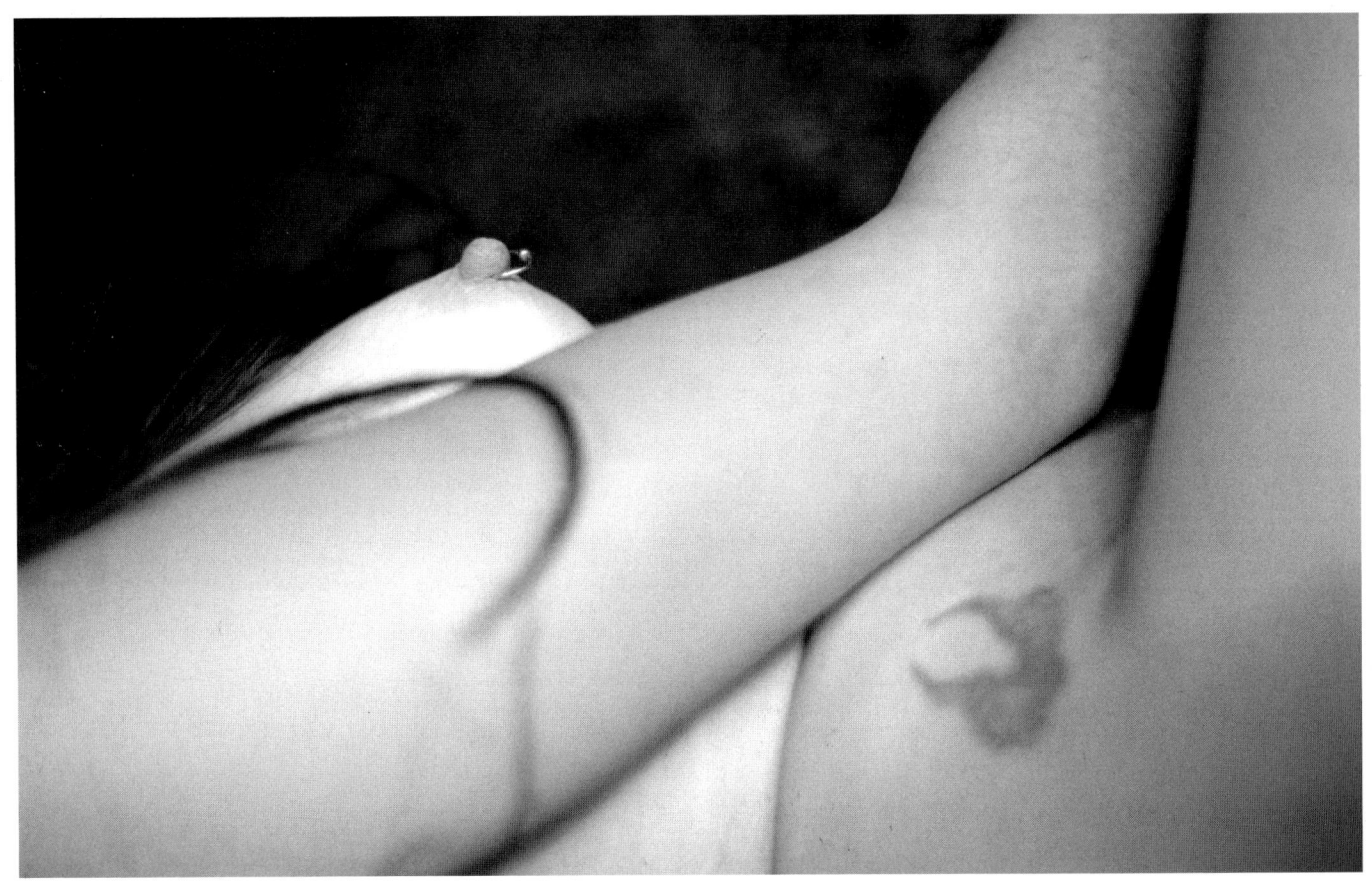

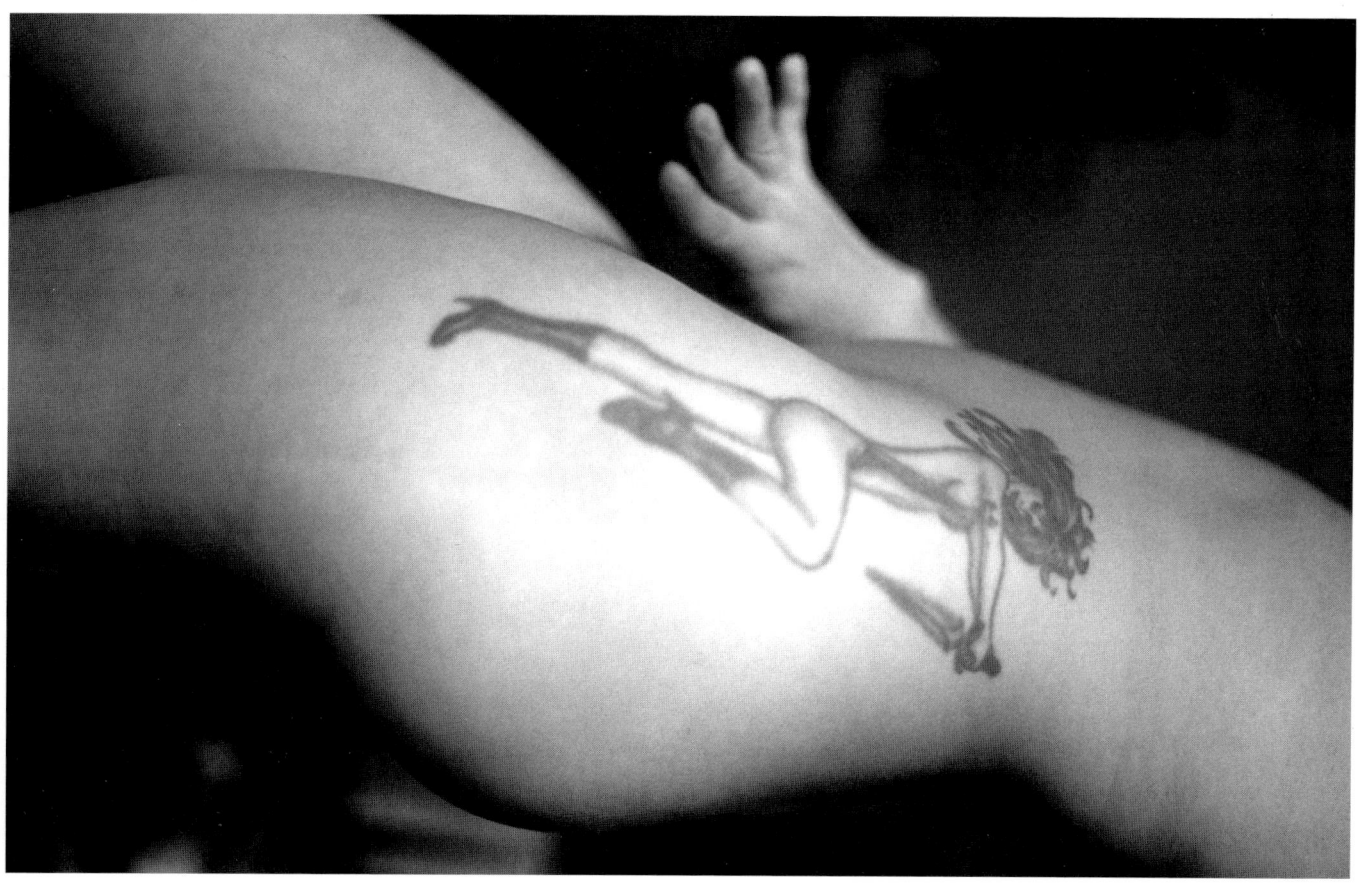

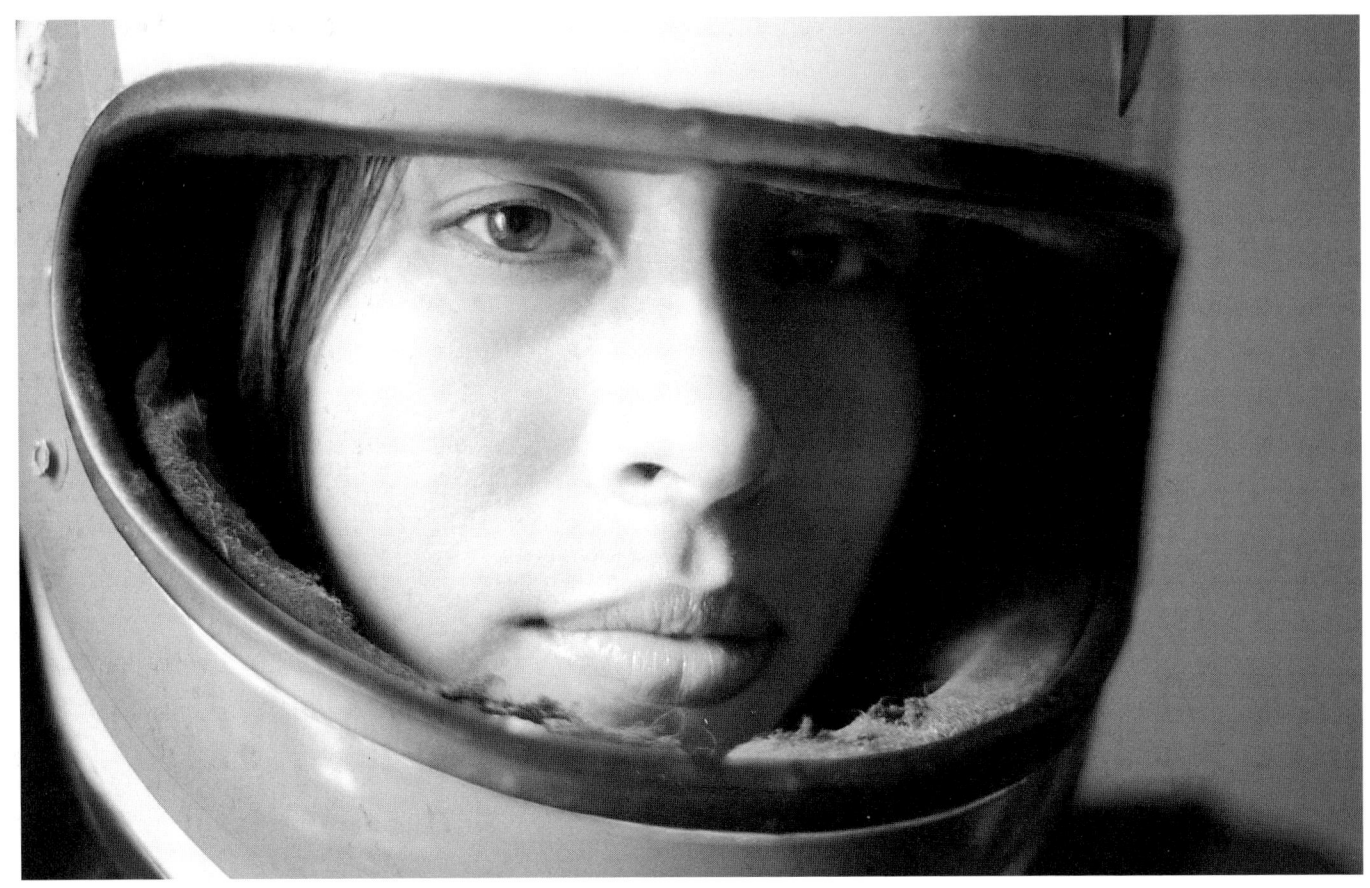

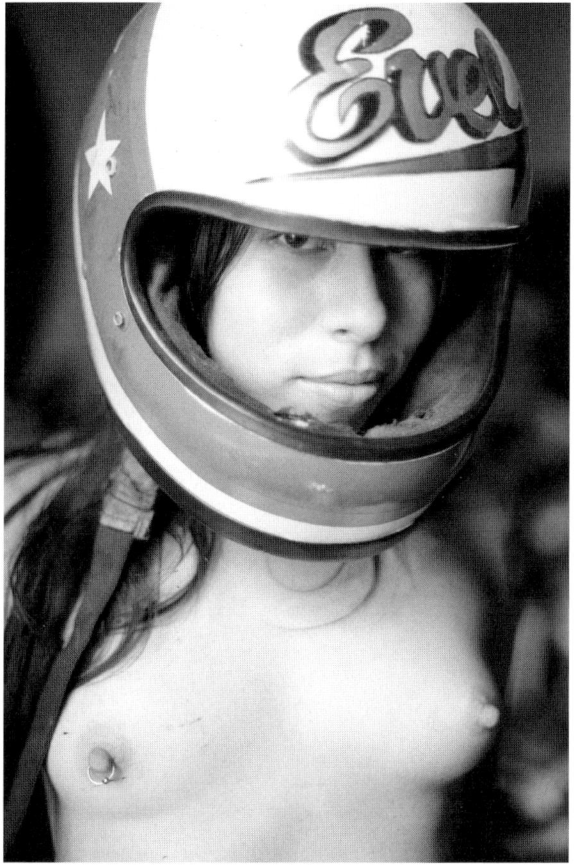

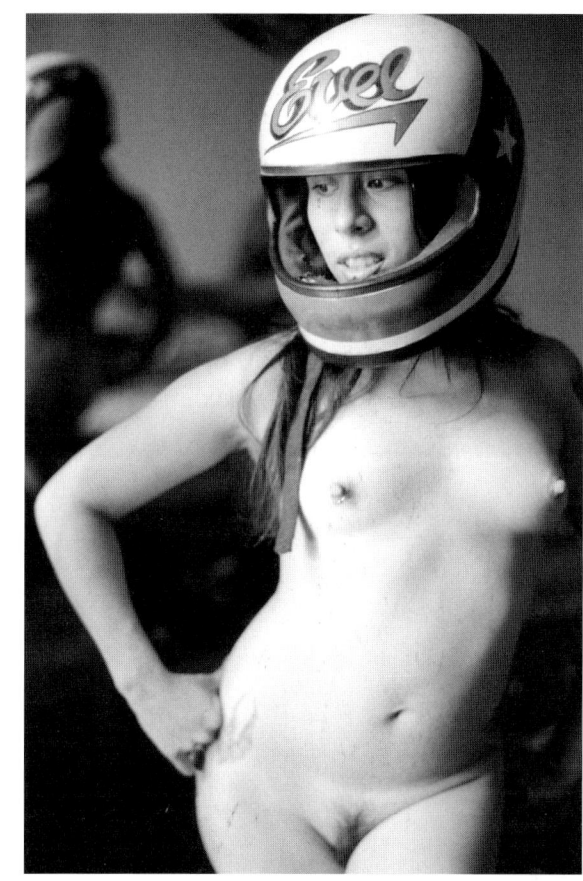

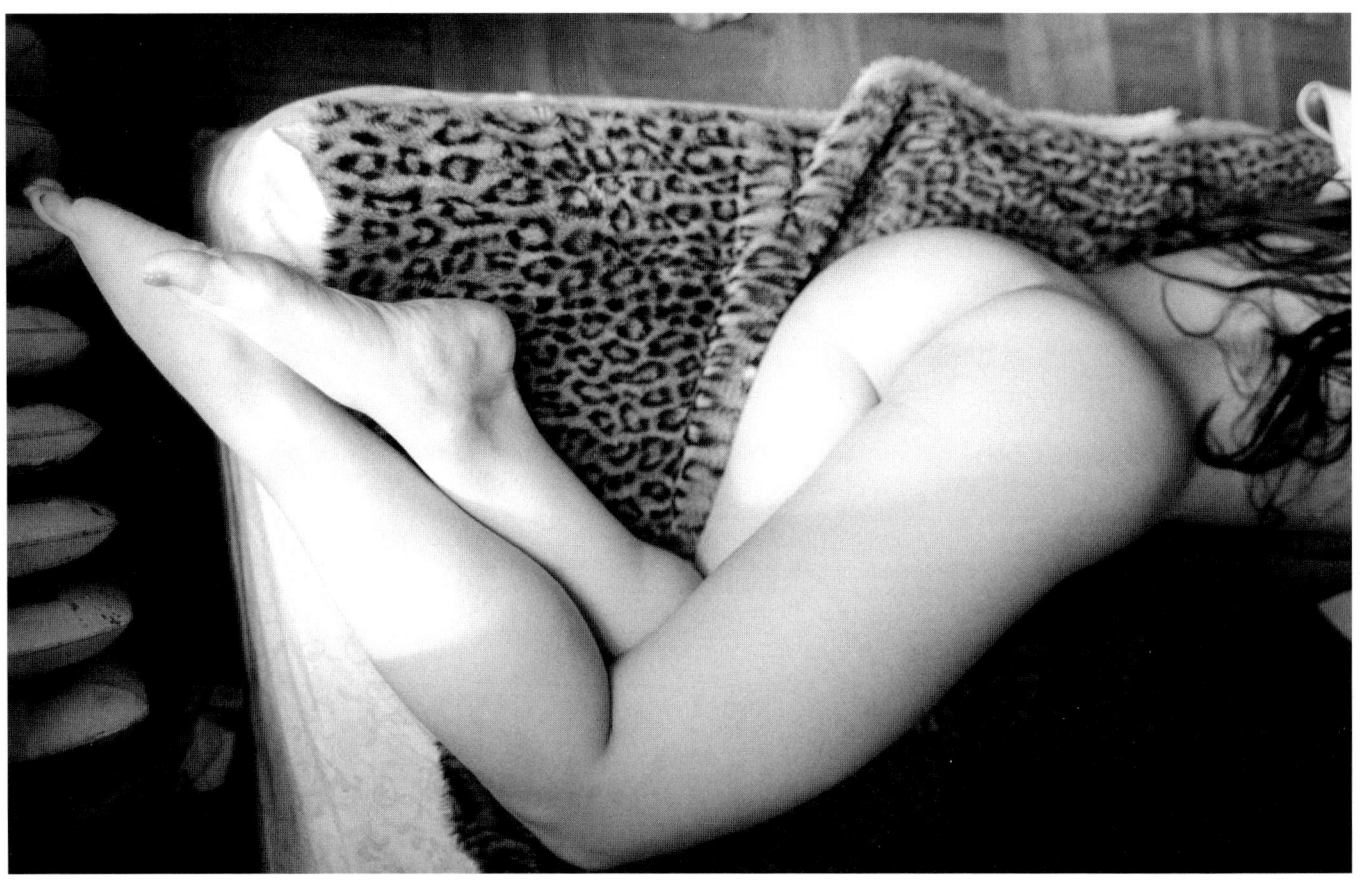

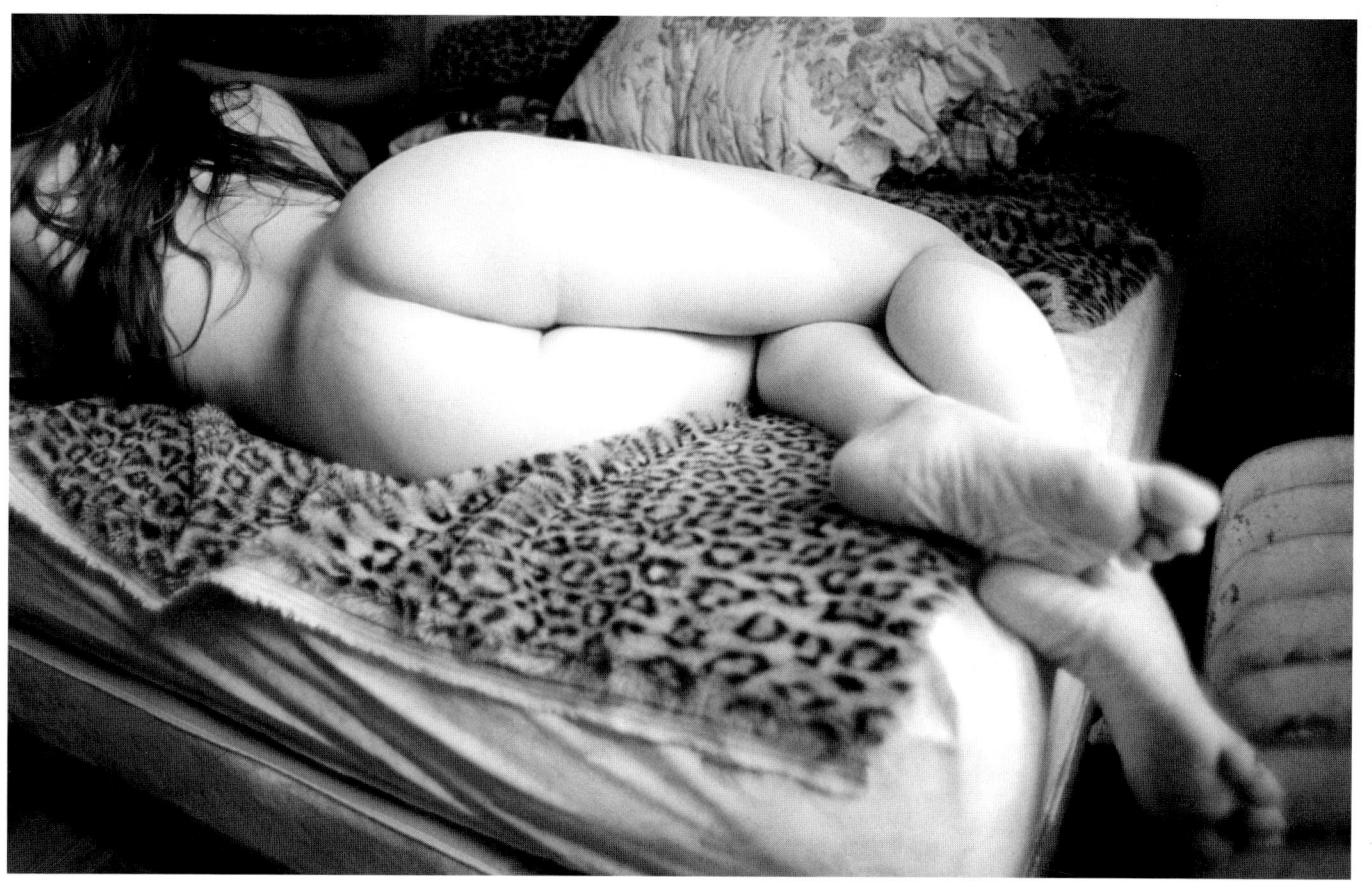

Chadia · I met Chadiya in Central Park, when she was dancing with a group for "Earth Day." Chadiya is Moroccan, but grew up in Germany. I photographed her in her Queens, NY apartment. As a dancer, she was great to photograph, because all her movements were artistic and graceful.

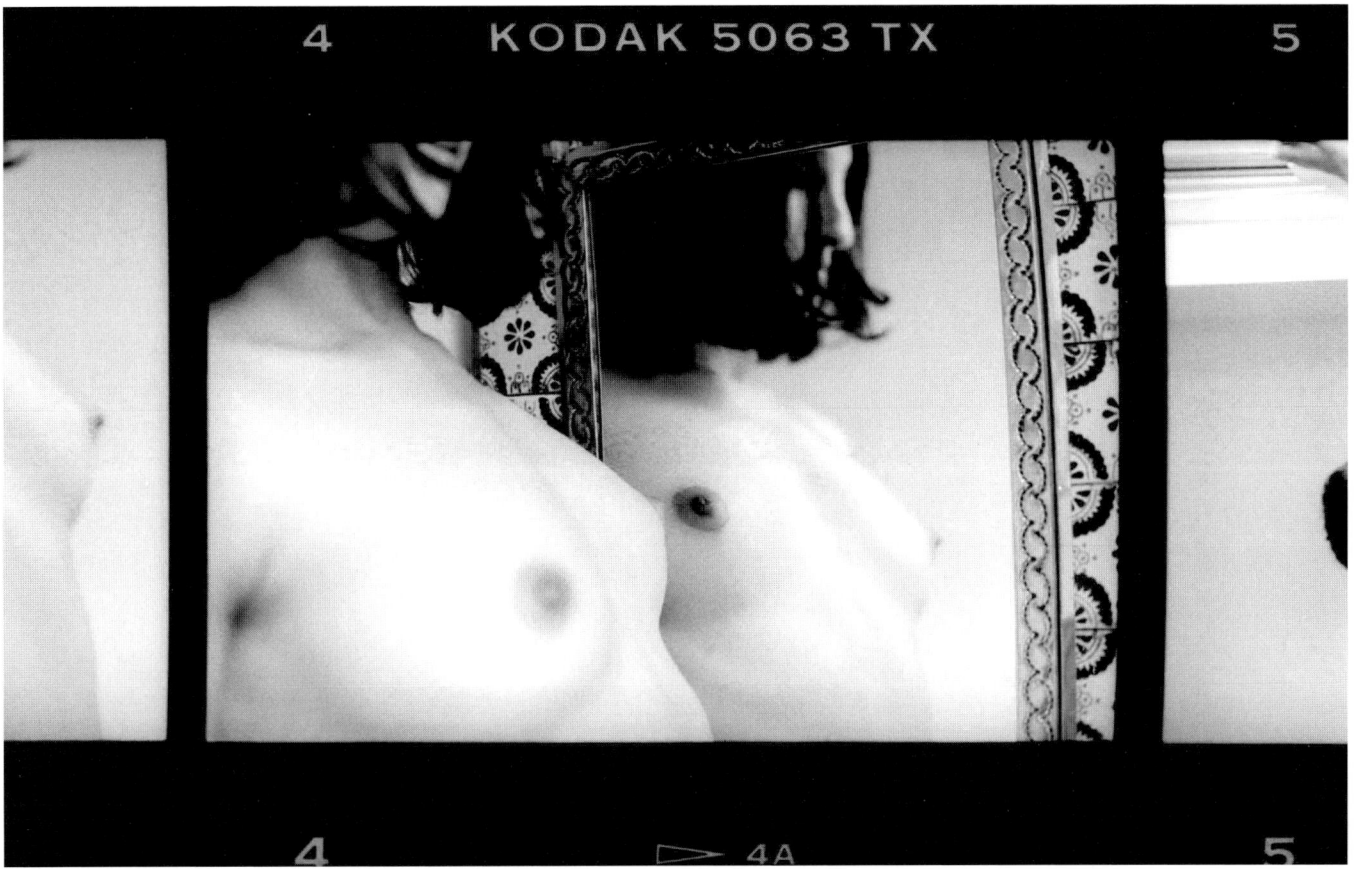

KODAK 5063 TX

4   5

4   ▷ 4A   5

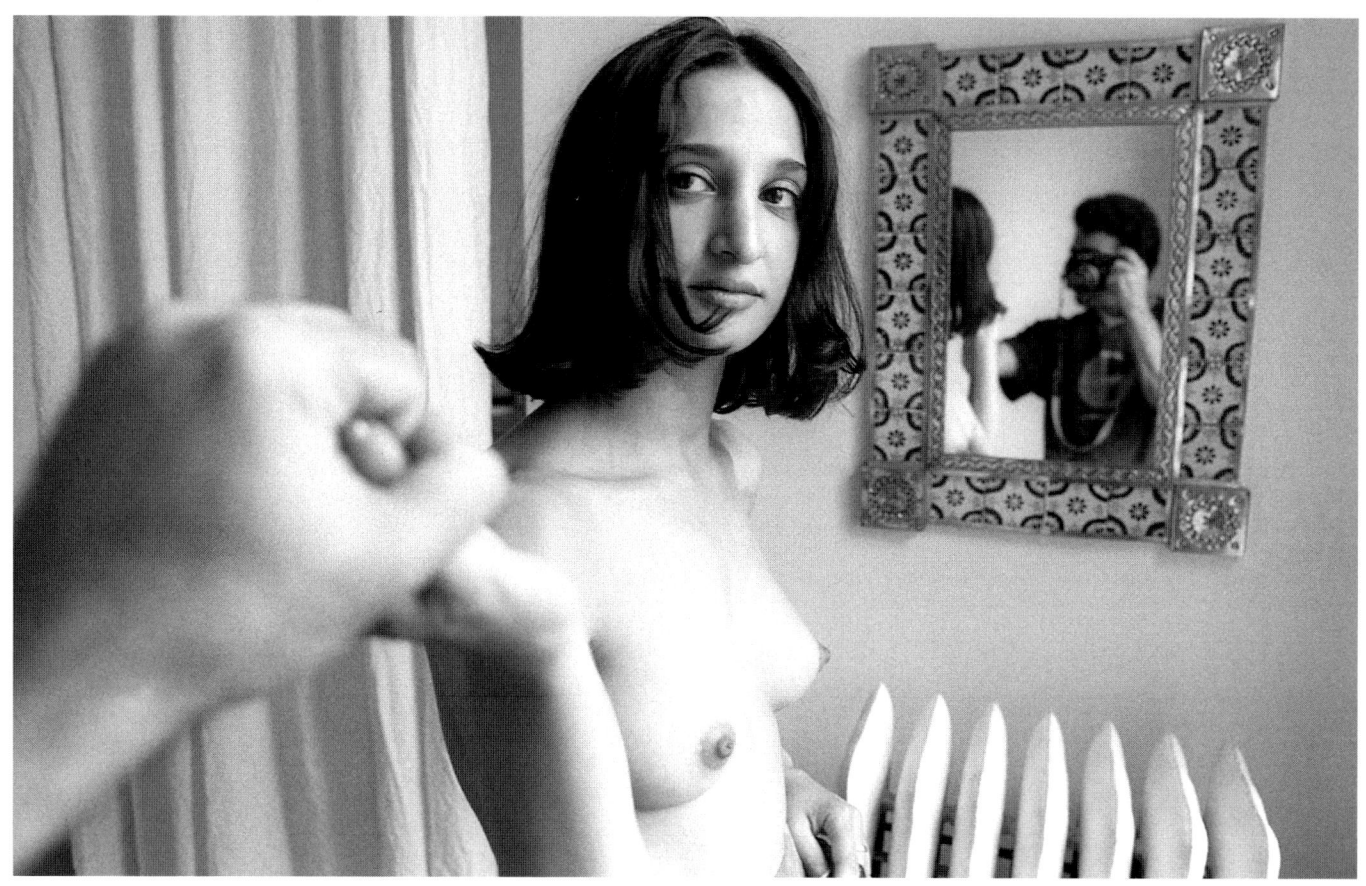

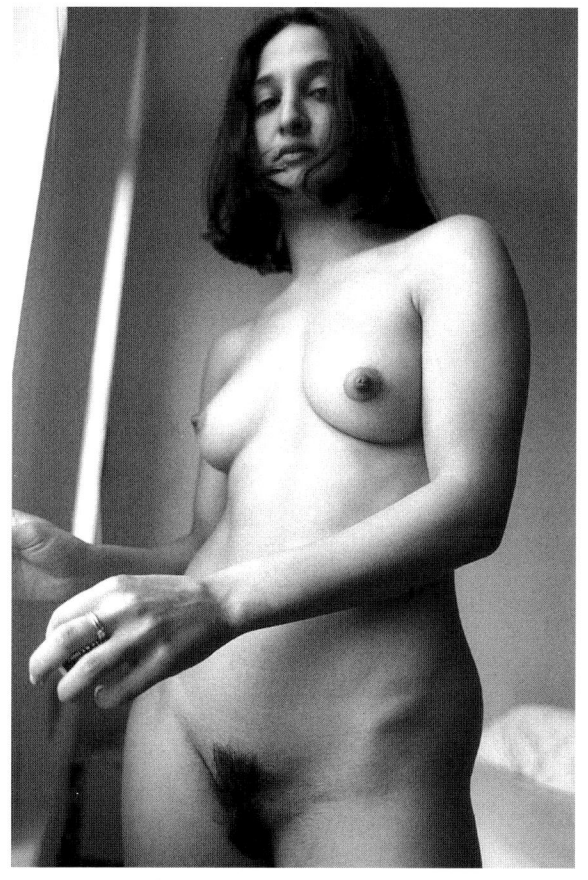
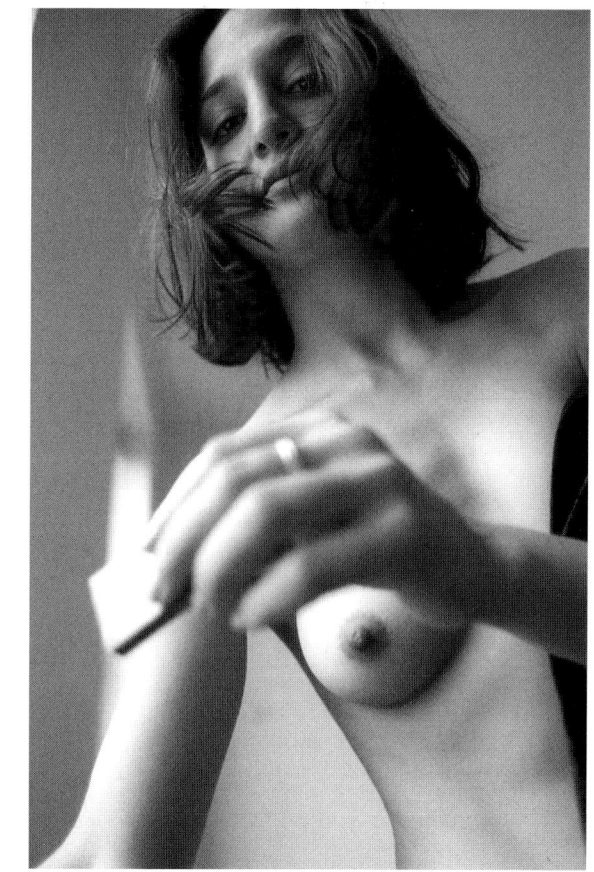

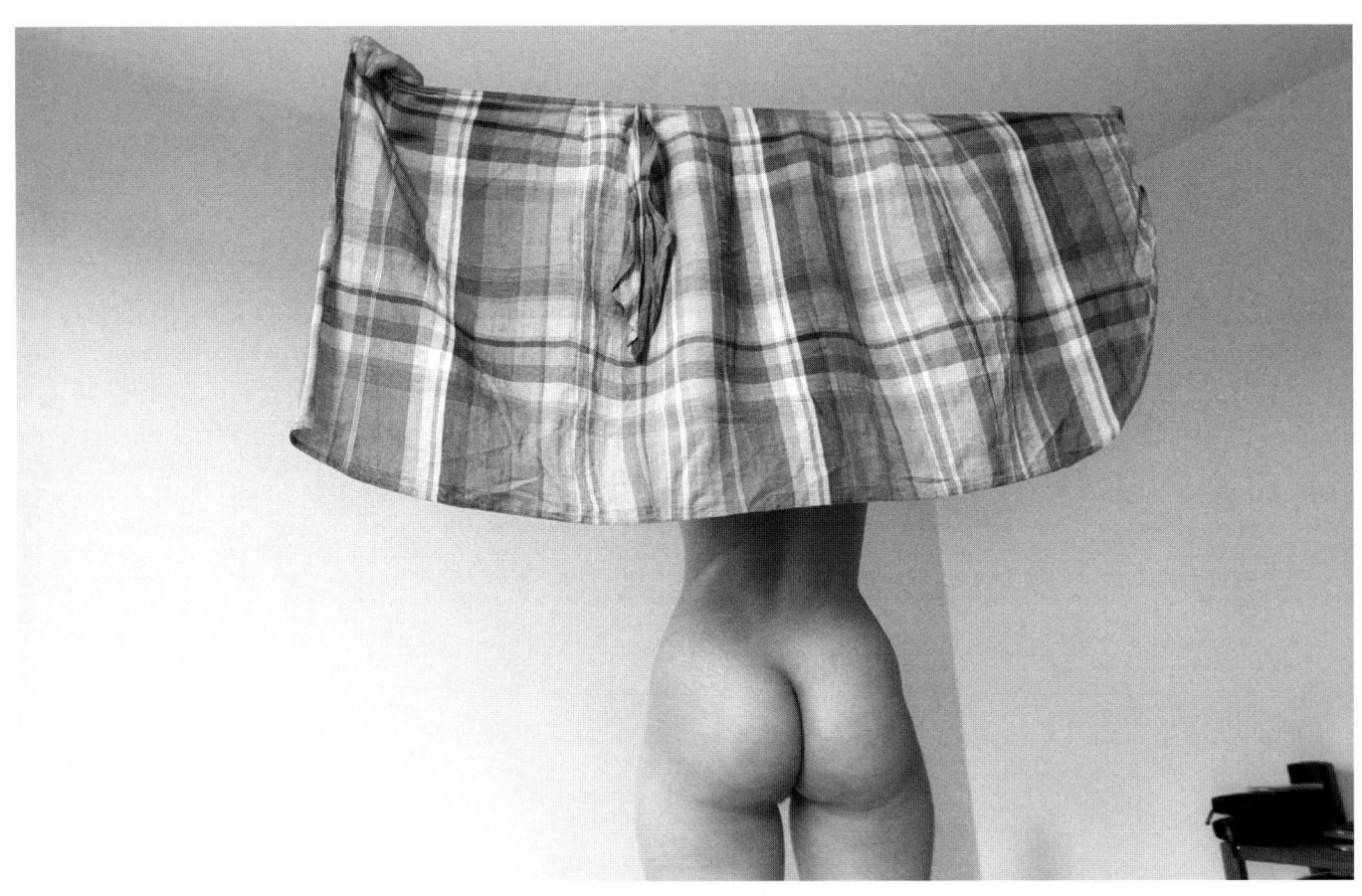

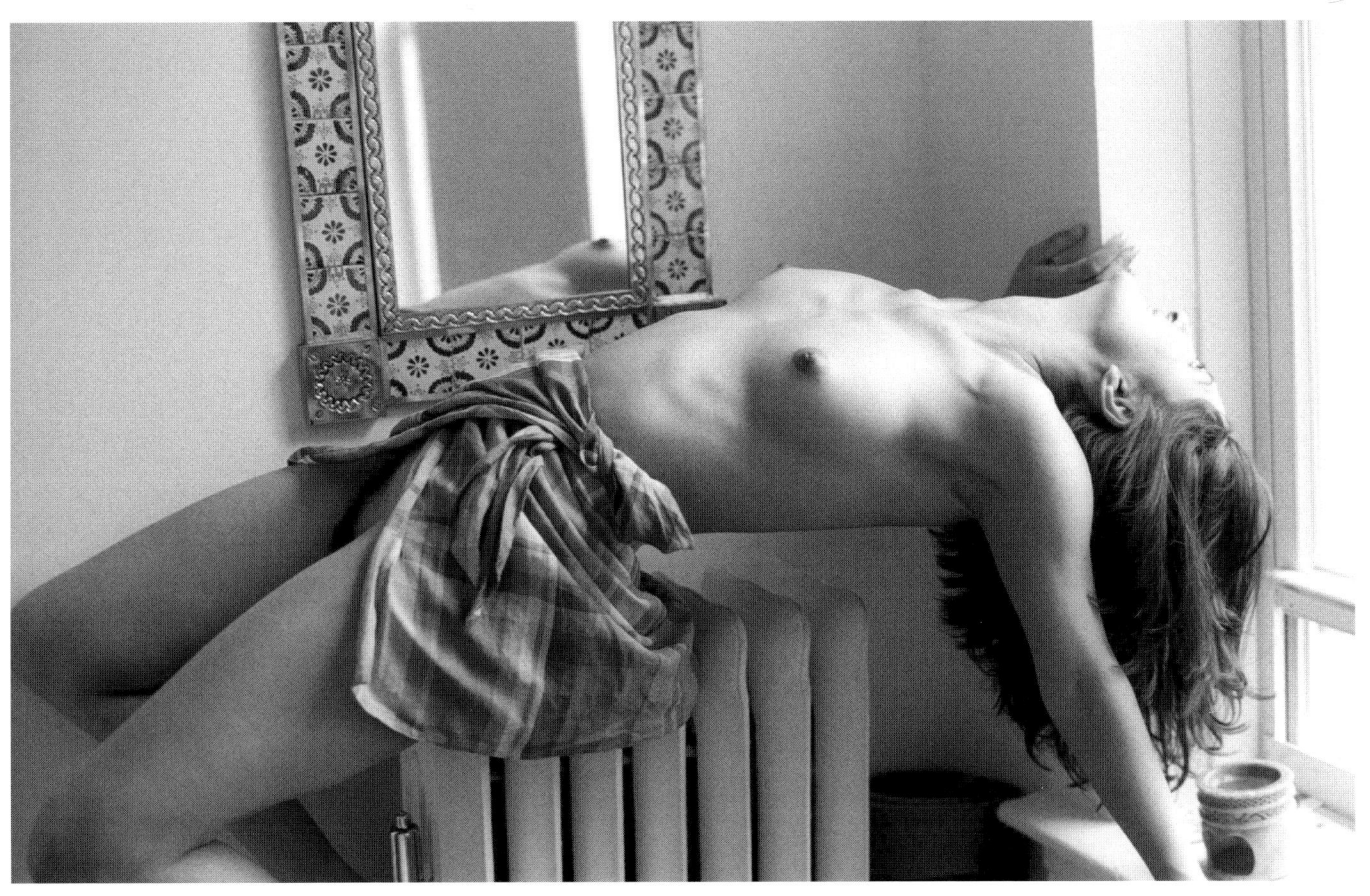

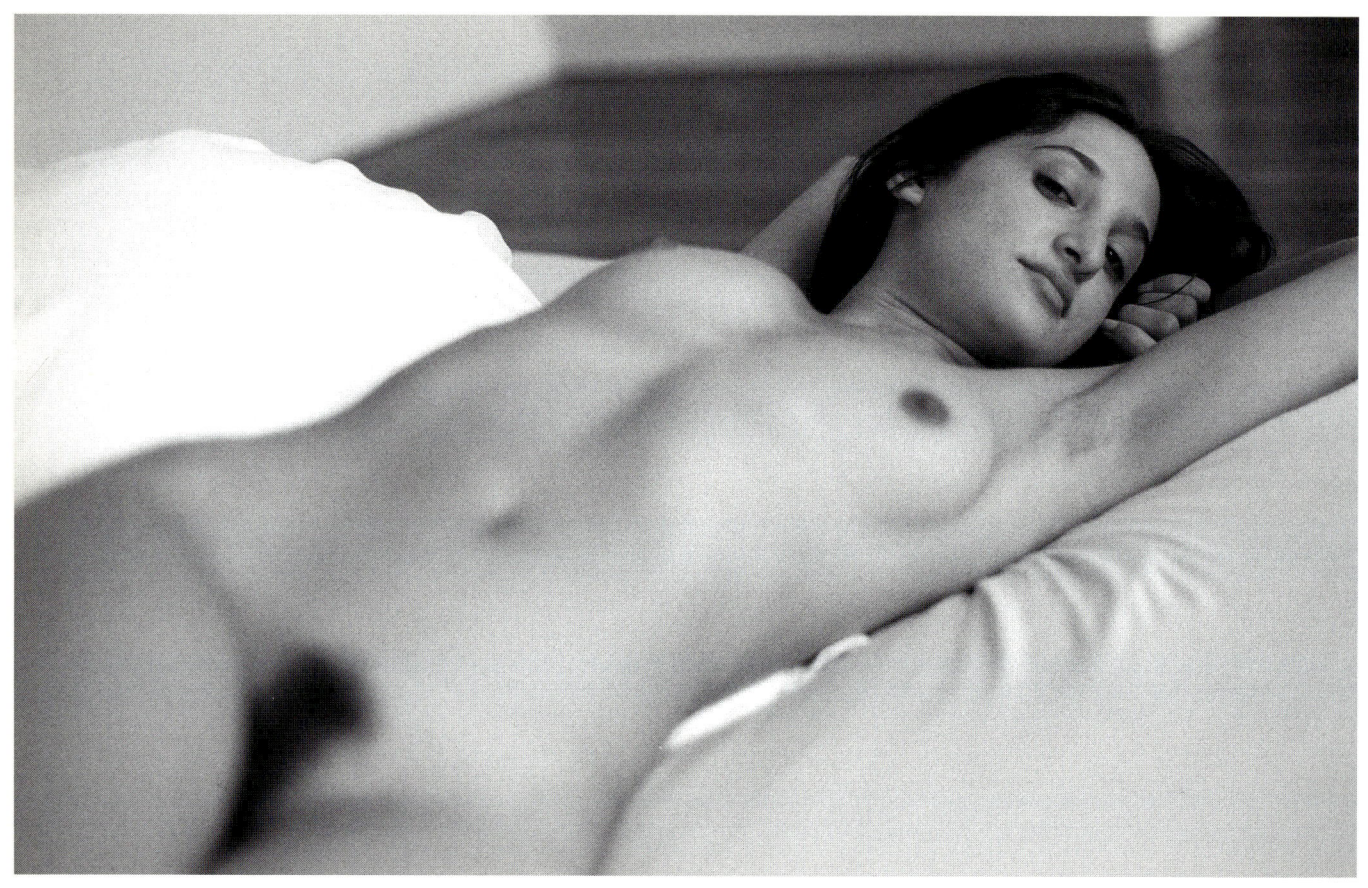

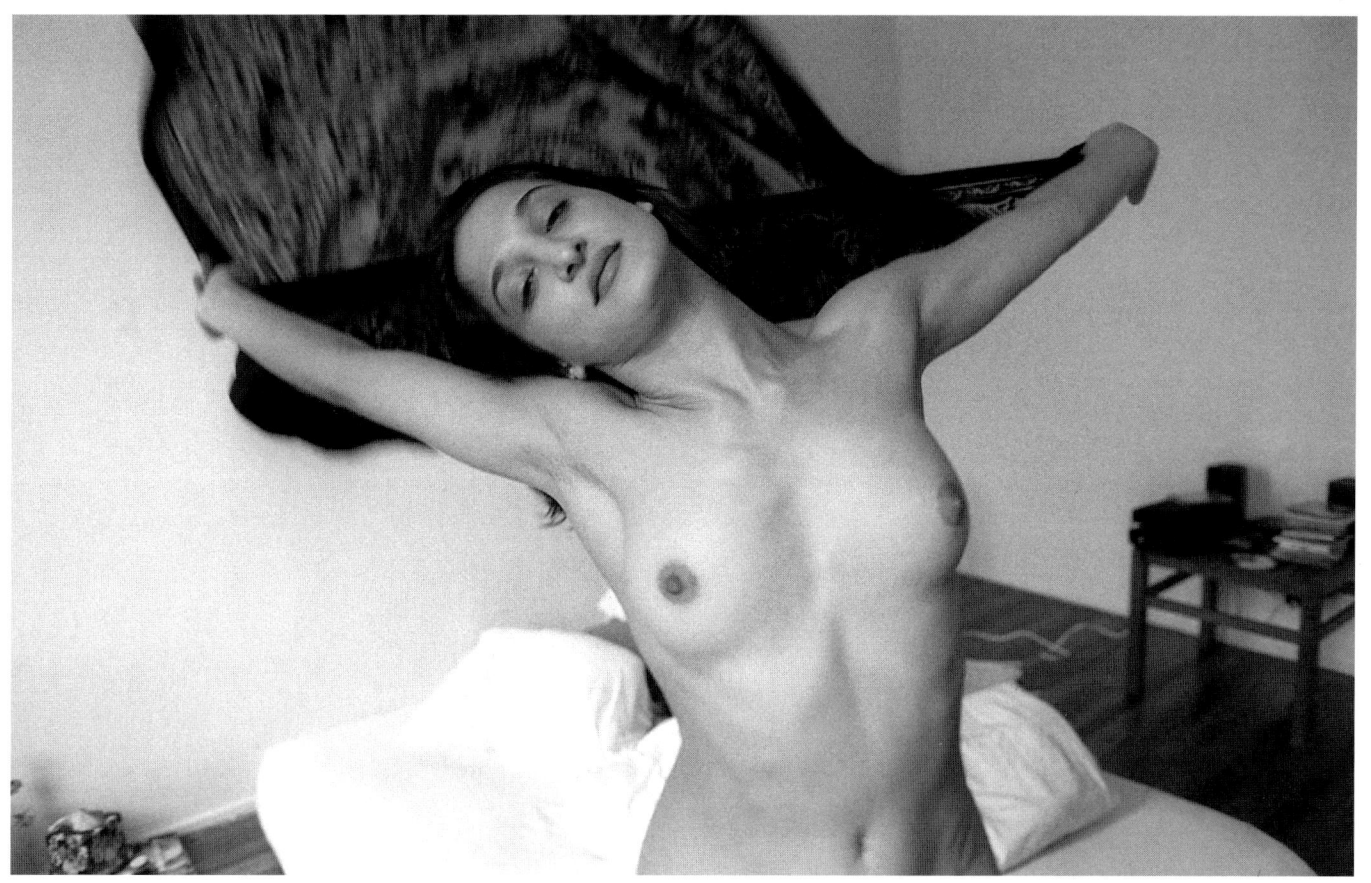

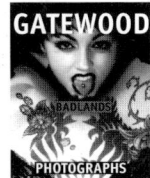

BADLANDS - Charles Gatewood
448 pages/410 photos
English / Deutsch / Francais / Espanol / Italiano
ISBN 3-9805876-4-9
Gatewood's world is **freakish, earthy, blunt, erotic** - most of all **terribly and beautifully alive.**

-A.D. Coleman, The New York Times.

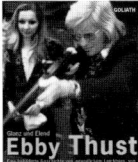

Ebby Thust - Glanz und Elend
192 pages/234 photos hardcover
Deutsch only in German
ISBN 3-9805876-6-5
Photo - Biography
Über **200 der besten Fotos** aus Ebby Thusts Leben. Mit Interviews über **Kindheit, Liebe, VIPs, Lifestyle, Boxen, böse Buben, Geld und Elend.**

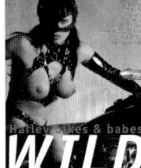

WILD - Horst Rösler
448 pages/400 photos full color
English / Deutsch / Francais / Espanol / Italiano
ISBN 3-9805876-5-7
Wild, wild bike! The illustrated book of the biker generation – 30 years after "Easy Rider"! 448 pages packed with **ball-busting photographs** of biker-events, crazy dudes, the **wildest chicks** and **hottest bikes** from all around the world. Simply: **WILD!**

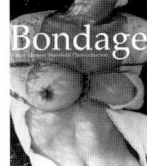

Bondage - Laura M.Stansfield
512 pages/500 photos
English / Deutsch / Francais / Espanol / Italiano
ISBN 3-9805876-1-4
30 years of **bondage photos**; over **500** pages and how it all came about; **unique.** One subject - one collection: **captivating, thrilling, provocative.**

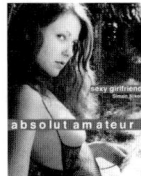

sexy girlfriends - S. Nikolai
absolut amateur 1
176 pages/150 photos hardcover
English / Deutsch / Francais / Espanol / Italiano
ISBN 3-9805876-9-X
Ready, steady, all go. "**Absolutely Amateur**", the new series of books purely dedicated to amateur photography, starts as it means to go on with **pure eroticism.** Here Simon Nikolai photographs his **fresh, natural beauties,** simply "sexy girlfriends".

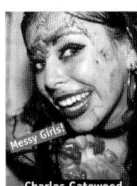

Messy Girls! - Charles Gatewood
368 pages/330 photos full color, hardcover,
English / Deutsch / Francais / Espanol / Italiano
ISBN 3-936709-00-9
MESSY GIRLS, the new book of famous Photographer Charles Gatewood, showing over 340 "**Sploshing**" color photographs of beautiful young fetish girls, naked and proud, smearing their nubile young bodies with pudding, honey and whipped cream, plus every messy substance imaginable.

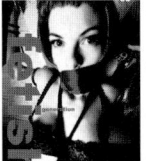

generation fetish - Lee Higgs
368 pages/330 photos full color, hardcover,
English / Deutsch / Francais / Espanol / Italiano
ISBN 3-9805876-8-1
„**Lush and evocative images...** Definitely a must-see for photography fans" *Dark Lady, AVN Online Magazine* „**Strange, beautiful and dangerous... sexuality like a sort of freak show,** something that David Cronenberg and William S.Burroughs visions" *Maxence Gruyer, Editor, Net-Zone*

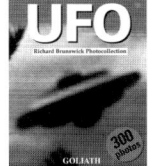

UFO - Richard Brunswick
320 pages/300 phots color and b&w
English / Deutsch / Francais / Espanol / Italiano
ISBN 3-9805876-3-0
Just landed! The ultimate picture bible for every UFO fan, the **most sensational and encompassing photo documentary** of the UFO century. Over **300** "never before publicized" **pictures** of UFOs, scenes, contacts, evidence.... Fantastic !!!

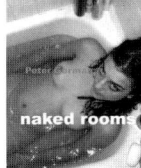

naked rooms - Peter Gorman
368 pages/330 photos full color, hardcover,
English / Deutsch / Francais / Espanol / Italiano
ISBN 3-936709-02-5
Powerful, playful and often completely exposed, Gorman's female nudes give new meaning to the phrase 'up close & personal. 'Prepare to discover what real women are really up to when they're getting naked in their own rooms. **An erotic tour de force.**

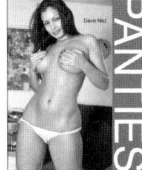

Panties - Dave Naz
368 pages/140 photos, hardcover,
English / Deutsch / Francais / Espanol / Italiano
ISBN 3-936709-01-7
Dave Naz is the Los Angeles photographer of all things sexual. He's quickly managed to soak up and regurgitate the dirty details of the secret lives of people in a star system that runs parallel to but outside of the Hollywood we all know from our local cineplex. This is **LA style!**

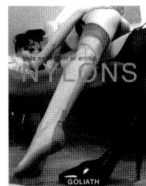

NYLONS - Uwe Fülleborn
512 pages/450 photos
English / Deutsch / Francais / Espanol / Italiano
ISBN 3-9805876-7-3
A stocking fetishist turns his obsession into a profession and photographs his "anonymous female neighbours" in nylons: **shy girls, upright housewives or uninhibited secretaries** present themselves over **512** pages "in all innocence" – girls next door in erotic nylons!

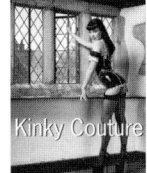

Kinky Couture - Emma D.Broughton
112 pages/100 photos full color, hardcover,
English / Deutsch / Francais / Espanol / Italiano
ISBN 3-936709-07-6
"Emma Delves-Broughton brings a fresh female eye to the modern fetish aesthetic, as can be seen in the beautiful work she has done for many of the rising stars of fetish fashion." *Michelle Olley 'Femmes' Carlton Books*

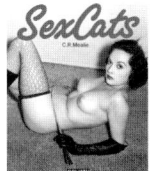

Sexcats - Christopher Mealie
368 pages/340 photos, hardcover,
English / Deutsch / Francais / Espanol / Italiano
ISBN 3-936709-03-3
"Sex Cats! is a collection of tawdry, yet titillating pictures from a sinful past. One would be hard pressed to find a greater collection of curvaceous kittens. Seductive, dark and always fun, over 350 fantastic images abound in this book of rare, vintage pinup and girly photos from the 1950s and 1960s. Purrrfect."

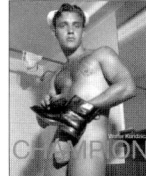

Champion - Walter Kundzicz
368 pages/350 photos, hardcover, color
English / Deutsch / Francais / Espanol / Italiano
ISBN 3-936709-06-8
"During the late 1950s and early '60s, in the world of male physique photography the name Champion became synonymous with images of handsome, athletic young men captured in vivid color. Walter Kundzicz, the photographer created a diverse **colorful and kitschy photographs** of scantily clad athletes.

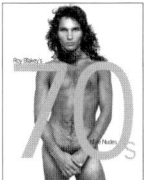

70s Male Nudes - Roy Blakey
160 pages/100 photos, hardcover,
English / Deutsch / Francais / Espanol / Italiano
ISBN 3-9807602-1-9
"The history of the male nude in photography cannot be written without acknowledging the important contributions Roy Blakey made to the genre. His 1972 monograph of male nudes, HE, was a revelation when it appeared.This stunning new collection -- lovingly edited and beautifully produced -- presents this important body of work and helps set the record straight."

366

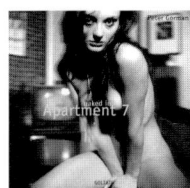

naked in Apartment 7
Peter Gorman

160 pages/152 photos hardcover,
English / Deutsch / Francais / Espanol / Italiano
ISBN 3-9807602-0-0
Who cares about time, desks, lamps and the other paraphernalia of life, the image seems to ask, when there's a sexually wired female spread out in the foreground? - *Inda Schaenen, salon*

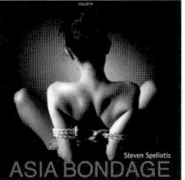

asia bondage - Steven Spiliotis

160 pages/150 photos hardcover
English / Deutsch / Francais / Espanol / Italiano
ISBN 3-9807602-6-X
Asia Bondage, a highly erotic, exciting and thrilling journey through the light and shade of traditional black and white photography. **An arousing shadow show of the senses.**

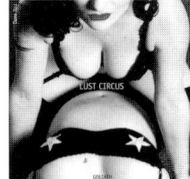

Lust Circus - Dave Naz

160 pages/155 photos full color, hardcover,
English / Deutsch / Francais / Espanol / Italiano
ISBN 3-9807602-7-8
„Gorgeous women beautifully photographed... Dave Naz manages to capture the deliciously erotic, seducing his delightful subjects into being playfully naughty. **Classy, sexy, hot!**" - *Lydia Lunch*

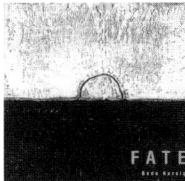

FATE • Bodo Korsik

108 pages/152 color pl./hardcover & dust jacket
English / Deutsch
ISBN 3-9805876-2-2
Unique visions about Fate in all its guises, in a unique game between five literary figures and Bodo Korsig's new encaustic works. All works were created in Garner Tullis' NYC studio, where artists such as Robert Ryman, Robert Mangold, Catharine Lee and Ken Kiff worked. Something to stimulate thought about oneself and Fate.

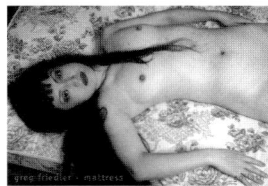

Mattress - Greg Friedler

size: 12 x 8,5 inches / 30 x 21 cm / Hardback
English / Deutsch / Francais / Espanol / Italiano
112 pages / 50 color plates
ISBN 3-9807602-8-6
How many naked women fit on a mattress? Greg Friedler solved this riddle in the same way as New York solved the problem of living space: one behind another on his bed, making it the smallest stage for an artistically, aesthetically and erotically wonderful pose for a photo!

Art / Photography - Charlie White

size: 12 x 8,5 inches / 30 x 21 cm / Hardback
English / Deutsch / Francais / Espanol / Italiano
112 pages / 50 color plates
ISBN 3-9807602-9-4
With an introduction by Ronald Jones, this generously illustrated book includes full color images and details of Charlie White's three recent photographic projects. This book is a must for all lovers of modern art and photography. **Definitely would become a cult book!**

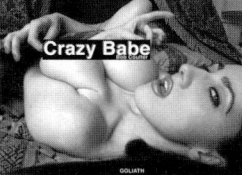

Crazy Babe - Bob Coulter

368 pages/350 photos, hardcover, full color
English / Deutsch / Francais / Espanol / Italiano
ISBN 3-936709-04-1
Crazy babes, nude and colorful, frolicking along pastoral lakesides, the bowls of New York City, and everywhere in-between. Finally, 360 of Bob Coulter's greatest hits off the infamous photographic website are available in book form. **WOW**

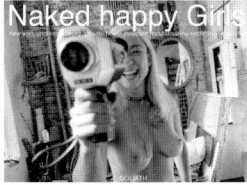

Naked happy Girls - Andrew Einhorn

368 pages/350 photos, hardcover,
English / Deutsch / Francais / Espanol / Italiano
ISBN 3-936709-03-3
Twisting and turning, lounging and laughing; I've never seen so many New York's girls, so happy to be naked at home. Andrew has a special way of bringing out the real hidden sexy side every New York girl next door. This book made me feel good.

For information about a **free catalog** of other Goliath books, **distribution** in your country, **dealer** information, or if you are interested in publishing a book with us as a **photographer** or **collector,** please contact:

Europe:
Goliath Verlagsgesellschaft mbH
Eschersheimer Landstr. 353
D 60320 Frankfurt/Main
Germany
contact@goliathbooks.de
www.goliathbooks.de

USA:
Goliath
P.O.Box 136
NY , NY 10035
USA
goliath@debitel.net
www.goliathclub.com

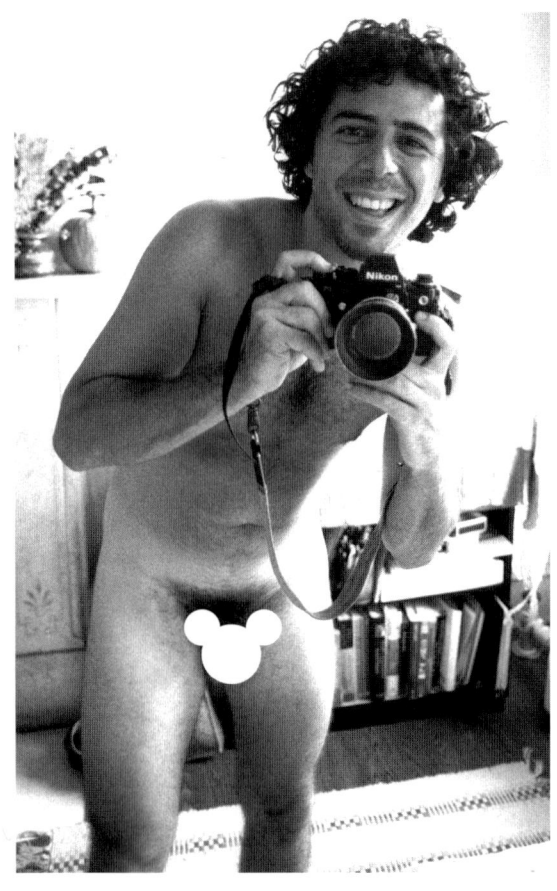

Andrew Einhorn was born in 1964 in Philadelphia, Pennsylvania. Originally interested in film and television, Andrew fell in love with photography at Temple University, where he worked on the school newspaper and yearbook. After five years as a photojournalist with the Philadelphia Inquirer, Andrew experimented with fashion, travel, and children's photography. In 1994, he moved to New York, and began shooting nude portraits of friends, and strangers alike, which were incorporated into a television show that he produced for seven years, called "Dog the Cat". Andrew still lives in Manhattan, and works as a photographer, videographer, editor, and comedian. He's currently working on several other book projects, and a television show that incorporates all his work.

Big thanks to Miki and Ana for their hard work, patience, and sense of humor, Spencer Tunick, Jon Porcelli, Cynthia Wang, and especially to all the models who gave me their time, trust, and laughter.
- *Andrew Einhorn*

You may contact
Goliath at contact@goliathbooks.com
-the photographer: Andrew Einhorn at Andrew@AndrewEinhorn.com